I0766988

K.A. KNIGHT
WRITING THE MONSTERS YOU LOVE TO HATE.

PRETTY LIARS

UNSTOPPABLE AND UNBREAKABLE DUET

USA TODAY BESTSELLING AUTHOR

K.A KNIGHT

Pretty Liars Duet

This is a work of fiction. Any resemblance to places, events or real people are entirely coincidental.

Written by K.A. Knight.
Edited By Jess from Elemental Editing and Proofreading.
Proofreading by Norma's Nook.
Formatted by The Nutty Formatter.
Cover Design by Moonstruck Cover Design & Photography
Art by Dily Iola Designs

TRIGGER WARNING

Please note, this is a dark book and as such contains scenes that some may find triggering. Mentions of sexual abuse, torture, murder, mutliation, death, suicide, sexual violence and much more can be found within, please be mindful if any of that may upset/trigger you.

If you have any concerns please reach out.

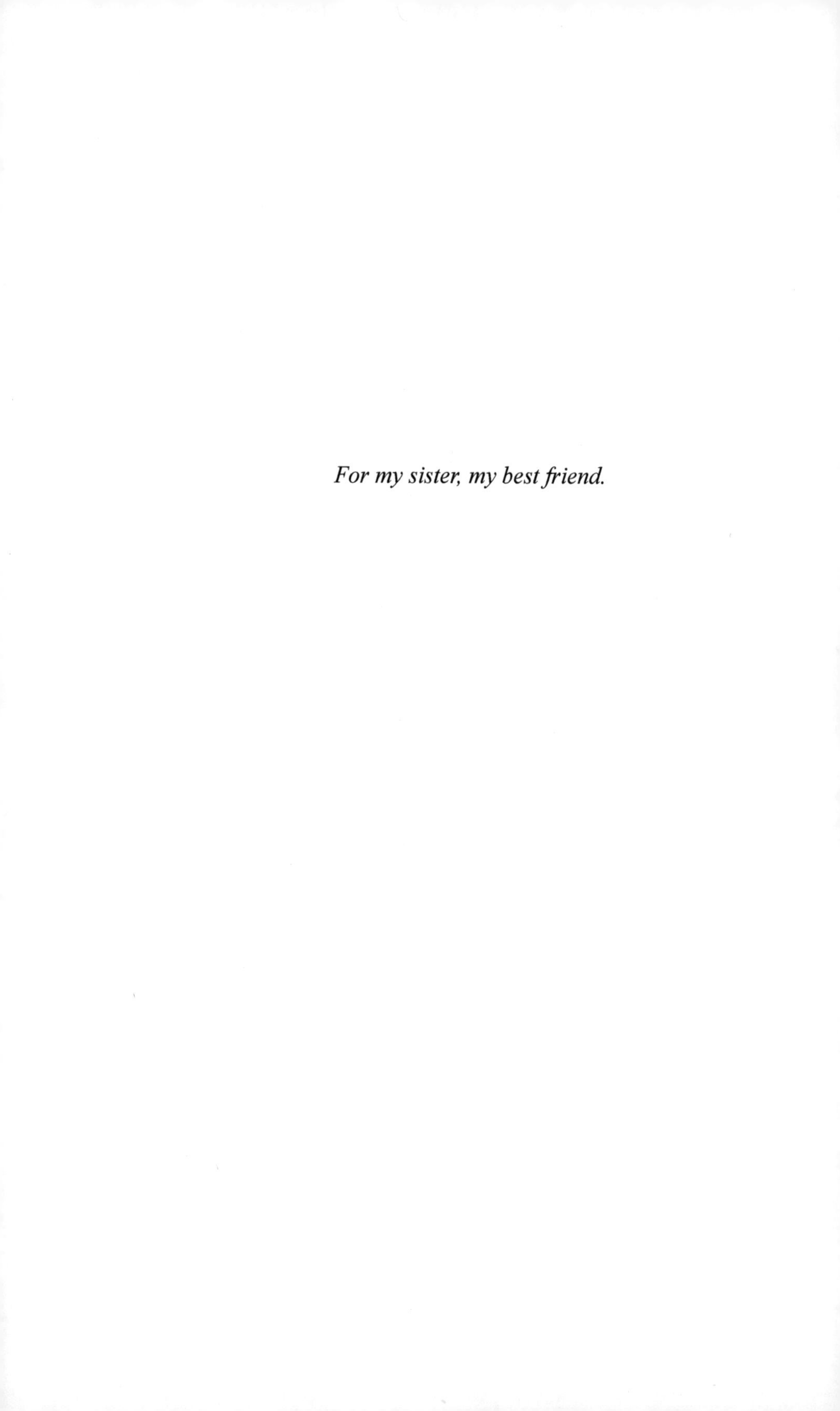

For my sister, my best friend.

UNSTOPPABLE

PROLOGUE

I fist my tanned, scarred hands, ripping the cuts on my exposed, bruised knuckles further. The shock of pain makes my heart race, chasing away the fog and tears.

My body shivers involuntarily, my hair still dripping wet. Today is about torture techniques, and he started early, breaking my weak body over and over. He said it was to test my response to extreme pain and how quickly a child's body could bounce back under immense stress. I didn't please him when I failed to react to the electric shock.

It comes again, and I jerk, my teeth clenched hard so I don't let any noise out. Doing so would either please or annoy him, so I try to distract myself and remain silent.

The sterile white room is thirty steps in each direction—I've counted—the ceiling has fifty-seven tiles, and the door has five locks. Counting calms my brain as the current finally passes through my body, then his distorted voice comes again as he watches me through the two-way mirror.

He's always watching . . . observing.

"Tell me how that feels."

I don't speak.

"Novaleen," he snaps, annoyed now. "You know better. You must answer for my research. How does your body feel?"

I still don't answer. It's a childish rebellion, but one I take pride in, especially when it breaches that cool exterior and brings anything other than cold disinterest to his voice—the voice that haunts my every waking and sleeping moment.

The shock comes again, jolting my body against the table I'm chained upon.

"Answer me!"

I don't, so he shocks me again, barely leaving me time to recover from the last one. He asks the same question again and again, followed by recurring shocks. I still refuse to answer, so he increases the voltage until I scream. The taste of my blood fills my mouth, and my bladder lets go.

"Please, sir, please!" I beg, but it's too late. He's punishing me and reminding me who's in charge. My high-pitched voice cracks and then breaks as my body heaves and twists, trying to escape the current burning through me and setting my brain and body on fire.

"Please, Daddy! Please!"

ONE

I jerk awake, coated in a cold sweat, with the sheets twisted around my bare legs. My tank top and thong stick to my body, and my long black hair is stuck to my skin.

Disgusting.

Pathetic.

Count, Nova, count.

I begin to count the specks of light filtering through the curtain, indicating it's sunrise, the bricks on the wall, and then the stains on the ceiling from my neighbour above watering her plants too often. I count until I can breathe again and his face and voice no longer haunt me. I realise then I can still taste blood, and with a sigh, I throw back the covers. I get up to stretch, waking my body before padding to the adjoining bathroom. Flicking on the fan and light, I lean into the counter and stare at myself in the rectangular mirror. My eyes are bloodshot, and my bones stick out from my lack of appetite. I'm getting worse the closer I get to . . . there.

Shaking my head, I push back my wet hair and spit into the sink. I run the tap, watching the pink, bloody water disappear down the drain. Sticking my tongue out, I see tiny puncture wounds from my teeth. I must have bit it in my sleep.

I turn away and crank on the cheap hotel shower. I didn't get in until late last night, and I have another day of driving before the funeral.

Funeral.

Even thinking that seems surreal. He's actually dead. The man who I thought was unstoppable, the man who I thought was invincible, is dead. I should be celebrating, I should be fucking rejoicing, but instead all I feel is lost. For so long, he's been the shadow following me, always one step away, and now . . . what am I running from? What should I do?

And Ana . . . What about Ana?

She's been by his side since I disappeared. What does she think happened to me? I often wonder if she remembers me. Does she even care, or did he brainwash her and turn her into his little clone? She was always so influenced by him, so eager to please. I wonder if he hurt her like he hurt me.

No, he couldn't have. I made sure of that.

But she will be at the funeral, so what do I say? Will she even recognise me? Will she even care?

It's been ten fucking years of running, hiding, and being nothing but a ghost thanks to him. I was just a kid when I left, only seventeen, but she was younger still. She was only fourteen, and that's a long time to spend with a monster like him.

My turbulent thoughts and worries won't help. He taught me not to jump to conclusions and that the only certain thing in life is reality, not the worries in my brain. The only accurate things are what you can taste, see, feel, and explain.

Facts.

Why jump to conclusions? Why worry about what you can't control? Focus on what you can. What can you analyse from the situation? Do better, notice more, and react without emotion.

The command floats into my mind unbidden, like it often does since I heard the news. I had gotten good at pushing the memories away and unlearning everything he taught me, even when it was an impossible task. I settled and even lived a normal-ish life, even if no one ever truly knew me. But then he died, and it was like opening a floodgate. All that fear and pain came back, drilling into my body until I couldn't even slouch without his annoyed command filling my ears like he was actually here.

I duck my head under the spray and crank the temperature higher, hoping the shock of the burn will wash away everything but the present. Grabbing the cheap soap, I lather it up and methodically wash my body, noting every raised scar—some of which have been dissolved thanks to his miracle serum.

Can't have a perfect being with scars, after all.

Everything had to be perfect and in its place. Everything was carefully controlled based on his whims, and I was designed to appeal to whatever he needed at the time—make me older, younger, more sophisticated, or a street kid.

My first rebellion when I ran away was to dye my once boring blonde, shoulder-length hair midnight black. Now it reaches my hips thanks to him not keeping it trimmed to his desired length. His opinion was that long hair was unkempt, and as I push it back, I see the shimmer of dark blue woven in the curly locks.

Continuing to wash, I run my hand over my defined abs. I could never escape the need for rhythmic exercises, cardio, and weights he trained into me, not to mention survival training and weapons expertise. Jujitsu and every other martial art still live inside my head like a routine I can't escape. At first, I hated the fact that I would wake up at 6 AM and need to run and work out. It was like I'd not escaped him, but now I revel in my strength, in the bliss and nothingness I find when pushing my body to its limits.

Reaching my tattoos, I hesitate. He would hate them and say they make me stand out when I need to blend in. It's the very reason I got my first one at just seventeen, the month after I left. Since then, I've covered my entire left arm in an intricate sleeve of lines, dots, flowers, and mandala, my hand too. Over my right hip, I have a gun, and a skull wraps around the top of my thigh before fading into the black and white piece stretching all the way to my toes. I have a few more here and there, like an under boob one and a piece behind my ear, but they were the most important and beautiful. The black ink stains my skin forever, reminding me I'm not that perfect creature he tried to create.

I'm real, right down to the chipped, black nail varnish on my toes, my nipple piercings, and the new, unhealed scar running diagonally across my foot from my new bike.

I'm not the same scared Novaleen who huddled before the man who was supposed to protect and love her.

I'm Nova, the badass bitch he created down in those torture chambers, one he could never contain.

I'm his biggest mistake, his loudest enemy, and, if he had lived, his death.

After conditioning my hair, I rinse it away before climbing out and wrapping a cheap, tiny towel around my waist. Swiping my hand through the condensation on the mirror, I stare at myself. I seem more determined and . . . free.

Is that the feeling?

Is that the glint in my emerald-green eyes?

Pursing my thick pink lips, I tilt my head as I analyse myself. I'm tall, like him, at nearly six feet. I used to be lanky as a child, but as I grew, I gained muscle and some curves, with a tight waist, flared hips, and double D boobs. I have long, lean legs, strong arms, and toned abs. Ana was always smaller, and I wonder if she still is.

Stop.

Focus.

Ignoring my invading worries and thoughts, I brush my teeth, comb my hair, and plait it back before putting on a bra and my tight black workout shorts. Moving into the other room, I push the double bed aside to create room, and then, like every morning, I conduct my warm-up routine to fully energise my body and get my adrenaline pumping.

I stretch first before doing cardio with running, jumping, and burpees. Next, I do my sit-ups, Russian twists, and push-ups. Once my workout is done, I stretch out my muscles, feeling the strength running through me as I cool down. I slowly work through some jujitsu, mixing it with Krav Maga and traditional karate. I can never be too prepared, and the moves are second nature as I work through all of my training, highlighting hold, attack, and defending movements.

Once I'm done, I take a moment to meditate and control my breathing.

When my eyes open again, I feel better, and I remember why I am doing this—for her, always for her.

Removing my workout gear, I change into tight black leather trousers and don my steel-toed military boots with knives in each one. I add a somewhat appropriate plain black shirt, which is loose to hide my holsters with small handguns, and as always, I slip my long, handmade necklace over my head then conceal it beneath my shirt—a habit from when I hid it from him so he wouldn't take it, crush it, or use it against me. It is a constant reminder of why I survived.

Of why I still fight.

Grabbing my tight leather jacket, I pack the rest of my duffle, and with one more look to check that I didn't forget anything, I head out of the cheap hotel room. I check out under a false name and a false credit card before heading outside to the one joy in this world I allow myself—my bike.

My Suzuki GSX-R750 is finished in black and fades to red. Riding is the closest I'll ever get to feeling happiness as I race through the world.

There is nothing like it.

Grabbing my helmet, I pull it over my head and crank up the volume of my rock playlist. Everyone else might be sad and mourning . . . but me?

I'm fucking celebrating. I just have to make sure the old bastard is really dead first.

TWO

"Are you sure this is a good idea?" Dimitri asks for the hundredth time.

Nico, who sits in the passenger seat of the big 4X4, just sighs and rolls his eyes. Turning in the driver's seat, I meet Isaac's, Dimitri's, and Jonas's eyes. They are all crammed in the back. Luckily, Nico was too big to fit back there, but those three aren't exactly small. In fact, Jonas is squashed up against the window looking uncomfortable. Nico faces them also, and when he sees them shiver, he turns away, his fists clenching on his thighs. I check him over to ensure he isn't going to flip out at the thought that it could have been him being touched, being near people, but he seems to have it under control at the moment.

"We have to," I remind them.

"What if she doesn't even turn up?" Isaac queries, always the logical one. His slight French accent is still fading after years of living there.

"She will," Nico confirms, and those two strong words are all he has to say on the matter.

"I wouldn't." Jonas snorts. "I'd be sunning myself somewhere with some hot girls and drinking to celebrate."

"She isn't like you." I grin, but it soon fades as I remember everything I read and saw on her. "She needs to be sure. She has to know it's true, that he's really dead."

"Not to mention her sister," Dimitri points out. "She will want to see her."

"Do you think she'll make contact?" I question. I might be the leader of this ragtag band of assholes, but I know when to trust their instincts and intellect. Isaac has a way of seeing people and getting emotional with them, but Dimitri? He can read them, know their thoughts and actions, and put himself into their shoes.

"I'm not sure. It depends on how safe she feels."

"But if you were her?" I press.

"If I were her?" He meets my eyes then, his expression stern. "I'd make contact. Ten years is a long time to be alone and on the run."

Jonas swears, knowing he's right. We all know the effects of extended isolation, anger, and hopelessness associated with being alone for so long. It affects your mental capacity, the way you think, and the actions you take. You become reckless, which he knows better than anyone after spending the most time locked up out of all of us.

"Then it's settled. We go. We keep a low profile and remember our mission."

"Her." Jonas nods, his gaze focusing on the still quiet church we are parked near. It won't be quiet for long. "The bastard who did this to his daughter," he snarls, looking back at us.

"She is like us," Nico states in his low growl.

Jonas nods but grinds his teeth before looking away. Any reminder of the man who changed us sours his mood and makes him unpredictable. His emotions are the very reason he was deemed a failure, after all.

In particular, his hatred towards the man currently awaiting burial in that church.

"She's not the enemy. We need her to finish this once and for all," I remind them, searching their eyes.

THREE

The drive to the church located on the outskirts of the small city only takes another hour. It's about thirty minutes from the manor I grew up in, and it's also the church where I was baptised, against my father's beliefs. He didn't believe in God or any deity, only in what he could see, but having unbaptised children made him stand out in such a tight-knit community, and he wanted to blend in. Thus, we were forced to have it done, and now he's forced to have a service and be buried in the very same hallowed grounds he disparaged.

My bike rumbles loudly as I pull into the uneven attached car park, and I make sure to choose a spot near the exit out of habit. Taking off my helmet, I see some older ladies and gentlemen in full military dress staring at me—probably due to the bike's engine—before they turn to greet the vicar waiting at the open double doors. The bells are silent, and huge stained-glass windows allow light to stream into what I know is a vast one-room church with big arched ceilings, old stone pillars with dates and names etched into them, and hard, uncomfortable wooden pews with colourful kneeling cushions tied to them.

Sighing, I turn off the bike before scanning the area and car park, searching for Anabel, my sister. I don't see her, though, and I wonder if she is inside already or if she didn't come.

I think she still likes Father, completely unaware of his monstrous actions, but I can't be sure. She stayed in contact with him and even lived there until about two years ago to save on medical school costs—after all, Father believed in making your own way. He wouldn't have paid a penny for it, no doubt teaching her to fend for herself. More than likely, he was disappointed she never went into research science like him.

She had the brains and the drive. So why didn't she?

I guess I'll find out. I just need to gather my courage, walk my ass into the church, and hope I don't set it on fire. The thought makes me grin before it fades. It's more likely that I'll be recaptured, seen, or stalked—hell, even killed. He could have left orders, and the friends he had could be on the lookout for me.

I don't look like the sweet, willing to obey Novaleen who ran away, however, and that works in my favour.

Hooking my helmet on my bike, I grab my shades and put them on as I swing my leg over, using the excuse to turn and check out the cars behind me. There are a few BMWs, some Audis, a Rolls Royce, a couple of Mercedes . . . and a black 4x4 that sticks out at the end of the row, but I shrug and decide to stop being a pussy and head to the church. If they want me, they'll have to kill me first.

Ducking through the wrought iron gate, which squeaks as I wander down the cobbled path, I join the end of the queue of mourners. When it's my time to enter, I nod at the vicar as he hands me a little booklet and then I flick it open with a snort.

Beloved father and friend. Doctor Davis was an inspiration to everyone he met, a hard worker, and a genuinely good person.

"Bullshit," I mutter.

"Excuse me?" the older vicar asks.

"I said, beautiful." I grin, and he nods but frowns, looking confused.

Heading through the ornate entryway, I scan the packed pews. I don't see the familiar blonde head of hair until she stands at the front, wearing a knee-length black dress, cardigan, tights, and flats. She is completely put together and perfect, right down to the gracious way she accepts condolences and greets people. I can't tear my eyes away from her, but I hear the door shut behind me, so I quickly duck into the end of an empty pew.

A man in the next pew looks over at me and gives me that sad smile everyone wears at funerals. "Did you know him well?"

"Probably better than anyone," I reply.

"I am sorry for your loss," he offers sadly.

"Don't be," I retort, leaning back and kicking my legs up onto the pew. I watch the vicar wander down the aisle to the podium at the front.

The man I was speaking to gawks before leaning in to mutter to his wife who then glances at me. I pull down my sunglasses and wink. She gasps before quickly turning forward, making me chuckle as organ music starts to play.

I almost fall asleep, but then the vicar starts to speak. He drones on about my father, his speech intersected with hymns and loving tributes, and then it comes to her.

Ana.

She stands with her hands clasped at her belly and heads to the microphone, her eyes sad and downcast. Her hands shake slightly, and I know she's nervous. She hates public speaking and being the centre of attention.

Ana clears her throat delicately as I notice her fine features are the same, just grown up. She has the same button nose, slightly round face, naturally thick eyebrows, and light lashes. Freckles dust along her cheeks and nose, and her icy-blonde hair hangs straight over one shoulder. Her makeup is simple, with nude lip gloss, brown eyeliner, and mascara, showing just how naturally beautiful my sister truly is. She possesses the type of beauty everyone envies, even me. Ana was always so graceful and soft spoken, but when she did speak, it was with a level of intelligence surpassing her age.

She is so perfect, unlike me.

"My father was a good man."

Fucking hell, Ana, really? I jerk like she slapped me and close my eyes.

"He gave his life to better this world, first in his service to the country, and then with his innovations in the medical and scientific fields. Given more time, he would have completed such great things. He was a good soul that was lost too soon. My family . . . My family is empty." Her breath catches. "After the tragic death of my sister when she was just seventeen—"

Fucking hell. He told her I died? I didn't expect it to hurt so much, but it does. Did she wonder what happened? Did she miss me like I missed her? At least she had closure and didn't have to wonder if I was out there.

"—my father was never the same."

"I bet he wasn't," I mutter. The people in front glare at me, and I stick my tongue out, but I hear a low chuckle and turn my head, meeting the dark gaze of a huge man on the end pew opposite mine. Four other men sit at his side, each more striking than the last.

They are too beautiful and too smiley to be mourners, so who are they?

Ana's words drag me from their gazes, and I quickly look away, wondering who they are. They are dressed differently than the mourners, more like me.

"And now that I am alone, the last of our legacy, I miss them both so much." A tear, as if she were a paid actor, rolls down her cheek, but I know it's not forged. She's too genuine to lie about something like that. No, she's trying to hold back her emotions, her voice choked. Ana always tried to be the perfect, sophisticated woman he wanted. They don't cry in public, after all, and in his mind, emotions were the mark of a weak or soft person.

"I ask that you remember him for his brilliance, for the love he brought into the world, and the great things he did as we stand together in his memory." She turns to the casket. "Goodbye, Father. May we meet again."

Oh, I fucking hoping we meet again too. I'll kick his ass.

The rest of the funeral is uneventful, and I lean on my bike as I watch them inter him in the ground. Good fucking riddance. My eyes stay on Ana the entire time. She's the perfect daughter—sad but not crying, polite, and quiet. She shakes hands, smiles sorrowfully, and talks with everyone until they finally leave. When she's alone, Ana turns and stares at the grave, then her shoulders finally slump. Her hands twist the material at her hips, showing a little weakness.

I push from the bike and head towards her, only stopping when I am standing silently behind her. My heart skips a beat. Of all the times I thought of seeing her again, of being together, this wasn't how I imagined it. Fear blooms inside me, fear she won't remember me . . . or worse.

"I'm all alone," she whispers, and I flinch.

I wish I could tell her that she's never been alone and explain, but I can't. It's better she never knows and safer that way. But can I do this? Can I step back into her life? And will she just let me?

My decision is taken away when she turns. She startles when she sees me and frowns before her expression clears, then Ana lowers her eyes respectfully. "I'm so sorry. I thought I was alone. Please forgive my outburst," she starts, her lips trembling, though she tries to hide it. She always was too caring.

"Outburst? Come on, Annie, you know I'm the outburst queen."

She gasps and her head jerks up. Her eyes widen as she freezes, probably from the use of her nickname—the one only I use. I see her confusion. Do I really look that different?

Pulling my glasses down, I smile, and she recoils. "Hi, sister."

"Nova?" she whispers before her hand comes up to cover her mouth, and then she steps back. I grab her arm quicker than she can react as her heel catches on the upturned earth and she stumbles. I steady her, and she jerks her arm away like I burned her.

"It's me." I nod solemnly, my fists clenched to keep in the warmth and softness of her skin that's so familiar and different from my scarred flesh. "Been a long time."

"You're dead." She shakes her head and squeezes her eyes shut as she pinches herself.

"I see you're still doing that." I chuckle, unable to help myself. "Annie, I'm not dead. It's really me."

"No, no, I'm finally going crazy. I knew it would happen," she rambles, her cheeks turning pink. She peeks out of one eye and squeaks when she sees me, and I can't help but grin wider.

"Annie, stop. You're not going crazy. I promise it's me. It's Novaleen."

"No, you're dead!" she yells.

"Your favourite colour is pastel blue. You mumble to yourself when you're tired or when you think no one is around. You like to talk your thoughts out loud. You like to wear heels to work so that people have to look up to you instead of down on you." I hesitate. "You're scared of thunder and always used to climb into bed with me—"

"Stop!" she begs, tears brimming in her big eyes before they fall as she stares at me. "It's you; it's really you."

I nod mutely as she continues to stare at me. "He said you died."

"He would." I snort. "I'm not—"

"But that means you left," she mumbles, thinking out loud, and her eyes jerk back to mine and narrow. "You left! I thought you were dead! I mourned you! What the hell is wrong with you?" she rants. "You just left . . . left me alone. Your own little sister. Not a letter, a phone call. Nothing. You let me grieve you and miss you. You left me all alone." Her voice catches, and I flinch. Pain blooms within me, matching what I see in her eyes before anger replaces it, tinged with sadness. "Why? Why did you leave me? Us? And why come back after all this time? Why today?"

"Annie," I start, stepping closer. She stumbles back and holds her hand out as if to physically ward me off.

"No! Don't do that."

"Do what?" I ask, frowning.

"Call me that like nothing has changed. You can't just fucking walk back into my life like you never left!"

"Annie—Anabel," I correct when she twists her lips in anger. "Please, let me explain. I never wanted to leave—"

"Stop!" she snaps, looking at me sadly now. "It's too late, Nova. I don't want your lies and excuses. For ten years, you had a chance to come back or reach out. No matter what happened, you made a choice to leave and start a life without us, without me. No, it's too late. Stay the hell away from me!" She flees, hurrying past me as if she's running from demons from hell, but not before I see the tears in her eyes.

Shit, that went well.

I want to hit something, and my eyes narrow on the overturned dirt. *This is your fault, asshole.* I spit on his grave and turn to follow her, but she's already gone. My shoulders slump as I head back to my bike. I'll have to keep trying. Now that he's dead, there's nothing keeping me from my sister, and despite my nomadic and scary life, I miss her.

Seeing her reminded me of how close we are—were, and how much I love her and want her in my life.

I refuse to let him ruin everything, even in death.

We watch her stride back to her bike with her head held high and lips turned down in anger. We catch a glimpse of her narrowed eyes before she pulls her glasses back on and swings her leg over her ride. She settles there and sighs before she looks to the sky as if searching for help. I can't help staring also, but not at the blue horizon, at her.

She's stunning.

She's the most beautiful creature I have ever laid eyes on. I know why we are here, but I can't seem to care as I watch her, analysing each wind-blown strand of dark hair that I ache to wrap around my fingers. The others talk quietly, discussing how to approach her. She's highly trained, which we already knew, but if we didn't, it's obvious in the way she carries herself, with purposeful fast movements and the weapons she clearly carries. She's just like us, and it's evident.

It's a look we have, something no other beings do.

Like recognises like, and this woman? She's just like me.

Her eyes drop to our car and narrow again as she looks at the darkened glass. I know she can't see us, but the motionless way she stares nearly has me fidgeting. It's unheard of. I can't look away, and the others stay quiet under her watchful gaze, as if feeling the intensity capture me and hold me in place. My breath catches, and my heart hammers until she releases me by looking away. She quickly fires her bike and guns it from the lot as if she knows she is being followed. She probably does since she's good. Really good.

This will be hard.

She will probably try to kill us.

The thought makes me smirk as the car starts, and I turn in my seat to face the front. Let her. It would be the most excitement I've had in a while—hell, the most fun on top of that. What we are doing is important, and we all know the costs of failure. It subdues my mood a little. She might be a beautiful, deadly woman, but she's also the reason we are here.

She's the key to ending all of this.

If only we can get her to listen before she runs or kills us.

I keep checking my mirrors for that SUV. Something about it didn't sit well with me. It didn't look like a mourner's vehicle, and why was it still there? It had no plates and blacked out windows. No, it was there for a reason. To watch me? Find me?

Is it him?

Fuck. I shouldn't have gone. I knew better. Gunning it, I speed back to the hotel to check in and lie low, but when I turn onto the double carriageway, I spot the SUV weaving in and out of cars to catch up. I pull my visor down and speed up. It's my turn to weave through cars. People honk and swear, but I move as fast as I can. When I look, they are right behind me, so I take a sudden sharp turn, and they do the same.

They are definitely following me.

Fuck.

It's clear I'm not going to outrun them, and as the road widens to an empty path into the outskirts of the city, I know I need to either lose them or hide. They could easily knock me off my bike or ram into me right here.

They keep pace with me the entire time back to the hotel, never losing me despite the crazy manoeuvres I pull. They don't hit me, but I feel the heat and the purr of their engine. Fuck. Sliding into the lot, I park and turn, ready to fight, but the car is nowhere to be seen. I search the road outside and the empty lot.

Nothing.

Shit, am I overthinking things?

Wiping my face, I spare another look at the area around me before turning back and heading up the stairs to my room. I take the steps two at a time, ready to be inside and away from prying eyes.

The spot between my shoulder blades starts tightening and sweating like there are eyes on me, and I make it to the second floor before I hear a slight scuff of a boot on the floor. Everything else is silent. There are no footsteps, but I know they are following me.

I keep walking, trying to discern where they are.

I feel them behind me and risk a small glance without them noticing: five guys, the same five from the funeral. I note several bundles of weapons, the tightening of their muscles, and the intent in their eyes. They are armed and dangerous. Fuck, I was right, and now I'm trapped. I purposely turn a corner and pull my gun, waiting. When they stomp around it, I slip behind them and silently aim.

"Who are you?" I demand. One starts to turn, but he spots the gun and stops before they all begrudgingly raise their hands.

"Who are you?" I repeat, glancing behind me, ready to leap from the two-story balcony and make a run for it. They have to work for my father to attend his funeral. Of course he would be watching. Stupid, Nova.

"Friends."

"I don't have any of those," I snap and start to back away. Obviously hearing me, though I don't know how since I am silent, they turn. The one who was speaking steps forward, and another grins.

"Well, that's lonely," he teases.

I swing the gun to him. "Laugh at me again, and I'll shoot your fucking balls."

He laughs and looks at the others. "I like her; you were right."

I run my eyes over them. I want no part of whatever is happening. Even though I can take on a lot, these men are highly trained, and I can tell when a situation is getting dicey.

Time to bail and regroup.

Keeping the gun on them, I slowly back away as they leisurely step forward. Once I am next to the rail, I put the gun away and smirk at them. "Tell the old bastard if he's alive, he'll have to kill me if he wants me." With that, I grab the rail, haul myself over it, and leap to the ground below. I roll as I land, hearing them swear. Getting to my feet, I glance up to see the others racing down the stairs, bar the biggest who takes a running jump off the balcony to follow me.

Shit.

I start to run, but they chase, and they are good. I don't risk the bike, knowing the seconds it would take to get on it would cost me and their car can clearly out speed me. No, it's better to lose them on foot, and there are more places to hide.

I wind through backstreets, around buildings, and over fences. All the while, they are hot on my heels. I'm usually the fastest person, so fast no one can ever keep up, but they do. Running and hiding isn't working, but I hate that choice anyway, so fighting it is.

I swerve into the street I'm in. Cars honk as I disrupt traffic, picking the alley I want. It's a dead end, so they can't sneak up behind me, and it gives me a better chance of winning.

I turn with my gun in my hand, aim it at the mouth of the alley, and wait. My heart rate slows, and my body relaxes and numbs just as it does whenever I fight, kill, or hunt.

I wait, my eyes open and unblinking. Between one heartbeat and the next, a head pops around the alley. With a slow breath, I fire, and it ducks back with a curse as I wait for the next one to try it. I can do this all day.

"Fuck!" someone yells. "She almost got me."

"I missed? What a shame. I won't with the next one!" I call with a shit-eating grin.

"She's crazy," comes a low mutter, the words carrying on the wind.

"Too right, so just leave, and I promise not to kill you for the insult," I retort.

It goes quiet then, and a hand pops around the alley. I shoot, and it yanks back with a groan. "Wait! Just wait and look!" comes a stern order. The hand comes back, slower this time, to produce a white piece of fabric that looks like . . . yep, underwear. "See? A white flag. We don't want to hurt you—"

"Shame, I want to hurt you," I reply, and I hear a laugh before there's a smack and a groan. My lips twitch involuntarily, and my hands begin to shake from holding my shooting stance. I can't keep this up much longer. I either need to get on with this or drop the gun. I know which option I'll choose.

The only way I'll drop this gun is when they are dead at my feet or if they shoot off my fucking arm.

"Still alive, hotties?" I call with a grin.

"Yep! Just thinking about your ass in that leather—"

I shoot the wall, and there's a chuckle, then a deeper voice asks, "What will make you drop the gun?"

"Nothing you have," I reply conversationally, but I know if I keep shooting, the cops will come, and I don't want that. It seems they don't either because I hear them talking quickly amongst themselves.

"Look!" one yells. "We know you. Your name is Novaleen Davis. You are twenty-seven years old."

I stiffen at that. "Public knowledge!" I shout.

"Your father was not the man everyone says he is. He experimented on kids . . . on you. He hurt you. I'm betting he even locked you up. Am I right? Shocked you? Tested you?"

I gawk silently.

"He did it to us too. He performed so many experiments, they blended together. I hated him so fucking much, hated what he made me into, what he made me do."

"Who are you?" I demand.

There's a moment of silence and then a man steps out. He's confident I won't shoot him, which I don't. "We are like you. Experiments. We are the other children."

My arm drops as I stare at him. "Other children?"

"You didn't think you were the only one, did you?" he asks, arching his eyebrow as the others spread out behind him. Their expressions remain serious as they stand in line, watching me with knowledge only someone my father experimented on could know.

"There were others, Novaleen, so many others. They are all dead now . . . apart from us."

"What do you want from me?" I demand, voice shaking. My mind is overloaded with questions and concerns, but I focus on what I can control and quickly pick the most important question. "Why are you following me?"

"Because we need you to help us finish this and stop what your father started."

"He's dead; it's over," I hedge.

"You know better," the one doing all the talking says. "It will never be over, not until all the research and facilities are destroyed. We can't do this without you, Novaleen—"

"Nova, my name is Nova. Only he called me Novaleen," I snap, and he holds up his hands and smiles.

"I'm Louis. It was what one of the only nice nurses called me way before your father got his hands on me. So, Nova, are you in? Are you finished running and ready to face your past? Or are you not the woman we've been told about?"

Well, fuck.

I drop the gun and stare into his eyes. "Fine, but you're buying me dinner while we talk."

"Deal." He smirks.

SIX

They lead me to the closest restaurant, their gazes never straying from me even as I hide my gun behind my coat. We are in public, but that doesn't mean I trust them.

It could be a trap.

Nevertheless, I follow them inside the little eatery.

I ignore the chair he pulls out and sit at another, yanking it in before he can assist me. Pulling my gun from my jacket, I make sure to keep it aimed at them as they choose seats around me. One of them watches me with a smile before another man drops into the chair next to mine.

He's attractive, that's for sure, but he knows it. He has dark, nearly black hair that's cut shorter on the sides and long in the front, so it sweeps across his forehead as he moves. His eyebrows arch over bright, baby-blue eyes that lock me in place, and his pink, puffy lips tilt as he watches me. His strong, square jaw is covered in stubble that's clearly a few days old, stopping at his sharp cheekbones. His nose has a small scar across the bridge, probably from being broken once or twice, and I spot a scar on his left earlobe too. He's a big bastard, not as big as some of the others at the table, but tall and packed with long, toned muscles. It's his eyes, however, that cause me to stare. They are cold but cunning.

"I'm Jonas." He smirks flirtatiously.

I nod in acknowledgement as Louis drops into a different chair. Slowly, all the others do as well, and I run my eyes over them.

The one next to Jonas is taller. He has to be nearly seven feet, with arms thicker than my body and thighs that would make a bodybuilder weep. His face is square and angular, both attractive and strong. He appears stern with his serious, deep-brown eyes, yet his black hair is neatly styled across his head. I spot a lot of scars and tattoos peeking out of his clothes as he meets my eyes.

"This is Nico," Louis informs me, and the big guy nods slightly at me but doesn't speak. He seems uncomfortable sitting in the tiny diner chair. Dressed in all black, he reminds me of an assassin.

"I'm Isaac," the one with the brilliant smile says, reaching over and shaking my hand gently.

He's not testing my grip, just genuinely happy to meet me. Weird. He's only a few inches taller than me, but he still clearly works hard at being strong. His muscles are well defined, but he seems friendly and easy-going. His eyes are almost a grey slate colour, which are filled with warmth where the others' aren't, and are surrounded by long black lashes. His lips are a rosy colour and tipped up into a smile, and they are so thick and pouty, I'm almost jealous. He's ridiculously handsome, that's for sure, and the longer I stare at his friendly face, the more I'm struck by his features. He has a sharp jaw and cheekbones, a short beard extending up over his lip, and nicely styled hair, which is clearly meant to look like he put no time into it but very obviously did.

Where Nico looks like a killer, this man looks like a model.

"Dimitri," the last man says, his thick accent rolling over his words. He sounds Serbian or Russian.

I analyse him like the others. Fuck, he's attractive too. What are they? A bunch of fucking runway models? His deep-brown and golden-streaked hair is pushed back carelessly and shaved at the sides. His eyes are a warm, honey brown and put me at ease. His lips are in a neutral line, not frowning nor tilted up. As I look at him, his long, scarred fingers tap on the table impatiently, as if playing the rhythm of a song I can't hear. He's the smallest of them, slim too, but there is a shrewd intelligence in his eyes that reminds me not to underestimate him.

I look at Louis again as he sits and scans the room. It's clear he's in charge of this ragtag bunch of men. I would have pegged Nico or Jonas as the leader, but as I continue to stare, I can see why. He's calm, collected, and clearly very smart. He almost emits a friendly vibe, which has me relaxing before I realise it.

He turns back to me like he can feel my gaze, his bright-green irises locking me in place. His hair is pale, almost an icy blond, which is shaved at the sides and then stands up on top in soft waves. He has rough stubble across his cheeks and chin, extending around his thick lips.

"So, what is this, *The Avengers*?" I snort, ignoring my own perusal of them and filling the silence just as a waitress comes up.

"Hi, what can I get you all?" she asks politely. She's a young girl, barely out of her teens. Her cheeks are red, and she doesn't look any of us in the eye for long. I can almost sense her nerves.

"I'll have a black coffee and a burger and fries. They are paying." I grin.

She smiles at me and winks. "I don't blame you, honey, and for you?" she asks the others.

"The same." Dimitri nods.

"I'll have a Caesar salad please," Isaac says, flashing her an award-winning smile that almost has her gasping, but he seems oblivious as she stares.

"I want something meaty, hard, and wet," Jonas purrs, looking me over.

"He'll have the chipolatas," I retort, making Louis laugh.

"I will have the pasta, please," he interjects, "and Nico will have the steak." With that, the woman hurries off to put in the order, and I lean back, crossing my arms.

"Tell me everything," I demand, not giving them any leeway.

"So needy," Jonas teases, leaning over to touch my arm. I grab his hand, twist, and slam his face into the table before letting go and sitting back again like nothing happened.

"Touch me and die," I warn.

Jonas groans but sits back. "Touché."

"Enough," Louis snaps and then looks at me. "I apologise for his behaviour. Like you, we spent a long time locked away. It makes our . . . people skills rusty."

Isaac grins. "Speak for yourself."

"You didn't track me down to reminisce about my dear old daddy and his favourite torture techniques, did you?" I question, ignoring the banter. I'm unsure how to react. I'm not used to having someone look at me and know my past. I feel unbalanced and unsure, like a wild animal backed into a corner, so I lash out with the only thing I can—words.

"No, Nova, we didn't," Louis replies. My coffee arrives, and he waits for her to leave before leaning in and dropping his voice.

Paranoid much? I listen carefully anyway. If what he said is true, and they are all like me, then I have questions. I thought I was the only one.

For some reason, the fact that I'm not helps, even though I know just what that means for their pasts and what happened to them. Besides the flirtatious idiot and the silent, angry-looking Nico, they seem pretty well adjusted. So, what happened to them, and why have they suddenly tracked me down if they knew about me before?

"You must have a million questions."

No shit.

"First, what I said is true, and if you agree to help, we will answer any questions you have about our pasts, what happened, and who we are. For now, I will give you a quick rundown. Your father is dead—"

"Stop fucking calling him that."

He looks confused, but Nico leans in. "She means Father." His voice is dark, low, and raspy, and I jerk my eyes to his. He stares back before I incline my head.

"I do. That monster was nothing but a jailor to me, but you know that."

"Very well. Dr. Davis is dead, but his research is still out there, and as we have discovered, it is still being used."

"Impossible," I snap.

"I'm afraid not. It seems he had a partner," Jonas mutters angrily, the flirtatious idiot nowhere to be seen, and in his eyes, I see such anger, such hate, that even I look away.

"And that partner is continuing with the work. We were locked up all around the world in different countries, always alone, but it appears there are more. These are not focused on children, but on grown men. In particular, soldiers. You see, Nova, he took the . . . research he did on us and proposed that if reduced to a serum and training, not only could it make the perfect soldier, but a super soldier. The child experiments were deemed a failure—too risky and too challenging on a young mind—but on a highly trained individual? It works. It makes them everything he wanted them to be, and he was doing just that. We need to find these facilities and stop what is happening before it's too late."

Blowing out a breath, I think over his words as the food arrives. "Why me?"

"You knew him better than anyone. You were his favourite, Nova, and the only successful experiment on children. We were all deemed failures and supposed to be terminated. He might have been a monster, but it seems he couldn't bring himself to kill children, so he kept us instead and raised us under lock and key. I escaped and hunted down other children. These are the only ones who are still alive. His partner does not have the same qualms about killing innocents. So, Nova, you ask why you? We can't do this without you. We need your insight, your training, and your mind to end this. We must go to the beginning, to the very first lab and experiment— your old house. We cannot get in, but you can."

"Fuck," I snarl as I grip my mug. "I vowed not to go back there," I admit as images of the horrors I endured there flash in my mind. I raise my gaze, allowing them to see the haunted shadows in my eyes. "If I do this, it will truly end?"

He nods. "We have to, you know that. No one should suffer like we did. He's dead, and it's time his research was too."

"So, it's this ragtag bunch of lost, abused kids to the rescue?" I scoff.

"We have some help," Isaac says with a grin and nods at my food. "You should eat." I sense his worry, so I grab the burger, take a huge mouthful, and start to chew with my mouth open to make a point. For some reason, it makes Nico's lips twitch, and I am entranced by the movement, but when I meet his eyes, they are empty again.

"Help?" I ask once I've swallowed.

"You'll see," Jonas answers, back to his smiling happy self. How weird.

"Eat, and if you still agree to help us, we will take you there," Louis offers as he takes a dainty mouthful of food.

"Fine." I sigh. "Looks like we really are The Avengers . . . just hopefully without the tragic deaths and terrible costumes."

"I don't know, you do look good in leather," Dimitri teases, making me snort as I grab a fry and throw it at him.

If Dad could see me now, he'd have a fucking heart attack, but it would be worth it.

My mind is still whirling over the fact that I am not alone, that there are others like me, and as they talk and laugh between each other, I analyse them. I wonder just what my dad did to them and why they were to be terminated.

I guess I'm going back down the rabbit hole.

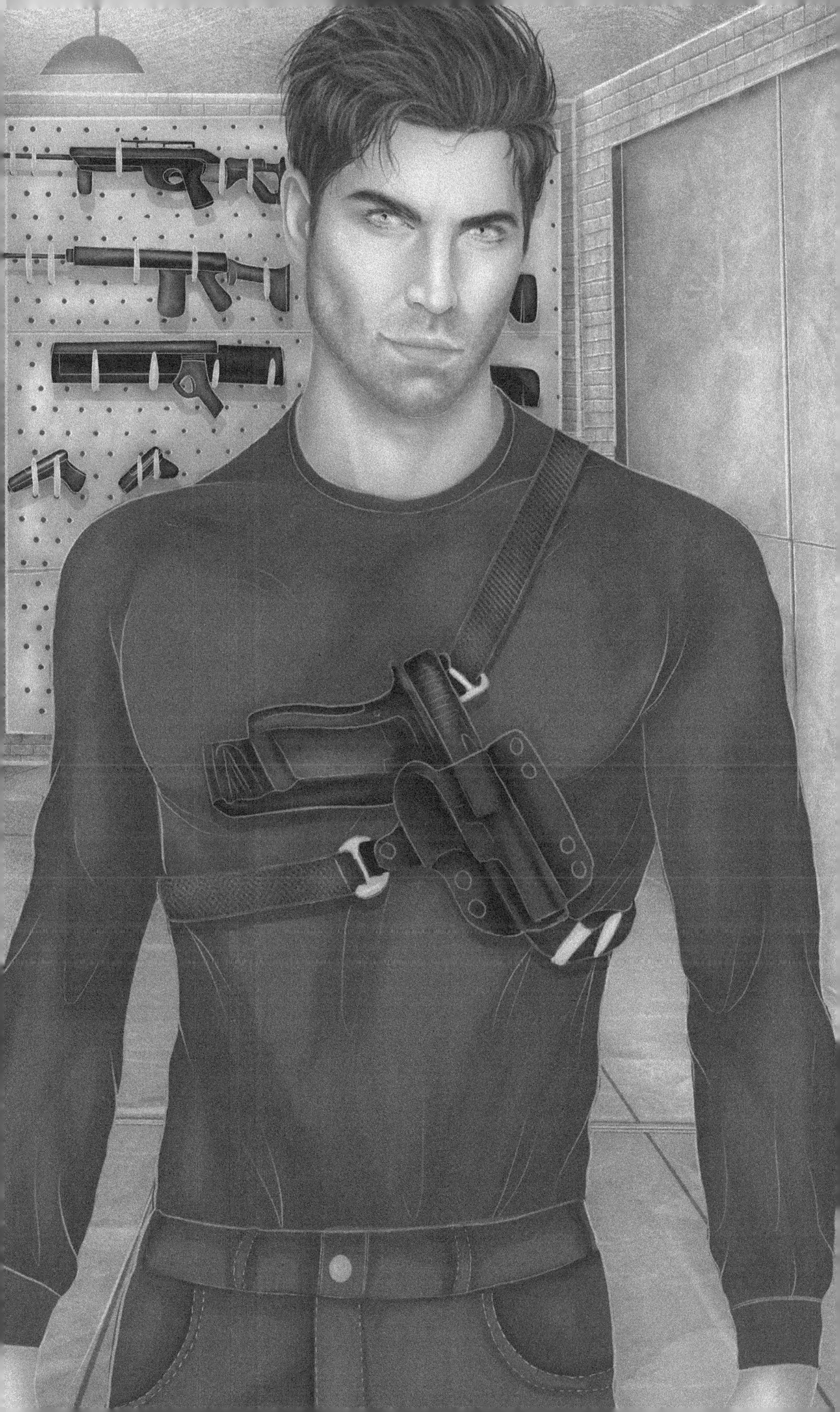

SEVEN

I watch as she finishes the whole plate, appreciating a woman who knows how to eat, and when she burps, I almost swoon. There's something about Nova.

She cools the anger inside me, especially when she gives as good as she gets. The others refuse to play my games, to tease or joke, but it seems her twisted, dark sense of humour is the same as mine.

It's probably a result of our fucked-up pasts. Her dad made me into a psycho, then he determined I was too fucked up in the head to continue on. He said I was consumed by too much anger and hatred, and that I couldn't be trusted.

Basically, I was a wild card.

A threat.

Therefore, I was not useful, as if spending fourteen years being locked in a bare, white room and being experimented on wouldn't do that to a kid. Seriously, what did they expect? A normal, functioning child? And they say they are the smart ones.

Isaac speaks, and I look at him. He has his own issues, for sure, but he seems more normal than the rest of us. He can even blend in with civilians, speak, laugh, and act normal. Underneath that soft, caring façade, however,

I know deep, lingering pain and anger festers insides him just like with all of us.

Nico feels it even more than me, Dimitri harnesses his, and Louis tries to control his turbulent hatred. Me? I give in to it and let it help me, but it does make my moods unpredictable. Maybe that's why her eyes keep flicking to me when I clench the silverware. With a smirk, I bring it to my mouth and lick it as she watches. She rolls her eyes and looks away, but I notice a flush on her cheeks—she liked what she saw.

I like having her eyes on me.

That's bad, but it's too late to care now.

She's one of us, and we are stuck together.

"We should get going if we want to get back before they wonder where we are," Louis says, wiping his mouth as he pulls out money to pay.

"You mean before they wonder if we have finally lost it and gone AWOL?" I snort and lean into Nova, careful not to touch her. I saw her eyes when I did it the last time, and I know she wasn't here with me. She was somewhere else, probably with the monster who fucked us all up. "They need us, you see, but they are also fucking terrified of us. It makes them uncomfortable that we can be so clinical and cold when on a mission. Oh yes, Nova, they need us, and they hate it."

"Enough," Nico snaps and stands.

Louis drops money on the table and nods at Nova, letting her go first. She ignores it and waits, so I stroll out first. "If you wanted to look at my ass, you should have just asked," I tease.

Something whizzes by my head, embedding in the restaurant door, and a laugh booms out of me when I see the knife and feel the slight cut on my cheek. She storms past me, plucks it out, and twirls it as she glares at me.

"I'll admit you've got a nice ass, but it's a shame about the mouth," she remarks and then pushes outside, leaving me gaping after her.

Isaac chuckles and follows her. He escorts to her bike while the rest of us pile into the car. Louis leans out of the window and calls, "Follow us."

"Believe I won't try to escape?" she taunts, straddling the machine, and my mouth dries as I imagine her straddling me like that.

"You are free to go. We are not like him, Nova, but I think you'll follow."

"Why is that?" she grumbles.

"Because you're interested now, and you hate what he did as much as we do." With that, Louis rolls up the window and pulls away.

I turn to watch out of the window, and a few seconds later, Nova turns on her engine and follows us out into traffic, making me smile. This may be business, and we may have his twisted experiments to end, but it doesn't mean I'm not enjoying our latest group member.

She's an improvement on these grumpy bastards, that's for sure.

I'll work *very* closely with her.

The drive takes over an hour and a half, the base set up as close to the old mansion as we dared without tipping them off—not that we had much choice. It was a military decision, the government's secret operation location. It's hidden, so if you don't know where to look, you would think nothing of it.

I can almost sense Nova's hesitation as we lead her through winding country lanes, with rolling hills on either side of us. There is no one for miles. I wonder if she thinks it's a trap. Probably, but the girl is fearless. She doesn't turn back, and when we pull into an old, abandoned barn to park, she follows us in before turning the bike off and walking over to meet us.

Her first question makes me laugh. She isn't concerned for herself but her bike. "Will it be okay here?"

"Yes, there are cameras and a fence, though you wouldn't see it, not to mention the sensors. This barn might look rundown, but it's maintained and made to look this way," Louis explains calmly before jerking his head at her. "Come, you can meet the people we work for. They are funding this operation."

"Yeah, real cheerful bastards." I laugh, walking backward to keep her in my line of sight. Nico rolls his eyes and trips me. I leap to my feet and swing, but Isaac gets between us, as always. Dimitri mutters something and rushes to catch up with Louis, probably antsy to get back to his computers and whatever shit he was doing on them.

Nico circles until he's behind her—a habit. I see her shoulders tense, but she doesn't protest, even as her eyes scan everything. She's probably spotting all the hidden cameras in the trees as we move through the scrapyard. It's a trap, of course. The cars and bits of metal are rigged with bombs, sensors, and even landmines. I did it myself.

You can never be too careful, and their security was almost laughable. Dimitri said even a child could hack it. They didn't like that, but they grudgingly took our help.

Nova stops abruptly, her eyes narrowing. "Let me guess—C4 hidden in the cars, cameras in the trees, and sensors all over the place."

That's so hot, I almost groan. "You forgot the mines."

"Of course." She nods and moves over to me, meeting my eyes confidently as my cock jerks. "I would have added a few hidden weapon caches and bail out bags." She strides past me, and I reach down to rearrange myself.

"I love her already," I mumble, and Nico glares at me, so I turn and follow her, my eyes locked on her ass.

Across the next hill is a sharp incline, which is easy for us. We cover the ground in under a minute, as does Nova, who effortlessly keeps up, but for some soldiers this is a struggle—pussies.

When we reach the top, she looks around. "There's nothing here," she snaps. "If this is a trap . . ." She draws her gun and points it at Louis.

He holds his hands up and nods at Dimitri. "Do it."

Concerned and looking for a way to disarm her, Dimitri moves over to the sensor. I move to her left, just in case she attacks, and Nico steps to her right. Isaac just sighs.

There's a buzz, and Nova's eyes narrow, but she doesn't move until the grass-covered panel in the ground parts in the middle and rolls back. She turns, dropping her gun to her side, and watches as it reveals a yawning abyss. I move closer, and she spins, aiming her gun at my head.

"Stop getting so fucking close, chuckles," she warns. "What is this place?"

"A hidden bunker. Our new employers are almost as paranoid as Dr Davis," Dimitri replies. "It's safe."

"Nothing's safe," she mutters, but she puts her gun away and moves towards the other guys. When the platform arrives, she steps onto it and turns to us. "Well, come on then. What are we waiting for?"

Even Nico grins as we all hurry on, surrounding her, and then Dimitri presses the button, causing the platform to descend slowly. The lower we go, the darker it gets, with only emergency lowlights embedded in the dark-grey metal walls. The circular chamber stretches deep into the earth, with the bunker built below, although *bunker* may not be the best word. The level numbers whizz by as Nova parts her legs, steadying herself. We finally slow and come to a soft stop before a ramp leading to the closed, bombproof bunker doors.

Stepping off the platform, I gesture at them as I wink at her. "Well, come on then, Nova, time to save the world."

EIGHT

The doors open, and a few soldiers nod at us. They don't like us, but they appreciate that we are here to help. They almost blend in with the walls in their black fatigues, and Nova pays them no mind as we lead her deeper into the labyrinth. The first room is a quarantine, questioning, and security room. After passing more doors and taking another elevator, we stop at the command room, which fills the whole second floor.

Louis nods at me, silently telling me what to do, then he looks at Nova, needing to speak to her since she hasn't been with us long. "Isaac will escort you. You will be given a chip to get in and out of the area and any rooms. Everything is open to us, but without it, you will be locked out. I'm going to debrief while you do that. When you are done, they will escort you back here to meet the people behind everything." Without waiting for her to respond, he merges into the hustle and bustle of the command floor.

There are about twenty computers all facing the wall of screens in the back, showing video feeds of active missions and other stuff. More soldiers are positioned at each, along with scientists. The generals are gathered in a glass conference room overlooking the entire floor, and that's where Louis heads with Nico following behind, ready to protect him. Dimitri and Jonas come with me, but they will undoubtedly split off to go train. Jonas is always on the move. When he's not fighting or training, he is cleaning and assembling his weapons.

I analysed his mental state when he was first brought in. I was more suitable than any of their medical staff to assess him after living as he did. Unlike myself, who compartmentalises everything that happened and looks at it logically, Jonas lets his anger control him, very much like Nico. Where Nico is scarred from his past, however, Jonas is fuelled by it. It means he's always moving, fighting, flirting, or fucking. He needs to move or he will think on it.

I have tried to offer them all advice and counsel at some point. Sometimes they speak to me—mainly Louis and Dimitri, though it is only when they have no choice—but we all prefer to fight our own demons. We were beaten, tortured, and made to believe that any weakness meant pain, and that's a hard cycle to break.

We return to the elevator, and Dimitri and Jonas get off on the accommodation and training levels. Jonas winks at Nova, who stands by my side. "See you soon, Nova. We can play then."

"I will shoot you," she threatens.

"Oh fuck, please do," he begs with his hand over his heart as the door closes.

"Please ignore him," I tell her with a friendly smile, trying to put her at ease.

"Trying," she mutters. "Plus, I'm used to much worse."

I tilt my head in consideration, using her words to ease into a conversation as the elevator lowers. "Is that so?"

She sees my obvious approach to get her to talk and sighs. "Let me guess—shrink?"

"Doctor." I shrug. "Habit, sorry."

She shivers at the word *doctor*, and I frown. "I'm not like him," I state, but there's a coldness between us, as if she has a basic distrust of the profession. I don't blame her, especially when all she has ever known from them is pain. I will earn her trust.

This makes it hard to complete my next tasks though. I need to check her out and implant the chip in the lab, where all my supplies are. If I give her any pain in the lab, it might only encourage her fear of doctors, as well as reinforce her anger and distrust of me and the other guys. Knowing I have no other choice, I lead her out once the elevator stops.

This corridor is lined with rooms, and our footsteps are loud on the metal as we turn a corner, the cameras watching her.

"This place gives me the creeps," she mutters. "Feels too much like my dad—Dr. Davis's fucking torture labyrinth."

"The others feel that way too," I share, giving her a bit of their weakness to gain her trust.

"But not you?"

"I guess I got so used to a clinical setting and living underground that it almost feels like home to me. Up there"—I point above ground—"is where I feel out of control and cornered."

I see her pondering my words, and I'm glad I could tell her that as we arrive at my lab door. The window to the left shows the interior, and her footsteps falter.

"What is this?" she demands, and I turn to see she has her gun out again. A siren goes off, but I hold my hand up to the cameras, indicating that I have this. The siren stops, but I know they are watching us, and it served as a reminder that she is surrounded and alone with us. I see fear and anger in her eyes, and I know she's thinking of trying to escape.

"You can leave at any time," I assure her softly, imploring her to trust us. "You are not trapped, not like before. This is for our safety so they can't find us."

"The lab," she snaps.

"It's where I work, where the chips are," I explain quickly. "Without it, you will be unable to walk around freely, and I don't think you would like that."

She stares me down, and I wait. It's her choice. I won't make it for her. She's been through enough, we all have, so her distrust isn't misplaced. It's built from years of pain and abuse, just like every single one of us. We might be what others consider superhuman—I hate that word, knowing it's a mix of nature, nurture, and genealogy—but we are still human. We still carry grudges, feel pain, and experience fear, but unlike others, our fear makes us dangerous and deadly.

Nova is no exception. She is a weapon, and right now, that weapon feels cornered.

I step back to give her more room, and the door opens. She stills and looks behind me. I know what she sees. I've tried to make it as calm and homey as possible by painting some of the walls, hanging posters and paintings, and dotting the space with sofas, chairs, and plants. Yes, there are computers and equipment, but it's more like a fancy office than a cold, sterile lab. I see her noting the difference, but it wars with her terror of the places she was hurt in.

"No," she snaps, stepping back, refusing to enter the lab.

I reach my hand towards her. "We all have to face our fears eventually, Nova," I murmur. "I used to hate labs too."

"Then why?" she croaks, true terror in her eyes mixing with the ghosts of her memories—the same ones we all carry.

"Because I refuse to hide from them." She flinches. "This is just a space. It can't hurt us. He did, not the equipment. This equipment saves lives. Think of it like a gun," I reason softly. "The gun isn't inherently evil. It's the user that chooses the path it takes." Stepping back, I wait. "Come in, and I will tell you more."

When she doesn't move, I leave her to think it over. I walk through the room, humming, trusting her not to shoot. I'm showing her I'm not afraid. I light some candles and prepare the chip as well as some needles and vials, since we need to do a blood test to ensure she is healthy and that *he* did nothing to her. One of the other children was purposely infected with a disease to see if it would change the way her body adapted to training.

I almost shiver in horror at the thought. He was a monster, a true monster. Doctors are meant to heal and protect, not hurt. It goes against everything I believe in.

I hear a noise but don't turn, focusing on my task as I hum until there's a deep sigh. "I don't know how you could become a doctor."

"It was easy," I reply as I turn and gesture to the seat near me, but she remains standing, so I shrug. If that's what makes her feel more in control, then okay. "I'm good at science. It made sense to me when human nature did not," I explain. "I like to help people and figure out problems. I hated labs for what he did in them, but I can understand the beauty and science behind it. It doesn't mean I agree with what he did, but I can understand the sophistication and work it took." I hurry on when her eyes narrow. "The things he did with research, however, were monstrous, and I'm sorry that ever happened to you," I offer softly.

She nods but doesn't look away, and I pick up the chip gun. "This will hurt, but only for a moment. It's an RFID chip that will be implanted into your hand; that is all. It's simply a key."

She nods and relaxes a little as I talk her through each step. When I get to the blood work, she snarls but stoically stands as I take the vials. I stroke her hand and squeeze it, talking about everything and anything until it's over. She's very much like Nico, who struggles with touch and medical equipment. It will make my job harder, but I find I like to comfort her, especially when her eyes soften a tad when she looks at me as if I am protecting her. Unlike the others, where it's my duty and what I'm good at, this feels different.

If I were Jonas, my chest would puff out, but instead, I have a dopey smile on my face.

The others hate my chatter, but she doesn't seem to mind, so I don't stop. "Other children?" she finally asks, interrupting my story of a time when Jonas shot up my lab.

"Hmm?" I ask as I analyse her blood.

"The other children. You said . . . Where are they? Are there any here?"

I round my shoulders and turn, playing with my coat. We had mentioned some had died, maybe it's hope that she's asking if any survived. "No." Pursing my lips, I think of the best way to explain it. "Louis is better at answering your questions—"

"Please, Isaac, I need to know," she implores, her eyes widening.

Whether it's her round, trusting eyes or the hand she places on my arm, I find myself answering. I am unable to say no to her. A dangerous thing, I know, but she has her father's magnetism, if not his streak for cruelty.

"They are dead."

She flinches but nods, probably already guessing that.

"According to his notes, some were . . . terminated. They failed some of the experiments, so he, um . . . Those that survived were pushed further. He would infect some with diseases or genetic impurities, as he liked to call them. Cancer, MS, or congestive heart failure were introduced into their bodies to see what effects could be created. Some died when they could have been saved. One I read about, a girl, killed herself at only thirteen."

"Fuck!" she cries, smashing her fist into the table. I surge to my feet and rub her back.

"I know, it's horrendous, but that's why we must do this. We need to stop anyone else from being hurt like us."

"Why me? Why us?" She tilts her head, and I see tears in her eyes. "When I thought it was just me, I could survive. I asked why all the time, but I survived . . . and the others . . . I didn't know. I left and ran like a coward while they suffered because I thought I was the only one. Fucking foolish. I could have helped them!" she yells, but then her voice breaks as she tries to hold back her tears.

Her pain calls to the caring part of me, the doctor part, though I know it's a lie—it's deeper than that. Her pain feels like a knife in my heart.

I wrap my arms around her. She's stiff at first, but then she relaxes, turning to bury her head in my chest as I stroke her back and hair.

"There is nothing you could have done, nothing any of us could have done," I murmur. "You were a child yourself, and you did the best you could to survive the unimaginable. We all did. We have a chance now to make it right, so do not let guilt change you, Nova. It was Dr. Davis who did this, not us. We are innocent, but we have a chance to avenge them and save others. Do not let the past fill you with hatred until you blindly fall into the madness like he did. Let it guide you instead. Learn from it, and let's do better."

She nods and pulls back slightly. Her eyes are rimmed red, and tears stain her cheeks, yet she's utterly beautiful. Then it hits me. I was looking at her like another patient, as if I knew when I looked too hard, I would see it, but now I can't not. I can't look away from her as my hands tunnel into her hair and touch her as if I can't get enough. My gaze drops to her lips then up to her eyes.

She's stunning.

She's so strong, beautiful, and intelligent.

It's a powerful combination that leaves me breathless, and for the first time in my life, I want to lean into another person instead of being the person they lean on. It makes me want to break all my carefully built rules and kiss her.

I can tell she feels the same because her eyes widen and her breath picks up, causing her chest to rise and fall against my own. Her hands clench the material of my coat, and a blush flushes her cheeks as we stare. We are both fighting the electricity between us, one that's so potent, I'm surprised we haven't set the room alight.

Something grows between us the longer we stare, and then I start to tilt my head down, unable to resist her.

Nova is one of us. I would never hurt her, not like other women, and it's that knowledge that has a slight groan leaving my lips as I finally give in. I lower my head, and she doesn't move away, making me believe she feels this too. Whether it's the desire to feel loved since we spent our childhood alone or she simply wants me as a man, I can't tell, and I don't care.

The spell is broken when we hear footsteps.

She jerks back, wiping her mouth like I kissed her, and looks at the door. I turn, my lips dipping into a frown as disappointment fills me. What was I thinking? She won't trust me if I force myself on her like that. I don't know what came over me. It's clear Nova is deadlier than we expected, considering I almost gave into the dark urges inside of me when I am usually perfectly in control and calm.

The beauty standing next to me nervously buzzes with embarrassment as Dimitri steps into the room. As usual, he enters farther than the others who would simply wait outside, as if by doing so he is telling his past to go fuck itself. He appreciates knowledge and computers as much as I do, though he hates how he obtained his interest for them.

I quickly turn back to the computer as I breathe deeply and pretend to analyse my notes.

"Louis is ready. Are we good to go?" he calls.

"Go?" I jerk my head up like I was consumed by work and not the woman next to me. I am no better than Dr. Davis at this moment, almost using her weakness to take what isn't mine. I close my eyes as hatred for myself builds. "Yes, of course. I need to stay and look at these results."

"Okay . . ." He frowns, sounding confused. "I'll escort Nova then."

"Yes, do that." I turn away quickly so he doesn't see the strong emotions in my eyes. I feel her looking back at me before she follows him out without a word. Unable to resist, I lift my head and watch her go.

With each step she takes, my heart slams, begging me to chase her and finish that kiss.

What is happening to me?

Was he right about the reason I was supposed to be terminated? Lowering my head, I press it against the screen to cool my overheated skin and try to ignore my body's urges. I will not become the creature he told me I would be, not even because of her.

And I have to work with her.

Fuck.

I follow Dimitri quietly, and he doesn't break the silence either. He seems nervous about my presence, flicking his fingers against his leg as we rise in the elevator. All the while, my mind goes back to what almost happened, what I almost did.

I almost kissed the doctor.

What a fucking idiot. He was obviously embarrassed after. He was only trying to be polite and professional, and I cried, raged, tried to shoot him, and then almost kissed him.

I'm a mess.

Poor man, no wonder he didn't want to come with us.

Feeling the need to fill the silence and escape my self-destructive thoughts, I glance at Dimitri. "Where's Jonas?"

"Stabbing stuff," he mutters, eyeing me before looking away. "I'm sorry. Next time, I will let them know you would prefer for him to escort you."

With that, he steps out of the doors when they open, and I tip my head back and groan. I'm so rusty at conversation and being around other people, I'm fucking this up. Great. Just great. Even though I know they don't have to like me, for some reason, it feels important, especially if what they say is true, because it means they are the only other ones in this world who knows what it's like to grow up the way I did.

I'm pushing them away by almost kissing and attacking them.

I'm surprised I wasn't terminated like the other kids, since it's clear I'm not as capable as these men here who have adapted to this world. Not only that, but they are actively using the training and strength my father gave us to make the world a better place while I just ran and hid.

Sighing, I follow Dimitri as he leads me through what they called the command floor. I analyse the huge screens that cover the back wall, showing this base as well as my old house. Scientists and soldiers are working everywhere, but Dimitri heads right to a set of metal stairs on the left that lead up to a glass room overlooking it all.

He opens the door without knocking and steps inside, holding it for me without looking at me. Great.

Inside, there is a giant rectangular table, a fridge, and a kettle on the counter at the back. The dark-wood table is surrounded by chairs, only two of which are in use. Louis sits in one, and in the other is a man in full military dress, with grey hair and sharp, cold blue eyes. It's clear he's a commander of some sort.

Just who are these people?

"Please sit, Nova," Louis offers, sounding friendly enough. I step inside, and Dimitri shuts the door harder than necessary, leaving me with them.

Before Louis is some water, and the other man has a mug. "A drink?" Louis asks as he stands.

"I don't suppose you have whiskey," I joke before sitting, automatically propping my heels on the table, but the commander glares at me, so I slowly put them down and cross my arms. "Water will be fine, thank you." I remember my manners, even though they irritate me, and Louis moves around as I glare at the military man. I refuse to be intimidated. He eventually looks away, and I want to whoop in pleasure, but I refrain and smirk instead.

Louis places a glass of water before me and sits. "Nova, this is General Smith."

"Of course it is," I mutter, making his eyes narrow further until he's basically just squinting. "I've been poked and prodded, and I followed you into a hole in the ground, so tell me everything now," I demand.

"Do not make demands, girl. You are only here because they believe you can help. We voted against this—"

"Well, whoopty fucking doo. I'm here because you obviously need me, so shut your trap and let the person actually in charge talk." I look at Louis then to see him trying to hide his smile behind his hand. He coughs as the general stands.

"You deal with this. Get her in line or it's all your asses," he barks and storms past me.

Louis sighs. "He really is in charge. This is his operation, and his team was the one that found out about the other experiments. We were brought in as . . . consultants because we know Dr. Davis's ways, his type, and, well, we are stronger and more capable than his soldiers."

"Then I'm here for you, not him." I shrug and put my feet back on the table. "And I'm running out of patience."

"Of course, well, you know the basics. Your father had an unidentified partner, and we know he's still running experiments—not on kids, but soldiers. We have to stop him. The government didn't know about his involvement or that he was conducting these studies, but they do now, and they want to put a stop to it—"

"I'm betting it's to save their own asses," I scoff, and he smiles sadly. "Oh, come on! If it gets out that one of their scientists knew he was experimenting on kids? Bad press."

"You're not wrong. They are doing this for their own reasons, the same as we are. We believe the best place to start is at the house where his main research was. Maybe there are hints regarding other locations or who his partner was. We have only found three additional old research facilities other than where we were kept, but they were all abandoned years ago. We are at a dead end, and that's why we need you."

"Why? Go to the old house and look," I mutter, feeling both annoyed and scared at the thought of going back there.

"Nova, he left the house to you. It's yours."

I flinch at that, thinking of Ana. Why me? But more than that, it means he did it as one last kick in the teeth. Here, have the place where I abused and experimented on you for years.

The dick.

"Not only is it illegal for us to go in, which, yes, we would do to stop this, but we couldn't find his lab. We tried."

I still at his words, going cold. "What?"

"It's there; we know that. You were a kid when you left, but I'm betting you remember the way in and out of it. It's clearly hidden, like this place, and we could spend years searching and never find it. We need you to get us in, Nova. Help us stop this and stop others from enduring what we did."

I get up and start to pace. Fury and terror fill me at just the thought of going back to that place. I vowed I'd never go back, ever, yet he's asking me to voluntarily go there. It doesn't matter that my father is dead. It matters that ghosts and memories still haunt that place.

"Fuck!" I snarl, smashing my fists to the table. "Even from beyond the grave, he's fucking me over."

"I'm so sorry, Nova. I wish we didn't have to involve you, but we do. We would leave you in peace—"

"I have never known peace," I mutter and close my eyes. "I can't remember," I croak.

"Try harder," he implores. "Calm down and focus. You don't even need to go there if you can show us on maps—"

"I can't. I'm sorry. I blocked so much of that place out. I would either be drugged through vents in my room and wake up down there or be blindfolded."

"Oh," he mutters, obviously disappointed, and for some reason, I hate letting him down, which is why the next bit spills out.

"I only saw it once. I can remember pieces, but not enough to direct you. I'm sorry."

He stands. "Don't be, we can work with that."

"We can?" I ask, eyebrow arched.

"Yes, come." He offers me his arm, but I ignore it, and he still smiles as he opens the door. "But first, you should rest. We will work on this tomorrow. It's been a long day, and I imagine you are eager to sleep."

Not really, I want to get this over with, but it doesn't seem to be up for discussion.

Louis spots Dimitri at the bottom of the stairs, working on a computer. "Dimitri," he calls, and Dimitri lifts his head, meeting my eyes before he looks at Louis. "Can you escort Nova to the spare room near ours?"

Louis looks at me then, not waiting for an answer, and I see Dimitri sigh. "Rest, and we will begin tomorrow. You're safe here, Nova." With that, Louis disappears down the stairs where Dimitri is now waiting for me.

"Come," is all he says.

Great.

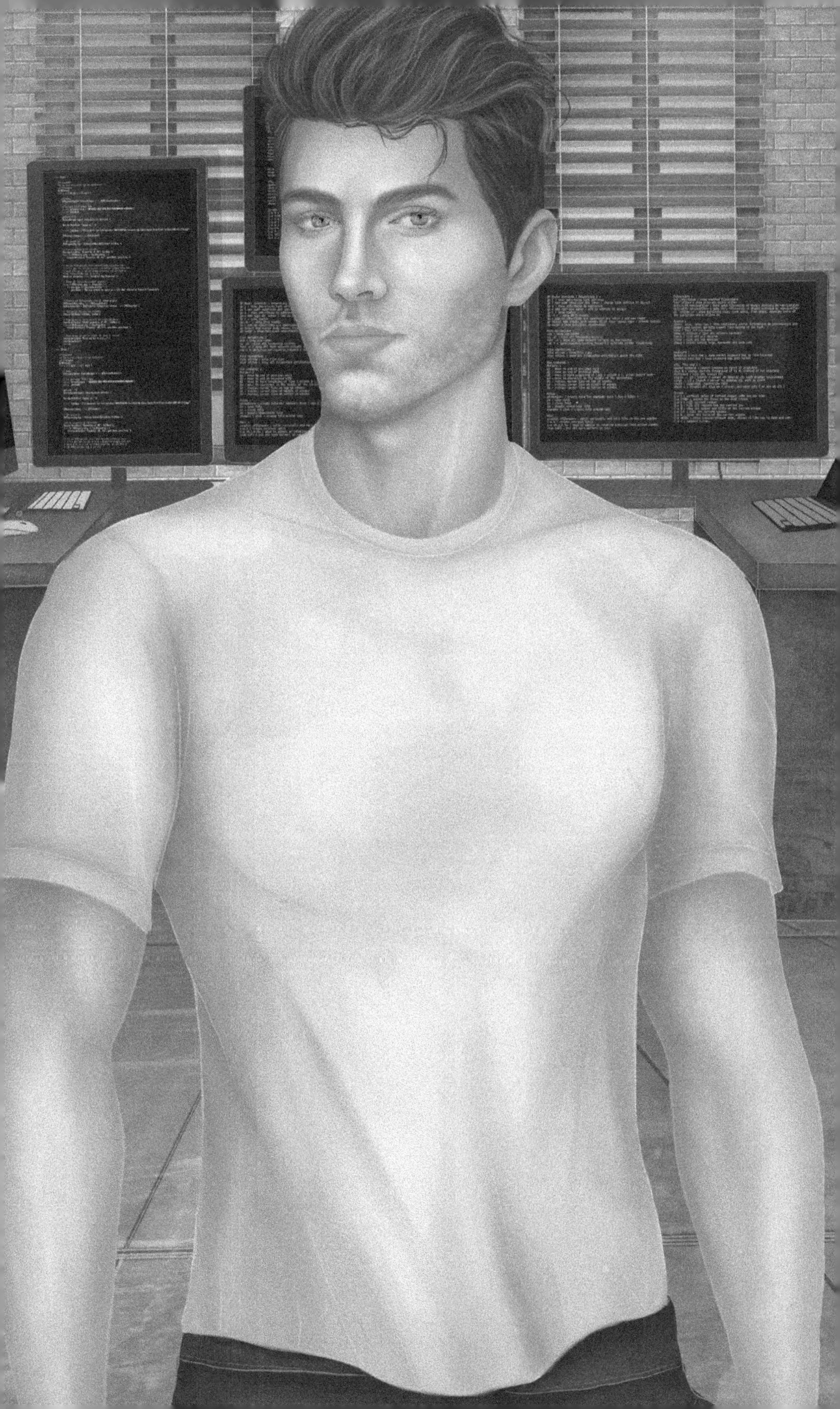

TEN

I feel Nova's eyes on me as I guide her back to the elevator, but I don't look at her. The first time I saw her, I was struck like an electric charge from a machine, and she restarted my cold heart. I don't know why. It's not because she's beautiful, she is, but it was something in her eyes, in her determination to survive.

She is broken, just like me, but she is also able to function.

It makes my fingers twitch to figure her out, to peel back her exterior like I would a machine and fiddle. Even now, I tap my fingers to resist touching her.

Once the elevator stops, I rush out, trying to escape her presence and her sweet scent, but then her voice splits the air, making me stumble. The soft, purring tone heads directly to my cock in a way it shouldn't, hardening it uncomfortably so.

"Look, I didn't mean it to come out the way it did earlier, okay?" she says, and I turn back to see her looking at me. "I don't prefer Jonas or any of you. I barely know you. I was just curious about this place and a little nervous. I want to talk and fill the silence. I'm sorry if that upset you."

Fuck, of course she didn't mean it that way. I don't even know why it's been bothering me that she asked for him, as if I weren't good enough. Like she said, she doesn't know us, so why did it hurt? Why do I wish she said my name? She's looking at me kindly now, not him. It doesn't make sense. Computers, cameras, and equipment make sense, but people? Not so much.

I don't even understand my own turbulent feelings regarding the beautiful woman waiting for a response, so I put those thoughts away to answer her.

"I understand."

She nods but seems to be waiting for more. "You're not a talker, are you?" she teases, grinning.

"I'm better at fixing things," I admit as she comes to my side, and we start walking again.

"Fair enough. So where did my dear old daddy keep you?" I flinch, and she winks at me.

"Prague," I mutter. "It was a nice city from what I saw of it."

"Exotic. I simply got a basement."

I can't help but smile. "I had no windows."

"Windows?" She gasps. "What a luxury! I had no bed, just a floor to sleep on."

"At least you had somewhere to lie down. I had to stand." I find myself teasing her, and we are both smiling. It's only then when I realise she put me at ease. How strange. No one, not even the others, can do that, and I've been with them for years.

"Come on, this way to the rooms. They aren't big or even comfy, but they are private, and there's a bed and pillows."

"God damn, you run a five-star hotel," she teases, walking next to me with strong strides.

"Wait until you see the food," I joke as we reach the room between Louis's and Isaac's. I open the metal door and let her enter first. There's a metal single bed to the left with the bedding folded at the end and a towel. A door to the left leads to a small en suite, with the wall caging in the bed. Each wall is made of metal, and there are no windows, just a bright white light above, a small desk to the right, and a wardrobe.

"Wow, there's so much room," she teases, sitting on the hard bed. "You guys really know how to spoil a girl."

"We do." I grin. "Your RFID chip will let you in and out. Try to get some sleep. I'll get some water and supplies delivered." I turn to leave, and she calls out.

"Dimitri?"

"Yeah?" I ask, looking back.

"Thank you," she offers softly, appearing happy.

"You're welcome, Nova." I shut the door after me, a smile on my lips as I turn to leave.

Maybe people aren't as bad as they seem.

here is my little Nova?

I'm annoyed at myself for getting distracted and not following Dimitri when he left. He came back to our training room, and after quizzing him, I learned she is staying in a room near ours, though he seemed annoyed at me asking.

Rolling my eyes at that, I slick back my hair as I make my way there. I haven't planned what I'll do when I get there, but it's pretty obvious Nova is as attracted to me as I am to her. Honestly, it's been too long since I've had my dick sucked, and never by a beauty like her. My cock hardens in my trousers as I remember the way she tried to kill us. I've never been with someone as dangerous as us, so I usually have to hold back, worried about hurting them. Our lives don't leave a lot of time for fun, never mind relationships even if I did want one, which I don't. Women are hard work, so I'd rather just fuck their brains out and leave them in ecstasy than deal with one all the time. If there isn't one about? Well, I always have my fist.

Speaking of, I stop at the next corner and slip my hands in my jeans. I palm my hard cock and give it a squeeze before stroking, recalling the fire in Nova's eyes and the expert way she held her gun. A groan escapes as I speed up my strokes.

When a soldier rounds the corner, stumbles to a stop, and gawks at me, I almost sigh. There's never any privacy around here.

"S-Sir?" he sputters, his eyes dropping to my cock before they slam shut. His face is bright red. Why is he embarrassed? Is it because my cock is a lot bigger than his? That must be it. It's very nice looking, after all. Or maybe he liked what he saw.

I pull my hand free and go to walk by him, slapping his cheek softly with the hand that just grasped my dick. "Sorry, I'm not into dudes, though never say never, but I feel like I would like mine prettier, you know?" I whistle as I walk away, happy to have set the record straight.

Maybe I should try sex with a guy, that way I wouldn't need to find a wet and willing pussy. I would miss it, but then I remember Nova has joined our team and perk up. She'll eventually come to me. How could she not? I'm the best-looking one, I can make her scream in ecstasy, and everyone loves a good quick, dirty fuck. I'll just make sure I'm available when she asks, like now, in case she needs to . . . let out any stress after the day she's had.

The only empty room in the dead-end corridor they placed us in sits between Louis's and Isaac's rooms. I slip into mine, which is opposite, leaving the door open. My room hasn't been touched, thank fuck, not since the first day when they sent someone in to clean while I was working out and I threatened to blow up the whole bunker. I mean, really, the person placed all my C4, guns, and knives in a box. A box! How dare they! They are perfectly placed, scattered around my room in what Louis calls chaos but I call order. I know exactly where everything is—

Shit.

I left a mine switched on.

Rushing to it, I turn it off with a laugh. That was close. If I had lain down with that under the pillow, it would have been bye-bye Jonas. I do a few burpees before taking a shower and changing into some shorts, nothing else. After all, I worked hard to have an impressive chest and abs, though Dr. Dickhead always told me vanity was illogical. I can't help but flex in front of the mirror before flipping off his ghost.

Suck my pecs, you dead bastard. I look good, more muscle for your daughter to hold onto as she rides me.

A few hours later, just when I'm about to get bored and knock on her door, I see it open. Perking up, I slide from my bed in the dark, not bothering to turn the lights on as she steps out, wearing skintight shorts and a bra. The sight of her is enough to have me coming in my shorts, and when she turns, I have to bite my fist so I don't call out. Her ass is peachy and round, and the shorts hug it perfectly.

Stepping out after her, I tilt my head when I realise she hasn't heard me as she treads softly down the corridor. She should be sleeping. The others will be working, but I promised to keep watch in case she needed help. It was an excuse to get close to her.

She reaches the steps that no doubt brought her to the room.

Clever girl.

Is she going to try and escape? I almost hope so. Tracking her, hunting her, and then fucking her into submission would be fucking amazing.

But no, she uses the chip to enter corridors and wanders aimlessly. I track her the entire time until she turns into a hallway. Speeding up, I turn the corner just as a leg darts out, slamming into my side. I tumble into the wall, the breath knocked out of me, and before I can move, an arm bands across my throat.

"Why are you following me?" she hisses.

Smirking, I let her touch as much of me as she wants. "I was curious. I was waiting to see where you would go. If you're bored, Nova, I could occupy you."

"I'm sure you would," she scoffs but doesn't let go. She seems unimpressed, so I need to show her how strong I am. I quickly grab her, spin, and slam her back against the wall, placing my arm across her like she did to me. Her breasts heave, and I lean in to try and look down her bra.

"Pig," she snaps and brings her knee up to hit my jewels.

I block it and step back. "If you wanted to spar, all you had to do was ask." I shrug.

"You have a training room, I presume?" she responds, straightening.

"Yes," I purr.

"Show me," she demands.

"Why? You'll be too scared to fight me and worried I'll kick that tight little ass." Her eyes narrow in anger, which is just what I want. It's clear she's unbalanced down here. I don't blame her; I hated it too. I loathed being confined underground just like that bastard did to me. Even the thought has my hands fisting at my sides. I know what helps me, and it should help her too. She's like us, after all, so I antagonise her.

"You couldn't beat me with two hands tied behind my back, though I don't think yours would fit around your muscular back," she growls.

I smirk. "So you noticed my muscles?"

Her hands go into the air. "Are you dumb or something?"

"Want to find out?"

"Fucking hell," she mutters, turning away.

"Come on, Nova, I'll show you, and you can take all that aggression out on me. Don't worry, I'll try to go easy on you."

That does the trick. She storms after me as I lead her to our training room. I don't tell her that having her under me is exactly what I want. I'm a greedy bastard, and I want to touch her. Plus, fighting always leads to other things, especially this time. I'll make sure of it. She needs to feel less alone, less scared, and more in control. I'll offer her that and whatever else she needs.

I can take it. I've had worse.

TWELVE

That cocky, egotistical, sexy—*wait, what?*

No. Not sexy.

He's an asshole.

It doesn't matter that his ass is tighter than a goddamn peach or that his arrogant, dangerous smirk has my heart clenching. It also doesn't matter that when he was pressed against me, it made me wet as hell. I left my room for a distraction after not being able to sleep, and I guess I found one in the guise of Jonas.

He leads me to a set of double doors and winks. "Ladies first."

Rolling my eyes, I shimmy past him, and he spanks me as I go, making me realise that was the only reason he wanted me to go first. That, and when I look at him, his eyes are locked on my ass hungrily. I can't help it. I smile. He's so forward with what he wants, and yes, definitely a little crazy as well, but aren't I also?

I guess we all are.

Thanks, Dad.

"Are you going to stand there fantasising about my ass or actually spar?" I joke, crossing my arms. His eyes quickly jerk to my breasts, and his tongue runs along the front of his teeth. I don't know why the sight is so sexy. Maybe it's the way his eyes sparkle or just that this bastard is hot as hell, but it has my pussy clenching. I appreciate a good fuck as much as anyone, but this one has strings, and I don't do strings or attachments. I only do strangers.

Jonas wouldn't be that.

He strikes me as the type who would want to fuck all night and then brag about it.

What is it about the cocksure assholes, though, that makes a clever woman weak?

He's clearly deranged and fucked up from his past, but damn if I'm not curious if he fucks as good as he looks.

"I'd rather have the real thing, but fantasies will do for now, unless you want to fuck instead of fight . . . or both?" He grins as he advances on me. I slowly step backwards, already having scanned the room when I walked in, so I know there are huge mats in the middle of the room which I lead him to now like a dog.

I ignore all the weapons on the wall, the athletic equipment to the right, and the assault course to the left—I'll explore those another day. For now, my entire focus is on Jonas. He could strike at any moment.

Once I feel my bare feet sink into the mat, I hop backwards, only stopping once I'm in the middle of a sparring ring. Tilting my head, I run my eyes down him, searching for weaknesses. I've fought a lot of people before, usually during training supervised by my father or on missions, but never one as skilled as Jonas. It's in every line of his body. He works hard to be the best, to be strong, just like me. It's probably another trait from our fucked-up childhood. It will make him unpredictable, wild, dangerous, and an actual challenge for once. The thought has me bouncing on my toes in excitement. Life has almost been too easy up until this point.

"Come on then, crazy, show me what you've got. Show me what I'm missing out on," I purr, widening my stance to prepare.

His eyes narrow, and his grin kicks up a notch as he steps closer. He begins to circle me, shirtless and shoeless, as his eyes roam over every inch of my body. I feel his gaze like a physical touch, but I focus on the shifting I hear, preparing for his first move. The anticipation has my heart slowing and going into business mode despite the electricity in the air. I'm not fighting to avoid punishment from my father or even for money

—no, this time, I'm fighting because I want to know exactly how dangerous the men I'm going to be working with are and to see if they can keep up.

I hear the whistle of air just before I see his arm darting past my head. I throw myself to the side, rolling away and to my feet, having to leap back to avoid his oncoming attack.

I move across the mat, on the defensive, as he kicks and punches. Weaving around me, he lands a few hits, winding me, and I bend over. With my eyes narrowed in anger, I meet his gaze. "You're dead," I hiss.

I lunge forward with all my strength, throwing him to the floor. I manage to get a few kicks in before he grabs my leg and pulls. Bringing my knee against his face, I hear his grunt of pain as I wiggle from his grip and get back to my feet. He climbs to his own, ignoring a trickle of blood running from his nose as I circle him.

"You're good, Nova, but not quite good enough." He flies at me again, mixing moves from different martial arts to try and throw me off. He should know better, though, because I'm Dad's first experiment. He taught me all the same and more.

We fight hard and fast, equal in each way.

He's harder, but I'm faster.

He staggers, and I take a shot, leaping into the air and circling my legs around his neck. I slam him down and quickly spin, my knees going to either side of his hips. I press my arm across his throat as I grin.

"Got you," I declare.

Panting, he stares up at me, and I watch as his shock melts to vibrant lust that I can almost taste. "Nova . . ." He groans. "If you keep me pinned much longer, I won't be responsible for my actions."

I know exactly what he's talking about. My wet pussy is sitting right on a steel rod.

He has a massive hard cock, and he's looking at me like he wants to do something with it. For a moment, I almost let my intentions sway and give into the desire between us before I lean down.

"Maybe next time. I've got a busy day tomorrow, and baby?" I purr, giving myself a moment of weakness to lick his lips, making him jerk beneath me. "You'd need hours to fuck and recover from me."

Rolling free of his body, I stand and give him one last grin. "Goodnight, Jonas. Try not to break your hand while you're thinking of me."

His groan follows me back into the corridor, as does the sound of his breathing picking up, and when I look back through the closing door, he has his shorts down. His heels are planted against the mat as he lifts his hips and thrusts into his hand, which is wrapped around a hairless, huge, hard cock with piercings glistening in the lights.

Swallowing, I force myself to leave before I go back in there and finish what we started.

THIRTEEN

I woke up early. My body is sore from sparring with Jonas last night, but that aching pain tells me I worked hard. It's addictive, and I stretch out my muscles before showering. Once I get back to the bedroom in a towel, I root through my bag for something to wear. The tiny towel almost slips, but half my ass and legs are already exposed thanks to the ridiculously tiny thing.

Just then, the door slams open without warning.

Instead of panicking, I grab the weapon I hid in my bag and turn. I drop the towel, uncaring about modesty as I hold the knife out, my body reacting before my mind could even play catch up.

Jonas stands there, his eyes wide before they narrow in desire and slide down every inch of my body. I spot Louis coming up behind him along with Nico. Great. Dropping the knife with a sigh, I glare at him. "Ever heard of knocking, asshole?"

"If I had, I wouldn't have gotten to see all this." He gestures at my body. "And god fucking damn, Nova, if it isn't a sight."

"Jonas," Louis snaps and politely brings his eyes to mine. "I'm sorry, Nova. We will give you a moment to dress."

Rolling my eyes, I place the knife in the bag, ignoring the obvious groan. I look back over my shoulder as I pull out some stretchy black shorts and a crop top. "No point, you've all seen me now. What's up?"

My eyes flick to Nico for a moment, expecting the silent man's judgement, but in those dark eyes I see . . . heat. It makes me shiver, and I quickly look away, busying myself with getting dressed.

Unlike the others, Louis doesn't seem fazed. "Okay, well, Jonas was supposed to *knock*"—Louis says it loudly as if to chastise the man—"and invite you to breakfast where we can discuss what will happen today."

"Okay, one sec." I pull on my shirt and straighten it on my chest. My nipples pebble through the material, but every person has them, so I ignore it. I don't get those weirdos who are so offended by nipples. It is a bit chilly down here, though, so I grab an oversized hoodie and pull it across my shoulders, but I leave it unzipped for now. I add some trainers, and then I'm ready to go, pulling my wet hair over my shoulder to dry. When I look back, they are all staring at me.

Louis quickly clears his throat and brings his gaze back to mine. I guess he's not as unaffected as he seems. "Shall we?"

"Lead the way." I wave him on, and as I pass through the door, Jonas leans into me.

"I'm going to wear out my hand tonight thinking about you, unless you'd rather just provide me with the real thing?" he flirts.

"In your dreams." I elbow him, and he laughs.

"Always," he calls as I fall into step with Louis.

Nico is behind us, and when I glance back, drawn by the feeling of his gaze, I see his eyes locked on my ass. When he realises I've spotted him, he doesn't have the decency to act ashamed—no, a small grin teases his lips before disappearing, as if it were never there.

Men.

A part of me is weirdly happy he was looking at my ass though. Being surrounded by so many attractive, strong men has my hormones going wild. I don't know if it's because they are like me and know my secret or if I'm just plain fucking horny, but I want them all.

Even cool and sure Louis.

I'd like to take them for a ride just once to see if they really are as strong as they look. After all, Dad was all about expanding the human mind and trying to make the perfect weapon. Did he succeed? Could one of these men actually kill me?

Why is that thought so thrilling?

No one else has ever gotten close, but I guess only time will tell. I don't trust them wholly, I don't trust anyone that much, but there's definitely a bond between us all since we share trauma and went through the same things. Maybe that's why I feel like I know them already and fit in so easily.

I remind myself to build my guard up though. Just because we have a common enemy and similar pasts doesn't mean they won't fuck me over when they get what they want. For all I know, they could want Dad's research to continue it, but I don't believe that. They seem too angry and fucked up by their pasts to want to inflict that on anyone else, but I don't trust the government, that's for sure, and they are pulling their strings.

I'll keep my distance for now, and I'll do what they want me to do so I can end this, even if it means killing them if they get in my way.

Before this, I was lost, but now I have a purpose, and I know it's right. I have to finish this. It started with me, and now it ends with me.

Louis leads us through the corridors and down a level to a cafeteria. "Go grab a seat over there with Dimitri and Isaac. I'll get your food."

I hesitate, hating that show of weakness, but then I nod and stride over, sitting on the metal chair opposite them at the long table. "Morning."

Dimitri smiles. In one hand, he has a book which looks like gibberish, and in the other, he has a spoon in some porridge. Isaac has a tablet in front of him showing charts, along with a full plate of fruit with toast to the side.

"Morning, Nova. How are you feeling?" he asks cheerfully, closing the tablet's cover.

"Oh fuck, you're a morning person!" I playfully groan, making him grin wider. Dimitri chuckles as he shuts his book.

"Holy shit, you got D to shut his book. It's the boobs, right, D?" Jonas asks as he plonks his tray down next to me, grabs his chair, and sits backwards.

Dimitri just rolls his eyes as he stirs his porridge.

"Maybe it's my winning personality," I deadpan, making Isaac laugh.

Louis places a tray before me. It has fruit, toast, cheeses, and a croissant, as well as some water and cranberry juice. Offering him a, "Thanks," I pick at the fruit as he sits next to me with an omelette. Nico sits next to Dimitri with a full English breakfast spread out on a massive plate. When he sees me watching, he sighs and offers me the plate, so I quickly pass him mine and take his, digging into the food.

"Did he just share food?" Jonas whispers.

A spoon flies through the air and hits Jonas right in the face, and I almost choke on my beans when I see Nico staring innocently at him, even though we all know he threw it.

"Children," Louis mutters. "Behave."

Smirking, I devour my food.

"Fucking hell, hungry?" Jonas nudges me.

I freeze as memories flash through my head, and then I drop my fork and turn my glare on him. "My father used to starve me to see how my body and mind would react under stress. I almost died more than once, and then when he would let me eat, he would make me so sick I hated it. When I got free, I was fucking poor and couldn't afford food either, so excuse me for enjoying it when I can," I snap.

His eyes widen and then narrow, filling with anger. "If he wasn't dead, I'd kill him."

"Join the fucking club," I mutter but settle down. When I glance back at the table, the others are staring, but luckily, there's no pity in their eyes, just understanding. I still hate all the attention. "So today?" I prompt.

Louis takes the hint, sipping his coffee and settling back. "We will hook you to a machine to help enhance your memory until we can figure out the entrance to the research area."

"Machine?" I arch my eyebrow. I didn't have a clue how they were going to do this, but Louis seemed so sure.

"Machine." Louis nods. "Dimitri."

"Anything in your past is stored in your brain. You only need the right stimuli to access it. Correct, Isaac?"

"Correct. The right triggers, words, or even sights or smells could help. The machine will assist with this," Isaac explains.

That's not what I was expecting at all, to be honest.

"This machine can help you access your memories. It was originally one of your father—Dr. Davis's creations, but Dimitri has since worked on it to make it safer, cleaner, and stronger. All you need to do is relax and trust us. We will be with you the entire time to guide you through it. If you want to stop at all, just let us know. I'll monitor your vitals too," Isaac says, looking worried even as he comforts me.

"Stop coddling her." Jonas snorts. "She's not a baby. She can handle this. She survived Dr. Dick and his experiments, so this is nothing, right, Nova?" He winks at me.

For some reason, that puts me at ease as well, and I grin. "Sure."

Dimitri squeezes my hand across the table, and Louis notices, his eyes narrowing in calculation and contemplation.

"Nico, take Dimitri to check the machine one last time," he orders, and Dimitri stands, blushing.

"I was just about to do that," Dimitri mumbles, throwing me one last look before hurrying away. Nico lumbers to his feet and follows him wordlessly.

I wonder what that was about, but I don't ask, too focused on what's to come.

What exactly will they see when we dive deep into my fucked-up memories?

My screams? My pain? My tears?

My hopes?

Or worse . . . my weaknesses?

FOURTEEN

Unable to eat after their explanation of what's going to happen, I wait for them to finish. Bile rises in my throat, and my memories crowd my mind. I'm unsure if they will be able to see them, but regardless, I'm betting that they will be able to guess what I'll see from my expressions, and that terrifies me.

Isn't it bad enough that I survived it and did what I had to do? For them to know what I did, though, and who I was . . .

The mere thought has me on edge.

I barely listen to their chatter as I am led to a room near the labs but off a different corridor. Once the door is opened, I freeze as fear rolls through me in waves. There's a metal chair in the middle of the room with a spotlight above it and a footrest swung to one side, with two padded armrests waiting for me to be tied to them. I can almost hear my father's voice. I have no doubt that this was his creation, but I can also see Dimitri's changes. There's a cushion on the back for comfort, there are no restraints, and the room is warm and comforting. There's also a computer to one side, but other than that, there is not much else.

"It's okay," Louis promises as he steps into the room. "We can stop at any time."

Dimitri heads to the computer and starts it up, and I flinch when it whirrs.

"We are not him," Nico states behind me.

I know it's true when they let me choose and don't drag me in. Instead, they wait. It's my choice, my body, and my mind. Taking a deep breath, I allow myself to be brave one more time and step into the room.

"Take a seat when you're ready," Louis instructs as he moves to the side. Just then, a screen I didn't notice comes down from the ceiling. "Through a lot of science that I won't explain to you because it will bore you to death, we are able to project some fragments onto this screen," he tells me as I slowly walk over and perch on the seat.

I am ready to leave at any minute, stiff and scared, but I'm also unwilling to let fear beat me.

"To do so, I have to implant this at the base of your neck," Dimitri murmurs. "It can be disconnected at any time, and I will numb the area—"

"Don't," I mutter and look up at him to see he's shocked. "I don't want to be numb. I'd rather feel it." Old fears, I guess.

He nods like he understands but looks at Louis who stares at me in contemplation. "It will hurt," Louis warns.

"I've survived worse," I remind him as I sit back.

"Do it," Louis orders, keeping his eyes on me. "If she says she can handle it, she can handle it."

Smart man.

The others spread out, watching and waiting. I almost feel comforted by their presence. Before, this would have felt like an experiment, but they have all survived shit like this, and I know no matter what the reason, they wouldn't let me get hurt. They are like me.

They are me—the experimental children of a mad doctor.

"Okay, I'm going to implant it. Take a deep breath for me," Dimitri instructs.

Isaac hurries over, takes my hand, and kneels. "Eyes on me," he orders, his voice soft and reassuring. Before, I had to grit my teeth through the pain and focus on the cracks in the wall, but now I focus on his caring eyes, on the way his lashes fall across his cheek, and the tilt of his lips—

Fuck!

I jerk, but the pain is over just as fast as it began. My head swims a little, and I feel sick as the chip wires into my brain like an octopus stretching inside and curving around the stems. My fingers tighten, gripping Isaac's hand with all my force, yet he doesn't complain. He kneels patiently, stroking my hand as I breathe through it. When I jerk my head in a nod, he stands and squeezes my hand once more.

"You've got this, Nova. We will be right here the entire time."

I nod again, feeling nervous now, before I turn my head to meet Dimitri's eyes. "Do we guide the memories? I have a, erm, lot of—"

"Nova," Nico says as I stumble over my words. I look back at him, and he smiles softly. "We all have a lot of bad memories we don't even want to remember, never mind want anyone to see."

Fuck, he knows. He knows that I feel exposed, vulnerable, and weak.

"We won't look. I promise you that. Your pain is your own, and your memories are too. We will only look when it's time," he promises, and I believe him.

"Okay, let's just bloody do this," I mutter, leaning back in the chair.

"I can strap your arms down if you want," Dimitri offers, and I snarl without thinking. "Okay, never mind, it was just to stop you from moving, but that's fine. Okay, we are going to inject you with a hallucinogenic to help. It's short-lived, so we have to be quick. Our metabolism burns them off too quickly."

"Too fucking right," Jonas mumbles, and when I spare him a glance, he frowns. "Doctor Dick created the serum using me as a lab rat."

Well, shit, that explains a lot.

"If you just roll with it, it'll be easier. If you try to fight it, it will hurt and make you sick for days," he cautions.

"Okay." I feel the prick, then an icy cold liquid moves through my arm and up my chest.

"Okay, Nova," Louis begins, his voice reassuring yet firm. "Take us to your home, to the estate. See it, smell it, and remember it."

I close my eyes, finding it easier than staring into their hopeful gazes, and then I do just that. I recall the way the rain would wash the huge gardens clean, and how it would fall through the big oak tree Ana and I used to play under, the leaves bowing under the weight. I remember how the fog would roll in through the moors, surrounding the old, red-brick building sitting in the middle of nowhere, giving it an eerie look.

There's a gasp, and when I open my eyes, the image, the memory I'm seeing in my head, is projected onto the screen. It's fuzzy, like a dream, and when I focus too hard on that, it falls away.

"Focus, Nova. Close your eyes. Go back to the estate," Louis instructs.

Taking a deep breath, I settle back.

Ana runs across the cobbled back patio, her dress flowing behind her as I chase her through the open back doors and into the cold, quiet kitchen, our bare feet loud on the cold tile.

She turns around to whisper, "Shh, we don't want to wake Dad."

Nodding, we sneak over to the fridge.

"Focus, Nova. Lead us to the entrance," Louis murmurs, his insistent yet soft tone piercing through the memory until Ana's face disappears.

Turning, I leave the kitchen. Like always, there's only minimal light out, and never enough to fill all of the unused, dust-collecting rooms. When I was younger, the dark scared me, until I grew to realise that it was what was waiting in the dark that scared me more.

"Good, where now?" Louis prompts.

I hesitate at the base of the grand wooden staircase. For a moment, I can't remember.

"You've got this," Isaac encourages, so I slow down and let my body lead.

I turn without thought, instinctively knowing the way. Slowly moving across the tile of the entryway, I see the huge double front doors are shut against the storm. I turn and peek at the stairs like I did when I was a kid. At the top, I see the flickering light from my father's study, and fear pumps through me, so I turn away and hurry on before he spots me.

Ana would be reprimanded for being out of bed late, but me?

I would be punished.

I come to the hallway, stilling before the cold darkness of it. The doors running the length of it mock me before I suddenly hear footsteps on the stairs. I turn slowly, and fear fills me until I'm choking on it.

"Focus, Nova. He's not there. You're alone, and it's daytime. You're okay."

The light he tries to bring to my memories is swallowed as I hear *him* heading towards me, and I know what is coming.

"Nova, have you been a bad girl?" The disembodied voice causes me to run.

Their voices become lost—no, that's me. I'm lost in my memory, consumed by snapshots of pain, screams, and torture. I see myself being drowned. I see the fire on my skin. I see the pain. I see the one I don't talk about before I skid to a stop.

I'm in the lab.

Oh God!

"Nova!" Nico snaps. "Pay attention, you're not there. Go back—"

It's too late.

Looming above me like a nightmare is my father with a gun in hand. I know what he's going to say before I hear it. "Kill him or I'll kill her."

I scream and fight. I hear the others trying to calm me down, and I try to change the trajectory of the memory, but then he's there. The man is tied to the chair, afraid and wide-eyed.

The gun is in my hand—

"No!" I roar as I lift it and shoot. The shot is deafening.

My eyes snap open, and I fall from the chair before scrambling across the floor. I press my head to the tile and try to breathe.

A hand touches my shoulder.

"Nova."

All I see and hear is him as my memory and the present fight each other. The feel of the warm, smoking gun and seeing the excitement and pride in my father's eyes is too much.

I jerk to my feet, knowing I look wild as I swing around before locking eyes on the door and sprinting through it.

"Fuck! Nova, wait!" someone shouts.

The corridors blur as I run through them, trying to outrun my demons.

My past.

My sins.

I run as far and fast as I can, trying to outrun my nightmares, my memories, but they are still there.

I skid to a stop, blinded by my memories, as I slap my hand out. It finds something cold—a wall, I think—and I press against it. My breathing is ragged, and my nails dig into my palms, drawing blood. I try to force the memories back into the box where they belong, but I opened it, and now they refuse to be forgotten.

"Nova." His mocking voice echoes around my head. I feel him behind me, waiting, so I spin and lash out, but someone catches my fist.

Their hand is hard, scarred, and warm.

It's not my father. He never had scars or calluses.

I blink, and light pierces my vision before the nightmares swallow me again.

"Nova, Nova, look at me!" I hear someone's voice, but it morphs into my father's. "Fuck, I knew we shouldn't have done this. Look at me, come back, you're not there. He's not there."

All I hear is him.

Father.

My torturer is coming for me again.

My hands are pinned to the wall as I try to fight them.

A dark, brooding voice barks, "Nova, stop, it's me!" but it's lost in the haze. "Fuck this," the voice mutters, and then suddenly something warm starts building inside me.

Hands drag along my sides, pulling me closer, and then lips are on mine. The shock of it causes me to freeze, and the softness invades my thoughts. The person deepens the kiss as they nip my lip, making me gasp before they sweep their tongue into my mouth. Each touch, each breathy moan and rub of their lips yank me back from my nightmares until I feel the cool tile of the bunker under my feet and the heat of a large body before me.

Thick hands caress my body until my clit throbs in time with my wild heartbeat. My head is tilted back, and something unmovable and hard is pressed to every inch of my front. The kiss pulls me from the abyss, and then it's over.

The person pulls away, so I slowly blink my eyes open.

"Nico," I whisper, and he pulls me closer, cradling my head to his chest.

"Thank fuck," he rasps, holding me.

I'm still dazed as my hand drifts to my lips.

He kissed me.

Nico kissed me.

Pulling back, he frames my face with his large hands and peers into my eyes. "Are you okay?" he asks worriedly.

I nod, and he frowns.

"I'm okay," I say, my voice hoarse. "You kissed me. Why?"

He swallows, his eyes drop to my lips for a moment, and when he speaks, his voice is silky and low. "It was the only thing I could think of to bring you back."

"That's the only reason?" I flirt, my lips tipping up into a smirk.

His own part in a grin as he holds me against him, letting me feel the evidence of his desire. "Maybe, maybe not."

"Nico! There you are! Is she okay?" Louis barks, and I hear the others running towards us, but I'm still trapped in Nico's dark gaze. His eyes tell me a whole story full of his worry and desire, and then he blinks, and just like that, a shutter comes down and he steps back.

I instantly miss his heat, so I wrap my arms around myself and turn to the others as they stop before us. They look me over before turning to Nico.

"I'm okay." I sigh. "I got lost in the memories is all."

"I know. We saw," Isaac hedges, wincing when I shoot him a look.

We become quiet then, none of us knowing what to say. After all, they just saw some of my deepest darkest secrets.

"Your dad was a real prick," Jonas finally says, breaking the silence.

I can't help it. I burst into laughter.

"Yes, yes he was," I agree.

FIFTEEN

She stands at my side, and her laughter fills the air, putting us all at ease. I thought we had broken her. I thought we had finally done what her own father couldn't. She was trapped there, and she didn't even see me—she saw him.

I know that feeling.

My own PTSD and nightmares are similar, and I learned how to bring myself back from them the hard way. I couldn't do that to her, and kissing her was the only idea I had, though a part of me can admit I've wanted to do it since I met her. I should feel guilty that I took advantage of the situation, but I don't. How could I with her sweetness still on my lips?

I look down at her. Her eyes sparkle with amusement, and her body shakes with it. She's just as beautiful as when I first saw her.

I knew back then she was like us. Some of the others wondered if Dr. Davis took it easier on her since she was his own blood, but he didn't. If anything, he was harder on her.

This woman at my side is a warrior. She has survived the unthinkable, and she is still able to laugh.

It astounds me.

She looks up like she feels my gaze, her laughter fading into a knowing smile that has my cock hardening. "Thank you for coming after me," she murmurs softly just for me.

"Okay, well, let's go take a break. We can try another day if you want to," Isaac starts.

Her head whips around, and before she speaks, I know what she's going to say. It's what I would do. Nova doesn't give up, especially with others depending on her. "No, we go back and try again. I think I can get there. It was just a shock is all."

He groans. "Nova."

"Nova," Louis calls. "We almost lost you. We can find another way—"

"No, this is the way. Everything I went through . . ." Her voice breaks, so she swallows. "It has to mean something. I have to do this. You understand that, right?"

We do. After all, isn't that why we are all here?

"It's her choice," I state, interrupting their bickering, and they all turn to me in shock. They are probably wondering why I agreed with her, since I'm the one always trying to outrun my demons. Here I am, however, standing with her as she faces her own. They all know parts of what I went through, especially Louis since he was the one who found me, and he looks at me now knowingly.

Swallowing, I allow some weakness to enter my words. "If I could help save people, even if it meant experiencing everything again, I would. I survived it once. I can survive it again." Looking at her, I nod then add, "They are just memories. They can't hurt you anymore."

"Thank you." She reaches out and squeezes my arm before rolling back her shoulders and stepping closer to them. "Then let's get back to it," she says, walking past them.

They all turn, eyeing her, but I see their pride and wonder.

I feel it too. Her strength astounds me.

We follow after her. Her father might have been our torturer, our enemy, but his daughter is our salvation.

She reminds me of what it means to be unstoppable.

Once we're back at the lab, she sits in the chair and waits with her chin tilted high in defiance, daring us to stop her. We won't. This is her choice. She knows her limits better than we do. After seeing hints of her past, though, I don't think there is anything she couldn't survive. Her father was an evil, cruel man. He did terrible things to me for most of my childhood, things that have left me scarred, but to do that to your own daughter . . .

It must be soul destroying to wonder why your father hates you so much. At least he was just a stranger to us, but to her, he was supposed to protect her, love her, and teach her right from wrong. Instead, he broke her over and over.

He tried to ruin her.

He did not succeed, though, because there is one thing his data could never tell Dr. Davis, and that's a soul's strength. Children like us are unbreakable. Unstoppable.

Just like his daughter.

She could choose to hide and spend the rest of her life in peace, healing from what happened, but instead, she's here, choosing to help us end this once and for all. And that is something he never could have explained with tests or genetics.

It's something you are born with.

"Are you ready?" I ask, knowing she won't back down, not when she has set her mind to it. It's an attractive quality, and my opinion of her triples tenfold.

"No, but let's do it." She grins, making Jonas laugh.

He blows her a kiss. "That's my girl."

She flips him the finger before closing her eyes and focusing on her past. The transformation instantly comes over her. Her eyes tighten in pain, her lips tilt down, and her cheeks pale. She looks like she's seen a ghost, which I guess she has.

Her father.

The man she was running from for so long, whom she's facing now for us.

Her first memories are the most painful, the ones she clearly doesn't want us to see, but our minds have a funny way of doing what we don't want them to. No one says anything. We just watch stoically as a little girl screams and begs her father to stop. As her memories progress, she becomes more silent in them. Her tears and screams fade into nothing, until all that is left is a broken little girl who realised asking for help did nothing.

My heart breaks at seeing her that way.

She is alone and so scared.

Memories of my own childhood filter through my mind—the very same memories we all try to push away so we don't have to live with their scars.

Seeing hers, however, brings all of mine to the surface.

I would scream until my throat bled and scratch at the walls until my fingernails broke and bled. Those were only the days when he locked me inside alone, wanting to see how starvation and darkness would affect my mind.

It didn't break me.

I refused to let it.

It was one of the nicer experiments he put me through, and better than the electrocutions, water, and gasses. Those haunt me even to this day.

Nova's gasp draws me back to her memories, pulling me from mine.

The torture and experiments she suffered fade, and then it's dark, but I hear Dr. Davis's voice clearly. "Remember, Nova, we focus on nothing but the darkness. This is a secret, isn't it?"

"Yes, Father," she whispers.

The lab.

He's leading her to the lab. She told us he blindfolded her.

When my eyes go to her, I realise she's counting something. Steps? Turns? It's all fuzzy to us, but she looks determined. "Nova, are you trembling?" I ask.

She nods, still mouthing numbers and words to herself before the blindfold is abruptly ripped away. Bright white light pierces her eyes, making her rear back in both reality and memory. She's in a white room, the one from before, and on the table are restraints and a machine I know very well —the shock machine.

The memory suddenly changes, and she's already in the chair, her body shaking with fear.

"Crank it higher. I want to see if she can withstand the same amount as before or more now that she is used to it," Dr. Davis calls.

"Nova, come back!" I demand.

"Can't," she whispers as the machine is turned up. The shock goes through her, and she jerks and screams in the chair.

"Turn it off!" I yell, rushing to her side. Isaac hits the kill switch, and she slumps.

I lift it gently, noting her closed eyes and parted lips.

"Nova?" I ask worriedly. Fear fills me at her silence, at how little she feels in my arms . . . breakable almost.

Isaac moves to my side, checking her pulse. "She's alive, just passed out. The sudden pain of the memories must have been too much. Let's get her to the lab where I can monitor her."

"Will she be okay?" I ask, even though I should be more concerned about the entrance to the lab since we have been looking for it for years. "Isaac," I snarl when he doesn't answer.

"I don't know," he admits nervously. "We could have fractured her brain. Only time will tell."

"Gentlemen, who cares? Did she get the information?" the general barks. All of us were so focused on Nova, we didn't see him come in.

Turning, I block his view of her. Jonas and Dimitri quickly move to my other side, doing the same, while Nico steps up next to Isaac and lifts her, hiding her from him. All of us are protecting her, and he sees it, his eyes twitching.

"Do not forget who is in charge here. She is nothing but a tool," he snaps. "I want that location in two hours or you are all let go."

Fuck.

"Understood." I step forward, feeling angry now. "But you will not interrupt again. You need us, and do not forget that, general."

His face reddens as he turns and storms away.

I slump slightly as I scrub my face. "We don't have long. Let's get her to recovery and make sure she is okay, and pray she remembered or we are all in trouble."

All our hopes are pinned on Nova now.

I watch the slow, even rise of her chest worriedly.

The things we saw in Nova's memories . . .

No wonder she ran and didn't want to help us. No wonder he kept her close. She wasn't just the first experiment; she was the worst. I can't even imagine everything she went through, but seeing those snippets was enough to know that this woman lying in the hospital bed before me is a fighter.

A survivor.

She deserves to be free of this life and her past, not dragged back to it, but that's her choice, and I won't make it for her. It might help her let go if she is able to destroy what he did, or maybe it won't help at all. Only time will tell, and I will keep a close eye on her to make sure her mental health isn't affected by this mission.

I have my own personal mission now—to save Nova and ensure she has the life she deserves.

It is clear her father, her family, or the world has never given her anything, but I will. I'll help her find her place and her happiness, even if it takes years. The doctor in me feels the need to give something back to this sweet suffering soul and prove the world isn't all bad. Nova craves love and a home. That much is obvious.

I'll help her get that.

I stand softly and check her blood pressure again. I gave her some fluids to counteract all the drugs she was given, and I've also checked her heart and head to make sure everything is okay. It is physically, but the mental pain?

I can't do much yet.

Now, we just need her to wake up. I kicked the others out, not wanting her to be overwhelmed when she wakes up. She will probably be embarrassed, and maybe even lash out because of that, feeling vulnerable and off kilter. I've also lowered the lights to change the room from something clinical to cosy. I spotted the layout of her father's lab from her memories, which is similar to this one. No wonder she didn't want to come in here.

It's probably a trigger for her, like chains are for me.

Her blood pressure is normal, so I sit back and double-check all the medical details I have on her while I wait for her to rouse. A lot is missing from her childhood, since only the public files are available. Hopefully, when I find her father's notes, there will be more. It leaves me blind, however, and wondering if she has any undiagnosed illnesses or broken bones. I wouldn't put it past him.

There was another one of us that we found as a child, who was left with chronic pain from purposely broken and unfixed hands, ribs, legs—not to mention all the internal scarring from procedures. Eventually, it got to be too much for him. I tried to help, and we got him morphine—well, actually, we stole it, and that's when we came up on the military's radar—but even then, it wasn't enough. He was in so much pain all the time. Not that he would admit it, but we saw it. It drained what was left of him, and he was unable to fight. He couldn't take it anymore.

He killed himself by stepping in front of a bus.

I close my eyes in pain at the memory. I was only a teenager, but I should have done more. There had to have been something, anything, other than just ending it.

I carry that guilt and blame, and I know the others do as well, especially Dimitri.

He made his choice, but we have to live with the consequences.

A slight change in Nova's even breaths jerks me from my memories, and I blink my eyes open, sit up, and push away all those thoughts so they aren't as obvious on my face. She needs me to help. They all do.

I need to be their rock, but they have no idea that I'm crumbling myself.

Her eyes slowly open, hazy and disoriented. Dragging her tongue across her lips, she tries to sit up and groans when she falls. I catch her then gently prop her up with some pillows.

"Slowly, Nova," I murmur, and her head turns as she meets my eyes.

The pain, embarrassment, and fear in her eyes undoes me.

I stare, unable to look away, until her lashes cover her gaze, and when she looks at me once more, her eyes are empty. Her guard is up again. "What—" Her voice cracks.

Turning, I grab water and press the cup to her lips, tipping it. She drinks as she watches me.

"Only sip a little. We don't want you to be sick," I caution.

Nodding, she pulls away and sighs. "What happened?" she asks, her voice clear now.

"The overload was too much for your brain, and it caused you to pass out. I'm so sorry about that. I have flushed the drugs from your system and helped rehydrate you. You may feel weak for a little while, so you need to rest." I sigh when she slides to the edge of the bed and arches an eyebrow as if to challenge me on that.

"You're not going to rest, are you?" I murmur even as a smile curves my lips.

"Nope, not my style, doc." She winks then stretches, groaning when her bones pop. It's obvious she doesn't like to feel weak, and resting in bed isn't Nova's style despite how much she clearly needs it. I wonder if she has ever let her soul rest or heal a single day in her life.

"Well, that was fun," she deadpans.

"Your sarcasm is intact, so you'll be okay."

She laughs. "That's your opinion, doc."

"It certainly is. Now—"

I'm interrupted when the door opens. I glance over and harden my expression, the teasing words dying on my lips. Sitting up straighter, Nova follows my gaze and stiffens. Every inch of weakness and embarrassment disappears, until only Nova the fighter exists.

The rest of my team stands there, their expressions a mixture of relief and worry as they stare at her—apart from Jonas who grins at her suggestively.

"Nice. Glad you didn't die before I got to fuck you."

I shake my head, and Nico smacks him. It makes her laugh, though, before the last person's voice interrupts—the general.

The asshole didn't care if she was okay. To him, she's disposable and only as useful as what she can provide. We all are, and he's made that very obvious, hence why everyone is on guard around him.

Louis's eyes tighten as he steps forward, ignoring the general's disgusted snort and obvious impatience. "Are you okay?" Louis asks.

"I'm fine."

Even if she wasn't, I doubt she would admit it in front of the general, whom she clearly doesn't trust or like.

"Great, now do you have the location?" the man in question demands, uncaring about her health. She ignores him and looks at Louis, which makes him smile.

"Do you remember the location, Nova?" Louis repeats kindly.

She shrugs. "I do."

"We have to know. Tell us," the general demands greedily.

Louis's eyes cut to him in a gesture only we would understand. Nova inclines her head slowly and looks right at the military man.

"I know it, but I won't tell you." He starts to sputter as she grins. "I'll show you."

Clever girl. She just ensured she has to come with us so we can guarantee everything is done properly.

It infuriates him, and he starts to storm away. "We leave in two hours. Make sure she is ready," he snarls just before the door shuts behind him.

Nova slumps. "Guess we are going on a road trip," she comments in the tension-filled room.

"Isaac, double-check her. If she isn't ready, we can wait. I will deal with him," Louis promises.

"I'm fine," she snaps, but he ignores her, knowing she won't admit if she's not. "I will get us all ready. Once we're on the road, we all stay together."

He doesn't say why, but it's obvious.

He doesn't trust them either.

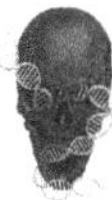

"You are completely healthy," I declare as I pull the blood pressure cuff off.

I knew she was, but I was hoping to find an excuse to give her some time to recover from what happened mentally before being pushed back into the very place where all her nightmares began.

"I could have told you that, doc," she teases, getting to her feet. She stumbles a little but holds up her hand to ward me off when I go to help her. "Dead legs," she explains, stretching. "Okay, where are my clothes so I can change?" She peers down at the ones she passed out in.

"Jonas selected some for you."

She groans as I point to the chair. "It's probably a thong and nothing else."

"I had Dimitri help him to make sure it wasn't." I grin, having thought that myself.

Nova nods in thanks as she grabs the clothes and starts to strip. I turn away to give her privacy, not that she requested it, but just because she is getting naked doesn't mean she's giving me the consent to stare at her body.

No matter how much I want to.

Instead, needing to distract myself from the thought of her naked, mere inches away, I repeat drug names in my head until I've calmed down enough to talk.

"You know what we saw doesn't change anything, right?" I don't know why it's what enters my head, but as soon as it comes out, I know I need her to understand this.

I hear her freeze, and I feel her eyes lock on me without even looking.

"I just mean . . . your past, Nova. It changes nothing. In fact, we think you are incredibly strong to have survived it—"

"So, you've been gossiping about my torture? Nice," she spits.

"No, not at all," I reply hurriedly before sighing. "There isn't much privacy down here or between us at all. We've all seen each other at our worst and best, and shared pain and nightmares. Yours are no different, Nova. What I'm trying to say is that we understand."

"Sure." She snorts, annoyed at the way this conversation is going.

Knowing I'm losing all my progress with her, I try a different angle and expose myself so she doesn't feel as embarrassed and, therefore, defensive. "Your father had specific experiments he did with me—"

"Isaac, you don't have to—"

"I do. You need to understand you are not alone." I turn to look at her then, keeping my eyes locked on hers and nowhere else. "He had specific experiments," I repeat. This isn't easy to discuss, even though I know it's safe with her and she needs to hear this. "It would usually involve playing with my genetics and digging in my head to see what made me tick. He knew I liked medicine and wanted to be a healer, so he would devise scenarios to test my morality and abilities. He would pit self-preservation against my need to save others."

"Isaac," she whispers.

"Some of the choices I made . . ." I shake my head. "I will have to live with them forever. They will haunt me, and I promised myself if I made it out of there alive, I would earn back my soul and help as many as I could."

"Isaac, we all did what we had to in order to survive. We were kids," she reasons. "We should have been protected and learning right from wrong, not holding people's lives in the balance."

"Still, I knew some of the choices were wrong. I should have died instead of saving myself." I let her see my pain, the one I hide. "I should have died before I let him hurt someone else. I never should have chosen my own survival over that of another. Child or not, I made those choices. Yes, he put me in those situations, and I will never forgive him for that, but I am the one who is haunted." Swallowing, I look away. "So, I understand more than you might think. We blame ourselves, Nova. We hold the pain and guilt while he gets to forget and move on. My body is riddled with his scars."

I pull back the sleeves of my shirt to show her the thick, mottled marks around my wrists.

"These are from his chains. He liked to take everything away but my brain. I hated it. I fought and got nothing for it but more pain. He wanted to expand the human mind, Nova, but all he did was destroy it."

"I know," she whispers.

"I survived, but at what cost? We all have these questions, these regrets, worries, and nightmares. I cannot begin to understand what you went through, but you are not alone. We all have our own horrors, things we wish we could forget but can't. Look closely, and you will see we all may be different, but we all carry the same scars."

"Thank you for telling me, Isaac," she murmurs, laying her hand on my shoulder. "I know you won't listen to what I'm going to say, because I wouldn't either, but you need to forgive yourself. You need to accept what happened and find a way to live with it. It's clearly still hurting you. Don't let him. He's dead, so the only way we can ever truly move on and let his pain die with him is to forget the ghosts he left inside of us."

"It's easier said than done, Nova. You know this yourself." I cover her hand and smile at her. She smiles back sadly, and for a moment, nothing else exists except this emotionally scarred, intelligent, beautiful, brave woman staring at me as if I'm the reason she's here—and then it's over when she steps back, realising she is still half naked.

Clearing my throat, I look away. I caught a glimpse of her body despite knowing it was wrong, and what I saw will stay in my mind longer than any bad dream or nightmare her father imprinted there.

"Well, at least he brought me a bra," she teases, and when I look over, she's slipping into a leather jacket. She looks unbelievably sexy and badass in skintight black jeans, a high lace bra under a white tank top, and boots.

I thought Dimitri was supposed to help Jonas.

The pervs.

"Good, then if you're ready, we should go." I stand and approach her. "If you can't do this, we will understand and fight against the general on your behalf."

"No, I can do this. I want to do this. Just . . . don't leave me, okay? I have a feeling this is going to be hard."

"Never," I promise, knowing how hard it was for her to ask. "We will never leave you alone again, Nova." I take her hand and kiss it.

"Then it's time to go home."

EIGHTEEN

When we find the others, they are waiting at the exit elevator, all geared up in black. Jonas wears a matching leather jacket —he winks at me when I notice—with some black leather trousers and no shirt. I see a lot of weapons on his body; he doesn't even try to disguise them. Dimitri is at his side in a long-sleeved black shirt, slacks, and trainers. Isaac nipped on the way to change, and now he sports a black denim jacket, trousers, and shirt. Louis looks every bit the commander in utility pants, which are tucked into black boots, and a black T-shirt that showcases his very hard muscles.

"We look like the Care Bear version of an assassin squad," I tease.

"Maybe we need matching uniforms with nicknames." Jonas smirks. "I would be BD, short for Big Dick."

"Enough," Louis snaps.

Turning, I see four soldiers heading our way in formation. At least they are dressed in plain clothes, but Christ, the way they move gives them away. They are all stiff, hard, and uncomfortable. It's clear they don't like working with us as much as the general.

Great.

"We have been ordered to accompany you," the one at the front says. He has greying hair, crow's feet around his eyes, and a mole above his lip.

He's also clearly older than the rest and in charge, if the sharpness of his order was anything to go by. "The general said there are to be no arguments. We are to report straight to the address here and then back to this bunker. No stops, no interruptions. Nothing but the mission." He narrows his eyes like he expects us to fight him on it.

"Sir, yes, sir!" Jonas calls, saluting him mockingly. "Would you also like to search my anal cavity for tracking devices?"

The man narrows his eyes and looks at Louis. "Control your people or I will report that they are not needed."

A tense staring match begins, so I step between them. "They are needed. If they don't go, I won't, and without me, you cannot access the estate or the lab. The general might have ordered you, but we are in charge here, so watch your tone, stay silent, and follow us if you must, but don't get in my fucking way, toy soldiers."

"Watch who you talk to like that, street rat, or we'll put you back where we found you," the soldier sneers.

That, of course, doesn't sit well with us.

I hear them all move, snarling as they form a line behind me. They stand at my back and side, defending me.

It's something I've never had before.

It's nice, even though my neck does prickle from their proximity. "Are we going to have a problem here?" Nico snaps. "Because we could easily . . . resolve that." The words hang in the air.

It's a clear threat.

Lines have been drawn.

The soldiers shuffle and actually reach for their weapons, but it's evident that fear passes through their eyes and bodies.

Just then, an announcement comes over the speaker. "No fighting, just get the job done, now," the general snarls.

"Guess we are working together for now," Louis mutters. "Men, weapons down." He includes me in his order, so I shrug and look away before Louis moves to my side, his voice lowered. "We will keep an eye on them. You don't have to worry, just lead the way, Nova."

It's time to go back to where it all started.

NINETEEN

O nce up top, we split up. Our cars are hidden in the old barn. I don't know where the soldiers go, but when we emerge onto the empty country road, they are waiting in two black SUVs. It alerts me to the fact they have a hidden cache somewhere they haven't told us about. I narrow my eyes at that, making a mental reminder to find it when we get back.

Even if it's just to play with their toys.

I knew the general lied when he said he had no nukes.

"Why do you look like you just hatched an evil plan?" Nova grumbles, scooting away from me. She's pressed between Nico and me, so I move over again, ignoring the empty space between me and the door, much preferring to have her plastered against me.

Nico sighs and presses against the door uncomfortably. I see his old ghosts rearing up, but when Nova looks at him and smiles, his eyes warm. His entire focus is on her now, and not the cramped situation.

In all honesty, we were all surprised that he volunteered to sit back here. He never does, always preferring to sit up front, and we never questioned it because we understand triggers better than anyone. He hopped right in today, however, and when he met our eyes, he said not to question it.

I see Louis in the driver's seat, throwing him worried glances and me harrowing ones, so I move back slightly, very slightly, to give them more room.

"Nico, Jonas is going to do bad things. If he gets his cock out, do I have permission to cut it off?"

"Why? You liked looking at it last time." I grin, reaching out to play with her hair. She smacks my hand away and rolls her eyes while the others gawk at my statement.

I let them think what they want, sitting back with a smug smile.

"If he gets it out, I'll cut it off for you." Nico grins at her, and they share a secret look that has my eyebrow rising. I meet Dimitri's eyes in the front passenger seat before he turns away, but I saw his envy. Interesting.

Isaac sighs in the back. "Please don't. That would be a lot of blood, and I'm wearing my nice jacket."

"Did doc just make a joke? Holy shit," I tease, looking back at him. His eyes are locked on a screen, and he flips me off without looking, making me chuckle as I lean into Nova.

"It seems you have them all on their best behaviour, trying to show off for you, Nova," I purr.

She shivers, but when she turns to me, her eyes narrow in fake anger. Under it, however, I see lust. She can't hide it from me for long. Oh no, Nova wants me just as much as I want her. "Or maybe they just aren't assholes like you, Jo."

"Oh, Jo! Are you giving me nicknames now? That's fine with me, baby, though I would prefer Big Coc—"

"Enough," Louis snaps from the driver's seat. "Don't make me come back there."

"Nice going, Nova. Way to get me in trouble," I tease with a wink, waiting for the hit to come from Isaac when Louis gives him *the look*, but instead, Nova reaches out and smacks the back of my head.

"Behave, and I'll let you show me your collection of toys."

I almost choke, and then she closes her eyes slowly. "I meant like weapons—"

"Can't take it back!" I shout, leaning in and wiggling my eyebrows. "I have this really long vibrating—"

This time, it's Isaac who hits me, but I see Nova chuckling softly, so it's worth the momentary pain.

"We know the location of the estate. We will be there in just over two hours," Louis informs us, the mood in the car sobering at the reminder of why we are here. I feel Nova stiffen, and before I can make a joke to help, Nico reaches out and covers her fisted hand on her thigh, offering her support.

It helps, and she leans into him, placing her head on his shoulder. I feel his shock ripple through the car, and ours also—both at him reaching out for her and for him touching another person voluntarily.

Nova is changing things, but is it for the best?

I end up napping out of boredom, and when I wake up, I'm curled around a grumpy Nova who pushes me away with a knife to my throat. Her and Nico are playing some weird game in Latin, Isaac is working, and Dimitri is playing with a machine while Louis drives.

"How much longer?" I whine.

"Ten minutes," Louis barks, cranking up the radio to ignore me.

Looking out the window, I realise we are winding through country lanes up a small hill in the middle of nowhere. When I look back at Nova, she's gone quiet and pale as she stares outside.

"Nova?" I murmur.

"It's been ten years since I ran down this road. It took me hours, and I tore up my feet. It was freezing, and when I finally managed to find someone willing to give me a lift . . ." She shakes her head. "Ten fucking years, and it still hasn't been long enough. I can already feel the evil he poisoned this place with leaking into the car."

"You're not alone though, Nova," Dimitri reminds her. "We face this together."

"D is right," Nico says, placing his hand on her shoulder. "Ten years is a long time, Nova. It's time to face your fears. That is all that exists there now: your own fear and memories. He cannot hurt you here anymore."

"I'm betting he will find a way," she mutters. "One last barb, one last ounce of pain wrung out of me . . . That was his style, and you know it." She turns away and looks out of the front window. "I swore I would never come back to this place."

Unsure what else to say, I reach for her hand, Nico takes the other, and Isaac's palm lands on her shoulder, offering support. Dimitri turns, setting his hand on her thigh, and even Louis reaches back with one hand, squeezing her knee for a second.

In that moment, we are like children huddling together in the dark, looking to each other for comfort from the big bad monster.

But we aren't children anymore, and at least now we have each other.

Louis stops the car then turns his head to meet her eyes. "Tell me to turn back now, and we will."

"What?" she asks.

"Tell me you can't do this, and fuck orders, we will leave. We will find another way. You're more important than what is in your head." There's an impatient beep behind us from the SUVs. They're probably wondering what we are doing, but Louis pays them no mind.

She jerks at that, her mouth opening and closing before she swallows. "I can do this," she finally answers. "I can. Just don't leave me, okay? We do this together."

"Of course, and any time you want to leave, we will." He nods. "Are you sure?"

"I'm sure," she responds, and without waiting, Louis turns forward and drives down the narrowing road to the driveway leading to the estate we can now see.

Within five minutes, we are before the huge wrought iron gates. The black paint is chipped and peeling in places, and the golden crest of Dr. Davis's family sits proudly in the middle of the designs. They stand close, with a guard station to the right which is empty.

"He never had guards because he never wanted them to know what we were doing here, not until the end, but I always knew there was no escape. He kept me here out of fear, not out of lack of freedom . . . fear for my sister." Her whisper reaches us all, and we jolt.

He kept her here by threatening her innocent, untouched sister. Nova endured all that pain and torture for her sister, Ana, and now she wants nothing to do with her for saving herself? For finally running?

Selfish bitch.

If she knows, then she's worse than her father.

The gate doesn't open, so Dimitri gets out, noticing a control panel. "Do you know the code?"

"It's the first four digits of pi," Nova snaps. "The pretentious bastard."

Dimitri nods and puts in the numbers, and with an audible beep, the gates start to swing open. The groan of the worn metal is loud as he gets back in the car. We wait for them to fully open before Louis drives through them, followed by the SUVs, which have been tracking us this entire time.

The drive winds through the estate's grounds. Upkept grass lines the driveway on either side with flower borders, and to the left, we see what must have been the servants' quarters in a separate building. When we turn into a circular gravel driveway, a large water feature with two small girls in the middle is switched off, the grey brick green from time.

Nova and Ana maybe?

Either way, it's nothing but a reminder for Nova as we park before the huge estate. Her hands clench ours, but we don't complain, as she stares at the old, towering brick manor where she was abused by her father.

She gazes at the large, ornate bay windows downstairs then the small balcony up top. Gargoyles are poised on the pointed roof of the three-story manor. The entire structure screams old British architecture, and the dark, ominous feeling about the place is only confirmed by Nova's fear of it.

It could have been beautiful once, but it seems like Dr. Davis didn't care about the upkeep, so he let it begin to rot away, like his mind.

"We don't have to go in," I start, but Nova climbs over me, kicks the door open, and slides out as if she doesn't do it now, she won't at all.

Nova is facing her fears head-on.

TWENTY

I don't wait for them as the other car pulls up. I can't, because even seeing this place is enough to send me running for the hills. I hate it here. The memories are already winding around me like fog on the moors that surround this hellish house. I can feel them looking for an entry, for my weakness. I can see my father's silhouette in the window the night I ran and hear my sister crying for me.

Can a place really be haunted by what transpired?

If so, this one is.

It should be burned to the ground and left to rot, but here I am, standing before the antique, ornate wooden doors with my heart in my throat like I'm a child again. Lifting my hand, I swing the gold door knocker and wait. A shiver goes through me as I remember that night.

The lightning crackled across the sky, followed by a clap of thunder as the harsh wind whipped around me as I ran and ran. My feet were muddy and slippery, and my dress stuck to my tiny body as a deep chill set in. It took weeks to stop shivering.

No one answers, so I try the door, and it swings open with a creak, admitting me to the entryway. The wooden spiral staircases rise before me, and the same rug lies over the cold tiled floor. To the left is a painting of my father, Ana, and me, which was painted when we were children. Step-

117

ping closer, I see the hopeless, sad look in my eyes as my father stands with his hand on my shoulder, like a threat. I was silently screaming for someone to save me, while Ana smiled happily up at him.

I fucking hate this painting. If I could, I would tear it down and burn it.

"Hello, M-Miss Nova?"

I hear a gasp and spin. The guys are hesitating at the door with the soldiers, but coming from the kitchen, wiping his hands on a tea towel, is Bert. He's older now, his hair thin and greying, and there are more wrinkles around his thin lips and kind brown eyes. He's hunched as well, when he used to stand tall and proud, but the ever-present suit is still in place.

"Bert," I whisper.

I thought he would be gone. Other than Ana, he was my only friend, my only confidant. Father hired him as a butler, but he was more than that, much more. He looked after the staff and house, and he helped Ana and me grow up. Bert was kind and caring. He even taught me to play the piano and read me stories when I couldn't sleep.

He was the father I always wished I had.

And I left him too.

However, he knew why—at least partially. At first, he didn't, but as I grew older and more withdrawn, he started to realise something was happening. He hated my father for how he spoke to us, and I know he saw the way Father watched me. He was also aware of the nights I wouldn't spend in my bed, and when I could make it to breakfast, I was usually in pain and tired.

He never spoke it out loud, but he knew. He tried to protect me as much as he could in those final months, talking to me so I didn't retreat inside myself, and the night I left, he was the one who helped me.

He brought me clothes, money, and supplies to set me free. The only thing he ever asked of me was to run and never look back.

"Nova." He shakes his head. "What are you doing here? You promised you would never come back."

"I had to." I move closer and take his hands in mine. "He's gone. He can't hurt me anymore."

He flinches and closes his eyes. "I'm so sorry, Miss Nova. I stayed to protect Ana. I often think about what happened. I should have done more."

I silence him by pulling him into a hug. "You did everything. You saved my life, Bert. I've been eternally grateful for it all these years. Thank you. I never said that."

He cups my cheeks and looks me over. "You grew up so much. Look at you. You are more beautiful than ever, but to me, you'll always be my little Nova chasing butterflies."

I can't help but smile. Someone clears their throat, and he drops his hands before straightening. "Oh, forgive me, I got carried away." He flushes slightly. "Are these your friends?"

"In a way." I smile. "Bert, I need my father's research."

"Why . . . ?I . . . It would be in his office," he begins, turning to the stairs.

"No, the kind of research he hid," I correct.

He frowns, not quite understanding, but he nods anyway. "Of course, this is your house." I don't correct him. After all, it's never been mine. "I will put some tea on. You know the way." He begins to turn before looking back at me. "I'm so glad you are okay. I have wondered about you every single day since that night, hoping you had a better life. Did you?"

I nod. "I did."

"Good, good, that's all that matters." With that, he hurries to the kitchen, uneasy with showing his emotions past his duty.

"Who is he?" Isaac asks as he comes to my side.

"An old friend," I reply, watching him go. "He saved my life."

"Then we all owe him a debt. Are you okay?" he whispers low enough for only me to hear.

"I-I don't know," I admit. "But I have to be." I turn to the soldiers and others, trying to fight off the emotions whipping through me like a gale force wind.

"I think the entrance is right down—"

"Who the—please move," comes a stern, feminine voice from behind the soldiers at the door.

Ana.

She slides through the busy doorway and stops, her mouth dropping open as she looks around at everyone before her gaze lands on me.

"Hi, Annie Bannie," I say softly.

"What the hell are you doing here, Nova?"

"I finally came home," I answer lamely.

She crosses her arms, her usually friendly eyes sparking with anger. "Get out. Get out now. You don't belong here. You're not welcome."

I flinch at the venom in her tone. "Ana," I murmur as Bert comes down the hallway.

"Miss Ana, how lovely to see you."

"Bert," she greets, softening briefly before looking back at me. Her face clouds with rage and betrayal again. "I don't want you here, and neither would Dad. Get out, this isn't your house."

"Actually, it is."

TWENTY-ONE

Both of us turn to Bert, confused and shocked.

"What?" we ask in unison as she steps closer, dropping her crossed arms as he smiles at us both. I didn't believe that I truly did own it after all. I thought it was another trick.

"It's so good to see you together again."

"Bert, please, what did you mean?" Ana demands. It's the harshest she's probably ever spoken to him, but he takes it in stride.

"I simply mean it is her home. It's in her name, Miss Ana. I know you haven't seen the will yet, but I was the one to witness it for him. Your father, well, he left everything to Nova."

The silence could be cut by a knife.

Shock fills me, then anger. It's just another way to get back at me, another fucking punch in the gut and a way to haunt me even as he's dead.

"You can't be serious." I laugh.

"Deadly, I'm afraid." Bert nods. "He expected you would be angry, upset even, but he told me to tell you one thing. Please excuse me if it's not verbatim, it's been many years. 'Novaleen, the house, the money, and the labs are all yours to do with as you wish. I hope they help you understand. I hope they set you on the path.'"

"What the fuck does that mean?" I snarl, throwing my hands up.

"I do not know."

"Dad knew you were alive? And he left everything to you? The kid who ran away?" Ana almost screeches.

"If you need money, you can have it—" I start as she snorts bitterly.

"I don't need money! I just didn't want my childhood home being destroyed or sold! It was all I had left of you, of us, and now him." Her face scrunches like it used to when she was sad. I reach for her, but she jerks away.

"I don't want it, any of it," I tell her. "I have my own life, my own things. It's all yours, I promise, I just need to get something—"

"I don't want it. Congratulations, Nova. As usual, you get all the attention and everything you ever wanted." With that spiteful comment, she flees, leaving me staring after her. Everything I ever wanted? All I ever wanted was to be happy, to be safe, and to be with her again.

My eyes lock on the retreating form of Nova's sister, my fists clenched at my sides. I wanted to chase after her and demand that she listen to Nova, but how can I make her see when she is so blind to the truth? So lost in the love of her father that she doesn't see the ghost of the woman he broke before her. When I glance back, it's to see Nova's stricken face before she shuts it down, turning that emotion inwards. I never had a family or siblings to care for.

To love and miss.

Nova did—does, and to see them turn their back on you? It must be indescribable. I want to scream at her sister and tell her what Nova went through to keep her safe, but as I go to chase her down, Nova's voice cuts through the air like a command.

"Don't."

I look back, and she shakes her head at me sadly, as if knowing what I was going to do. "Let her go. She has every right to feel the way she feels. She owes me nothing. It's probably better if she hates me anyway."

"She doesn't know," I snarl, getting angry on her behalf. For a moment, I see sadness in her eyes before they turn cold again, but she can't fool me. I saw the hope, pain, and heartbreak written there.

"And she never will. It would break her heart more than I ever could," she replies before sighing. "Let's just find the fucking lab and leave this bloody place so I can burn it down once and for all."

"We must insist you find the lab also," a soldier sneers, uncaring about the fact that Nova is clearly upset and already feeling triggered by being in this fucking awful horror house.

Louis throws them a withering look as Isaac moves over to Nova, whispering in her ear. She smiles slightly, and jealousy pounds through me for a moment before I toss it aside. There is no room for jealousy here, and I'm glad he got her to smile. When he leans back, she nods, squeezing his shoulder.

"It's down here, if I remember correctly." She turns and freezes for a moment, blinking at the dark, empty corridor. We all move closer, knowing the signs—after all, we struggle with them too.

"Nova?" I murmur.

"Yeah, sorry," she whispers, but her voice is shaky. "Fuck, I hate this place."

"We do not have time for memory fucking lane," one of the soldiers snaps.

I turn to knock him out, but Nico beats me, fisting his hands in the man's shirt. "You do not get to fucking speak to her. You know nothing of what we survived. If I hear one more word come from your mouth, I'll rip out your tongue and give it to her as a gift," he snarls, and then with an effortless move, he launches the man across the reception area and right out of the front door, where we hear him hit the car. The alarm sounds as he groans. Turning back to us, he winks at Nova.

"Just taking out the rubbish."

I can't help but laugh, and she does too, even as the other soldiers start barking orders and surroundings us.

It's going to be a long day.

TWENTY-THREE

I stare at Nico, extremely turned on by that display. I shouldn't be, since it was angry and chaotic, but I hear the man scream, and shit, it has my pussy clenching as I look at his bulging muscles. It's only when another soldier clears his throat as the others leave to fetch their comrade when I turn back around. I shake my head, remembering that there is no time for flirting or even figuring out if Nico would throw me like that.

My steps are slow as I make my way down the corridor. I feel their eyes on my hunched back and sense their worry, and it only fills me with shame. They think I'm weak and stupid—

No!

It's my father's voice and insecurities rearing their heads, so I push them back, knowing they are only concerned about me. There is something about shared trauma that bonds people. I trust them more than I ever knew was possible because we are the same—same wounds, scars, fears, and hopes. They would never judge me, only support me, and that level of trust and support has me standing up taller, knowing I can do this. I have to so I can find peace, not just for me, but for them. We also need to finish this and stop what my father did, so it can end with us.

My steps become steadier, my hand dragging down the wall as I walk.

The shakiness disappears once I realise their strength is my strength and that I'm not alone anymore. My father's ghost can't hurt me here. They won't let it.

The hallway turns darker the deeper we go, and memories assault me from every corner, but I grit my teeth and force myself through them. They cling to me like the cobwebs in this house. Those silky strands wrap tighter around me until each step is heavy and dragging.

His grip tightens on my too young hand, tugging me down the corridor. I dig my feet in, not wanting to, a wordless whine on my lips. My eyes dart around behind the blindfold desperately, seeking help.

Seeking something that won't come.

Someone to save me.

He throws my hand down like a petulant child, and I feel his fingers on my face as he moves closer. The heat of his body makes me shiver, and the faint smell of whisky on his breath as he spits his words makes me recoil as far as I can. Pain already racks my body, but it is nothing that will compare to what is to come now that I have tried to defy him.

A useless rebellion.

In the long run, it will only hurt me longer if I fight.

"Now behave, Novaleen. You know why I do this. It's to help you and to better mankind. It will expand the human mind . . ."

Panting, I lean into the wall, pushing through the memory. It fades away with a mocking laugh. For a moment, I'm still that young, scared, pained girl who's lost in the dark, reaching out desperately for someone to save me, only for my hand to be taken by the monster.

Betterment of mankind? It's such bullshit.

All of his research was utter bullshit. All he did was scar children and force them to become wounded adults. Yes, we are stronger and faster, and we have higher IQs and survival skills. That part of his research might have succeeded, but everything else?

It failed.

We aren't supersoldiers. We are too broken for that.

"Nova?" Louis's soft voice pierces the haze of anger and resentment, reaching for me in the dark.

They aren't coming to save me from my father, but instead, they are right here in the darkness along with me, and their hands are in mine as we face our demons together.

"I'm fine," I mutter gruffly, pushing away from the wall, shaking yet again.

It's just a place, Nova, just a fucking place. Get over it and man the fuck up.

With that thought repeating in my head, I lift my foot and take one step, and then another. The world around me is a blur, my racing heartbeat roaring in my ears as I focus on my feet and nothing else, like that will stop the memories from reaching for me again.

Flashes of them move past my eyes, but I ignore them as best as I can as I lead them to the lab.

"No, Daddy, please, I'll be good. I swear!" My young self struggles to walk as he pulls me down the corridor, sighing in disgust before slinging me into his arms and carrying me into the lab. It's the only time he ever carries me.

Next, I silently walk down it. I'm older and not even reaching out anymore. I'm just silently and numbly walking after him.

The years pass through those memories, from a sobbing, begging child to a stern, dead-inside teenager. My understanding of the world evolved alongside my understanding of the father who only saw me as an experiment, and never a child. Once upon a time, I loved him. I used to stay awake at night, begging for signs to tell me what I did wrong to make him hate me so, before I realised he didn't. He never loved me either. He didn't have children for that purpose. We were just another scientific research opportunity for him, nothing else. It made it easier when I realised he didn't hate me but, instead, felt nothing, so I made myself the same, hoping it would be easier.

It wasn't.

In that numbness, cracks formed in the dark as my silent hopes for a family, for love, tried to break through and pierce the shadows.

I finally stop, and when I do, I realise I am just above the steps and the hidden door to the lab. My hand reaches for the knob, but I snatch it back like it burned. The wood warms, screams fill the air, and hands reach under the door for me—familiar hands.

Mine.

I stumble back, turning to look at the others, seeking them out amongst the madness.

"I can't . . . I can't go down there," I mutter, my voice shaking. I hate to admit that one weakness.

"It's okay. We've got it from here," Louis promises, stepping up to my side. He places his hand on my shoulder, grounding me. When my eyes meet his and I nod, he passes. The others squeeze through, putting their bodies between the door and me. I move farther and farther away, and with each step I take, my breathing gets easier, freer, and lighter, until I'm leaning into the wall, almost sagging in relief.

"It's locked!" Louis calls, and a part of me relaxes at not having to face whatever demons are lying in wait in that torture lab.

"Open it!" a soldier commands me.

"I don't know how," I mutter, not looking at them. "It was always open."

"Figure it out now!" the head one orders, his hand reaching for his weapon again. I'm feeling too vulnerable for this, and not like my usual, argumentative self. Luckily, Jonas slides before me, his arms crossed.

"It's a fucking high-tech security lock. She wouldn't know how anyway, so back the fuck off before I decide to play Nico's game and see how far the soldiers can fly."

The soldier stands down but doesn't look happy, and we spend the next twenty minutes in uncomfortable silence as they work on the lock. I stay as far away from the door as I can. Jonas is before me, grinning suggestively at me as he blocks my view of everyone and anything but him.

"I bet I could make you shake harder." He winks.

It's so out of the blue that a laugh escapes me and a true smile crawls over my lips as I face him. That rat bastard, he's never going to let me live it down.

He grins, wiggling his eyebrows. "Knew I could make you laugh. How about next I make you choke—"

"Jonas!" Dimitri snaps, making me grin wider.

"How's it going?" I call out, and he grunts.

"Bad," he mutters, so I quiet down and leave them to it.

The time passes slowly. Bert silently comes out with drinks, and I smile in thanks but can't bring myself to drink anything. A phone rings, breaking the silence, and we all turn to the soldier who pulls it from his pocket.

"All phones must remain on silent for the performance," Jonas jokes.

He ignores us and answers the phone, barking answers. His face twists in displeasure at the conversation before he hangs up. "Move out, men."

"You're leaving?" I ask, my eyebrow arched.

He grinds his teeth and looks at Louis. "There's an emergency back at base, so orders have changed. We are to leave, while you are to remain here and get into that lab. We will be back to help with the collection of the research, understood?"

"Aye, aye, captain," Jonas jokes.

"Understood," Louis snaps, unhappy with the order, but when the soldiers leave without another word, we all relax without their presence.

"Thank God, finally." Dimitri sighs.

We all turn to him as he straightens from the lock, blinking as we gawk.

"What did you do?" Louis sighs.

"I just set off a few alarms and sprinklers at the base with a tiny fake fire to get them to leave." He grins, and all of us laugh. "Hey, I hated them as much as you. Plus, I don't like the way they spoke to Nova."

My heart warms, and I smile at him. "Thank you, Dimitri," I tell him sweetly.

"No problem. Now let me crack this baby," he mutters, focusing on the lock as if no one else in the world exists, and to him right now, no one else does. His single-minded focus is sexy as hell. I wonder if he focuses on other things . . .

No, don't go there.

Not wanting to just stare at him and knowing it might take a while, I push from the wall. "I'm just going for a walk. Don't worry, I'll be okay," I call before they can ask. Instead of going outside, though, I decide to walk upstairs. I feel their gazes on me as I reach the top and turn right. Once out of sight, I allow myself to show a little weakness. My hands drag along the walls as I walk like I did as a child when we were playing.

Flashes of my and Ana's laughter have me smiling as I stop before a closed door.

My room.

I shouldn't, but I can't resist as I reach for it and push the door open. The wood creaks from years of disuse, and my nose crinkles as stale air hits me. I guess they didn't want to keep this room open. When I step inside, nostalgia fills me.

It's smaller than I remember.

The single bed with the princess curtains sits to one side, all made and clean. Teddy bears are perched on the seat under the window with the books I read when I got older. The mix of my childish room and collection of stuff as I grew makes me wrap my arms around myself.

There are still boy band posters hung haphazardly on the wall, CDs piled up on one side, and my old iPod too. There is no TV, since Dad said it was bad for the brain before bed. Clothes are also folded in the drawers and hung in the wardrobe. Everything is how I left it.

It's like I never disappeared.

I wonder if Ana ever came in here and if she missed me as much as I missed her.

All I ever wanted was to love and grow up with my sister to keep her safe, and now we are strangers.

It's so odd how you can go from knowing everything about a person to knowing nothing, from best friends to strangers. The love you have for them is still there, but there is a chasm between you, filled with everything that has happened, and both sides fight not to fall in.

Sighing, I throw myself down on the bed like I had done countless times in my childhood. My hands automatically go up and under the pillow, but I freeze when the fingers of my left hand touch something. Flipping, I lift the pillow and slowly extract the slip of paper.

It's a torn out, lined page that's haphazardly folded. Sitting up cross-legged, I slowly open it. The edges are jagged where it was ripped out of a notebook, but the sloppy handwriting is more familiar than my own.

Ana.

I miss you, Nova.

That's all it says. I reread the sloppy, black inked words over and over. The paper is yellow from age, yet it still has the power to break me.

My heart cracks, and the yawning abyss finally takes over as tears fill my eyes and slowly slide down my cheeks.

Gripping the page, I hold it to my heart and close my eyes.

"I missed you too, Ana bug," I whisper brokenly. "More than you could ever know."

TWENTY-FOUR

Not wanting to leave Nova alone here, especially after we forced her to come back to a place that hurts her, I venture upstairs. The place is dull, over the top and filled with stuff, but dull. There's no life here, and I can almost feel the pain and heartache. At the top of the stairs, I hear a little noise and turn right, following it. I stop at the doorway to her bedroom where she sits on the bed, holding a crumpled piece of paper with tears in her eyes, and I swear internally.

Feeling like shit for interrupting, I begin to turn away when she wipes her tears and her head jerks up to find me. I lean harder into the door, crossing my arms. I won't let her see my worry or my pain—pain caused by hers, the very same one we all carry.

Her agony is so much more, though, because she lost her sister in the process. We had no one to lose, but she did.

"Are you okay?" I ask softly.

Swallowing, she folds the note in her hand and looks down at it before her shoulders slump. That usual, cocky force of nature persona is gone, and in its place is the scared, broken little girl her father created here. "No, not really."

"Can I do anything?" I inquire honestly, and in this moment, I would do anything to see her smile again and help her rebuild her walls. If I could tear this place down for her, I would, but we know how to endure pain for the greater good, and that's what she's doing right now: enduring her nightmares to stop this and save others, even as her shoulders sag from the weight of it.

Shaking her head, she wipes at her face before standing, pocketing the piece of paper, and looking around the room. "It used to be my sanctuary. He wouldn't come in here. It was the only few hours of peace I ever had. Ana and I played here, and I read her bedtime stories. I used to do these elaborate voices and act it out for her. Sometimes, it was the only thing I would say all day. This was the only room in this house where I was happy. Now it's just cold and empty like the rest of this fucking torture mansion." Looking at me, she smiles sadly. "I shouldn't complain. At least I got a house and a sister, while you guys—"

I shake my head and move closer. "Do not compare pain. Ours doesn't detract from yours or vice versa. We were hurt by the same sick man, and we are allowed to hate him and what he did, to suffer from it in whatever way we need to survive." I place my hands on her shoulders, and she leans into me. "But you do not have to do it alone anymore."

Looking up at me through her lashes, she searches my face, and the expression painted across her features kick-starts my heart until it's racing as I stare back.

"What if we can't stop this?" she finally whispers.

"We have to," I murmur equally as soft, our whispers creating a barrier around us. "We are the only ones strong enough to. We didn't get to pick our lives, but we can still take a stand to stop this and save others. Afterwards, we can be whoever we want."

"But that's not true, is it?" She sighs and looks away for a moment, and I instantly miss her eyes, almost slumping from the force of her gaze being removed from me, searching my very soul. "We will still be the same fucked-up, overtrained people. There's no place in society for us, so where do we go then? Where do we belong in a world we protected from an evil they didn't even know about?"

"Together," I reply instantly, not even knowing where it came from.

Her eyes jerk back to mine, searching them in shock. I meant all of us, but deep down, I also meant that she belonged at my side. I don't know if it's our trauma that is pulling us together or the strength she exudes that makes me unable to leave her, but since the moment we met, I haven't been able to stop thinking about Nova. This mission is the most important thing to me, as well as keeping my men alive, but she snuck her way in there, winding through my body and heart so quietly, I didn't even notice until I couldn't stop thinking about her.

I have shouldered the burden of leading our people, of protecting them in any way I could, since I was young, but with her, I feel like a man, just a man, standing before a woman he likes.

A lot.

With her, I am not Louis the leader, the freak the military fears, or the experiment her father saw. I am just a man, and she sees him like no other ever has. For a moment, I allow myself to be weak, and my eyes drop to her lips, which part on an inhale. I wonder not for the first time what it would be like to kiss this wildcat, this living tornado, and taste the pain and beauty on her lips.

"Boss man!" The echo of Jonas's voice has me stepping back and dropping my hands to my side.

The desire pushes back and is replaced with a business-like demeanour. Her lashes close for a moment, and when her eyes open again, the same determination I feel is reflected there.

"I thought you would want to know we got in, but if you need thirty seconds to finish like normal, then we can—" There's a grunt, no doubt someone hitting him.

"We better get down there before they start killing each other," I murmur as I offer her my hand. "Shall we?"

Nodding, she takes it, and I squeeze hers, letting her know that whatever she'll face down there, she won't do it alone.

TWENTY-FIVE

I grip Louis's hand like a lifeline as he leads me downstairs, lending me his strength. The others wait at the bottom, watching me carefully, so I give them nothing. I don't want them to think I'm weak. It's just a place, just a fucking place, and my father can't hurt me anymore.

I repeat it silently as Louis turns us to see the open door that leads to the one place in this world I never wanted to go again. Darkness mockingly creeps out of it, its tendrils reaching for me. Releasing Louis's hand, I step forward, my chin notched back.

Breathing slowly, I force one foot in front of the other, my hand curled around the lingering heat of Louis's palm to remind me that I'm not alone. It's easier than before, and once I'm in the doorway, halfway between worlds, I close my eyes against the darkness before me.

The feel of my father's orders washes over me, as does the way my heart would always stop when I stepped over this threshold because of the pain I knew was waiting. Lifting my foot, I step willingly inside for the first time ever.

I still then, my nose twitching at the slightly old smell of the place, as if it hasn't been touched in a while, but under that is the antiseptic cleaner my father used meticulously, the one that would always follow our sessions.

Swallowing past the ghosts that want to take over my body, I walk farther inside, knowing the way in the dark better than in the light.

I feel the others hesitate, but I don't stop, my feet automatically taking me through the space. It's as if my father is right there at my side, his commanding presence filling me with fear more than safety. I can almost see him out of the corner of my eye, but I shake my head and stop, knowing it's inches away.

Lifting my hand, I stroke the glass that separates me from the room where some of the most horror-filled days and nights of my life were spent.

"Light, anyone?" someone mutters.

"To your left, there's a bank of switches, two steps," I murmur, remembering every inch of the layout. After all, I used to count the bricks and study the tiles, anything to forget the pain rolling through my body every time I was here.

There's a moment of searching, and then I hear the click. The lights bloom to life with a buzz, long ones attached to the ceiling and walls, washing the area in a bright white light that's also too painful to look at. I blink past the sting and then look at the room beyond, one that hasn't changed. The metal chair is still neatly tucked under the table as if it's waiting for me. No doubt the scratches in the cushioned leather handles from my nails are still there too. The table is spotless and clean, and the chains are neatly coiled in the middle. The floor and ceiling are still immaculately tiled—a hundred exactly on each.

The cot in the corner is made up and waiting for the other types of experiments, and the cameras in each corner no doubt turned on with the lights. I don't need to look behind me to feel their shock and horror, nor do I want to.

"Holy fuck," someone whispers.

I couldn't agree more. It's so clean and perfect, yet I remember the walls being covered in my blood, the echo of my screams filling the space, and the smell of burnt skin and melted plastic. I recall the sight of the burns on the table and floor and the shattered glass on his worktables, a consequence of his anger. I remember it all.

Thousands of memories converge on me as I close my eyes and press my hand to the glass. I can see her, the younger me, doing the same, her eyes filled with tears and exhaustion, and her forehead resting against the glass as I do the same now.

"Please, help me," I would beg.

It's as if I can touch her, can reassure her that we will get out, but I can't. She turns away, dropping her hand, leaving a slight smear in her hopelessness. With her back to me, her head drops back as she screams and screams, letting out every inch of her pain and agony.

It will never echo around the house, though, only down here, haunting me even now.

"I'm sorry," I whisper. "I'm so sorry it took me so long to get us out," I murmur, needing to get it out. "I'm sorry it still hurts, and sorry we are still just as angry and lost."

"Nova?" someone calls behind me.

With one last look at my past, I open my eyes and pull away from the glass, leaving an identical smear across it as I turn to them. They are standing at the door and watching me with sad, knowing eyes. I see no pity there, only horror and anger on my behalf.

Turning, I scan this side of the office. It's still the same, and everything is exactly in its place. The rows of books on the small shelf in the corner are all perfectly lined up with the edge—his notebooks. The filing cabinets are locked and spotless, and the corner desk holds three computers, ready and waiting. To the right is his whiteboard with mathematical and scientific equations I could never follow, no matter how much I tried. His equipment sits before it, like the centrifuge. I look at it all idly, numbly.

Nothing has changed.

In all the time I've been gone, I changed nothing.

"It's so . . . normal," I mutter. "It shouldn't be this empty, as if this place didn't destroy me."

"Once we've searched it, you can rip it to pieces," Nico tells me, coming closer and stopping before me, blocking my view of the room. "You can destroy it all for all we care."

Nodding, I turn back to the room and hit the switch on the wall. The door to the left of the glass slides inwards, and I step to it. Nico follows me, not asking me if I'm sure but silently supporting me. Moving deeper into the room, I stop next to the table, sliding my fingers across the metal I used to trace over and over.

A shiver rolls through me. I feel so weak just being here. My breathing starts to pick up, and a scream lodges in my throat. I can barely see, can barely hear. I'm losing it. Fuck! But Nico notices. He turns me and cups my cheeks hard, the slight pain bringing me back from the edge.

"Focus on me, on my voice. Count with me, okay? That's it, slow breath in, slow breath out. Focus on breathing, nothing else." With him instructing me, I work on getting myself back under control until I'm blinking before him. I feel tears in my eyes as I meet his stricken gaze. I know he struggles too, but only someone who has flashbacks would know how to bring you back so quickly and recognise them so easily.

What haunts Nico?

What does he see when he closes his eyes?

"You are safe. He's not here. He's dead. You are safe, you are alive, and we are here. Nothing in here can hurt you unless you let it, baby," he murmurs, pulling me against his chest, the steady thump of his heart grounding me. "That's it, breathe for me and remember who you are, not who you used to be."

His low, calming voice grounds me like nothing else, and I stand in his arms with my face pressed into his chest, gripping his shirt as I finally let out all the hurt, pain, anger, and hopelessness. I scream into his chest, the sound ragged and filled with horror, as tears flow down my cheeks.

He holds me steady, whispering to me and stroking my back as I sob and scream. Other hands join his, stroking me, and they add their voices until they drown out my own thoughts and turbulent emotions.

I don't know how long I stand there before I lift my head and look around at the men standing with me in my solitary pain, the men who are quickly becoming family and something so much more. Their hearts echo my pain, and yet they are ready to defend me, their eyes filled with their own tears.

Their own pasts.

Suddenly, I'm better, feeling emptier than I ever have before, like I've cried it all out. I have no doubt it will happen again, but I do feel better getting it out. Dimitri reaches out and strokes my face, wiping away my tears as I swallow.

"Thank you," I whisper.

"That is what family is for," Isaac murmurs, squeezing my hand I didn't realise he held. "We all break sometimes, but we are here to hold each other up when the darkness becomes too strong."

Smiling at him sadly, I step away, needing a moment to rebuild myself. There's a noise that has us all whirling around with our weapons raised before we realise who it is. It doesn't escape my notice that they move closer to me as well, far enough away to fight if need be but close enough to protect me, but it's only Bert.

His eyes run over the room in horror, his hand pressed to his mouth. The sound was a tray of tea shattering on the floor. When his eyes meet mine, his entire body shakes. "I never knew it was—"

"I know," I murmur, putting away my gun and stepping over the threshold. I kneel before him and start to pick up the broken pieces of china. Standing with those pieces in my hand, I stare down at the beauty of their jagged, shattered edges. "It will never be the same, but you can fix it with a little love and patience," I murmur, knowing he understands I mean more than the china as I carefully place it on the tray he now holds. "It might even be stronger than before, and different, but still as beautiful as the others."

"The broken ones always are because they are different and they stand out. Their healed wounds are a mark of their inner strength," he whispers, his hand covering mine. "I should have killed the bastard."

It's so out of character for him, a laugh barks out of me as I pat his hand. "Well, he's dead now, so let's focus on better things, like that amazing chocolate cake you used to make."

Smiling, he leans in and kisses my forehead. "Anything for you." He begins to turn before hesitating. "I am glad you found a family, Miss Nova. A real one, I mean. You always did have the biggest heart I had ever seen. Whatever your father—the doctor did to you here, it doesn't define you. He was a monster, but you are better than him in every way. Remember that." With that, he hurries away, leaving me staring after him.

"Nova, we need to start looking. You don't have to help," Jonas says, sounding serious for once.

Shaking my head, I turn to face them. "I want to help. Let's get this over with." I head over to the cabinets as they share a look.

One of pride.

I start with the folders as Jonas works on the cabinet locks. Dimitri works with Louis on the computers, while Isaac goes through folders near the medical station. Nico paces, watching everything and everyone with gritted teeth—mainly me, as if he's worried for me, but I keep my head down.

When I find anything that could be relevant, I mark it and add it to the pile in the corner. I'm working my way up to my father's journals, knowing they will hurt and trigger me, but once I shut the final folder, I can't put it off any longer. I feel them watching me carefully as I select one at random and flip it open.

His messy scrawl covers every page with diagrams, equations, and even pictures. It falls open on a page, and I inhale, closing my eyes for a moment. Nico is there instantly, placing his hand on my shoulder, so I show it to him, and he growls. Ripping it from my hands, he stares at the picture as if he wishes he could destroy this whole place for hurting me.

But they can't protect me from my past.

"It has already happened," I remind him.

"What is it?" Isaac asks worriedly.

"Just a picture." I pull it out of the journal, holding it in my hands. I stare down at my own sad, tear-filled eyes. I was young, and it was one of the first months I spent down here. The white gown I have on falls from my too slim frame, my face is pale and scared, and my hair is shaved off—a mental test.

My hand reaches up now to touch my head before I drop it and trace the photo instead. When I see the machine behind me, I sigh. "I remember this. It was one of the first times I realised my father truly didn't care if I lived or died. I was broken-hearted."

"What did he do?" Louis asks slowly. He knows if I'm talking, he should probably ask, but he doesn't want to make it worse.

"EST," I murmur. "Electroshock therapy, though it wasn't therapy. He wanted to see how I would react to extreme pain and how it would affect my brain waves at such an early age. More than anything, it was a test to see if I could endure it. It was this night he told me he was proud of me for the first time, and that I would be his best yet. It only got worse from there." I go to tuck the picture away, but Nico takes it from me and places it in his pocket.

"To remind me," he murmurs.

I don't know what to say, so I flip through the notes. "It's just his thought processes and findings on some of his early experiments." I clear my throat before I read his notes out loud. "If we are to expand the human mind and reach all it is capable of, then sacrifices must be made. We have already established a baseline that pain can help trigger these changes. Extreme stress, exposed at an early age, is helpful in unlocking the brain's secrets." Shaking my head in anger, I carry on. "I am hoping constant exposure to both fear and pain will develop the brain in further ways, mouldable at such a young age. Coupled with training usually given to soldiers, and learning equivalent to those given with high IQs, we can reach the results we need to prove my theory correct—that the human brain can be changed and expanded. That we can be better, stronger, faster, smarter, and more capable. A new race of beings, unmatched by any. By manipulating the brains of our children and selective breeding, coming generations will be nearly superhuman." Shutting the journal with a sneer, I toss it to the floor.

"Bullshit. That might have been his aim at first," I scoff before turning away. "But he began to like the pain he caused and the experiments he conducted. It wasn't just to make us better, as he called it, but to satisfy his sick urges and theories. It was never as simple as proving that theory. It was to test our humanity and how much we could endure."

"Nova?" Dimitri whispers.

I shake my head again. "Sorry, I'm okay. I'll keep looking."

"Never apologise," Louis orders. "You are right. Your father might have started as a scientist, but he broke his oath. It was about so much more than creating the perfect human, and we will prove that."

I hope so.

TWENTY-SIX

I keep my eye on Nova as I hack the doctor's terminal. I have to leave some programs running to try and crack some of the encrypted notes and locked folders, which could take weeks, but I also search the computers and hard drives for anything I can get to.

Minutes turn into hours, and all of us are still working.

We hoped it would be easy, but we should have known better. That doesn't make us give up, though, because we are destined to stop this once and for all. If not for us, then for Nova and all the children who didn't make it. None of us deserved what he put us through, but we can make it right. We can't change the past and what we endured, but we can stop it from happening to another. We just need to find the right pieces of the mad scientist's puzzle.

Louis forces everyone to take breaks except me, knowing he wouldn't get me to no matter what. Nova sits with me every now and again, talking and joking, distracting me from the screen even just for a few minutes. She doesn't get it though. I'm determined to find the information for her.

I need to do this.

It's all on my shoulders. Even Louis is trying to help, but none of them are as good with computers as I am. I feel that heavy weight until my eyes sting, my hands cramp, and my back aches, but I still keep going late into the night. The others stay with me, and food is brought but it remains uneaten. We all continue to push forward, refusing to stop when we are this close.

Then there's a ping. We cracked a folder. I quickly navigate to it, saving it in case there's any kind of virus or trap. It's labelled with a date, and there are video files inside. I stiffen when I examine them, wondering what they are and if I should play them.

"Louis," I murmur, and he turns from the screen next to me. "Should I play them?"

It must catch the others' attention because they crowd us, and I feel Nova's hand on my arm. "Play them," she orders.

Louis nods, so I pick one at random. It loads quickly, and we all swear. Nova freezes, and I wish I could protect her. I try to close it, but she knocks my hand away.

On the screen is a screaming Nova. She's young, an early teen, and her hair has grown back, but it's stuck to her skin with her sweat. I can't see what is being done to her, but she's screaming, and her father is watching her from the corner while making notes. I close it and open another, only to see her at another phase in her life.

She's curled into a ball, sobbing on the cot.

Another one has my eyes closing. There's a gun between her and a man on the table.

All of them are of her torture, her experiments, and all the while he's there, watching and making notes. Closing them, I lean back and scrub at my face. Those images will haunt me now as well.

What she endured . . . *Fuck.*

I'm more determined than ever to make them pay, but when I look up to her, I find her eyes still locked on the screen. "I-I need a break," she murmurs and hurries from the room, wrapping her arms around herself. We all track her worriedly.

"Don't," I murmur when I feel Nico begin to move after her. "She needs a moment. She will feel raw and weak with us all seeing her pain. Give her a moment alone." I hate it as well, and he hesitates before sinking heavily into a chair, holding his face.

"How could he do that to his own daughter?" Isaac murmurs sadly. "How—" He shakes his head, looking away.

"Because he believed it was a necessity." I hate that I think like him. "Love is a useless sentiment, a useless feeling, remember? He never loved her or cared beyond her purpose in his experiments. She was just like us—a thing to use."

"Save them all and any others you find. We will all watch them so we know what she was forced to survive and to remind ourselves why we are doing this, but she will never see, do you understand me? Not ever again. We cannot protect her from her past, but we can protect her from this," Louis orders, and we all agree.

She shouldn't have to watch them again, not when they still fill her every waking and sleeping moment, but I will watch every single one, even when it fills me with hatred and helplessness. I will keep them with my own memories and pain, so whatever happens next, I'll remember why we are doing this now.

Not just for us and the other nameless faces, but for her.

Nova.

TWENTY-SEVEN

Louis forces us to rest, but I can't sleep upstairs, and the others seem reluctant, so Bert brings in sleeping bags and sets them up in the unused living room I have no memories of. They take turns sleeping. Louis checks in with command. They aren't happy, but they understand that we need time to go through all the findings and research for what we are looking for.

Everyone sleeps but me and Dimitri.

He never stops or moves from the computer.

Slipping from my sleeping bag, I tiptoe past a snoring Jonas and over Nico, who's near the door. I spot Louis at the front door, staring out, and Isaac in the kitchen, so I move back to the computers and Dimitri. From the doorway, I see his hunched over form. His eyes are red and raw, and the light from the screen gives his face a hollow look.

"You should rest," I murmur, and he jumps like he didn't hear me creep up. Blinking, he rubs at his eyes as I move closer, pulling a chair over to sit at his side. He looks back at the computer with a grunt, so I cover his hand on the mouse. "Dimitri, you need to sleep, you know that. Your brain needs rest."

"I'm fine." He shrugs off my hand, and I debate walking away, but something is bothering him. "I can't stop, okay?" he finally says as I stare at his profile.

"Why?" I murmur, needing to know.

He turns to look at me, his gaze pained and dark. "Because I need to do this for you!" he rages, tugging at his hair. "I can't stop what happened, but I can do this. I can find the information that will help them, you, and us stop this. That might give you peace and a better future. I'm doing this for them as much as you. How can I sleep when I know that with each minute I wait, another child could be hurt, and that you are stuck in this place that haunts you?"

He's doing it for me.

I sit back, blinking as I stare at him, and suddenly I can't stop myself. Leaning forward, I cup his face and the stubble there, and I kiss his warm, soft lips. He freezes as I pull back, pressing my forehead to his. "Thank you," I murmur. "I do hate it here, but I would hate it even more if you were to get sick because of me. I can endure this. It's . . . better with you all here. I know how important this is, I do, but so are you. Do not kill yourself for answers. They will come when we need them. Louis and the others need you for the long run, not just for your mad computer skills." That makes his lips curve, and mine follow as I search his eyes. "I need you, okay? So please, sleep and eat."

The smile drops, and our breaths mingle. "You need me?" he echoes.

"I do," I admit, my voice hoarse, "in more than one way, but right now? I need you to sleep, please." I lean in and kiss him softly again before standing, then I offer him my hand.

He swallows, glancing at the computer before taking my hand. "Just a few hours," he concedes, making me smile wider.

"Fine by me." Squeezing his hand, I lead him from the room. Louis is at the door, and I almost stumble, but there is no judgement or jealousy in his eyes. I only see gratitude. I nod and lead Dimitri to my sleeping bag, where I tuck him in like a child as I brush his hair back. "Sleep, the computer will be there when you wake up."

His eyes start to close, but then his hand moves to squeeze mine. "I need you too," he whispers, and just like that, he's asleep.

I sit back on my heels and watch him before forcing myself to stand

and move to the kitchen, unsure what to do with the feelings inside of me. Isaac is staring out of the kitchen window with his hands wrapped around a mug, and he appears to be miles away. I slip inside, and he jumps, turning to look at me before getting to his feet.

"Let me get you one." He quickly pours me a mug, and I sit opposite him, drawing my knees to my chest as I balance the mug that's filled with some kind of herbal tea. I raise my brows, and he grins sheepishly.

"It's good for the soul," is all he says.

"Okay, Dimitri is resting," I tell him, taking a sip and almost groaning as the warm, comforting taste sinks into me. Isaac's eyes are wide.

"And how the hell did you manage that?" He gapes, making me laugh. "Seriously, we've been trying to learn how to for years. Tell me your secrets."

I lean in and look around like we are being watched. He does the same with a grin, and I crook my finger until he comes closer, then I press my mouth to his ear, ignoring the pulse of desire it sends through me as his scent wraps around me. "Feminine wiles."

Sitting back, he chuckles. "Well, we never stood a chance then."

"Nope, sorry." I wink while taking another sip.

"How are you doing, really?" he asks over his tea.

"Probably about as good as anyone would be," I admit, not wanting to lie. "But I've survived worse."

"Yes, but you're not alone anymore," he murmurs, eyeing me.

"I know, I know." I wave it away. "There are just some things you have to deal with alone."

"I can understand that." He nods.

"What about you?" I ask, tilting my head. His eyebrow arches, and I laugh. "Oh, come on, this can't only be affecting me, so how are you, Isaac?"

"I, um, I don't think anyone has ever asked that," he says quickly.

"Then I'll ask every day. Come on, you have all seen my deep, dark secrets," I joke.

"Truly, it's not easy," he admits as if he's ashamed to share it. "It reminds me of my own . . . imprisonment," he hedges.

"In France, correct?" I ask. He still has a slight accent.

He nods. "Not that I saw the place. Maybe I will go back and visit one day just to see the beauty I knew lived above my prison." He sips his tea, his eyes going far away. "My cell wasn't quite as grandiose as yours. It was in the basement of a house on the outskirts of the city. It was surrounded by land, though I never saw the sun much. I was kept in a room bigger than that one, with a bed, a toilet, and a shower. That was it." I reach for his hand, and he takes mine with a sad smile. "I spent so many years there, I thought I would go mad, but I didn't. Instead, I filled the time by learning everything about medicine I could. I thought maybe it would impress him, but I would also be able to look after myself."

"And did you?"

He nods, squeezing my hand before he stands and pulls his shirt up. I inhale when I see the healed marks on his chest, and then he peels back the sleeves, where there are scars raised around both wrists. "For years, he was obsessed with capture, with chains restricting my movement to see if it would help my brain grow if I couldn't focus on my body." Sitting, he takes my hand again. "To this day, I hate them . . . when I see them on the table." He looks away in shame, so I force his face back to me. "The only reason I didn't sink into my own memories was because I needed to be there for you."

"Isaac." I swallow. "I'm sorry. These words feel inadequate, but they are true. I'm sorry for what he put you through, but I'm not sorry it brought you to me."

"No?" he asks. "You might be soon."

"Nah." I squeeze his hand with a wink. "All families are dysfunctional. No matter what, though, he cannot take away your achievements, your good heart, and how you take care of everyone else. When do you look after yourself?"

He swallows, and I smile sadly. "Exactly what I thought." Standing, I round the table, take his tea, and put it down as I sit on the table before him. "You need to look after yourself and give yourself that chance to heal. You do not have to bear the brunt of all the weight alone. That's why we are together. Right now, I'm betting you are in here worrying about them all out there"—I jerk my head towards the other room—"and how they are handling it, while coming up with plans to reduce their stress without even considering your own."

He's silent, but he knows I'm right.

Leaning forward, I capture his chin and force his eyes to mine so he can't look away from me this time. "You can't save anyone if you don't save yourself first," I tell him before I stand. "I mean it. I will ask how you are every day, and I want the truth. Now get some rest. As a doctor, you should know how sleep deprivation works on the brain."

"Is that an order?" He laughs as I put the mugs in the sink.

"You bet." I grin at him and smack his ass as he walks past. "Go sleep, doc. I'll keep watch."

Once I've cleaned up, I move through the house, seeing them all resting except for Louis. I find him at the computer, and I sit at his side. He meets my gaze with a grateful smile.

"Thank you for getting them to rest."

"Any way I can help." I shrug it off, but he turns my face back to his.

"It's a big deal, Nova, thank you." I hate the kindness in his tone, so I clear my throat and look at the screen, blinking. "What is that?"

"That," he begins, and he seems pained. "Is something that would destroy Dimitri."

I flinch, and he nods.

"That is Bassel, Bass for short. He was one of us."

"The one Isaac spoke of," I mutter. "He . . . He killed himself, didn't he?"

"Yes, when the pain became too much." The young boy on the screen looks so lost and sad, my heart aches for him. "Your—the doctor didn't just do mental experiments, but physical. He wanted to see how life-long chronic pain could affect you. He carved up his insides so badly, there wasn't a day when he wasn't in agony. We supplied him with morphine as much as we could, and he was constantly high on it just to be able to sleep or breathe. It's why we got caught in the end, but before we could help him too much, he walked in front of a bus. He left us a note that said he couldn't do it anymore, couldn't fight the pain, and that he was sorry."

"Fucking hell," I murmur softly. "Dimitri—"

"And he were lovers." Louis smiles. "They were so close, they were inseparable. It hit Dimitri hard when he died. He buried himself further into his love of machines, losing himself in them and pulling away from all of us. He had no drive for anything but revenge, and then you came, and you reminded him of friendship, love, and a future. I cannot thank you enough for that. We were going to lose him like we lost Bass, but you are saving him."

"I'm not doing anything," I reply worriedly.

"You are. You just don't know it."

"Will you tell me about him? Bass?" I ask, changing the subject. I want to know more about the man who could have been a friend, who went through what we did.

"Dimitri knew him best, but he had this laugh that would light up the room, and he was so creative. He would tell us stories and act them out. He liked to paint . . ." For the next hour, Louis lets me fall in love with a friend. It's easy to see how much he cared for the man, and how deeply they are all connected. The stories make me laugh as much as they make me cry, and when he trails off, I'm almost desperate to know more about someone I will only know through them.

Someone I couldn't save.

Someone my father killed.

TWENTY-EIGHT

I get a few hours of rest once Jonas comes and takes over, and I wake to the sound of grunting. When I open my eyes, I realise Nico and Jonas are sparring right there in the hallway. A nervous Bert flits around them, making sure they don't break anything. Sitting upright, I feel my mouth dry at the sight of their huge, glistening muscles as they move with precision and speed that rivals mine.

That's when I realise I haven't trained or sparred in a few days, and it's evident from my turbulent emotions and nightmares from being back here that I could use it. Rolling out of the sleeping bag, I rip my long shirt over my head, leaving me in a sports bra I fell asleep in and biker shorts. I tie my hair back, grinning when Jonas spots me. His eyes widen before they simmer as Nico lands a hit that sends him flying back into the wall.

"No fair! Her tits distracted me!" Jonas groans.

Nico whirls, his eyes widening as I move towards him with purpose. "I think they would distract anyone," he murmurs. "You want in?"

I nod, rolling my shoulders back. "Both of you against me. I could do with a challenge." I smirk.

"Oh, she has a death wish." Isaac sighs, leaning against the wall as he comes from the kitchen.

"Or maybe I'm just that good." I wink at him, ducking below a hit from Jonas, who wasn't really trying. They circle me as I stand there.

"Are you sure about this?" Nico asks, giving me a way out.

"I've fought bigger and faster opponents." I grin. "Killed them too. Bring it, baby."

"When I win, I'm going to fuck her." Jonas laughs.

"Master Jonas!" Bert snaps.

"Sorry, Berty." Jonas winks as I give him a grin.

"If you can beat me, I might just let you," I murmur. He didn't expect that, and I use it. I launch myself at him, tackling him to the floor before rolling to my feet as I smirk down at him. "But fight properly."

"I won't hold back," Nico warns, his voice a whisper behind me as I duck a punch and spin to face him, sliding back.

"Good, then neither will I." I smirk at him, seeing the flare of desire in his eyes.

Glancing over, I see Jonas push with his hands and flip back to his feet. "Oh, this will be fun." It's the only warning I get before he comes at me. He's fast and feral, with no rhyme or reason to his movements. I duck and weave around him, managing to land a few hits before I'm kicked back into the table with a grunt. The vase there tips to the side in slow motion, and we all watch it drop to the floor and crack. All eyes go to Bert, whose eyes narrow before he looks at me.

"Kick their asses."

I can't help but laugh as I nod and throw myself back into the fray, ignoring Isaac's, "Now you've done it."

Nico manages to grab me from behind, but I use his body and height and throw myself back, flipping over him and taking him down. He rolls back to his feet, though, and then they work together. One is always behind me, and one is always in front. But what I said is true—my father and his mentors used to blindfold me and throw me into the ring with their guards.

I am used to being outweighed and outnumbered.

It's fucking thrilling for me, in fact.

Adrenaline courses through me until I can't help but laugh as I spin away from a sweeping leg. Despite their words, they are still going easy on me, so I decide to up the ante and force them to take this seriously. They wouldn't go easy on each other, so I won't let them go easy on me.

As Jonas chases me, I race towards the wall, kicking off it with three steps before I flip over him, then I wrap my arms around his head and bring him down in a headlock as he snarls, elbowing me. I grunt from the pain and hold tight with my hand on my wrist, tightening my hold.

There's a cheer, and when I glance over, I spot Dimitri and Louis watching from the hallway leading to lab room. I grin as I release him and roll, avoiding Nico's silent sneak attack I sense coming up behind me.

"About time." I grin, and then there's no room for talking as they turn and come at me faster than I thought possible. They aren't normal guards, and this isn't typical fighting. I should have remembered that. They are like me—stronger, faster, and harder—but fuck if that isn't a turn-on. It's an actual challenge for once. I don't have to hold back the strength of my punches. I split Jonas's lip, where that blow would have knocked someone else out. Nico's punch to the gut only winds me, where it would have taken anyone else down.

Jonas kicks out the backs of my knees, and the pain is sharp. I fall forward, hitting the floor with my bare hands and rolling as they follow me. I roll back and forth to avoid their kicks before stopping in front of Nico. I grab his foot as he brings it down, grinning up at him. I twist, and he growls, having no choice but to turn with it or break his foot. He spins away, and I sweep Jonas's legs out, watching him tumble as I climb to my feet.

I'm panting slightly, and my body is lit up with excitement. For some reason, a thought flickers through my head

If this is how they fight, imagine how they fuck . . .

That idea distracts me enough that Jonas manages to grab me and lift me into the air with a hand on my throat, squeezing so hard I gasp. I slam my hands down in a V, but it doesn't affect him as his eyes smoulder up at me. "I think I'll let them all watch as I take my prize," he says before he throws me.

Instead of hitting a wall, I hit a solid chest as arms catch me midair.

Nico.

His mouth meets my ear, and somewhere along the way, this fight has charged with sexual tension strong enough that I could cut it with a knife. I feel his very hard, very big cock pressed against my ass as he holds me, letting me feel just how much he is enjoying this.

"Maybe I'll join in," he murmurs into my ear before bringing me down in what I can only describe as a WWE move to the floor. Groaning, I stumble to my feet and wipe my mouth as my heart skips a beat.

"Fine, you want to play like this?"

"Oh shit," someone whispers. "It's about to get good."

"I think I should leave," Bert mutters.

"Good call," someone else replies, but I focus on Nico, who's coming at me again. They want to win just as much as I do. It's not in our nature to submit or give in, so I fight back, even though I'm starting to realise the odds are stacked against me.

They are fucking superhuman.

They don't stop.

I try to tease them like they teased me, but it doesn't work because they are so focused on winning.

I dodge one attack, only to fall into another. I do manage to bust Nico's ribs and take them down to the floor, but they just get back up. I can tell they feel the same as we dance around the foyer. They are both panting, covered in cuts and blood, as I get back to my feet again despite the pain and exhaustion flowing through me.

"Fuck, you can take some punches," Jonas remarks breathlessly, his hands on his knees and head bent down so his hair falls into his face. He straightens with a groan and cracks his back. "Come on, let's finish this."

"My thoughts exactly," I retort.

Nico nods, blood running from his nose. They share a look again, and then we are back at it, clashing in the middle. I duck their punches and jump over their kicks, giving as good as I get. One movement slides seamlessly into the next, mixing martial arts together. I bust open Jonas's nose, and Nico splits my lip. I kick Nico back to a wall and take Jonas down, grabbing a piece of broken vase and pressing it against his neck with a grin. "Submit."

"You," comes a growl, and I feel a sharp edge of a glass vase pressed to my own neck.

Laughing, I toss the glass away and get to my feet as Nico does the same. "Well, shit, it's a draw." Louis sounds shocked.

"Good fight, boys." I hold out a hand to Jonas, who is grinning madly at me. He accepts it but pulls me down so I sprawl across him with a groan. Gripping my head, he gives me a hard, swift kiss that leaves me breathless and clears all thoughts from my head.

"Since I didn't win, I at least get that." He smirks and then rolls us to our feet, putting me on mine as I gawk at him. "Well, look at that, I finally shut her up."

Rolling my eyes, I swallow my shock. I'm about to walk away when Nico grabs me, spins me back to him, and tilts his head down. I freeze, thinking he's about to kiss me as well, but his tongue darts out and traces the cut on my lip, tasting my blood. The stinging sensation makes me gasp as he pulls back slightly.

"I'll collect my kiss when I'm ready," he whispers and then spanks me. "Go get washed up, it's time to eat."

Unsure what the hell just happened, I blink and accept the clothes Dimitri holds out to me. "I've never seen anyone lose against either of them separately, never mind together," he tells me, stroking my ego, which is bruised.

"He's right." Louis nods. "Now back to work." He claps.

I nod at them with a small smile, happy they aren't watching me strangely after Jonas's kiss and Nico's near miss, before I hurry to the stairs where Isaac is standing.

With my clothes tossed over my shoulder, I stop beside Isaac as he hands me a warm mug. I meet his eyes over it. "Are you okay?"

His eyes widen before a soft smile curls his lips. "Yes."

Nodding, I turn and head upstairs, feeling all eyes on me and not minding one bit.

TWENTY-NINE

"Bert, I said I'm sorry!" Jonas whines as I step into the kitchen. My hair is still wet and hanging over my back, and I'm dressed in skintight black yoga pants and a crop top. I lean into the door and watch as Jonas follows an angry Bert around like a kicked puppy. With his lips pursed, Bert sniffs, ignoring Jonas as he cooks.

"Please, my man, I just want those epic pancakes you made," Jonas begs. "I'll go and clean up the vase. I'll even get you a new one!"

Shaking my head, I stride to the table and take a seat next to Dimitri, who smiles at me. I grin back and knock my shoulder against his as we turn to watch the show, but then Nico comes in and steals all of my focus. My mouth becomes dry, and my thighs clench together as desire pounds through me.

He's shirtless, wearing low-rise grey joggers that do nothing to hide his thick thighs and slightly hard length. I scan his impressive abs and Adonis belt, leading down to the joggers and then back up to his huge pecs. I get lost in his muscles before there's a whisper in my ear.

"You're drooling," Dimitri teases.

"And you wouldn't?" I mutter.

"Oh, I do," he purrs.

I throw him a mock glare and wipe my mouth, even as my eyes jerk back to see Nico grinning at me, flashing straight white teeth, as he purposely heads over, leaning over the table to kiss my forehead. "Good fight. Next time, don't hold back so much. You can't hurt us."

I swallow and nod, not trusting my voice when his man boobs are so close and I have the irrational urge to flick his nipple. Fuck it. I tweak his nipple, laughing when he jerks back. "Same goes for you." I ignore the looks thrown my way, especially the dark, hungry one Nico gives me as I grab a plate and start to load it with fruit and pastries, whistling happily.

"Fucking hell," Nico finally mutters as he sits opposite me, bringing his pecs back to my line of sight as I munch on fruit. There is a crash, and I jerk my gaze up to see Jonas on his knees before a shocked Bert, who dropped a pan.

"Please, Bert, I'm not into guys, but I'll blow you if that's what you want."

I frown at the panic winding through Jonas's tone. Looking at Louis, I see him sigh, scrub at his face, and nod at Dimitri.

"Dr. Davis used to starve him as an experiment and withhold his favourite foods as punishment and to taunt him," he whispers sadly. "When we found him, he was half dead and crazed. He panics about food."

"Fuck." I climb to my feet and head over, my hand going to Jonas's shoulder. He looks up at me sadly with haunted eyes, completely broken. Getting to my knees, I lean into him as I stroke his face, comforting him as tears fill his eyes. He's terrified that someone will let him starve again and tease him with what he wants but can't have. "Go sit down, baby, okay?"

He still seems concerned, but he stands, and with sagging shoulders, he heads to the table, not meeting anyone's eyes. I look at Bert who tracks him with a shocked, saddened gaze.

"We all have our issues from my father. Do not ever withhold food from them again, do you understand me? I know it wasn't meant as a punishment, but we've been treated as lesser humans since we were kids. Everything you can imagine was used as punishments. Don't do that to us, please," I beg when he looks like he's about to cry.

"I swear, Miss Nova, I didn't—"

I grab his hand and squeeze. "I know, my friend. I'm just explaining.

Now, how about some pancakes?" I say happily. I meet Jonas's eyes. He looks hopeful, like a child perking up.

"I will fill the entire house with them whenever you want, sir," Bert tells Jonas, his back straightening and eyes determined, as if he would cater to his every whim to not see that look again. Turning, I sit next to Jonas, placing my hand on his thigh under the table. He jumps but settles into my side as I fill his plate.

"Eat for me," I murmur, and he quickly dives into it as I meet Louis's grateful gaze.

Not ten minutes later, a plate stacked so high with pancakes I can't see Bert over it is placed before Jonas, who looks lost for words. Tears actually well in his eyes. "The doctor was a cruel man. I am not him. I'm sorry, Master Jonas. I meant no disrespect. You are always welcome in this house and in my kitchen, so never hesitate to ask for what you need. A friend of Miss Nova's is a friend of mine." With that, he bows to Jonas and goes back to making more pancakes, as if he truly will fill the house with them.

Jonas just stares at them, so I lean in and break the moment, knowing he will hate that we all saw his weakness. I would. "Are you just going to stare at them, or are you going to eat them before I decide I want them?" I tease.

He blinks when he turns to me with a bright, unguarded smile on his lips. He looks so innocent for once that it stops my heart. "Thank you," he tells me, squeezing my hand before taking a pancake. I stare as he eats, and something shifts inside me. A barrier falls before this equally damaged, crazed man, and a sense of protectiveness roars through me, the force of it scaring me. I return to eating but make sure to watch him as he carefully eats and treasures the pancakes as if they are a gift.

And in a way, they are from Bert, to show Jonas not everyone in this world is the same.

When Jonas sits back with a groan, I see the usual mischievous sparkle in his eye and relax a little. He's back, and he's not lost in the past anymore. "Next time, I'm going to cover your entire body in them and eat them from you," he warns, closing his eyes before he cracks one open when I laugh. "Hell, maybe I'll even fill your cunt with syrup and drink it from you."

"Jesus," Louis mutters, making us all laugh, but mine is tense and filled with desire.

Jonas hears it, his grin knowing as he strokes my thigh under the table, heading higher and higher until I scoot my chair back suddenly. I am not ready to go there, not with him. I fuck for fun and never remember them. I know it wouldn't be like that between us, and I don't want to lose them.

I like them. They are starting to feel like family, and I don't want to do anything that will ruin that, even if I know it would be amazing—okay, better than amazing. Fucking spectacular.

"I suppose we better get back to work."

A flash of hurt echoes in his eyes as he turns away. Licking my lips, I look away and meet Louis's concerned gaze before he stands.

"You're right, back to work. Let's find these bastards."

After five hours of helping everyone that I can, I go for a dinner break that Louis orders with Dimitri at my side. He's teamed us up since he told us Dimitri listens to me. Jonas says I have some kind of weird pussy power over them.

That got him a smack, even if it was the first time in hours I cracked a smile.

I don't know how they manage it, but they bring me back from the brink when I'm in there, and I'm grateful for it. They keep the atmosphere light and teasing, and if it wasn't, I think we would all sink into the depths of what we are looking through and handling.

Bert makes us a basket for dinner and shoos us outside, saying he needs to clean and we need sun and fresh air. Grinning, Dimitri takes it from him, and we head out back. I lead him to my favourite spot. I used to read and hide out here all day if I could to avoid my father. Bert reminded me of it with a knowing look, and although I've never taken anyone there before, even my sister, I take Dimitri, knowing he will understand why I needed it.

I don't anymore, but it's nice to share those places with someone who will understand and not judge you.

Crossing the huge back garden and walking past the pool that haunts me, I smile back at him as we reach the tree line and I duck under a low branch. The leaves crunch under my boots as I lead him deeper into the woods.

"If you are taking me out here to kill me, can I eat first?" he jokes from behind me.

Laughing, I hold a branch for him. "If I were going to kill you, I would have brought a shovel." I shrug. "Plus, I'm too hungry to kill."

"Good to know," he mutters. "Always keep her hungry."

Shaking my head with laughter, I duck under the two huge stones that lead into the dark crevice between. "Oh, this isn't sketchy. She's definitely going to murder me," I hear him say, but he follows me anyway, and when we come through the other side, he gasps.

"This is my favourite place in the world," I tell him, looking out at the land that has remained unchanged. "It's where I used to come to get away from it all." Stepping over the soft grass, I kick off my boots and wiggle my sock-covered feet into it with a sigh. The sun filters through the trees, warming us against the slight chill. "I would spend hours up here, reading and imagining I was the characters in a book. I would pretend like I was in a different land, envisioning a prince coming to rescue me," I admit as I look back at him to see he's listening carefully.

"Here, I was in a different world, and for a few hours, I was just a child, and I could be anything." I turn to face him as I spin. "A pirate rescuing his love from a stolen ship, a wizard going to school for the first time, a high priestess winning the war for her people. I could be anything, and I was. When my world came crashing back down, I took their strength and lessons with me to survive."

"Thank you for showing me this place," he murmurs, crossing to me and cupping my chin, forcing me to meet his eyes so I can see the truth in his gaze as he speaks. "I know that wasn't easy. I am so happy to be here with you, in the place that saved you, so I could meet you. Let's eat, and we can read for a while for old time's sake."

"I'd like that," I murmur softly with a smile just for him. I hope my place can become his and help him when he needs it. It can be his escape from the reality of the harsh, uncaring world we live in.

For a moment, we just stare at each other from inches away, and his eyes drop to my lips before he clears his throat and steps back. I turn to hide my disappointment, knowing it's for the best, and look out at the place I've brought him.

The cliff overlooks a raging river below where you can spot deer sometimes. The sun shines brightly through it, almost making it ethereal, and on foggy days, it transports you to a different world. The trees make natural arches above us, creating a barrier from the summer sun and keeping it warm in the winter. The grass is soft and dotted with flowers that have me grinning. There are also some rocks worn from age that I used to lounge on under a tree for shelter, soaking in the sun glistening across the worn grey space.

There's just something so beautiful here, and since it remained untouched by the horrors of my life, I found solace in its unreserved neutrality and softness. It reminded me that there was good in the world if one looked hard enough. Probably an idiotic thought as a child, but I did whatever I could to get through. Crossing the distance, I sit with my back to the natural seat of the rock, and he does the same opposite me, opening a basket similar to the ones Bert used to sneak to me when he knew I was coming out here.

Dimitri laughs, and I see why. Inside are little sandwiches cut into squares with the crust off. "I hate crusts," I admit. "He remembered."

"He loves you." He shrugs as he takes some for himself. There's a spread of different flavours—ham and cheese with honey mustard, garlic cream cheese and red pepper, egg mayonnaise, and BBQ pulled chicken. He's made a feast. Dimitri also pulls out scones with homemade jam and clotted cream, little cakes, and crisps.

"Wow," he mutters.

"He doesn't like people to go hungry." I shrug as I unwrap the sandwiches and dig in, gratefully taking a napkin and paper plate from him, and then he divides it out and begins to eat himself. As we do, our eyes wander to the land around us.

"Did you have a place like this?" I ask, curious.

"Not really. I escaped into the never-ending line of computer code," he replies. "If I focused enough, it swept me away from my body and the pain in it, as well as human emotions such as loneliness, hunger, and sadness."

It makes more sense why he loves anything that has to do with technology. It's like my meadow. That's where he feels safe and happy.

"Then I found it in a person as well, and he became my safe place, my hope." He swallows and looks away as I slump, saddened by his pain.

"Bassel," I murmur. He jerks in shock, and I smile sadly. "I saw a picture, and Louis told me a little. I'm so sorry, Dimitri."

He swallows, his face pale as he looks away.

"Did you love him?" I ask. I shouldn't pry, but he needs to talk. I can see that he's keeping it bottled up, and that won't help. I know.

"With every fibre of my being. He was my best friend, the only one who understood . . ." He looks back nervously. "I love the others, and they are my brothers, but they are stronger than me. They understood the violence or the beauty in the science. Me? The world didn't make sense to me, and Bassel was the same. He didn't get people or the world. He floated in pain, wanting to escape. We found it together. I tried drugs with him once, but I didn't like how they felt, too out of control. With him, though, I was in control, and I was strong. Someone needed me, and I wasn't alone. I still wake up expecting to see him there."

Tears roll from my eyes, and he reaches out and captures one, bringing it to his lips to kiss.

"He would have liked you," he murmurs as I smile.

"Really?"

He laughs. "He would always say, 'Trust the crazy ones, they know something we don't.'" I laugh with him, and he grins. "He had this unique way of looking at the world. He said the broken were beautiful and that we understood something no one else ever could. He told me one day I would understand that love could be as healing as it could hurt. It did hurt with him because I loved him, Nova, but he loved the pain meds more. He couldn't exist without them, and I saw him withering away before me. I would wake up to a ghost, a stranger, towards the end. We were so young, so lost, and clinging to each other. He told me once it wasn't a partnership, but a necessity for us to survive. It was a love created out of desperation and pain, not friendship and need, but it was what we had. In the end, I lost him, and the pain was too great."

"He killed himself?" I ask, knowing sugar-coating it won't help.

He nods. "I found him," he admits.

"Jesus, Dimitri, I'm sorry." I reach for his hand, and he looks down at our intertwined fingers as he speaks, as if he's gathering strength for his words.

"At first, I was so angry at him for leaving me in this fucked-up world. He left me alone. Nova, I was furious with him and hurt. I even hated him a little for it and thought it was selfish." He peers up at me as if he's expecting recrimination, and guilt fills his eyes.

"I think that's normal," I hedge. "You are allowed to feel however you want. You lost someone you love, so you have to just feel it."

"That's what Isaac said, but more . . . technical." We both laugh then. He's bitter and sad, so I slide closer, and he rests his head on my shoulder as I stroke his back.

"Then I just missed him so much it broke the last parts of me your father wasn't able to."

I swallow my own pain and tears. This is about him, not me.

"Now I can hardly remember him or the sound of his laugh. It's like he's fading all over again, and that scares me."

I cup his face and force him to look at me. "No one is ever truly gone. They live on in our memories and our love for them. You may forget some things with time, but you won't forget the way he made you feel and the love you shared. You won't forget the important things—that you loved each other—and in the end, that's enough."

"You think?" he asks, searching my gaze hopefully.

"Yes, and you'll see him now and then in other people, in places and things you shared, and be reminded of that love. Like now. You remember him as you tell me about him, right?" I smile, wiping away the tears that fall. "So, tell me everything you remember about him, and I will remember him with you. That way he will never be forgotten, and if you start to forget, I will remind you."

"Promise?" he whispers.

"I promise," I say solemnly with strength infused in my voice. "He was so loved, Dimitri, and sometimes that isn't enough, but you have to know you did everything you could. Now you need to live for both of you. Let him live through you. Sometimes . . . Sometimes people aren't meant to be here. I believe it happens for a reason, despite everything I have survived. It's not about being strong or weak; it's about nature. It takes the best of us, and Bassel? He sounds beautifully brilliant. He had to be for you to love him. Forgive him, Dimitri, for leaving. It's time. He was human and imperfect. He felt like he had no other way out, and I have no doubt that, in the end, you were with him, and he wasn't scared because of that. He was happy to go into the light knowing one day, you will join him."

"Do you think it hurt?" he asks, sounding like a child seeking comfort.

"No," I answer seriously. "I think for the first time in his life, it was probably the only moment he wasn't in pain or afraid."

It seems to settle him, and he leans into me. I hold him as he cries and lets it all out. When his tears dry up, the birds chirp above us as if signalling a fresh start. He leans back, and I clean his face, and then we start to eat again.

Here, in my meadow, in my safe space, he tells me about the man he loved, and I keep him in my soul with the man next to me, remembering and loving him for both of us.

THIRTY

After leaving the meadow, Dimitri kisses my cheek and hurries back to the computers. For a moment, I let my hand linger on my cheek, wishing it had been on the lips. I've been so starved for contact that these men, these ridiculously attractive men, have driven me wild with their teasing touches and looks.

I have lady blue balls, in all honesty. Remembering the way their sweaty bodies pressed to mine as we fought and the promise in their eyes . . . Yeah, it has me hurrying upstairs to my bathroom. I need to blow off some steam so I can focus on why we are here.

Kicking the old wooden door shut, I stand before the mirror above the sink, one of my hands holding the porcelain edge. Usually I would turn away, but the spark in my eyes has my breath whistling from my lips. It's something that wasn't there before . . . .They were always dead.

Cold.

Now they are burning up.

My black hair is mussed from the wind, and my face is bright with happiness. Is this what this feeling is? Closing my eyes, I let my hand slide into my jeans, tracing over my knickers before slipping under. Widening my legs, I spin so my back is against the sink as I stroke my pussy.

I'm wet from thinking of them.

From chaste kisses and teasing looks.

Fucking hell, I'm like a teenager, but it doesn't stop me from flicking my clit with a muffled moan. With my other hand, I nudge my top up and cup my breast through my bra, rolling and tweaking my nipple. Pleasure explodes through me as I pant, my finger rubbing my clit quickly, but for a moment, I imagine it's not me.

I imagine it's them.

Their hands cupping my breasts and playing with my nipples. Their mouths sliding across my skin and marking it up. Their hands inside my jeans, touching me, sliding down my wetness to push inside before moving back to my clit. Their mouths pressing to my ear. No doubt Jonas would whisper dirty promises, Isaac would keep a watchful eye, Dimitri would hold me up, and Nico would destroy me and make me his all the while Louis watched on. All working together to make me come.

I don't have time to think about how fucked up it is. I'm imagining all of them fucking me, and my imagination gets the better of me. I visualise Nico on his knees before me, gripping me meanly as he jerks me closer, his mouth sealing over my pussy and dominating it. I see Jonas at my side, stroking my breasts as he whispers in my ear. I imagine Dimitri on the other side, doing the same, while Louis watches it all with his hand on his cock and Isaac stands next to him.

Shit, shit, shit.

My clit throbs in time with my racing heart as I speed up my fingers, needing to come so badly but not wanting this fantasy to shatter.

"Good girl, I told you I would claim my kiss."

Nico's voice echoes in my head, and a gasp leaves my lips as I slide my hand down my dripping pussy and thrust two fingers inside myself, pretending they are his. I widen my legs farther as I thrust in and out of my pussy, hitting my clit with the palm of my hand each time until I'm almost coming, my back arching and mouth falling open.

A noise has my eyes opening, and at the sight of the peeling wallpaper, reality comes crashing down and embarrassment chases away the desire.

I pull my fingers from my pussy, about to berate myself, when there's a husky groan. My head turns, and my eyes clash with Jonas's bright, lustful gaze. He's poised at the door, his fists clenching the wood as he watches me, his nostrils flaring.

"Don't you dare fucking stop," he growls, stepping into the room and kicking the door shut behind him. "Watching you touch yourself is the most beautiful thing I've ever fucking seen. The best fucking torture I could have ever endured."

"Jonas . . ." I lick my lips, unsure what to say, but when his eyes drop to my glistening fingers and his body shudders, I slide my hand back inside my jeans. "Like this?" I murmur, playing along. He's igniting my lust again, only this time I can't control it. It storms through me like a wildfire as I hold his gaze while I stroke my clit.

"Fuck," he groans, reaching down to rearrange himself. My eyes lock on the huge bulge in his joggers, and I remember the sight of him fucking his hand. I moan and my pussy clenches. I'm dying to know what that magnificent cock would feel like inside me.

"I did watch you." I rub faster, my other hand gripping my breast harder as I rock my hips, fucking myself. "I watched you touch yourself. I was so fucking wet I could barely sleep."

His eyes narrow, neck straining. "I came harder than I ever have in my life, and I had to stop myself from hunting you down and forcing you to your knees to taste it. I wanted you to see what you do to me, baby."

Groaning, I speed up, and his eyes drag over my body possessively, hungrily, but I'm about to come, and I don't want to yet, so I pull my fingers free and suck them clean, moaning at the taste of my desire.

He snaps, lunging for me, grabbing me, and turning me.

He presses me to the edge of the sink as his hands slide down my body to grip my hand again. "Don't stop. Watch yourself as you come, watch as you touch yourself for me." He quickly unzips my jeans and pushes them down so he can watch, his hard cock pressed to my ass.

His fingers nudge my knickers aside to expose my glistening pussy to his hungry gaze. He grunts, his hips jerking forward as he pants. "Fucking hell, look how wet you are. You better touch yourself before I decide to eat that pussy until they have to rip me from you."

"That's not a threat," I purr, even as I touch my clit.

"Like that?" he murmurs in my ear, licking and biting it. "Is that what gets you off?"

I nod jerkily, rolling my hips as I rub my clit furiously before sliding my fingers inside myself. His eyes darken, almost turning black, as if they are sucking all the light from the room so he can watch me. One of his hands grips my breast for me, pinching my nipple hard.

I cry out as I speed up my fingers, so close to coming again. "You're close. I can almost see it." He groans, rolling his hips into my ass, humping me. "Fucking hell, I've never been so turned on. I haven't even got my hands or mouth on you yet, and I'm about to come in my joggers."

The idea of him coming from watching me has me picking up speed and closing my eyes, but he twists my nipple so hard, they shoot open.

"Eyes on us," he snarls, biting my neck. "You will always keep your eyes open when we fuck, baby, so you can see what you do to me. So I can watch you come apart and see all those walls come down as you explode."

"Holy fuck," I whisper, desperately rubbing and flicking my clit now, and with a knowing smirk, he bites down on my neck at the same time he pinches my nipple.

I shatter, and explosions rock through me. My legs shake from the force, and a moan is trapped in my throat as I fight to keep my eyes open through the crashing waves of pleasure.

As he rocks none too gently into my ass as he watches me come apart, I can't pull my eyes away from the man behind me—the man framing me like I'm a fucking masterpiece painting and he's simply been made to hold me up.

"Good girl." He pets my oversensitive pussy, making me jerk before he steps back and laps at the palm of his hand, tasting me. Snarling, he pushes at his joggers as if needing to touch himself just from the taste of me. I turn and almost fall, having to hold myself up as I watch him. I redress as my tongue darts out to wet my dry lips. My pleasure ebbs, even as my pussy clenches at the sight of the man before me. He's wild, panting as he tries to find his own pleasure after helping me find mine.

It's that thought that has me stepping forward. Reaching up, I drag his head down and slam my lips onto his. He freezes for a moment, not even breathing, before he groans into my lips. Gripping my hips, he jerks me closer, trapping his hard length against my belly and rocking into me like he can't help it. I slide my tongue across the seam of his lips, and when he opens for me, I sweep inside, tangling with him. Both of us become lost in the other.

His kiss turns feral and hard, just like I expected. Our teeth clash, almost drawing blood from my lips, and I still can't get enough. I have to rip myself away to breathe, and when I do, I shove my hand into his joggers, curling it around his cock. His hips jerk forward, and his eyes close for a moment.

"I want to watch you this time. I want to watch you make yourself come for me," I order him, gripping him hard as I stroke him. "I want to see how you like it."

A noise invades for a moment before I ignore it, focusing on him as I stroke his length. His head falls back, his eyes closed in bliss and agony. His neck strains, his veins throbbing with his pleasure. He loses himself to my hand, but another noise distracts us, and I jerk my head around, listening.

It's shouting.

"Jonas . . ." I stop, looking at the door. The need to rush down there and confront the situation wars with the fact that I *need* to see him come.

"Let them fucking kill each other," he growls, thrusting into my hand. I laugh, I can't help it, and then I press my head to his chest, hearing his racing, thundering heart. "Hell, let the whole world burn around us right now, and I wouldn't give a fuck."

Smiling, I reluctantly remove my hand from his joggers and press a kiss to his chest before stepping back. "Later, baby. Then you can feel how frustrated I've been since you chased me down." I wink and move to the door. He grabs me, spinning me and slamming me to the wood. His lips come down on mine, hard and fast.

He gives me a brutal kiss before he presses his forehead to mine, both of us panting and fighting the need to tear each other's clothes off. "Now, we are even," he murmurs, his voice like gravel, echoing around me. He grabs the handle and rips open the door. "Let's go save the idiots so I can kick their asses."

Taking his hand, I let him tug me downstairs, trying and failing to ignore the desire storming through me again.

Unleashed by him.

I have to try and focus on the shouted words as I hurry downstairs, hand in hand with Jonas. I still feel the heat of his cock warming my palm, and my knickers are drenched with my own cream from our encounter, but as soon as I reach the bottom step, all that pleasure and afterglow fades, and my throat clenches in panic and something else . . .

Hope.

At the front door, unsure and hesitant but standing her ground, is my sister. Ana wears an expression that echoes one I usually wear, although it's slightly more nervous, and she has her arms crossed as she stares them down.

My men.

Standing together, side by side, Nico, Dimitri, Isaac, and Louis create a barrier as if to protect me from her. After all, they all saw how much her anger and hatred of me killed me last time, but she's my sister. Squeezing Jonas's hand for strength, I carry on until I stop next to them, sparing her a look. "What's going on? I heard shouting."

For a moment, all eyes are on me. Louis's eyebrow arches at my flushed cheeks and rumpled clothes, but it doesn't faze any of them as they return to glaring at Ana. What did she do? She jerks her gaze to me and looks me over as her lip curls.

"Oh yes, she's clearly so fucking traumatised," she spits haughtily.

"Huh?" I frown, confused. "Someone fill me in."

"We were trying to educate your sister"—Nico spits the word like a curse—"about exactly who you are and what you went through."

"You what?" I snap.

They know they have fucked up because they won't meet my eyes, but Nico does. "I couldn't stand her insulting you like she did. I didn't tell her everything, just some bits."

"Oh yeah, because she was clearly fucking abused," Ana snarls.

The urge to run consumes me, but when I meet their eyes, I see their confidence in me and the strength they are offering. They want me to tell the truth and stop protecting her. After all, that's what I'm doing. I am protecting her from the truth, but she's not a child anymore, and she deserves to know, even if she won't believe it.

That actually terrifies me, but with her note burning a hole in my pocket, I stop before her, blowing out a breath. We are night and day. Two very different sisters.

"Of course you wouldn't think I was. I protected you from it, Ana," I tell her softly. She jerks and meets my eyes with derision. I rush forward, knowing she's the only person in this world who could flay me alive anymore. The anger in her gaze makes me raw.

I want her to believe me, but I made my decision, and now she needs to make hers. I will give her all the facts, knowing she will need them. Her scientific brain is unable to accept anything but evidence.

"Father hurt me, Ana." Her mouth opens on a rebuttal, but I surge ahead. "For years. He was not the man you knew, sis. He wanted me to feel like this. He wanted me to feel isolated, ashamed, helpless, and alone. I was scared to tell anyone, scared to tell you because I needed to protect you, even if it meant hurting myself in the process. He knew that by separating us, it would turn us on each other. Ana, you know deep down what I'm saying is true. You know he was capable of being cruel and cold if it got him what he wanted. You must have noticed the changes in me. I tried so very hard to hide the evidence, but I know you saw it, even if you didn't understand it."

"Stop," she demands, shaking her head. "I can't believe you are trying this."

"What?" I ask, frowning. I feel the guys step closer behind me to protect me.

"To disparage his name and make me think he was evil. He was a good father. It's not his fault you are a selfish bitch who skipped out on her family. You can't come back and spin these lies now because you aren't the favourite anymore. Did you know that? You were always his favourite. Whatever I did was never good enough and could never hold his attention while you were around. When you left, it was like you died. Those were the best years of my life because he finally paid attention to me."

Fear pounds through me at the fact that I might have missed him hurting her like he did us, but when she carries on, I realise he didn't.

"He finally loved me," she confesses. "Just because you messed up, that doesn't mean you can concoct these stories. You are probably doing it for money."

"I don't want money, Ana," I reply sadly, rubbing at my aching heart. "I just wanted you to finally know the truth because I hate this. I hate you thinking the worst of me. He knew you would. He encouraged it, knowing that even if I was protecting you from afar, he was driving a wedge between us. It was a final blow to me, the only way he could hurt me anymore. I never should have left you with him, Ana, and I'm sorry. I ran because I was scared. You're right. I was scared he was going to go too far and kill me, but I protected you. I promise."

"I don't need your protection!" she screams.

"You did! He was a monster!" I yell, ripping up my shirt to show her the scars he left behind.

"Those could be self-inflicted. You are so delusional." She looks away.

I realise she will never believe me, too blinded to what truly happened, or maybe her mind is rejecting it to protect herself. Nothing will change her mind, unless . . .

My shoulders sag at what I'm going to have to do. I was a fool to protect her from this for so long, but I refuse to lose her again. I refuse to let him win on this. "If you don't believe me, then let me show you."

"Nova," Louis snaps and turns to me, searching my eyes. "You don't have to prove anything to her. If she doesn't believe you, then that's on her. She knows deep down what her father was; she just doesn't want to see it. She doesn't want to confront the fact that she let you be hurt over and over and did nothing about it."

I cup his hands, leaning into him for a moment. "I have to do this. She has to see. She deserves the truth as much as we all do." I look back at her. She's watching us with a confused expression. "Give me five minutes. If you still don't believe me, you can leave and continue to hate me. I will leave you alone."

"Five minutes," she agrees. "Lead the way."

I turn and find Bert there. He steps forward and takes my hand. "For what it's worth, Miss Nova, I never doubted you, but Master Louis was right. I was scared to tell the truth, for it meant that I was involved in something so terribly vile. My excuses and apologies don't matter. I let him hurt you, and I never did anything. For that, I will spend the rest of my life apologising."

I shake my head and kiss his cheek. "It only would have gotten you hurt, my friend," I admit honestly. "I often begged for someone to notice, but I was selfish because it would have ended their life. You do not take responsibility for the vicious, cruel nature of that man, do you hear me? We are all victims here." When he nods, I look back at Ana, who looks unsure.

Bert straightens. "I can help you now." He looks at Ana then. "Miss Ana, everything Miss Nova is saying is true. Please do not make her relive this for your own peace of mind. She has already suffered so much. If I could protect you both from this, I would."

"I need to see," she responds, and he sags. I pat his hand as I pass, heading to the lab.

She follows me, as do the others, and at the door, she hesitates. "I didn't know this was here."

"No, he never wanted you to. This is why you never saw or heard it. This is the place of my nightmares," I tell her coolly as I step inside. I don't look around as I sit at the computer and pull up what I need, but when I look up, I see her staring at my cell in dawning horror. When she looks around and then back at me, there is fear on her face—a child's fear that the man she loved, the man she looked up to as a hero, was actually a villain.

I have to burst her bubble, but I nod at the screen. Slowly, she steps behind me. I meet my guys' eyes in the doorway. They crowd the entrance, offering me their friendship and love.

"I don't want your pity or sympathy, sis, only for you to believe me. You are the only person in this world I care about believing me. After, I will answer everything you want to know." I hesitate before pressing the button. It's a random video file of me. My dad is there, talking and introducing it before it pans to the cell.

Ana gasps, the pure horror in the sound making me curl into myself. There is a surly, angry teenager strapped down to the bed. My head is turned as I glare at him, and he stops before me, device in hand. My eyes spit fire at him, even as he touches it to my chest and my body jerks with the shock, a scream leaving my lips.

I pause it, but she pushes me aside, her hands shaking as she clicks another. I don't watch what's playing, and instead, I watch her. Her face is pale, and horror and agony are written across her features as she watches video after video of me being tortured by our father. I was experimented on under her nose. I watch the moment her life crashes down around her and all the lies are unveiled. Her eyes dart to mine, filled with tears, as her lips quiver. Her gaze silently begs me to protect her from this.

For a moment, she's the little girl I used to hold as she slept. She's asking me to protect her from the monsters in the dark again, but I can't, not anymore, because the monsters are real, and they got me.

"Ana, it's okay—"

"How can you say that?" she screams, but it has an edge of hysteria to it. "I can't breathe. Oh my god. I need to get out of here." She rushes to the door where my men are. They look at me as she beats at them blindly, trying to get them to move. When I nod, they step aside, and she rushes out. I hurry after her in time to see her burst out of the front door. I step out after her as she falls to her knees, gripping the gravel like a lifeline. An anguished scream rips from her throat.

The sound burrows into my heart, another scar to add to my collection.

I stop before her, kneeling as her tear-stained face and hopeless eyes lift to see me. "I-I didn't know," she whispers, her voice ragged. "I swear, Nova, I didn't know."

"I know you didn't." I take her hands in mine, brushing off the gravel and rubbing them to stop them from hurting—an automatic response to her pain. "I never wanted you to. I thought by not knowing, I could protect you from it. From him."

Her eyes close for a moment. "Everything was a lie."

Leaning in, I press a kiss to her head like when we were kids. "Not everything, sis. Not us. Never us."

I simply hold her as she cries into my chest, her hands pulling me closer as another piece clicks into place in my heart. I look at my men who are gathered at the door, protecting me from afar.

And since I arrived, I smile for the first time.

THIRTY-TWO

na's hands shake as she grips the mug and takes a sip. Her face is still pale, and she's in shock. Her eyes go to Nova, as if she's worried she will disappear. I know the feeling. She sits in silence on the sofa. I'm opposite her on the other one, and Jonas is stretched out next to me, still glaring at her.

I know that feeling too. He's still angry at the woman who hurt our Nova, but she was a child, and she didn't know better. Then I remember how adamantly she fought her, and how she didn't even believe her for a moment, and that anger does not fully dissipate. Nova might love her, but that leaves her open to getting hurt, so we will protect her from everyone, even her sister.

Nico blocks the door, as if worried she will run again. Isaac watches her worriedly before looking at Nova with open admiration. Dimitri is tapping his fingers in the corner, clearly wanting to be at the computer but staying for Nova, who hurries back in and wraps a blanket around Ana, protecting her yet again.

But did she ever protect Nova?

No.

After five more minutes of silence, Ana lets out a breath, places the cup down, and turns to her sister. "I need to know everything."

"There is a lot. Ask whatever you want. I have no secrets." Nova sits opposite her sister on the sofa, one leg bent up with her arm thrown over the back. She appears casual, but I see the tremble of nerves and the tightness of her body. I wish I could lessen what she's feeling.

"Do not harm her more than you already have." I lean forward, and Ana jerks her gaze to me. "Remember, Nova still has to live with this, so do not make it worse just to settle your curiosity."

"Louis." Nova sighs, but I shake my head.

"No, I don't care if she is your sister. She doesn't have our loyalty; you do. We will protect you, even from her." I want her to realise how serious I am, and the smile that curls up her lips steals my breath.

"Then let's start with who they are," Ana says, nodding in understanding at me, so I settle back. If she takes this too far, she's gone.

Nova hesitates and looks at us, so I incline my head, telling her to let her in on the secret. "The other children." She blows out a breath. "I wasn't the only child Father experimented on. He had children all around the world, from different walks of life, but they had one thing in common—no one cared if we were hurt or missing."

"But why?" Ana asks.

"He wanted to expand the human mind," Nova repeats before she shakes her head. "But the truth is, he used us, experimented on us, for his own gain. For research. He liked playing God. There were more, but they didn't make it. For the last few years, I've been on the run to avoid him and his clutches, just trying to survive and keep you safe, but with his death, a chain of events was set into motion. They found me"—she grins at us— "and chased me down to prove who they were. Together, we are going to stop his research once and for all."

"But he's dead. It's stopped," Ana protests.

"No, it hasn't. It's still happening. Children are still being hurt, and we are going to put an end to that. We are going to destroy it all, and his name will go down in the history books for what he truly was. That's why we are here, in his lab, looking for our next location, our next research facility."

Ana looks shocked and seems to be absorbing it before she looks around. "He hurt you all too?"

I incline my head. Nico grunts, and Isaac offers a gentle, "Yes." Dimitri just looks away, and Jonas snorts. "Quick on the uptake." He looks at Nova, his eyes softening. Later on, I need to address where they were and why they came out looking rumpled. Jealousy roars through me before I seal it up. "Are you sure she's your sister, baby?"

Ana blinks. "Baby?" she repeats.

Nova flips Jonas off, but he just laughs. "Questions, Ana," she reminds her.

"Right." Ana sits up, flicking off nonexistent lint, and I see the calculation in her gaze. She's now the scientist, not the scared child.

For the next hour, Nova answers question after question about the science, their father's co-workers, the experiments, and everything and anything in between. I butt in when it gets too hard for her, and Ana deftly avoids those conversations. That's when I realise something else. She recognises the signs of PTSD and abuse now, and she seems to know how to deal with them. *Strange.* Why didn't she notice them before? Or was she purposely blinding herself to them with her hatred?

Ana finally sits back, drained of questions and looking exhausted. "I just can't believe"—she shakes her head—"that he did this, that he got away with it. That I never noticed."

"He was good at playing the perfect, doting father," Nova comforts her, easing her guilt when she shouldn't. Ana was a kid, that's true, but so was Nova.

"So what now?" Ana asks.

"Now?" Nova repeats in confusion. "Now nothing, you go back to your life—"

"I can't do that." She sits up, forcing Nova to blink. "I can't. I need to help. I need to make this right. Our father—he was a monster; you're right. We need to stop what they are doing."

"We?" I repeat, looking her over. "You have no skills that are of use to us, and everything you know is from us. You don't know the locations or anything of use. You aren't as fast, strong, or capable as us. Go back to your life."

"No." She meets my eyes, and I see a spark of Nova there. "I will make this right. I will protect my sister."

"Ana," Nova starts, but I lean forward, a tiny spark of respect starting to form for the younger woman. She might not have known then, but she does now, and she's choosing to help us.

"I can read my father's research. I worked with him for years—not on this, but I can read it. I can help," Ana reasons. "Please, let me make this right."

I can see Nova doesn't want her involved in this and wants to protect her, but she deserves the same rights as us. "Fine, you can help with the research, but that is all, understand?"

She nods quickly, determination on her face. "I can help." She seems to be telling herself that.

"You won't get in the way, do you understand?" I demand, and she nods again. I see fear in her eyes as she looks at us. Good, she should fear us because her sister is quickly becoming our whole world, and we won't lose her, and anyone who stands in the way of that or jeopardises that won't have our mercy. "What kind of scientist are you?"

"I work with the brain." She blushes. "Mainly the effects of war and PTSD. I work with veterans . . . ," she trails off. "Ironic, I know."

Tell me about it.

Nova looks at her sister with nothing but pride as I sit back. "Dimitri, show her to the lab."

He turns to face me, not looking at her. "I won't work with her there," he snaps.

"D, please." Nova stands, going over to him.

"No, Nova," he retorts. "She hurt you. She didn't believe you. I won't."

Ana looks like she's about to cry, but we all watch as Nova stops before D and their heads bend together. They whisper before she sighs and looks back at me, defeat in her expression.

"Fine. Ana, you will take the research to your room here."

Ana nods, looking at Dimitri in shock before bowing her head, shame in her expression. I stand, and Dimitri slips from the room. I follow him before nodding at the others. I need to talk to him. He's hurting, and he's protective of Nova, but I can't let him get lost in his grief again. Not like with Bass.

"Nova." I look back at her, silently communicating for a moment before speaking. "Look after them for a moment." I narrow my eyes on Nico and Jonas. "Do not kill her sister; it would hurt her."

It's the only thing that would appeal to them. I know that. If I'd said it was wrong, they would have laughed. If I'd argued she didn't know, they wouldn't care.

They will do nothing to hurt Nova, however, and I see my order hits its mark, even as Ana pales, realising she's surrounded by killers.

"Now, back to our mission. We have information to find, so let's not waste time." I slip from the room, intent on protecting my family.

Including Nova.

THIRTY-THREE

I watch Louis go, my heart racing from the look he gave me. It told me he would protect me no matter what. I look around and realise they all would, even from her. Dimitri was so adamant about hating her for what she did to me, he refused to listen to reason, and even gentle Isaac doesn't seem happy with her.

"Would . . . Would they really kill me?" Ana asks, fear in her voice.

"Yes." I won't lie to her. "So don't give them a reason to." I move to Nico and meet his angry gaze. He eventually looks at me. "He's right. If you kill her, you will ruin me in a way my father never could." He flinches, and I kiss his cheek.

Jonas watches me stride towards him, his eyes hazy with madness and lust. I straddle his lap, uncaring who's watching, as I grip his chin and force his head back to meet my eyes. I need to penetrate that fog and make him understand. After all, he's the wild card.

"You touch one hair on her head, and I will chop off your dick."

"I knew you liked it." He grins, gripping my hips and tugging me over his hard length. I try to swallow my gasp as I narrow my eyes. "Though chopping it off to keep for your pleasure is sexy as hell, I'll admit to liking it where it is."

"Jonas."

"Nova." He grins, and I have to fight my own as I grip his chin harder, making his eyes smoulder from the pinch of pain.

"Please," I beg, and that makes him jerk, his eyes turning serious. "Please don't hurt her."

"I would do anything for you," he replies, and I don't know what's scarier: his madness or the fact that when he says that, his gaze is clear and serious for the first time since we met. Sighing, he looks over at Ana. "Fine, you're safe from me. Thank your sister for that." He leans up and kisses me quickly. "Now, if you're not going to ride my dick, let me go so I can deal with this hard-on."

For a moment, I debate it before sliding off his lap. He stands and stretches, and Ana quickly averts her eyes as Jonas winks at me and then wanders off, leaving me shaking my head.

"He scares me," she murmurs.

"He should." I look back at her. "I'll go get the research for you." I look at Isaac then, and he nods, letting me know he'll watch her as I stand. Although I am thankful for him, I still hurry. They watch me, but I force myself to head back to my sister and hand her his books to start with.

Holding them tight, she nods at me, taking this seriously, and hurries off as well. I watch her go before looking at Nico and Isaac. "Well, we are all on break, right? So what shall we do?"

Nico groans as Isaac laughs. "I have an idea."

I wiggle my eyebrows, even though I know that's not what he means, but it's nice to see them both grin. To be honest, I'm exhausted from this conversation and from seeing my sister hurt, and as usual, Isaac notices, so when he leads me outside into the sun, I turn, wondering what he's doing.

"Let's play hide and seek." He grins, jumping on the spot. "I could do with some exercise, and I never got to play it as a kid."

"Me either." Nico frowns. "What do we do?"

"You never played hide and seek?" I stare, open-mouthed. I know they are doing this for my benefit, and it makes my heart melt as I grin. "Oh, this will be fun."

"What are the rules?" Nico demands seriously.

"I count to thirty, and you hide while I do. We will limit it to the trees and property here. No going too far or out front. If I find you, you're it."

"I'm so going to win." Isaac grins. "Cover your eyes, sweetheart." Laughing, I do as I'm told and spin around, starting to count. I hear them racing away, and I can't help but laugh, just like they knew I would.

When I've finished counting, I drop my hand and look up for some reason, spotting Ana at the window of her room, watching us. She looks so alone and so lost that I hesitate, but with a determined grit of my teeth, I turn back to my men, knowing they did this for me. They are right. I need some laughter and fun. She's made her bed, so now she must lie in it. I can't protect her from everything, and it's time I started living for myself.

I run into the forest, leaving her behind to find her own way, and a weight I didn't even know I was carrying lifts with each step I take away from her and that house.

THIRTY-FOUR

Grinning, I press my back to a tree. I don't really want to hide, since I want her to catch me, but I want to listen to her giggle as she searches. Her steps are loud despite the fact she knows better. She's enjoying this. This is exactly what she needs, and honestly, so do we. We've been working so hard that we haven't just had fun or enjoyed life in far too long. Nico needed a distraction from his anger at the world and her sister, and I did as well, so this seemed like the perfect thing to do.

The sun shimmers through the trees. It truly is a beautiful estate, despite everything that happened here. I can't hear or see Nico, but I know he will take this very seriously. I have different plans, and I don't even realise it until I hear her draw closer.

Seeing her coming down the stairs with bruised lips, mussed hair, and a glowing expression was enough to cause feelings, such as jealousy and possession, that were so strong, it scared me. I told myself I wouldn't make a move on Nova, not after the kiss, but I can't resist.

I really can't.

She makes me want things I have no right wanting, and I'm tired of hiding my desires and trying to be her friend when she clearly doesn't want that. She crossed the line with Jonas, but that doesn't mean she's willing to with the rest of us, and yet I can't hold myself back from chasing her now.

I'm hunting her even though she's the one searching.

I'm leading my prey into my trap, and I'm not bothered by that in the slightest. She giggles, and I tilt my head, realising she's close. Suddenly, she jumps out from behind the tree, her grin wide and carefree. "I got you!"

"No, I got you." I smirk as I tackle her, lifting her over my shoulder. She laughs, and when I throw us down on the leaf-covered ground, her eyes alight with happiness.

She's so fucking beautiful.

I must say it out loud because her laughter tapers off, and her eyes turn dark with desire, dropping to my lips. She wants me to kiss her as much as I want to. Her legs frame my hips, and our bodies are completely pressed together, so I can't hide my rapidly hardening cock from her. When she feels it, her mouth forms a perfect O, and she doesn't pull away.

"This isn't in the rules," she teases as her hands stroke up my arms and loop around my neck.

"We make our own rules," I murmur as I lean down, unable to resist feathering my lips across hers.

She groans. "I like our rules better."

Laughing, I swipe them across her chin and cheeks. "Me too. So what do I get for letting you catch me?" I purr as I lift my head up. Her pink little tongue darts out and traces a path across her lips.

"What do you want?" she flirts, playing the game, but I'm done with games.

"You," I snarl and drop my lips to hers.

Tangling my tongue with hers, I swallow her moan as I tilt her head back and dominate her mouth, taking over every corner and tasting every inch until she's panting beneath me and rolling her hips, dragging her warmth across my hard cock. I nip at her lips as I pull back, grinning at her.

"Hold on," I order as I kiss down her chin and neck, nudging her shirt down to place a gentle kiss on her rapidly beating heart. Moaning, she tightens her hold on my hips, lifting her own to roll her cunt against me. I move slowly, taking my time. I want to remember this, the taste of her skin, the feel of her silky warmth, and the sounds of her moans, so when the darkness takes over again, I can push it back with this.

She watches my every move as I push her thighs apart, pull off her trousers, and settle between her legs. Her knickers are wet with desire, and I press my nose against them before inhaling deeply, filling my lungs with her sweet scent. Groaning, I dart my tongue out to taste her before looking up. Her head is back, her neck arched, so I bite down on the soft, silky material and tug them aside to expose her pink, glistening pussy.

"So pretty," I murmur as I stare at her, reaching out with shaking hands. I part her lips and lick my own, staring at her swollen clit and pretty hole that's begging for me to fill her.

"Isaac." Hearing her moan my name has my throat thickening with desire and something much deeper.

Swallowing the words I want to say, I drag my tongue along her pretty pink cunt.

The gasp she makes has me doing it again and again. I love her reactions and need them all. I watch her carefully as I stroke, lick, and explore her pussy, noting what makes her sigh and what makes her cry out, and then I use it against her.

I need to feel her come for me and be as crazed for this as I am. I'm not as wild as Jonas, but I have the insane need to taste her pleasure and to make her mine. Panting, she drags her hands up her shirt, tugging at her nipples as I watch.

"Fuck, you are so beautiful, Nova," I tell her, kissing her clit in that maddening way she both loves and hates. "So bloody beautiful, and you taste so good. I could eat you all day."

"Jesus, Isaac," she calls out, looking down at me.

"Don't believe me?" I dip my fingers into her tight, wet heat, stroking them inside her as she rolls her hips to fuck them, and just when she has a rhythm, I pull them out. Ignoring her cry of anger, I lift my fingers to her. "Taste yourself, taste your desire for me."

With her eyes locked on mine, she leans up and wraps her lips around my fingers and sucks, tasting her own desire for me. When she moans and drops back, I smirk.

"Told you, darling, you taste like fucking heaven, so be a good girl and lie back and let me enjoy my new favourite meal."

"Don't let me interrupt you," she mumbles, but then she moans when I suck her clit into my mouth in punishment.

I tease the swollen nub as she lifts her hips and grinds into my face. Releasing it, I nip and lick at it until she's panting heavily and widening her legs. Grinning, I switch between licking and sucking her pussy, teasing her, then I drive her higher by dipping my tongue inside of her before flicking her clit as I thrust two fingers into her tight channel.

I grind my hard cock into the ground, and the pain and pleasure mixes together until I'm nearly spilling in my pants just from tasting her.

"Isaac!" she yells, gripping my hair and tugging me as she rolls her hips. "Shit, I'm so close."

"Let go," I murmur against her sensitive skin, turning my head to nip her thigh. "Let go for me. Let me watch you come, Nova. Let me feel it against my tongue."

My words send her off the edge. Flattening my tongue, I lap up her release before plunging my tongue into her clenching pussy as she cries out and writhes beneath me. I lick and lap at her, desperate for more of her addictive taste, and I don't stop until she tugs my hair until it hurts.

Letting her pull me up her body, I meet her blazing eyes.

"Fuck me right now," she orders, lifting her legs to wrap them around my waist.

"Anything for you." I chuckle as I lean down and kiss her, letting her taste her release. Swallowing her moan, I reach down and pull my hard cock free, stroking my length before settling between her thighs and dragging it up and down her cunt. I let her feel the blunt end of my cock as I nudge her clit over and over.

"Isaac," she warns as she pulls back, biting my lip until it hurts.

Grunting, I line up with her pussy, lifting one of her legs higher as I kiss down her cheek to her ear. "I can't wait to feel you wrapped around me. Fuck, I've thought of nothing else since I first saw you, and how pretty you would look beneath me, taking every hard inch."

"Fuck," she groans, closing her eyes as she lifts her hips, trying to take me inside.

Grinning, I nip her ear. "Hold on, beautiful." Then, without warning, I slam inside of her, unable to go soft or slow. I still once I'm balls deep, closing my eyes at the tight, hot feel of her gripping my cock. She feels like a fucking vice, making me tremble with the need to move. Her hands claw at my back as she rolls her hips, trying to get me to move, but I wait, savouring the first thrust, the first moment of her.

I know there will never be another that feels this good, whom I want this much.

"Isaac." My name on her lips is my undoing, so I pull out and slam back in, filling her before speeding up my thrusts. Both of us need to come, even as much as we want this to last.

I lose myself in her body, kissing her while I do, and she fucks me right back, meeting me halfway, encouraging me to go harder and faster in the dirt.

"God, you feel so fucking good," I rasp when I have to break away to breathe, my head pressing to hers. "So fucking good, Nova. How can you feel so fucking good? Like heaven, Christ, I could spend the rest of my life inside you and die a happy man."

Her eyes round as she stares at me. "Don't say shit like that to me. We don't get forever; you know that."

"Then I'll take what I can get, which is right now, with you dripping beneath me, begging for me," I promise as her hands slide down my back and tug my pants lower.

Her hands grip my flexing ass, and her nails dig in until I groan from the flash of pain. One of her hands flops to the ground next to us, gripping at the dirt and leaves as she cries out for me, her eyes wild as she meets my gaze.

Glancing up, I spot Nico half hidden behind a tree. His dark eyes are lit with hunger as he watches us. Smirking, I slam into her harder, making her scream, and then I look back down at her, watching her take my cock and give as good as she gets.

Her hands drag up my back to my neck, and without warning, we flip. Grinning down at me, she lays her hands on my chest and starts to bounce on my cock.

"Fuck," I murmur, watching her amazing tits sway with her movements. "Goddamn, Nova, you are too fucking sexy. You're going to make me come before I even get you off again, and I consider myself a fucking gentleman, darling, but with that hot body riding me? All that goes out the window."

Her head falls back as she winds and rolls her hips, chasing her own release.

"Use me to come, fucking ride me until you do," I growl, gritting my teeth against the pleasure storming through me. My balls are heavy, and my abs are tightening, but I hold back, feeling her tight, wet cunt engulfing my cock over and over until she grinds herself deeper and screams her release.

Then and only then do I flip us. I pull out of her as I press her front into the dirt and wrap her hair around my fist. I pull her head back, arching her for me as I slam back inside of her dripping, milking cunt. I hammer into her, chasing my own release. She claws at the ground, pushing back to meet my thrusts as I take her brutally, knowing she can handle it.

I need to fill her with my cum, and I can feel my release approaching. Pleasure bows my spine until I can't hold back anymore. Yelling, I explode, filling her with my release as she cries out, coming again and gripping my dick, milking it of every drop of my release. Moaning, I fall forward, resting my head on her sweaty back as I bury my cock deeper, wanting to keep my cum inside of her so she'll think of me later.

Breathing heavily, she falls forward against the ground, and we just lie here before I gently pull out of her and roll to my back next to her. A smile I can't stop curls my lips. I'm almost giddy, and I am so happy, my heart feels like it's going to burst. When she reaches over and takes my hand, I almost declare my feelings for her there and then, but I don't, knowing it will freak her out.

Nova is like a wild animal. She craves freedom, not chains, and I will never contain her like her father did.

I turn to stare at her, and she watches me with knowing, smug eyes. Finally, I start to shiver from the cold, and so does she, so I dress and help her into her clothes before rolling her onto her back once more and kissing her, needing that connection.

It's the only time I've ever felt grounded and like a man, not anything more.

With her, I am not a freak, an experiment, or even the doctor they all rely on.

"I suppose we better get back to reality."

"I guess." Brushing hair from her face, I drop a soft kiss there as she grins mischievously up at me. "What?" I find myself smiling.

"Hey, Isaac, are you okay?"

My smile turns molten as I stare at the incredible woman below me. "Better than okay. I'm incredible right now."

THIRTY-FIVE

"Dimitri," Louis calls after me, but I ignore him, not wanting to talk.

My emotions are too messy, too volatile, to speak to him, and he'll want me to talk it out. That never works. Instead, I'm going to lose myself in the one thing that still makes sense—computers—but I should have known he wouldn't let me. He follows me into the lab as I sit.

"D," he begs, "talk to me. What's going on?"

I shouldn't respond, shouldn't unleash the tornado of fury inside of me. I should focus it and never let it out, as her father would say. Emotions make you weak. I try, clenching my hands on the desk and closing my eyes to count like I was taught.

"Is it her sister?" he questions, hoping to understand.

One mention of her, and I'm turning with a curled lip, my nostrils flaring with the fury I can't contain. Not when it comes to Nova. For so long, I lived in nothing but code and flashing screens. There were no emotions and no connections, I was just adrift online, but then she came and she yanked me into real life, sending me tumbling around with things I haven't felt in years. Memories, pain, happiness and hope are all tangled up inside of me because of her, yet she also settles it. Her soft smiles, stolen touches, and comfort anchor me to this world and give me a chance to breathe.

Is she right? Is Louis? Do I retreat into computers because it's easier not to feel anything? If so, it's the coward's way out, yet aren't I doing that again? Afraid of the true depths of my feelings for this woman we only just met?

Bass would call it fate. His smile would crinkle up in that adorable way, and he would chuckle at my uncomfortable thoughts and my bumbling attempt to express what is happening in the vortex in my head. He would tell me to go for it, to take the leap, because even if you hit the bottom and crash, the fall would be worth it.

Is Nova worth it?

Yes. I know that one hundred percent, which is why I'm so angry on her behalf.

For so long, my life was carefully filed inside of my brain, locked away in folders with passcodes, but now, she's the virus infecting them, and I can't even be mad about it.

"D," Louis demands, sitting next to me and turning to me as I sort through my muddled feelings.

"I hate her," I finally admit.

"Who?" he asks, his brow furrowed. He's dragging the words from me and leading me to a confession. That's how Louis operates. He sees what we don't inside of ourselves and finds the best way to coax it out, whether it be potential, trauma, or hopes. He protects us by knowing everything he possibly can, taking the blows for us, and keeping us together by pure grit.

"Her sister," I snap, trying to control my anger. It's not directed at him, after all.

He watches me carefully, the only one who knows what I'm truly capable of. "D, breathe."

Nodding, I count, and only when I feel like I am on stable ground do I carry on. I'm still angry, but I'm not about to go out there and wring her fucking neck. "Okay, why do you hate her sister?" he asks slowly when he sees I'm calmer.

I give him an exasperated look, and he grins. "I know why I hate her, but D, why do you hate her?"

"For hurting Nova and not believing her. Fuck, you've seen Nova, Louis. She's loyal to a fucking fault, and even after all these years, she protected her sister. I saw her face when Ana"—I sneer the name—"said she didn't believe her. It broke her, Louis, in a way even her father wasn't able to. It fucking killed her. She's been betrayed, used, and hurt by her own family for so long, yet she still protected her. How fucked up is that?" Swallowing, I look back at the computer and close my eyes. "I would have done anything to have someone willing to protect me like Nova protects her sister, and yet she doesn't even care. She threw it all away."

"I know. I'm angry too. All we can do is be there for Nova and protect her because fuck knows she doesn't protect herself, even from her sister."

I nod, drumming my fingers on the desk.

There's a scuffle outside, and Louis jerks up. After peering out, he shrugs at me and sits down heavily. His eyes are still locked on my profile, and after my outburst, I just want to go back to what makes sense, like finding answers on this hard drive, but I know he won't let me. He has something else to say. I can feel it. He was like this when Bass . . . well, yeah, then.

He was worried I was going to explode and watched my every move.

He once told me people fear Nico and Jonas because they look like they are willing to kill because of the darkness in their gazes, but they should fear me because I would destroy the world and stand in the flames before they even realised I was a threat.

I guess that's not wrong.

We are all a little fucked up, even Isaac who plays the perfect, doting doctor, and our fearless leader has a dark side, not that he lets it out often. That iron control was built to contain what lies within.

"You're letting her get close," Louis finally comments, and I almost laugh at the absurdity of it. If I wasn't, I wouldn't give a shit about her weak sister.

"And you're not?" I retort, lashing out in my own anger, but he doesn't react to the barb. He simply sighs and sits back. His response only deflates me and makes me feel like rubbish for taking my issues out on him when he's only trying to help.

"I am, and that's what worries me," he finally admits, sharing a shy grin with me. "She is magnificent, isn't she? When we suggested finding his daughter, I never thought we would find *her*." He shakes his head with a laugh. "Who knew such an incredible woman could be born from such cold hatred."

"Diamonds are crushed, not made," I reply simply, and he laughs, nudging me.

"Maybe tell her that." He winks, and I can't help but smile. The phone rings, and we share a look, understanding washing through us. It's a reminder of our duty and what we are doing here, and all traces of amusement disappear as he extracts it from his pocket and answers it with clipped greetings.

He barely speaks, and I can only hear the vague hum of words on the other end, but we all know who it is. When he hangs up, his expression is closed down and serious.

I raise my brow, but he just scrubs at his face, and it's then I realise he looks tired. Not just now, but always, as if this life is slowly draining him. Was I so self-centred and locked in my own world that I didn't notice my friend, my brother, was suffering too? I want to ask, but I know he will just close down further, so instead, I file it away for now.

"Same shit, different day. We need to find something soon. They already don't trust us as it is, and I don't trust them not to lock us up and throw away the key. Humans are good at that, hurting those they are scared of."

Just then, there's a beep on the computer. If I were a man who believed in fate, I would have said it was exactly that, but instead, I know it's just a coincidence. Turning back, I raise my brows at what I've got.

"Well, we might have something. I'm finally into the encrypted files, so let's take a look at what the good doctor felt he had to try and hide."

Grinning, I let Isaac chase me to the main house. Nico catches me halfway, slinging me over his shoulder as he strides into the kitchen. Laughing harder, I smack his ass, and he does the same to me.

"Oh, hi, Bert," I hear him say.

Mortification fills me as I lift myself to peer over at Bert who is just smiling like this is a normal occurrence. "Is anyone hungry?" he asks us.

"Starving," Isaac replies, smirking over at me. The desire I see in his eyes makes me shiver where I'm perched on Nico, who spanks me again.

"I could always eat, especially something sweet," Nico teases, but Bert is oblivious.

"I could make a fruit cocktail for you." He looks around seriously. "Five minutes."

"Add peach if you have it," Isaac replies, licking his lips as he moves closer to me.

Okay. I slide from Nico's back before they can cause me to self-destruct, and with withering glances at them both, I hurry away, but I can't help but smile when I hear them bantering and laughing with each other. I soon sober up, though, as I move upstairs, heading to the shower, knowing

I have leaves and dirt in my hair and clothes. At the top of the staircase, I hesitate and move to Ana's bedroom door, peeking inside.

I need to check that she's still here and that she's okay.

She's hunched over on her bed, with folders and documents spread out in an order only she'll be able to understand. Her hair is pulled back in a clip, and her face is bare and locked in concentration. For a moment, I don't see her now, but as she was when she was a kid. She would focus so hard on her homework to be the best and to understand as much as she could, always hungry for knowledge. Briefly, she's not Ana, the grown woman, but Annie, the little girl I ached to protect from ever seeing the evil in this world.

Slowly, I shut the door and move away. After calling down to make sure Bert will send her some food and drink, I force myself into the bathroom. She's not a little girl anymore, and she doesn't need me there making sure she sleeps and eats. She needs me to trust her, and after I demanded that she trust me, I can offer her that much . . . right?

Once in the bathroom, I quickly strip and put my clothes in the basket. Turning on the shower, I wait for it to warm up as I look at myself in the mirror. There are leaves and twigs in my hair, my cheeks are flushed, and my eyes are bright. I look happy.

I look healthy.

If my dear old dad could see me now . . . With a self-deprecating snort, I hop into the shower, cranking the heat up to the point where it almost burns off my skin, and only then do I sigh, my eyes sliding closed as I just relax under the punishing spray.

My head is tilted back, and water sluices over my tired and aching muscles, and that's when I feel it. I jump and try to spin, but hands grab mine before I can attack the intruder, and they are slammed to the wet tile of the bathroom wall.

I kick out, but a warm, hard naked leg wraps around mine, trapping me, and I freeze. Warm breath blows across my neck as the water continues to pound down on me, almost obscuring my vision as I blink away the water droplets.

It's one of the guys, I know that, so I relax a little more. The force of his groan shakes my body as he presses against my back, letting me feel every hard inch of his body, including a massive hard cock prodding my ass.

I almost smirk, having my suspicions on who it is, but I play along, letting him lead this time.

Curling his hands in mine, he drops his head, his tongue darting out to lap at the water on my neck before he licks up to my ear. "Now, where were we, baby?"

I shiver at the hungry words.

Jonas.

"Well, by the feel of your cock, you were hoping to bend me over and fuck me, I'm guessing," I tease, pushing my ass back to rub against him. I shouldn't. I just fucked Isaac while Nico watched, but there's a madness in Jonas that I crave. While Isaac softens me, and Nico encourages me, but Jonas? He frees me, meets me head-on, and I find myself licking my lips in anticipation. A savage hunger races through me so suddenly, it steals my words.

"Or maybe I was imagining just slamming you up against this wall and fucking that tight little cunt until you scream for me again." He grunts, bucking his hips against my ass. "But I'll take you how I can get you, baby. So tell me, Nova, are you wet for me?"

"Why don't you find out?" I taunt, but my words are breathless. Anticipation floods through me, making me tremble with the need I feel for this man and a hunger they all seemed to have awakened.

Don't get me wrong, I love sex, but it's never felt like this before. Maybe it's because I know I can fully let go with them because I can trust them.

The chuckle he lets out is edged by madness. He slaps my hands harder against the wall. "Do not fucking move or I'll just slam into your cunt and fuck you until I come and leave you wet and wanting." The threat hangs in the air, and it turns me on more than it should as his hand slides up my arm and down my body, making me suck in a breath when he purposely catches my tightening nipple and then covers my mound. He grips it as he bites my leaping pulse.

"Oh yeah, baby, you're wet for me. I should be nice, taste that little cunt, and make you break apart, but if you want nice, you should have fucked the others. Me? I'm fucking mean, and I don't give a fuck if you aren't wet enough for my huge cock. I'm going to fuck you so hard it will hurt, and you'll love it, won't you?"

"So much talk," I snap. I want to turn on him, but I don't because I want what he is offering more. "Tell me, Jonas, are you all mouth?"

His hand slides back up my body to grab my neck roughly, and his teeth meet my ear. "You know I'm not, but how about I remind you, baby, since you seem to have forgotten? You think being a bitch will make me fuck you faster? Just for that, baby, I'm going to be mean. Keep your hands there the entire time or I'll walk away." With that, he reaches up and grabs the showerhead. I blink, wondering what the hell he is doing, but he kicks my legs open and, with a mean laugh, aims the spray right at my cunt.

Fuck.

The pressure hits my clit, and he moves it closer until it's just beating at it. "Let's see how long you can last, shall we, baby?" he taunts. "Let's see how quickly you'll come for me, so desperate to ride my cock."

"You're a prick," I snap, even though I roll my hips, that relentless spray making me cry out despite my words.

Laughing, he slides his hand down and circles my trembling hole. "You can lie to me all you want, but your body tells me the truth. It tells me how much you want this, how much you want me, Nova."

Narrowing my eyes, I kick back, but he just laughs. My eyes close, and my hips rock into that spray, but they fly wide open when I feel something hard, round, and cold at my entrance.

"Jonas!" I snap, but then I scream when he pushes it inside of me, forcing me to accept it. I stiffen, but he presses the showerhead right against my clit until I moan loudly, my pussy relaxing against the invasion and taking it deeper. It's wide, impossibly wide, but fuck if it doesn't feel good. My hips kick without me meaning to, sinking me deeper onto it, and when he finally stills, I look down. My head hangs between my trembling arms, which are still pressed to the shower wall, to see his hand wrapped around a bottle of what looks like shampoo.

He's fucking me with a shampoo bottle.

Oh fuck.

"Get that out of me now," I snarl, feeling embarrassed. When he starts to pull it out, the pinch of pain is eclipsed by the pleasure, and I whimper.

Laughing, he slams it back inside of me, setting a steady, brutal pace as he fucks me with it.

"Nah, I don't think I will. I've got to get you nice and stretched for my cock. Now watch me make you come, baby. You think you can resist this?" he growls into my ear, grinding against my ass. "Yet here you are, letting me fuck you with an inanimate object because you are so greedy for my cock."

"Fuck you!" I snarl, but he just laughs and speeds up, slamming it inside of me, and despite my protests, my abject horror at what is happening, I find myself pushing down to take it, letting the beating of my clit push me over the edge, and without even wanting to, I come hard, right as he slams the bottle inside of me and presses the showerhead to my clit.

My hips jerk, and he groans into my ear, grinding his cock into my ass. Sagging, I press my head to the wall, and he takes pity on me and pulls the showerhead away, the bottle too, leaving me whimpering at the almost painful pressure of it. A moment later, his hand is there, cupping my pussy. "Next time, be a good girl, and you'll get my cock instead of this."

He pulls away, but fuck that. If I have to submit, then so does he. I didn't let him do that to me, no matter how good it felt or how much I liked it, just so he could walk away. I pull my hands from the wall and spin to him, kicking him back. He looks shocked but laughs. I fling myself at him, and he catches me with a groan, his hands going to my ass and hoisting me up as our lips meet.

The kiss is hungry and desperate, and then I'm suddenly slammed back into a wall again, only this time it's my back that meets it hard enough to force the air from my lungs and pull me from his greedy mouth to suck in lungfuls of air. I wrap my legs around his waist and reach between us, gripping his hard cock and slamming myself down on it.

His eyes widen as he moans, his hand slapping against the wall as he holds me there. "Fuck, Nova," he yells. "Are you trying to kill me?"

"No, baby," I taunt. "If I was, you'd already be dead. Now be a good boy and fuck me."

"God fucking damn it, we are going to make some incredible babies." He groans, lifts me, and drops me onto his cock.

"They would be psychopaths," I retort as I reach out and grab a fistful of his hair and yank his head back. "Now stop fucking talking, you crazy bastard, and fuck me."

For once, he listens to me, his lips curling in a snarl as he slams me back into the wall with the force of his thrusts. There is no room for talking as he hammers into me. His huge, pierced cock hits that spot inside of me that has me raking my nails down his back to grip his flexing ass, urging him on as I slide down his dick to take him faster and harder, until there's nothing but jagged breathing and moans between us. I hit the tiles with each hard thrust, and I feel them crack, break, and cut my back, yet I don't care.

I want more.

Like walking a tightrope, I'm ready to fall at any moment, only this time he'll be coming with me. "Jonas," I moan, and it only urges him on. He grunts as he fights my fluttering cunt, gripping me roughly. There's nothing but madness in his eyes, and I love how focused he is on me, how he doesn't care if he could hurt me.

He just fucks me, hammering into me like it's his life's mission.

With his next thrust, he grinds into my clit, and I tumble from that tightrope, falling with a scream. My nails cut into his ass to keep him inside of me as I writhe on his cock. Fighting my tight hold, he flexes his hips twice more before stilling with his own shout. His cum splashes inside of me, almost too hot to handle as I fight his hold, nearly causing us both to fall.

Finally, the pleasure ebbs, leaving me exhausted, satisfied, and boneless in his arms. I feel his legs shaking as he holds us up, leaning into me to pin me to the wall so we don't fall.

"Holy fucking shit," he whispers. "I would say I went to heaven, but we both know I would end up in hell. I guess that makes you my punishment, baby, and I am so fucking okay with that."

I can't help but laugh, and it isn't long before he joins in.

Fucking hell, if we are supposed to stop and save the world, then we are all fucked.

THIRTY-SEVEN

The screaming finally stops, and with a forkful of fruit held midair, I trade a smirking, knowing glance with Isaac. Bert is blushing hard, and the radio is cranked up to drown it out as he moves around the kitchen.

Poor man.

But I'm glad to know she's a screamer.

Finishing my meal, I sit back and look at Isaac, who ducks his head slightly. "Got to be honest, doc, I didn't think you'd be the first to crack."

He rolls his eyes, delicately eating his fruit just like he ate her cunt in the woods while I watched. "I couldn't help myself," he finally admits.

"Yeah, I think we are all feeling that way when it comes to her," I respond as my gaze goes to the ceiling again, wondering if we will survive her.

"We have something. Grab the others," Louis calls to us before hurrying back to the lab.

I share another look with Isaac. "Rock paper scissors for who goes and gets them?"

"Fuck no, he will murder me. You go," he replies instantly.

Rolling my eyes, I get to my feet. "Pussy."

"Nah, that's what I got earlier." He toasts me with his bowl as he stands, and I can't help but laugh.

Shaking my head, I thunder upstairs, letting my footsteps be heard to give them warning. I see Ana peek out of her room, but when she sees me, she ducks back inside quickly with a pale face and fear in her eyes. I almost snort. Smart girl, that one.

Rapping my knuckles on the bathroom door, I swing it open, ducking the knife I know will be coming as I do. It sails over my head as I grin at them, noticing Nova's flushed cheeks and half-dressed state. Jonas is naked and proud, but I blink.

"Where did you pull the knife from? Wait, I don't want to know." I groan, rubbing my head. "Louis needs us in the lab. He found something." That sobers them, and Nova gulps, but her back straightens.

That's my girl.

Turning, I pluck the knife from the wall and toss it to Jonas without looking as I head back downstairs, giving them time to get dressed. At the lab, Louis is pacing, Dimitri is rubbing his head, and Isaac is leaning back against the wall, his face closed down. I arch a brow but lean behind the computer and wait.

A moment later, Jonas saunters in naked with a pancake in his hand. When he sees us all watching, he grins. "What? I worked up an appetite."

Nova comes in then and smacks him as she goes past. "Idiot," she mutters, but she's nervous as she moves around to stand near me. "What did you find?"

Louis looks at me, and I lean back, wrapping my arms around Nova and bringing her into the shelter of my chest. She's stiff for a moment before she melts, propping her chin on my arms as she looks between them.

"Just tell me," she finally snaps, and a grin flits across Louis's face before it locks down.

"We don't know. It's a video file addressed to you. We haven't watched it yet," he answers.

She becomes rigid against me, and she's barely breathing, so I lean down and kiss her ear, unable to help myself. I hate the anxiety spiralling through her. "Breathe, baby," I remind her.

She lets out a low breath and sucks in another, shivering against me before straightening. She's strong and brave, such a fucking fighter. "Then play it."

I hold her up as much as she holds me up, especially when the bastard's face comes into view on the screen. The room is silent, memories no doubt crowding all our minds of when we last saw him. She pats my hand, comforting me, even as she fights her own demons.

He's older than the last time I saw him, wrinkled, and appears weak, but he still has those sharp, cold, evil eyes. As I see him now as an adult, and not from a child's body and mind, I can't believe I was ever scared of him. He's just a man.

That's all.

He's just a man, despite how we built him up in our minds. His brain made him seem immortal and invincible, but he's not. He's just a man, well, now a dead man, but that doesn't mean he isn't fucking with us from beyond the grave, and I hate that she has to face him again.

"Hello, Novaleen." She startles, so I tighten my hold, even as the others move closer as if they can protect her from his ghost. A slight smile curls his lips, and she shivers. I don't blame her. It's a cruel, mocking smile. I don't think he is even capable of a real one. "If you are watching this, then I am dead."

"No shit," Jonas mutters as he blows out a breath.

A chair creaks on the video from where he is filming in this particular room, exactly where Dimitri is sitting. He must realise it because he stands in disgust and backs away, as if not wanting to be tainted by being near where he was. "I know you hate me, I understand the emotion, but I want to explain myself. I did what I thought was best for mankind. I thought I was bettering humanity and I could play God. I truly believed it was for the best of our people, and a few sacrifices and suffering, including yours, daughter, were worth the end result, but I see now that I was wrong, very wrong. In the name of advancement, I hurt you, and I stole yours and many others' innocence, and only now, at the end, are my sins catching up with me." He lets out a cold, bitter laugh. "Strange how you think about the beginning at the end. I did love you. I need you to know that, Novaleen. You were brilliant, the very best of me and the world. The capacity for greatness you have was revealed in every experiment I have ever conducted. None ever compared."

"Bastard," she mutters.

"But you threw it away. If you are watching this, it means you're back, though, and despite what you think of me and my research, there are some things you need to know and do, if not for me, then for those like you—those still out there enduring the same treatment as you. There are other children, lots more. Some are grown, and I hope you find them, but some are still young. It's bigger than the children now. I needed help, Nova, and that was my first mistake. I needed funding, and I sold my soul for that. The man who no doubt killed me and will be searching for you now is the very same man still conducting my experiments, and despite what you think about me, he is evil. He doesn't want this for advancement, nor to help people. He wants to hurt them, use them, and profit from them. I did this for knowledge, but he does not. There are no lines he won't cross. I'm afraid I have once again put you in danger, but I know you are smart and strong enough to stop him."

He moves closer, his face filling the frame.

"And you must stop him, daughter, otherwise not only will my research be corrupted, but it will be sold to the highest bidder. It would destroy the world as we know it. I can never ask for your forgiveness for what I did to you and the others, but in my last act, I am trying to make things right as much as I can. All of the lessons I taught you will come in useful now, Novaleen." His eyes narrow as he drags that out, like it's important. "You will need them all. Find the others like you, tell them, and let them help you stop this. At the end, I hope you find peace." He sighs, scrubbing at his face in an unfamiliar sign of stress and exhaustion. "She doesn't know, Nova. She doesn't know what I did, and she doesn't know what you are, that you're alive somewhere out there. She doesn't know the deals we made to keep her out of it, but she must be included now. You will need her."

"Ana?" she murmurs, confused.

He glances behind him, then, before looking back at the screen. "I don't have long, but I will not run and hide. He will kill me, Nova, which I'm betting you will be glad about, but heed my warning—he will stop at nothing to protect his secrets. You think I am the devil, daughter, but you are wrong. You are going to meet him, and I wish I could see you all in action, but it is not meant to be. Stop him. That's my last order to you." Then he's gone.

A picture of a notebook flashes on the screen for a split second, and then the video cuts off.

"If he wasn't already dead, I would kill him." We all jerk our heads up, not realising Ana had joined us. Her expression shows she is heartbroken, and anger flashes in her eyes.

"That's the first smart thing you've ever said," I mutter, and she throws me a glare before blowing out a breath.

"He knew you would need my help. That picture at the end of the message . . . play it back. Yeah, there, stop," she instructs Dimitri, glancing over the gibberish. "I can decipher his notes. These are locations."

"Locations?" Louis demands.

"Yes, it seems so. Locations and numbers . . . No, wait, ages, I think. Fuck, you think these are other labs he . . . experimented at, don't you?" she whispers, looking at us.

"Only one way to find out," Nova grinds out. "We hit them all and destroy everything he has. Ana, you stay here and keep working. None of this leaves this house. If anyone tries to take it, you kill them." She steps from the circle of my arms, moving towards her sister. "I'm trusting you to do this."

"I won't let you down," Ana promises, her back straightening. The two sisters, night and day, face each other.

Nova looks us all over. "Pack your bags, boys. We are going on a road trip." With that, she storms from the room, and Louis watches her go before nodding.

"You heard her, pack up. I want wheels up in an hour." He follows after her, pulling his phone out.

"I guess that means I need pants," Jonas grumbles, making us all laugh despite what we just saw.

THIRTY-EIGHT

NOVA

There is no time to waste, so I pack as quickly as I can. As I stare down at my bag, his face flashes before my eyes, and my hands curl into fists. Anger, resentment, hope, and fear fill me.

I hated him, but seeing him brought back all those childhood feelings of wanting to be loved, and I hate that more. I hate that even at the end, he's still playing me, using me, and ordering me around, even going so far as to involve Ana, knowing I would have no choice then.

Whoever this mystery man is, he killed my father, and for that I'm grateful, but if he is doing worse, I'll kill him myself and bury his body right next to my father's grave.

Determined, I zip the bag closed and toss it over my shoulder, finding Louis in the doorway, watching me.

"Just wanting to check your state of mind."

"Pissed, hateful, and wanting to kill someone," I reply, and he grins.

"Good." He pushes away from the doorframe.

Shaking my head, I drop my bag in the foyer as Bert comes in, holding a bag in his hands.

"I packed as much food as I could." He hands it over to Nico, who stops next to me, his own bag slung over his shoulder. "I've also included pancakes for Master Jonas."

"You da best, Berty boy," Jonas calls as he leaps from the balcony and lands next to us with a smug grin and kisses Bert's face.

He blushes and grins at Jonas before looking at me. "Please be safe, Nova."

"Always," I promise, kissing his other cheek. "Take care of Ana for me."

"I will." He nods solemnly. "We will be here when you get back, all of you." He looks around at them as the others come in with their belongings packed up. "None of you are to get hurt or killed, do you understand me?" he orders, and we all nod like naughty children. "Good, and if you get arrested, call me." He steps back, his eyes glassy with tears just as Ana hurries down the stairs. She throws the guys a nervous glance before she hands me a journal.

"Here's as much as I've found so far, as well as the locations. I have Louis's secure number. If I find anything more, I will send it to him."

"Be smart and safe." I hate it when I almost repeat my father's words. "I will be in contact when I can. Stay here with Bert." She nods, and we share a look, unsure what else to say, the years still arching between us. I sigh and grab my bag as I head towards the door where the others are already loading the cars.

"Nova," she calls. I turn back, and Ana races towards me, wrapping her arms tightly around me. I freeze for a moment before melting and wrapping my arms around her as well, kissing the top of her head.

"I'm so sorry I hurt you as much as he did, but I'm here now, and I will make this right. I will help, even if none of you believe me. I'm . . . I'm just so sorry. I love you, Nova, I always did, always will. Come back home soon." She steps back, dashing her tears away.

I nod at her, unsure what to say, so instead, I pull out the note that was folded under my pillow. "I know. I love you too," I tell her, and Bert steps up, placing a hand on her shoulder as I throw my bag in the car and get in.

"So where to? I'm betting the secret military peeps won't be happy about this." I smirk.

"What they don't know won't hurt them." Louis grins over his shoulder. "I just told them we have a few leads and are going off grid."

"And how did they take that?" Isaac asks curiously.

"Started shouting, so I hung up, but we should get going before they track us. Your sister will be safe, but us? We might get locked up."

"Then let's go." I nod, sitting back next to Nico. Jonas and Dimitri are in the other car behind us.

I flip through the journal and pick a location at random. "The first coordinates are somewhere in Berlin. Wait, how are we getting there?"

They share a look before laughing as I frown.

"Wait, what's so funny?"

That just makes them laugh harder as we pull away.

THIRTY-NINE

ow I know why they were laughing. Two hours later, we pull into a private airstrip, and sitting on the tarmac is a private jet. The stairs are down, and the lights are on inside. The cars stop before it, and I lean forward.

"Erm, okay?" I say to no one in particular, but they laugh and get out. Hoisting my bag up, I follow them onto the plane. They are all comfortable and instantly settle in. Louis talks to the pilot and assistant while I just stand there looking around.

Behind me is a small galley and the cockpit, and before me is something out of a movie. It sure beats the shit hole hotels I stay at, that's for sure. To the right is a full-on sitting area, with a sofa along the plane's wall covered in cushions and blankets, perfectly decorated. Two huge reclining leather chairs sit opposite on either side to create a square, with a table in the middle with a fruit bowl on it. The carpet is soft and fluffy under my dirty boots, and I cringe, feeling out of place.

Behind the sofa is another one where Jonas sprawls out, his arm behind his head and feet kicked up. To my left are two reclining chairs that are facing each other with a table between them, and at the back are three more chairs. All are done in luxury prints and leather. I feel like a dirty thief. The curved ceiling is filled with warm LED lights that are dimmed to create a soft atmosphere, and it smells expensive in here. Hell, there is even a full-length window in the ceiling, which I stare at incredulously.

There are two closed mahogany doors at the back. I'm guessing they are for the toilet, but I don't dare explore. I hesitantly sit on one of the chairs. Dimitri sits down heavily on the sofa and pulls his laptop out as Nico takes another chair at the back and instantly kicks back, going to sleep. Isaac grins at me as he passes and takes the spot next to Nico, reclining it and taking out a book.

They seem comfortable here and used to it, which has me frowning as Louis comes back to us and sits in the chair opposite me with his legs crossed. A very beautiful stewardess in a suit closes the door and smiles at us before moving back to the galley.

"Take off in ten. Refreshments will be served in an hour or so," Louis tells me.

I've bitten my tongue enough. I have to know.

Leaning across to Louis, I narrow my eyes. "Who the hell does this plane belong to?" I hiss.

FORTY

He grins, and there's a shuffling sound at my side. I turn my head to see Dimitri ducking his head in embarrassment. "What?" I ask, confused.

"It's Dimitri's," Louis explains, sparing a clearly worried Dimitri. "He made some money online, and he is very good at it, but he always felt like he didn't need wealth, so he shared it between us to help keep us afloat and not dependent on doing things with our skills—things like this plane so we can get around uncontrolled."

I blink, looking at Dimitri and then around again. He bought them a plane?

Dimitri feels my gaze and sighs, looking up at me. I lean across and take his hand, squeezing it. It doesn't change how I feel about him. He freezes, searching my gaze. With or without money, I care for them all, but in all honesty, I would feel more comfortable sleeping on the floor together again, and he must sense that because he smiles softly at me.

"Money is just another necessity, like food or shelter. You need it to survive, and anyone who says differently has never had to be without it. I simply made us some so we didn't have to exploit ourselves and could fly under the radar, same as the military, to protect my family," he explains logically, and I swear my heart actually melts for this man. He simply found a way to make money to protect his family, to provide for them, and to offer safety the only way he could.

Money changes people, but not these people.

"The plane's nice," I comment with a shy grin, "but I prefer the shitty hotel you found me in."

He cracks a smile but still seems worried and embarrassed. Sitting back, I keep my eye on him as we take off, and once we're in the air, he still won't look at me.

Blowing out a breath, I meet Louis's gaze, silently asking him how to fix this and assure D that I don't care. Louis nods, and I follow his gaze to the back of the plane and the doors there. Frowning but trusting him, I stand and hold out my hand to Dimitri.

He doesn't notice at first, and then he seems confused, but he trusts me and takes it. I haul him up and tug him behind me. Ignoring Jonas's knowing look, I take the first door, but it's a huge bathroom with a shower. The second door leads into a bedroom, and my eyebrows rise. I almost whistle but know it will only upset him, so I don't say anything about the emperor-sized bed made with silk sheets, the mirror along the wall, and the dimmed light fixtures and glass ceiling. Turning, I drag him in and shut the door.

A plan comes to mind, and I know how to show him how much I see him, how much I appreciate him.

It's something that has been brewing since the meadow, if I'm honest.

"Nova?" he asks, sounding confused, his eyebrows furrowed. Smirking, I plant my hand in the middle of his chest and push. He stumbles back to the bed, his legs spread.

Kicking them farther apart, I drop to my knees between them. His eyes widen, his mouth drops open, and lust blows his pupils as he stares at me.

"Dimitri, baby, if you didn't have a private plane, I couldn't do this," I purr as I slide my hands up his solid thighs to his waist and unbuckle his belt.

"Nova," he whispers raggedly. "You don't have to—"

"I want to," I promise. "I want to taste you and see you come apart for me. I need to be in control as much as you need to let go." Leaning up, I press my lips to his and nip at his lower one. "So let go, baby."

Moving back down, I slide his belt out, the slick of it loud, and he groans. Smirking smugly at the uncontrolled desire smouldering in his eyes, I flick open his trousers and slide my hand inside.

He moans when I grip his huge, hard shaft. He's massive and so hard it has to hurt. "Poor little Dimitri, so needy," I purr as I pull him out. He helps me push his trousers down, his eyes wild as he watches me. His chest heaves with his ragged breaths, and I've barely touched him.

This will be fun.

Grinning, I drop my eyes to his cock and lick my lips at the sight of him.

"Fuck, Nova," he growls, watching me, but damn, he's got a pretty cock. That's not a word I use lightly, but Jesus. He's long and thick, veiny and hairless, but when I spot the ink on his cock, I raise my eyebrows.

He grins shyly. "A dare with Jonas," he mutters.

I lean down so I can see what it says, then I laugh when I realise it says, "Ride me."

"Oh, don't worry, I will," I promise with a wink before dragging my tongue down his veiny length, tasting the musk that is all man and Dimitri. "Lie back, baby, and let me have some fun."

Tugging at his hair, he falls back, his spine arching as I suck him deep. "Holy fuck!" he yells as I take all of him to the back of my throat and hold him there before pulling my mouth away and licking down his length.

"I can't wait to have this inside of me," I purr against his skin, rubbing the tip of his leaking cock across my lips. I taste his precum as he watches me with dark eyes. Locking my own on his, I swallow him down again before lifting my mouth and bobbing on his cock, sucking hard and fast. I wrap one hand around his base to hold him still for my exploring mouth, twisting harshly.

Moaning loudly, he grips his shirt and lifts it to expose his tanned, cut abs, making me suck him harder, and his hips jerk up.

I dig my nails into his abs and scrape down, making him cry out as I suck him down hard and fast. My head bobs faster now as his hips jerk, forcing my mouth lower on his cock. He fucks my mouth, his hand darting down to grasp my hair and drag me down his length, but I don't let him take over.

I slow until he releases his tight grip slightly and lets me do what I want. "Please, Nova," he begs. "Your mouth is too fucking good. I'm going to spill."

Pulling my lips free, I slide my hand up his abs and down again as he watches me. "Then spill, but it will be down my throat because I want to taste everything you have."

"Fuck," he groans, falling back onto the bed. I can almost taste his desperation to come, but he holds back. His other hand fists the bedding as I play with him, licking and tasting before sucking him down again.

I bob faster and harder until he's slamming down my throat, his loud moans echoing around me.

Cradling his balls, I suck him all the way down to the back of my throat before I squeeze. His cock jerks in my mouth, and his release spills down my throat as he writhes. I suck him dry, only pulling my mouth away when he sags back, breathing raggedly. I clean every inch of him with my tongue as I wait for him to open his eyes.

"See? Private planes are good."

Watching such a brilliant, strong man come undone just from my mouth empowers me like nothing else ever has.

He watches me, his chest heaving and cock dripping in my saliva, like I'm a dream, and I start to wiggle, trying to ignore my wet pussy. Desire coats my cunt from the taste of him and the way he gave in for me.

He sits up, and I almost fall back, but he grabs me, throws me onto the bed, and is on me in seconds. He flips me so my face presses against the comforter and drags my pants down, then his hand presses to the back of my head, keeping me there as he jerks my hips back.

"D," I pant, but it turns into a scream when two fingers spear inside me. "Holy fuck!" I shout, pushing back as he starts to fuck me with them.

"It's only fair," he tells me, his voice dark and rough. "You got to taste me, and now I get to taste you and see you come apart for me. Damn, look how wet you are from sucking my cock. You love it, don't you? You loved tasting me, loved swallowing my cum like a dirty girl."

"Yes," I say without hesitation, pushing back to take his fingers deeper. My pussy pulses around them as he grinds his hand into my aching, throbbing clit.

"I can tell." He groans. "It's so fucking sexy. Look at you. Your pretty wet pussy spread for me. Fuck, Nova, I've never seen a prettier pussy," he praises as he adds a third finger. It's my turn to grip the silk bedding as I moan, pushing back to fuck myself on his fingers. A release is already building inside me, the slick sound of him pumping into me turning me on more.

"I wonder if you taste as good as you look," he purrs.

"I know I do, so why don't you find out?" I taunt. He doesn't reply, but a moment later, he pulls his fingers free of my clinging channel, and there's a wet sucking sound and then a groan.

"Fuck, you're right. You taste delicious. I need more. Be a good girl and let me lick this cunt."

I'm about to reply, "Be my guest," when he grips me tighter.

He yanks me up higher, and one hand slides under my body to press down on my stomach, while the other holds me still for him, and then he seals his mouth onto my cunt.

All forms of niceties are gone, and in the place of a shy, unsure Dimitri is an animal. His tongue thrusts inside of me until I cry out. "Fuck!" I yell, and knowing the others can hear me only has me crying out louder and grinding against his face.

Pulling his tongue from my pussy, he laps at my clit until my hips jerk. "Scream, let them hear, let them all sit out there with stiff cocks, imagining what I'm doing to you in here," he growls against my pussy, the vibrations making me cry out.

"Then make me," I retort, spreading my thighs wider.

"Oh, I plan to, pretty pussy Nova." Without waiting for a reply, his talented mouth returns to my pussy, licking from clit to ass like he can't get enough of my taste. He circles my clit before dipping inside of me.

He does that over and over before I push back impatiently. Chuckling, he grips my hips, keeping me still for his mouth, and sucks my clit, making me scream for him just like he wanted. I almost come, but just as I'm about to, he stops, leaving me panting, dripping, and unsatisfied. His fingers stroke over my pussy like a caress.

"I didn't say you could come yet, Nova," he warns.

"Fuck you," I snap, frustrated.

"Not this time. Next time, I'll have you under me with those claws in my back. This time I plan on licking this cunt dry," he says, and when I slump, he licks my cunt again. Desire explodes through me as he twists his tongue around my clit, giving me the right amount of pressure. I push back, and this time, he thrusts his fingers inside of me, letting me fuck myself on them as he licks and sucks my clit.

It's too much.

"Now, Nova. You will come now," he demands, and without waiting for a retort, he sucks my clit again.

I come with a scream, my thighs clenching and pussy clamping. I come so hard I see stars, and he laps up my release. His tongue dips inside of me alongside his fingers to taste every drop until I'm spent, and I fall to the bed with his fingers still inside of me.

Slowly, he pulls them out, and when I blink my eyes open, they are next to my face. His thick digits glisten with my cum. "Suck them clean, Nova, and taste how hard you came for me."

I open my mouth, and he thrusts them inside, watching me as I suck and lick them clean just like I did with his cock. When he pulls them free, I groan and roll onto my back, watching him. His cock is hard again, and his other hand is wrapped around it, stroking leisurely as he takes in my spread thighs covered in my cream, my breasts that are almost falling from my shirt, and my eyes heavy with pleasure.

"Fuck, I've never seen such a beautiful sight," he growls, his teeth sinking into his lower lip as he speeds up his hand on his cock. I can't help but watch, my gaze darting from it to his eyes until, a moment later, his cum spurts across my spread pussy and thighs, making me whimper.

He pumps his cock, squeezing every last drop of cum out before slumping next to me. His hand goes to my pussy and rubs his release across my oversensitive flesh before dipping his fingers inside me.

"Next time I come, it will be inside you," he murmurs.

"Fucking hell, I've unleashed a monster." I laugh as I turn my head. He grins, looking relaxed and happy now, as he pulls me against his side. I go willingly and burrow closer, watching the sky above us in the ceiling window.

"I like this plane now," he declares, and I can't help but laugh.

FORTY-ONE

By the time we have cleaned up and changed, we are landing.

"I've never been to Berlin," I comment as I lean forward to peer out of the window. "What's it like?"

"Beautiful," Louis murmurs. "I've been once for work, but the snippets I saw were stunning." Standing, he offers me his hand. "Let's do this, Nova."

Nodding, I take his hand, and with our bags slung over our shoulders, we disembark the private plane. There are two taxis waiting outside, and Louis pays them a heavy sum to keep quiet about what they saw. It's not foolproof, but we leave as little of a paper trail as we can as we speed through Berlin.

I don't know where we are heading, but I soak up the views. Tourists flood the streets, and the shops and cafes are full and bright with light. Seeing the modern amenities mixed with the old, historical elements almost entrances me.

"We would usually stay at a shitty hotel with a don't tell policy, but since it's your first time in Berlin, why not go big?" Louis winks down at me. "If they are going to find us, they will anyway, so it doesn't matter where. Plus, they will be expecting us to fly under the radar. Instead, we will blend in by remaining in plain sight."

"What do you mean?" I ask, drawing my gaze away from the window to him.

"Luxury, baby. We are spending our time here in luxury, just like you deserve." He winks, and I swallow as I look back out the window. Not long after, we have to get out and walk down a huge shopping district called Ku'damm. There are restaurants, cafes, and shops lining every corner and side of the street. He's right; we easily blend into the crowd. We stop before a massive, six-story building placed between two equally large buildings, the hotel name boldly displayed at the top.

"Zoo?" I ask, and Louis grins as he heads inside.

I follow after him, gawking when we plunge into a different world. A sumptuous, darkly lit interior greets me with epic decorations, and a dramatic tiger rug leads to a reception area. I find myself gawking at everything as Louis heads right up to the desk. I barely hear what he says, but I notice it's in German, which makes my eyebrows rise. When he comes back, he slings his arm around me and leans in as if to kiss me. "We got the penthouse, baby," he purrs then looks to the guys. "You are in rooms next to us."

"Bastard." Jonas grins but winks at me. I let them lead me to a bank of elevators, and from there, we head up. The guys are, in fact, in rooms next to us. When I walk into the penthouse, I freeze. I'm used to shitty hotels with questionable bedding and dirty old bathrooms.

Not here.

Light almost blinds me from the floor-to-ceiling windows with views of a courtyard below. Sofas and chairs sit to my right with a table between them. A partial wall with a fireplace is to my left, and when I peer through, I can see into the bath. There's a dressing room, a huge king-sized bed, and a bathroom that almost makes me weep with an epic tub and huge shower big enough to fit four people. There's also a minibar and so many amenities, I don't know where to look. I just wander around in awe.

Louis lounges on a chair with his chin on his chest, watching me. "Like it?" he murmurs, and I swallow as I turn to him, my back to the windows.

"I love it, but are we—"

"Don't worry about it." He stands smoothly and pads towards me, taking my chin and lifting my head. "Just enjoy it. Yes, we are here under horrible circumstances, but it's time you saw that the world has more than death and darkness. A little bit of luxury won't hurt you. It might even do you good." He winks before sobering. "We are as safe here as anywhere. There are plenty of entrances and exits onto a busy area of Berlin that we can get lost in. I did my research and set up backup meet points, but for now, we set up shop. Everything here is soundproofed, so we use this as base." Just then, the door opens. He doesn't break apart from me, just watches me. "And we prepare."

I nod, and only then does he step away. The others make themselves comfortable, with Jonas peering through the fire and then back at me. "I know where I'll be spying," he teases, making me roll my eyes.

"Nico, order room service and check the floor. Jonas, help him," Louis orders. "Dimitri, get set up. Isaac, check the room."

"For?" I ask curiously, crossing my arms.

"Bugs and cameras, wiretaps, anything." Louis grins at me. "You can help him."

Isaac takes my hand, and we start in the bedroom, working our way through the entire suite. By the time we are done, food has been delivered on a silver trolly they rolled in themselves, not wanting staff to enter the room. "We are good." Isaac nods as he sits and picks up a lid, munching on some fruit while Jonas grabs a handful of chips and starts eating.

"Good, then let's begin."

Stretching out my back, I walk to the windows and look out at the darkening city before me, the lights stealing my breath with their beauty. Sometimes it's easy to forget how big the world is, and how beautiful and crazy it can be with so many unexplored places. Especially when you are so focused on the present and the little places around you.

But seeing it now steals my breath.

Nico snores, making me turn with a grin. He's cramped up on a tiny chair, snoring happily away, with his head back and one leg bent up uncomfortably. His other leg is thrown over the edge, and one arm hangs down. The other is under his head. Jonas shakes his head and goes back to cleaning the weapons. Dimitri and Louis are on the computers, checking our trail and locating the next stop as well as hacking security cameras and planning in case anything goes wrong. I was helping out, but my eyes are almost crossing. I'm not made for computers. Shaking my head, I grab the blanket that's neatly folded on the sofa and drape it across Nico, tucking him in before wandering to the bedroom to find Isaac curled up there, fast asleep.

We are supposed to take turns sleeping, and it's not mine, but I need a break from the screens and from . . . everything. It's all so much. I feel like I've not had a moment alone since they invaded my life, and although it's been for the better, and we have important things to do, I know I need some quiet time and space to regroup. I need to build up the barriers around myself again that protect me from being hurt, the very ones they have been smashing down since day one with soft smiles, teasing words, and protective hands.

They make it very hard for a girl not to fall for them, but I can't. I know that. We can have our fun and enjoy every moment until our pasts catch up with us, but people like us aren't made for love, and we don't get a happily ever after. We just get now.

Reminding myself of that, I slip into the bathroom and decide to run a bath to ease my aching muscles.

There are fancy ass toiletries on the side, so I fill the bath with them before stripping and stepping into the hot running water. I groan as I sink into it, my head falling back as I drape my arms on either side, letting the warm water wash away today and my worries.

Once we destroy everything my father built, we will go our own separate ways, right? If I am not careful, I will miss them something fierce. I'm not used to being alone anymore. I look for them in the silence, letting their laughter wash over me and their smiles ease my concerns.

I lean on them and trust them, and when they are gone, I will be alone again, which means before then, I need to protect myself so when they leave, it won't break me. I can admit to myself that they could destroy me in a way Father never did. With their kind eyes and friendship, they filled a hole in me I didn't know I had, and although they wouldn't mean to, they would break that last part of my soul and take it with them. But they deserve to live and find happiness when this is over, and this cannot last.

We were brought together by my father, by our trauma, but it won't be enough to stay together.

I will only have me at the end, and I remind myself of that over and over, even when I hear Jonas laughing with them and Nico's snores.

Slowly, my thoughts settle as I turn off the tub, just soaking and allowing myself to rebuild as the night passes.

My eyes open, and my heart freezes when I see Louis turned in his chair, his eyes locked on me. The whole world falls away as I stare into his eyes that are so hungry, I actually shiver in the tub. Dimitri is oblivious, and so is Jonas, so it's just Louis and I locked in a stare before his eyes very purposely drop to my exposed breasts and then crawl back up to mine.

When he turns away, I gasp and slump, free of his gaze. Shaking off my lust-filled thoughts, I submerge myself under the bubbly water, trying to remind myself to protect my heart from them.

Even if they are set on stealing it.

FORTY-TWO

"**G**et some sleep," Louis orders the others. "We begin in the morning."

Groaning, Jonas drags Dimitri out, Nico following with a yawn. Isaac smiles at me and kisses my cheek.

Louis turns to me. "We will take the first watch. I'll keep an eye on the hallway cameras, and you can keep watch on the target location. Let me know if anyone comes or goes."

I nod and sit next to him, curling up in the long shirt I stole from one of them. My wet hair is plastered to my back as I focus on the screen before me. Nothing much happens, just the same old building we have been reconning all day, and an hour or so later, Louis brings me coffee, and we keep watch, protecting our family.

Staring at the screen eventually gets boring, so I look at Louis, watching the play of light on his handsome, sharp features. His hair looks darker in this light, and his eyes appear tired.

He feels my gaze, and his lips quirk up, but he doesn't look at me. "Problem, Nova?"

"Just looking." I grin, unable to help it. "Seems only fair since you got a good look at me."

His head swings to me slowly, his eyes gleaming with amusement and lust that he doesn't even try to hide. His gaze drops to my body again. "You wanted me to watch."

As soon as he says it, I realise he's right. "Maybe, and you want me to stare, talk to you, and tease you, or you would have had any of the others in here with me."

"Maybe I was just keeping an eye on trouble." He grins, flashing white teeth as he leans in. "And you are trouble, baby, down to the core."

"Yet you can't stay away," I murmur knowingly. He leans back, glancing at the screen before turning slightly to take both me and it in.

"Maybe not, or maybe I just want to keep you away from them." I flinch, but he doesn't hold back. "I see them with you, and, well, you are a part of this family, and I will always protect you, and them, from this."

"This?" I swallow, confused at the turn this took.

"You." He takes my hand and won't let me drop it when I try, yanking me closer. I fight him, and he lifts me and pins me between his body and the table.

Stilling, I glare at him. "I don't want to hurt them. I'm not my father," I snarl, darkness clawing at me.

As if he can see it, he pinches my chin until I focus on him and his words. "I never said you were. I know you are nothing like that monster, but you don't see it, Nova. We were just heartless men searching for purpose, and you have given them hope. You bind us tighter than ever before, and yes, that terrifies me. Not for me, but for them. It is my job to protect them. I pulled them from their cells and promised them revenge and protection, and I will always protect them, even over my own wants. You have the ability to hurt them, Nova, and you know it."

I nod but lick my lips, the truth spilling free. "But you have the ability to hurt me too," I admit, and he flinches, searching my gaze. "I was just thinking that you all strip me bare. I'm used to fighting alone, living alone, and then you all come and fill me with life. You remind me how to laugh, and you show me joy and friendship. It scares me because what happens when you leave and I'm alone again? You say I'm a threat to them, but the truth is, Louis, it's all of you who are the threat to me."

"Nova," he murmurs, his grip on my chin turning soft as he pulls me close and wraps his arms around me. I press my head to this throat, just breathing in his scent. I should pull away and focus on the cameras, but I can't. He strips me bare, revealing all my fears, hopes, dreams . . . everything. It's like he can see them clearly, even clearer than I can.

"How about we promise never to hurt each other?" he finally responds.

Pulling back to see his face, I search his gaze. "Just like that?"

"Just like that. We have had enough hurt to last a lifetime. Who knows where this mission will take us? Instead of wondering and fighting what's all between us, let's just give in and promise not to hurt each other."

A naïve promise? Maybe, but it's a desperate edge we are both clinging to.

The electricity returns between us as his eyes darken. "Promise?" he murmurs, his voice rough.

"I promise," I whisper.

"And I promise not to break your heart, Nova, but I never said anything about your body." He slams his lips onto mine, pushing me back to the table. He grabs my hips and drags me farther down his lap until I'm perched over his very hard length. Groaning, I run my hands up his shoulders to his hair where I grab on and kiss him back, giving as good as I get. Pulling back slightly, I can't help but smile. "Is that another promise?"

"Baby," he warns, his eyes narrowed, "it's a threat." He yanks me back to him, kissing me so hard I can't remember the hurt or anything but the taste of him on my lips and the feel of his hands roving possessively over my body.

Snarling, he lifts me and walks us across the room, slamming me into the wall there.

I watch him through simmering eyes as he kisses down my neck and then back up, nipping my lips as he nudges his thigh between my legs, rocking the hard length against my pussy. I moan his name, watching his eyes blow as I do, and his grip tightens until it hurts, so I do it again.

"You'll be screaming my name in a moment, Nova," he promises against my skin as he slides his lips across it. "You'll see just how mean I can be, and you'll love every hard inch I give you. Fuck, baby, I've never forsaken my position, but right now, I will, so keep your eyes on those cameras for me while I taste what's mine."

Dropping to his knees before me, he holds me effortlessly in the air, keeping his eyes locked on mine. "Cameras," he barks, reminding me. "Or I'll stop and let you sit with wet underwear all night, imagining my cock and tongue inside you."

Huffing, I drag my gaze to the monitors, groaning when he rips off my underwear with his teeth before he attacks me with his mouth. He tears down my defences as he drags his tongue from my clit to my ass and back again, tasting every inch of me. I grab his head, trusting him to keep me up, and narrow my eyes on the screen. I try to concentrate as he attempts to rip me apart with pleasure.

His wicked tongue circles my oversensitive clit before lashing it, making me buck and cry out. My eyes slide shut for a moment, and he stills with his tongue against my clit. He only carries on when I open my eyes again.

"Good girl," he coos, the vibration of his voice making me cry out and tilt my hips. Chuckling, he drags his tongue down my pussy and circles my hole before thrusting into it. I rock and ride his tongue as one hand holds me up, and the other circles my clit in a maddening pace.

The screen is fuzzy as pleasure arcs through me, my panting loud. Louis does what he does best and takes control, giving me the freedom to let go as his tongue circles back to my clit and his fingers slide down my wetness and thrust inside me. He stretches me around his digits as he starts to fuck me with them. "You taste so good, Nova." He groans, licking his lips as he watches me, fucking me with his fingers until I'm reaching for release just from his touch. "No wonder they all need this pretty pussy. You're enough to make a sane man wild, Nova, and drive any man to distraction. Are you still watching those cameras, baby?"

"Yes, fuck, yes," I call out, my eyes locked on them like a lifeline, fighting the urge to look down. His lips wrap around my clit, and he sucks.

The pressure is too much, but I'll be damned if I don't grind against his face as I come. Pleasure explodes through me, and I basically drown him in my cunt, but I somehow manage to keep my eyes open while doing it. He continues to lick my pussy before sliding back up my body. His face is coated in my release, and as I watch, he wipes his face with his hand and drags his tongue down his palm, tasting every drop of me.

"Fucking delicious," he growls, the wild look in his eyes so unhinged.

This is so unlike Louis, and it makes me desperate. Grabbing his shoulders, I wrap my legs around his waist and snap, "Fuck me so we can work."

"Such a pretty, dirty mouth, baby." When he leans down to kiss me, I taste my own pleasure, and then his hand is on my throat, pinning me to the wall as he squeezes. "You move those eyes from that camera one more time, and I'll bend you over that computer and take that pretty perky ass until I fill it with my cum and then leave you hurting and wet. Understood, baby?"

"Bastard," I hiss, hiking myself higher. I glance back to the cameras as I reach between us to stroke his cock. "You can have my ass later, now shut the fuck up and get inside me."

"Such a sweet talker," he purrs, smacking my hand away and freeing himself. He's still fully clothed, and both of us know that this is a quick fuck to get it out of our systems. We need the release or we will be useless, yet the freedom I find in his touch is like nothing else I can explain.

I've been in control my entire life, meticulously aware of every action. I never even drink just to be safe, and now with Louis, I can fall because I know he will catch me.

And I do.

I keep my eyes on the cameras and trust him to give me the pleasure I need. Praising me, he lines that huge cock up to my pussy, and with a squeeze of my throat, he slams me down on him. He takes me rough and hard, forcing me to stretch around him. I cry out, almost shutting my eyes before I remember.

Snarling, I lean into him, biting his shoulder through his shirt to keep him inside of me and my eyes on that screen. With a yell, he pistons into my cunt, taking me rough and hard, slamming me back into the wall with each thrust.

His cock is huge, and it borders on painful, but it's absolutely perfect, and those little cameras become my everything as he steals my body one thrust at a time.

"Fuck, you feel so good, baby, too tight, too fucking wet." He pants into my ear, the sound so sexy I clamp around him. "Fuck!" he roars, hammering into me. Gone is the cold, unemotional leader, and in his place is a wild, lust-driven man. "Don't fucking do that, Nova," he growls. "Not unless you want me to come in two pumps like a teenager," he threatens, and even though he tries to slow down, he continues to pound into me.

"Louis," I snap, "please." It's a plea, a demand.

"Hold on, baby. I've got you," he promises, and the hand that was on my throat slides down and circles my clit. "Come for me, let me feel it on my cock. Scream so they all hear and they all know that you're mine right now. I bet they are in the other rooms, listening and stroking themselves, wishing they were me, but they aren't, and you're all mine. It's my cock you are riding so good, my cock you are drenching, and mine you will come on until you pass out," he purrs, and fuck it that isn't the trigger I need.

I come on command like a cum slut, clenching around his cock, and my eyes close with the force. He either doesn't care or doesn't notice, fucking me through it.

The other guys, the cameras, the mission, everything is forgotten in the pleasure Louis is dragging out of me, draining every last drop. The orgasm turns into two and then three, flowing through me, and he still doesn't stop.

"I can't," I whisper, but both of us are too deep to stop. "I can't, another—"

"You can and you will," he demands, slamming his lips to mine. He swallows my sobs as he fucks me, and I feel the wall dent behind me. His hands hurt where he holds me, and my cunt drips so much I bet it's on the floor. My clit throbs painfully, and yet when he snarls, chasing his own release, I come alongside him.

I scream my release into his lips as his hips stutter, and his cum splashes inside of me as he groans my name.

We stay locked like that, both breathing raggedly as we shake from the aftershocks. He kisses me softly. "Shh, baby, I've got you," he promises. "You did so good, so fucking good, Nova. Jesus, you feel amazing. It's never been that good. No one has ever made me want to forget everything before," he murmurs, pressing his forehead to mine.

A noise has us both looking behind him.

Panting, I look around to see Jonas watching the cameras and us, holding popcorn in his hand. "Don't let me stop you," he drawls, making me groan and drop my head to Louis's shoulder, which shifts with his chuckle.

I'm just about to shout at Jonas for being a perv when something on the camera catches my eye.

"Movement, there's movement!"

FORTY-THREE

We watch the cameras until morning. All we saw was a hooded man leaving the front door and slipping into an idling car before it pulled away. No one came back, and no one else went in.

It's been hours, and nothing.

"It's time," Louis finally says. "Get ready, we are going in. We need to find the research there and destroy it."

"And if there's a kid there?" Isaac reminds him softly.

"Then we save them and get them somewhere safe, somewhere far from their reach," Louis commands, giving us all a pointed look, so without any more conversation, we all jump up and get ready.

We are going in as soon as the sun sets and need to be ready to find out just what my father was hiding around the world. Is it another kid? More torture in the name of research? If so, who was the man who came out of the house, and why has he not been back?

I guess wondering won't change anything. Instead, I dress in my usual black jeans, tank, and zip-up bomber. I plait my hair back and grab the cap on the table and tug it down, then I add some knives, avoiding guns. I could use them; I'd just rather not.

I lean back and watch the guys get ready. They are all wearing black, and seeing them like this makes my mouth dry. Tight black T-shirts cling to their muscles, black cargo pants are tucked into boots, and their holsters are hidden under their jackets. Seriously, they look sexy as hell. Louis is perfectly dressed, while Jonas is mussed and his shirt gapes slightly to show his pecs. Isaac's outfit has more pockets for first-aid supplies, Nic has more weapons strapped to his body, and Dimitri is carrying a laptop. When they all check themselves over, I can't help but smile.

It's an important mission, but jeez, they look cute, like toy soldiers but oh so damn sexy.

Shaking my head, I clear my throat. "Let's go."

We wait until the sun sets to make our move, watching from bushes both in the front and rear of the house. No one comes or goes, and there's no movement at all. A bad feeling starts building in my stomach, but I keep it to myself as the instructions come through my earpiece from Louis, who's in the front with Isaac and Dimitri. I'm with Jonas and Nico in the back.

"Five minutes, and then we move. Set watches." I hear Nico doing it and trust him to alert us. Jonas is busy drawing dirty stick figures in the mud, and when I glance over, he wiggles his eyebrow, pointing at an elaborate sexual position.

"This is for us to try later," he teases.

"Jonas, you perv—wait, is that even possible?" I tilt my head, looking over the diagram as I feel Nico's eyes on me.

"Yes," he grunts, and we both swing our heads to him, wearing twin expressions of shock. His face is cool and collected as he watches us back.

"Well shit, you dirty dog, Nico. I didn't know you had it in you." Jonas almost whoops as Nico rolls his eyes, but when I wink at him, a grin tugs at his lips as his watch counts down.

"Remember your position and check the corners. Dimitri has disarmed all alarms and cameras. The main focus in the house is the mainframe and command centre. Get any research or data before it's wiped. Ours is to check every other room in case there is a . . . subject being held here. Understood?"

"Yes, boss." I salute, making Jonas grin.

"As long as I get to be behind Nova, I'll behave." I realise that is exactly why they put Jonas with me. Jesus, I'm like a psycho's babysitter, if the baby was an almost seven-foot, built, weapons expert with enhanced senses and intelligence.

"Louis, am I with Jonas to make him behave?" I mutter as I look back at the darkened house.

"Yes," he answers without shame, making my eyes narrow.

"And Nico?" I hedge.

"To make you behave." He chuckles. "Sorry, baby, but we all know if anything goes down, you and Jonas are firing first."

"Touché," I mutter, even though I'm annoyed and, yes, slightly turned on that he thinks that much about me. Grinning over at Nico, I wiggle my eyebrows. "I guess that means you get to punish me if I misbehave."

"Oh fuck, me, me, let me!" Jonas shoots his hand up, and without looking, Nico knocks it down.

"No, that's my job as this unit's commander for the mission." The heated look he gives me makes me want to misbehave just to see what he would do. As if reading it on my face, he moves closer in his crouched position and wraps his hand around my neck, twisting my head back until it hurts, and I meet his gaze.

"But if you're a good girl, you'll get a reward too, and trust me, baby girl, the reward is better," he promises, his lips almost touching mine.

"Fuck, you two would make beautiful babies," Jonas randomly remarks, his eyes wide and confused. We both turn, so our cheeks touch, and stare at Jonas, who is just grinning at us, and then we glance back at each other and laugh.

Just then, his watch beeps, and he transforms back into commander mode. "Thirty seconds until we move. Stay low, silent, and keep your faces hidden just in case. Watch for traps, and be aware of what is within." With that, he moves to the edge of the bush, gun in hand, as he counts down silently. I slide behind him, palming a blade while Jonas pats my ass from behind me, sighing dreamily.

"If I'm good, do I get to eat your ass later?" he whispers in my ear.

"We both know you'll prefer the punishment," I murmur, and then Nico starts to move, and Jonas quiets down as we hurry in a crouched run to the back door. It's a seemingly normal house in a rural area, but we all know it's a lie. The windows are dark on both the second and first floor. I peeked in the one next to the back door earlier that leads to a kitchen and a hallway. Dimitri found some blueprints, but we all know it has probably been modified by now. However, it did show a basement.

Which is where we are assuming everything is.

I move past Nico to take my position at the door, quickly picking the lock and grabbing the handle as he counts down with his fingers. On three, I rip it open, and he rolls in, sweeping the room before a whispered, "Clear," comes. I hear Louis and the others coming in the front in my earpiece, but I focus on keeping them safe. It never mattered before, when it was only me.

If I messed up, it was only my life, but now it's theirs too, and I refuse to let them down.

I follow Nico as he sweeps the room, and Jonas brings up the rear. We move through the silent, empty house. There is a layer of dust everywhere and old furniture covered in sheets, but the dirty floor has booted footprints leading to the hallway. We follow them and see Louis shadowed by Isaac and Dimitri. Isaac breaks off with Dimitri, and Jonas and I break off. They sweep upstairs, and we sweep the rest as Louis and Nico watch the door. Every corner must be checked before we go down there. We don't want to be crept up on.

When it's clear, I call it out and move back to the door to see them hurrying downstairs. Once there, Nico points at Jonas and at the ground. I feel him grumbling, but he agrees to stay and watch our backs while we head downstairs.

Nico opens the door for Louis, who strides in. Nico and I are next, followed by Dimitri and Isaac. The stairs creak as we walk down them, and we flick on our torches, lighting the way. It's deeper than I thought possible, but I'm betting they built the house to conceal this. At the bottom, the corridor runs left and right. Louis points right and heads that way with his team, while Nico and I go left. There's a corner up ahead, and I peek around it before rolling and coming up with the knife just in case, but there's no one there, so I wave and move on. Nico moves past me, his eyes sharp as his torch lights up the white walls that make me shiver in memory.

This place is definitely one of my father's locations. It has the same clinical feel to it. Recycled air and pain almost circulate in the air. The corridor ends at another set of stairs. These are metal and only have a few steps, and once we are down them, we freeze side by side in a huge laboratory and observation room. There are computers and workspaces everywhere. Notes are scattered all over the floor, half-trodden and destroyed, and each computer seems like they were broken in a hurry.

"Fuck, boss, they knew we were coming. Everything has been ransacked," Nico informs the others as he walks through the room, which extends both left and right, but I move straight ahead to the glass window running along the whole front wall.

When I look out, I see nothing but white. I follow it down, and what I see makes my heart skip as a scream claws at my throat.

Spinning on my heel, I find the entrance to the left and hammer on the red button. The door opens with a hiss.

"Nova!" Nico growls, but I ignore him as I race to the other door and smack the button, turning to see it close the outer one before the inner one opens. Putting my knife away, I rush down the metal steps, my booted feet loud as I land on the tiled floor, sliding in the blood there.

I don't breathe until I'm next to it. My fingers hesitate before I press them to the body's neck, knowing he's already dead. When I don't feel a pulse, I let my head fall back and scream.

And scream.

There are panicked questions coming through the comms, but I rip it out as I swallow my pain and glance down at the boy. Just a boy. Just a fucking kid. No older than fourteen, he wears a hospital gown like I used to wear. His head is shaved, and his bright blue eyes are locked on the ceiling. His hands and feet are chained to the operating chair.

The whole room is a fucking sterile operating theatre and prison, but I can't look away from him, noting his slightly parted, bruised and cut up lips. A scar runs across his forehead and down to the slit neck.

The blood is dried there, pooling onto the floor. His body is cold and going into rigor. He's been dead a while, I know that, but it doesn't stop the agony from forming a ball in my chest and mixing with my fury. He was just a kid, just a fucking kid, and they slit his neck like he was an animal.

I hear them then as they come into the room, and I turn to face them. I don't know what they see on my face, but they still, worry in their eyes as well as pain. "He's dead. He was just a kid. He's dead."

Isaac moves closer, taking my face and searching my eyes before examining me. "She's in shock, but she's okay," he tells the others before moving to the kid.

I don't watch as he examines him.

"From the wound and rigor, I'd say he's been dead about seven hours," he murmurs.

"They killed him today. They knew we were coming, and to hide it, they killed him rather than let us save him." My voice sounds weird and faraway.

Dimitri steps into the room, staring at his phone. "Everything has been wiped, cleaned out entirely—" He jerks his head up and stops, his face paling when he sees the kid.

"They knew," I snap at Louis and storm past them. I need to move, to do something. In the other room, I ball my hands into fists, and then with an anger-filled scream, I yank on one of the desks and throw it. Once I start, there is no stopping.

I throw chairs at walls, smash beakers, and crumble equipment in my wrath. Computers are destroyed and paperwork is ripped up until I just rage and take it out on the room. When I stumble back, my chest heaving, I don't feel any better, but the room looks like how I feel inside—a destroyed mess of pain.

Arms wrap around my waist and turn me. I sink into that warm embrace, pressing my head to a solid chest. I feel their heartbeat as they try to soothe me, stroking along my back. "Collect what you can," Louis orders, and the chest in front of me sighs.

"Shh, I have you," Nico murmurs, and I realise he's holding me.

Once again, he came after me and brought me back, and when I lift my head, I meet his knowing eyes. He glances down at me, flicking glass off my shoulder. "We need to move quickly. Are you okay?"

I nod and step back and look at the glass before glancing away. "We bury him," I tell them, leaving no room for argument.

"Nova, we can't," Louis starts, and I whirl to him. "We can't. I want to, but we can't. If his body is found, there will be questions we can't answer. Plus, it will expose us all. We have to burn this place to the ground, so no one ever finds it."

"He deserves better than being burnt to fucking ashes and forgotten," I yell, knowing I'm being irrational and taking it out on him when it's not his fault.

"He's dead," he snaps meaningfully, making me flinch.

"Boss," Nico snarls, but Louis narrows his eyes on him, silencing him as he steps before me.

"He's dead, Nova. He doesn't know or care anymore. I will not risk my family or you to bury the boy, no matter how much I want to. I vowed to protect you, and I will. He burns with all this, and I fucking pray that wherever he is now, he's free of this hell."

"He was just a kid," I whisper, my lip quivering.

"So were we. We will get the bastard who did this, and when we do, he's yours. Until then, we need you to keep it together. Can we count on you?" He searches my gaze as I breathe through the pain and anger until I feel more whole.

"Yes," I mutter and meet everyone's gazes, but they look away, working quickly to take anything that might be useful. Embarrassment heats my cheeks as I clear my throat and look back at Louis. "Yeah, I'm here."

"Good." He squeezes my hand as he passes. "Then let's do this and get out of here."

FORTY-FOUR

After clearing the house of anything useful, we find some gasoline in the shed outside and fill the house with it. Standing in the back garden, I toss the lighter inside, watching as flames engulf the house of horrors. We stand side by side and watch it burn away all evidence of the evil done here and the boy's body within.

Closing my eyes, I say a prayer for him, something I've never done. I pray to a god I don't believe in to protect him and give him the happiness he deserves in life. When we hear the sirens, we disappear back into the darkness.

We don't know where to go, and we're unsure of our next move.

Luckily for us, we have Louis who barks out orders. We grab our stuff from the hotel and check out. If they know we are in the city, they might come for us, so we need to move fast. When we load into the plane and take off with no direction in mind, we are all feeling angry, hurt, and lost.

Dimitri spreads out the papers and computer parts he saved, giving us a purpose. It keeps my mind off what happened and the boy, even though I know I will see his body every time I close my eyes. Instead, I sort through the papers while Dimitri and Louis pick at computer parts.

An hour later, Dimitri's head jerks up.

"I have it!" He hurries off to the cockpit, and when he comes back, he grins at us. "They tried to wipe all of the hard drives, but in their rush, they didn't corrupt them enough. I managed to save some documents on another location, another experiment, which they were comparing this one to."

"That's great." Louis sighs, clearly relieved, the only sign that he was as worried as us. "So where to?"

"We are going to Scotland," Dimitri tells us as he shuts his laptop and stretches. "We might as well get some rest and then we'll hit the ground running when we get there. The notes on this one are odd."

"Odd how?" I ask, and he looks at me, not with pity, but understanding.

"The age . . . It isn't a child."

Unsure what we will find when we land in Scotland, I spread out across the bed in the back of the plane. Right now, I'm grateful Dimitri's money was able to provide this. We are all drained after this mission. We knew it would be bad, but we never expected that. We should have.

My father is dead, though, so then who killed the boy?

And why?

How did they know we were coming?

I have so many questions and not enough answers, and my turbulent thoughts only quieten when Isaac slips into bed next to me, taking my hand. "Are you okay?" we say at the same time and share a grin.

"No," I admit, and he nods.

"Me either," he murmurs.

Closing my eyes, I turn and lay my head on his chest, sliding my leg over his.

He sighs contentedly and wraps me in his arms. "We have to do this, Nova. I just wish I could make this easier for you, for all of you."

"We do this together," I mutter, listening to the steady thump of his heart. "I should have expected . . . but yeah, I guess I didn't. It made it so much more real again, that's all. That poor boy, what he went through . . ."

"We all did. Part of me is happy that he at least escaped the future we had, but either way, we cannot change what happened. We can only prevent it from happening again, and we will. No doubt there will be more horrors the deeper we investigate, but you are right. We will do it together, and when there is nothing left but the ashes of your father's research, we will mourn them."

Lifting my head, I meet his eyes. "You are amazing, you know that?" I tell him, and he blushes even as his eyes drop to my lips. Leaning in, I allow myself a little weakness and kiss him softly. "So amazing," I whisper huskily against his lips as the bed bounces, rolling me into Isaac.

Grinning, I pull back and turn to see Louis stretching out next to me, closing his eyes. "Don't mind me," he murmurs, even as his hand snakes out and tangles in my hair. He sighs and settles down as if he just needed to feel me, so I snuggle between them, not even cracking an eye when I feel the others climb on, and we lie in a tangle of legs and arms.

There is a grunt and a smack.

"That better be your gun," Nico snarls, and when I laugh, Jonas does too.

"Nah, I'm just happy to see you."

There is a yelp, and when we look, Jonas is on the floor. He glares at Nico before pouting at me as he climbs up and lies on the full length of my body, burying his head in my chest. "He's being mean, baby," he whines.

"Nico, be nice." I grin as he huffs, wrapping his hand around my ankle. Dimitri's head is on my leg, and something settles deep inside me as I look over them.

"Sleep," Isaac commands. "Dream of good things," he whispers in my ear.

Closing my eyes, I can't help but smile and feel protected and loved. I'm not alone, I know that, but there are people out there who are, and they need our help. I cannot afford to break, not now, but I know with the guys by my side, I never will.

FORTY-FIVE

By the time we catch a taxi into Scotland, we are all ready to stretch our legs and walk around. The air is cool and fresh, and the castle casts a beautiful shadow across everything we pass. The mixture of old and new buildings is incredible. I've never been to Scotland before, and my eyes are wide as I try to drink everything in. I know we are here for work, but it doesn't stop me from bouncing in my seat, wanting to explore the little shops and climb to the castle and do the ghost tours. The taxi takes us just off the main road to a side street of houses. Once there, I pay and slip out, stretching my arms up into the air. I giggle when someone tickles my side and smack their hands away, then I turn and glare at Jonas who just winks.

"Guess this is home for a few days," I comment as we stare at the three-story house.

Isaac hoists his bag into the air and takes off towards the front door. "Yep, I made sure we could just let ourselves in so we didn't have to meet anyone. It's private and gives us the cover of tourists we need. So get settled, but keep your bags packed. Dimitri is going to work on the next location information."

"Does that mean we can explore?" I almost bounce up and down.

Louis looks back at me, his eyebrow raised, and when I glance over,

Nico and Jonas are at my side. Jonas is pretending to pray, but Nico just rolls his eyes. "Actually, I set up an automatic system to work on the encoded information. It could take hours, so there's no point in watching it," D calls and smiles at me. "How about we all explore, and get some good food and some drinks? I'll get a notification on my phone if anything comes up."

"D—" Louis starts, but when he looks all of us over, his resistance crumbles. "Fine, a few hours, no more!"

Grinning, I jog over to him and kiss him. "Thanks, boss man," I purr, smacking his ass as he turns and unlocks the door for me.

"Bloody woman is going to get us all arrested. I can feel it," he mutters, but I ignore him as I head down the long hallway. There is a living room to the right, and beyond that is a dining room, kitchen combo with huge glass doors that open to a beautiful Zen garden with swinging chairs, bean bags, artificial grass, a pizza oven, a grill, and even a hot tub. Jesus. Heading back the way I came, I leap up the wooden stairs two at a time. On the first floor are three bedrooms and a bathroom.

"You're on the top floor!" Louis calls up. Listening to him, I hurry up the second set of stairs, hearing the boys fighting over the rooms on the floor below me. There's only one bedroom up here. It has an en suite, and it takes up the entire top floor, with a bed big enough to fit us all and skylights that let in the beautiful soft daylight. The carpet is white and fluffy, and there is a sofa to the left under one of the skylights, a flat screen TV, and a glass partition into the bathroom with a huge waterfall shower, golden clawfoot tub, and matching his and her sinks.

There's abstract art above the bed, but the decor is all very simple and pretty. Throwing my bag down, I strip off my jacket and stretch, needing to loosen my muscles.

I hear footsteps but don't turn. "This room is pretty big for just me," I call out to whoever is there.

"And me," Louis replies, surprising me. I glance over as he tosses his stuff next to mine and winks at me as he lies back on the bed. "Perks of being in charge, I get to pick the rooms." His tongue darts out then, licking his lips as his eyes run down my body. "Are you sure you don't want to stay and explore here?"

"As tempting as that is," I purr as I crawl onto the bed and up his body, "I need food."

"I could feed you, though I am starving too," he admits, making it clear by the stark hunger in his eyes it's not for the same thing I am.

Laughing, I smack his chest and go to roll off him, but his arms wrap around me and flip us, pinning me facedown on the bed. "I think I'll eat my fill first," he purrs into my ear as he captures my hands and holds them against the middle of my back. He kicks open my legs and covers my jean-clad pussy with his hand, making me groan.

I could get out of this position, but why would I want to?

Especially now that Louis is finally playing and giving in to this heat between us.

"Louis," I mumble into the bedding, faking a struggle to at least pretend like I'm fighting it. Arching my back, I try to buck him off, but he simply grips my pussy harder, making me still.

"Good girl," he praises and starts to stroke me through my jeans, digging the seam into my clit and making me gasp as I push my ass back into his hands. I give up. Who am I to complain if he wants to make me come? Especially since my knickers are already wet.

"Whoa, we didn't get invited to this. I want in!" Jonas calls, his footsteps silent so I didn't even hear him come upstairs. "Guys, come look at this!"

"Make sure to leave no traces of ID, check every window and door, and put up the cameras and alarms," Louis orders, all the while stroking my pussy through my jeans. It shouldn't be so hot, but it is, and I wiggle below him. I'm needy as hell now.

"Seems like we have time for me to eat that sweet little cunt like I've wanted to every moment of every single day since I met you. I'm tired of fighting it, Nova. I'm tired of holding back, so be a good girl and scream for me."

"Louis," I murmur, "I need to help them—"

"Shh." He smacks my pussy and keeps me pinned with one hand. With the other, he starts to wiggle my jeans down my ass, leaving me in a lacy thong with my ass in the air. His hand strokes up my leg and over my cheeks, ignoring exactly where I need him to touch me. "Fuck, you are way too beautiful. Look at that." His voice is soft as his fingers feather across my pussy and the thong there, feeling how wet I am for him. "So strong and certain until I touch this little pussy, aren't you? You are probably going to destroy us all, but I will enjoy every second of it. Life is too fucking short not to have what I want, and Nova? I want you so badly. Fuck the rules. Fuck everything but this need."

"Shit," I mumble. "If you don't—"

His hand lands on my ass in a rough slap. "Shh, Nova. You're not in control here, I am, and I'll taste this cunt when I damn well want to. First, I want to look at you." His mouth moves closer, and I hear him inhale deeply. "Fuck, you're a masterpiece."

"Louis," I beg as he hoists my ass into the air, the heat of him behind me making me shiver.

I never beg for anyone, but for him?

Fuck, I might just learn to.

"So demanding," he teases as his thick fingers stroke along my dripping folds, avoiding where I need him most. "Such a beautiful disaster, Nova."

"Fuck you!" I go to flip over, but he slaps my ass hard, making me groan as his fingers thrust into me, giving me what I want.

"Behave, and you'll get exactly what you need," he promises. His fingers curl and stroke inside me, making me moan as I push back and fuck myself on them. He lets me, his thumb rubbing my clit. Pleasure slams through me as he shows me what a reward would be like.

And then his fingers still.

"Are you going to behave?" he murmurs slowly, like he has all the time in the world.

I squirm on his fingers, and pleasure arcs through me so much, I want to say fuck it, turn over, and make myself come, but I don't want that.

I want him.

Clenching my eyes shut, I breathe slowly before nodding.

"Words, Nova," he demands, his mouth almost touching me now.

"Yes! Fuck, I'll behave," I snarl.

Uncaring about my angry tone, he darts his tongue out and flicks my clit, making me gasp. "Good girl."

I fall forward when his mouth seals on me, giving me the pleasure he promised. He takes no prisoners as he methodically decimates my cunt with his tongue, his fingers stroking inside me as he licks and sucks every inch of my pussy.

He leaves no inch untasted in his conquest to destroy me.

I moan and writhe below him, pushing into his mouth and fingers as he sucks my clit before moving away and down. He doesn't give me enough to get me off, only winding me up more.

"Louis!" I practically scream, rolling my hips to try and move him higher.

He ignores me, taking his time and learning what makes me moan, but he never lets me come.

"You taste so good, baby," he purrs as he laps at my entrance while he thrusts his fingers in and out of me. "How can someone who has experienced such pain, bitterness, and sin taste so fucking sweet? I could eat you all day. In fact, I just might."

Shit, shit, shit.

I'm so close, I can feel it, like when you are standing on a mountain and about to drop down the other side. My whole body shakes with anticipation, and my pussy clenches on his fingers.

"Boss, you want the cameras on the back too? There's no entrance point that I can see, but I want to be sure," Dimitri calls, his voice closer, and I feel his eyes on me. The fact that they are talking business while I'm almost coming on their leader's face is ridiculously attractive.

Louis lifts his mouth from my cunt to speak. "Yes. Better to be safe than sorry."

I want to scream. I was so fucking close! Louis chuckles like he knows my thoughts.

"Got it, enjoy your snack." D laughs as he walks away.

"Oh, I will. Now where were we?" he purrs, sealing his mouth back to my cunt.

"If you don't make me come, I'm going to fuck myself," I snarl, knowing I'm being a brat.

"Is that right? I don't take well to threats, Nova." His words vibrate my pussy, making me gasp. "But luckily for you, I want to see you shatter more than I want to punish you." His fingers slam into me, fucking me hard and fast as he lashes my clit and sends me spiralling over the edge with a cry.

"Again," he demands.

I shake my head, falling forward, but he hoists me back up. "I can't—" I'm too sensitive. I try to push him away as the aftershocks of the orgasm tear through me, but he licks me through it and out the other side, forcing me to reach for another one.

"You can and you will," he orders. "Now be a good girl and come all over my tongue for me."

"Louis!" His name is practically a scream. His other hand holds my cunt open for him as he sucks my clit, scraping his teeth against it until it almost hurts, and despite my protests, I come again, all over his fingers and tongue, and he laps up my release.

"Good girl."

Collapsing to the side, I turn to see him, his mouth and chin dripping with my cream as he licks his fingers clean, watching me. I roll to my knees and grab his head, kissing him deeply, tasting my release on his lips. I slide my hand down his body to his hard cock and grip it through his jeans, but his other hand circles my wrist as he pulls from my lips.

"No, darling, this was about you, not me. I don't need you to think you have to touch me to make us equal. Making you come was more pleasurable than even your talented hand." He kisses me again. "Go get ready so we can go explore like you want to, but remember, Nova . . ." His other hand slides around my throat, gripping it tightly and tilting my head back until my eyes open and lock on his determined, hungry gaze. "When you come back to this bed tonight, you're mine, all fucking mine, and I plan on spending every minute between those pretty thighs as you scream for me. It's your choice. I'm done fighting this tension between us, and I plan to give in to you completely, so this is your last warning, baby. If you step into this room after nightfall, you won't be leaving until I've fucked every single inch of you."

Fuck me.

I almost come just from the threat. He tightens his hand on my throat, using all of his strength. Dominance pours from him in waves, and usually

I would fight it, needing to be in control, but something about Louis gives me the strength to let that go and just be in the moment, trusting him to keep me safe and happy.

That terrifies me, and he watches the emotions play across my face before leaning in and kissing me softly—a promise of what is to come. He won't let me back away or hide.

Not this time.

As much as whatever is happening between us all scares me, the thought of living without them now terrifies me even further.

Louis leaves me after that, no doubt checking on the others.

He leaves me to my muddled emotions and clenching sex.

After changing out of my plane clothes and taking a whore's bath in the sink, I slip on some ripped black jeans with a white top tucked in loosely, and then I add a belt and some black boots. I even brush my hair and apply lip gloss and grab some shades, just in case. As I'm about to head downstairs, my phone vibrates, so I sit on the bed and accept the call from Ana.

"Hey," she says then hesitates. "I just wanted to check in and see how you are." I pull the phone away with raised eyebrows before putting it back to my ear.

"Yeah, we are all okay," I admit slowly. I am unsure what to say, not wanting to make her mad again.

"Okay, where are you now?" she asks, clearly nervous and trying to start a conversation.

"Scotland. We got another hit. The last one, well, they were dead, and it was all ruined. Let's leave it at that. How are you getting on?" I find myself lying back, feeling awkward at first, but as the conversation goes on, I smile, missing this connection between my sister and me. Although we have a lot to work on to trust each other again, this is a start. She reached out, and that makes me beyond happy.

"Hard," she grumbles. "His writing is worse than a doctor's—oh, wait." She laughs, and I laugh with her. "But I'll get there, I've been sending anything I've managed to translate to Louis, which isn't much yet."

"You'll get there; you always do. Let's be honest, you're smarter than me or Dad, so there is nothing you can't do if you just put your mind to it." I find myself needing to comfort her. I love my sister, and everything I've done is for her. Although I'm starting to put myself first and I'm still upset about what happened, I can't just stop loving her.

She will always be my Annie.

"Why are you always so nice to me? Nova, for so long, I pushed away memories of you because it hurt too much. I was angry, but under it was pain. I forgot how you used to tuck me in every night and make up these elaborate stories. I forgot you would hold me when I cried or clean my cuts or create these incredible worlds for us to play in so I didn't feel lost and alone when Dad ignored us, which was always."

"Annie," I murmur, the old nickname just slipping out, but she interrupts me.

"No, you need to hear this. The point is . . . I forgot. I forgot everything you did for me out of my own selfishness, but I'm remembering now, and I'm so sorry. I am so sorry I ever doubted the girl who promised to protect me, who fought off bullies and protected me from falling from that stupid old tree." I smile, remembering that day. "I'm sorry I didn't believe you. I will be for the rest of my life, and I'll make it up to you because I missed you, Nova, so much. If you are willing to, I'd like us to be sisters again. I'd like to have a family again, with you."

I remain quiet, and she swallows. "I—sorry, I shouldn't have—" She sounds dejected.

Life is very much like the weather. You get some good days and some bad. When it's sunny, you forget about the rain, and when it rains, you long for the sun. No matter how much she has hurt me, she will always be my sister, and she's offering me something I've wanted for so long—to be together again.

Everything else is just rain. It's beautiful and sometimes painful, but in the end, the sun always comes out.

"I would like that," I admit softly. "It's all I've ever wanted."

"Me too," she replies.

I hear Jonas yell, and I grin. "I have to go, there's work to be done, but I'll talk to you later, okay?"

"Okay," she replies softly.

"Make sure you eat and sleep, Annie," I order as I stand.

"Yes, Mum," she mocks like she used to when we were kids, the nostalgia quickening my heart rate as I rub the aching organ through my skin. "Love you, Nova."

"Love you too, kid," I reply before hanging up. There's an extra bounce in my step as I head downstairs. Now I just need to destroy all of Father's research, and everything will be good.

I find all the others waiting in the kitchen. D is in front of his laptop, which he closes and brings with him. I notice the temporary cameras and alarm systems and smirk. "Let's do this, team!" I call, clapping my hands. They all groan, but they are grinning. I head for the door and out so we can go explore.

We end up walking around the centre of Edinburgh, window shopping and taking pictures. We even climb to the castle where I ask a tourist to take a picture of us all. The guys pick me up and hold me sideways, making me laugh, and the picture has me smiling as we finally find a small pub and sit down for some beers and food.

For a moment, I just sit back with an unrestrained grin on my face as they all laugh at a story Isaac is telling. The food is good, the beers are cold, and the happiness in my chest is something I'm so unfamiliar with, I don't quite know what to do with it, but as I look around at their laughing faces, I know it's because of them.

Because of this team.

This family.

I don't think I could ever give it up now, and when D slings his arm around my shoulders and brings me back into the conversation, something close to love fills my chest.

After spending hours just enjoying our time together, we decide to wander back to the house. Along the way, Jonas spots a shop, and we all follow him in, only for him to buy a kilt. It makes me laugh, but I'm also ridiculously turned on as I imagine him wearing it.

Once we're back at the house, I grab a bottle of water and head outside, watching the sky while the others check the perimeter and D opens his laptop. Downing the bottle, I head back inside and bid them goodnight as I go up the stairs. Each step I take is slow and deliberate, as I know what is waiting for me up there—Louis and his promise to make me his tonight.

Shivering, I stop on a step and wonder if I'm really going to do this. Part of me knows it will change everything. I know he's giving me a choice to choose him—them.

It's an important moment, and it feels like something huge is on the horizon. My breath is shallow as I take the next step and the next, until I reach our bedroom to find him lying on the bed, his arms behind his head and a cocky, knowing smirk on his lips.

"Good girl, I knew you would come."

FORTY-SIX

"And what do you plan to do about it?" I find myself asking as I lean there.

Smiling wider, he rolls from the bed in a smooth move and prowls towards me, hunting me before he cages me against the wall. His muscular arm comes up next to my head as he leans in. His chest is bare, and his muscles clench deliciously with his movements. His joggers are slung low on his hips, showcasing that incredible V, which has me licking my lips before I drag my eyes back up to meet his shining, knowing gaze.

"I plan to reward you," he murmurs, making my heart stutter and my breathing pick up. "All night."

He steps back, and I almost slump, as if I were released by him. Louis has this overwhelming magnetism. Before, I was always dominant, but he makes me submissive, and I find myself loving it, so when he barks a command, I jump to comply.

"Undress, love."

I don't just rip my clothes off though. I might like what he orders, but let's face it, I always have to rebel.

Even a little.

I drag my shirt over my head and kick my trousers off before strolling towards him in nothing but my lace thong and bra.

"All of it, Nova," he demands.

When I reach him, I slide my hand down his chest to cup his hard cock through his joggers, making him groan as I squeeze and lick his nipple. Suddenly, his fist is in my hair, yanking my head back.

"I said all of it," he grits out.

"Then make me," I challenge him.

Snarling, he turns me until my back hits his chest and then rips away my thong and bra, making me jerk before I moan. I rub my ass against his hard length, my nipples tightening in the cool air as his hand moves down to grip my throat.

"If you wanted to be punished, baby, then all you had to do was ask," he purrs in my ear as he wedges one leg between mine, pressing his thigh against my pussy. His free hand grips my hip and rocks me until my clit hits his solid muscle, sending sparks of pleasure spiralling through me.

My eyes close at the friction, and my lips part on a moan.

"Is this your idea of a punishment?" I mock.

"No, I'm just getting you nice and wet." He smirks, licking and sucking at my neck as his other hand strokes up my body, twisting my nipples meanly. He continues to work me up until I almost come just from this, and like he feels the pulsing of my pussy, he pulls away, leaving me cold and frustrated.

Before I can turn, I'm pushed down and my ass is dragged out.

A hard smack jiggles my ass, the pain heading straight to my clit. His hand soothes it away before gliding over the ink on my hip. "I love your tattoos. They look so fucking sexy." His tongue replaces his hand, stroking over the ink and then up over my stinging cheek. He trails his fingers over my parted ass to my pussy, where he plunges them inside of me before pulling back once more.

"You taste so fucking sweet, baby. Do you know that? All these hard, sharp edges, yet your pussy gives you away, sweet and soft and wet, begging for my big cock." There's a rustle, and then I gasp when his length drags down my pussy. "Do you want this big cock, Nova?"

Fisting the sheets, I push back, but he pulls away.

"Words, baby," he orders.

"Fuck! Yes, I want it!" I scream, throwing him a venomous look over my shoulder. I moan, watching as he grips his wet shaft and drags his fist up and down his length as he watches me. He's so fucking long, I actually shiver from the look of him. He's slimmer than the others, but fuck, he's so goddamn long, I know it's going to hurt in the best way.

"Good girl, and you'll take every hard inch . . . but not until I've had my fill." He steps back between my thighs and drops to his knees, slanting his mouth over my pussy as my eyes slam closed and my back bows in ecstasy.

His tongue flicks with expert movements, tasting my pussy before circling my hole and moving back up, teasing my clit until I'm humping his face. I push back rapidly, rocking and reaching for my release once more, but just as I'm about to come, he stills.

"Louis!" I groan.

"Beg me to make you come, Nova."

"Never," I hiss.

"Then you don't get to." He grins against my thigh as he licks and sucks at the skin there.

Panting, I squeeze my eyes closed before forcing the words out. "Please, Louis, please make me come."

"How?"

"With your tongue." I groan. "And then your cock. Please, just fuck me!"

"Good girl. If you behave, you get what you want." His mouth seals over my cunt once more, and within seconds, I'm screaming my release and coating his tongue as he laps me through it. Holding me against his greedy mouth with one hand, he keeps tonguing my oversensitive flesh.

"No more."

His hand comes down in a smack on my ass as he nips my clit, making me jerk from the pain. "Not until I've said so. Now come again."

"I can't," I grind out.

"You can and you will. I want you squirting on my tongue, Nova," he orders, slipping his fingers inside of my still fluttering channel and stroking me before adding another, all the while he nips and sucks my oversensitive clit until I'm rocking into him.

He holds me there, between pleasure and pain, until he adds another finger, and then another. The pinch of pain as he stretches me is almost too much. "Good girl, take my whole fist."

I jerk, going to pull away, but he holds me in place as he adds his final fingers before pulling out and thrusting his fist back inside me.

His tongue drags over my pussy to my ass where he licks my asshole, all the while fucking me with his fist. The burn of pain and the stretch is too much, and with a scream, I come once more.

He pulls out as I fall forward, writhing in ecstasy from pleasure that's so great, I almost pass out.

When I can finally breathe again, I find him stroking his cock over my pussy, and without warning, he lifts me and impales me on it, like a rag doll.

The noise that leaves my lips isn't even human.

"So fucking beautiful, Nova. Such a good girl. Next time, you'll get my cock in your ass and my fist in your pussy," he growls, and it turns me on, making me grip his cock.

"Oh, you like that, don't you, you naughty girl?" He groans as I clench around him again. "You fucking love it."

"Asshole," I spit, even as I push back, finally recovering enough to move.

"You love it," he retorts. "Now be a good girl and take your man's cock. Let them all hear you fucking it like a good girl. No doubt they wish they were in here, and they are probably stroking their own cocks, fisting themselves in bed while imagining they're in this tight little cunt."

Shit, shit, shit.

Gripping my ass, he starts to speed up, fucking me harder. I grip onto the bed as I take it, his name a plea on my lips as he pounds into me from behind. Each brutal thrust rocks the bed into the wall in time with my moans. His huge length spears me to the point of pain, dragging across those nerves inside and making me wild.

One hand releases the globe of my ass and slips between my thighs to play with my clit, curling and flicking.

Over and over.

"Come for me, let me feel you gush on my cock, darling," he growls.

"Let me feel you explode. That's it. You're so close, I can feel it. Fuck, you should see yourself. All hard muscles yet soft fucking cunt gripping my dick, begging for it. You're so fucking beautiful, my girl. That's it, good girl, come for me. Milk me."

Oh fuck.

He slams inside of me at the same time he flicks my clit, and it sends me over the edge once more.

I come all over his cock like he said. He strokes me through it as my legs quiver, my body locks up, and my pussy clamps around his cock.

"Good girl, such a good girl. Look at you, look at how prettily you came for me, wetting my cock like such a greedy girl." His words of praise fill my ears as he blankets my body, holding me until I slump, and then he slowly pulls out of my clenching cunt and flips me.

Breathlessly, I stare up at his possessive, lust-filled eyes.

Gripping my hips, he yanks me to the edge of the bed and lifts my ass from it, placing it against his stomach as he slides back inside of me like he belongs there. I press my feet to his shoulders and reach up, gripping the bedding as he starts to fuck me once more.

He moves with slow, purposeful thrusts until I throw my head back and my hands slide up to grip my swaying tits as he watches.

"Fuck, Nova, you're killing me," he growls.

I sit up and lick the sweat on his chest before falling back and lifting my hips to meet his thrusts. Snarling, he hammers into me now, watching me bounce with each thrust.

"Fuck, I've never needed someone as much as I need you. I've never been able to let go with anyone like this. You drive me mad."

"In the best way," I tease, sliding my hands down my body where I stroke through the wet mess of my pussy to grip his cock at the base as he hammers into me.

Grunting, he speeds up, his arms shaking and abs flexing with each brutal twist of his hips until he turns his head and bites my thigh, making me cry out as I come once more.

This time, though, I drag him with me, a roar leaving his lips as he pummels into me before stilling.

His release splashes inside me until he finally collapses on top of me. His sweaty body slides against mine as I wrap my legs and arms around him and kiss him, tasting the pleasure on his lips.

"That was only round one, baby," he murmurs, placing a soft kiss over my hammering heart.

I'm a wet mess, and I can't help but smile.

"Bring it on."

He does. I wake up later to his face buried between my thighs, and he orders me to come so many times, I actually pass out. The next time I wake up, it's with his fingers buried inside of me, which he quickly replaces with his cock, rocking into me from behind until I scream and he fills me with his cum.

I'm exhausted and fall straight back to sleep until the sunlight hits my face, slowly waking me up.

His hands explore my body, mapping every inch and stroking across the muscles in my stomach, over my slightly rounded hips, down and up my legs, over my toned back and shoulders, then down my breasts and back again.

I wake up wet and panting.

"Louis," I groan, burying my face in the pillow, even as I part my legs to give him better access to explore.

"I warned you, baby." He chuckles as he laps at my pussy before I feel his cock sliding into me.

He leans down to kiss me as he slowly rolls his hips, taking mercy on me and fucking me gently, each slow drag of his huge length making me gasp into his mouth. He swallows the sound, his own grunts making me feel giddy.

To have such an effect on such an incredible man?

Yeah, it's addictive.

My hands slide across his shoulders and down to his flexing ass, where I dig my nails in as I lick and suck at his lips, tasting his pleasure there.

"Shit, you're so fucking good like this. I don't want to blow just yet, baby, and if you keep kissing me like that, like I'm your fucking everything, then I will," he murmurs into my mouth before pulling from my body, leaving me blinking and unsatisfied, but I shouldn't have worried because he rolls down beside me and lifts me right onto his face.

My hands fall to his chest as I bow over him and he seals his mouth over my pussy, licking and sucking, using everything against me until I'm coming across his lips and tongue. I lean farther down and swipe my tongue across his hard cock, watching it jerk for me.

"Good girl," he purrs against me, the vibrations making me jerk away.

Chuckling, he drags me down, bringing his knees up to prop me up as his hard cock presses into me once more and he thrusts up from behind, spearing me on it.

He holds my hips as I face the stairs. "Ride me, Nova. Let me see that pretty pussy swallowing my cock."

Sighing in pleasure, I roll my hips before using my thighs to ride him with his help, while his fingers stroke my skin once more before grabbing my ass and parting it to see better.

"Fuck, I've never seen a more beautiful sight." He moans behind me, giving me all the control. "That's it, baby, take me, fuck me, use me for your pleasure."

I do, winding my hips and doing what feels good until a slow, rolling orgasm washes me away. I feel him sit up, changing the angle, and press his face to my neck, where he nuzzles and trails kisses as he bounces me on his cock, chasing his own release. The lazy thrust of his cock leaves me defenceless against this man, and he knows it.

He knows how to pull me apart and put me back together again, giving me no choice but to surrender his control.

It's so easy to see why the others follow him and trust him implicitly, and right now, so do I.

He fucks me right into another release, my name on his lips as he grunts and stills, pumping me full of his cum once more.

When the pleasure finally abates, he pulls free of my body, making me wince, and then tugs me into his arms, kissing my face and lips. "You did amazing, Nova, so fucking good. When I can walk, I'll bathe and feed you."

"Asshole," I murmur, even as I snuggle closer.

The chuckle makes his chest lift against me as he strokes my back. "No, that's for next time, baby."

Oh fuck.

FORTY-SEVEN

I roll out of bed, finding the other side cold. Louis is gone, but there's a T-shirt folded on his pillow with a note on top.

> Wear this. Let them all see whom you belonged to last night while I remember the way you came for me so prettily, baby. See you downstairs.

Flipping onto my back, I bite my lip to hold back my smile, feeling like a giggling schoolgirl. Hell, it's not a sweet, loving note, but damn, it's perfect for me and for them. Dragging myself up, I force myself to shower, wincing at the soreness between my thighs. It's that special kind of ache that reminds you that you've been good and fucked. I don't bother with knickers or a bra, and I leave my hair wet and my face bare as I pad back into the other room and slip on the shirt. I fold the note and shove it into my jeans pocket to keep. Not that I'll admit that to myself.

Walking downstairs, I hear them in the kitchen, their banter reaching my ears even on the second floor. It doesn't stop when I walk in, which makes me grin wider. Louis winks at me as he adds bacon to a pan, while Nico pushes him out of the way, eggs in his hand. Isaac is nursing a cup of tea and watching it all unfold with a paper folded before him, and he grins when he sees me. D is flipping sausages in a frying pan, and Jonas is doing push-ups on the deck outside.

"Morning, beautiful," D calls as I pass him, kissing his cheek as I head to the fridge. Nico beats me there, handing me a mug of coffee.

"Juice is on the table. Morning, baby." He kisses my cheek so close to my lips, I stumble for a moment, and then he whacks my ass with the spatula. "Go get Jonas and sit down. Breakfast is nearly ready."

When I pass Louis, he leans in and murmurs, "You look awfully good in my shirt, Nova." The promise in his tone almost has me skipping to the table. Putting my mug down, I pop my head outside.

"Hey, hot stuff, breakfast is ready!" I call.

Jonas stops mid jump clap push-up and grins up at me, his eyes bright. "I'll be right there—wait, get on my back. Let me use you as a weight."

Not needing to be told twice, I hurry over and sit on his back cross-legged. He doesn't even grunt at the added weight as he continues doing push-ups. The others look out and just shake their heads, and when Jonas is done, I climb down and offer him my hand. He takes it, and I hoist him up.

"Ew, you're sweaty," I tease, wiping my hand dramatically.

"Yeah, how about I make you all sweaty?" he flirts, and I point my finger at him.

"Don't you dare. I just showered," I warn, and his eyes narrow.

"Run, Nova," he teases.

I hurry back inside with him chasing me, laughing. I drop into Isaac's lap and wrap my arms around him. "I claim sanctuary!" I yell.

Isaac just wraps his arm around me and continues drinking his tea. "Leave her be, Jonas."

"Nah, now you'll both get sweaty." Laughing, he wraps us both in a sweaty, meaty hug, and when he pulls away, Isaac is sighing, but I see a smile twisting his lips. Kissing the top of my head, Jonas flops back into my chair and starts to pick up my coffee as Nico comes over to put a plate on the table and extracts it, handing it to me.

"Get your own," he tells Jonas.

"Rude, just because she has a vagina," he whines.

"Yup." I wink.

"Sexist," he tells me as he gets up.

Turning on Isaac's lap, I smile at him as he peers down at me with soft eyes. "Morning, how are you?"

"I'm fine," he replies as he holds me closer, pressing his face into my neck and inhaling. "Better now." His voice is husky, and it sends a shiver through me. It also doesn't escape my notice that something hard is pushing against my ass. I wiggle to be a brat, and he smacks my thigh.

"Unless you want me to bend you over this table and fuck you before breakfast, behave," he warns.

"No sex on the table, I just set it," D calls without even looking.

"Party pooper!" Jonas accuses as he sits back down with a mug. "There should always be time for sex before breakfast. It's like that fancy word for starter."

"Hors d'oeuvre? Appetizer?" I suggest, making him grin.

"That one. See? I knew you were a genius, Nova," he purrs, licking the rim of his mug while he watches me.

"Behave." Louis smacks his head as he passes to pop two plates down before Isaac and me. "And you need to eat. You burned a lot of calories last night." The satisfied smirk he wears tells everyone how I accomplished that, but they just laugh, not the least bit bothered that I'm fucking Louis now too.

No judgement, no hate, just pure acceptance, and I feel myself glowing as I tuck into the food, turning to share some with Isaac, who takes it gratefully, kissing my lips after every bite. When I look back, I find the others watching me with knowing, happy grins, and I just roll my eyes.

"So what's on the agenda for today?" I ask when the plates are clear. It's my turn to wash up, so I drag my feet, trying to distract them.

"I'm still waiting on any new information, so this morning we'll train and rest," Louis replies. "I want at least three hours of drills for everyone. We have been slacking while we've been on the road."

"Oh, does that mean I get to watch you all sweaty and half naked?" I bounce on Isaac's lap, making him groan again and grip me tighter.

"It means we get to watch you in skintight workout gear." Nico grins, making my mouth pop open.

I gasp. "You are supposed to be the well behaved one!"

"Oops," is all he says, sparking a surprised laugh from me.

"Wash up and then meet us outside," Louis orders, not letting me get away from my part in the group, even though I blew his mind last night.

"Can't I just suck one of your cocks and get you to wash up for me?" I grin.

Isaac laughs as he pushes me up, spanking me to get me moving.

"Oh, mine, mine!" Jonas calls.

"Deal—"

"No, wash up," Louis commands, shaking his head. "Lads, back outside."

They all grumble as they file outside, and I mutter as I clear the table and start to wash up, but I really shouldn't have complained because I get a free show as I do. I watch them strip their shirts off and warm up before working through Louis's drills. He does them with them as he calls them out, and I stop what I'm doing and just drool over all the tanned, exposed muscles.

I gawk, watching them do burpees, when Louis catches me and raises his eyebrows. Coughing to cover my awkwardness, I wash the pots as fast as possible and hurry upstairs. I change into some shorts, a sports bra, and a big T-shirt that I'll take off after warming up. Once I get back downstairs, I lace up my trainers and meet them outside. I stretch and focus on warming up my body while they work on their sets, and when I'm ready, I start with the drills they did—push-ups into burpees into jumping jacks. After I'm done, I pull my shirt off and put it on the table before stepping into the sled zone which they have fashioned out of the chairs with one of the guys lying on it. I pull it back and push it, barely breaking a sweat, and then Louis pulls off the kid gloves.

He doesn't go easy on me at all. Oh no, he pushes me to see how far I can really go, testing how strong, fast, and agile I am. Two hours later, I collapse onto the grass, breathing heavily with that elated feeling I get after a great workout, the likes of which I haven't had in a long time.

"Need a hand . . . or some new lungs?" Nico grins down at me.

"Sadistic bastards. All of you," I retort, even as I groan and sit up, accepting the cold water he hands me. "But damn, that was good. I haven't worked that hard in too long."

"Oh, I don't know. I think you worked pretty hard last night," Jonas teases, wagging his eyebrows. I throw my water at him, making him laugh as he catches it and takes a big gulp.

Louis is about to respond when a buzz goes off, and all of us turn to the kitchen where D's laptop sits. Sharing a look, we scramble to our feet and race inside, hoping for the best, for more information to lead us to the next step.

FORTY-EIGHT

We all gather around the laptop as D works through the information, but when he starts to get annoyed with us hanging over his shoulder, Louis barks at us to shower and hydrate. Realising it will be while, I kiss D's cheek to let him know it's okay and head back upstairs to shower once more.

I take my time and dress in a comfortable but moveable outfit in case we need to go out, sticking to my jeans, boots, and a jumper before grabbing my jacket and taking it downstairs with me. I hear bickering on the second floor.

"We do not share showers!"

"Then get out!"

"Get your dick away from me! Nova, help!"

Laughing, I shake my head as I head to the bottom floor. Louis is on the phone, shirtless with his workout shorts still on and coated in sweat, looking fucking delicious. His eyes heat and turn hungry as he looks me over, even as he carries on talking without even a hitch in his breath.

The possessive lust in his gaze makes me lick my lips before I turn to D and sit next to him. "Everything okay?"

He nods, typing away. I lean back, letting him work, but he blinks and looks over at me. "I'm sorry. I just get so into—"

"Never apologise." I lean over and drop a kiss onto his lips. "You want a drink while you work?"

He blinks at me slowly before a wide smile crawls over his face. "Coffee, please."

"You got it, babe." I wink as I stand, and when I pass him, he grabs my waist and hauls me back, tugging me down so he can kiss me properly. When I break away, breathing heavily, his eyes are molten. "I forgot to tell you that you look beautiful today," he purrs and then smacks my ass and goes back to work.

As I start making everyone coffee, Louis hangs up with a disgusted sneer on his lips. "Fucking soldiers and their sticks up their asses," he mutters as he leans back next to me. "Where are the others?"

"Last I heard, it sounded like Jonas was trying to scare Isaac out of the shower with his dick." I shrug, and we share a grin as we hear their thundering feet upstairs. "So, the usual."

"You are too good to us," he murmurs as I hand him a coffee.

"Don't forget it. Now go shower," I order.

His brow arches as he leans in. "Don't like me all sweaty, baby?"

"Oh, I do," I purr as I lick a long line up to his ear, tasting his musk. "But if you continue standing there shirtless, I'll end up fucking you and getting you all distracted."

"I wouldn't mind that," D calls out absentmindedly, making Louis and I chuckle as we break apart.

"Next time," Louis promises and drags himself away from me. I hear him heading upstairs as I turn back to the coffees, making them to each individual person's tastes.

"Fucking hell, Nico, get the knife out of his balls!" I hear him snap a moment later. "Behave, all of you. It's like living with animals. Jonas, stop chasing Isaac with your cock."

He sounds exasperated, and I giggle as D laughs.

Just as I'm laying out some biscuits and snacks, Nico comes in, wrapping his arms around me from behind and burying his face in my neck. "Save me from the madness."

"Nope, sorry." I pat his hands, leaning into him for a moment before dislodging him and handing him a coffee. "But here's a peace offering."

He takes it and sips it before his eyes close. When they flutter open, they are blazing as he backs me into the counter. "Fucking perfect."

"Yeah? Is it good? I've never tried that roast," I find myself asking.

With his eyes on me, he takes a big drink before grabbing my face and kissing me, letting me taste the coffee on his lips and tongue. When he pulls away, he's smirking. "Well, do you like it?"

"You're right. It's good," I rasp, my eyes wide.

"Either fuck or don't, but you're distracting!" D calls, making us both chuckle as we separate.

"Sorry, D!" we both call in unison.

We drink our coffee in peace until the others come down and wait with us. Ten minutes later, D leans back and blows out a breath before he chugs his coffee and wipes his mouth. He looks over at us and blinks before he blushes slightly, as if only just now realising we are here and watching him. "We have a location, but you might want to check with our bosses," he says mockingly.

Louis heads over and sighs before nodding, getting his phone out, and walking away. "It could be a while before we get permission, so today is an off day. Go have fun."

He doesn't have to tell us twice.

We spend the day wandering around Edinburgh before heading back to the house. D and Louis are busy with work, and Nico decides to go on a run with Isaac, leaving Jonas and me unoccupied, which is truly a bad idea.

We share a matching grin. "What bad things can we get up to?" he purrs as he prowls towards me, and I back into the garden. He thinks he's cornering me, but in reality, I'm leading him.

I glance away, scanning the garden before coming up with an idea. I step into him and press my hand into his chest, sliding it down. "I can think of something," I purr and kiss him, nipping his lips before stepping back once more.

His eyes are closed, and when they blink open, they are dazed and euphoric. He watches me as I grab my jumper and strip it off along with my jeans, socks, and boots, leaving me in nothing but a lacy bra and thong. With a wink at him, I hurry to the hot tub, lift the lid, and climb in, sinking into the hot, bubbling water with a sigh.

My head tips back as the heat warms my chilled body, and then I move to the back row of seats and drape my arms across the edge as I lick my lips and meet his hungry gaze as he stands frozen, still watching me. "Well, what are you waiting for?"

He rips off his shirt and tosses his trousers away. He's naked under them, which I should have guessed. His huge, hard, pierced cock bobs as he walks towards me and climbs in. Pushing through the water, he doesn't stop until he's pressed against me, and I wrap my legs around him, grinding my cunt onto his cock.

I know D and Louis are just inside, and we are within view of them and the neighbours, but I don't care, especially when Jonas leans down and licks a trail of wetness between my breasts. Tugging my bra down, he uses it to push my breasts up before he nips and sucks my nipple. Keeping those dark eyes on me, he turns his head and sucks and nips the other. Pleasure arcs straight to my throbbing clit, even as the jets pound into my back, starting a lazy, hazy pleasure. My head tips back and my eyes close as his hands bracket my breasts, pushing them tight as he sucks and bites them. The stings of pain are followed by pleasure so great, I grind and moan against him without a care.

"Jonas." His name is a cry, and it drives him wild. He grinds his cock into my thong-covered pussy as he bites my nipple so hard, I jerk and scream. When he raises his head, I see he's drawn blood. Panting, I grip his hair and drag him up, kissing him.

Our tongues tangle as he reaches down into the water and rips my thong away, tossing it to the grass as his hands slide across my thighs to my hips and tilt me back so my clit hits his cock every time I wind my hips.

"I knew the moment I met you that I was yours," he murmurs into my lips, forcing me to swallow the words and sending them straight to my heart. "Knew I would worship you, that I'd be on my knees for the rest of my life if it keeps you at my side. I saw you, Nova. I fucking saw you and knew you were ours."

Fuck.

I moan into his lips, digging my teeth in and letting the pain flash through him until he grinds harder against my cunt, nearly making me come from that alone.

"But we are just as much yours." He groans. "So let them see that."

He grabs me and flips me around so I'm hanging over the edge of the hot tub, my tits pressed to the side and pushed up indecently. My nipples drag across the smooth plastic as his hand fists my hair and tugs. His other hand grips my hip and yanks me back onto the seat so I'm kneeling with my ass out for him, and then he lets go. I pant, feeling him moving in the water underneath me, and then he chuckles evilly.

Using my hips, he holds me tight and slams into me, taking my cunt the way I want him to. I close my eyes in agonised bliss as his hard cock fills me. The water churns around us as he pulls out and hammers back inside me.

"Let them hear you scream. Let them see the way I fuck you. You were made for all of us. We've been so lost, Nova, so fucking lost, and now that we have you, we'll never be again." The noise that leaves my lips is inhuman, his words ripping apart my heart. "Fuck, you feel so fucking good, too fucking good. It drives me crazy. It's all I think about, Nova: your pretty pussy. I'd be chained to your side and eating it every day all day if I could, begging for a taste, for the honour to be inside you. Look how well you're fucking taking me." His dirty words have me pushing back and impaling myself on his cock, and he bites my neck like an animal, making me cry out again.

His hand slides down to my throat and jerks my head up. "Eyes open, Nova. Look at what you do to us," he snarls, and my eyes pop open to see the others watching—all of them, their eyes hard and hungry.

Fuck!

I sway back harder, crying out, and then he repositions me, and I wonder why, but then I feel it.

A jet shoots right at my clit, making me writhe and scream. The intense feeling is too much, and I explode, coming around his cock, but he doesn't stop. He fucks me through it, keeping me pinned in place. The pressure on my clit is almost too much, and my eyes roll into the back of my head as he hammers into me.

"Ours, you're fucking ours, Nova." He grunts. "Look how you bring us together, how wild you make them. They never understood my madness until you." His voice is tight, harsh, as he bites and nips my skin, fucking me so hard, my hips slam into the side and I know I'll bruise.

The water splashes over the sides as my eyes open once more, meeting with those hungry ones of my other men as Jonas roars and hammers into me, forcing me tighter against the jet until I come alongside him. I cry out so loudly, everyone hears as I jerk and writhe on his cock and he pumps his cum inside of me. When I slump, he covers me, kissing my skin as his softening cock slips out of me, leaving me whimpering.

I almost slip into the water, but he holds me up as my legs twitch and my heart skips. "I love you, Nova."

I freeze and turn my head to meet his serious gaze. I was expecting it to be a joke, but there is nothing but sincerity in his eyes as he softly pushes the hair from my face.

"You don't have to say it back. I know you struggle with love, with trust, but this is enough for me, and even if I never get any more of you, that's okay. You hold my heart, though, all of it. I'm yours until the very end, and I'm not going anywhere. Where you go, I go. I will never betray you, never hurt you, and never leave you like everyone else, and with time, you'll believe that."

Tears fill my eyes as he voices all my fears. Leaning in, he kisses me softly.

"And one day, you will believe that I love you. I will wait for that day."

"What if it never comes?" I rasp.

"It will," he vows, his forehead pressed to mine. "Because we plan to show you every day just how worthy, important, and perfect you are so you'll finally see yourself as you are. Until then, I'll hold the shattered pieces of your heart and soul with mine."

FORTY-NINE

After what I'm calling Hot Tub Fun, we spend the rest of the day checking our equipment and relaxing. It's strange, and we even watch a movie. We are waiting on confirmation from the military bros, as Jonas calls them, so in the meantime, we lie low.

When Dimitri suggests a BBQ, everyone seems excited. I don't help much with cooking, more moral support from the bean bag I'm reclining in with a beer. Louis and D are bent together over the grill, Jonas and Nico fight over setting the table, and Isaac sits next to me in the same double bean bag, sipping his beer and watching with a content smile.

I slip his arm over me and grin up at him as he directs that smile down at me, which only seems to grow and soften. That one look alone makes my heart skip and my voice hoarse when it comes out. "Are you okay?"

His grin turns smouldering as he starts to play with my hair and kisses my forehead so gently, so softly, my eyes close on a hard swallow. "Perfect now that you are here," he murmurs, his voice lowered to create our own little bubble.

"Good," I whisper, opening my eyes and meeting his.

Something passes between us, and breathing becomes hard. Our legs are intertwined, and our bodies are touching, and I realise I'm practically sprawled over him as lust pulses through me. Licking my lips, I watch his eyes blow with desire as he watches the movement, his teeth catching on his own.

"Nova." The way he breathes my name has me leaning up as Isaac leans down.

He meets me halfway, our lips coming together in a soft, loving kiss—one that burrows into my soul and takes root. His hand cups the back of my head as he tilts me backward so he's practically covering my body as he chases my lips. I part them for him, and he thrusts his tongue into my mouth, tangling it with mine.

What started as a soft, chaste kiss soon turns heated and wild.

I claw at his shoulders desperately, tugging him closer as he swallows my moan of pleasure. I nip his lip, and I feel him shiver against me, making me bolder. Pushing him back, I throw my leg over him and straddle his waist, all without breaking the kiss as I taste his hunger for me.

His hands grip my hips to help me before sliding down to my ass and hauling me closer, perching me on his huge, hard length. Grunting, he pulls back, his eyes blown wide with desire as he watches me.

Our hearts hammer in sync.

The others watch as they cook, and yes, we are having a nice family day, but I want to rip off my clothes and ride Isaac so I can feel him shatter below me as he keeps those loving eyes locked on me. Isaac makes me feel powerful, strong, sure, and in charge. He offers me comfort and happiness, and right now, I want that so badly, it almost hurts to stop.

So why should I?

It isn't anything they haven't seen before. Fuck the BBQ, I'm hungry for him, not the meat.

Biting his lower lip, I pull back and pop it free before sliding my hand down his chest and gripping his cock. "I'm hungry, and I can't wait," I murmur, and when he swallows, I grin, sliding down his body until my knees hit the grass. He slumps back into the bean bag, watching me with wide eyes as I tug down his joggers enough to free his cock.

I spit into my hand and slide my fist up and down his hard length, watching it jerk and leak for me as he groans.

He reaches down and tangles his hand in my hair. "Nova, you don't have to."

I blow over the tip of his cock, watching him writhe for me. "I want to," I murmur as I suck his tip into my mouth and moan. Desire hums through me, but I focus on his pleasure, knowing he never does.

"I guess she really wants his meat," Jonas jokes.

I flip him off as I roll my eyes up to Isaac's, watching him as I hollow my mouth and swallow his length. His head falls back, the veins popping in his neck as it strains. I watch his Adam's apple bob as he swallows hard, and then I feel his hand flex in my hair, tugging me closer.

God, I love this, love sucking cock and seeing the power I have over someone else. With Isaac, it's a heady feeling knowing I'm looking after the man who never lets anyone else look after him.

Only me.

Moaning, I grip his base and pull back, licking his length and tracing the veins there before sucking on the tip as his hips jerk. "Fuck, Nova!" he yells, making me grin as I pop his cock free from my mouth. The musky taste of him coats my tongue as he drips for me.

"Do you want me to stop?" I flutter my lashes innocently, but my smile is wicked.

"Oh, God, please, no!" he begs, tugging me back down.

Laughing, I go willingly and swallow his huge length all the way to the back of my throat, and then I linger there as he shakes beneath me. His thighs become taut as I pull up and then bob back down on his cock, speeding up and fucking him with my mouth. I keep my eyes on him the entire time, seeing the wild desire, love, passion, and friendship he feels for me as he watches me wordlessly.

Humming, I let him feel the vibration as I pull back and suck on his tip again.

"Oh fuck, I'm already close," he warns, his hips jerking. I swallow him all the way back, letting my throat close around him, and he cries out, thrusting his hips and widening his legs until he explodes with a yell.

Cum spurts down my throat. I swallow and pull back, letting it spill across my mouth, tongue, and lips as he watches.

"Nova." My name is a ragged cry as he reaches down and jerks his cock, spilling more cum across my tongue, and then I swallow as he slumps back, his cock wet and spent, and his face flushed and slack.

Sitting back with a smug expression, I use my finger to swipe up the mess on my lips and chin as he watches, moaning as I suck my fingers clean of his release.

"I'm full," I purr.

"Fuck, do you know how hard it is to cook with a stiff cock?" Dimitri calls, making me grin over my shoulder at him as I toss my hair back.

"I bet it's very *hard*." I pout over the word. "You should have let me help with that." His face heats as he watches me. "Or maybe you should help me." Turning, I press my back to Isaac's knees, and he reaches down and pets my hair as I watch the others. I spread my legs and drag a hand down my body.

Four sets of eyes track the movement, the food forgotten. A plate crashes from Jonas's hand as he lifts it into the air. "I volunteer."

"It's my turn to taste her cunt!" Nico snarls at him.

Louis watches it all with an arched eyebrow, but nobody notices D tossing his cooking utensils down, ripping off his shirt, and then prowling towards me. Grinning, I cup my pussy and grind into my hand through my shorts.

He drops to his knees several feet away from me and crawls forward, stopping to lick up my legs and across my shorts until his mouth covers my hand. "Fuck cooking, I'd rather eat," he whispers, rolling his eyes back up to mine, waiting for my decision.

Moving my hand, I cup his chin with it and sit up to kiss him softly. "Then lick my pussy until I come, baby," I order and sit back, letting Isaac pet my hair as I spread out between his legs. Dimitri instantly rips my shorts off, leaving me bare from the waist down.

Licking his lips, he grabs my thighs and tosses them over his shoulder.

"Fuck," Nico and Jonas say at the same time.

Louis turns off the grill, grabs a chair, and drags it to the side where he sits back with his legs spread as he watches us. Shit. My eyes close at the first touch of D's eager tongue. He laps at my cunt, tasting me as he slides his hands to my ass and lifts so he can access every inch of me.

"Fuck!" I scream as he sucks my clit before he drags his tongue down my pussy and spears it inside of me. I'm already dripping and on edge from blowing Isaac.

My head drops back to Isaac's thigh, and his thumb slides into my mouth, so I suck as Dimitri eats my cunt so good, I'm already close to coming.

His talented tongue fucks me before licking my clit in the way that drives me mad. My eyes open when he nips my clit, the wet sound of him going down on me ridiculously hot.

"Fuck, he's good at that. We should take lessons," Jonas comments, judging Nico.

"Speak for yourself." Nico grunts, smacking his back. My eyes dart to them before landing on Louis, who is smouldering, his hard cock outlined in his trousers.

Oh fuck, fuck, fuck.

My head falls back again as I grind and twist, chasing my orgasm, and when he pushes three fingers inside of me and curls them, I come all over his face with a scream. Holding him tight against my pussy, I ride out my release and then slump back, panting while Isaac pets my face and tells me how good I was, but I don't want to be a good girl.

I want to be bad.

Dimitri sits up, his face covered in my release, as he grabs his cock through his trousers and squeezes it, taking in my spread legs and my pussy that's on display.

"I want to fuck you all while you watch," I say, totally unashamed.

"You don't have to ask me twice," Jonas calls, hurrying forward.

Louis holds up his hand, and everyone freezes. "Are you sure, Nova?" His eyes hold a plethora of questions, but I simply nod. "Then we will do this my way. Nico, you have not had our Nova yet, have you?"

"No," he murmurs, watching me with unrestrained lust.

"Then you'll get her mouth. The first time you'll feel that incredible cunt will be alone. Jonas, you get her pussy, but don't make it hurt too badly because after you fill her with your cum, she'll get D's and mine."

Holy fucking shit.

Why is the thought of that so hot? Why is Louis taking charge and telling them how they are going to fuck me turning me on so much?

I don't know and I really don't care, because I get what I want—them for as long as I can have them—and so much pleasure I know nothing else will ever compare.

There are no secrets between us, and no lines we can't cross. We are all the same, a fucked-up little family, and I plan to fuck and keep every single one of them if they'll let me.

I'm flipped as Nico replaces Isaac. "Nico . . ." I swallow, knowing he doesn't need to.

"Open that pretty mouth and swallow my cock, baby," he orders, his head tilted to the side as he watches me, his eyes dark and hungry. "He's right. I get that sweet pussy when we are alone, not together, but for now, I want to fill that teasing mouth with my cum until you choke on it."

Well, fuck.

How could I resist?

Hands slide across my hips, yanking me up—Jonas.

Nico watches me as he pulls out his huge cock. My eyes widen. He's fucking massive. I knew he would be, but fuck. I don't think all of it will fit into my mouth. As if hearing my thoughts, he narrows his gaze. "You can and you will. You'll take me all the way down that pretty throat until all you can taste is me."

"Yeah, Nova, be good and suck his cock," Jonas taunts as his hand smacks my pussy, making me jerk and fall forward right onto Nico's waiting cock.

He fists my hair, and tears fill my eyes. Snarling, he presses the tip of his cock to my lips and then looks over my head, and just as I feel Jonas's tip at my pussy, I open my mouth, and both of them slam into me at the same time.

I jerk between them, the invasion too much, but they don't let me do anything except take it. Nico bottoms out in my throat, making me gag, but I dig my nails into his thighs to hold on as Jonas grips my hips painfully, pulls out, and pummels into me.

Moaning, I pant as Nico withdraws and thrusts into my mouth. Unlike Isaac, who let me take control, Nico takes what he wants, fucking my mouth as I choke and relent.

A loud slap rings out and I jerk, taking Nico deeper as Jonas's hand lands on my ass. Stinging pain comes after, and I whimper around Nico's cock as he rubs it in, my pussy clenching around him.

"Shit, Nova, I love how tight you get when I hurt you." He groans. "You should feel it, Nico. She clamps like a whore, watch." He smacks me again, the pain making me do just as he described as it explodes through my body.

"Is that right, baby?" Nico growls, his face feral as he thrusts up, taking my mouth hard and fast. "I wonder . . ." His eyes narrow further as he yanks me down, forcing me all the way to his base.

It hurts, yet I clamp around Jonas so hard, he groans. "Fuck, man, she really liked that."

I wasn't prepared for them both to work together against me, and it's so fucking hot that when Jonas spanks me again, I come so hard that Nico has to pull out of my mouth as I writhe and groan on Jonas's cock. He holds still, letting me come around him, and when I slump, he yanks my thighs back, pummelling into me as Nico thrusts into my slack mouth.

"You look so good taking their cocks," Louis comments, making my eyes widen as I simmer. "Doesn't she?"

"She does," Dimitri replies. "It would be even better if there was one in her ass too."

"Next time," Louis says.

"Look at her pretty tits practically spilling out," Isaac adds.

The fact that they are all here watching makes me push back, and I meet Jonas's feral thrusts. Hands slip across my body, one softer than the other as they slide over my skin, stroking me as I'm fucked by their brothers.

There are so many hands, the sensations are too much, and I practically squirm, but they hold me between them as they fuck me, each chasing their release. I can feel Nico's thighs quake below my fingers, and I know he's close. I want to feel it and taste him, so I lower my head all the way to his base and suck hard.

Fingers start to play with my nipples from both sides, tweaking and rolling, and I whimper, causing Nico to snarl before he comes with a roar, pumping his release down my throat. I swallow, but it spills over. Jonas growls, pummelling into my pussy before groaning, and then I feel his forehead hit my back as his hips jerk and he comes.

I slump down as Jonas pulls free, my body spent and wound up at the same time, but I don't have a moment to breathe because I'm turned.

"Sit that pretty pussy on his cock," Louis orders as I find Isaac lying back with one hand loosely stroking his cock. His length makes my mouth water as I crawl up his body, greedy for more.

Cum drips down my thighs and mouth, and yet I stop and lap at the tip of his cock, watching as his back bows.

Oh yes, this will be fun.

"Now, Nova," Louis snaps.

Giving him a pout, I slide up Isaac's body and place my hands on his chest, lining myself up with his hard cock, and then I sink down. Both of us groan as I wiggle, lift, and drop until I'm settled deep on his cock. His head lifts as he searches for my mouth, and I lean down and kiss him as I start to move.

I wind my hips, rocking and riding him as the others watch.

A hand slides up my back and to my hair, pushing down until I lie on top of Isaac, kissing him. I moan into his mouth as that same hand slides down my spine and wraps around Isaac's cock as it spears me.

Dimitri.

"You should see how good you look right now with him stretching you like this. It's almost as good as you will look with my cock in your ass." Biting Isaac's lip, I take out my desire on him as he groans and jerks below me.

A mouth slides across my ass, and a tongue slips down my crack to trace my hole, making me shiver. "I fucking love eating ass as much as I love fucking it, but that will be for later. For now, I'm going to get my cock all wet with cum so I can sink in deep and stretch you between us."

Oh shit.

I rip my mouth away, panting as I wiggle back. "Then do it," I demand breathlessly.

Louis chuckles. "You heard her, Dimitri."

"That I did." He grins against my ass and then he pulls back, taking his heat with him. I whimper, clenching around Isaac's cock. Suddenly, the thick head of Dimitri's cock is there, pushing in alongside him.

I fall forward, and arms wrap around me, holding me still. "Shh, it's going to feel so good," Isaac promises. "That's it, my good girl, take him as well. You know you can."

His praise has me wiggling, and Dimitri slips an inch deeper into my pussy. The burn is almost too much, and I let out a pathetic whimper as fingers slide down my dripping pussy and play with my clit. Desire roars back to life, quick and fast, and he sinks deeper.

Dimitri just sits there, letting me stretch around them as he circles my clit until I grind back, and then, in time with his fingers, he slides in deeper and deeper.

Finally, I feel every hard inch of him stretching my pussy to the point of pain, pressed to Isaac's cock.

Hurt and desire mingle together as he continues to flick my clit, and then they rock slowly, and, before I know it, I'm moving with them, chasing another release.

It builds inside me, and just as I'm about to topple over the edge once more, they stop. I cry out as Dimitri slides his cock free, leaving me sagging and unsatisfied.

"Good girl," Isaac praises, dotting kisses along my face as I shake frustratedly, until Dimitri's cock presses to my ass. Holding my cheeks in his hands, he pulls them open and slams into me.

The release that was fading away comes roaring back, and I shatter around them with a scream.

Dimitri turns my head and kisses me hard until I'm panting and barely able to breathe. "Fuck, your ass feels too good, Nova," he growls against my lips. "So fucking tight with him in your pussy too, and when you came, I nearly lost it."

"Fuck me," I beg.

"Oh, we are going to," Isaac promises with a wicked look, and he glances behind me before winking at me.

Dimitri keeps my head yanked up as he pulls out of my ass and slams back in. Isaac withdraws and thrusts in, and then they find a rhythm. They use me, both my ass and pussy stretched to the limits, as they hold me between them.

"You look so good right now, Nova," Jonas calls out. "Shit, I'm going to add this to my spank bank forever."

"I'm bloody hard again already," Nico grumbles.

"Good girl," Isaac praises, cupping my breasts, and Dimitri pushes me down, feeding them into his mouth. He sucks and licks my nipples until I'm gasping and writhing.

"Shit, she's close again," Dimitri growls in my ear. "I won't last if she keeps gripping me like this."

"Then don't," Louis replies. "Let her feel it, and fill her with your cum."

"You want that, Nova?" He groans long and loud in my ear. "Do you want us to make you come again as we fill every hole with our cum?"

"Fuck yes," I cry out, arching between them as Dimitri's fingers return to my oversensitive clit, the pleasure bordering on too much.

My heart hammers so fast, it scares me, and when D rubs my clit and Isaac bites my nipple, I come apart with a scream.

Dimitri hammers into my ass before stilling, his cum spilling inside of me and over my ass cheeks as he pulls out.

Moaning, Isaac fights his release, but as I keep clenching and riding the waves of pleasure, he finds his own, holding me tight as he grinds me down onto his length, and his cock jerks inside me.

I slump between them as Isaac moans my name and strokes my sweaty hair, and Dimitri rubs his cum into my ass before he moves away.

I'm limp.

Maybe even dead.

"My turn." Louis's voice startles me, and then hands are on me once more.

Louis lifts me with my back to his front, and then he slams me down on his cock. He tilts my head with his chin, nudging it to the side as he licks and nips my neck. "Look how badly they want you, Nova, and how crazy you make them." My eyes open and meet the others' gazes.

He's right; they look wild.

"Isaac, come lick this pretty pussy until she comes on me," Louis demands.

His hands shove my thighs wider as he thrusts up into me. Isaac readily drops to his knees and seals his lips over my cunt, uncaring about the fact Louis's cock is inside me.

"Good girl. Look at you, Nova. You are so goddamn beautiful and so powerful, you have us all on our knees for you," Louis croons in my ear, one hand on my throat and the other gripping my breasts as Isaac eats my pussy.

Louis leisurely fucks me like he has all the time in the world.

Nico is on his knees, watching me, and his huge cock is hard again as he licks his lips. Jonas strokes himself as he observes, and Dimitri is lying down with his gaze on me.

All of their attention is on me.

The power I feel makes me clench around Louis. "I can't come again."

"You can and you will," he retorts, biting my throat until I cry out. "You'll come all over Isaac's pretty face, and then you're going to come all over my cock."

"I can't." I shake my head as his hand tightens on my throat.

"You will," he warns dangerously, sliding his hand up until his thumb slips into my mouth. "Show me how you sucked him, baby. Show me how you sucked him so good, he couldn't help but come."

Groaning, I close my eyes as I suck his thumb, all while he keeps up his slow thrusts, driving me higher as Isaac's expert tongue circles my clit. Their touches are driving me wild, and even though I thought I couldn't, I come again, shouting around his thumb.

"Good girl," he croons as Isaac moves away with his hand on his cock.

Arching into me from behind, Louis speeds up, fighting through my clenching cunt as he growls dirty words in my ear that I can barely hear over my racing heart.

His heartbeat matches mine, echoing through my back as he takes me.

Claims me.

Fucks me.

With a snarl, he pushes me down onto all fours, grips my hips, and just hammers into me.

My head hangs down, and my body is limp in his grasp.

I am his—theirs.

He jerks, filling me with brutal thrusts before yelling out his release and dragging me along for another that makes me black out.

When I come to, I'm curled into him, my body covered in cum. My muscles are sore, but in the best way, and I have a smile on my lips.

"I think we burnt the food," I mutter as I flop back to the grass, making them all chuckle.

"Fuck the food," Louis mutters, and we laugh in shock.

Fuck the food indeed.

Even as I laugh, though, my heart skips a beat, and I know that when this mission is over, I might have to give them up. I don't know how I'll go back to life without them.

Without this.

This . . . unstoppable love.

FIFTY

E ventually, we eat, since we were able to save some of the food, and then we all sleep in a big pile in the living room. I wake up early the next morning, grimacing at the sticky, nasty feel of my body, and I steal the first shower.

I am dressed and pouring coffee before they even start to stir, so when Louis's phone rings, I pick it up so he can rest. "Nova," I answer.

There's a moment of silence. "Put Louis on the line," a voice snaps.

Ah, the general.

"He's sleeping. What's up?" I purposely piss him off as I lean back, blowing on my coffee. Louis stumbles into the room, scrubbing at his adorable, dishevelled hair. His eyebrow rises, but he doesn't make me hand over the phone. Instead, he takes my coffee as he slips between my legs and holds me as he listens.

"Fine, tell him the location has been approved and to report his findings." He hangs up the phone.

Rude prick.

"Good morning to you too, asshole," I mutter as Louis yawns. "You hear that?" He nods, so I lean around him to see Jonas's naked ass on display as he bends and stretches, making Nico hit him with a pillow while D just watches with a chuckle.

"Get ready, boys. It's time to hit the next location," I call, and that causes them to switch to work mode.

We are ready and on the road in twenty minutes flat, heading out of Edinburgh as we make our way towards the old abandoned military base we found.

I lean back in my seat, watching the world go by as Louis drives. D and I are in his car, while Nico and Jonas are in the second vehicle with the equipment. The radio is on low as we drive farther into the middle of nowhere, but I trust them to know where they are going, so I close my eyes.

I jolt awake when we pull to a stop and sit up.

"Morning, Sleeping Beauty." Louis winks as he turns. "We are here."

Leaning forward between the seats, I frown as I survey the land below us. "Here?"

He nods. "Here."

The old base is surrounded by a new chain-link fence, so it would make sense, but the old grey buildings are mostly boarded up and falling down. The timeworn hangars and runway are empty and overgrown, and it looks deserted.

That's probably a good thing.

Sliding from the car, I stretch and twist, jumping on the spot to wake my tired muscles as the others get out and prepare. Rounding the back, I accept a bag from Nico and slip the backpack on. Next, I put in the earpiece and strap on the camera. D is going to set up in the first building we search so he can watch our backs since there are so many buildings to check, which also means that we all need to be prepared and on point.

Excitement races through my veins as I check the guns and strap them on before adding knives to my holsters. After putting my torch on my hip, I check everything once more before nodding. "Ready."

The others are equally strapped up, even D, who has his laptop in a case at his side, is holding a pistol. "Okay, so we know the plan. We take the gate after checking for alarms and tripwires. There is an inactive mine-field to the left and right, so we need to ignore those. Once there, we take the security outpost. D, you set up and hack into any cameras if there are any left. If not, keep tabs. I will take Building L. Nico you take J, Jonas K,

Isaac P, and Nova Q. Keep in contact at all times. If you think you have something, call it out. We sweep and clean, boys . . . and, erm, girl. Let's do this."

"Fuck yeah." Jonas lifts his arm, and they all smash it, even me.

We don't speak after that as we carefully make our way down the hill, coming from the side so we avoid the main road and signs beyond. At the chain-link fence, D carefully cuts the padlock and slides it back. No alarms go off, and the cameras there don't move. We cut another one farther in, and then we are on the base.

We turn right, heading to the closed door of the security outpost. It's barely two rooms, and once we kick the door in, we can't all fit inside it, but the newer equipment here makes me frown. It has updated screens and monitors, and the desk is clean and tidy with a coffee cup growing mould in it. It's clearly been used recently.

"It couldn't have been too long ago," I murmur.

"No, so be careful. D, set up and let's see what we are working with. Until D lets us know, get into position." Nodding, we head out across the base. I move to the building in the back on the south side that has two floors. When I get there, it's labelled "Bunks."

I wait and scan the horizon as we let D work.

"I can't access the cameras. We are going in blind," D says.

"Got it. In three, two, one." I breach the door at the same time the others do.

The entrance is a simple hallway, with stairs on the right and doors all down the corridor. I sweep each corner, noting vending machines, a sofa, and a living area to the left. The doors all lead into bedrooms and bunks. I check every one meticulously before heading upstairs.

"Base level clear—nothing. Heading to second level," I call, keeping them updated.

"Copy, sweeping the third floor," Louis replies.

"Mine is empty, no sign of life for a long time," Nico responds.

"Same here," Jonas mutters, "apart from mouldy food and benches."

I don't reply, focusing on moving around the corner. I freeze at the top of the stairs. There are booted footprints in the dust. I follow them down the hall, stopping to check more bunks and showers. The trail leads to the very last closed door. "I might have something. Hold," I murmur, and the line goes quiet.

Grabbing the handle, I twist and shove it open, going in ready to fire.

There's a rumpled bed, a used shower, and discarded clothes and toiletries, but nobody is inside it, and it looks like it's been a while. "The room here has been used, but not recently. Maybe a week or two," I murmur. "My building is clear." I drop my weapon and head back downstairs and outside.

"Clear," Jonas calls.

"Clear," Louis says.

"Clear too," Nico and Isaac announce.

"That's the infirmary, bunks, armoury, cafeteria, and offices all clear. Maybe we were wrong?" D mutters.

"Maybe," I respond.

"There has to be something. Keep looking, D," Louis barks.

I step outside and eye the base, wondering why here.

Why? What makes this place special?

Wandering around the back of the building, I check out the view of the Highlands. The mountains are beautiful. My eyes drop to a dip in the terrain that is not easily visible until you are right on top of it. Heading towards it, I realise it's a depression covered in grit, but hidden away is a bunker with the door shut and clean.

"D, you seeing this?" I murmur into my comm.

"I am. It's not on the maps. Guys, we have a bunker. I think this is it. Meet southside. Nova, wait for us."

"Copy."

I wait even though I want to go in, but we don't know what's in there, so we need to do this together. It's the only place we have not cleared. This has to be it, but I know deep down what we will find.

More death.

It doesn't take them long to converge on me, and I move to one side of the door as Nico steps to the opposite side. The others spread out behind us, and when I nod at Nico, he rips the door open and I go in first.

"Clear," I murmur, feeling them moving behind me. I don't glance back, trusting them to protect my rear.

The bunker door leads into a small air lock with another door fifty feet in. I peer through the glass, but nothing except a darkened chamber waits on the other side. The emergency lighting is on, but it doesn't provide enough for me to see from here.

"I got it," D says as he moves to the panel and works his magic. Jonas and Isaac aim their guns out the bunker door, while Louis and Nico stand with me in case anyone is waiting on the other side of the second door.

There's a beep, and then D steps back, swinging his laptop around to pull out his gun. "Door opening in five, four, three, two, one."

It swings open, and we surge in as a line of three. I go forward, with Louis on my left and Nico on my right, as we sweep the entire room.

"Clear."

"Clear."

"Clear."

Relaxing slightly, I nod as Jonas hurries to the double door leading to a corridor beyond and takes up guard as we scan the room. It seems to be an entrance chamber, with computers, cameras, a locked metal weapons cabinet, and even labelled lockers. My eyebrows rise at that as D moves to the computers and starts to access them.

"This was on a different system, so I couldn't find it before . . . and I'm in. Okay, it seems we have power and lights. They are just all turned off for some reason. It's like it has all been powered down but the generator is fine. All the doors should work, and I can see there are some utilities still running. The cameras, however, are off. I'll stay here and try to get them back on."

"Good, do that, and turn any alarms off. I want no surprises. Who knows how big this place is? Isaac, you stay with D and guard the outer door. At the first sign of life, you lock it and call us in. I don't want to be trapped, but it's better to be safe than sorry. Nico, Jonas, and Nova, you are with me. If we come to any splits, Jonas, you are with Nova, and Nico is with me. We sweep this place. I want every room, every fucking nook and cranny, searched. I want no surprises." It's clear Louis doesn't like this situation, and I feel it.

An unknown bunker underground with a weapons system and separate locks in an abandoned military base? Yeah, not to mention the super creepy feeling I'm getting.

D turns the lights back on, flooding the place so brightly, I blink, and then I continue to look around warily.

This is our job, I refuse to back out, but something is telling me this place is important. They wouldn't have gone to such lengths to hide it if it wasn't, not to mention the systems are still running and someone was clearly here recently.

No, this is it.

I can feel it.

A change in our mission.

Lifting my gun once more, I stride to Louis's side. Jonas steps up behind me, and Nico takes his position at Jonas's back, ready to find out the truth.

Finally.

FIFTY-ONE

The corridor is long, the floors under us are a spotless white, and the walls almost curve like the entryway. There are no windows, but bright lights flood the place, showing us the long, empty hallway leading to another set of closed double doors. When we reach them, I count down and open one, letting Louis and Nico sweep in before Jonas and I follow.

We communicate with looks and hand gestures, not wanting to alert anyone of our presence the farther we venture into the bunker.

The place seems to stretch, becoming wider and taller. The echoing chamber is almost the size of the base itself, and it makes me wonder if it runs under the entire structure. Probably. Maybe that's why they built the base here, to cover it.

Either way, it's too big to stay together, so we break apart. I move to the right, Jonas following me, while Nico and Louis take the left. In the middle are machines, generators maybe, and at the back, I spy a metal staircase leading up to another level above us. It's one giant room, where we can't even see the end. At first, the doors are opaque and labelled— toilets, kitchen, lounge, and bunks. It's clear they lived here or maybe even stayed here in shifts.

The doors to our right change, and I still. The wall turns into a glass, showing the labs beyond, and the farther I move, the more I see.

They are all fucking labs, which are empty, clean, and full of state-of-the-art equipment, waiting to be used.

"What the fuck?" Jonas hisses. "Do you think this is where they did all the experiments?"

"I don't know, but I don't like it," I murmur, and when I glance over, I see Louis and Nico finding the same labs on the other side.

It's like one big laboratory, and it is totally empty. There are no signs of life, not even any poor experiments like us.

Where is everyone? Were we wrong? Feeling dejected, I keep moving, speeding up with each empty lab I pass. Jonas doesn't protest, even though I know I'm being reckless. When I reach the stairs, I hurry up them, needing to see. A sharp command from Louis rings through the comm, but I ignore it.

There are more labs on this level, but they are bigger, with two on each side, taking up the entire place. The first two I pass are empty, with metal tables with bindings left forgotten and undone. I move across the metal walkway to the other side, finding the other labs unoccupied.

Dropping my gun, I lean over the edge to look down. "Clear. It's all fucking empty. Maybe they knew we were coming again?" I call.

"Maybe," Louis replies, looking around suspiciously. "Keep searching. Check everything. I want no surprises."

I nod, and after checking the labs up here, Jonas and I return to the ones downstairs, each going into one alone.

There aren't many places to hide, and even though I feel my ghosts rearing their heads at the stale air, the bright lights, and reminders of what I went through, I keep moving. Otherwise, I'll break down.

We need to find the research and destroy it, but how can we when this man seems to know our every move? When he is prepared and already gone?

Dad was right, he's dangerous, but we are fucking deadly, and we will end this. I have to believe that or we are fighting for nothing.

We search lab after lab, each one only making me more furious. It's clear they have been used. Was my father here? If so, then why couldn't he just give me a fucking list of places to destroy if he really wanted to make this right?

Is this all one big game?

I'm tired of fucking playing.

I want to win.

Past the labs, I check the kitchen, finding half-eaten food and water on the table and counters. A door clicks behind me, and I swing around with inhuman speed, my gun raised.

There, with one hand on the door and the other gripping a bloody knife, is a man.

He's dressed in army fatigues and coated in blood and sweat. His short blond hair is sweaty and stuck to his head, and his face is pale. His eyes are wide, but with pain, not fear, and something else.

Shock, I realise.

He's tall, taller than even me, and built like a Mack truck.

It's clear he's military from the way he moves and the clipped bark that comes. "Who are you?" he demands, his voice thick with a Scottish accent.

"I should be asking you that," I respond calmly, still looking at him down my gun.

I could call out, but he could attack faster. I can take him, and he's obviously injured and weak. Who knows how long he's been here? He could be half crazy, but I'm faster and stronger, so I drop the gun and arch an eyebrow.

"I'm here to find out what the fuck they were doing here," I say, telling him the truth.

Laughing, he drops the knife with a groan and slides down the wall with an audible thump. His legs are oddly bent, like he can't move them anymore. It's then I spot the first-aid kid to the side, used and covered in blood.

"Then you found it . . ." He gestures at himself and then promptly passes out.

Shit!

"Guys!" I yell as I rush to his side. I press my fingers to his clammy skin, focusing on the steady thump of his pulse. Pushing up his shirt, I search his chest, finding multiple wounds and even a surgery site. It's clear he tried to close them and fix himself.

I sit back and eye him.

Is he an experiment?

Are the fatigues even his?

The door bursts open, and Jonas instantly aims his gun at the man. "Don't," I command sharply as Louis storms in. I look up at him. "Get Isaac, he's dying."

"Shit," Louis calls out and then comes closer. "Are you okay?" he asks me as he regards the man carefully.

I nod, looking back at him. "I think he's like us. I think he's an experiment, and they left him to die."

We wait nervously while Isaac works on the man. Louis helped carry him to the closest lab, and once there, they stripped him and quickly started working on putting the soldier back together again. He has so many incisions, and he had sewn himself so badly, Isaac actually swears. He spends hours putting in drips, fluids, and sedatives before cutting and sewing him. Isaac cleans his wounds and dresses them before checking him over.

We wait the whole time, and when Isaac comes out, exhausted and coated in blood, I straighten. "Well?"

"He'll live, but barely. I have no idea how he survived what he did. He has been tortured and experimented on, and the bastards must have left him cut open. He tried to close the wound. He's dehydrated, in shock, and his body is shutting down. If we didn't find him when we did, he would have been dead."

"Did he say anything to you?" Louis asks me.

"Only that we found what we were looking for," I murmur, my gaze on the deathly still man. He looks massive on the table, and I turn to Isaac. "You find anything?"

"Dog tags and a tattoo. He's military alright. Since when do they experiment on active soldiers?" he snarls.

"I don't know, but we need to find out. I want someone on him at all times in case he wakes and attacks. I also want Isaac here too. The rest of us will gather everything and start to figure out what the fuck happened here," Louis orders.

"I'll stay." I nod when Louis arches an eyebrow. "I'll be fine."

He pulls me in and kisses me quickly before barking orders, and the others hurry to their tasks. Isaac sighs, and I melt into his side for a moment.

"What did they do to him?" I ask softly.

"What didn't they do? I don't even know how he's alive. He's one tough son of a bitch, that's for sure. I hope he survives. I really do."

"Me too," I murmur, squeezing his hand as he goes back in to keep an eye on his patient while I take up guard in the corner of the room, but I don't think he's a threat.

Not from the anger I saw in his eyes when he fell.

He's just as much of a victim as us, and he hates it.

FIFTY-TWO

"Do you think he'll wake up?" Annie asks through the phone, worrying her lip and even in the tiny screen I can sense her anxiety.

I'm sitting on an uncomfortable chair with my legs thrown over the side, the unconscious soldier still sleeping soundly despite Isaac stopping the sedative hours ago. We decided to stay until he wakes, and then we will be able to move him without hurting him. It means we are all on high alert, sleeping and patrolling in shifts. I refuse to leave the soldier's side, though, knowing he'll need a familiar face when he wakes up.

I glance back at his sleeping form and sigh. "I'm not sure. He is clearly strong if he survived what they have done to him."

"Poor man." Annie frowns with tears in her eyes. "What are you going to do with him if he wakes?"

"I don't know," I admit honestly. "He will need to be debriefed, but he's not good to us like this. He needs to heal somewhere safe, where they can't get to him."

She nods, her eyes hardening as she straightens in bed. I see her laptop and work spread out around her, and there are circles under her eyes. I'm worried, but she ignored my question about her resting. "You should bring him here. I can look after him. After all, it's my specialty. I can help him heal and work through his PTSD."

"Annie." I sigh. "It's dangerous. They will look for him—"

"Then they will have to go through me," she snaps before scrubbing at her face. "I need to help."

"You are," I murmur.

"More than this. I can do this, Nova. It's who I am. I heal. Let me heal him. Our father did this to that poor man, so his daughter should save him. You can't, since you need to be out there stopping this, but I can, and this will be the last place they'll look."

I follow her logic and sigh. "I'll propose it to the others, but no promises. The military will probably want him back."

She scoffs then, her eyes flashing with fire. "And you know what they will do. He will go missing." Her blonde hair flips as she glares at me. "Over my dead body."

"When you're mad, we are awfully similar." I grin, and she barks out a laugh.

"God, I hope so." We share a grin as I look her over.

"How are you really, Annie?"

"I should be asking you that." She arches an eyebrow at me. "Though in all honesty, despite the anger you are clearly feeling, you look . . . good, healthy, and happy." There's clearly a question in her words, and I look out of the glass door but see none of the others.

"I am," I hedge.

"Tell me!" she gushes, flipping onto her stomach, and I can't help but grin.

Is this girl talk? Sharing stories about boys with my sister?

I can't help the twinge of happiness that goes through me despite the situation.

"Come on, spill the dirt, which guy is it? They are all very attractive, if not terrifying." That makes me laugh, and I lower my voice.

"All."

"All?" Her eyes widen before she laughs, smacking the bedding. "Fuck yes." She pops her hand over her mouth at the curse before grinning. "You never did anything by halves."

"I guess not." I grin.

Her cheeks redden as she looks at me. "All of them . . . together?"

"Sometimes." I wink as she blushes. "But it's more than that, Annie. They fill something inside me I didn't know I needed. I was so lonely and so scared all the time, always on the move, and they . . ."

"Fill that," she murmurs knowingly.

I nod. "They make me happy. They make me laugh. They make me forget about my past, even for a moment, and they happily use my skills and support me. They hold me through my nightmares and fight at my side. I've never felt something like this before, never mind for more than one person. It can't work, surely."

"Who said so?" she snaps. "People have multiple wives or partners. Do whatever the fuck makes you happy, Nova. God knows you deserve it."

"I—" I look away, and she calls my name. When I look back, she wears a determined expression.

"Do they make you happy?" she demands.

"Yes," I reply without hesitation.

"Do you love them?" she asks.

"Yes." I shock myself with that answer, and she grins.

"Then that's all that matters. Fuck what anyone else thinks. You all need each other. I saw that when I met them. They need you, and you need them. Together, you're just . . . stronger. Stop fighting that and accept it. Some love is just meant to be unconventional, and you might have been brought together by a common cause and traumas, but it will be love that keeps you together. You'll have to fight for it, but you've always been good at that."

"When did you get so wise?" I croak.

"I always was." She winks.

I lick my lips. "What if they don't love me back? What if they leave?"

"You cannot control how others feel or what might happen in the future, only what happens now. Are you going to let your fears and doubts stop you from finding happiness, even if it will possibly end in the future?" I shake my head, and she nods. "Good, then stop doubting yourself and getting in your own way. You're brave, Nova, so be so now. Plus, I saw those men. They are head over heels in love with you. You're never getting away, so stop worrying and just enjoy it, and let your little sister live vicariously through you."

I laugh at that. "I have missed you so much."

Her eyes soften once more. "I missed you too. Now get back to your hunks and keep my patient alive. I'll speak to you soon, sis."

"Bye." I hang up, my eyes going back to the patient. She's right. She's the best place for him.

And my best place is here, with my men.

It's time I stop running so hard and embrace this. It might be forever, but even if it's not, it's going to be one hell of a good time while it lasts.

FIFTY-THREE

I don't let her know I listened to her conversation with her sister.

I stop in the kitchen with a frown marring my face. Louis is there, making food for everyone, and Jonas is sprawled out, snoring, or pretending to. Isaac is asleep, and D is working.

Louis freezes when he sees my expression. "What?" Jonas is instantly up, but I wave away his concern as I debate if I should keep it to myself or not.

She loves us.

How could she ever doubt that we would feel any different?

Have we not shown her? We need to every day.

From the moment I laid eyes on Nova, I knew she was ours. I knew she would be my everything, but I never could have imagined the depths of my feelings. I can barely breathe without her in my sight, and every smile and look she shoots my way steals another piece of my soul.

"Nothing. I overheard Nova talking to her sister."

"Good, they should heal their relationship." He stares at me though. "What is it?"

"I . . . Do you love her?" I ask, needing to know. I will protect her, even from my family.

"Nico," he snaps. "What is it?"

"Do you love her?" I question more forcefully, staring him down. He searches my face with a perplexed expression before sighing.

"Well, I was hoping the first time I said it, it would be to her, but yes, I love her, as do you."

"Me too!" Jonas adds helpfully.

"You are in this forever and not just for now?" I press.

He carefully puts his spoon down and meets me head-on. "When do I ever do anything halfway? I am all in with her. We all are. I tried to resist to keep us safe, but we both know that didn't work. She's mine, and I'm hers. Now tell me."

"She loves us," I croak, and I hear the disbelief in my voice.

"Of course she does. We are amazing and have great dicks," Jonas says.

"How can she love us?" I whisper, and Louis sighs as he squeezes my arm.

"Because we are worthy of it—*you* are worthy of it, and if you let her, Nico, she will prove that to you. But how do you feel about it?" There's our leader, always trying to protect us.

"Like I've won every fucking lottery in the world," I growl. "Like I don't deserve it, but I'm going to take it anyway and hoard it, never letting her go."

He grins then, a wicked one. "Then I guess we better keep our girl happy." Turning, he bowls her some soup and hands it over with a spoon and a water. "Let's start with this. She gets grumpy when she is hungry." I nod and take it, still humbled as I head back to her.

How could I do anything else? I need to be at her side at all times.

"Oh, and Nico? Don't let her know you listened in. Respect her privacy. She will tell us when she's ready. I do believe our Nova is more stubborn than us," Louis calls.

Jonas waves me on, and when I head back to her, I quicken my steps.

I need to tell her or, better yet, show her, so she never doubts us again and she stays with us forever.

I know she's not used to a family, but she needs to get accustomed to it quickly because we won't let her go, even if she wants us to. We won't chain her like her father, but we will follow her anywhere.

"Hey," she says softly as I enter, her eyes sparkling. Her hair is tied up in a bun, and she's looking way too fucking beautiful. For a moment, I freeze and just stare, feeling unworthy and far too scarred for her, but then she pulls a chair over for me and pats it. I sit beside her and hand over the food.

She arches a brow but takes it. "Thanks." She starts to eat as I nod. Nova watches me, probably realising something is wrong.

Think, Nico. Speak before she finds it weird.

I have nothing.

All I need to do is prove I love her.

The way to do that is to lay myself bare so she knows every part of me, even the parts the others don't.

"I hate tight spaces," I blurt, and her spoon pauses before she swallows.

"I know," Nova says, and I stiffen. "I notice things."

I look away for a moment, but her soft hand lands on my thigh encouragingly. Her touch is so soft and warm, it thaws my bitter, cold soul. "He used to lock me in them, and they were so small, I could barely breathe, couldn't move, in the dark."

"Nico." She puts her food down and before I know it, she's on my lap, cupping my face. I press my forehead to hers. "You don't have to tell me. We all have our issues from what they did, but all that matters is the future."

"I know, but I want you to know all of me," I admit softly. "Not just who I am now."

She kisses me, and when she pulls back, I grip her hips, tugging her close to give me strength as she straddles me.

"I hate the dark."

She shrugs. "I hate labs."

"I'm terrified of tight spaces and being locked away and forgotten."

"I'm terrified of needles," she admits.

Her confessions give me strength. "My favourite colour is black." I grin, and she laughs.

"Mine is red. How boring are we?"

Smiling, I stroke her back. "I'm still scared of your father, even though I'm an adult now."

"So am I, and he's dead," she replies, as if daring for me to keep going and try to tell her something that will change her feelings.

After all, isn't that what I'm doing? I'm admitting shit because I'm scared that once she finds out about it, she will stop loving me.

"I love cupcakes even though they are usually cute and frilly. I hate scary movies and I listen to Taylor Swift more often than I should admit to," I blurt.

"I love Taylor Swift; only psychopaths don't." She giggles, running her lips over mine. "Cupcakes are incredible, we can get them together, and I love scary movies so you can hide behind me."

"I'm scared I will never be enough for you."

She gasps, her nails digging into my cheeks as she brings my gaze back to hers. "Do not ever fucking say that again."

"I am," I whisper brokenly. "I'm scared I'm too fucked up for you to ever truly love me. That one day you'll realise it and leave."

"I will never leave," she snarls. Her eyes flash with that fire that gets me hard. "They would have to drag my dead body from you. I am here forever, Nico, and nothing you could ever tell me would change that. Fuck, you could tell me you dress up as a unicorn for fun or that you like plain vanilla ice cream and it wouldn't change how I feel. We are all fucked up, Nico, but that's why we work so well together."

"But what if you change your mind?" I ask, laying my fears bare. My fingers tighten at the idea of her trying to run. "I don't think I could let you go, even if you wanted me to."

"Good, don't, not ever," she purrs, licking my lips until I part them for her, and then she bites down on my lip until I shiver in pleasure. "Stop doubting yourself, Nico. I don't, and neither do the others. We will figure this out together, but I'm all in. We are in this together, and I'll remind you whenever you need me to."

Swallowing, I search her gaze before my hand grips the back of her head, spanning most of it since my hands are so big, and I slam my lips onto hers. I swallow her moan as she presses her hot chest against mine. My other hand kneads her ass and rocks her against my hard cock as I tangle my tongue with hers, showing her everything I wish I could say.

Telling her I love her too.

There is a groan behind us, and we pull apart, both leaping to our feet as we hurry to the soldier's bedside. His eyelids are fluttering, and I quickly move to the door and call for the others.

"Where am I?" he rasps.

"You're safe, hold on."

"Not safe, coming. They are coming." He gasps and begins to struggle.

"Who's coming?" Nova snaps as Isaac slides into the room.

"The ones . . . The ones who did this to us," the soldier grits out before passing out.

"He's out cold," Isaac observes. "Should have been for hours—"

We look at Louis then. "We have to trust his word, even if it's wrong. Doc, get him ready. We are moving out and moving out now."

FIFTY-FOUR

I keep him stable as we load him into the plane, and after a few hours, we land near the mansion again and transport him there. When we arrive, Ana is ready, and the lab has been changed into a medical room. She helps me hook him up as I explain what he needs.

She's clearly smart and capable, and I finally trudge upstairs, trusting her to care for him. Stripping, I jump into the shower.

The plane is going back for Louis and Nico, who stayed to pack our stuff, but we had to move fast just in case what he said was true. D did set up some cameras so we could keep watch, but so far nothing has happened, so I take the time to wash.

I watch blood swirl down the drain as exhaustion tugs at me. This week started out so well. I was happy and in love, surrounded by my family and my girl, and now I wash off the blood of an almost dead soldier who has been experimented on.

I know that the feeling of being lost and so far behind the man who is responsible for all of this is weighing on all of us.

I feel like a failure for not figuring it out and keeping the man down-stairs safe.

For not being able to protect my family.

Like my misery calls to her, Nova wraps her arms around me from behind, her wet, naked, hot body pressing against me. I shiver and tears fall from my closed eyes.

"Are you okay?"

"No," I admit, my voice choked. "Not at all."

Turning me, she pulls my head to her chest, but I drop to my knees and press my forehead to her stomach. She strokes my hair and back as she whispers comforting words before falling to her knees and wiping my tears away. "You did everything you could."

"Did I?" I whisper, searching her gaze.

I feel raw and weak.

"I feel like I failed everyone. We keep fighting, but is it enough? People are suffering, and I can't save them."

"You cannot save everyone," she retorts, making me still. "We save who we can, but I will not let you lose or destroy yourself to selflessly save the world."

"But—"

"No, you are used to looking after everyone else, but I will look after you, Isaac. I will take care of you when you won't. You did everything you could, and that's what we will continue to do, but not at the expense of your happiness and soul. So tell me now, and we will stop and turn our backs."

"We can't—"

"We can if that's what saves you and what keeps you with us," she argues, her eyes gleaming like she would fight the fires of hell for me.

I think she would, this damaged, scarred warrior. I think she would fight everything to protect us.

"I love you," I admit without shame.

"I know." She grins. "I love you too, and that is exactly why I won't let you self-destruct."

Pulling me close, she holds me as I break, and then she washes me before drying my body and helping me into some clean clothes. Nova sits me on the closed lid of the toilet as she brushes my hair, and the entire time, I keep my head pressed to her stomach, listening to her thumping heart.

I rebuild myself while she takes care of me, and I have to admit, it's nice to have someone looking after me. When she tilts my head up and kisses me, looking me over and nodding, my heart swells.

"Perfect," she declares.

I lose that last little part of me to her, to my Nova, my protector.

My love.

"You decide your future, Isaac, and wherever it is, your family will follow. We can't do this without you."

I know she's right and the others look to me. I might not be the strongest or even the fastest, but I'm the healer, their confidant, and friend.

"I-I need to see this through. We do. I just had a moment of weakness."

"We all do," she murmurs softly as she strokes my face lovingly. "But you will never have to go through them alone."

I smile then, pulling her close and kissing her until there is a knock at the door. "Plane's here." That is all that's said, the voice knowing, and I wonder if he heard it all. D is good at that.

"The plane is here," she whispers. "We have to keep going so we can end this. That's how we save him and all the others. Are you with me?" She holds out her hand and without hesitation, I lay my hand in hers.

"Always."

FIFTY-FIVE

"So where to?" I ask as I kick my feet up onto Nico's lap and press my head to Nova's. She grins down at me, stroking my hair as her eyes refocus on Louis as the plane door shuts.

"We have one more location, somewhere Ana was able to decrypt from the doctor's message—Greenland. We are going to Greenland."

"Never been." I look up at my girl then, watching her eyes flitter over all of us before landing back on me. They seem to soften, and a grin tugs at her lips that mirrors my own and makes my cock hard. "Have you, baby?"

"Nope. I guess there's a first time for everything."

"I guess." I snuggle closer when Nico groans and pushes my feet off.

"Dude, your boner is near me!"

Nova giggles as I wink at Nico.

"Wouldn't be the first time. You remember when—" Nova covers my lips with a laugh, and Nico's lips twitch. Louis shakes his head with a roguish smile, D laughs, even Isaac grins as he kisses Nova's cheek as he passes.

Her eyes track him for a moment before she looks at Louis. "Then let's hope we find something. I think we all could do with that."

"Yep. Get your rest because we'll hit the ground running."

After a few hours of annoying the others, I flop onto the bed in the back, huffing. I've always hated being bored, so when Nova sneaks in with a wicked grin, I sit up. My cock is already hard as I reach for her.

"I'm bored," she whispers, since the others are sleeping.

"Me too. Want to play?" I tease, making her laugh as she bounces on the bed. I quickly grab her and pin her beneath me. Her eyes sparkle as she grips my hair and pulls me down for a hard kiss, stealing everything, including my soul.

"Jonas," she murmurs as I slide down her body.

Sitting up slightly, she tugs off her top and bra, making my mouth water as I stare at her breasts before wagging my finger at her. "Behave," I warn as I slip off her jeans and thong, sliding them down her thick thighs. My cock twitches at the sight of her laid out below me, naked and beautiful.

She is a work of art, all tatted skin, long lush hair, and sexy muscles, and she watches me hungrily. She parts her legs for me, knowing exactly what she wants and not shy to ask for it.

"Well, are you going to make me come or just stare?" she taunts, her lush lips curved up in a mocking smile that makes me want to go to war for her.

I'm utterly obsessed with everything that is Nova, but when she gives me that look, I feel like I could take on a million armies just to crawl between her thighs and toss them over my shoulders.

With my eyes on her, I seal my mouth to her cunt and suck. The force makes her back bow, and her hands tangle in my hair and tug. Her moans bounce off the walls as I finally release her and lap at her clit as she pants.

Her flavour makes me snarl in hunger, so I slide lower and thrust my tongue into her, searching for more of her addictive taste. Her legs tighten as I attack her pussy, switching between thrusting my tongue inside and lapping at her clit. It leaves her unbalanced and before long, she cries out, coming so prettily on my tongue.

I lick her clean, wanting another taste, but she drags me up. Grumbling, I stop to lick, bite, and suck her nipples before kissing her, letting her taste her cum as she whimpers below me.

I pull back. "I fucking adore you."

"Back at you." She grins, rolling her body against me until my cock can't be ignored anymore. I need her.

It's almost loving, something I'm not used to. It feels right when I flip her. She arches, wiggling her sexy body against mine as she pushes her round ass into me, urging me on. Gripping her hair, I push her head down with a snarl and drag my cock along her dripping pussy.

"Jonas," she begs.

"That's it, baby, call my name for them all to hear," I demand, leaning down to bite her perky ass. She groans, and I grin as I lean back, seeing my teeth imprint there. I press my thumb to the bite mark and she jerks. "I might get this tattooed. Now scream, Nova."

"Make me," she demands, pushing back.

"Oh, I plan to." I fist her hair with one hand and grip her hip with the other, then I slam my cock inside that taunting wet heat. Both of us moan at the sensation. The feel of her tight, wet cunt gripping me makes me wild. I hammer into her, taking her roughly now. I need to hear her screams, and I love the sight of her clenching the bedding as her beautiful body pushes back to take me.

It's always so perfect between us, the mix of pain and pleasure making us crazed. "That's it, beautiful," I purr. "Fuck, look at how sexy you are, split open around my cock."

Grabbing my phone, I live stream it to the others, hearing them beyond the door as they get the video. Moaning indecently, she swallows my cock with her tight pussy, arching back as I fuck her.

I slide my cock out to the very tip and then drive in so hard, she finally screams. Her body contorts around me as her cunt milks me with her orgasm, and I still fuck her, watching as she squirts around my cock and stains the bedding.

"Fuck, just like that. Again. Squirt," I demand, driving in harder and dropping the phone to rub her clit. I release her hair and slide my hand down her back to press my thumb into her asshole. I fight off my release, feeling it building. Lightening sparks down my spine, and my balls tighten.

Fuck, she feels too good.

Fighting to get her to come again, I make the mistake of giving her everything, and when she screams once more, squirting around my cock, I yell my own release as it takes me by surprise. She groans, and when the pleasure releases me, I slump into her.

"Made you scream," I croak.

"So did I." She smirks as she rolls onto her back, her delicious tits swaying with the movement.

Leaning down, I lick her juices from the bed. She laughs and tugs me up and into her arms.

Our sweaty bodies press together, and we hold each other with lazy satisfaction and love. I don't let her go back to the others, even though I feel time passing, and I keep her with me until I can't anymore.

"Come on, assholes, we are landing soon. Time to get to work."

"Oh, asshole? Next time, I get yours." I wink, making her laugh.

NOVA

We land on an airfield in the middle of nowhere and disembark. We have to rent some off-road vehicles to get to the location, and it's over a day's drive. We continue into the night, switching drivers until Louis calls it and we hunker down.

The next morning, I'm stretching my legs when my phone buzzes in my pocket. I move away from the cabin we rented for the night and sit in the grass, and then I answer the FaceTime. Ana is in the lab, and she smiles softly at me when she sees me. She still looks tired though.

"I'm glad you got there safely," she greets.

"How's our patient?" I ask.

"See for yourself?" Grinning, she tilts the camera, and I see the soldier sitting up. He waves at me with a wink.

"I wanted to thank you for saving me," he begins. He glances at Ana. "Both of you." His eyes seem to soften and almost heat when he looks at my sister, and my eyebrows rise. "I never told you my name before I passed out. It's Sam, Sam Danes. I was a soldier before I was recruited to be part of a clinical trial. We were never told what it was for, and by the time we were in, it was too late. Most of my unit died from what they did to us. Only I survived, and just barely." Ana moves closer, and he offers me a stern look. "I know you are going after them. Make them stop. Make them pay."

"That's the plan." I nod. "Ana, look after our patient. Sam, look after Ana and make sure she sleeps."

"I will." He grins, and Annie ducks her head with a blush.

"Let us know when you find anything. We will be here," Annie says.

"Of course. I'll let you get back to it." I snigger. "Bye, love you."

Her eyes widen as they fill with tears. The words had been an instantaneous reaction, but I don't regret them. "I love you too, Nova. Be careful."

Dropping the phone, I see the others loading up the trucks, so I head over to help them.

I am ready to get back on the road and to this next location, hoping it holds something since they never went to the location in Scotland like Sam thought. It seems we have to hunt them ourselves, and that's just what we will do.

It's time to end this once and for all.

"You have got to be kidding me?" I groan as I sit at the side of the road, scanning the maps on my laptop. "It seems we have gone past it. The bloody roads all look the same here."

Louis sighs when he peers over my shoulder. "They want it hidden. It's a good sign at least." I nod as I stretch and accept the water Isaac hands over. Nova is stretched out on the truck's roof, sunbathing, with Jonas next to her, and for a moment, my eyes linger on her.

Like she feels my gaze, she lifts her head and gives me a wink. "You find it yet, babe?"

"I think so." I know I'm blushing, especially when she does an incredible roll and flips off the truck to land on her feet before she heads my way and kisses me softly.

"That's my boy," she purrs and looks at Louis. "Well, let's go then. What are we waiting for?"

Once we're back in the trucks, I keep a careful watch on the satellite phone and navigate us through winding hills and topography. Louis is right; they want this hidden and hidden well.

Is that a good sign or a bad one?

LOUIS

"There's life," I murmur, watching through the sniper rifle's scope.

Our earpieces are in, and D is back at the trucks, trying to access their systems. Nova is with Nico on the other side of the hills, hidden behind foliage, Isaac is protecting D, and Jonas is with me.

The location is right in the middle of mountains, completely hiding it from view. We had to hike to get here, and I wanted as many angles as possible. Passing the scope to Jonas, I grab my camera and shoot as many pictures as I can, needing them to come up with a plan. I know Nova will be doing the same.

But there's life.

I see planes on a runway, bunkers with doors open, and buildings with soldiers and scientists streaming in and out.

We've finally done it. We've finally found their main location.

This is our chance.

"Okay, let's regroup at the trucks to make a plan. We'll observe tonight, and then tomorrow, we'll attack."

I leave Jonas to keep watch as I climb back down and meet at the trucks. An hour later, Nova appears, leaving Nico in position as well, just in case.

We all look through the pictures. It's a fortress, that's for sure, with electrified fences and gates. Soldiers guard the perimeter in shifts, and cameras are placed strategically around the area . . . and that's only the stuff we can see.

It doesn't matter, though, because we need to get in there and find the truth, destroy the research, and end this.

"Okay, we switch at five. Get some rest. I want to know everything about that place before we go in."

"We go in tomorrow, right? I think under darkness would be better. They would be less likely to see us," Nova murmurs.

"Maybe. Give me a few hours, and I'll have a plan."

"Yes, boss." She winks. "Then I guess I'll get some sleep."

My eyes wander to her ass as she climbs into the back of the truck before I turn away. I need to concentrate despite the fact that I want to curl up behind her and hold her close, because I know one thing—we aren't coming out of there unscathed.

FIFTY-SEVEN

I switch out with Jonas and watch the base for most of the night. The moon is shining down on it, and no matter how much I try, I see no weakness.

It's impregnable, but if anyone can do it, it's us.

We just have to get in. I'm almost frothing at the mouth to.

When Isaac comes to relieve me, I head back down to hear the plan, eating the canned food we pass around as Louis stares down at a map D made from the pictures. His eyebrows are deep slashes, and there are bags under his eyes. He clearly hasn't slept, and I have no doubt that the same thing we are all thinking is keeping him up.

How are we going to get out of there after?

And if we do, will we all be in one piece?

It's Louis's job to keep us safe, or so he thinks, but it's time I showed him he doesn't have to.

"Talk through it out loud," I call.

Louis's head jerks up, and he looks around at us and then back at the map. Scrunching his face, he sits back heavily, his shoulders rounded with his responsibilities. I need him to smile, so I head over and sit on the ground between his thighs, feeling him soften. When his voice comes, though, it's hard.

"We could disarm the alarms, if possible, and cut a hole in the fence, but it might be too noisy. We could try to talk our way in, or we could bust our way in. They all have cons and are too risky. I don't like the odds."

"You never do," D says softly.

Looking up at him, I mull over his words. "There's one more option."

"What's that?" he asks, looking down at me hopefully, almost begging for another way to do this.

"I think we can draw the soldiers out, set a fire or something and trigger the alarm system that lines the mountain side. When they come, we can knock them out, steal their uniforms and vehicles, and drive ourselves back in, Trojan horse style."

For a moment, he just stares at me, calculating the odds, and then his mouth drops open. "Fucking hell, that just might work." He yanks me up and slams his lips onto mine. Blinking, I meet his smouldering gaze. "You are too fucking clever, baby. When we finish this, I'll remind you of that with my tongue in your cunt."

"Erm, can I join?" D asks, making us laugh and break apart breathlessly.

"So that's what we'll do," he murmurs. "It just might work. Okay, D—"

And so the plan forms.

There are still downsides and things that could go wrong, but we have to try.

None of us can live without succeeding.

We wait for nightfall to make our move.

Everything is set, and everyone knows their positions. I wave up at D, who's watching our backs with a sniper rifle. Nico and Jonas are on branches above the position we chose, waiting to pounce, and I'm crouched behind a rock. Isaac is farther down to alert us of their approach, and Louis is ready to light it up.

We all know what's at stake. Nothing can go wrong, and when Louis's call comes, I tense, ready for this. I'm dressed casually, so it will be easy to strip off and get into their uniforms. My gun lies across my lap, and I have a knife at my hip. I don't need much more since I am a weapon.

The fire is small and contained, but it will draw their gazes since this area is abandoned, and ten minutes later, Isaac's signal comes. Two minutes after that, I feel the thrum of their engines, and the next minute, I hear the rumbling of a truck. They have to stop at the edge of the trees just beyond like we planned. We didn't want them running or ramming us, after all.

A few minutes of silence pass, and I remain motionless. I am like a statue, and unless you were looking for us with our exact location, you would never see any of us. I see them creeping through the trees in formation—ten of them, and they aren't messing around at all. Their guns are up, the torches on top sweeping the area.

We wait.

And wait.

Five of them step towards the fire to investigate, while the others break off and head into the trees just like we wanted. I turn away, letting Nico and Jonas handle those near the fire, and then I pick through the bush and sneak up on a male. Pressing my back to a tree, I barely breathe, and when he passes, I step out behind him and break his neck before he can turn. Catching his body, I lower it gently to the ground, switch off the light, and move back into the darkness as another approaches.

"Simons," the person hisses, straining to see right until they stumble over the body and fall. I pull my knife, and I'm on them in an instant, slashing his throat then covering his mouth. I watch his eyes drain of life before clicking off his light too.

I don't see any others, but I do look over in time to see Jonas and Nico drop down from the trees, right on their prey. Jonas simply rips through his two, blood going everywhere. Nico knocks one out, and he snaps the other's neck.

I let out a whistle to let them know I'm clear, and the others respond, so I stand and drag the bodies into the clearing. Louis comes out with two more, and D strolls in with his sniper rifle slung over his shoulder and puts out the fire as Isaac emerges from the dark.

We silently strip the men and finish off the ones that are still alive, tossing them into a ditch we found and covering them so they aren't discovered right away. We check their weapons and then we change, having to pick the uniforms without any blood. The trousers are too big for me, so I have to roll them up, but the shirt is loose enough not to show my breasts, and with the jacket I slip on, I look like a slim man. I tie my hair up and stuff it under a cap, then I pull the cap down, shielding my face. I stand to see the others are also ready in their fatigues. Louis has a radio, and he checks the scene before grinning at us.

"Good job, team. Now let's waltz into the enemy's lair."

The truck is easy to find, with the doors open and lights on. There's one man still in there, shifting nervously, and D slips in behind him and slides a rope around his neck. Within moments, he's dead, his body tossed aside as we climb in. I huddle in the middle seat, concealing myself, while Nico drives, grumbling at how tight the pants are. Louis sits in the front seat next to him.

Jonas leans into me. "You look hot in cargo."

"So do you." I grin, gripping his hard cock. "But lose the hard-on. They might find that odd."

"Then don't look at me, touch me, breathe . . . or even exist." He chuckles, and the others laugh as I huff.

D snickers at my side. "I second that."

"Third," Isaac adds.

"Fourth." Nico winks back at me.

"Fifth," Louis says.

I cross my arms and slump down. "I'm dressed like a dude, and it's doing it for you?"

"You could be in a bin sack covered in shit, and I would still want to fuck you," Nico replies, making my mouth drop open.

"True." Jonas chuckles.

"You are all insane. Madmen, I tell you."

"I guess that makes you our madwoman," D purrs in my ear, sliding his hand up my inner thigh as we drive through the trees.

"Behave, all of you." I smack his hand away, but he just puts it back, and a smacking contest begins when Jonas joins in.

"Children." Louis laughs. "The gate is coming up, behave."

"Yeah, behave." I stick out my tongue, and D leans forward and bites it, making me moan.

When he releases it, he licks my lips. "I will when you do."

They settle as we approach the gate, the lights shining into the forest. "Showtime, boys."

"If it all goes wrong, we'll just shoot them," Jonas adds helpfully. "God, I hope it goes wrong."

Yep, insane, the lot of them, and I might just be the worst because I agree as I tug my gun out.

FIFTY-EIGHT

When we pull up to the gate, we slow down and try to look as relaxed as possible, even though we are all stiff with tension.

A bored-looking guard heads over, shining his torch in the truck, but he doesn't seem to recognise us or care. "What was it?"

"Some brush caught fire, but we put it out. Nothing to worry about," Louis murmurs.

"Okay, head back. It's time to switch shifts anyway." The guard barely contains his yawn as he waves us in and the gate buzzes. He either didn't care or was dumb or both, but it works in our favour.

Having studied the layout of the base, Louis drives slowly towards the hangar that's farthest from the rest of the compound. We all step out of the truck and into the darkness to gather our thoughts. Jonas grabs some explosives and places a few around the truck, and then we head to the building that we've seen the most activity at.

We slowly march through the darkened base, placing explosives in a few places so we can set them off when we need to.

The car charges will go first, causing a distraction to get us into the buildings, and the others are in case everything goes wrong.

We'll blow this place sky high—an agreement we all made.

We manoeuvre into place down the side of the huge, two-story brick building with two guards posted outside. D works his magic, and when he nods, I know he has control of the power and cameras, which is just what we need.

Jonas lifts the handheld detonator, and with a mouthed, "Boom," he flips it. The car we were in explodes into a fiery ball, lighting up the sky. Alarms immediately blare as soldiers rush to the car from every corner—except for the two at the door. Nico nods and moves around the building to the other side, and when I peek out, we slip out in sync. I drive my knife into a man's chest, pushing him to the wall and covering his mouth as D kills the lights and cameras. Nico does the same, and with a matching grunt, we tug the bodies behind the building and into the darkness.

They will eventually be found, but it gives us time to get in first, especially since the alarm still shrieks, drawing everyone on the base to the burning truck.

"Let's move; the clock is ticking. We go in low and use the element of surprise. D, I want those cameras off inside as quickly as possible, and you are in charge. Nico and Jonas, you are the battering ram. Isaac, stay in the back with D. Nova, you're with me." We all nod, and when we step in front of the doors, Jonas pulls the pin on something and tosses it inside before slamming the doors.

There's a flash and some groaning, and then he opens the doors and we peer through the smoke to see disoriented soldiers as Nico and Jonas rush in, knocking them out as they go.

I follow them in, wincing at the smoke, but we push through into an entryway where soldiers are scrambling about. I don't hesitate to kill them because if they are here, then they know what's being done.

They know, and they helped hurt their own.

And children.

It's what keeps me going as we move as a unit, never faltering.

The element of surprise works for us. D blocks the door after us so no one can get in or escape, we find a security office where we quickly dispatch the guards, and Dimitri sets up shop. Isaac stays with him as we keep moving.

The building is a maze, but D quickly barks instructions in our ears after locating us through the cameras and taking them over so no one else can see us. "There are four giant labs on the second level. First level is living and relaxation. Third level does not have as many cameras but seems to be an office of some sort, and there's motion inside."

"We take the labs and keep as many subjects alive as we can, and whoever is here? Let's hope he's in charge," Louis murmurs, and we all agree.

We form a square as we move through the first floor, which includes reception areas, kitchens, lounges, and even some bedrooms.

We engage with more guards, but they are either unprepared or just not fast enough. Others are highly trained soldiers, and I can appreciate their sharp eyes and quick movements, but they are not quick enough for us.

I watch the moment of shock on their faces when they realise what we are before we end their lives.

It's almost too easy.

We sweep room after room, leaving bodies in our wake, but they hear us coming now and they are prepared. At the back of the first floor, they have created a barricade of tables and chairs, the tops of their heads just peeking above them when they start to spray fire across the hallway. I roll to the side and into the open doorway of a room, yanking Isaac with me as he groans. Pushing him against the wall, I scan him for injury. He's focused on the others who are all ducked into side rooms, but my focus is on him when I see he's bleeding just above his pants. Ripping up his shirt, I find a single bullet wound.

Glancing down, he blinks in surprise. "Oh, I didn't even feel it. I'll be okay. It will heal." He peers over his back. "It looks to be a through and through, so just leave the shirt to tighten on it and collect the blood. Nova?" He peers down at me worriedly as I stare at the blood dripping from the wound on my love.

On my healer.

On the man who has been tortured his whole life when he just wanted to help.

Something snaps in me, and before Louis or the others can call for me to stop, I'm moving out into the corridor with a snarl on my lips. Power surges through my body, making me faster, stronger, and smarter, just like Father wanted.

He wanted to see what I'm made of?

He wanted to see what perfect soldiers we could be?

Well, that's what he gets.

I shoot as I move, sliding across the hallway to avoid their fire. I shoot twice.

One shot into the man spraying the hallway, his head exploding as he falls back.

One into the man peeking up over the edge, firing straight through his eye.

I run towards the wall and flip off it, firing as I go. I spray the whole other side of the barrier before I land and roll, pulling two blades as I drop the now empty gun. I rush the barrier as more guards and soldiers try to pull the dead away, flinging my body over it with a snarled yell.

"They. Are. Mine!" I tear into their masses with my blades, spinning faster than they can track as I cut throats and disembowel others.

I sense the moment a gun is aimed towards me, and I turn, throwing the blade with such strength, it impales the man in the throat and throws him back into the wall, pinning him there like a trapped butterfly as he dies.

Yet I still feel more strength in my body, more anger, so I let it loose.

I release all those years of bottled rage, pain, and fear for the first time ever, my tight grip on it easing, and those would who blindly protect the person willing to kill, torture, and maim children and men pay the price.

I let them see just exactly what they are protecting.

I show them I am unstoppable.

I spot some trying to retreat, but I don't allow it. Picking up a weapon, I cut them down, and when it clicks empty, I swing it like a bat, smashing their faces in. Bodies fly through the air, but I don't hear anything over my thundering heart and breathing. When I swing around, searching for a target, holding a blade I picked up midair, a hand catches my own.

Snarling, I try to rip my hand back, but I'm suddenly backed into a wall, even as I fight, until lips descend onto mine.

I gasp and still, and then they slowly pull back. I blink away the haze I seemed to be under to meet Louis's hard, hot eyes. "Finished, baby?" he purrs.

Swallowing, I search his gaze as his eyes crinkle with a smile.

"While I think watching you hack up bodies with a blade is hot, I have no intentions of it being mine. You like it too much, so behave, and let's keep moving."

"Sorry," I pant, peering over his shoulder. I'm mortified when I see at least twenty dead bodies splayed around, looking like they have been torn apart by a wild animal. I close my eyes and hide, barely able to meet the others' watchful gazes.

I don't want to see the horror and reproach.

"What did he do to me?" I whisper.

"Nothing, baby, you are perfect," Louis promises.

A hand cups my cheek, and I turn into it, dropping the knife as I let Louis pin me there so I don't hurt anyone else.

"Look at me," comes a sharp command. I squeeze my eyes shut, and the fingers clench my jaw until it hurts. "Now, Nova."

I open my eyes to find Isaac before me. I worriedly search his gaze for disgust, but I simply see love. "You would never hurt one of us," he murmurs knowingly. "You did that, all of that, because they hurt me—because they hurt your family."

"I—" I shake my head, feeling lost and raw despite where we are. "I don't trust myself," I finally admit.

"Well, we do," Nico snaps, crowding behind Louis as Jonas moves to my other side.

"You were fantastic." He sighs lovingly, making me smile slightly.

"When we found another dead kid and we first came together, I lost it," Isaac tells me.

"And when Nico was hurt while we were hunting your father years ago, I tortured four men to get answers," Louis says.

"I just like to kill everything . . . everything but you guys." Jonas grins.

"You might be dangerous, deadly, fucking wild, and messed up, but we all are, Nova," Louis tells me, "and you would do anything to keep our family safe, just like we would. This just proves it, so trust us. We will always be right behind you, watching your back."

"And feel free to use your blade on me anytime." Jonas chuckles.

Sighing, I close my eyes and bang my head back against the wall. "Are they all dead?"

"Oh yeah, baby." Nico chuckles. "They are very fucking dead, but we are going to be too if we don't start moving," he reminds us.

D's voice sounds in my ear. "Nova, listen to them. What we do to protect our family is nothing to be ashamed of, nor is what you are and what you're capable of. If you are a monster, then so are we, and I love that you fight every day just to survive. After all, not everyone could." I feel the name on his lips.

Bass.

"But Nico is right; we need to keep moving. Soldiers are trying to bash through the doors right now, and we need to get to the labs before they end any of their experiments or anyone makes a getaway."

"I'm here. I'm okay." I shake it off and straighten, and Louis searches my gaze before nodding, trusting me.

"Then let's do this." Louis plucks the blade from the ground and hands it over, while Isaac offers me my guns which are now reloaded. I take them carefully, blood coating my hands and arms.

Isaac leans in and kisses me deeply. "I love you too," he murmurs, "and when this is over, I'll show how much that meant to me."

Smiling, I push from the wall and step over the bodies, not sparing them another look.

Maybe it should haunt me and killing should be harder, but it's not.

It's almost too easy when it's for my men and to stop what my father started.

Shaking my head, I refocus as we head upstairs and into a whole different level. This one is filled with labs and hiding scientists. I see some running, but I pay them no mind. They won't get far, and they can't hurt us.

Not now.

I keep to the middle to allow my heart to slow as we break into pairs without orders. The first lab is empty, bar a partially cut open body of a soldier on the bed, which makes me snarl. I grab a sheet and cover him gently, which is the least I can do for him for now. The next room has a scientist, and he throws us a panicked look as he plunges a needle into the neck of an unconscious soldier who's tied down.

"No!" I yell as I rush him, shoving him away. I grab the needle and lift it. It's half full. "What's in this?"

He tilts his head back, even as his eyes dart around for an escape.

"Tell me," I roar in his face.

"It is to kill him. It's painless. The research is to be destroyed rather than taken," he stammers.

"Research? Research? He is a person!" I scream before lowering my voice. "Let's see how truly painless it is," I sneer and stab it down into his neck, depressing the plunger. He falls back with a yell and yanks it out, covering the wound with his hand as I watch with a cruel twist of my lips.

It doesn't take long. He drops to his knees, his mouth opening and closing as he wheezes like he can't breathe. His entire body shakes before turning into full-blown seizures, causing him to froth at the mouth before he stills.

"I guess not very," I spit before turning. Nico is standing with his fingers pressed against the soldier's neck, and when I ask silently, he shakes his head.

Grinding my teeth, I hurry to the final lab, meeting Louis and Jonas there.

I need to save just one person from this hellhole.

Only, there is just a scientist standing there in his white coat, and his eyes are hard as he watches us.

Louis moves over and picks up his badge. "Lead Scientist Tyrion. Are you in charge?"

"Only of the labs," he murmurs, shooting us worried looks. "You are them, aren't you?"

"Them who?" Louis asks.

"The children. The first experiments. His legacy. We heard you had been sweeping labs, and we were on lockdown. You are magnificent," he whispers, "just like he said."

"Oh, looks like we're famous." Louis turns to us with an arched brow as we all laugh humourlessly. "Then I guess you know what comes next," he tells the man.

"Please." The first sign of fear breaks through his facade, his voice warbling. "It's just a job."

"Not to us," I spit, stepping to Louis's side. "Not to those dead soldiers out there or the countless dead children."

"I had nothing to do with you or the other kids!" he yells. "I swear, I was only brought on a few months ago before your father died. I didn't even know what it entailed until I took the position, and it was too late."

"Lies," I sneer.

"Please," he begs, holding his hands up as tears well in his eyes. "I was only following orders."

"You all were," I scoff. "History is filled with men and women simply following orders and committing horrendous crimes. You made your choice. You did this, and now you should suffer the consequences."

"Please, I have a family," he babbles. "I did it for them. I never wanted to, please. You'll never hear from me again."

Dropping the gun, I jerk my chin at him. "Get out of here, and if I see your face again, you're dead."

I show him the mercy that was never shown to us, and I hope I am right in doing so.

"Nova?" Louis asks.

"Leave him. He's not worth it." I whirl and leave the labs, heading to the stairs at the very end of the hall.

Hopefully, we'll find the man in charge because I have some things I'd like to discuss with him.

The stairs have a closed, locked door that D opens for us.

"I've got you," he murmurs. It feels wrong to be doing this without him, but then again, he's right there, in our ears, watching us.

We surge up the stairs, knowing that with each second that passes, they could escape.

This might have started with my father, but it will end here with this man—the one tugging at a door as we rush into an ornate office. There are bookshelves to the left filled with pictures of him and military commanders, and even a fucking president. There is a sofa to the left, and a huge desk taking up the back placed in front of some windows. Beyond is a plane gearing up to depart.

The man tries to escape through the locked fire door as he glances back at us with purpose and hatred.

He's not what I was expecting, but then again, I guess the bad guys never are. After all, he's just a man. Just a fucking man. Nothing more.

He's middle-aged and moderately attractive, with salt and pepper hair. His face is angular, with bright blue eyes, and his body is encased in an expensive three-piece suit. He's neither tall nor short, fat nor slim.

He would be forgettable if it weren't for the shark-like smile he aims at us when he swings the door open. "He's making a run for it!" I yell and sprint across the office to see him leaping into the plane.

We have to roll when he looks back and pulls out a pistol, aiming badly, but it keeps us down as the plane starts to lift.

"Shit! He can't get away!" Louis roars.

Putting my gun away, I throw him a narrow-eyed look. "Then let's stop him." Without waiting for his approval, I push into a sprint, aiming for the plane.

We can't let him get away.

I pump my arms faster.

This has to end.

I duck my head.

He dies today, giving us freedom.

With a roar, I leap into the air.

I manage to hit the closing back door and turn to see the others running. Louis makes it, Nico too, then Jonas and Isaac. D breaks out of the door and sprints across the deck. With my hand stretched out towards him, I let the others anchor me as I reach for him, unwilling to leave him behind.

We end this together.

"Hurry!" I yell at him.

Eyes glittering, he moves like lightning just as we take off into the air. Our hands slap together, and I grip him tightly as he swings. Staring into his determined eyes, I haul him up, and we fall into a heap in the plane's belly.

Panting, he rolls off me, and Louis helps me up as I pull my gun. He nods at me. "D, you're with me. We'll get them to land safely. Everyone else, check for soldiers and secure the leader."

He sneers the word, echoing our feelings as we climb up the ramp and into the small plane. He's there, banging on the cockpit, and when he sees us, his nostrils flare as he takes aim once more.

"Not a good idea," I call. "Sure way to crash the plane." I shrug.

"Maybe, but it might be worth it," he replies. "Unless you want to find out, weapons down."

Playing nice for now, I slowly lower my gun to the floor and leave it there as I straighten, smiling at him. "I don't need a weapon to kill you."

"No, you wouldn't, would you, Nova?" He arches a brow.

I look him over as he steps closer, still aiming his gun at me. Nico and Jonas slide down each side to circle him.

"I don't know you."

"Oh, but I know you. I watched you be born. I watched every moment of his research on you. He always told me you were the future, you kids, his pet project. I believe differently, but here you are. He was right. You are incredible." He shakes his head. "We could have done such amazing things together if you hadn't grown a conscience."

"Who are you? He never told me your name."

"He wouldn't. After all, your father plays the long game. Name's William Moss. I was your father's silent partner from the beginning. The money, the operations, nothing would have happened without me."

"And that's something to be proud of?" I distract him as the guys move closer.

"I would say so. Just think of everything we can achieve and how much money we will make. I will obviously have to kill the men who are with you, since they were all failed experiments and we don't need that pollution, but you?" He shakes his head. "Perfect. You are the perfect blend, and we can work on your obedience."

"Never," I spit.

"Ah, stop or she dies. We might all go down, but you'll watch her choke on her own blood first," he sneers at Nico and Jonas. "Yes, Nova, this isn't the end like you want it to be. This is just the beginning."

"When I kill you, it will be the end. It will finally be over, and your precious research? I'll destroy it all and let it burn with your body."

"And then what?" he asks. "You'll live happily ever after? A normal life isn't for you. You are a weapon. All of you. You couldn't exist any other way. You need the adrenaline and the fight to stay alive. Tell me that you haven't felt the best you ever have while following his breadcrumbs."

"Shut up," I spit, moving closer.

He just smiles "And you followed it so willingly, so happy to do exactly what he wanted while showing just what you are capable of—the final and best experiment. The final test."

I still, searching his eyes. "You mean your test."

"His." He smiles slowly.

"He's dead," I state bluntly.

"Is he?" He grins. "Then yes, my final test, and you passed with flying colours, though we never anticipated you would form such a close bond with the others. That will be severed though, not to worry, since we need you clear-headed."

"Shut up!" I roar as I press against his gun. "Kill me and be done with it."

"Oh, Nova, you still don't get it, do you? All of this was to bring you home. No, you won't die, but they will." He swings the gun, ready to fire, before I slam my arm down, breaking his.

He falls back with a roar and the shot goes wide, hitting a window.

The air is instantly sucked out, and the plane rattles and nosedives for a moment before it straightens. I'm about to end this, to end him, when the hole gets bigger and the chairs rip from the walls and slam through the windows. I grab the wall and hold on.

"D! Cockpit!" Louis roars as he tries to get to me.

D crawls past me, ripping open the door and slamming it shut. Looking out of the window, I watch a chair hit the engine, and we start to nosedive again. I feel D struggling to try and right the plane. He yells that the side of the mountain is rapidly approaching, and I know we are going to crash.

Whipping my head back around, I leap for William to end this just as we hit.

We are all thrown about as we hit. D manages to straighten us as much as possible, and that's the only thing that saves us. Even so, I feel my shoulder pop out of place and my ribs crack. My head smacks into the side until Nico catches me as I fly about and pulls me into his arms, wrapping himself around me as we hit once more, and everything goes dark.

I open my eyes with a groan as I feel his arms slipping from around me. Rolling, I see Nico's out cold. Panic instantly takes hold, but his chest is rising and falling. Isaac is groaning and clutching his bullet wound on his side. Louis is on his knees, coughing. Jonas holds onto a rope that was once on the side and not the ceiling, and he lets go and falls to his back with a thump.

Staggering to my feet, I rush to the cockpit, ripping open the door to see D in his chair, wiping at a head wound but alive.

My eyes then swing to William.

He's groaning and holding his stomach, where a metal bar is speared through his gut, pinning him in place. Dropping to my knees before him, I watch the blood pool around his hands as he tries to staunch the flow. He blinks repeatedly, his mouth moving.

Shock.

Gripping my shoulder, I pop it back into position with a grunt. There's not much I can do about the other aches and pains, but we are all alive, and that's what matters.

William, however, is dying, and I let it happen, surrounded by his creations, his experiments, and his enemies as he does.

Forgotten and unimportant.

"Is that all the research back there?" I demand, needing answers.

"Yes, in the vault, the other . . . The others are at your father's house and lab." He coughs, splattering blood on his lips and chin.

His head falls back, but he holds my gaze. "I guess we all think we are so invincible, so immortal, until the end," he jokes bitterly. "But you? You truly are unstoppable, like he promised."

I don't speak, and he smiles, his teeth and lips covered in his blood as he chokes on it, just like he threatened to do to me.

"He's alive." He coughs, the force racking his body.

Snarling, I grab his shoulders and slap him until he focuses on me again.

"Who is?" I demand as he groans. "Who is?" I yell.

His head lolls back as his eyes start to close, and his whisper comes out half broken and dead. "Your father. Your father is alive."

"No," I whisper.

"This . . . This was all his plan." He coughs again, the sound wet and rattling. "To get you back. One last experiment."

Then I watch as he takes his last breath.

"Nova, it could be a lie from a dying man, one last way to hurt you," Louis murmurs. I didn't even know they were close.

I can't speak over my panic because deep down, I believe him.

There's one way to . . . Reaching forward, I search through his pockets until I find his phone. Using his thumb, I unlock it and scroll through his call list and hit the last number.

The only number he has rung.

The ringing is loud, even over the groan of the plane and the flames licking at it.

"We need to move," Louis says. "It's over, Nova. Let's go!"

I don't move, don't speak, as it rings in my ear.

There's a click.

"Hello?"

My world falls apart as I hear my father's sharp and commanding voice.

One I would know anywhere.

One that sends shivers of fear through me.

"Hello?" There's silence then. "Novaleen, is that you?" He sounds way too overjoyed about it.

"You're alive," I croak.

"And you found him for me. Thank you for that. I wish I could have seen it. Is he dead?" he asks curiously.

"You're alive," I repeat.

"Do not state the obvious, girl," he admonishes, his usual cold tone snapping me from my shock as I tighten my blood-soaked hold on the phone.

He's alive.

The bastard is alive and has been playing us this entire time.

"I'm coming for you. Nowhere is safe," I snarl, and before he can answer, I crush the phone in my grip then turn to see five shocked faces.

"This isn't over. Not yet." I stand and storm from the plane, ready to hunt my father down.

The man who started all this.
The one who's supposed to be in the ground.
I thought I was unstoppable, but what if it was all a lie?
What if it was all a pretty lie . . .

For my mum, who walks through the darkness with us

...and also because she was jealous that my sister had a dedication. There, you happy now?

UNBREAKABLE

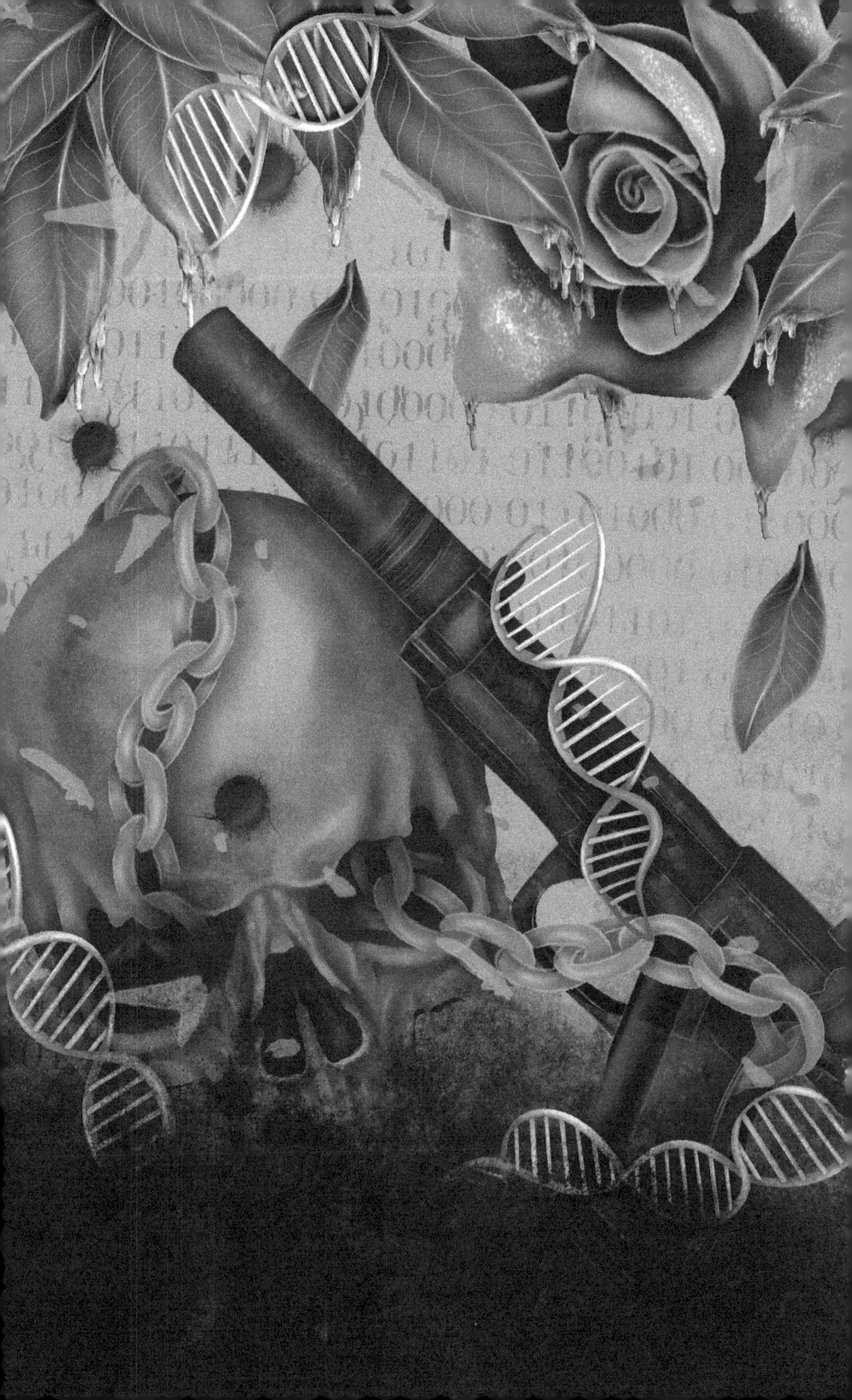

PROLOGUE

Gritting my teeth, I swallow the taste of my own blood, my nails breaking as I claw at the rails of the bed. My legs thrash against the restraints, my arms too.

My head is thrown back in agony as it blisters through me like a flame.

The blade slides deeper into my stomach, and I lift to watch the blood well on my abdomen before I glare at the scientist above me.

He doesn't spare me a glance.

"You're dead," I warn, my voice choked.

He ignores me as he plunges his hand into my stomach, making me fall back, and finally, the trapped howl of agony rips through the lab before I pass out.

When I wake up, I feel him above me, watching and judging.

He pulls me apart just to put me back together again like a cat playing with a spider. Forcing my swollen, grimy eyes open, I find my stomach stapled, but I'm still tied down and coated in sweat and blood.

My father stands there with a pen poised above a notebook. "How do you feel, Novaleen?"

"Fuck you," I croak, my voice raw from screaming.

His eyes narrow impatiently before he repeats the question harder.

"How do I feel?" I echo, my tongue thick. "Like when I get free, I'm going to rip you apart to see how you like it."

Dropping the pen, he leans in with a cruel twist of his lips. "Oh, but you won't be getting free, will you? Not again." With those parting words, he departs.

He leaves me screaming and fighting, trapped again.

Once again, I have been reduced to an experiment.

ONE

S tumbling from the plane crash, I vomit whatever is left in my stomach onto the grass. Hands rub my back, hold my hair for me, and pass me water. I accept it all as I straighten and wipe my mouth, and when I turn to them, I know my gaze is ice cold.

The same ice moves through my veins.

Numb.

"We need to go back to the base and search for signs of my father, gather all the research, and destroy what is left," I order. Louis watches me worriedly but nods, and then I sweep my gaze over all of them. "And we need to see to Isaac's wound."

"I'll be fine," he mutters, but he's favouring one leg, his face is shiny with sweat, and his eyes are pinched in pain.

"If we are going after my father, we need to be better than fine," I snap before I soften my voice, stopping before him. "Please, I can't lose anyone else. I can't deal with anything else right now."

He searches my gaze, those grey eyes worried, before nodding. "We've got you," he murmurs. "Are you okay?"

"Not one fucking bit, and I won't be until my father is dead." I grab my gun, throw it over my shoulder, and pick my way through the plane crash, heading back to the base.

I know they will follow.

They are worried, I sense it, but I can't put them at ease. I can't even speak anymore, not without wanting to scream. I thought . . . wondered if he was really dead, but after seeing the video and then hearing nothing from him, I thought he truly had passed, that he was buried and I was safe.

I was so fucking wrong.

My father is alive, and not only that, he orchestrated this whole thing. I am nothing but a puppet once more, my strings being pulled by him. He brought me home, ensured I met the other fucked-up kids like me, then sent me on missions to stop his partner who clearly still worked with him.

I wonder if his partner knew that was the endgame or if my father lied to him too.

Either way, I'm done playing his games.

I'm done being an experiment.

I'm going to find him, and when I do, I'm going to kill him once and for all. This time, there will be no doubt, no burial, just his rotting corpse at the end of my gun. I'll free us all, I'll keep us safe, and I'll do whatever it takes because this isn't just about me anymore.

Or about us.

This is about every single person he has experimented on. He was right, this brought us together, but he should have realised then that he fucked up because we won't rest until he's stopped. The very same super soldiers he created will be the ones to end his life, and there is nothing he can do to stop that.

It's a quick journey through the forest, as the plane didn't go too far, and with our enhanced speed and strength, we are back in a few hours. The sky is starting to lighten as we approach the base.

"Nico, Jonas, Dimitri, sweep the whole area and look for any soldiers who have not fled or been killed yet. We want no surprises. Nova and I will help Isaac," Louis orders.

I let him take charge because I wouldn't know what to say right now.

I'm not reliable.

My anger conflicts with my disbelief.

My idealistic future, the happiness I had felt was just on the horizon, was ripped from me. I should have known it would happen. People like us don't get happily ever afters, and to think that just makes us pretty little liars.

Pain is a constant, Novaleen. It is how a person deals with it that interests me. Some conquer it and wield it, while others crumble and fall.

So tell me, daughter, when I make this hurt, and I will, are you going to conquer or fall?

His voice in my head makes me gnash my tongue until I taste blood as old memories and wounds resurface—ones I thought long since buried.

He's right, though, pain is constant, but I will conquer it. I will never fall, not with so much on the line.

The pain he instilled in me will be wielded as the blade for his death—he can bet on that. He wanted to watch his experiments in action and see what we are capable of? He's about to, and he has no idea what I am truly willing to do to finally stop the man who started all this.

I will end this with one of us in the grave.

I don't enter the labs. Instead, I sit just beyond, watching Isaac instruct Louis on how to help him. They check the wound for bullet fragments before stapling it closed and dressing it. He also takes some antibiotics and pain relief. I admit he looks better, but we leave him to rest a little. Louis comes out to stand near me, drying his hands, as I watch the stairs, protecting their backs.

His bright blond hair is tinted with blood and ash, and it's streaked down his face as well, but those bright eyes are sharp and locked on me.

Tossing the towel away, he crouches before me, places his hands on my knees, and says nothing. I am unable to meet his all-seeing, bright-green eyes for too long, so I glance away, scared of what he will see.

"Nova," he says, our unit leader demanding attention.

I can't give it to him.

"Baby," he pleads, changing it up. The worry I hear in his voice has me looking at him.

I feel my lip tremble before I bite it, refusing to fucking cry. I won't be so goddamn weak. "He's alive," I whisper.

"I know, and he won't be for long," he vows. "I will fucking kill him for what he did to you and my brothers. I'll bring you his fucking heart on a goddamn platter if it will stop this." I must look confused because he slides his hands up my body to cup my face. "This vagueness, this nothingness, you pulling away from us to protect yourself and drive off the hurt—guess what, Nova? It hurts, so fucking let it. Do not shut everyone out just because you're scared."

"I'm not scared." I get to my feet, pacing away.

"You are. We all are." That makes me stop as I turn to look at him. "You don't think I still have nightmares about him? I see his face every single day of my fucking life. I wear his cruel intentions on my skin as scars, and my heart is heavy with dread and the idea that he could hurt those I love again."

"I failed," I admit, finally acknowledging what is wrong.

I was so sure I was right and that it would end, but now I've failed them, Annie, and the soldiers.

The whole fucking world.

"You didn't fail, Nova," he begins, but I shake my head. "You didn't. I did!" he yells, and when I turn to face him, his eyes are brimming with tears. The sight shocks me into silence. I've never seen Louis cry, nor did I think I ever would.

His hands are fisted and his chest heaves as he watches me.

"I failed," he repeats.

I step closer, and he reacts as though he doesn't believe he deserves comfort. Wasn't I thinking the exact same thing when I pushed him away?

"Louis," I start.

"I failed them, Nova. Don't you see?" he rants. "When Bas died, I couldn't protect D, and he withdrew, not feeling anything. He was like a machine, and I couldn't stop that. You did! You brought him back! I couldn't stop Jonas from descending into madness, but you did. I couldn't stop Nico from blaming and hating himself, cutting himself up every day, but you did. I couldn't get Isaac to look after himself and let the guilt go, but you did. I couldn't figure out what I was doing wrong, and yet, you did."

Ignoring his retracting steps, I pull him to me as tears drip down his handsome, heartbreaking face.

"And you couldn't begin to look in the mirror and maybe see that it's not all on you to save them? That you can't protect them from everything? You were so focused on saving them, you were losing yourself." I grip his face. "I see it, Louis, and I refuse to lose you, so I'll fucking fight for you, for them, but don't you ever lessen what you did for them. You've looked after them. They are alive and a family because of you. Neither of us has failed, nor are we to blame, and together, we will do this. You're right, I was withdrawing, but I won't. I won't hurt you like that. I'll endure the pain for you, for them, because I love you."

He gulps, his Adam's apple bobbing.

"What if I don't deserve your love?" he murmurs.

"You do, and the fact that you even ask that proves you do," I retort, gripping his face harder. "You deserve to be loved and so much more. We all deserve to be happy, but we know we have some things to do before then and we will. When we survive, which we will, we'll do it together. It isn't all on you, Louis. We follow you because of our trust in you, but that doesn't mean it all weighs on your shoulders. Let us help. Let your family share the burden."

I feel them before I see them, and Nico, Jonas, and D silently press to Louis's back as we hold him.

"Let us help you, my love," I murmur as Isaac stumbles in, probably waking from our shouts, and wraps his arms around us.

All of us stand together, holding Louis as he sobs.

I don't know what flipped in me. Maybe it was seeing such a strong man break before me, believing it was all his fault and all on his shoulders, but now I am confident and strong once more.

I refuse to lose him or anyone else.

"She's right. We let you take on too much, but it's not on you, Louis. This is a burden we share," Nico murmurs. "You are not in charge of saving us. You never were."

"He's right," Jonas says seriously. "No one blames you for anything. We owe you our lives. You brought us together."

"You made us a family," D murmurs. "And what Bas did is not your fault. It's not anyone's. No one could have saved him, Louis. No one."

"We will always have each other," Isaac adds.

"And we will never lose another," I promise as I kiss away his tears. "We will protect this research, we will destroy my father and the legacy he built, and we will do it together. Wherever this road takes us, I know that for certain."

He nods, blowing out a breath. "I guess I take on too much."

"You think?" I snort, making him crack a grin.

"Want me to suck your dick to make it better?" Jonas asks, making us all laugh.

"Hey, you never offered to suck mine." Dimitri grins, making Louis's grin grow, which is why they are doing it.

"I was trying to make him feel better! I'm not good at lovey-dovey shit, but fine!" Jonas drops to his knees, pushes his hair back, and smacks his lips, making D laugh as he shoves him away.

"Give me the dick!" Jonas yells, crawling after D, who runs away laughing.

"Boys," Louis and I say at the same time, and we share a secret grin. "Go get packed up," Louis finishes.

"Nico, you help them. Isaac, go back and rest."

"Yes, sir!" Jonas leaps to his feet, dragging D with him. "I will if you want me to, though I think Nova is better at it."

Nico sighs and gives us a look as if to say, *I'm stuck with these idiots?* before he lumbers off after them. Isaac squeezes us both before moving stiffly back to the bed to lie down until we are ready to leave.

"He's right. It might cheer you up. Want me to suck your dick?" I grin.

Louis rolls his eyes as he drags me closer, kissing me softly. "Later, baby. For now, let's get our family out of here." Nodding, I help him start to pack up.

The more I find, the darker my mood gets.

All joy disappears as I remember what happened to us and what will continue to happen.

Louis begged me to not shut down, so I don't, and I feel every hard, sharp edge, even as it cuts me to ribbons on the inside.

I endure it for them—for him.

When we are done and all loaded with bags, Jonas sets explosives on the compound to destroy everything else, meaning my father can't come back here and no one else can find this.

As we leave the base, there's an explosion on the horizon. Turning my head, I see the plume of smoke coming from the direction of the plane, and I watch it wind throughout the trees and into the sky, knowing it's burning the evidence of what transpired.

Of us, of my father, of it all.

I want someone to find it, but it would only make them hunt us. I know it's for the best. Turning away, I meet the shadowed eyes of my men and know they feel the same. They are anxious for what's to come, even though they are determined and ready to do whatever it takes.

"Let's go," I murmur, glancing back at the smoke once more. "We'll get this research back and then we'll hunt. We'll hunt him to the ends of this fucking earth, and we'll stop him."

"Too fucking right." Jonas grins, his expression wicked and filled with anger.

"I'm with you," Isaac offers solemnly, but I see hints of anger in his gaze directed at the man on the phone—my father.

"We all are," Dimitri responds.

"We will do whatever it takes. We are the only ones who can stop this, and we will," Nico adds with a glance at me.

"Let's end this," Louis agrees.

After all, they have their own pasts with my father, their hatred matching my own.

Hiking back to our trucks, I hold onto the hatred, letting the anger in my heart warm me and keep me moving so we can stay alive.

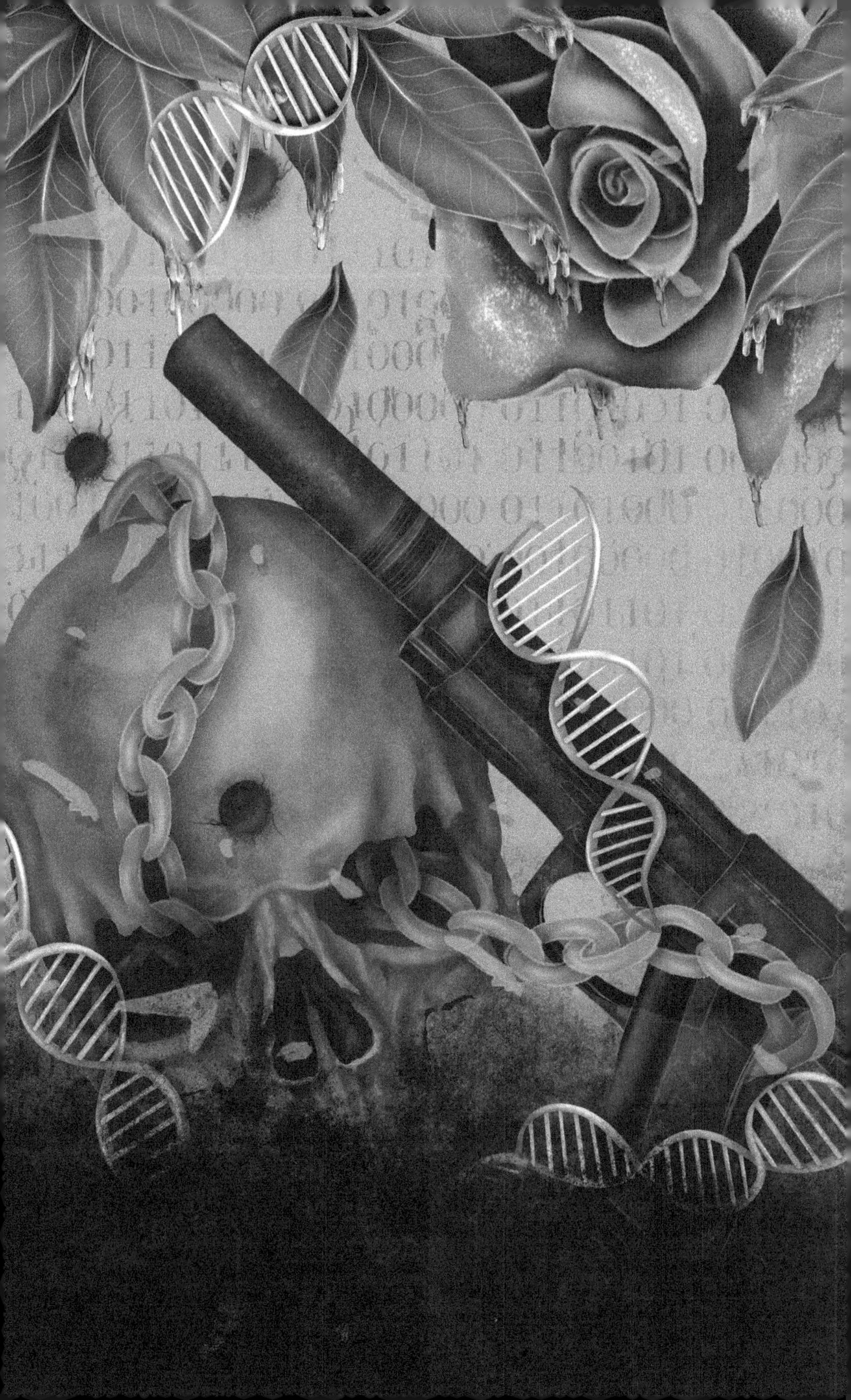

Even the plane ride home is quiet, all of us lost in our own thoughts—or exhaustion from the marathon we have been on over the last few weeks.

"Where to?" Louis asks, seeming as lost as all of us, and when I speak, my voice is hoarse from not using it.

"We go home to my sister. We regroup, lick our wounds, and seal his research away. Then, we kill him."

Louis nods, but I sense his worry. I ignore it as I head to the shower. My head hangs as I wash the blood and death away, only it ends with me sobbing on my knees.

I thought it was over.

I thought we were safe.

I was wrong and all along, I was so sure.

It was just another test, another experiment.

I willingly walked into his lab, but this time, I'm not a child.

That's how Jonas finds me. Water sprays down on me as I cry, my arms locked around my knees as my bruised body shakes with my sobs. I lift my head and meet his forlorn eyes.

He slowly steps into the room and shuts the door, holding his hands out like I'm a spooked animal. I have to bite back my cry as he crouches before me. "I've got you," is all he says. Reaching up, he switches off the shower and lifts me out, holding me tight as he dries me off and dresses me. All the while, I cry silently, leaning into his strength.

With a soft kiss on my forehead, he carries me to the bed, where he lays me down and carefully covers me with the duvet before curling around me. "I've got you," he repeats, and I know he does.

The door opens, but I don't even lift my head, knowing they are all there. Jonas must silently communicate and I let him, choosing to close my swollen, raw eyes as they join us, sprawling around me. All of us touch each other, needing the comfort for what is to come, remembering what the man we now hunt is capable of.

What he did to us.

What he has continued to do.

"I fell for it," I croak sometime later, the hum of the plane's engine almost swallowing my words. "He did it to bring me out of hiding, and I fell for it."

"We all did," Dimitri murmurs.

I sniff. "I hate him."

"I know. We will find him, Nova. I promise that. We will end this. He will not get you. Not ever," Nico states firmly, his hand squeezing my ankle.

Why does some part of me feel like he already has and he's already won?

Ana and Bert stand at the front door as we pull up, and I'm out of the car before it stops moving. She's nervous but smiling. However, when she takes a look at my face, it falls away.

"Nova, are you okay? What happened?" she demands.

Stopping before them both, I search them for wounds. "He's alive."

"Who is?" she asks, sounding confused.

"Dad," I mutter. "Dad is alive."

"Nova, we buried him," she scoffs.

"I spoke to him." That falls into the silence like a lead weight as I hear the car doors slamming behind me. "He was behind this all along. It was to bring me back, to bring us back, and to experiment on us once more. We fell for it. He's alive, Ana."

She's pale, and I spare Bert a sad look before I focus back on her.

"And I'm going to stop him. I'm going to kill him for good this time." Unable to watch the twisting emotions crossing her face, I move around her and head inside.

I never thought this place would feel like home, but as I step into the foyer, I'm almost glad to be back.

Despite the horrors and the bad memories here, I have good ones too—of Annie, Bert, and my guys—and I need that. I will need all the strength I can muster for what is to come.

Heading straight to the kitchen, I grab a bottle and pour myself a healthy helping of whisky, grimacing at the taste as it goes down.

"I'll make some tea," Bert murmurs as he joins me.

I just nod jerkily until his hand lands on my shoulder, making my eyes close as the alcohol burns down my throat.

"I am sorry, Miss Nova, but you are not alone."

"Thank you," I murmur as I turn, watching him move around to make some food and tea. Annie comes in and sits heavily at the table, staring at it. Dragging the bottle over, I pour her a glass and push it to her. Without sparing me a look, she tosses it back.

She groans at the taste before meeting my eyes. "Part of me is angry, disgusted, and sad, but part of me is glad, Nova." She searches my gaze as I flinch. "I'm so sorry."

Reaching over, I take her hand. "You are allowed to be happy your father is alive, Ana."

"But how can I be after what he has done?" she sobs.

"Because he is still your father, and you can't shut off love just like that."

"You did," she whispers.

"No, he beat it out of me through years of pain. There is nothing but anger for him in my heart, anger and hatred, but you need to know, Ana, that I can't—won't save him. He has to die, even if that means you'll hate me."

"I know," she says, taking my hand and holding my gaze. "You have to stop him, Nova. You have to."

And so we sit, with a shared bottle of whisky between two sisters who don't drink.

One who just wants to heal the world, and the other who only ever wanted it to leave her alone.

THREE

"**S**am, this is my sister, Nova."

"The one who helped save me." He slides to his feet with a wince, and Ana moves forward, holding him up with a grunt.

"Sit down now!" she reprimands him.

"Yes, doc." He grins cheekily at her, watching her as she helps him sit and then fusses over his blankets and IV drip. The look in his eyes can only be described as soft, even as she tells him off, and for a moment, I want to turn away and let them have this moment, but he glances up at me. Some of that softness remains, but it's different. That look was for her alone.

I know because I see it in my men's eyes every single day.

After a few drinks with Ana, where we mourned what has to come, I felt the need to get moving and she needed to check on Sam, so here we are. She's obviously been taking good care of him, and there is clearly a bond between them.

"Thank you," he offers. "Did you get them?"

Sighing, I lean into the wall. "Not all of them, but we will."

"Annie told me all about your father."

"Oh, has she?" I grin as she blushes and ducks her head, the nickname seeming familiar on his lips. Despite my frustration, my turmoil, and the emotions I feel about what has happened, I'm almost giddy about the shared look they exchange.

"If I can help in any way, please let me know," he finishes sombrely.

"You need to rest, not help," Ana hisses. "Otherwise, I'll chain you to the bed."

"Kinky." He winks, making her blush brighter, and I grin as I push away from the wall.

"I just came to check on you, but it's been a long few days so I'm going to rest."

And leave them alone, but I don't say that.

He nods, but they are both lost in each other as I saunter away. The whiskey still burns my stomach, since I'm not used to drinking. We had a few more and some of Bert's tea and sandwiches before she brought me to see Sam, but now I'm exhausted.

My legs almost drag behind me as I head upstairs, unsure where my guys are but knowing they are close. They are probably checking the perimeter since we now know my father is about and could be, and probably is, watching our every move.

I should do a million things, but instead, I find myself stopping at my sister's room, needing comfort. I slide between her sheets fully clothed and close my eyes as I breathe in her scent. The familiar fragrance fills my lungs.

My heart aches, and my emotions are all over the place, but I'm so very tired.

When the bed moves, I crack open my eyes to see her. She slides in opposite me, taking my hand and holding it in the bed between us. She doesn't have to say anything, she just holds my hand as I close my eyes once more.

She's supporting me, just like when we were kids and I would sneak into her bed when she had nightmares. Only now, it's her turn to protect me from the very real nightmares I know are still to come.

"I've got you, Nova, sleep," she whispers.

And I do.

When I wake up, the room is dark and moonlight streams through the window, illuminating Ana's sleeping face. Her hand is still in mine, holding it tightly like she will never let go, and the sheets are twisted around us.

So I don't disturb her. Knowing she hasn't been getting enough rest, I slide out of bed, pad around it, and stop above her, looking down at her too young, too innocent face. Tucking the blankets around her, I brush her hair back and lean down to place a kiss on her forehead. "He won't hurt you. I promise," I murmur before slipping from the room, pressing my back to the door, and sucking in slow breaths.

At least one good thing came of all of this—we are back together and a family once more, even if it is dysfunctional and healing. Pushing from the door, I use the bathroom before heading downstairs in search of everyone.

I expect them to be asleep, but I should have known better.

They are in the dining room with the research spread out around them, organised into piles. Louis is on the phone arguing with someone, and D is on his laptop.

"What's happening?" I murmur as Bert comes in with a tray of mugs, which looks like it's not the first time. He smiles when he sees me and hands me a coffee. Taking it, I warm my hands as I meet their gazes.

"We are finding your father and any kids or soldiers who may still be alive," Nico replies as if it's simple, and maybe it is. I told them we needed to, so now they are.

"But you need to sleep—"

"And you need answers and for this to end," Jonas retorts as he accepts a mug. Bert leans in and lays a gentle kiss on Jonas's head like a father would before sneaking him a plate of pancakes that puts a wide, childlike smile on his face.

"You did this for me?" I murmur.

"We are a team, a family. It's what we do," Isaac says as he pulls out a chair for me. I sit with my mug, and he hands me a folder. "Here, look for anything helpful. It's not easy reading, so if you need a break, we understand."

Looking around the table, I can't help but tear up. "I love you all."

"We know." D winks, glancing up from the laptop.

Louis hangs up and comes to me, leaning down and kissing my forehead. "We love you too, now get to work," he teases.

"Yes, sir." I grin, opening the folder and diving in.

Hours later, my head hurts and all of my good feelings have disappeared into nothing but anger and hatred. Shoving my black hair into a bun, I lean back to stretch, ignoring the looks I feel thrown at me.

I know they are worried about how I am taking all of this. After all, I thought we were so close to stopping all of this and finally destroying everything my father built, only to be right back at the beginning. It's hard not to feel dejected and angry, but I try to hide it from them, even as I plunge myself inside those feelings, knowing I will need to survive what's to come.

After all, what I told Annie is true: I will have to kill my father.

Despite everything he has done, there is a price for taking a life, and it will be steep, but I will gladly pay it to protect children and soldiers and to stop the abominations he calls experiments.

"Here, Miss Nova." Bert places a plate next to me. "You must eat."

I lift my head, and he frowns at whatever he sees there. "Please," he adds, his face contorted in worry. "I will go check on Mr. Sam to make sure he is okay so Ana may sleep."

"Has she not been?" I find myself asking.

He grins. "Like you, she is unable to rest when there is a job to be done, but you cannot do that job when you're exhausted, hungry, and weak, so eat." He infuses his tone with a command, the same one he used on me as a child, and I smile but turn back to the folder, feeling too sick to eat.

What they did to this man . . .

It's a crime against humanity.

Acts of pure evil disguised by the word "science."

I always knew my father was evil and that what he did was wrong, but I never really understood the extent of his reach and ability to hurt others to get what he wanted.

"Nova, eat," Nico snaps.

"I can't," I retort, glaring at him as he leans into me, ready to fight, his nostrils flaring.

I know it's only because he cares, but that dark part of me lights up at the prospect of releasing some of these emotions through a fight. Suddenly, Louis stands and rounds the table, kicking my chair back.

"Come on," he demands. "Nico, you too."

Expecting us to follow, he heads outside, and with nothing else to do, we file out after him. He turns to us, rolling back his sleeves as he watches me, and then gestures to the grass. "Well then, if you want to spar, then go ahead. If you want to fight us and take it out on us, then go ahead."

"I don't know what you mean," I mutter in shame.

"Nico, you're in," Louis orders, keeping his eyes on me. "Yes, you do. You need to fight. Nico does as well, so you are not the only one. Reading all that is not easy, and it leaves you feeling frustrated and useless, so get it all out, and then we will get back in there and you will eat." He grabs my chin. "Even if I have to force-feed you, you will fucking eat, baby, and then we will figure this out. You are not alone, Nova. You will never be alone, so stop acting like it. We are in this together, my love. You will remember that or we will remind you every single day we are alive."

Swallowing, I search his gaze. He lets me, shielding nothing and letting me see his own anger, frustration, and horror at what has been done.

"We've got you, baby. We've got you. If you need us to hold you while you cry, if you need us to burn the world at your side, or you just simply need this to help you work through your emotions, then we will. We will do anything because we are a family. We don't just get the happy emotions, but the bitter ones too. Nothing is ever too much for us, so stop shielding us and pushing us out. We want it. We want every brutal, raw edge. We can take it."

"What if I can't? What if I can't take it? What if I'm not strong enough?" I admit.

"Then we will be strong for you," he promises, stroking my cheek. "But, Nova, you are the strongest person I have ever met. Strength isn't measured by how tall you stand, but by how beautifully you break and get back up, and you, Nova, have been broken so many times, only to put yourself back together and keep going. You still believe in good, in love, in hope, and right and wrong despite the world never doing anything for you. Despite only seeing evil, you fight for good. We all do. We are all this world has."

"Then it's fucked," I joke, "because I'm not a hero, Louis. I never was. I'm just a scarred, angry woman trying to get back at her father."

"Maybe you started as that, but now you are so much more," he counters, angry at me tearing myself down. "Now you are one of us. You saved that man in there. You saved every single one of us. You walked into gunfire with our family to stop the experiments no one else cares about. You are magnificent, Nova, and not in the way your father always wanted you to be, but in the way that makes me love you more. You are real. You're flawed, emotional, and stubborn as hell but so fucking strong, I feel awe just being around you. No matter what is thrown at you, you never stop fighting, and that, Nova? That is what he can never take away from us or understand in all of his experiments. He wants to better humanity, but he didn't realise that by torturing you, by destroying you and letting you be reborn in the flames, he had already achieved that. You, Nova, are the best person I've ever and will ever meet. Now get your sexy ass on that grass and fight it out with Nico so we can get back to work, because like it or not, you're the only fucking hero this world fucking has, and we have to stop this. Together."

"Come on, beautiful, show me what you've got," Nico taunts, and I turn to see him shirtless and waiting. I know he needs this as much as I do. Both of us are angry at the situation we have found ourselves in once more, feeling dejected and let down, and we need an outlet. This is it for us, a healthy way of expressing it, and Louis is right. They can handle it. Nico can handle it. I need to stop testing them and pushing them away because I expect them to leave. It's easier for me to create distance so it doesn't hurt as badly.

But I'm beginning to realise that pain is the whole reason we live.

We hurt and love and do it all over again. Otherwise, why are we fighting so hard every day to make the most of the life we have? Love doesn't have to be grand and beautiful; it can be this, a man willing to fight for you, willing to show up every day and put in the work.

Life isn't perfect—fuck knows I know that better than anyone—and it hurts you over and over, but I truly believe it never throws more at you than you are willing to endure, and you'll find a shred of happiness in the chaos. You just have to be strong enough, brave enough, to hold on tight and fight for it.

Even if it hurts like hell to do so.

Even if in the end, you are giving them the power to hurt you back.

Trust, I'm finally understanding, is the scariest thing of all.

It's so easy to break but so hard to earn.

I have theirs, though, and they have mine, and if I let them . . .

I think they just might save me from myself.

"Come on, Nova," Nico teases.

Rolling my eyes, I step onto the grass and face him. He doesn't wait—there's no clean sweep here. No, he comes at me, swinging his fists. I duck his first hit and sweep my leg out, which he jumps over, and then there is no more thinking.

Louis is right. I let out all the emotions taking me away from them, and I use them to make my movements faster and hits harder, and Nico takes it all. His eyes are bright with glee as we spar, moving around the grass. We are evenly matched because what he has in bulk and weight, I make up for in speed and attitude.

I manage to connect a hit, and he stumbles back.

There are cheers, and when I look up, I realise everyone is gathered outside, even Annie with Sam leaning on her shoulder. "Kick his ass, Nova!" he calls, making me chuckle, but the distraction is all Nico needs.

He holds nothing back, hitting me like a freight train and knocking my breath clear out. I feel a rib crack as I slam to the ground. Grinning down at me, he blows me a kiss. "You getting slow, baby?"

"Nah, you're just getting bigger," I tease as I throw my legs up and flip back to my feet, circling him.

"You'd know." He winks, making me burst out laughing even as I fling myself at him.

The movements come easily to me as I fall into old practice routines, but Nico is just as good as I. I'm definitely more martial arts focused, whereas he fights dirty, but it works. We both take hits that would make the others fall and we keep going after each other, knowing we can take it. We exhaust our bodies and minds until we both start to slow.

I see an opening when his left hand drops. Slipping under his guard, I sucker punch him and sweep my other leg out, knocking him back on his ass, but just as quickly, he kicks my legs out and I fall beside him.

Panting, sweaty, and grinning, I turn my head and meet his eyes. "Better?" he whispers.

"Yeah, you?" I ask as he reaches over and takes my hand.

"Much." He squeezes as I hear footsteps approaching and look up to find Louis clapping.

Crouching over me, Louis pushes my hair back. "We are not your enemy, Nova. We love you, and we can take everything you throw at us. You can always work out those emotions with us without worrying. We feel it too."

He holds out his hand, giving me a choice to keep fighting alone or to let go and be with them.

I take his hand and let him pull me up, choosing to let him save me.

I'm able to eat, as if all my emotions have settled, and Louis kisses my head as he passes to take my now empty plate away. "Good girl," he coos, making my thighs clench as heat builds in my core. He knows exactly what he's doing.

Jonas grins at me, flipping a knife in his hand as he reads. D is lost in his computer, Isaac is helping Ana with Sam, and Nico is showering. I could rest, but I don't want to. We need to find something, anything, that links my father to this.

Louis has to debrief with command for a few hours, so I spend that time searching the notes and experiments, looking for his handiwork.

"Jonas," I murmur as I read one experiment. "Does this seem familiar to you?" I hand the file over, certain I experienced the exact same experiment, but it's more than that. The writing looks familiar, but I don't remember why. It's not Father's, that's for sure.

He takes the folder and scans it before I see him shut down. "The man who wrote this is dead. Move on."

"Really? I recognise it—"

"He's dead!" he roars, his eyes wild, and my head jerks back automatically as I prepare for an attack.

D looks up. I nod to let him know I have this and stand carefully, like I would with a wild animal. I round the table with my hands out, ignoring my adrenaline to focus on him. His chest is heaving, and his eyes dart everywhere.

He's been triggered. I know the signs.

Crouching to make myself smaller, I keep my hands to myself and just let him see it's me. "Jonas, it's okay, babe. It is just me. It's just your Nova."

"He's dead," he repeats. "Dead. Dead."

"Okay, this file is dated a while ago," I say, and he nods jerkily.

"Dead, he's dead," he repeats.

I share a worried look with D as Louis comes into the room. D urges me to carry on, so gently I lay my hand on his thigh. He jerks and grabs me, slamming me to the table with his hand on my throat.

It happens in a split second, but I ignore my instincts and relax into his hold.

I hold up my other hand to the others who want to break us apart, stopping them. Jonas is attacking but not killing, and he doesn't see me. I need to make him see me before they hurt him.

"Baby, come back to me," I purr, feeling his hand tighten on my throat as mine drifts up his chest to his face. He shakes his head, but I hold on tight, digging my nails in. "It's me. It's your Nova."

"No," he whispers raggedly.

Leaning up, I lay kisses along every edge of his face I can reach. "It's me," I promise. "Come back to me."

His hand slowly loosens as he blinks, and I see realisation dawn in his eyes. I don't let him pull away in shock or fear, instead wrapping my legs around his waist and holding on as I continue to kiss him. "If you wanted to choke me, all you had to do was ask." I grin, teasing him.

He smiles shakily as he lifts me and sits heavily. Curling up on his lap, I stroke his chest and hair and whisper teasing comments to him as he works through this. The others relax slightly and at my nod, they drift out of the room to give us some space.

"Sorry, so sorry, baby," he mutters, burying his head in my neck. "I'm usually okay and better prepared for the triggers, but the writing took me off guard."

"It's okay," I murmur. "I understand, you know that. You could never hurt me, not really."

"I could though. I could kill you." He shivers, clutching me tighter.

"We would never let that happen. Trust me, Jonas," I murmur, lifting his head so I can meet his eyes. I hesitate. I don't want to push this, but he needs to talk about it. I need to know what to avoid so I don't trigger him again. "What happened? You said they are dead."

I see the vulnerability in his eyes. Whoever this person is, it's someone he fears, which is not something I ever thought I'd say about Jonas.

"I killed him. I hunted him down. The others helped, knowing I needed to. I couldn't sleep knowing he was still out there. He was my first kill. I was seventeen."

"You killed him because he deserved it." I have no doubts. "He's dead. He can't hurt you."

"But he did so badly, Nova. He was my tormentor. When they left me to go insane, it was on his orders. Your father left him in charge of me. He was not a good man. He was not in it for science or experiments, but because he liked to hurt people. He was cruel, Nova, and he broke me. I still barely cling onto my sanity. Sometimes, I wake up thinking I'm back in the cage like the animal he called me."

"But you aren't, you are here with me, and they can't have you ever again. Do you understand?" I demand.

"He watched me, beat me, tortured me, left me alone in a pitch-black room for days, and shocked my brain over and over. Nova, what if he truly did ruin me?"

"Then he ruined me too," I snarl. "You, Jonas, are not ruined. You are fucking perfect, and I love you. You believe that, right?"

He nods sadly.

"Good, and I don't love someone who doesn't deserve it. Fuck what they did, fuck them, fuck them all. I'll kill every single one if it will help you sleep." I lean in. "But you have to stay with me, fight with me. He's dead, Jonas, and soon they will all join him for what they did. I can't change the past and what happened, but I promise I will never let them hurt you again."

"Promise?" he whispers trustingly.

"I promise. I promise you all. I will never, ever let them hurt you." I search his gaze until he nods. "Come back to me," I plead, still sensing the distance and hating it. I lean in and kiss him. When he kisses me back, I pull away, watching him rebuild himself.

Sometimes I forget how fragile Jonas can truly be. Unlike the rest of us, something in his mind shattered from the torture, and he fights every day to not let it consume him, but sometimes it wins, and I'll be there every time to help bring him back and put it back together for him.

The writing . . .

As I hold him, I realise where I've seen it.

The same man had come here once, writing on his pad and observing my father. When my father left, he leaned into me and promised we would have some fun.

Jonas was right; he deserved to die. I only had moments with him and I saw the evil in his gaze. I'm glad Jonas got to face him in the end and take back that power, but I couldn't hate my father more than I do right now as I hold the man I love.

The others slowly trickle back into the room, and I spend the rest of the day on Jonas's lap, teasing him and making him laugh until he's somewhat back to normal.

I feel the others' worry for him, for us, for me.

For what is to come.

I feel it, too, like we are on a precipice and none of us know what is coming next.

It won't be good, so we hold onto the moments we have in hopes that it will be enough to get us through.

"Nova, I don't care if you're getting freaky, get dressed! We are having a family meal!" my sister yells up the stairs.

I, in fact, was getting freaky, or about to, with Jonas pinned under me, chained to my bed.

He snarls, "Ignore her."

"Now!" she yells.

"She will just keep yelling." I grin.

"Then we can be quick," he says, tugging on his chains to try and get to me.

"If I come up there and see some stuff that scars me, I'm blaming you. Come on, everyone is coming. It's a family meal like we used to have."

Well, shit, the guilt trip gets me moving as I ignore Jonas's complaints. He peers down at his hard cock sadly. "Sorry, little J, maybe later."

Laughing, I throw his pants at him and quickly unchain him before I slip into my loose shorts, a tank top, and a cardigan before walking downstairs to meet my sister. "Bad timing," I mutter.

She grins at me so widely, it makes me grin back. "I don't care, come on. When was the last time we had a family dinner together?"

Taking her hand, I follow her after. "Long time," I admit.

"Yep, well, we are having one, all of us."

I let her pull me into the formal dining room, where everyone else is already seated. The table has been laid with candles and fancy china and more food than even my guys can eat. They all grin as I sit with Ana to my right, Sam next to her, and Louis to my left. Jonas comes in with a groan, rearranging himself as he glares at my sister.

"Not the right way to get us to like you," he complains as he huffs and sits down, but then he spots the meal and claps like a kid. "Yay, chicken!"

Laughing, I watch Bert bring in more plates. "That is everything. I hope you enjoy."

"Uh-uh, sit down, Bert. You are family," I order.

He freezes at the door, searching our gazes. Louis instantly moves from my side, patting the empty seat. "Come on, she's right. You're family."

Tears form in his eyes, but he blinks them away as he carefully sits next to me. Grinning, I lay a napkin in his lap and start to dig in. He scans everyone, watching them laugh and talk before a soft smile curves his lips.

"You are correct. You are my family."

Squeezing his hand, I smile up at him. "You are ours and always have been. Thank you for taking care of us."

I feel him watching me as I eat, but I let him work through his emotions, knowing he needs to. The food is delicious, and the conversations flow. Everyone is having a good time. Sam tells everyone stories of his army days. The others chime in and all the while, he holds Ana's hand and keeps putting food on her plate.

I wink when I catch her blushing, and she flips me off, making me laugh.

It's honestly one of the best nights I've ever had. My entire family is in one place, and after taking down the amazing desserts Bert brings out, we all just lounge around the table, too full to move, and enjoy each other's company.

"Oh, I forgot. Something came for you earlier." Bert drops an expensive white envelope before me as he begins to clear the table with some of the guys' help. Frowning, I turn it over to see a red-wax seal. I rip it open, and a thick piece of cardstock drops out, clearly letting me see my father's handwriting.

Everything screeches to a halt inside of me as I stare at the note.

"Nova?" Isaac calls, noticing my silence, and everyone else turns to me.

"It's from my father," I murmur, and you could hear a pin drop at the sudden silence.

"What does it say?" Ana asks.

Swallowing, I pick it up, already feeling sick.

I don't want to read it, I really don't, but that won't solve anything. Being brave, I clear my throat and begin to read it out loud.

Dearest daughter,

For all of my wrongdoings, I have done something right. You. I watched you become the very thing I was aiming for, and now it's time to come home to me—where you belong, where you will only ever belong. Only I can understand you. The others are just holding you back. Think of all the things we can do, Novaleen. Ana was my control group and she has failed me. I no longer need her or the others.

Only you.
So come to me before it is too late.

Yours,
Father

Looking up, I see Ana wrapped tightly in Sam's arms like he can protect her from his words. Louis is already on his feet, and the others are coming towards me.

"It's a threat, a promise," I whisper, looking around. "If I don't go to him, he'll hurt you all."

"He won't be able to," Louis snaps. "You are not going to him."

"Maybe I should?" I suggest. "But not in the way he wants. We will all go to him to kill him."

"Did he say where?"

I shake my head and Louis sighs.

"Then it's moot at the moment. He thinks you can figure it out, though, so think hard, Nova. Meanwhile, I want patrols. Two of us need to be awake at all times, and no one is to go outside of the grounds alone. We watch each other's backs, stay close, and ride this out until we figure out our next move."

I nod, but my eyes go back to the note.

Before it's too late . . .

What is he planning to do?

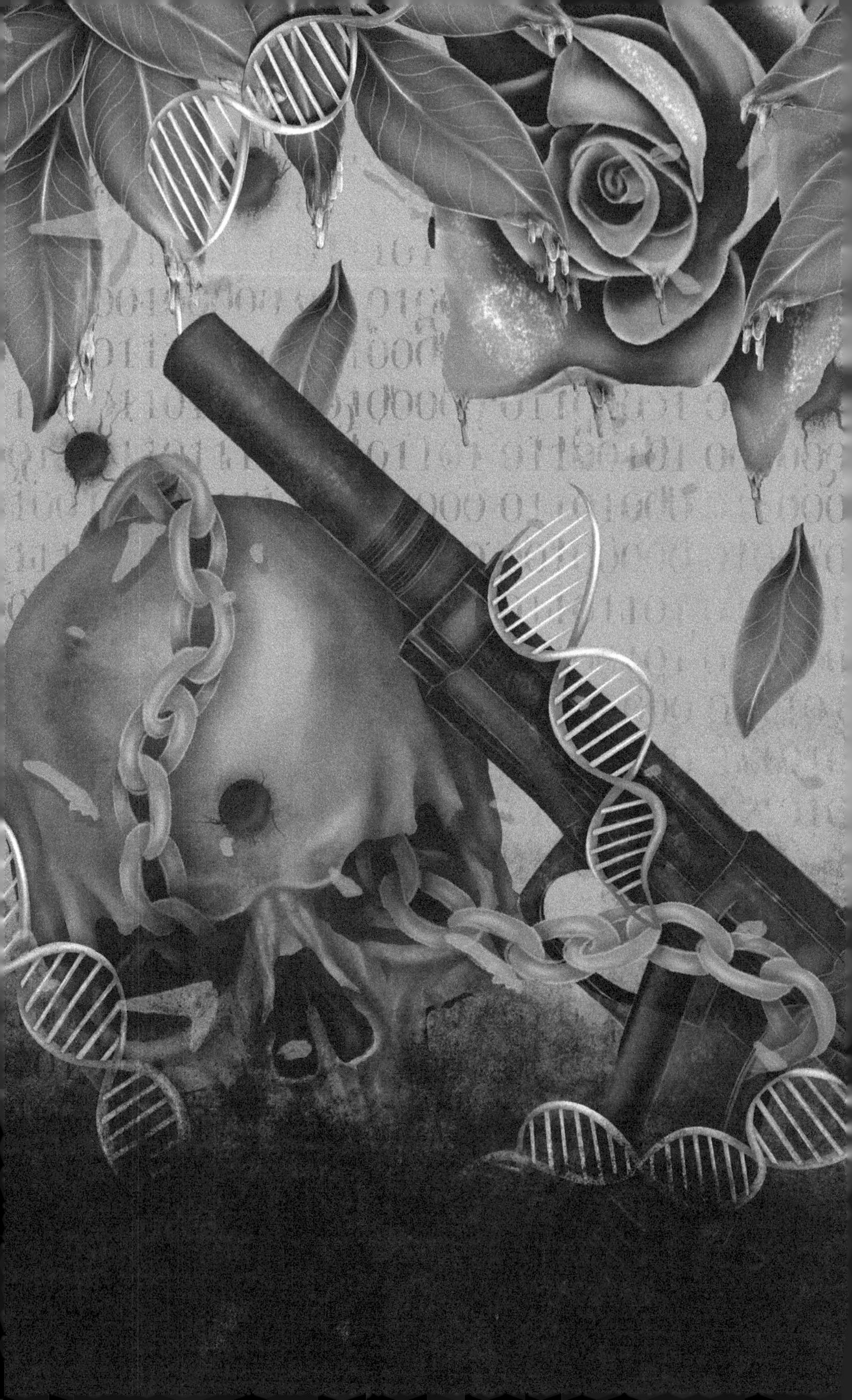

FIVE

My father's letter hangs over my head the entire day. I barely slept the night before, debating his meaning and trying to figure out where he is, but it's no use. Clearly, he thinks I can, but I'm drawing blanks.

Not only that, but he ruined the family meal we were having, the atmosphere becoming tense afterwards. All that laughter disappeared into stone-cold determination. We put the house on lockdown, and now we are taking turns to sleep and patrol.

I feel responsible. He wants me, while the others are merely in his way. I know how he thinks. He will hurt them to get to me, so I need to figure out his riddle before that happens, but my mind is blank, hence me beating up the punching bag.

I've been down here for a few hours, beating the shit out of this bag and taking my frustration out on it.

I did my patrols this morning, and after lunch, I came down here, and here is where I will stay until I can figure it out.

Sweat pours from me, my black plaited hair slapping my shoulders with my movements. I watch the others come and go, checking on me, before Nico stops the bag and jerks his head. Without a word, he takes a fighting stance, and we spar. There is no laughter, teasing, or flirting.

We don't hold back, trying to hurt each other. Both of us are annoyed, frustrated, and feeling useless, so we take it out on each other until he pins me with my leg thrown over his arm, his other arm banded across my throat as his lips tilt up in victory.

His dark eyes shine with triumph before desire sparks in his gaze, something neither of us will act on while so much hangs over our heads. "Better?" he asks as he releases my leg.

"Not really," I admit, closing my eyes as my head hits the mat. "I can't find him, Nico."

There's a sharp inhale. "Nova—"

"No, don't comfort me. I'm failing. He basically fucking spelled out his location and I can't find him! I can't even save my own fucking family or protect you."

"Shut the fuck up." His hand covers my mouth as my eyes snap open, filled with fury, and meet his own angry ones. "This is not just down to you. Even if you knew where he was, we wouldn't let you go. It's not on you to save the world, Nova. When will you realise that? Think it through. Your father loves to play games, and this is just another one. We were playing along unknowingly, and enough is enough. We don't play anymore. We break his fucking rules and play by our own."

"How?" I murmur against his palm.

"We change it up and do the unexpected. He wants us to find him and expects us to react to the threat, so instead, we'll lie low. We'll wait and watch, and when it's time, we'll kill the bastard. Stop putting the world on your shoulders and locking yourself down here. It's not good."

"It helps," I mutter.

Sitting up, he holds out his hand. "I know, but we worry." He smiles. "Plus, I'm sick of dealing with Jonas. It's your turn."

Laughing, I let him haul me up, and together, we go back upstairs. I have a new pep in my step. He's right. All this time, we were playing my father's game without even realising it, and I refuse to walk into another one. Instead, I'm going to play my own game.

He wants a perfect soldier? He'll get one.

It will be the last thing he sees.

Days pass the same way, filled with patrols and silence as we work hard to figure out the riddle. We are all determined to work through this. I try not to take it all on my shoulders like Nico said, but with each day that passes, the darkness inside of me grows.

I become restless from the sense of impending doom we all feel, and even Ana is affected.

She's been working around the clock, going through his notes with D and Louis. Nico, Jonas, Isaac, and I take most of the patrols, knowing they need as much time as possible to come up with answers. No more letters arrive, but the first sits proudly on the table.

It's a mocking reminder.

I'm lounging in my bedroom, debating what I could do to pass the time before I'm on patrol, when there's a knock at the door. It opens before I answer, and Jonas ducks inside, laughing to himself. I smile, knowing whatever he's up to will be trouble. Tilting my head, I watch him as he turns, and then my eyes drop to the object tied around his waist.

"Where the hell did you get a strap-on?" I demand as Jonas models it for me.

"Unimportant." He smirks. "The question is, do you want to play?" He wiggles his eyebrows as I continue to stare at him, a slow smirk curling my lips.

Getting to my knees on the bed, I crook my finger, and he walks up to me. "You want me to fuck you, Jonas?" I purr, dragging my hand up his chest and gripping his neck. His eyes flare, and his lips part in hunger as I tighten my grip. "Is that right, baby? You want me to shove this massive cock up your ass and fuck you with it?"

"Baby, I want you every way I can get you." He groans. "Ride me, use me, fuck me, claim me, do whatever the hell you want. I'm yours."

"Is that right?" I purr, leaning up until my face is level with his. "How about we test that out, shall we?" Dragging my lips along his, I bite the bottom one before falling back with my arms and legs spread. "First things first, we need that cock nice and wet, don't we, baby?"

The smile he gives me is wicked. "That we do, so be a good girl and come all over it for me. I want your cream in my ass while you fuck me."

"Make me," I taunt, tilting my chin up.

With a flick of his wrist, he produces a huge knife and advances on me. He presses one knee to the bed and with his eyes on me, he cuts through the thin material of the biker shorts I wear. I don't flinch, not once, and the heat in his eyes only grows. As he drags the sharp edge of the blade across my exposed stomach, I quiver under his lethal touch. My eyes drop to track the movements as it wiggles under the edge of my sports bra.

"I love it when you look at me like that, all needy and demanding." He groans. "I love it even more when you're all marked up for me." With a quick twist, he cuts my bra away, and it flutters to either side of me, freeing my breasts. Groaning, I arch my back, offering them to him.

My frustration turns into desire. It's what he wanted, and what we both need to keep us occupied.

The hard edge of the metal slaps one of my nipples, making my eyes close as I cry out. Desire surges through me as he teases my nipple into a stiff peak with the cold edge of the blade, only to do the same to the other.

"So pretty, so needy, you love this, don't you, baby? You love the threat. You love that you never know what I will do next."

"Yes." I groan, arching higher, begging wordlessly. My thighs clench together and rub for friction.

One of his hands delves between them and rips them open as he drops between my splayed thighs, the cool rubber of the cock pressing against my overheated, wet pussy. He lays it against me as he toys with me, the sharp edge of the knife circling my nipple.

His hips move slowly, nudging the strap-on across my pussy until the blunt edge hits my clit with each shallow thrust. Pleasure builds within me as my eyes snap open and meet his wild gaze.

Glancing down, I see the pink marks across my breasts from the knife, and I can't help but moan and reach for him, but he slaps my hands aside. "I'm playing, behave," he snarls, "or I'll turn you over and slam this cock into your ass instead."

Huffing, I drop my hands and roll my hips to grind against the fake cock, the rubber warming with my body until we find a quick rhythm. I hump it as he plays with my breasts, tweaking my nipples until they are sore and achy from the attention, but he still doesn't stop.

"Nova, baby, you're so goddamn beautiful. I love you like this, begging for me to make you come. You are all soft curves, hard edges, power, and muscle, and yet you are so pliant for me, wet and wanting. You're such a good girl when you want to come." He groans, moving faster as he winds me higher and higher.

"I fucking love you. I knew it the moment I saw you, but I fall harder each and every day. Our life is going to be like this, baby, with me coming to you with toys and you dripping to play with them. Fuck everyone else. Fuck normal. This is us, baby, and I'm loving it, so be a good girl and come for me so you can bend me over and I can feel you fuck me."

I writhe below him, jerking with my pleasure, and it causes the blade to slip. The quick slice across the top of my breast makes me scream as my release slams through me, leaving me gushing over the rubber cock. Jonas snarls, and while I'm still fighting the aftershocks, he shoves my thighs open farther and thrusts the fake cock inside me.

My hands scramble at the bed, gripping it as I try to move away, but his arms pin me in place as he starts to move, fucking me with the toy. I tilt my hips until it hits that spot inside of me that has me crying out wordlessly.

"Fuck, baby, look at you, taking these ten inches so well. You're getting it nice and wet for me. Goddamn, you're so beautiful. You love this, don't you? Love me fucking you with this dildo. Love coming all over it for me, knowing you're going to use it on me."

"Jonas," I purr, reaching up to grip his shoulders. Tearing at his shirt, I pull him down and slam our mouths together. He kisses me hard and wild, our tongues tangling. It's sloppy and delicious as he works between my thighs faster, deeper, and harder, making me lift my hips rapidly to keep up. The wet slap of our bodies is loud as he takes me, and the bed creaks with the force as he rips his mouth away. His lips are puffy and red from my attention, and his eyes are crazed as he slaps the knife across my heaving breasts. Groaning at the sight, he does it again and again. The sharp sting fades into a pleasurable burn, almost sending me over the edge once more.

It's only when I lift my leg and wrap it around his hips to take the strap-on deeper that he shows me he was only playing. His thrusts turn brutal, almost pushing me from the bed with the force. He snarls above me as he rains hits down on my breasts until it hurts too much and feels too good.

I scream his name as a release rolls through me, taking my senses with it until all I feel is pleasure.

When I come down from the high, I'm twitching and moaning beneath him. Leaning down, he laves my sore tits with his tongue before slowly pulling that huge fake cock from my body. Groaning at the almost painful feel, I lift up on shaky arms to see it dripping with my cum.

He slides his fist down it then drags it along my messy pussy with a moan. "Fuck, baby, you come so prettily for me."

"I love you too," I rasp as I push myself up, forcing my muscles into action even as my legs spasm from how hard I came. I tug him back down and kiss him as I roll my hips, sliding my pussy over the length to get it nice and wet. When I pull back, he's panting harder. "Now be a good boy and get on all fours for me. You wanted my cock, and now you'll get it. No safe words, no backing out. You'll take it and love it until you come so hard, they all come up here thinking I'm killing you."

"You better." He reaches behind himself and something clicks before the strap-on falls off, then he stands. With his eyes on me, he reaches back and rips his shirt off, exposing his exquisite chest. "Keep looking at me like that, baby, and I'll come before you're even inside me."

"We don't want that, do we? Pants too," I order.

He shoves his shorts down, his huge, hard cock springing free. Biting at his lip, he fists his length and strokes himself as he watches me.

Climbing onto shaky feet, I smack his hand away. "Uh-uh, the only way you get to come is with my cock in your ass, darling. Get on all fours now or I'll make you suck it instead."

He quickly drops to all fours, his perfect peachy ass pointed towards the door. Smirking, I quickly strap the cock on, liking how it feels. Moving towards him, I drop to my knees on the hardwood floor, ignoring the sting as I part his cheeks and rub the dripping head across his ass.

He jerks forward, so I grip a hip and pull him back. "Now I get what you mean. I love seeing you like this, begging for it and so easy to control. You want this cock inside you, babe?"

"Yes." He groans, his head falling to the floor as he pushes back. "Please fuck me, Nova."

"I didn't hear that," I tell him, dragging the cock across his ass as I reach down and palm his balls, rolling and squeezing them until he cries out. "Louder."

"Fuck me!" he snarls. "Please, baby, fuck my ass and make me come."

"Since you asked so nicely . . ." I release his hip and part his ass farther. "Now, just like you all say to me, relax and take it." I slowly start to push the huge, wet length in.

He jerks, trying to escape, but I pull him back and work his tight asshole around the length a couple of inches before pulling out.

"I promise it will feel good, babe. Just relax for me and take it."

"Shit, shit, shit." He relaxes slowly as I work it back in again, a few inches at a time, until I reach down and palm his cock. I stroke and squeeze it to the point of pain, just like he likes it, until he cries out, and then I slam the cock all the way inside him. My hips meet his ass as he shakes below me, his cock jerking in my hand.

"Not yet, baby," I coo, leaning down to kiss his back. "You're doing so well. It's all in. How does it feel?"

"Good, wrong, good." He groans. "Move, please fucking move."

Chuckling, I release his cock, grip his hips, and start to move. It is hard to find a rhythm at first, but when he starts pushing back, I get the hang of it. I pull out until just the tip is seated inside him, and then I slam back in as hard as I can. Each time I do it, he moans, and I see his precum dripping to the floor below as he fucks the cock, his arms and legs shaking.

He's already so close and I've barely started.

"You like it, baby?" I purr.

"Yes, there's a spot . . . Oh God, it feels so good."

I make sure to twist my hips and hit that spot that has him screaming and clawing at the wood.

There's a noise, and I turn to see the door opening. Isaac stands there, and his mouth drops open. With a confused chuckle, he starts to shut the door. "Nope," is all he says and then he's gone, so I focus back on Jonas, on fucking my lover.

Reaching down, I palm his cock and make a circle with my hand so he's fucking into it as I take his ass. He whines, his precum spilling over my fingers as I speed up. He screams, and his cock jerks in my grip as his cum shoots out, spilling over my fingers and onto the floor. I see his asshole clenching around the cock as he yells, still fucking into my hand and pushing back onto the cock until, suddenly, he stills.

"J, did I kill you?" I tease, but he doesn't reply.

Frowning, I pull the cock out slowly, hearing him moan, and then I flip him. His eyes are closed, his mouth is slack, and drool runs down his chin. His chest is heaving and covered in sweat, and his whole body shakes.

"Jonas!" I slap him, and his eyes slide open lazily.

"We are doing that again," he mutters with a full body shudder.

Laughing, I unclip the cock and crawl into his arms. He tries to wrap them around me but they fall back to the floor with a thump. Kissing over his racing heart, I lie beside him, just soaking in his warmth. "Sure thing, baby, you can take my cock anytime."

The distraction with Jonas only worked for so long before I found myself in the gym again, working my body to forget my anger and frustration.

Just like the last few days, I'm sparring with Nico, but today, we are both frustrated. We are all on high alert, and it is taking its toll. I'm snappy and I know it, and he's reacting to it, his hits coming harder and faster.

"Pay attention," he orders.

"I am," I retort.

"No, you're daydreaming," he growls.

"Asshole," I hiss as I slam my foot into his side. He blocks my second attack and spins me away.

"That's right, baby, I'm an asshole, an asshole who's kicking your ass. Come on, is that really all you got?" he mocks. "Want me to be blindfolded?" He covers his eyes and with a snarl, I throw myself at him. It is clear he was expecting an attack, but not like this, so he stumbles and falls back. Despite it, he quickly wraps his arms around me to stop me from hurting myself, and once we hit the mat, he flips us.

Gritting my teeth, I slap my hands out, but he quickly catches them and pins them above my head, his thighs holding mine down. Even as I buck and twist, I know it's useless. Nico is a powerhouse and he pinned me. His eyes are hard and hungry as he watches me fight him.

"Finished?" he asks when I slump.

"Never." My eyes narrow before I flip the switch. I won't win outright on strength, so I play dirty. Lifting my head, I slam my lips to his, swallowing his groan as our tongues tangle. My chest presses against his bare, sweaty one. For a moment, I forget my plan as desire courses through me, mixed with my anger, but his hands slowly loosen on mine and I wiggle them free. Sliding my palms across his shoulders, I rip my mouth away and twist us. My knees land on either side of his head, and I grin down at him, his hair mussed, his eyes tight, and his lips puffy from my attack.

"You got me, baby. Now what are you going to do to me?" His hands slide up my thighs, tugging me down until I'm almost sitting on his face. "I know, how about you sit that pretty pussy on my mouth? I'm fucking starving."

"Fuck you," I snap angrily, still fighting my emotions. I go to stand, but he sweeps my leg out and I tumble. My face hits the mat, and my arms are twisted into my back.

"You're too angry, too worked up. I think we need to work some of that frustration out," he mocks, grinding his cock into my ass. I can't help it. I push back even as I wriggle to try and get free of his hold.

"I'll fight you every step of the way," I growl.

His mouth meets my ear as he pins me once more. "Good. Fight me all you want, baby, but I'm still getting my cock deep inside this wet little pussy until you scream, and we both know it, so thrash, scream, and fight because it won't matter. You're mine, Nova."

"Asshole." I throw my shoulders back as he pulls away before I make contact.

"You love it." Keeping my hands pinned, he lifts up slightly and tears off my legging and knickers, tossing them aside so I'm bare below the waist. I manage to flip to my side, and he quickly turns me over and pins me once more, grinning down at me.

His huge erection tents his workout shorts, his tattoos stark against his tanned skin. His dark eyes remain locked on me as I lift him, wanting him badly, even as I'm angry at myself, at everything.

"There she is," he purrs. The sports bra I'm wearing has a front zip, and I narrow my eyes as he reaches for it. My hands are pinned under my back and his weight, so I kick out at him. He grunts as my foot hits his side, but he still unzips it, my breasts tumbling free under his hungry gaze.

Panting beneath him, I narrow my eyes on him. "Don't you dare—" I groan as he leans down and sucks my nipple into his mouth. He either doesn't notice or care as I fight him, sucking hard on it before popping his mouth free and blowing his warm breath across it. I fight the pleasure blooming inside me, the ache of my pussy, and my throbbing clit. I focus on my anger and he laughs against my skin as he turns his head and gives my other nipple the same treatment until they are both hard and aching.

With one hand, he pushes my breasts together and licks and sucks them both, leaving bites across them as my eyes close. I stop my fight as he presses his thigh against my bare pussy and rubs it back and forth.

"I wonder if I could make you come like this," he murmurs against my breast. "I think, considering that you're dripping on my leg, I could. Don't you, baby?"

"Shut up," I snap, and he hums, biting my nipple. I cry out, arching up without meaning to. The pleasure is too much, and he's right. I'm already on the verge of coming, which annoys me. He easily changed my feelings from frustration and anger to need and want.

"Good girl," he purrs. "Ride my thigh and make yourself feel good, and when you've come enough, I'll give you my cock and let you fuck out your tantrum."

"Bastard," I mutter as I roll my hips into his hard thigh, whimpering at the feeling. I'm going to do exactly that and love it. Nico and I have never really been alone to fuck, and I'm so excited and ready for that huge cock.

Frustration ebbs from me, turning to blazing desire as I roll my hips into his touch, chasing my release as he chuckles meanly. He edges and taunts me with what I want. "Say please, Nico, make me come."

"No," I grumble, and he stills, his mouth hovering over my breasts while his hand pins my hips so I can't even get the friction I need. "Nico," I whine.

"Say it, baby, or I'll leave you here naked and wet," he replies.

"Then I'll find one of the others," I retort, fighting again.

"No, you won't. I'll warn them. The only way you are going to come tonight, baby, and get a cock is with me. So, say please and be a good girl for once."

Smashing my head back, I try to move my hips again, but he has me well and truly pinned. He's just that fucking strong, and he waits patiently. Grinding my teeth, I blow out a breath. "Please, Nico, make me come," I mutter.

"Was that so hard, baby?" he purrs, sliding his lips over my nipple again. He pulls his knee away, and I go to shout at him when his hand covers my pussy. "Fuck, you're so goddamn wet for me, but you're going to need to come a few times to take my huge cock. I don't plan on fucking you softly, baby, so come for me." He slams two thick fingers into me and rubs my clit with his thumb.

I tumble over the edge with a scream.

"Good girl, keep going," he purrs. "That's it, milk my thick fingers and show me how good it's going to feel being buried deep inside you. Shit, baby, look at you, so goddamn pretty."

Groaning, I shake from the force of my release until it ebbs. I open my eyes and meet his dark gaze.

Grinning, he slides down my body. "If you behave and don't fight me, I'll lick this pretty pussy until you scream."

"Fine. Only because I want your tongue," I retort with a small grin. Chuckling, he presses my thighs wider and tosses them over his shoulders.

"Whatever you say, Nova," he murmurs, rubbing his nose up and down my wet pussy with a groan. "You smell so fucking good, baby. I can't wait to have you dripping down my throat."

"Then you better make me," I order, reaching down to grip his dark hair, tugging at the roots. He groans, and it vibrates through my pussy. Luckily, he doesn't taunt me this time because both of us are too needy now. His tongue lashes out, lapping at my pussy as he moans.

My head falls back and my eyes slide shut as I grind into his mouth, those two thick fingers working in and out of me before he adds a third. My moans reverberate around the gym as I lift my hips and grind into his face.

His other hand comes up and pins my stomach down for his attack as his tongue sweeps down and around my asshole before moving back up to my clit. "Nico," I whisper, riding the pleasure that's growing once more.

His tongue speeds up, lashing my clit as his fingers fuck me, sounding wet and loud in the gym. It's so fucking filthy, I groan. My heart skips a beat as I tumble over the edge once more, screaming my release as my thighs clamp around his head, keeping him against my pussy.

He licks me through it, keeping his fingers inside me until I relax. I push him away, my pussy oversensitive.

Sitting up, he pulls his fingers and mouth from my pussy and pushes his shorts down, fisting his hard cock. "Say thank you, Nico."

I narrow my gaze, and he smirks as he strokes his huge length, making me lick my lips hungrily.

"Say thank you, Nico, and you can have my cock like we both know you want."

I know he's serious, and my need for his huge length outweighs my pride. I'll beg if it gets me what I want. I need him inside of me so badly, it feels like I might die if I don't get him. "Thank you, Nico, now fuck me."

Shoving his shorts farther down, he strokes his cock as he crawls over me, his other hand grabbing both of mine and pinning them to the mat above me as he nudges my thighs wider. He rolls his hips to tease me, and I'm about to start shit when he presses to my entrance and slams into me.

I cry out his name as he slides all the way inside me. It hurts so fucking good, my eyes cross and my legs wrap around his hips to take him deeper.

"Baby." His head drops to mine as he starts to move with slow, rolling thrusts that have me gasping before he speeds up, his hips slapping into mine. Each time, he hits so deeply inside of me it hurts, but it's so good.

"Faster," I demand. "Harder." I need everything he can give me.

I manage to get my hands free, so I reach down and grip his ass to urge him on. He pushes them away, so I slap him hard. His head snaps to the side, and when he slowly swings it back to me, he's snarling.

Oh shit.

Flipping me onto all fours, he slams his hand down on my ass. "You want to act like a brat? I'll fuck you like one."

"Nico—" My response ends in a scream as he hammers into me, pushing me across the floor with the force, his hand slapping my ass again.

"You want to slap, baby? Then you'll get the same." He smacks me harder, making me clench around him.

"Please." I claw at the mats, pushing back. His hand comes down harder, and I know it will bruise. He fucks me hard and fast, hitting that spot inside of me that has me seeing stars, and then his hand comes down across my clit.

I scream as I explode, milking his cock for his release.

Groaning, he works through my fluttering pussy, fucking me as I pant. I collapse forward after the pleasure releases me, my pussy, ass, and tits aching.

Still recovering from the release, I remain boneless as he flips me again and slams back into my pussy. He hitches my leg up as his other hand pins my wrists above my head, keeping me restrained for his attack. He fucks me hard and fast, his teeth gritted and his veins bulging in his neck.

It's too much. I can't take it.

I feel him losing control, moving with wild, erratic thrusts, so I turn my hand and lace my fingers through his. "Nico, I love you," I say, and it sends him over the edge.

He roars his release as he spills inside of me, shoving his cock as deep as he can. It triggers me again, and I am close to blacking out as I clench around his huge, invading length.

When I can finally breathe and see again, I'm panting below him. He is breathing heavily and covered in sweat as he leans down and presses his lips to my forehead. "I love you too, Nova. Feeling better?"

"Much," I admit. "Thank you."

"Always, baby," he murmurs as he collapses, half on me and half next to me. "Just give me some time to recover."

I laugh, and we both groan at the feel of the vibrations. Closing my eyes, I wrap my arms around him and just hold him. My mind is quiet for the first time in a long time, so I soak up the peace, knowing the real world will invade soon.

But not yet, not here with us.

Sam is still healing, but he begins to train in the gym while I beat the shit out of the bags, growing angrier every day. He watches me with an impressed arch of his eyebrow, so I start to train with him. I have to take it easy since he's still seriously injured, but when he's tired or hurting, he sits out and watches, giving me pointers and refusing to leave me alone. I find that I don't hate it, however, since it distracts me from my eternal struggle.

Taking a break, I sip my water as I stretch out my muscles. He holds his side with a wince. "I hate being this weak."

"But you like Ana babying you," I tease, making him grin widely.

"That I do." He chuckles. "She's something else, your sister. She's . . ."

"Annoying." I laugh.

"Incredible," he adds. "I've never met such a strong, smart, sexy woman."

"You like her," I tease, nudging his foot, and he rolls his eyes.

"More than that. I don't know, it sounds crazy, but it's like I knew who she was to me when I met her. I think she feels the same too," he admits.

"It doesn't sound as crazy as dating six mostly crazy men," I reply, making him chuckle. "Ana has always known her own mind. She's already made her decision, but as her big sister, I have to warn you—if you hurt her, I'll kill you painfully, and we both know I can make that happen."

"I'd be disappointed if you didn't." He nods seriously. "But I have no intention of ever hurting her. It would be like cutting into my own chest. She's been my rock through this which reminds me. I better go check on her. She's been working too much and not eating."

"Whipped," I cough just as Isaac appears with a plate of food.

Sam eyes me. "You were saying?"

I kick him, and he laughs as he slowly climbs the stairs, holding his side.

Isaac comes over, handing me the plate of salad, cheese, and bread. "Just some snacks. It's been hours." He eyes me worriedly. "It's my turn to ask you if you're okay."

"I am now that you are here," I tease. Tugging him closer, I kiss him before melting into his chest. He wraps his arms around me tightly and holds me. "I'm scared," I admit softly.

"I'd be worried if you weren't," he replies, the vibration of his laughter causing me to shiver and hold him tighter. He pulls back and frames my face, searching my eyes. "Whatever happens, Nova, we do it together, okay? You're not in this alone. Tell me you understand."

"Together." I nod as he kisses me softly before deepening it. I moan, the plate falling to the floor as he reaches down and hoists me up. Desperation and need dance between our lips as I claw at his shoulders, but then there's a crack and the lights go out.

Isaac drops me to my feet, and we both sprint for the stairs. I've just reached the top, breathing heavily, when the sound of a crash comes again.

"Find the others, I'll bring Ana!" I yell at Isaac. Sliding down to the lab, I grab the knife I set on the table earlier. Trusting Isaac to check in, I peek around the lab. The house emergency lights flicker on, throwing us into a dim glow that's barely enough to see by but enough to clear the hallway.

There's another crash upstairs, followed by the sound of shattering windows, footsteps, and yelling.

I ignore it, trusting my guys, as I duck and roll into the lab. There's a scream when I come up swinging. Ana is huddled under the desk, clutching a book, tears streaming down her face. Covering her mouth, I cock my head to listen.

I was sure I heard something beyond her screams.

Creak.

It comes again.

I press my finger to her lips and she nods, sniffling. Leaning in, I kiss her forehead in reassurance and move silently to the door in a crouch, peeking around into the corridor beyond.

I watch as booted feet appear at the end, coming from upstairs. It's a tall man, and he has goggles and a mask on. Wearing all black, he holds a gun in his hands as he sweeps the entryway. The house is silent now, and I know my men will be hunting. They trust me to get Ana and myself to safety, just as I trust in them.

I watch as the man turns to the corridor and heads down it, his flashlight sweeping around.

Pressing my back to the wall, I wait and count his footsteps. I feel calm and prepared and very much in my element.

When the man walks past, I pounce. I slap one hand over his mouth and slam the knife into his jugular with the other before dragging him into the lab as he fights and screams. I wait until he stops moving and lower him softly to the floor. Glancing back at Ana, I hold out my hand. She drags her eyes from the body and scrambles towards me. I keep her behind me as I check the corridor and slide out, keeping her to the wall.

"Nova, who are these people?" she whispers. "Are we under attack?"

"Yes," I murmur, glancing around the entryway. They haven't breached the front door, which makes sense. Who walks straight into an enemy's lair? I'm betting they came through the upstairs windows, maybe even repelled down.

I hear a soft thud upstairs and nothing else.

"I don't know who they are, but I need to get you to a car before I return for the others."

"No, I won't leave you or Sam," she hisses, trying to push me. I slam her back to the wall and wait as I hear footsteps pounding across the landing. Once they are gone, I get in her face.

"We are all trained to handle this and you are not. Ana, I can't concentrate when you are in danger. I need to keep you safe so please, let me look after you."

She wipes at her face, glancing around. "No, we face this together. Give me a weapon. I'm not leaving you."

"Ana!" I hiss, but she snaps her hard gaze back to me.

"No, together. Weapon." She holds out her hand. A familiar gleam of determination enters her gaze, and I know it's pointless to fight her on this. We are only wasting time.

I hand her my only knife and tell her to wait there as I go back, grab the semiautomatic rifle the attacker was carrying, and check that it's loaded. When I return, I nod at her. "Stay behind me at all times," I order. "I mean it or you're out of here."

"Fine." She nods as I swing around the stairs and keep low, moving silently up the steps. I hear her breathing behind me but other than that, she controls her panic, her feet only making a soft slap on the stairs as she watches my back.

At the top, I crouch lower, putting my hand up to stop her, and swing my weapon each way, searching. When nothing jumps out, I move and press my back to the wall, tugging her with me.

Heading down the corridor, I check each room as I go. Nearly every window is broken, making it hard to guess how many men there are or where they are.

I don't like this, I don't like that Ana is here, and I definitely don't like that I can't see the others. I've just stepped past the doorway of a room I thought I'd cleared when a gun swings out, aiming for my face. I barely duck it in time, but when I jerk up, there's a knife embedded in the man's chest. I glance back to see Ana's shocked face.

"He was going to hurt you," she whispers.

Nodding, I slam my gun into his face, pluck the knife free, and hand it back to her. "You did good," I praise her.

I drag the body away and we keep moving, but at the next door, a hand wraps around my mouth and jerks me in. I slam my foot back, and I hear a grunt before I break free to see Jonas, his expression showing his annoyance.

"How many?" I hiss. "Where are the others?"

"I don't know. They pulled Nico and Louis through the window before I could get to them and dragged them away. Sam was trying to find anyone else, me too."

"Isaac?"

He shakes his head as Ana moves hesitantly into the room. He looks at me and I shrug. "She's helping. She saved me actually."

"Okay, they seem to be coming from this floor's windows. We'll work together, take them down, and find the others," he suggests.

"Sounds good." I lift my gun and grin. "You got a weapon?"

"Baby, I am the weapon." He smirks but shows me his pocket, which is filled with a knife and a . . . yup, a grenade. "Let's do this. Oh, and Ana, nice knife."

"Thanks," she squeaks.

"Make sure to keep it out of us," he offers softly, warning her. "I'll take the back, you take the middle, and Nova, you're in front. We work as a team. You're one of us now, kid." He ruffles her hair, and she smacks his hand away, smiling slightly, and I know that's why he did it.

I mouth, "Thank you," and then head to the door, needing to move and make sure the others are okay. Louis, Nico . . . God, I hope they are okay, but I know they would want me to keep moving, so I do. I focus on saving my family, on keeping them safe.

That's all that matters now. I should have trusted my instincts before and got us to safety, but that's moot. It's in the past, and all I can do now is keep moving forward and remind them why they should fear us.

They'll regret coming after us, and my father will regret standing against us.

He wants proof of the effectiveness of his experiments? Well, he'll get it tonight.

This house will be filled with screams and run red with blood like it did when I was a child.

I move down the corridor. In Ana's room, my trainer-covered feet crunch over glass, but beyond that sound, I hear breathing that isn't ours. Smirking, I turn and joke, "Clear," before heading to the door. Once there, I slam it shut and leap over the bed, slamming into the man crouched there.

He's out before he even saw me coming. Grabbing his gun, I toss it to Jonas, hearing him catch it, and then I tie up the bad guy before standing and opening the door again.

Ana is blinking and shaking her head. "I didn't even see you move," she whispers.

"Kind of the point, babe. Super soldier, remember?" I tease as we head out into the corridor again. Each room has more broken glass, and I can't help but think about how annoyed Bert will be when he sees it.

Bert . . . I hope he's okay. Hopefully, he's hiding in the pantry or something.

I have no time to worry, though, because as we approach the next door, I get a bad feeling and nod at Jonas. He moves me out of the way, flipping open a knife, and with a wicked grin, he stabs through the wood. There's a groan as the door swings open, and Jonas descends on the man like a wild beast. He beats the shit out of him before plucking his knife out and throwing it at a man sneaking through the window. Once there, he rushes to the window and looks out. "Ropes," he mutters as he tugs it down and throws it at me. I use it to tie both men together, taking perverse pleasure in their sixty-nine position. It will be a nice surprise when they wake up.

Chuckling, Jonas kisses me on his way by. "Good one, baby. Two more rooms."

I nod, and luckily, the next two rooms are clear, but there are more ropes, meaning there are more men somewhere. At the end of the hall, I gesture to the attic, and Ana and I crouch as Jonas sweeps it.

When he returns, he's brushing the cobwebs from his hair. "Nothing but spiders."

"Then they are downstairs," I grumble, throwing him a narrow-eyed look, "probably with the others. How about we switch up this game?"

He grins. "What do you have in mind?"

Dropping my gun, I nod to the side. When he sees what I'm looking at, he winks. "Fuck, you're a genius."

It's a tight squeeze as Jonas and I head down in the dumbwaiter first. Once there, we yank open the door and roll out into the kitchen. As we sweep it, we find the back door is open, and there are tracks leading out. They are probably checking the perimeter. Locking the door, we wedge a table before it to give us notice when someone tries to get back in.

A bang makes me spin to the cupboard next to me and yank it open. I find Bert hiding inside, a frying pan in his hand. "Miss Nova," he whispers gratefully, looking me over worriedly.

"Stay in there, okay? We are going to get them all."

"Miss Nova, I saw them take Isaac and Samuel past. I am sorry I couldn't stop them."

"Don't be sorry, but I need you to wait for Ana to come down here, okay? Keep her safe," I instruct him.

He nods seriously. "Of course, Miss Nova, be careful."

Jonas picks up a butcher's knife, and we move out of the kitchen, ready to sweep the rest of the downstairs and find our family.

Oh, and kill the bastards invading my fucking house.

SEVEN

The entryway is empty. Jonas and I sweep every nook and cranny and find . . . no one. There are no footsteps or people. Sharing a confused and slightly worried look, we head to the closed double doors of the living room.

As soon as I touch the wood, I know something is behind it. I shoot Jonas a look and he nods, lifting his gun higher to watch me. Taking a deep breath, I rip open the doors and roll inside in case anyone starts firing. I might be fast and strong, but a well-placed bullet could still take me down, and I don't plan on dying today.

Nobody is.

No one shoots, however, and when I jerk my head up, I freeze as fear pounds through me.

Dimitri, Louis, Nico, and Isaac are lined up in a row of chairs, tied up and gagged. Their eyes are wide, and Nico shoots fire at me with his gaze. Louis's expression is demanding, Isaac looks worried, and Dimitri seems sad. Jonas slides inside behind me and pulls out a knife, hurrying over to them as I climb to my feet and look around for Sam. I don't see him. I hope he got away.

I don't know how they captured my men, other than taking them by surprise and drugging them, which is possible since they look sluggish, not to mention the number of bodies in the house.

"Get them free, and let's get the others. We can regroup—"

I blame my own stupidity and shock.

Dumb, Nova, so fucking dumb.

"I'm afraid that won't be happening."

His voice is like a boulder, slamming me back to reality, and I actually gasp as I spin to see him. Every bad memory, nightmare, and moment I have thought of him pounds into me until I stagger back.

He is just a man, but the power he has over me is that of a god. Fear and pain return until I no longer feel like Nova, their Nova. Instead, I feel like that scared little Novaleen, staring at her father.

"Hello, Novaleen." He grins at me. Four masked men stand behind him, their guns aimed at us. "Sorry to drop by like this, but it is my house, after all."

"Father," I spit, finally finding my voice. "I would say it's good to see you, but I preferred you dead." I grin. "Not to worry, though, I can rectify that." I raise my gun, and he yanks something—no, not something, someone into view, holding them before him like a shield.

Ana.

Fear dawns on her face as she watches me, her eyes searching the room for Sam. Panic threads through me, but I try to mask it and come up with a solution that will get us all out of here alive.

"Uh-uh, we need to talk, Novaleen. Do not be so brash." He huffs, his eyes narrowed in displeasure as my hand with the gun hesitates.

"It's over," I spit and look Ana over. "Are you okay?"

"I'm fine, but Bert . . ." Sobs rack her body. "I think they killed him while he was trying to protect me."

I startle, resisting the urge to kill them all as I breathe through the grief of losing a man who was never supposed to be more than staff but took in two little girls and tried to make their miserable existences worth living. The gun wavers and falls as I stare at a shaking Ana.

"That's a good girl. Behave, Novaleen, or should I say Nova?" he spits. "Though I must say I much prefer your true name."

"Yeah, well, fuck what you prefer," I retort, feeling Jonas moving behind me.

"Tell him to stop, Nova, or I will kill her and the others." He grins, and the expression is slightly deranged, but the intensity in his eyes shakes me to my core.

"You won't kill your daughter," I hedge. No matter how much of a monster he is, Ana is still of his blood.

"Try me," he replies, and for a moment, we just stare at each other in a test of wills before my shoulders sag. I'm unable to put any of them at risk, least of all my sister. "Jonas, stop."

I hear him stop instantly. "Baby," he murmurs.

"Don't," I snap at him, glaring over my shoulder.

He nods in understanding. I will not risk my sister or my men, knowing how sadistic my father is. He would relish our pain. More than that, he would cause it to understand the aftermath then study us.

"You did this all to talk?" I gesture around. "Then talk."

He releases Ana, thrusting her towards me. I grab her hand and haul her behind me, but she stops at my side, gripping my fingers in support and fear. We are two sisters standing together against their father. His men stream into the room, taking up position, their weapons aimed at my men to make sure I do not go back on what I said.

"Look at you." His eyes move over me as mine move over him.

The sharp edge of panic and fear disappears the longer I'm in his presence. The projected version of the man from my childhood fades, and standing in his place is an older man. His hair is grey, short, and styled. His eyes are the same, sharp blue, but surrounding them are crow's feet that weren't there before. His lips have sagged slightly, and they are surrounded by lines. He's plumper than he was before, maybe stress eating, and his shoulders are slightly rounded as if from stress.

He looks older and weaker.

It just reminds me that he is nothing but a man, and something about his decaying appearance makes my chin tilt up as I face my maker—the man responsible for all of this. I always worried about how I would react, but I truly feel nothing except . . . pity for him.

"Look at you. You're older, a lot older. You look weak." I see him flinch and know I've landed a hit. For all his research, all his gifts, he cannot stop himself from aging.

"And you, you look stronger every time I see you. You are impeccable, everything I imagined and more. I cannot wait to see what is going on in your body." His eyes go far away for a moment. "Though you are surrounding yourself with . . . strange company."

I ignore that, unwilling to let him land any more blows, even as I search for a way out of this, inching us back to my men. "I feel sorry for you," I comment, trying to distract him as I tug Ana with me.

"For me?" He laughs.

"Yes, for you. All these years, you wasted your life on research that even your own government has turned its back on. You have no one to trust, no one to share it with. You are completely alone. These people follow you out of fear or obligation, nothing more. Everything you have done will be for nothing. No one will remember you, and no one will mourn you. You will simply disappear like specks of dust in the light."

"Oh, that's where you are wrong, Novaleen." He grins, and alarm bells sound in my head. That smile would appear right before he would do something so horrible, I cannot even think about them. "They will remember you. They will remember I made you, created you, and changed everything. And you? You're the key to that."

"I will never help you," I snap. "This is my family. This is where I stand. You'll have to kill me."

"Never." He shrugs. "I need you, like you pointed out; however, I don't need them."

Fear stabs through me, but I tilt my head back at his bluff.

"You won't turn us against each other. We stand together," I snap, squeezing Ana's hand.

One sister who just wanted to heal the world and the other who wanted to watch it burn are finally united and standing together.

Father sees it, and with a cruel grin that sends shudders down my spine, he looks to Ana. "Look at you, Ana. You are incredible. I have been following your research. It is very good, but think of everything you could do. Join me and help me finish my research, and we can change the world. We can help those who need it, heal them, and make them better so no one ever has to suffer again." It's a lie, but he's appealing to her soft caring side and he knows it.

For a moment, I panic, thinking she will try to help him simply to defuse the situation or protect me, until she looks up with a determined expression. I realise the days when Ana trusted or would help our father are long gone.

"Never. I'll never help you. You are nothing but a psychopath who craves power and fame. You split us once, but it won't happen again. I'm with Nova every step of the way."

Pride fills me as I stare down at my little sister.

"Then you are useless to me," he spits.

I see it too late.

For all my training, for all my strength and abilities, I'm too fucking late.

The gun flashes in the dark living room, and I watch in slow motion as the bullet heads for Ana. I throw myself towards her, but when she screams, I know I'm too late.

Too fucking late.

Too fucking slow.

We slam to the floor, where I cover her with my body as Jonas lunges at my father. A scream escapes my lips when one of the men slams their gun into his head and he collapses in a heap. Lifting up, I meet Ana's gaze as she blinks rapidly.

She's alive.

"You're okay," I whisper, cupping her clammy cheeks. My mind screeches to a halt, my heart frozen. "You're okay."

"Nova?" she whispers raggedly. "I'm cold."

"No, no, you're fine," I promise as I sit back, but everything freezes inside me when I see the bloody state of her stomach. There is a large hole in her clothes and skin. Pressing my hands to it, I feel tears dripping from my eyes. "You are okay," I tell her as I apply more pressure, making her whimper. I lift my head, searching for something. Anything.

"Help me!" I scream at my father.

"Nova," Ana whispers, her body shaking underneath me.

"Fucking help me!" I beg him as he stares at us. "She's your daughter!"

"She's useless to me," is all he says.

"No, no, no," I say. "I'll do anything, please, please fucking save her. Please don't take her from me, not now. I just got her back. Please!"

"Nova." Ana's voice is firmer. I swing my head down to see her smiling shakily. "I love you."

"Don't you dare say goodbye," I snap. "I can save you. I can—"

"Nova." She reaches up with a bloodied, shaking hand and cups my cheek. "You can't save everyone."

"I can save you," I protest, lifting my hands and whimpering at the blood pooling around the wound. I turn my head to see Isaac fighting in his restraints. "Tell me how!" I tell him.

"Nova, stop it," Ana demands, a wheezy breath rattling her lungs. "It's okay. I love you, please know that. I'm okay with dying to protect you. Tell Sam . . . Tell him I love him too," she pleads as I hang my head, sobs racking my body. For all my power and all my strength, I'm lost and useless in this moment.

"Tell me how to save you," I whisper to her.

"You can't. It tore something important. Even if you operated now, it would be too late," she admits with a cough, wincing in pain. "I don't fear death, Nova. You taught me that, but please don't let this break you."

"I can't lose you. I just got you back," I sob, lifting her into my arms. She's so fragile and pale.

"You'll never lose me," she whispers, blinking rapidly as her face pales even further.

"Don't you fucking dare close your eyes. Stay with me. Please, stay with me." My tears drip into her face, mingling with her own as her body shuts down.

I know the signs.

"Sorry . . . Love . . . you," she gurgles, struggling to breathe.

"I love you. I love you so much, Annie," I croak, holding her tighter and rocking her in my arms. Her blood covers us both.

I wish I could say it was quick, but she struggles to breathe before her body gives out. All the while, I plead to a god I don't believe in not to take her. I feel the moment she dies, the moment she lets go, her hand dropping between us as her head falls back.

I rock her back and forth, singing to her like I did when she was a child. When the song ends, I squeeze my eyes closed. "No, it's not real. Please, please, don't leave me all alone. Please don't leave me, Annie."

"Nova, it is time to go or I will kill the rest," Father snaps, tired of me.

I drop my head back on a ragged scream, then I gently lay her down, brushing her hair from her face as I position her arms and legs so they are straight. "I'm so sorry, Annie. I'm so very sorry. I love you so fucking much." Leaning down, I press my trembling lips to her forehead, my tears splashing into her unseeing eyes. "I will make this right," I tell her softly before turning away.

Blinking through tears, I turn my head to my father, no longer scared. I feel empty and cold. "You're a dead man walking."

He opens his mouth to respond when there's a roar and a body flies into him, smashing him to the side. Sam scrambles to his feet, his chest heaving and blood coating his head, but then he spots Ana.

"Ana, no!" he croaks, stumbling towards her. He falls to his knees next to her unmoving body, and I choke on my tears as I watch. "No, baby, wake up. Look at me!" He slaps her face before looking up at me. "Why aren't you doing anything? Save her!"

"I'm sorry," I sob.

"No, no, you're okay. You're okay, baby." He pulls her into his arms, kissing her face as I cry. "Please, baby, I just found you. Please, don't let me lose anyone else."

"Sam," I murmur, reaching for him.

He screams and pulls her away from everyone as I stumble to my feet, his back bowed as he cries, trying to get her to wake up.

Everything in me is cold and broken at the same time.

It's as if I can't breathe and I'm swimming underwater.

I can see my guys fighting to get to me. I see my father raising the gun again and hear a shot go off. It hits Sam, but he doesn't move except for a flinch and a yell. He shoots again.

Four more bullets are shot until Sam slumps over Ana, their blood mingling together, and I still can't move.

A girl bound to heal, a soldier bound to die, I think idly.

My eyes are locked on their bodies. Someone screams my name, but I don't move as the soldiers board the windows and something starts pumping into the room to knock us out.

Let them kill me.

What is the point of living without her?

I look at Sam and for a moment, fresh agony spills through me before it, too, is swallowed up.

My grief is not loud like his.

It is silent, deadly, and cold.

"It's time to go, Nova." Father holds his hand out to me. He took her from me. "I'll kill them, Nova."

That's what jerks me back to reality.

"If I go with you, you'll leave them alone?" My voice sounds strange, even to my own ears.

"Yes," he promises. "I never needed them, only you. They are failures. I will let them live if you'll come with me now."

For a moment, my eyes go back to Ana's unseeing ones. "No more death, not for me," I whisper as I turn. I can't bring myself to meet their gazes.

Nico roars behind his gag, his chair creaking with his struggles. Louis pleads with me, his eyes darting around as he tries to look for a plan. Dimitri is silent, watching me with understanding. He is the only other person who has felt my grief. Isaac cries as he reaches for me. Jonas, still slumped on the floor, remains silent.

Six men who love me and would give anything for me.

They would die for me.

"No more death," I tell them as I step back to my father. "No more."

Turning away, I put my hand in his as he grins down at me. "We are going to do great things, Novaleen."

At the threshold, I look back, meeting their eyes. "I love you. I love you all. I can't watch anyone else—" For a moment, emotions slam through me before I lock them away. "Stay alive." With that, I let my father lead me from the house in a daze, and when he injects me in the car and knocks me out, I welcome the oblivion, drowning in the darkness and hoping I never wake up.

My eyes start to water, and my body tries to give into the toxins being pumped into the room, but I refuse. I fight against them to get to her.

I am so fucking angry at her, I want to tan her hide raw for sacrificing herself for us. I know why she did it . . .

Nova. I hear the engines as they speed away.

Fuck! I rock harder, trying to break the chair, when I hear a cough. Jerking my head up, I see Bert opening the front door. He stumbles into the living room, batting away the smoke and shoving open the windows to clear it. When he sees us, he squints, his eyes watering too.

His mouth is twisted in agony, and his hand is pressed to his chest where he's bleeding. He's pale and clearly in danger, yet he heads towards us. "Nova?" he croaks.

I try to shout and warn him, but I can't, and he stumbles over Ana and Sam.

Falling to his ass, he sees the bodies and screams before covering his lips with his hand.

I shout his name, trying to get his attention. With each second that passes, they take Nova farther away, but his eyes are locked on Ana as he cries. "Ana . . . Oh, God." Turning his head, he throws up.

Somehow, I manage to work the gag down. "Get us free!" I roar. "Nova!"

Nodding, he crawls to us as he cries, grabbing a knife from my boot and slicing my bonds. After, he moves back to Ana, stroking her face. I leave him there as I cut the others free, all of us rushing out the front door to go after our love.

Our girl.

However, our cars are destroyed.

"No!" Jonas roars, going to run, but I grab him.

"Don't," I snap. "We need a plan."

"No—"

"We will get her back!" I yell at him. "Isaac, get Bert and check him over. Everyone else, clear the building now!" I see them hesitate, and I turn on them. "Now!" I roar, and they rush inside as I turn to stare at the drive-way. "We're coming, Nova, I promise."

"I failed her," Bert whispers, his sad eyes focused far away. "I failed Miss Nova, and I failed Miss Ana."

"You got us free so we can rescue her."

"Ana is dead. I should have protected her better. I should have protected them both better."

"We do not have time for regrets," Jonas snarls.

"Jo—" Isaac starts, but he shakes his head.

"We don't! Each moment we waste puts him that much farther away from us. Regrets don't change what happened, only actions do."

"He's right," Bert murmurs. "Go get her and bring her home."

"How the fuck do we do that? We have no cars."

"There's one in the garage." Bert sits up, wincing in pain. "Bring Nova back. I will not lose them both."

"You need blood and surgery," Isaac begins.

"I need my girls!" he snaps, angrier than I've ever seen him. "Screw me. Leave me to die and go get her. That's an order."

"Isaac, stay with him," I demand.

"No." He stands. "I'm going too."

"I need you to keep him alive," I implore. "Nova loves him. She can't . . . I won't let her lose anyone else."

The weight of my failure sits heavily on my shoulders, but I push through it, knowing I need to be smart. They need answers and a leader. They need me, so I don't break, not yet.

Nodding, Isaac sits back down.

"Everyone else, grab your weapons. Let's get our girl."

Storming from the room, I load up. Dimitri pulls the SUV around front, where we all hop in.

"Which direction?" Dimitri asks nervously.

"Drive," is all I say, because honestly, I don't know. I need to think.

Where would he take her?

It can't be close. He'd want her far away from us just in case. "Airport," I mutter. "The son of a bitch will either take her to a boat, which is too far away, or a private jet. Clearly, he's moving around with them, so get us to the airport."

"Step on it," Nico growls, the only words he has spoken.

"Louis," Dimitri whispers, sharing a look with me as he guns it.

"Don't. We are getting her back," I snap at him. "Now focus on driving."

We are all alert, watching the road as he drives like a madman, covering the distance in half the time we did last time. Leaping from the car, we sprint through the building, only to see a plane taking off with a car parked before a hangar. I hurry over and search inside, freezing when I see a note on the seat.

I unfold it, only to realise it belongs to Nova.

I miss you—Nova.

"She was here." Slamming the door closed, I look at the plane. "She's on there."

"Fuck!" Nico roars, punching his fist into the car before whirling on Dimitri. He grabs him and slams him into it too. "Work your fucking magic. Track her!"

"I need my laptop."

"Nova," Nico roars.

"Nico!" I demand. "We need to calm down. We need a plan."

"Fuck your plans!" Jonas hisses, clenching and unclenching his hands. "Look where it got us."

I slam my fist into his face before he can react, and everyone freezes. "I am just as lost as you," I tell them honestly. "I am just as scared and panicked, but right now, Nova needs us, and acting like buffoons will not help. Instead of fighting each other, we need to work together to bring her back. We will find her," I promise. "We will bring her home, but right now, we need to take care of Bert, look at Jonas's head, regroup, and come up with a foolproof plan to get our girl back."

"And then?" Dimitri asks.

"Then we kill her father."

My heart hurts.

I've lost the only woman I have ever loved, and more than that, I couldn't even save her sister for her. The one time she actually needed me, I couldn't do anything, but I can save Bert for her. I can and I will. I refuse to let another person she loves die.

It's the least I can do.

He's knocked out at the moment. Luckily, he didn't need surgery, but it's going to take a long time for him to heal. He's had two blood transfusions, and I'll keep him sedated for a while to make sure he doesn't spring up and hurt himself more.

Scrubbing my hands of the blood, I hang my head as tears fill my eyes.

Her screams echo in my brain.

God, I saw the moment she broke and actually felt it in my soul. Tied to the chair, I could do nothing but watch the love of my life lose everything, shut down, and give up. I hated the defeated expression she wore. I hated the fact that she was struggling to even breathe and talk.

Even then, though, she protected us and made a deal to keep us alive.

She should have let him kill us because living without her is not possible.

The only thing that is worse is knowing she's out there somewhere, all alone and hurting. I failed her. I failed them all. I should have seen this coming when they knocked me out, but I did nothing. I let Bert get hurt. I let them kill the sister of the woman I want to spend the rest of my life with, and then I let her leave.

That moment haunts me as I finally break. Sobs rack my body as I remember the dead look in her eyes as Ana's blood coated her cheek and hands.

She looked weak and raw—not words I would ever use to describe Nova.

Now, she's with him, the man willing to kill one daughter and hurt the other, and she's all alone and hurting. Yet here I am, feeling sorry for myself. I smash my fist into the wall, and the throb of pain cuts through my self-pity.

It feels good, so I do it again and again.

Even as my knuckles split and my bones crack, I keep on hitting the wall, letting it all out until I fall to my ass, cradling my broken hand. My heart hurts as I pray the others have found her and that they are coping better than I am.

Usually, I'm the one in control, helping and containing them, but not now.

Not this time. I cannot even think clearly.

When they come back empty-handed, I know we failed. One look at their heartbroken expressions and I know we've lost her.

"He took her on a plane," Dimitri says where we stand in the foyer, covered in blood. "We will find her. I'm going to right now." He rushes away, no doubt heading to his laptop. I turn to track him when my eyes catch on Ana's and Sam's bodies curled around one another.

Sharp, piercing agony rips through my chest for everything my girl has lost.

"We should bury Ana," I whisper. "It's not right that she's lying there. We should put her to rest and give her peace. Nova would want that and a place where she can go to see her sister."

"We will," Louis replies softly. "We'll bury them both."

"Together. They'd like that, I think," I say.

"Together." He squeezes my hand.

NICO

I need to keep it together for the others because they are falling apart. Guilt, agony, and stress wreck them. I have to be strong.

Jonas and I dig the graves. We picked a spot under a big apple tree we think Nova would like. I take Ana into my arms and carefully carry her over as Jonas holds Sam. Bert drags himself out front as we bury them, knowing we can't call the police or offer them a proper burial without drawing too much attention to ourselves.

We can do this, however, for our girl.

Once they are in the ground, we silently cover them up, and then Bert clears his throat. "We should say something." Tears stream steadily down his face as he stares at the side-by-side graves.

"Miss Ana . . . She was a force to be reckoned with. She was kind, funny, and very talented. When she was a kid, she would come up with the most profound things, and I knew she was going to change the world." He hiccups but straightens with purpose. "She saved me, an old man with nothing to live for. Those two girls became my world. I watched her grow into an incredible woman who was so kind, generous, smart, and determined, but she was aching. She missed her sister. I never saw her happier than when she got Miss Nova back. They were always destined to be at each other's side. Without her, there will be a hole. I'm so glad I got to see you grow up, Miss Ana, and fall in love and stand for what you believe in. I'm so very proud of you. I have loved you since the moment you took my hand and declared us friends when you were four years old, and I will love you until the moment I lie in the ground at your side. I will find your sister, our Nova, and I will bring her home. I will uphold your dying wish. I hope that in the next life, you find the peace and happiness you deserve with Sam, Miss Ana, and now I will wait for the day when I pass on and into your waiting arms."

I know we all wear matching expressions of pain. We barely knew Ana, but we know how much Nova loved her. Stepping forward, I clear my throat. I hate speaking, I hate being vulnerable, but for my girl, I will. She can't be here to offer peace to her sister, so I will do it for her, and when she comes home, she can say her goodbyes and I will be there to catch her.

"Nova loved Ana more than anything in the world. Everything she ever did was for her sister, to keep her safe and give her a chance at a normal life. I never knew what true love was until I saw them together."

Bert starts to sob, and Jonas catches him, holding him as he cries.

"I will never forgive myself for failing you, Ana, or your sister, but your death will not be in vain. I promise you that. We will make them pay, and I will spend the rest of my life trying to heal your sister's broken heart with every ounce of love inside me. We can never fill the hole you have left, but we will keep her happy and loved until you two meet again."

"The world is a cruel place," Dimitri says. "I hope now you have peace. If you can hear me, find a man named Bas. He will love and protect you, and when our time comes, we will meet you both on the other side."

"Love lives on in those who love you, who outlive you. I know Nova will never let your love or your life fade, Ana," Isaac adds softly.

Jonas nods. "I'm sorry we couldn't save you, but we will save her."

"Together," Louis adds.

We stand around her grave, each saying our goodbyes and offering her our hopes and apologies until, with a wince, Bert gently lays a flower on each of the graves. "I will stay here with you until the very end," he vows, and then he lets Jonas lead him back to the house.

"We need to find her," I say as I watch them go. "We all know what he's doing to her right this moment." I focus on Dimitri. "Find her." I stomp off, needing a moment to hide the tears in my eyes, the horror in my soul, and the fear that I have lost the love of my life.

TEN

I wake up slowly, feeling groggy. Every inch of my body hurts, but it's the pain in my soul that has me crying out. Once, where my sister existed, there is nothing. She was ripped away, and the pain is so acute, I pass out again.

I'm dying from a broken heart.

She's gone.

I drift between consciousness and sleep, struggling with the pain.

She's gone, and I don't want to wake up again. I don't want to live in a world without her. Out of all the things my father has done, he finally did what he always wanted—he broke me.

I would gladly beg and give everything I have to get her back. All the pain I endured as a child was to protect her, and now she's gone, and it was all for nothing. We changed nothing, and we saved no one.

She's gone.

I can almost hear her laughter here and feel her chasing me through the woods. I want to stay here forever with her in this place where she exists, where she didn't die for me. We are happy here, and we have a normal life.

The world doesn't give a fuck about my pain, though, so it drags me back, kicking and screaming. I wake with a gasp, jerking upright before struggling against something binding me. Panic slithers through me as I twist and turn blindly, fighting whatever it is.

"You are going to hurt yourself if you do not calm down."

Lights blare to life, and it's then that I realise I'm strapped to an operating table. The room is sterile, half empty, and clinical, and my father stands at the door. He watches me with an impassive expression as he wanders over.

"You killed her," I whisper.

"She was useless to me. Let that be a reminder, Nova. Do not become the same. If you want to live, then do as I say and we won't have a problem, little girl." The smile he gives me is pure evil.

"Did you ever love us? We were your children," I ask numbly.

He hesitates, his gaze going far away. "I suppose I did, in a detached sort of way. I loved the attention you brought me, the normality, the cover, and the accolades. Is that the same thing? I suppose not. I always knew I was not capable of such emotions. They are a hindrance, after all, but if it makes you feel better, Nova, I will miss Ana. She had a very capable brain."

"She was your daughter!" I scream at him.

He watches me struggle against my restraints with a patient and cold expression. "And now she is dead. It is a pity. Had I known the strength of your attachment, I would have kept her alive to make you more . . . compliant. Nevertheless, we will find a way."

"Fuck you! I will kill you all!" I scream, the numbness morphing into pure fury for a moment.

"I hope you keep your fight because it's most entertaining," is all he says. "Now, shall we carry on where we left off?" He picks up a collar, and I close my eyes in horror.

I'm dragged, limp and covered in my own blood and vomit, down the white tiled corridor. It's dark and when we step through each section, bright overhead lights flicker on. I cannot even lift my head, legs, and arms as I hang between two men who haul me over to a door, grunting as they open it.

Every part of me hurts just as much as my soul aches. I deserve it, and it almost takes away from losing her. I wish I passed out, but I didn't. I felt every incision and test he ran on me. I felt it all, and now I'm suffering from my father's cruel touch.

The door beeps and unlocks, and they drag me in, dumping me unceremoniously onto a single cot screwed to the back wall. The room is small, barely enough to walk in, with just a bed, the door, and another door to the left, which is open to reveal a small bathroom. A camera blinks its red light in the corner, pointing at me.

"I don't understand the fascination. She broke as easily as the others," one says with a laugh as they step out. The door slams shut with a click, letting me know it's locked, and then the lights go out, plunging me into darkness where I can finally break.

I bet they are listening, so I cry silently, tears tracking down my face as I turn and bury my head against the wall. Grief and agony rock through my body as I drag my legs to my chest and bury my head in my knees as I shake and cry.

I don't even know if the guys are alive or if they are okay, and the thought sends my heart plummeting to my stomach. What if he killed them? What if they are all gone?

What if I'm all alone in the world once again?

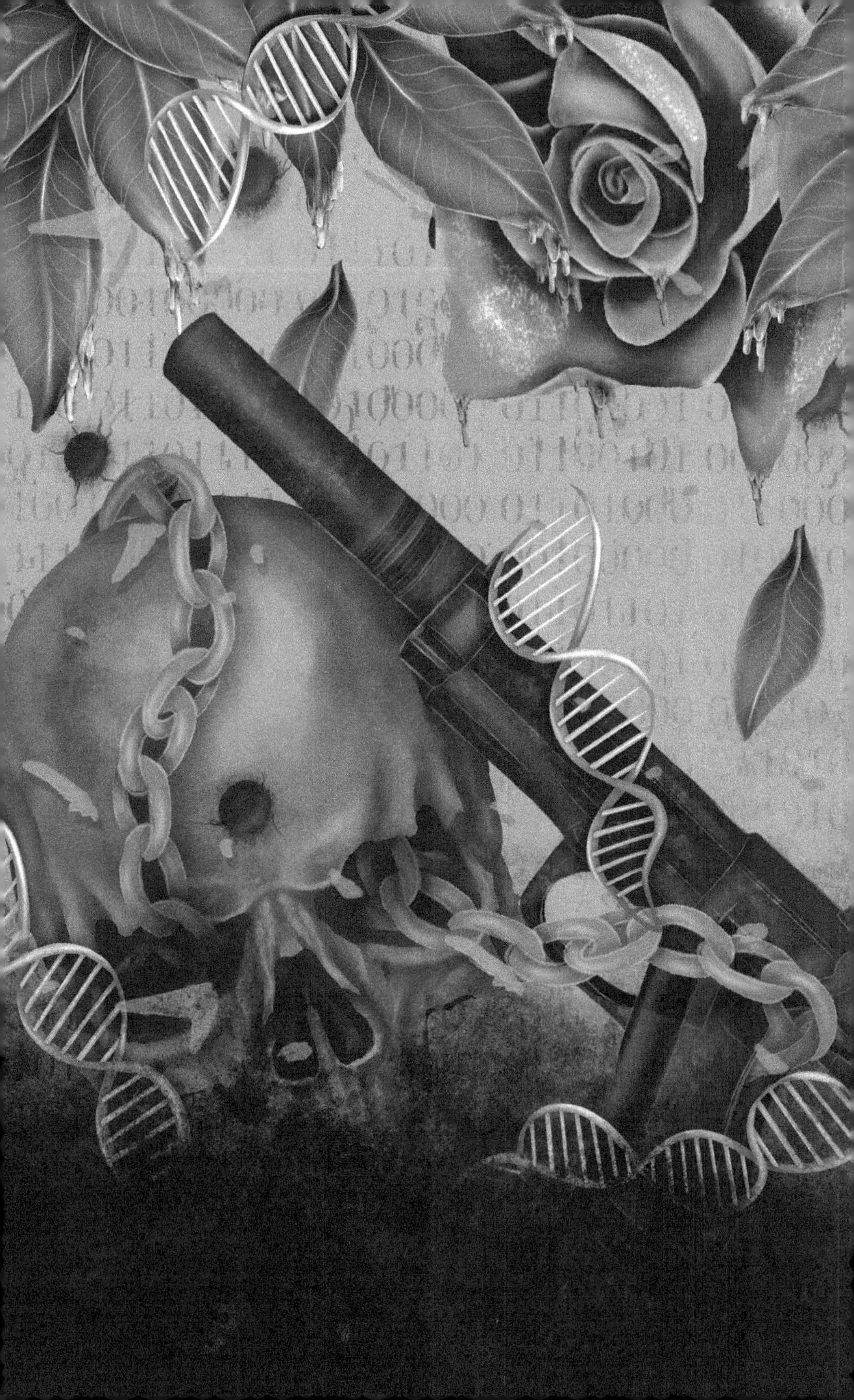

ELEVEN

The plane isn't registered, but to take off or land, even on a private airstrip, they have to let somebody know. It will take some searching, but I'm confident I will find where they are flying to. I just hope it's in time.

I don't sleep or eat.

I leave the others to clean the house so Bert will rest. They want it to be perfect for when she comes home. Jonas even makes him pancakes. They are all confident in my abilities to find her, even when I'm not. If I find where she flew out to, they could have travelled again, yet I know I have to find her. The look she gave us when she left haunts me, and it's all I see.

I can't lose her, not like I lost Bas.

I refuse to let another person I love drift away when I can stop it. I know the pressure is mounting on me, but I keep moving. I have four computers open, working at all times. One scans any international data with her photograph, looking for her, the second looks for her passport— which is a long shot but worth trying—and a third searches for her father's.

"Anything?" Jonas demands from behind me.

I ignore him, using the fourth computer to search through the data of all incoming flights today.

"Dimitri, anything?" he snaps.

"Not fucking yet!" I spin. "Just fuck off and let me work. I'm trying my best."

"Hey, we know you are." He moves over, crouching before me and taking my hand. "We know. This isn't all down to you."

"I have to find her," I murmur, dropping my gaze to the floor in shame. "I have to. I couldn't save him, but I can save her. I can. I will."

"We will," Jonas promises. "This isn't like Bas. Nova will fight to get back to us. She's so strong, stronger than any of us. We have to trust in that just like she has to trust in us right now to find her, but blaming yourself will not accomplish that, okay? So focus, find her, and give me a fucking target to destroy because right now, I'm fucking useless and I hate it."

"Scan the bodies." I jerk my head up. "If we can find out who they are, we can trace their payments back to the source and we might just find her."

"Got it, I'll do that." He stands. "You good?"

I nod, even though we both know it's a lie. "We're going to get her back," I murmur.

"We are, and when we do, we'll burn the fucking world for her."

JONAS

I feel useless as I pace near the front door. All the bodies have been checked, and we are running their IDs to see if we can find any links. We are tugging at every thread, unravelling the game he has set before us so we can find our girl, yet there is nothing more I can do. There is nothing I can shoot and nobody I can fight. I'm stuck waiting while my girl gets farther and farther away.

It's clear we are all feeling the pressure. Isaac is working around the clock to get Bert fixed and back to health, as if making sure he's absolutely fine will bring her back. Louis is on the phone with every military contact he can think of, screaming at them. Seeing him lose control really hammers home just how fucked we are.

Nico is in the gym, beating the shit out of the equipment to stop himself from going on a killing spree, and Dimitri? He's barely slept or moved, his eyes are bloodshot, his clothes are rumpled and stained, and he hasn't moved away from the computers since the moment he woke up.

And me? I'm standing guard, as if they will come back. I know they won't. He doesn't want us. No, he wants her—the only experiment to succeed. He wants his daughter and what her mind holds, and the idea of what they could be doing to her right now makes me feral.

I'm like a wild animal, but the only person who is able to soothe me is gone.

They have backed us into a corner, but don't they know that only makes us more dangerous? After all, we have something to fight for now, which we never did before—our family, our heart, our reason to live.

I remind myself that she's survived his treatments before as I pace, ragging at my hair. She's survived so much pain at his hands. We promised her she would never be taken again, but we broke that promise. I hate it, and I hate that she's alone again. I hate that she's hurting, grieving, and in agony, and we aren't there to hold her.

I need my Nova, and if I have to kill every single person who gets in my way to get her back, I will, and when I find her father?

I'm going to torture him to death for hurting the love of my life.

TWELVE

The days pass in a cycle of pain and passing out. I don't know if it's night or day, and the rest I do get only occurs when my body gives in and I fade into the darkness. When I wake, I never feel better. My body is slowly breaking down, and every inch of me hurts.

This is so much worse than ever before, as if he knows he's racing against a clock and needs to get what he can before it's too late. Is my father worried? It's the only thing I hold onto. He's worried he's not as safe as he thinks and that they will come for him.

My family.

They will come for me.

I don't want them to, though, because all I want is revenge. I want to wring the life out of my father's old, wrinkled body for what he took from me—my sister.

Even thinking of my sister has my eyes closing in pain. Doesn't he see that no matter what he does now, he can never replicate that kind of pure horror and agony again? He took the only person in this world I have ever risked everything for and loved so completely. I'm a shell, existing in nothing but physical pain. I revel in it, however, because it's better than the pain in my heart.

I don't know what he expects to gain from this experiment, but I no longer care about the thought process of his sick mind.

All I care about is killing him and joining her once more.

I lie on the bed—maybe for the fifth time, but it's hard to tell—and my body won't move on command at the moment. It's due to the sedative that is still in my system from the last test. I don't know what they did, only that I fought them before the needle went into my vein and then it was lights out. When I woke up here, I had a new incision on my back and agony racing through my spine. I don't bother asking since they won't tell me. The scientists here are butchers, nothing more. I spotted other cells when I was dragged back here. They didn't seem to be occupied, but that doesn't mean they aren't now or haven't been in the past. Knowing them, this place, wherever it is, was or is full, and they are just running one giant experiment ring.

It's clear all their attention is on me at the moment. My father thinks I hold the key to his successful research or some shit. It means I'm important, which means I get the brunt of his attention and experiments. I guess that's something.

The door opens, and I don't even bother looking up, knowing it will be the guards once more. They sent five to begin with, but now I'm too sluggish to even lift my head, so they only sent two. It's insulting and pisses me off. I want them to be afraid of me. I want them to be scared.

They should be.

I'm going to rip every single person here to pieces and then burn it down with me inside.

Grabbing my arms, they drag me from the room. I don't fight them, but I let my anger grow until it blinds me. I let it push away the numbness, exhaustion, and sleepiness in my body until I'm practically on fire with it. Now, they are dragging a loaded weapon without even realising it.

My father wants a weapon? He wants a soldier?

Then he got one.

It's time to show him that. It's time to make them all pay in any way I can.

I don't even look where we are going, since I know it will be a lab of some sort. When I get inside, I see it's not the operating lab, which means no sedative. That provides me with more opportunities to hurt them. They don't even bother tying my wrists down, as if expecting me to be compliant. They band my shoulders, waist, and legs and, with sneering looks at me, they leave me there.

I wait and roll my eyes as I look around the room, mostly out of boredom and to stop my mind from wandering to anything else.

Boom.

I watch her fall again before squeezing my eyes shut and pushing the memory away. Torturing myself by watching my sister die over and over won't help. I need to stay focused. I need to keep my mind sharp. I can't give in, not yet.

And the guys . . .

I can't even think of them. The last time I saw them haunts me even in my sleep. I love them more than I've ever loved anything apart from Annie. They gave me a family, they gave me a home and a purpose, and now I will never see them again. I tell myself it's for the best because this is my problem to handle. I can keep them safe, and I can end this, even if it means I die.

They still have a future.

I just hope they understand that and let me go.

Focus, Nova.

I snap back to attention, scanning the room once more. The table I am on is metal and resembles every other one I have been tied down to. There is a computer on a desk to the left with files spread out across it. I'm too far away to see what they say, but they won't help me anyway. There's a surgical tray to the right filled with tools. It's too far to reach for now, but I note the scalpels and scissors that could be useful. The wall before me is glass, and not much else exists here.

Pure white.

I can't wait to see it splattered with blood.

Just then, the door opens, and a scientist in a lab coat comes bustling in. He doesn't even look at me. His grey hair is combed back perfectly, and his bright-blue eyes are hidden behind thick-rimmed glasses. He's fit, clearly in shape, and slightly smaller than me, but right now, he's in charge and he knows it—not that he looks up from his tablet as he moves around the room, muttering to himself. My eyes track him like he's prey, and when he stumbles and knocks into the tray, I almost smirk in victory. It spins closer to me, and he rubs at his hip as he moves to the computer. Keeping my eyes on him, I reach out as far as I can, my pinkie catching on the edge of the tray, and with gritted teeth, I pull it closer until I can reach the top and grab a tool. It happens to be a medium-sized scalpel, but I grip it tightly, sliding it up the inside of my arm to hide it as he lifts his head and frowns at me.

I simply raise my eyebrow as he stands, heading my way. "Shall we begin?" he asks formally, as if I have a choice in the matter. I want to say as much, but he's already turning away again, so I take my shot. I swipe out, stabbing the scalpel into his middle. He falls back with a scream, blood gushing from the wound. His face is pale and sweaty as he stumbles around, shouting for help. The idiot yanks the scalpel out and blood spurts everywhere.

I guess I hit an artery.

Good.

Ripping the bindings from my body with the last of my strength, I grab the dying man and slam him into the glass as the alarm sounds. The door locks as the guards fight to try and get in. Grinning as my father appears, harried and confused, I slam the gurgling man into the glass. His blood splatters across it, and with my eyes on my father, I rip out the scientist's throat before dropping him to the floor. I step back, covered in blood and gore, wearing a maniacal grin on my face.

"You are behaving like a feral animal!" Father yells as the alarm cuts off.

"That's what I am," I sneer. "You caged and tortured me, and you expect me to be civil? No!" I scream. "You wanted an animal? Now you've got one."

Slamming my hand into the glass, I laugh when the guards jump, my bloodied handprint remaining behind like a promise. Laughing, I grab one of the bone saws when the door opens and the guards stream in.

I throw myself at them, fading into the anger and ignoring everything else, even the pain in my heart and body, as I hack and kill. They are trying to subdue me, but I'm trying to kill them. I see them drop, I hear their screams, and I feel their blood splatter me, but I still don't stop.

Not even as I'm thrown onto the table once more and pinned down by five of them as I twist and laugh, seeing their shocked expressions above me.

I see a fist heading towards my face, along with their shock, their horror, and their dawning understanding.

They underestimated me.

They won't ever make the same mistake again.

I pay for what I did. Father calls it conditioning, but I know the truth. It's punishment. He's angry he underestimated me and that I fought back instead of being the good little experiment he always wanted. He can never dull the spark of rebellion, but he sure tries. He keeps me awake for two days with drugs and pain until I'm delirious, but I still continue to laugh and struggle, even as they torture me until, finally, he gives the order and I'm tossed back into my room.

I lie where they threw me on the floor, and my laughter finally turns to tears. Curling around myself, I push through the agony and focus on my memories.

I'm back at the dining table with everyone laughing around me.

Annie is sitting on Sam's lap, love in their eyes.

Bert is smiling at me.

Louis is holding my hand, and Nico is under me. I'm safe, and I'm warm. Dimitri winks at me, Jonas throws food, and Isaac watches me. I'm loved. I'm safe. I'm happy.

I lose myself in that memory, uncaring that my body is slowly wasting away. Let it, he can have it, but he can never have this. He can never take away the love and happiness I found in a short amount of time.

He can never have them.

They are mine, my secret, and the reason my mind doesn't break.

In there, I am with them, and they are holding me tight and telling me they love me. I think of what our lives could have been like had it been different. We'd have a farm somewhere warm, with no more fog and rain in that manor. No, the sun would shine, and we would work the land. Our lives would be simple, but they would come home to me every day. We would live in the kitchen, dancing and singing. Bert would be there with us, making pancakes for Jonas. There would be horses and goats and maybe a dog or two. I'd never be in pain. I wouldn't even know what that is. I'd be so loved, I would choke on it. Their bodies wouldn't bear the scars of their past, and they wouldn't know what it means to lose everything. They'd be happy.

That's all a dream, but I hold onto it to get me through this.

To give me the strength I need to endure.

To survive and finish this.

Maybe they will get that farm one day, and maybe they will find peace. I'll make sure of it.

I'll make sure, even though I won't be there, that Dimitri won't have to stare at the screen anymore. I'll make sure that Isaac never has to worry about not being okay, that Jonas gets the passion and room he needs, that Nico finds peace, and that Louis is finally unburdened.

I'll make sure of it. I have to.

Even if I burn in the ashes of what I desire, I'll do it for them.

I know I can do this. I can do anything—anything but go home to them.

I stay inside my dream. It's the only time I will be home with them ever again.

THIRTEEN

I find myself in her old room. It's sparse. Other than a few books and clothes, there are no pictures or anything else to indicate it was her room. I hate it, yet it's the closest I can get to her right now, so I stride in and drop onto the bed, sucking in her scent. I finally break, and the tears fall.

I failed her. I failed them all.

I cannot even breathe around the guilt and pain I feel. I don't let the others see, knowing they will worry, but here, I cry silently and beg for her forgiveness. I couldn't stop him from taking her sister and I should have been able to. What's the point of all this power and strength if I can't use it to stop the one person in this world I love from suffering any more than she already has?

I need her. I need her so badly.

I need her in my arms. I need to hold her tight and reassure myself she's safe.

Instead, I feel sick, knowing she's out there right now and probably in pain.

My heart aches so much I struggle to breathe. It's my job to protect them, to keep her safe, but I failed, and now she's all alone.

I stare out of the window and wonder where she is under the night sky.

Can she see the stars? Is she thinking about us too? I inhale her faded scent, needing it to calm me. My heart won't stop breaking or hammering until she's back in my arms, but this will have to do for now.

For a moment, I close my eyes, imagining she is here with me—her soft hands sliding across my body, the smile she gives me that ruins me. She is strong, but she needs us.

Needs me.

I often wondered what it would be like to lead a normal life, but I know with certainty now I would take all the pain, torture, and imprisonment just to have her again and be given a chance at happiness by her side. She's worth it.

My eyes open, and I look at the stars again. "Stay strong, my love. We are coming for you," I promise her. We will not stop until we do. This isn't the end of our story. Our girl will get the happy ending she deserves, and she'll get the peace she needs. I'll make sure of it.

We all will.

She might be willing to give her life for us and her sister, but so are we. Every one of us would die for her without hesitation, and without her here, we have nothing else left to live for.

"Nico, she needs you to be strong," Louis murmurs behind me. It's a testament to how lost I am that I didn't even hear him come in. I stiffen and don't turn to face him, not wanting him to see my tears, my weakness.

The bed dips and arms wrap around me, offering comfort, and I struggle to pull myself together. "Break now, then tomorrow you will be strong again. We are going to get her back, we have to, but I need you to do that."

"I failed her," I croak.

"No, *we* failed her, and it won't happen again," he replies. "We will get her back, and then we will kill every single one of them for taking her. We will beg for her forgiveness and spend the rest of our lives following her around, but for that we need you."

"What if I'm not strong enough?" My eyes lock on the stars. "What if he was right about us . . . about me? What if I failed his tests because I'm not good enough."

"That's fucking bullshit and you know it, brother." I turn, and he grips my chin, pressing his forehead to mine. "He failed us because we didn't fit into his little perfect box—nothing more, nothing less. Our girl thinks we are fucking perfect, and we will not dishonour her by proving otherwise. He thinks we are failures, so let's show him we're not." Wiping the tears from my face, he smiles sadly. "Then after, we can deal with all this. Until then, let's shove it all in a fucking box, okay? It is the only way I—we can keep moving."

I realise then that this is for him, not just me. He's faltering and he needs me.

Wrapping my arms around him, I hold my brother as we break in our love's bed, our silent promise drifting to the stars. We are coming for her.

Nothing will stop us.

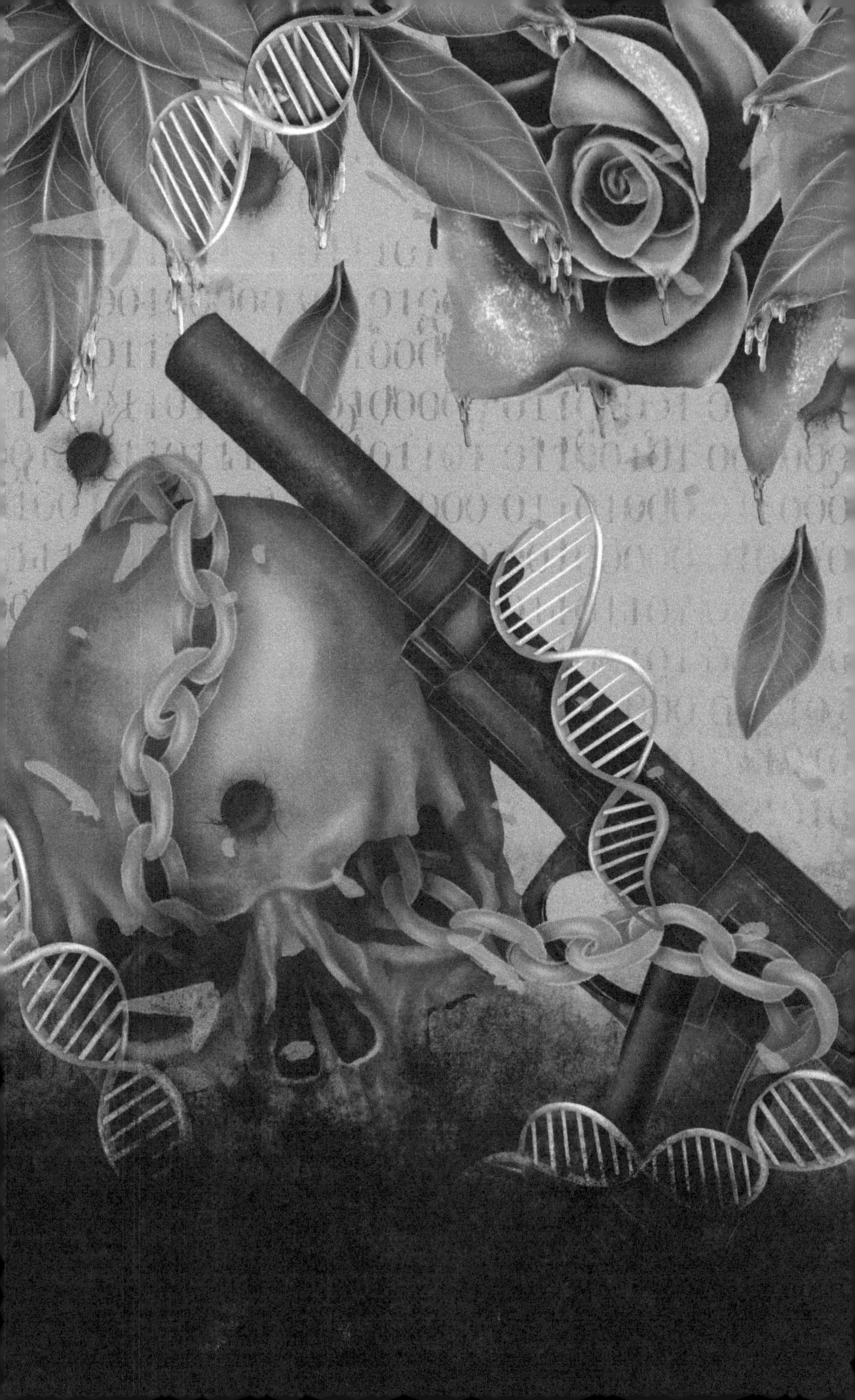

FOURTEEN

I t's like my rebellion broke that last line between prisoner and captors. They are brutal with round-the-clock experiments. Father is almost frantic, his hair out of place and dark circles under his eyes. Is he feeling pressure or guilt?

I almost laugh at the idea.

Since I'm not a child, he's not holding back, and the idea that he held back previously scares me—not that I will ever show him that. I slowly lose myself in planning how I will bring this place down. I go through many plans and ideas. I hear Louis's voice in my head, making me discard ideas that won't work. I can't just outright escape because there are too many guards. I would be drugged or knocked out instantly, and then I would lose my shot. No, I need to let them relax again and think they have broken me. I need maps and schematics, and I need to hack into the cameras and alarm systems. Then and only then can I make a move. It seems insurmountable from my position, restrained to a table as they run electrodes across me. An armed guard points his gun at me, but all I have now is time.

Time and nothing else.

I bare my teeth at him like an animal and watch in satisfaction as his eyes widen in fear.

"Now, Novaleen, that is not very nice, is it?" my father calls through the two-way mirror.

"I was never the nice one. That was Annie. You know, the daughter you killed," I retort, and his expression turns cold.

"Today we are going to be testing your mental fortitude and how it affects your body—"

I tune him out, imagining leaping across this table, taking that fucking tablet he holds, and shoving it up his ass.

Two hours later, I find out what he really meant—mental torture to see how my body reacts and if my emotions heighten my strength and speed.

Snarling, I lunge at him, but the chains hold me down. He makes a tutting noise. "It seems your past is a trigger and heightens your skills. I wonder what else is? It's evident your emotions are tightly tied to it. Would speaking about Ana be one as well?"

I freeze, my heart slamming in my chest, and the machines note it for him. Not even my pain can be my own. I had been playing with him and winding him up for hours, but now I stare, begging him with my eyes not to go there.

Not to rip out whatever remains of my heart.

But of course, he does.

"How did her death make you feel?" he asks, sounding clinical and cold.

"Don't," I snarl, but even I hear the devastation in my tone.

"Did it bring up those instincts in you?" he continues, ignoring me completely, his eyes going to the machines. I see my heartbeat race on them, just like it pumps in my chest. Each breath is agony until I'm raggedly breathing, my hands shaking where they are chained to the table. I want to rip off the lines, smash the machines, and cover my ears like a child, but I cannot protect myself from this, just like I couldn't protect her.

"Novaleen, we require your answer. When you felt her dying, what happened inside your body? Can you talk me through it?" When I just stare, fighting back my anger, he frowns. "It was almost too easy to kill her, you know?" He switches tactics. "She was so trusting and still expected her father to protect her. She never could understand the need in me to succeed no matter what. It never mattered how many degrees she got or how much she succeeded in our field, she could never turn her emotions off. She was soft. It got her killed. I felt nothing as she fell—"

"Stop," I beg, whining like an injured animal.

"It was nothing to me, like watching the results of an experiment. I suppose I did expect to feel something, but I didn't. She was useless to me. She was corrupted by you, and she outlived her purpose, but you loved her anyway, even when she hated you. Did she know you protected her all those years?"

My heart is exploding out of my chest, and my head aches and spins. "Did she understand how much of a martyr you were and how easy it was to get you to do what I wanted? I just had to threaten her. It's why I kept her all those years. I knew you would never leave her, not really. Did you tell her, Nova? Or did you just let her hate you? Did you think you deserved it?"

I fight against my restraints but it's useless. Baring my teeth, I feel my anger and pain explode as I yell at him wordlessly.

"Did she die hating you, Nova? Or did she forgive you? Did my bleeding-heart daughter die thinking you would save her?"

Closing my eyes, I try to block out his words, but it's useless. They burrow into my brain, ripping every part of me to pieces. Ribbons of my heart and soul die from his sharp-edged prodding.

"I think she did. I think, even at the end, she expected you to save her and you couldn't. At that moment, you wanted to kill me, so why didn't you? I would like to understand."

I try to breathe through it, choking on my blood and pain. For a moment, there's silence as he watches the monitors.

"Interesting. That simply breaks you down. It's a weakness. Let's switch gears then, shall we, Novaleen?" My eyes flutter open, and even that small act hurts because he's right.

She expected me to save her and I couldn't.

I have to live with that, but not for long.

"What about the others? The failed experiments you had grown so attached to?" I become ice cold all over. "Maybe I should bring them here to be used as . . . incentives."

I lift my head slowly to meet his knowing eyes.

"Do you think you are more inclined to love them because you are so desperate to be loved since you were not as a child? Or are you simply so desperate not to be alone, you convinced yourself to love those people like yourself?"

No, he does not get to ruin this.

He doesn't get to taint them and what we have.

"Do you think you are more likely to keep losing all your hair because of stress from your experiments never working out? Or is it from the realisation that you will never again be able to accomplish anything?" His eye ticks, and I grin evilly. "Does it upset you that no one will ever remember you? That all of this will become nothing but a warning to those who come after you? That everything you have done is for . . . well, nothing? You're old and weak, Father. You're slower, your brain is not connecting like it used to, and your skin is wrinkled and sagging like cottage cheese. Who knows what lies in your future? Wouldn't it be ironic if you lost all your memories or something as simple as a mortal disease killed you before anything could ever be finished?"

"Novaleen, let us get back on track," he says, his voice tight.

"Oh, I am on track. Do they all know that you are legally dead and you are slowly losing money? Do they know that no one will ever support you and this vision you have? That's why you are so desperate to finish this now and find the answers, isn't it? Do they know it keeps you up at night, wondering if the scientific community will ever accept it?" I know I'm on target when his knuckles turn white on the tablet, gripping it tightly. The guards shift slightly. "Do they know you sold your soul to the devil only for it to mean nothing?"

"Enough! Punish her!" he yells and turns to depart.

"Do they know how weak you are, and that's why you crave my strength?" I scream after him before descending into laughter. I even welcome the pain as the guards close in around me, needing it to forget his words, his truth.

"Hello, boys, ready to play?" I jangle the chains. "How about you take these off and we play fair?"

One sneers at me. There are two types of guards here—ones who are desperate for the money and look the other way and others who enjoy their orders and dish out pain. Luckily, I get the latter today. Their fists smack into my head on the left and then the right. Laughing, I spit my blood onto the table, watching in satisfaction as it drips across the brilliant white floor.

Let it stain it like it stains my soul.

They pummel my body, the temporary physical pain briefly driving back the heartache until it comes roaring back.

You couldn't protect her.

I bare my teeth. "Is that all you got?" I demand, needing them to knock me out so I don't have to think or remember for a little while.

"Oh, I'm going to enjoy this," one spits, and then his hands wrap around my throat. He adds more and more pressure.

Black dots dance in my vision and my lungs scream. On the verge of death, of passing out, and I race towards it, needing oblivion.

"P-Pussy," I croak out, and he grips tighter, then my vision fades out.

All I hear is the trapped fluttering of my heart and then nothing.

I go with a smile on my face.

When I wake, I know I'm not alone. I turn slightly to see Father sitting on a chair, watching me. Groaning, I flop onto my back. "I haven't had enough sleep to deal with your fucking face," I sneer.

"Does your hatred keep you happy?" he asks, observing me. I swallow, and he watches the movement. "You loved me once," he declares as if it confuses him. "Even though you knew you shouldn't, you loved me."

"I was a kid," I whisper, staring at him, "just a kid. You were supposed to love me."

"I did in a way."

"Someone who loves you wouldn't have done what you did. I feel sorry for you. You'll never know loyalty, love, or friendship."

"No, just riches and great success. How horrible of me. Nova, think of the great things we could do together if you only helped me. When I get the information I need, I can let you go back to them if you wish."

For a moment, I'm tempted to give in before the reason for his presence dawns on me, and then I laugh.

"You're desperate. You can't get what you need. Really, Father? A bargain? Pleading? It's below you. Pathetic," I spit.

"If I have to hurt them to get what I need, then I will, Nova," he snarls.

"You will never find them." I smile. "You will never get your hands on them. They are safe from you and so much fucking stronger than you could ever believe." As I talk, my sore throat starts to fade back to normal thanks to my healing. I know by tomorrow, the only evidence of my brush with death will be the bruises on my neck.

"They were failures." He frowns. "They didn't meet the required—"

"That's your problem, Father." I force myself to sit up, not wanting to be lying down before him. "All you see is data and numbers, not the person. You failed them, not the other way around. They are stronger than I am and better too. They are the very things you have been working so hard for, and you let them go. Don't worry, though, because I found what you never did—their souls, and they are mine. Rip me apart, burn me, cut me, or shoot me, but you will never have them. You can't." I bare my teeth.

"We shall see about that." He stands, looking me over. "Rest. We need you to be strong, not weak like you are now. I shall allow you a day to recuperate."

"How fucking kind," I snap.

"You will remain here and sleep." The door shuts and locks after him, and a plan starts to form, leaving me grinning.

I have a whole day. I can do a lot with a whole day.

FIFTEEN

Two days have passed, and I'm having a hard time keeping it together. I struggle to eat and sleep, but I know I need to. I check in on the others all the time. Bert is doing better, but it's clear he's struggling with the loss of Ana and Nova. Those two were like his daughters, and I cannot imagine how he feels. He's back in the kitchen, cooking up a storm as if they are going to walk through the door at any moment and will need food. I think it gives him something to focus on. Jonas and Nico take turns eating all the food, making themselves sick, knowing Bert needs that. Isaac keeps checking on him, too, and like Nova would want, I check in on Isaac, but it's Dimitri whom I'm the most worried about. His skin is bleaching from being indoors, and staring at the screens day after day is creating purple bags under his bloodshot eyes. He's jittery with all the caffeine he has consumed, but he won't listen to me. I know I will eventually have to ask Isaac to sedate him so he can rest before he kills himself.

He's worried, and he can't physically handle losing someone he loves again.

Not like Bas, not when he feels like he can do something, so for now, I help as much as I can. When he snaps and gets annoyed at me, telling me I'm doing it wrong, I don't take it personally.

Like now.

"D, calm down."

"No, you are doing it wrong. We will lose the file," he snarls, his eyes narrowed on me. "Are you that fucking dumb?"

"Dimitri, breathe," I order.

His nostrils flare before he covers his face, scrubbing it with his hands and turning away. I see his shoulders droop. Disappointment and guilt are in every line of his body. When I move in front of him, his eyes are filled with mortification. "I am sorry, Louis. I know you're only trying to help."

"You need to sleep."

"Not yet. I'm so close. I can feel it."

"You cannot help anyone if you are bedbound and sick because you did not rest and eat."

"Not yet," he murmurs, dismissing me once more.

"At least have something to eat and drink," I demand, pushing the plate at him. The forgotten ones have been taken away. "Nova needs you to be strong." It's wrong to use his love for her, but it works. His eyes close for a moment before he snatches up the sandwich and starts chewing, not even tasting it.

"Good. I'll come back in a bit. I want it all eaten. I am not playing anymore, Dimitri. I will keep you alive, even if it makes you hate me." I go to check on the others, knowing he needs a moment. I do as well because even mentioning her name hurts.

I miss everything about her—her laughter, her sarcasm, and the way her eyes would glint as she challenged me. I miss the way she loved and supported me. I miss the way she kept my family together.

She belongs here, with us.

If this is just a snippet of what our lives will be like without her, then we won't survive it. It will break us, and our family will wither and die without our heart.

I'm just planting flowers around the graves when Nico jogs over. "Dimitri needs us."

I jerk to my feet. Fuck, I knew I should have pushed him to rest. Nico must see the panic in my eyes because he claps my shoulder and says, "He's fine. It's good news. I think he's manic. We could barely understand what he's saying, he's so excited."

"Then let's not keep him waiting." We jog inside to find Dimitri pacing in the living room. A worried-looking Isaac watches him from the sofa, and Bert flits around Jonas with a plate of pancakes, watching Dimitri with interest.

"You're here!" he practically yells when I enter, and I know my eyebrows rise. "Sorry, sorry, this is important. Sit."

I do, perching on the edge of the sofa and exchanging a worried look with Isaac. His eyes let me know that he will take care of Dimitri after this. I hate putting that on him, but it might do him some good to have someone else to fuss over.

"Dimitri, take a breath and talk to us," I tell him.

His hands shake as he closes his eyes and calms his breathing. "Sorry, sorry, but I found something. You see, I was looking into his bank accounts to see if we could follow the money trail as another avenue, but then I started to think he's too smart to use his accounts. I thought maybe blind funding, but then I checked Ana's name just to be sure and there, in bank accounts she would never know to check, were purchases, so I started to track them down." He speaks so rapidly, it's hard to follow, but I try. "I've managed to track one all the way back to the source. It's a manufacturing company based in China. He spent a considerable amount there. When I looked into what they manufacture, it seemed to be lab equipment. If you weren't looking for her father, you would assume she bought it for her own research," he finishes with a grin.

I blink, and it finally clicks. "You think it's the equipment for whatever lab he has taken Nova to?"

"It was made just a month ago when Ana was with us, when he was dead. Yes, I think so. If we go there and put some pressure on them, we can figure out where the equipment was shipped to or at least find the next step. I have the guards' IDs and their friends' and families' funding, as well as trying to decrypt the other purchases, but it's somewhere to start, right?" He deflates then, looking anxious, but I grin and nod.

"You did good, Dimitri. Let's get the plane fuelled and go check it out before he realises we are onto him and tries to cover his tracks." Slapping his shoulder on the way past, I offer him a nod. "You did good, brother. Get it all started and then sleep on the plane. That is an order." Turning to the others, I clap.

"Pack up, brothers. We are going after our girl."

"Finally," Jonas cheers around a mouthful of pancake.

SIXTEEN

Like Father promised, they leave me alone. It's clearly the middle of the night, and the lights are out. I crawl from the bed and into the bathroom, where there are no cameras. Why would they be necessary when there is no escape route? Or so they think.

Shutting the lid on the toilet, I ignore the ache in my body. Above the toilet is the vent for the room. It's a square that will fit my body at a squeeze. I'm taking a guess that the air ducts are beyond, but it's worth a shot. I need to get around without being seen.

I stare at the screws for a moment until I spot the shampoo bottle. Ripping off the lid, I twist the plastic, and with frustrating patience, I slowly undo the screws. When enough are out, the top swings down. I leave the bottom attached in case I need to hide quickly and recap the bottle of shampoo, even if it is bent, and then I peer into the vent. Well, here goes nothing.

Gripping the edge, I lift myself up and into it. It's a tight squeeze, and I think about Nico and how he would freak out right now. Pushing thoughts of them away, I use my arms to crawl through the vent as quietly as I can. It's straight for about three feet before it branches left and right. Closing my eyes, I remember the hallways I was dragged through and choose right.

The motions allow my mind to settle. If they find me, they will punish me, but they already are so it doesn't bother me.

I peer down the first open vent I come to and see a corridor, so I keep going. I stop over the fifth vent when guards sweep the corridor, relaxed and chatting away. I wait as they pass, not wanting to give my position away. When it's quiet again, I carry on, coming to a four-way junction. I haven't seen a control room on this floor, and I've seen a lot of it, so I'm guessing it's either up or down. If it were me, I would have it near the entrance, so I head that way. I squeeze and twist until I can stand up, and then I press my back to one of the metal duct walls and my hands to the other, watching it dent slightly, before I begin to climb. I grit my teeth as my muscles strain, thanks to the beatings I have been taking and the lack of exercise, but the burn is good because it clears my mind and takes it off my itching throat and worry for my guys.

Sweat beads on my forehead, but I continue to climb until I come to a junction once more, this one going left and right. I pick left this time for no other reason than I went right last time. It's a squeeze as I wiggle up and into the tunnels. I hit some of my bruises and cuts and have to breathe through the pain, but it keeps me alert and awake, so at least that's something, I shimmy down the tunnel, and it eventually stops at a dead end with a grate. I peer through the slats to the room beyond. It appears to be empty, so I open it and drop down onto an unmade bed. It cushions my fall, and I roll onto my feet, glancing around.

I got lucky. It seems to be an unused medical room with another two-way mirror. Moving to the door, I look out to see the numbers in the corridor. This one seems to be empty, but there's a camera in the upper right-hand corner. Blowing out a breath, I look around and find what I'm looking for. Grabbing a metal pole, I open the door a crack and swing the opposite door open, activating an alarm, and then I wait. Not too long after, guards come surging down the hallway, opening the door and stepping inside. With them distracted, I hurry out and along the corridor. When no alarms blare, I figure they are focused on the room. I make it to a junction, looking left and right, and find what I want at the end on the right—a nearly white door with a word saying, "Security."

Bingo.

The door is slightly open, so I hurry inside and shut it. The guards must have gone to the room to investigate. There are rows upon rows of monitors, and I quickly memorise the camera locations before moving to the unlocked computer.

Idiots.

I scan through the contents as quickly as possible, finding the alarm map. It shows me the layout of the building we are in, which seems to be a three-story industrial unit above and a bunker of five levels below. I memorise it and click it all shut before focusing on the cameras. I carefully turn some just a few inches to create blind spots, knowing I might need them in the future. Without much else to do, and knowing I'm running out of time, I slip out and into the closet room just as the guards storm past, muttering about idiot newbies. I dart out after them and back to the room I climbed out of. Jumping, I catch onto the vent, haul myself up, and shut it after me.

It's like I was never there, unless they watch the cameras.

They seem almost bored with this job, however, thinking it's too easy, so that works well. As quickly as I can, I make my way back to my room, shutting the vent. I use my fingers and nails to slide the screws back, but not all the way. My fingers bleed after, and my nails are jagged and broken, but I wash them and ignore the pulsing pain and ripped skin as I slide back into bed.

They will come to check on me soon.

It's almost all too easy.

This is going to be fun.

Not five minutes later, the door opens, and a guard peers in before it shuts again.

I lie back in bed and wait, knowing I need the rest, so I shut my eyes for a few hours.

I wake up with a groan when the door opens. My eyelids are heavy, and my body is sluggish from the lack of sleep and the round-the-clock torture and experiments, but I force myself to sit up as a guard throws a tray on the bed next to me. I glare at him until he huffs and leaves, then I pick up the tray. I know they could have drugged the food or done something to it, but I also know I need to eat or I won't be at my full strength, and that outweighs the other risks.

There's chicken with mixed veggies, some bread, and yogurt. It's not Bert's cooking, but I use my hands to eat it because obviously, why would I need cutlery? Fucking assholes. I have to use the lid of the yogurt for a spoon, and when I'm done, I toss it at the door, watching it clatter, the mess bringing me great joy.

It's the little victories.

The same guard comes back and cleans it up, glaring at me the entire time before he stomps off. He lets the door swing shut behind him, but I hurry over and put my foot in it. When he doesn't reappear, I peek out to see the corridor is empty. The camera here is one I moved a few inches to give me a blind spot, so it will work when I need it to. Not right now though.

Ripping the bottom of my shirt, I ball it up and stick it in the lock, so the door shuts but won't lock properly. Unless they look closely, they won't notice, which is exactly what I want. I begin to stretch out my body, flipping off the camera as I loosen up, and then fall into a usual routine—one I haven't used since before I was alone and moving constantly. Jumping jacks turn into burpees then sit-ups and push-ups, and then I stretch out my body and do it again. I'll need to keep my strength and speed up. I finally collapse onto the bed, panting and covered in sweat, with that telltale burn in my muscles.

I eventually manage to drag myself to the shower and wash off all the sweat and dried blood. Watching it circle the drain, I trace the bruises across my body. There are older, yellowing ones and bright black and purple ones. I let the shower spray hit the laceration on my side and peel off the gauze. It's healing well, and I shouldn't need it anymore, so I gently wash that before doing the same to the one on my hip and then turning to scrub my back. I wash my hair a few times to get the feel of their hands and leers out of it, and then I stand under the spray, letting the lukewarm water take me away to a different shower, where hands slid possessively across my body.

Jonas loved joining me in the shower. I press my hands to the wall, wishing he were here touching me, loving me, and making me laugh.

I wish they were all here.

And Ana.

Fuck.

The tears start, but I let them fall, washed away by the shower until there are no more, and then I dry off and slip on some grey shorts and a matching shirt they provided before collapsing onto the bed and turning away from the camera.

The lights go off shortly after, and in the dark, I imagine a body behind me in the bed, never letting me sleep alone. I envision their comfort and lov and not for the first time, I wonder what they are doing. Have they stopped looking? Have they let me go?

Fuck, I hope so. I would hate for them to end up trapped here once more. I'm not worth it. I want them to trust in me to finish this and find the life they deserve, but even as I think that, I know they won't. They are loyal, and they love me. They have proven over and over that we are in this together and that they will always come for me.

I just hope that when they do find me, it's not too early.

I want them to arrive when this place is up in flames and understand it's over. Then, they can mourn me and move on.

I hope they find the happiness they deserve. I send it as a prayer as I stare into the darkness.

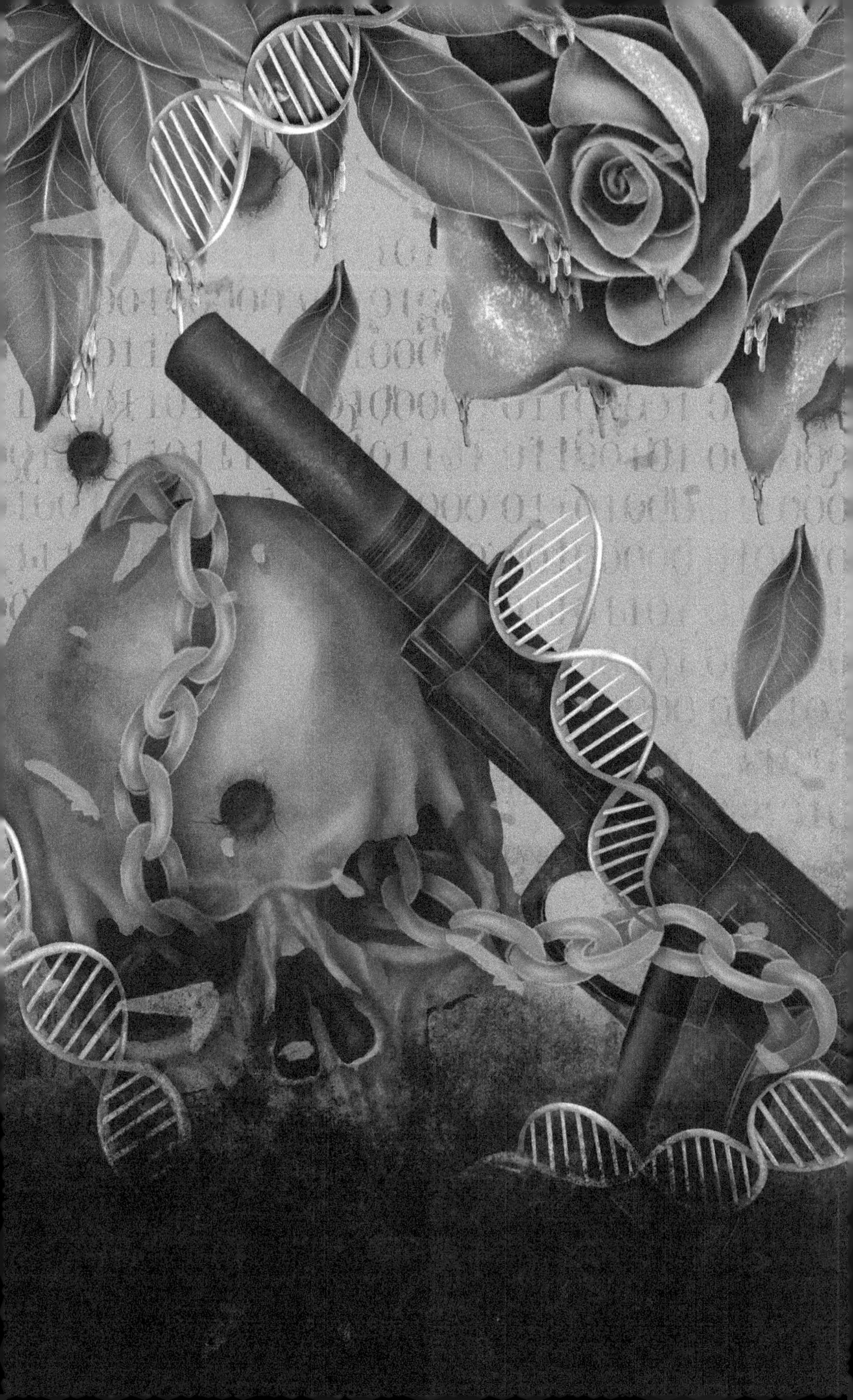

SEVENTEEN

Morning comes all too quickly, and I know my day of rest is over. The lights flicker on, and I sigh as I turn over, knowing they'll be coming for me soon. I quickly use the toilet, wash my face, and brush my teeth before tying my hair back, slipping on some trainers and socks as I wait on the bed. I place my hands on my knees like a good little girl, even as my heart fills with fear and determination.

As soon as the door opens and the guards step forward, I know today will be different. They have cuffs, so I hold out my hands, letting the guards chain them together before they silently drag me into the corridor. We don't go to the labs, and I quickly work through the map forming in my head from my days here and the cameras to figure out where we're going, but I draw a blank. I soon realise why when we head down two levels in an elevator and through a secure door.

I've never seen this section before.

Yay, this will be fun.

"Oh, spooky and dramatic with the long hallways and cameras. Would it kill you to put some art somewhere? Haven't you ever heard of happy worker—" I grunt as an elbow meets my gut, making me double over, then I glare at the guard. "Touch me again and I'll break your arm," I hiss in warning.

I might have a plan, but that doesn't mean I'll take their pain.

With a sinister smile, he slams his arm into my gut again, only this time, I let him, and instead of doubling into the pain as the air whooshes from my lungs, I use it. I lunge for him and grab his arm, and even with my cuffed hands, I manage to slide behind him and slam his arm down over his shoulder. I hear the bones snap before he howls and drops to his knees, cradling his arm.

I hold up my bound hands as an alarm is triggered. The other guard points his weapon at me, glancing between me and the downed man who has tears falling down his mottled face. Through gritted teeth, he says, "You are fucking dead!" He surges to his feet, but more guards pour down the corridor with their guns pointed at me, blocking him.

I smile sweetly at all of them. "I warned him what would happen. Now, shall we continue on? We all know Dr. Davis doesn't like to be late."

For a moment, nobody moves, so I just smile with my hands up as the broken-armed guard is led away cursing. I'm the most dangerous person here, and they all suddenly realise it. Their eyes are sharp and wary, and their guns are held aloft, ready to be used.

They are truly understanding the depths of the experiments now and just what I'm capable of.

"Well?" I sigh like they bore me.

A guard slowly moves toward me, circling me and pointing his gun at the back of my head. "Walk," he barks, and I do just that, surrounded by a platoon of guards.

That's how we enter the giant room I am led to, with the guards blocking most of my view bar my father who turns and spots us with a frown. "Is that really necessary? Novaleen, you will behave, won't you?" he questions.

"Of course I will." I practically ooze sincerity.

"See? Put the guns down. You don't need them." When nobody moves, his face clouds in anger.

"Oh, you've done it now," I whisper. I know that look.

"I said now, unless you want to be on the next garbage rotation!" he yells. All too quickly, the guns are pulled away and the guards step back, melting to the sides of the room. Their eyes remain on me, and they are ready to act, but they are following orders.

"Good boys," I purr and hold my wrists up to my father. "Can we get these off now?"

"Yes, of course," he replies like we are civilised people, and he moves over to grab the key as I look around our location today. It's not a lab, that's for sure, and as I see what's in the room, I get a really bad feeling and all my cockiness evaporates.

There's a giant mat covering most of the space, clearly for sparring and training. To the left is a gym with floor-to-ceiling mirrors, and to the right of the mat is an extreme obstacle course.

There is a man in the middle of the mat I don't recognise. He has on army cargos and a black T-shirt, but his feet are bare as he does push-ups. He's well-muscled with a buzzed head and intense black eyes. I watch how he moves, fast and hard, his body a well-oiled machine. That would give him away if his clothes didn't.

He's a soldier, not a guard, and he's clearly fast and capable.

"Ah, I see you've noticed Sergeant Joel," my father comments as he undoes my cuffs, and I flex my hands. "One of the successes of that batch. I believe you met or found some of the other unsuccessful members of his unit."

I swallow hard as I eye him, thinking about Sam. This man knew Sam? When he leaps to his feet and rolls out his muscles, his eyes land on me. They are cold, dead, and cruel. This man is nothing like I am, and he's embraced whatever they have done to him.

"Yes," is all I say.

"Good. He will be part of your testing today. You are always asking for more of a challenge, so I figured someone on your level would be more beneficial for your results. I'd like to see the difference between the outcomes of the experiments from adulthood to childhood."

"How?" I ask, knowing the answer deep down.

"By testing you against each other, of course," my father answers, turning away to grab his tablet as I eye Joel. He's tall and built like a brick shit house, and he clearly likes what he's being ordered to do.

I don't know if they suspect it was me last night, or if they simply want to punish me, but I have no choice but to perform for them. I can't endure another punishment so I need to be smart. I need to make them relax.

I need my father to think he's won.

That means defeating Joel. A spark of excitement rolls through me. I've had to hold back for so long, even with my guys. I worried about what I would become if I let go, but with this sergeant, I won't have to. He's changed, like me and my guys. He can take it, and unlike my guys, I have no loyalty to him, and getting rough and winning is what I need to do to survive.

He moves closer, nodding at my father, but his eyes are all for me.

Like recognises like.

He sizes me up like I did to him, and there's a gleam in his eye I don't like as he surveys me. It's hard to pinpoint, but when his eyes drop to my body, I almost shudder in revulsion.

"So, you're the prodigal experiment?" he sneers. "You don't look like much." He has a thick Irish accent, and sure, he's attractive, but that gleam? I watch him more carefully. "In fact, you look like a lost little girl. Is this really who you are pinning all your hopes on?" he asks my father, ignoring me.

"She has shown the best results under pressure and seems to have accessed more of her brain than any other, including you, even if she wastes it," he tells Joel without even looking at me.

"Happy to waste it." I salute my father, and Joel throws me a glare.

He grinds his teeth, but like a good soldier, he ignores me and focuses on my father. "Orders?"

"I want her fully tested. Push her to her limits."

"I'm right here," I mutter, but they both ignore me.

"And past them. Show me exactly what she is capable of, and I will make my decision about how this will proceed." My father looks at me. "I am rooting for you. You were my hope for the future, for what we could become, but if you fail me again, I will allow Joel to put you down and proceed with his strand of research. Is that understood?"

I swallow hard. So far, my father's need for me has kept me alive, but he's telling me that if I fail today, it won't. I need to push harder than I ever have because I know Joel will not let me do anything else. This will be a true test. I'm not a child anymore. I'm a full-grown adult with abilities others could only dream of.

I hate what my father has done to me, so I never explored the full depths of my abilities, and the darkness in my brain scares me, so I always shied away from discovering exactly what I am capable of. I only ever pushed as hard as he made me and never any further, truly scared of what he had done to me.

When I'm pushed, what if I'm not even human anymore?

I guess we are going to find out.

Joel nods and smirks at me. "Gladly. Start on the course, and we will compare times. Go," he orders.

I hesitate, wanting to smash in his smug face in and ignore his orders, but I have no choice. My father is watching me right now, and I am at their mercy. I need to play nice and give into the side of me I fear to survive.

I remind myself I am doing this for my men as I turn to the obstacle course, Joel sharply on my heels. He is almost silent as he moves, but I can feel him behind me. I stop at the beginning of the course and eye it, my brain working a mile a minute to plan the best route for the fastest time.

"Begin when you're ready," Joel snaps. I bend my knees slightly, closing my eyes for a moment as I centre myself. I imagine his smug face if he wins and know I can't let that happen.

He thinks I'm nothing, and my father is expecting me to fail.

I won't just to prove them wrong.

When my eyes snap open, I give myself over to that force deep inside me. Strength surges through me, as does speed, purpose, and determination.

I let all my worries and thoughts flee until there is only action.

Adrenaline pumps through my veins as I push off the floor and leap at the first piece of equipment. A rope hangs down to help me climb the wall but I ignore it, leaping up and grabbing the lip of the vertical wooden block. I hang there for a second, easily six feet in the air, and then I haul myself up and roll over, flipping to land with one knee down on the ground, then I'm moving again. There's a rope strung between two poles, and I quickly ascend the ladder to it and drop forward. I use my hands to pull me across it, with one knee pressed against it while the other hangs.

When I reach the other side and descend, I race across a small sprint section to a cargo net suspended twenty feet in the air. Pushing off, I grab the ropes and climb diagonally, since I noticed they are shorter distances for my shorter legs, and it makes the ascent quicker. I can feel them all watching, but I ignore them as I reach the platform at the top and race across it. The platform ends, and there are twenty-foot poles dotted at random intervals to a bridge on the other side. I leap across them and race down the slope back to the ground.

The next piece has four poles in staggered heights before each other. I duck under the first, climb atop the second, and hop to clear the other two. After all, he never mentioned rules; he just said to get through it the quickest.

Before me are monkey bars and I jump, grabbing onto the first and swinging easily to the second. With my legs locked together, I keep up the momentum, moving so fast I barely see the bar before I move onto the next, and then I drop to the ground at the other side.

There's a tire with a line at the end. It's huge and easily weighs six hundred and fifty kilograms. I crouch and flip it, grunting at the weight, but then, just to be an ass, I pick it up and with gritted teeth, I carry it to the end, knowing even most army people would struggle to do so. The next obstacle is a round sprint track, and I push myself to run faster, and then, without stopping, I drop to my knees, crawl through the tunnel, and pop to my feet on the other side before I sprint back to the first wall I started at. I race up it and drop down on the other side, sliding to a stop beside Joel who has a watch in his hand.

Smirking at him, I fight back the need to bend over and pant, but then I realise I don't actually need to. It didn't even wind me. What the fuck?

"Well?" my father calls, and there's a smugness in his voice that tells me he knows the answer.

"Twenty seconds faster than me," he reluctantly admits, and my father's laughter fills the air.

"It's not over yet," Joel snaps, dropping the watch. "Weights next."

Joel forces me to lift the weights he does, watching my form carefully. Next, he has me run on the treadmill next to him. When he ups the speed, so do I, always doing one better. After that, I'm forced through cardio until he finally calls it quits. I sip the water I'm given and watch him talk with my dad before nodding and heading back my way.

"Last test of the day," he mutters, glaring at me. He's clearly angry that not only can I keep up, but I can beat him.

"Sure, what is it? Want me to lift you until you cry? Or maybe beat your ass on the course again?"

"No. This time, I'll be beating your ass." I narrow my gaze, and he grins. "It's time to test your combat skills."

Great, he literally meant kick my ass. For a moment, Nico's face is on top of Joel's, smiling at me and urging me to fight him before it's gone. Nico is nothing like Joel. Joel wants to hurt me. This might be a sparring session, but it will be no-holds-barred. He will break bones and rip me apart if he can. It's in his eyes and the tension in his muscles.

Dropping my water to the floor, I kick off my shoes and step onto the mat. I shake out my arms before taking up my stance. I'm heavily trained in mixed martial arts, but I can already tell from the way this man moves that he knows exactly what I do and maybe more, which means I need to play dirty, and I will do just that.

I have to win.

He circles me, and I watch him carefully for signs of his moments, but unlike most, he gives nothing away. His arm just suddenly swings and his fist catches me in the chin. My head whips to the side from the strength of his punch, which is so much stronger than I have ever felt. I almost go down. My chin instantly aches, and my whole mouth locks up as he smirks.

"You're weak and sloppy. You care too much about being normal to fully give in. You will never win." He launches at me, holding nothing back. I have to fight just to stay on my feet, blocking his fists and feet. One connects with my ribs, and I feel the healing bones crack again. A fist hits my shoulder, and it goes numb as I stumble back under his assault. My heels almost catch on the edge of the mat because he's pushed me back that much.

I hear my father sigh. It's one sound filled with resignation and disappointment, but coupled with the glee in Joel's eyes, it ignites something within me. Something clicks, and I duck his next swing, leaping at him. I wrap my legs around his neck and flip us both, getting back to my feet and circling him as he stands and watches me.

The predator just became the prey.

He's right. I do hold back because I am so worried about what is inside of me. I am scared of myself, not my father, but I can't hold back, not if I want to survive this.

I have to let go.

Cocking my head, I smile slowly. "My turn," is all I say.

This time, I drive him back. I attack him with more speed than I've ever used before. Each movement is clean and so fast, he can't anticipate it. Years of training and honing skills flow back to me until he has to dance back out of my reach. His chest heaves slightly, while I'm not even sweating or panting. After all, brute strength isn't everything.

I'm faster than him, I realise, when I duck under his punch and come up behind him, kicking out his knees. He stumbles forward, but he flips back and over me, wrapping his arm around my throat. His muscles bulge as he squeezes, almost breaking my neck. Most people would struggle, so he's expecting that, and when I relax and go limp, he loosens his hold enough for me to slam my elbow back into him. I hear something break, and then I drop completely. He wasn't expecting that, and I'm free. I slam my hand up, right into his nose, and it explodes as he groans and steps back.

Ignoring the blood and busted nose, he comes for me again, but this time, his movements are wild with aggression. It makes him unpredictable and as fast as I am, so a few of them catch me. We both fight without holding back, each of us landing hits. Blood splashes across our skin, and bruises and broken bones make us cry out in pain.

His fist catches me in the face again, but the force of it knocks me down and he's on me in an instant. I narrow my gaze on him as his hands wrap around my throat.

"Why?" I ask him, voicing what I've been curious about this whole time, even as I wrap my legs around him and buck, trying to dislodge him. "Why are you helping him despite what he did to your unit?"

"Do you know how many soldiers die on duty, or even after? He can help stop that by making us harder, stronger, and faster. Why wouldn't I want to protect my people by doing that? We can be better."

"He will sell it to every army, and then you'll still be in the same predicament," I snarl as I thrash.

"I do this for my people. Why do you still fight, lost little girl?"

I meet his eyes as my nostrils flare and my lips curl in disgust. "For my people." I smash my head into his and roll out from under him, leaping to my feet and then kicking my foot into his balls. "And you will lose."

He falls forward with a cry, cupping his balls, and I smash my elbow into his head. He hits the mats hard, knocked out.

Panting, I look over at my father, feeling my split lip pour blood. One of my eyes is swollen, and one ankle aches.

He smiles at me, and I hate the spark of pride I feel at that. "Take Joel to the infirmary," my father calls, then he picks something up and heads my way. "I knew you could do it. I was always betting on you. We just have a few more things to test and then you can rest, okay?" he says kindly, but I grind my teeth. He gestures for me to turn and I do.

A blindfold wraps around my head, blocking my sight. Blowing out a long breath, I loosen my stance, my arms hanging at my sides as I wait for instruction.

"Please show us your senses so we may test each. You will face multiple opponents," my father says, and I hear him move away.

I hear more movement as guards come towards me, and I wait as they spread out, and then it's silent.

Finally, there's a squeak, a scent, and I move quickly. I am fast, but so are they.

There has to be at least three of them. One knocks my leg out, but I jump back up and slam my own into something hard. There's a grunt, then arms wrap around me from behind. I kick and smash into another body coming from the front. They fall back, and holding onto the arms around me, I push off and up, rolling to my feet.

I lose myself in the fight. I can't see, and the darkness seems to unlock something inside me.

It's as if that darkness was always waiting to come out. I hear more than I ever have. I hear the air whooshing in and out of their lungs, the beating of their hearts, and I can almost smell their fear as I attack.

I lose myself in the rhythm. There are at least eight of them now, and I know as soon as I knock one out or hurt them too badly, they are dragged away and replaced by another. There are no words, just actions. I don't know how long I fight for, but after what feels like hours and I start to slow, a punch lands that I wouldn't have let make contact before.

My body is tiring. I'm still healing, and it's taking its toll.

Another punch slips through, then another, until I'm finally kicked down. Suddenly, several booted feet slam into my body. I drag my knees to my chest as they slam into me over and over. I groan, managing to crawl from them and get back to my feet, but then something hard hits the back of my head.

The last thing I see as the blindfold slips away is my father turning away in disappointment.

The flight to China was uneventful, and we find the manufacturing plant easily enough. We survey it for a while, watching the workers come and go. The trucks leave and arrive, and D tracks each one in case we need to know where they go, and then we wait for Louis to give us orders and let us know it's time.

Bert was worried when we left, but he was also determined. His final words reach me even now. "Bring her home!"

We will. We have to. This is a good lead, I remind myself, even as I shift for the hundredth time. I need to move, to do something, anything. As the clock ticks, I can't help but wonder how much more damage is being done to the woman I love while we sit here.

"Soon," Jonas reminds me. He is struggling too. I feel it as he sits next to me, crammed into the car. Louis is at the store opposite the plant, Nico is on the roof of the store for a better angle, and D is in the front of the car with his laptop open.

"Not soon enough." I scrub at my face, no doubt messing up my hair, but I don't care.

"I prefer it when you're the happy-go-lucky doctor," Jonas grumbles.

"Well, tough shit. Not everybody is happy all the time, Jonas. I'm allowed to be upset," I snap, and he watches me with wide eyes. "Sorry," I mutter.

"Don't be. I've been waiting for that outburst. It's good. I like it when you're happy, but this? This is real. I was getting sick of you holding it all back," he mumbles, glancing out of the window to make sure we are not compromised.

"What do you mean?" I feel my brows draw together in confusion.

He snorts and grins at me. "Come on, Isaac. You act so calm all the time, so put together and like you're ready to face everything. You take in everything we do and say and never complain. That takes its toll, and I always saw it lingering under the surface. I'm glad it's finally coming out."

"What?" I whisper.

"Madness," he says calmly. "It's the same madness we all have, including Nova. Let it out, brother. We are going to need that to get her back."

He turns away like he didn't just drop a bomb. Is he right? Nova always asked me if I was okay. She worried about my reactions and how I was dealing with everything. What if I kept such a tight grip all along because I was worried about what would come out?

Jonas wears his madness proudly, Nico channels it, Louis embraces it, and Dimitri fights it, but me? I hide it.

What if I've made it worse?

Is he right? Do I need to embrace it and therefore burn myself?

Have I been holding back who and what I am?

Yes, I realise with sudden clarity.

"Who knew you were so smart?" I mutter as I stare at his profile.

"Nova." He shrugs. "She sees us all clearly."

Isn't that the sad truth?

Taking his hand in mine, I squeeze it. "You're right. Maybe you can teach me how to embrace it better and I can teach you how to be calmer, brother."

"Nah, she likes me when I'm manic, and so do I." He winks. "But welcome to the club."

Louis slides into the car along with Nico and turns to us. "We'll wait for most of the workers to leave, but not the boss, and then we'll go in. I want as few witnesses as possible. We go in silently. I want no alarms, no police, and no footage of us being there. We do not give the doctor any reason to suspect we are on his trail. Is that understood?"

We all agree since we don't want to do anything that could jeopardise us not only getting to Nova, but also keeping her alive. He's right. We have to do this silently and carefully without tipping off her father.

We wait until the shift ends to make our move. I go with Louis right through the front door. D is at the electrical board outside, cutting off cameras and alarms and fielding any phone calls that might happen from mobiles. Nico repels in from the roof and slips through the open top-floor window on the right, while Jonas is on the left, although we all hear him squealing softly in our earpieces as he goes. We are covering all of our bases. We shut and lock the doors behind us. The warehouse is massive and filled with shipping containers and lab equipment in the process of being made or tested. We move past them, looking for any stragglers or workers.

"Security guards are up top, Nico, coming your way," D says.

"Got them," Nico murmurs, and there's a barely audible grunt down the mic. "Taken care of."

"There are three workers on the late shift coming in early in the canteen. I can auto lock the door from here, but avoid it so they don't see your faces. They haven't noticed as of yet, too busy talking and drinking coffee."

"Got it," Louis murmurs down the mic as we move to the stairs. They lead up to the second floor. Nico is already there, and all of us converge on the office on the second floor. The door has no window, so Louis smashes it open and we surge inside. Nico instantly shoots the phone as the man jerks up from a nap, imprints of the wood from the desk across his cheek.

His eyes widen in fear, and he leaps up, but I push him back down into his chair.

"Sit," I demand.

"What do you want?" he asks in English.

"Just some information," Louis replies, sitting in the opposite chair. "If you tell us what we need to know, we won't harm you, but you will forget we ever existed. In fact, we are more than happy to pay for this information." He smiles charmingly, and the man relaxes but glances at Nico and pales. He plays the part of muscle well—not speaking, just glaring.

"What information?" the man finally mutters.

"Just about one of your buyers and where the last shipment went. That's all." Louis lifts the bag he is carrying and throws it on the desk. The man glances at it and slowly reaches out and undoes the zipper, seeing the bills inside.

He blinks owlishly at us. "I have a family," he says randomly. "You can have the information you want. I'm just trying to provide for them."

"We know, hence why we did this here and not at your home. You're innocent in this," I reply softly, "but you're supplying equipment to a very bad person, and we want to talk to him. No one will hurt you or your family so please, just tell us what we want."

"Okay, can you tell me the date? I will find out for you," he asks, sitting up taller. I'm surprised by how easily he wants to help us, but when I glance around, I see why. It's in the hard glint in our eyes. Anyone can see we are getting that information one way or another, and he's simply choosing the best way out.

Smart.

Dimitri informs him and watches carefully as he pulls information from a cabinet. It's paper, which surprises me, but he hands the folder over. "That's everything we have on the buyer. It was his first time with me. I remember speaking to someone who mentioned their usual supplier did not have what they wanted. It's the credit information as well as the delivery address. I remember because it was very far and random. Do you need anything else?"

"He hasn't bought again?" Louis asks with a frown.

"No, only that once. I guess he went back to his regular supplier after," the man replies with a sincere tone.

"Thank you so much for your help." Louis stands then carefully tucks the chair under the desk. "Forget you saw us. I would hate to have to come back and visit you and your family. Here, take the money and our apologies." Louis turns, and we all follow him out like we were never here.

Dimitri turns the cameras and alarms on once more, unlocking the door like nothing happened. For a while, we watch the man in the office, but he doesn't make any calls or ask for help. He stares at the money. His shoulders slump, and he seems both resigned and relieved.

"He won't tell," I murmur as I watch him, noticing the signs. "He needs the money too much."

"Are you sure?" Louis asks, looking over at me in the car.

"Yes." I watch the camera, but I'm sure, and then I look at Dimitri. "Do we have it?"

"Yes, he's right. It's a weird delivery address. It's an airstrip. Give me an hour and I'll have more information."

An airstrip.

Fuck, are we still on a wild-goose chase?

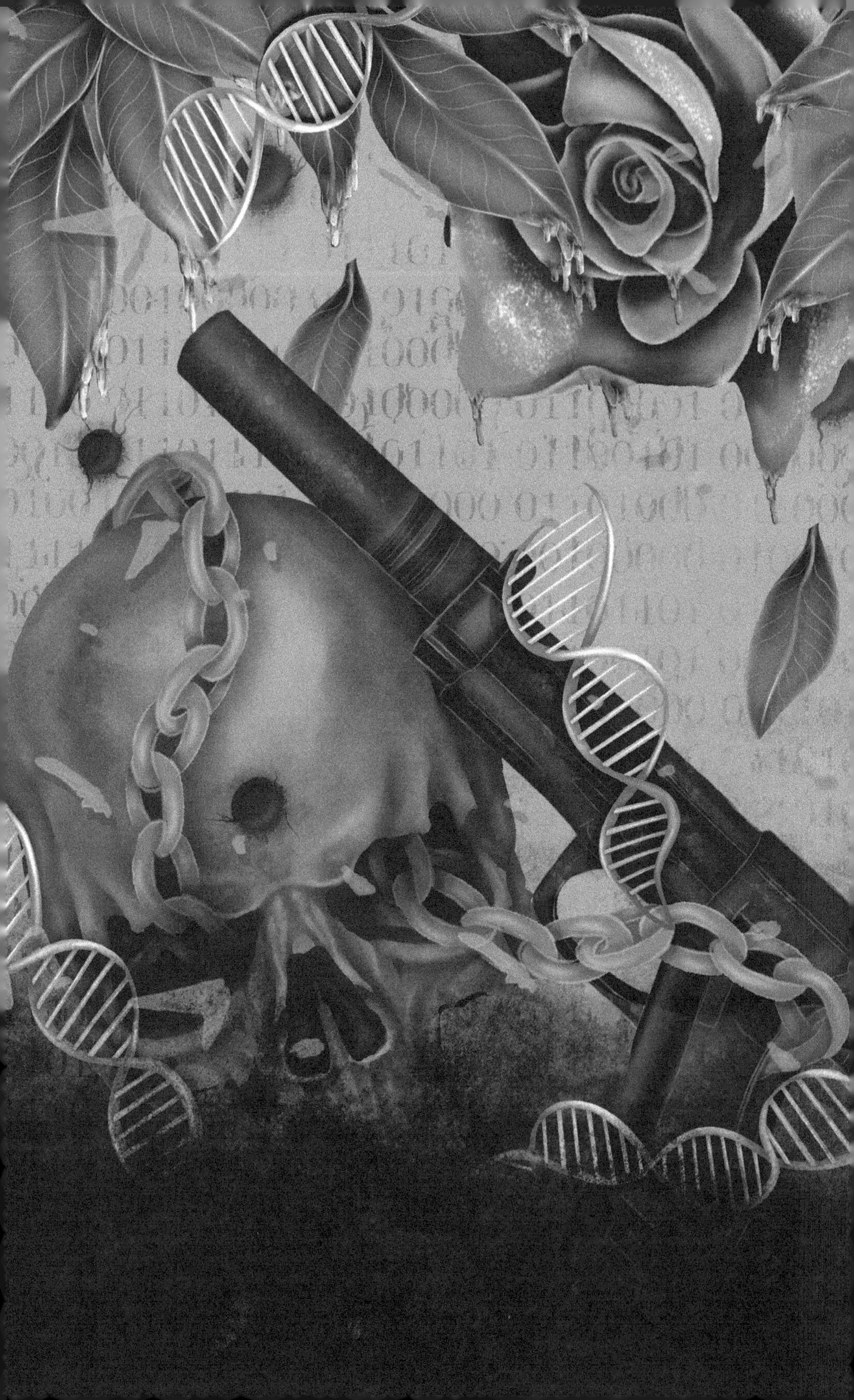

NINETEEN

When I wake up, my whole body aches like one giant bruise. I trap a groan in my throat, just feeling out my situation. It wouldn't be the first time my father has taken advantage of my passed-out state, and it feels a lot like that now. I'm lying on something cold and hard—a medical table perhaps. There's that air-con noise that only happens in the lab and the whirring of machines. I'm not in the gym anymore, but I'm also not tied down.

That's a plus, not that I'll need to make a move yet. I need to play the long game.

I take stock of my body. Nothing is broken. There may be a few fractured ribs and some bruised bones, but nothing feels completely wrecked, which is good. I undoubtedly look like shit, but I don't care about that.

I'm about to open my eyes and scan my surroundings when I hear booted feet entering the room. I relax my body despite the fact I want to stiffen, keeping my breathing nice and slow. It's a moment when they might give things away unintentionally.

As expected, someone comes over and checks on me. I feel them hovering above me before they wander a little farther away. "Dr. Davis." I almost snarl at the voice. It's Joel. I guess I didn't kick his ass hard enough if he's awake.

"Feeling better?" my father responds, and there's a thread of disappointment in his voice. I want to laugh.

"Much. I will not make the mistake of misjudging your daughter again. She is a lot stronger than she looks."

"That she is. Watching you two spar, though, gave me the results I expected for you, and it also gave me some ideas," Davis murmurs, and a horrible feeling starts to build inside me, like the moment before a car crash when you see the vehicle coming towards you. That's how it feels. I want to knock myself out. I want to run. I know it's going to be bad, but instead, I lie here and listen.

"An idea?" Joel queries.

"Hmm, yes. I always thought Nova would be the start and end of my research, the key to it all, but what if she is in a different way? She reached peak human potential, and she has begun to access her mind more than any other. It is changing not only her brain, but her physical abilities and structure. She is adapting, to put it mildly, but she started out like the rest of us, and that will give her some limitations. If we were to use that and create a being, a child, perhaps, born from two individuals already enhanced through experiments, then the possibilities would be endless."

My heart freezes.

"Are you saying what I think you are?"

"Yes, you and Nova will breed. You will make me a child, which will be the future of us all. Just think how strong it would be with two almost perfectly enhanced parents."

"I . . ." Joel hesitates, and for a moment, hope fills me that he won't agree and he sees how wrong this is.

"You can do this, yes? She isn't bad looking. If not, we can offer stimulants. She will, of course, have to be sedated, and although there are other ways to do it, this would be the fastest."

No, no, no.

"I-I can do it. Of course." He sounds unsure, but I know that won't stop him. "The child, what will happen to the child?" I guess he's not as big of a monster as I thought. My mind is numb to what I am hearing.

They want to impregnate me.

No, they want to rape me and implant a child in me, which they will use as a test-tube baby.

"It will become the next step of my research. The first one or two always have mistakes, but Nova is in her prime, as are you, so we have plenty of time to get it right."

Annie, he's talking about Annie. Calling her a mistake.

I'm almost sick at the implication of what he's saying.

He's going to force me to breed children for him to experiment on.

My eyes snap open, but the men are too focused on each other. My head is turned to face them, my cheek pressed to the metal table. A tray, as usual, is next to the metal table, ready for his next sick experiment.

I can tell by his face he means it. He'll do it.

Oh, God, no.

I'm numb and cold as he turns and finds me awake. I can see his mouth moving, but his words don't register. Other doctors join us, and my head turns to look up at the ceiling. Something cold touches my stomach, but I still don't move or make a noise. I can't or I'll scream.

Or I'll break.

Something sharp pierces my stomach and starts to drag, causing red-hot agony to shoot through me.

They are cutting me open.

It's like everything snaps back into place, and the noise in the room comes rushing back with the agony. Air fills my lungs with a gasp. I lie here as he cuts me open, and when he turns back, I stare at the man I thought I couldn't hate more but do.

Looking into his eyes, I know he'll do it. He will force him to breed with me or worse. I can't have that. I won't. I will not become a vessel for his sick games. That child would be a pin cushion, tortured and ripped apart like me. I will not put another person through what I went through, but I cannot stop him. I'm weak, powerless . . .

Or so he thinks, but he doesn't understand the lengths I will go to in order to stop this and make sure it never happens to another, even at the risk of my own body.

He will never get my womb or get a child from me.

I'll make sure of it, even if it ruins me for life or kills me.

It's better than the alternative.

There is a table next to me holding the hot sealing prong they use to cauterise my wounds. I don't think, just act. Grabbing the red end of the prong when he looks away, I slam it into myself, into my open stomach wound, screaming in agony. My skin is on fire, and the pain courses through me, but I carry on. I fight them off when they try to pull me away. It's only when I start to pass out that they manage to rip it from me, but I know the damage is already done.

I smile shakily as I begin to die.

That wasn't my aim though. My womb is ruined. I smile at him. "Now you'll never get what you want. Now you will never get my children."

Then, once more, everything goes dark.

I welcome it like an old friend.

We watch the private airfield for hours. Only one flight comes in all day and by the looks of them, they are not your regular businessmen. No, this is a don't ask, don't tell kind of place, which means there will be no records.

It's another dead end . . . until we see her.

A tiny, curvy blonde leaves the building after locking up. A manager maybe? "Follow her," I instruct, and so we do. This town is small, so there isn't much, and she heads right to a bar.

Dimitri follows her in, reporting that she's sitting alone at a table in the corner.

"Find me everything you can on her," I demand. She was the one meeting the clients, so maybe she knows something.

"On it," he murmurs through the phone, and a few minutes later, a document is on my screen. I scroll through it as the others spread out to watch the back. Jonas remains at the airfield with Isaac, searching just in case.

Lives alone, thirty-five, divorced, and has worked there for five years. She has a huge bank account, one dog, and one cat. No family, nothing else. She's also alone on a Friday night in the bar looking lonely. No listed address, shit.

She's the only link we have, the only choice.

She's lonely and desperate for attention. I hate it, but I know what I'm going to have to do to get the information we need. It makes me feel sick.

"I'm coming in," I tell him. "I'll get the information."

"How?" he asks, but I hang up, ignoring the clenching in my gut and the deep feeling of betrayal. If Nova found out, she would kick my ass, and the thought makes me smile as I cross to the bar. I'd let her since I'd deserve it, but I have to do whatever it takes to get my girl back. After that, she can beat me and then kiss it better. Taking a deep breath, I paste on a fake, overly friendly smile. I hang around the bar for a while, ordering a beer and taking a sip before approaching her. She's reading a romance book, and when I stop before her table, she is so engrossed she doesn't even notice at first.

I clear my throat, and her head snaps up, her eyes widening and cheeks heating. She looks around nervously.

"Hi." I grin. "I'm Reggie."

She blinks and then blushes harder. "Oh, God, I'm sorry. Hi, erm, hi, yeah, I'm Sarah," she blurts out.

"I'm new to town, and I don't really know anyone," I tell her, leaning in like this is a secret. She smiles and giggles as she looks around. "Can I join you? I really don't want to sit alone, drinking my beer."

"Oh, of course."

I slide into the booth opposite her before she can change her mind. Her eyes scan me and heat, and when she meets my gaze, I see desire and curiosity. Good. I can use that, even as the sight of another woman lusting after what belongs to Nova makes me want to gag. This body is hers, every inch of it.

"What are you reading?" I ask, leaning back and purposely flexing my arm as I drape it on the back of the booth. Her eyes follow it like I knew they would. "Sarah?" I murmur silkily. I hate this. I hate every fucking second of this.

I can feel Dimitri judging me, but I'll do anything for her.

"It's just a romance novel." She ducks her head. "I love them. They always get their happy ending. I don't know why I said that."

Laughing, I reach out and eye the cover. It's of a lady and a dragon, and

I make a note to read it to Nova later. She would probably love it. "I love happy endings. I'm hoping for my own," I say softly. "Is it sexy?" She laughs nervously, and I chuckle. "I take that as a yes. I'm curious, do you enjoy reading it? The sex scenes?"

"I . . . Yes," she admits, eyeing me through her lashes. "Most women do."

"How come?" I ask with genuine curiosity and no judgement.

"I guess it's how we want to be loved. It's more than the mind-blowing sex they get, which if we are honest, not a lot of women get, but it's the love. Did you know romance is the biggest selling genre in fiction? Let that sink in. Women are so desperate to be loved right that they buy books about it because they know it's the only way most of them will get it, and men? They make fun of it. They make fun of women wanting to read a book about being loved and cared for like the idea is ridiculous."

"Because men are idiots. You want to be loved?" I ask.

"Everyone wants to be loved, Reggie," she replies, sitting up straighter, bolder in her passion. It's cute. "Every single person, no matter what they say, wants that. They want to be loved deeply and stop being hurt over and over. They want a happy ending without pain. Many don't find it, so they find it through this, fiction, until they do find their happy ending. Other people already have it and love relearning the feeling through others. Some simply want an adventure. They get it through books. Like me, a small-town girl, I've got to visit the stars, see other planets, and go to the deepest depths of the oceans. I'm a soldier, a sailor, a mermaid, a pirate . . . I can be anything I want in these books, and for the hours that I indulge and read, losing myself between ink and paper, the shitty world around me doesn't exist. I'm free."

"That sounds amazing. I never thought about it that way. I guess I never really gave myself the time to explore reading. I'm always so busy planning for the future or what comes next."

She smiles. "You should."

"I will." I'll explore it with Nova, if she desires to find the kind of freedom pages can offer. She will always have that deep love this woman loves reading about, but I like how happy it makes Sarah, and I want that for Nova.

She's a lovely woman, and she deserves to find happiness. She's clearly smart, kind, giving, and optimistic, but she isn't my Nova. There is only one woman for me, and I'll use and hurt this kind woman if I have to.

I take a deep breath, hating myself for what I'm about to say. "If you want, I could help you find that freedom."

"How so?" she asks obliviously.

Smiling secretly, I stand and offer her my hand. "How about you take me back to your place and I'll show you? We can even act out some of those scenes."

Wrong, so wrong, so very wrong.

She hesitates, but then she lays her hand in mine. I pull her to her feet, and she clutches her bag as I lead her to the door.

I tell myself to hold her hand. Even if it looks odd, I drop it in the ruse of opening the door. She hesitates again but ducks through, and I wipe my hand on my trousers, the wrongness of it sticking with me. I need Nova to replace it. Sarah's hand was too hot, and it didn't fit right, not like my Nova's, which fits perfectly.

At the parking lot, I look around and back at her with a smile, draping my arm around her coat-covered shoulders so I don't have to touch her.

"You drive?" I offer. "I don't have my car."

Liar, but that way Dimitri can follow us.

"Of course." She fumbles with her keys, and I grin. When she gets them, she blushes and leads me over to her car. It's a nice brand-new model, and I slip into the passenger seat as she hits the ignition, and then we are on the road. I glance into the side mirror to see lights a few cars behind us. They are not noticeable to anyone else but me.

Dimitri.

I make small talk until we pull up in front of her house, and then I get out and follow her up to it.

Her house is adorable, a single-story cottage set before the woods. The lights are on, and there are flowers bordering the stone paths to the door. Once inside, we are greeted by a purring black cat and she blushes. "This is Romeo." She laughs as I chuckle.

She heads in, strips off her coat and bag, and drops them onto a side table. There is a kitchen to the left, a farmhouse style one that's cut with a few steps into an open-plan living room. Sofas face a huge fireplace with bookshelves on either side, and the back windows are floor-to-ceiling to show the forest.

It's cute.

"Do you want a drink?" she asks nervously.

"Sure, a drink would be great," I reply.

I wander around, pretending to look at things, but really, I'm scanning the house. Beyond the kitchen, there is a door that clearly leads to a bathroom. There's also a short flight of stairs to an open loft up top with a bedroom and an office. That's where the information will be. Maybe locked?

"Here." Sarah offers me a tumbler of what smells like vodka and something fruity. "Oh, let me just let Juliet out." She blushes again and calls, tapping her leg, and an older Labrador trots in. Juliet spares me a glance as she goes outside. I use the opportunity and pour the drugs into my cup, using my finger to stir, and then I swap mine with hers, which sits on the table, all before she turns back.

"Sorry," she offers, and heads over.

I sit on the sofa, and she copies me, clearly nervous.

"So, what's your favourite book?" I ask, sitting back on the sofa, trying to gather as much information as I can in case we need it.

She hesitates. "At the moment or in life?"

"Both," I reply, and she seems to struggle for her answer.

"Right now, probably *Touch of Frost Queen*. I don't think I could pick one in general because there are so many good ones." She grins. "What about you? I don't know much about you, so tell me all there is to know."

"There isn't much," I answer, and she looks worried. "I live a pretty boring life." I take a sip, but she doesn't. "We can spend all night talking if you want, or we can spend our night having fun. Which one would you like?"

"Fun," she whispers.

"Good." I smile. "Down the hatch." I wink. "And then into the fun."

She quickly downs the drink and reaches for me. I let her straddle me, but just as she leans in to kiss me, her eyes grow fuzzy. Thank God. I don't think I could stand feeling her lips on mine.

It doesn't take long before she's out, and I turn so she falls into the sofa.

I lay her down slowly and cover her. Romeo jumps onto her chest, purring. Her dog, Juliet, barks at the back door, so I let her in, and she snarls at me but moves over to her owner. Juliet whines and nudges Sarah, and then she crouches before her, snarling at me when I get too close.

"Good girl," I tell her and move to the front door and open it, finding nothing but darkness. Dimitri slowly materialises, glaring at me before slamming his fist into my stomach, and then he steps past me. "You deserve that." He stops at the sight but turns away, scanning the house as I rub at my aching abs.

"Search upstairs. There's an office there, get everything," I demand.

"What if the information isn't here?" he mutters.

"Then we wait, and when she wakes, we get it out of her," I snap.

"Seduce it out of her, you mean," he retorts angrily.

"You think I enjoyed that?" I go toe to toe with him, snarling. "I hated every single fucking minute, but it if gets us closer to our girl, I will. I will do whatever it takes, and then I will beg on my fucking knees for forgiveness."

"I can't wait to see her kick your ass." He smiles, and I smile back.

"Me too. Now go, we don't have very long." My phone rings and I answer it. "Report," I tell Jonas, ignoring the other missed calls from the general. I don't have time to deal with him. I've debriefed him as much as I can, and he's angry, but there are more important things than handing over the research.

Like getting my girl back.

"Nothing here, boss, only a few flight numbers." It's clear he's frustrated.

"Text me them all, you never know."

"Got it," he offers as I hang up.

"Anything?" I call to D.

"Give me a second!" Dimitri snarls.

I wander to the kitchen and do the pots while I wait—it's the least I can do—then I fill up the cat's and dog's water dishes since she will probably feel groggy.

"Nothing." Dimitri comes back down.

"Fuck." I slam my fists down, and my eyes go back to where she stirs. "Then we go to plan B."

We wait for her to wake. Dimitri leans against the wall, and I sit on the coffee table. When her eyes flutter, I wince. She sits up groggily and rubs her head. When she sees me, she frowns. "Reggie, what happened?" she slurs, looking around. When she notices Dimitri, she screams and scrambles back on the sofa.

"We will not hurt you, Sarah," I promise. "I'm sorry about drugging you."

"You drugged me? What the fuck? God damn it, I knew it was too good to be true. A ridiculously hot man hit on me then drugged me. Come on, what the fuck? You couldn't just live with your mother or something?" She seems to be talking to someone else, maybe God, so I ignore it.

"I need information," I begin, and she laughs hysterically.

"You could have just asked like a normal person," she snaps. Is it bad that it didn't even occur to me until she mentioned it? Maybe.

"You wouldn't have told me. You would have screamed and called the police, and it would have cost precious time," I reply logically with my hands splayed, showing I'm harmless.

She watches us carefully. "Get out," she demands.

"I can't. Please, we just need your flight records for this date." I show her the date, and she frowns harder, her nostrils flaring.

"Get out before I call the police or worse." She tries to throw herself over the sofa, so I move quickly and block her, sitting her back down. She slumps, realising she is outnumbered. I can see how terrified she is, but she holds it in check well. She's brave, this girl.

Very brave.

I hate that I'm doing this too. She is a good person and doesn't deserve it.

"I should have taken that Italian mobster up on his fake marriage offer," she mutters. "But no, I had to be independent, and look where it got me."

"Please, Sarah," I plead. "You can hate me and call the police, but I need the information. Not for me. For her."

"Her?" She hesitates.

"My girl. The love of my life. She was on that plane. She was taken. You said you read about men doing everything they can for their love, and that's what I'm doing. I love her more than anything in this world. She's my family. She's my everything. I can't lose her." I know my voice cracks, but I let her hear the truth. "Please, Sarah, I just need to know where she went, I have to find her."

"I'm fucking crazy," she mutters as she stands and moves over to a small bookshelf I didn't notice. She roots around for a while before ripping a paper out and handing it to me. "I don't ever want to see you here again; do you understand me? And if this girl isn't who you say she is, I hope she hurts you badly."

"She will, no doubt," I admit. "She's crazy like that." I chuckle. "Thank you, Sarah. I mean it."

She simply nods, and it's clear it's time to leave.

As we head for the door, she calls out, "Reggie, or whatever your name is, I hope you find your happily ever after."

"So do I, Sarah, and I hope you find yours too," I reply as I shut her front door and look down at the note. "Ready the plane. We are wheels up. It's time to get our girl."

Hold on, baby, we are coming. Just hold on a little longer.

TWENTY-ONE

"Is he sure this is where his contact is meeting us?" Louis asks for the hundredth time. I scan the busy market, on the lookout for any threats. The sunglasses and scarf wrapped around my head obscure who I am, but I'm still on alert, waiting for Davis's men to pop out. Jonas is inside the bazaar a bit farther up, and Dimitri is in the van with Isaac, while Louis and I are close in case this goes wrong.

"He's sure. We need the weapons before we get there," I reply, and Louis nods, knowing I am right. Not only is Jonas's contact going to sell us everything we need gear-wise, but they will also get us the false identities we need to get into the labs. Obviously, with one look at most of us, Davis will know who we are, but that's an issue for another day.

Picking up the small, green-quartz elephant figurine, I let the sunlight catch it. "Do you think Nova will like this?" I ask Louis.

"Here he is."

"Louis," I demand, "do you think she will like this?"

He blinks, coming out of his work, and looks at the elephant and smiles. "Why does it matter?"

"It matters," I say as I look down at it, curling my fingers around it. "I want to show her we didn't forget or let her go. I want her to know that I thought about her every minute of every single day and that she will never be alone."

He's silent for a minute. "It's perfect, Nico. She will love it."

Nodding without looking at him, I hand over some money, and we get moving again, scanning the streets as we wait for word that Jonas got what he needs. A plan has started to form from the location information we received from the airfield. It's going to be next to impossible to break in and free her.

We need to be smart, hence this meeting.

This won't be an overnight job. We are planning for every possibility so we never lose our girl again.

We wander around the market for hours before Jonas finally joins us. "All good," he says, carrying two duffle bags over his shoulder and another two on his wrists. I take some, and so does Louis. "Let's get going." We weave our way back to the van, and as soon as we are inside, we head back to the plane, ready to get to the location.

Once onboard, I sort through the weapons with Jonas, my eyebrows rising at the explosives inside.

"You never know." He shrugs.

"Jonas, this is enough to blow up a city," I say carefully, knowing he's always a little unhinged, but since Nova has disappeared, he's become very unhinged.

"Good." He nods.

I share a look with Isaac but shrug. Jonas is good with explosives. He won't blow us up, right?

"Okay, now that that's all sorted, we have one last decision left. Who's going in?" Louis asks as he joins us.

Everyone volunteers, but I wait for them to quiet down. "It has to be me. I was one of the first to fail, which means their files on me are old. Davis didn't pay much attention to me along the way or even at the house. He would probably recognise me up close, but I won't let him. It has to be me. I look the part and can act it. Dimitri needs to be on the outside as our point of contact. Louis, you need to direct us and put us in position. Jonas would end up killing too many people, and he needs to be our backup plan.

Isaac is too kind and would try to save everyone. It has to be me." I know I'm right, and as they share a look, it's obvious they clearly know it too.

"It means going into the belly of the beast, Nico, and probably facing a lot of your past and fears," Isaac remarks carefully.

"I know." I nod. "I'll be fine. I have to be, for her. Beast or no beast, nothing will stop me from getting to our girl."

And that is what it comes down to.

I would face every single bad memory, fight a million armies, crawl through a million tiny spaces, or face torture and imprisonment again if it meant freeing my girl and kissing her.

Isaac said the belly of the beast, but they haven't seen a beast, not yet, so I'll show them one.

And they took the beast's girl.

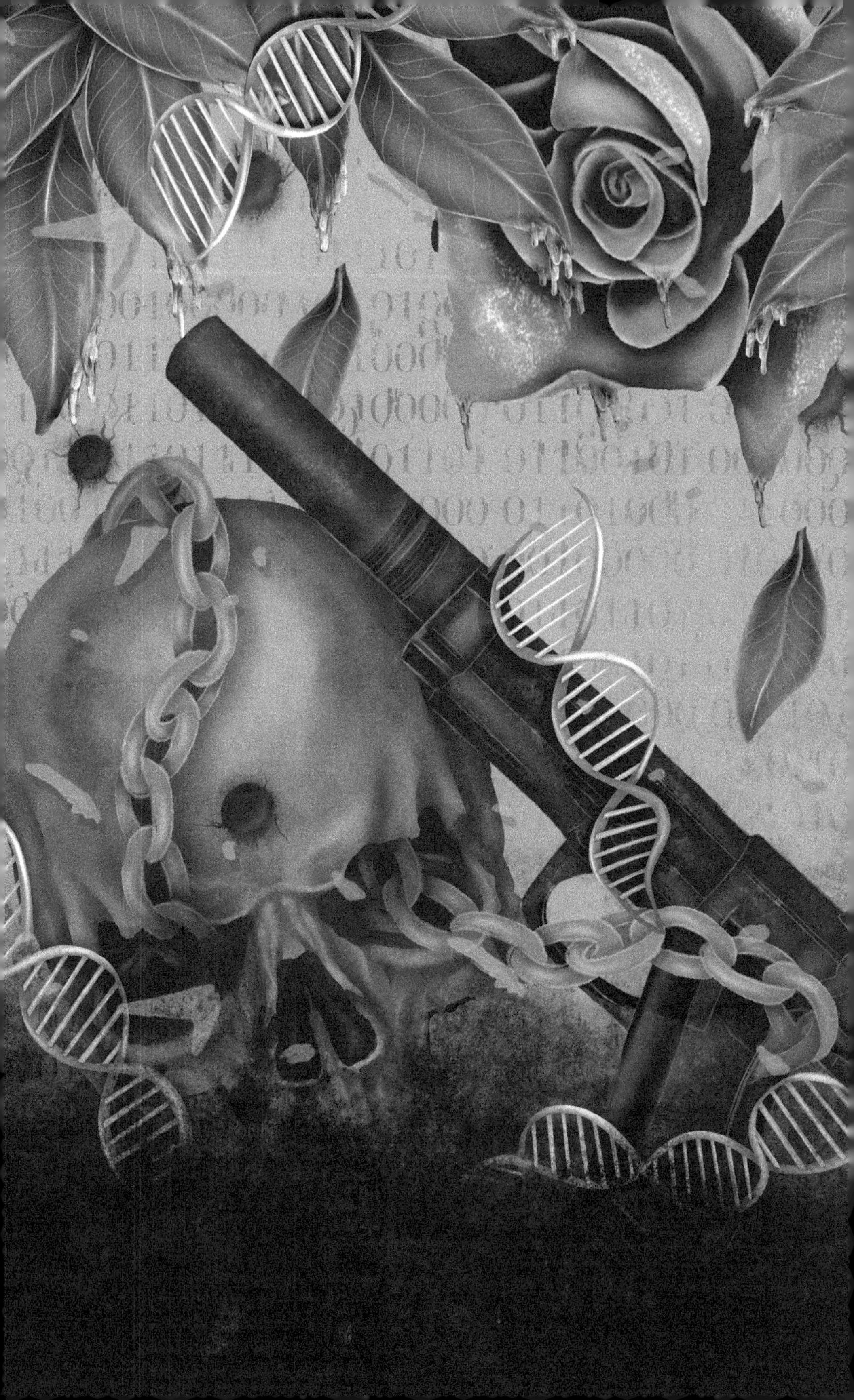

TWENTY-TWO

I don't know how long I'm out for. I vaguely remember waking as my father screamed for his surgeons, his doctors, everyone. I remember masked men running in, IVs, and sedation. After that? Nothing.

I'm in one of the side rooms now. The bed is uncomfortable, and my wrists are manacled to the bed. It's dark bar the light through the gap in the door to the corridor, and I'm alone, the beeping of the machines attached to me the only sound filling the room.

My whole body, from chest to pelvis, feels raw and pulverised, but whatever drugs they have me on are keeping me a little numb to it for now.

I remember what I did. I even remember why, and suddenly, the ramifications of my actions take root in my brain. My eyes lock on the plain ceiling above me as my heart rate speeds up, the beeping growing louder as panic winds through my chest.

I ruined my body. I no doubt destroyed any chance of ever having kids.

Good, that means he can't use me to hurt them. They will be safe. He will have to find another way. I protected many innocents from having to go through what I and the others experienced.

I can't have kids.

I never thought I wanted to bring a child into such a fucked-up world and a fucked-up family, not to mention I would be a terrible mother. No, I was better going without, but as my hand covers my stomach, tears fall silently from my eyes, rolling into my hair as I bite back my pain. At least I had the choice, the chance, and as my eyes close, the images of tiny versions of Louis, Nico, Jonas, Dimitri, and Isaac fill my head, running around with a smile. It's something I will never have.

Our world is crazy and dangerous, but it doesn't stop the bone-deep longing from suddenly appearing because I will never be able to give them that now. I don't regret my choice. I did it to save the child that would be born into a test tube, even if it meant my death, but it doesn't stop the pain.

I seriously maimed my body and my future to save something worse from happening, and it hurts.

It fucking hurts.

Haven't I given enough?

Haven't I suffered enough?

When is it my turn to be happy?

How much more can I truly give?

Grief for a child I will never have now aches alongside the grief for the sister I lost, and I hold onto it as I sob silently, my body racked with pain. I thought I was so strong, and I thought I could handle anything, but for the first time, I don't know if I can survive this.

I don't know if I want to.

I'm so alone, so very alone, and so very tired of being covered in shit I can't scrape off. I struggle to even breathe and open my eyes. I'm so very tired of being alive.

Is this how Bas felt?

It would hurt Dimitri and the others to lose another like that, but the thought to end this all is there. Almost selfishly, I realise I wouldn't have to be around to see it.

I already planned not to make it out of this alive and to end this once and for all. Maybe it would be for the best because they wouldn't know I didn't try to make it out. They would only know I died stopping this, and that might make them hate me less.

I know I'm spiralling and going to a really dark place, but I can't help myself.

I can't pull myself out this time.

The door opens and my father stops above me, a scowl on his lips. "Well, I hope you are happy and got what you wanted. You will never be able to have kids, Nova. Do you know what you have done? You have ruined my research!" he hisses as he leans down. He wipes away my tears, and I flinch, knowing it wasn't an act of comfort. He eyes them clinically and then smiles. "There are other ways to make you into what I need though, and now you have removed any barrier that meant I needed to keep you healthy." He turns and leaves.

When the door shuts with a click, I allow myself to sink deeper into that dark hole.

I did it. I stopped him from getting my kids.

It doesn't matter what happens to me.

That's all that matters. They will never hurt innocents.

Only me.

I deserve it.

It's good because it means they might finally kill me, and I will be free of this pain. This world is a shitty fucking place but for a moment, I had hope for a better life. I got a glimpse of happiness and love, only for it to be taken away, and I can't keep pretending I will get it back.

Wherever the guys are, they are safe from him, and that's good. They wouldn't want me now anyway.

I'm not just broken this time.

I'm ruined beyond repair.

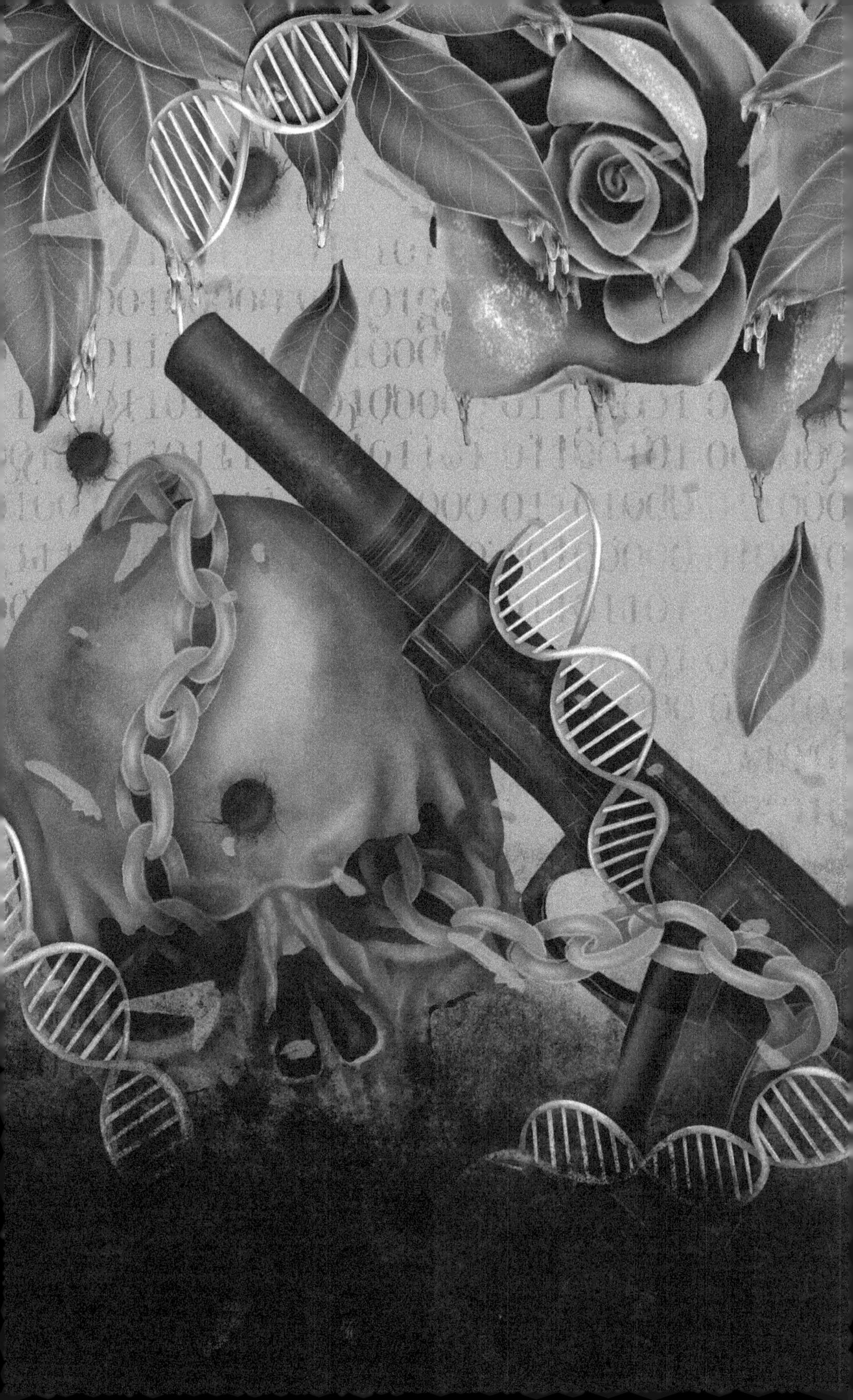

TWENTY-THREE

They leave me alone for several days to heal. I'm checked on every few hours by a doctor who refuses to look or speak to me properly, and I am forced to eat and drink as if they think I will try to kill myself that way, which lets me know how bad I truly look. On day five, I've had enough, so I slide out of bed, crumpling to the floor in pain. Gritting my teeth, I stand and bring my IV with me as I shuffle to the toilet, hating the weakness and the pain.

I cannot stand another day lying in that bed and pondering how much I hate life and how unfair everything is. I'm over it. I'm over the pity, and I'm just angry.

Flicking on the light, I shut the door behind me and take a steadying breath, then I turn to the LED lit mirror. I wince at my reflection. The lighting is harsh, but I look like death warmed over. Hanging my head, I close my eyes and pull in deep breaths, trying to pep myself up. I need to look on the positive side. I've had days to rest, no torture, and three meals a day, and the food could be worse.

It falls flat, and I look back at my reflection with tears in my eyes.

There are purple and black bags under them, my lips are chapped and raw, and my skin is pale and lifeless. My hair is greasy and hanging in unbrushed strings around my face. I can't do anything about the wound or the pain or even about my situation right now, but this? This I can fix as much as I can. Maybe when I look like the old me, I'll have more confidence too.

I turn to the walk-in shower cubicle. There isn't a curtain, like they think I might hang myself with it—or them, I can't decide. Looking down at the IV line, I think about ripping it out, but I know better. Instead, I tug off the tape, slowly slide the needle out, and then toss it away. As I strip off the gown, I don't allow myself to look in the mirror to see the gauze covering my wound.

I flick on the shower and don't even let it heat before I step in, the sharp iciness making me gasp in a good way. It wakes me up and reminds me that I'm still alive. With my blood pumping faster, my heart awakens from its slumber, and I slick back my hair and just stand here, letting the water wash everything away—my tears, my defeat, and my hopelessness.

I finally turn and start to wash my body. I carefully avoid the gauze and wash my hair twice before deciding to tackle it. It needs to be changed, so it might as well come off, but am I prepared for what lies underneath?

Refusing to look won't change anything, but I still just stare as if that will make it better. It's best to see it now when I'm alone, I rationalise, so that he can't monitor my reaction and use it against me. *Just do it, Nova*, I tell myself, getting annoyed all over again.

I despise weakness, so I reach for the gauze.

The water dampens the gauze as I peel it off, and I stare at the scar while the spray hits my back. A choked noise escapes my throat, and I cut it off instantly. I know why I did it, and my sacrifice is proven on my body by a mark. I am strong, but that doesn't stop the agony I feel at seeing my raw, red skin stretching from either side of my belly button and carved into my abs. It's almost clean, but it's going to scar badly, and there is nothing I can do about that.

I remind myself that I have many scars, and all are proof of my victories and survival, but it doesn't stop me from mourning the loss of innocence with each and every one that mars my skin, and this is no exception. It hurts more because of what it stands for and because I realise the guys haven't touched this one and made it better. For the first time since we have been separated, I no longer look like the woman they love—another connection to them severed. This isn't skin they have kissed, tasted, and loved. This is raw and brutal. Like me.

I carefully wash the edges. Despite how fresh the wound is, it looks weeks old thanks to my healing, so I guess that's something. Once I'm done, I get out and dry off, putting on a fresh set of grey underwear, joggers, jumper, and socks that were left in here. I have to roll the joggers down so they don't press on the wound and they sit on my hips, and then I shuffle back into my room, exhausted just from that movement after days of being bedbound. I shuffle over and slowly sit, refusing to lie back down and choosing to rest just for a little bit to catch my breath.

I need to heal faster. I can't exercise because it will rip the wound, but I need to do something, anything, rather than just sit here with my pitiful thoughts.

As I'm about to get up and figure out a plan to keep myself busy, the door opens. I freeze when I see who it is. Instantly on alert, I search for a weapon. He holds up his hands in a placating gesture, his expression cold. "I'm not here to hurt you."

"Then why are you here, Joel?" I snap.

He steps inside and shuts the door, keeping his back to it as he watches me. He ensures there is space between us since I'm practically vibrating with tension and the need to act. I shift closer to the IV pole, ready to use it as a bat if he comes closer.

"To talk," he answers simply. I just carry on glaring, and he glances at my stomach. "How are you feeling?"

I fight not to wrap my arms around myself protectively, feeling sick at his presence. After all, he was going to rape me on my father's orders to create their super babies or some shit. When I don't respond, he sighs. "For what it's worth, I'm sorry it has come to this and that you saw no other way out."

"Apology not fucking accepted," I snarl. "Now get the fuck out."

He ignores me and moves closer, walking around the room as he inspects everything. I keep my body tense, ready to move, tracking every tiny movement just in case. They can't use me for my womb anymore, but my father has made it clear that my life will be hell and this man is his sidekick, his minion.

"It won't change anything, you know," he finally murmurs and glances over his shoulder at me, not surprised that I'm watching him so intently. He turns and moves closer. He's fast, with controlled, coiled movements. Pure soldier.

"What won't?" I find myself asking, and then I snap my mouth shut to stop more questions from coming out.

"Your sacrifice." I flinch at his words, but he carries on. "He's just going to take it out on you even worse now. You thwarted his plan. He needed you alive and somewhat functioning before, but now? He will make it hell for you."

Tilting my head back, I smirk at him. "I've lived in hell since I was a child. Bring it on."

He watches me carefully before a smile curls his lips. "Good. I was afraid your spirit had been broken. Where would the fun be in that?" He moves towards the door then stops to glance back at me. "There's nothing to save you anymore, girl, so I hope you are ready for the repercussions." Then he's gone and I slump.

All my adrenaline vanishes, becoming bone-deep exhaustion, and despite my mind screaming protests, I curl up on the bed and close my eyes, hoping to leave this place the only way I can—in my dreams.

He's right. There is nothing to protect me now.

There is nothing to save me.

I won't leave this place alive, but neither will they.

I'm escorted back to my room that night, and there is a terrible glint in the guards' eyes, like they know something I don't. I hate it. Alongside dick-head's earlier warning, I know tomorrow will be very fucking bad. It's time to move my plan up and fast.

Ignoring the agony ripping through my stomach, I pull myself up and into the vents again. I crawl towards the control room once more and wait for the guards to grow lazy, drifting off into a nearby room where I hear them making food, the fools.

I drop down, wincing as each step sends pure agony splintering through me. My stomach is healing faster than humanly possible, but it's still not fast enough to be doing this.

Once inside the control room, I quickly turn off the camera and the alarms, and then I head back down the hallway. The only issue I'll have is if I run into guards, but still, I don't hide. I walk like I know exactly where I am going, and maybe I do from the map I've been creating in my head. I find what I need on floor four, and I know I need to hurry before they find out what I've done and turn it all back on. Opening the unlocked door, I slip inside, scanning the shelves with a grim smile before yanking down the chemicals I need.

I feel my stitches rip, and blood starts to drip into my trousers, soaking the material. Glancing down, I see it seeping through the grey fabric, turning it red, but I still keep going.

I mix most of the chemicals together in the steel mop bucket, and then I drop the last one in and hurry back to my room, racing against the cameras. Once there, I quickly shimmy under the quilt to hide the blood on my clothes that show I've been moving.

Ten, nine, eight, seven, six, five, four, three, two, one . . .

I count down in my head and right on schedule, the chemicals mix together and explode. Alarms start to blare, and I hear running feet as they try to contain the fire. My main mission is to cause chaos and make them suffer before I kill them, and that starts tonight.

Just like I expected, my door slams open and a guard peeks in. I tilt my head towards him. "Problems in paradise?" I tease.

He points at me. "Behave." He slams the door.

Grinning, I slide the sheet off and hurry to the bathroom. Peeling the bloody clothes off is harder than I expected, but I manage to get them off and soak them to get as much blood out as I can before replacing the grate and checking the wound. It's red, raw, and angry, and I nicked the skin and popped a few stitches, but there is nothing I can do about it now. I cover it with more gauze and redress it before slipping into another top and pants, and then I climb back into bed as the alarms continue to blare.

I smile as I close my eyes.

One step closer.

I'm one step closer.

TWENTY-FOUR

It's a testament to how much the wound knocked me on my ass when I'm jerked awake as hands grab me. I didn't even hear them come in or see them turn on the lights. I was sleeping, and it pisses me off. I start to fight before agony slams through me from my wound, and then I stop. I can't do any more damage to myself than I need to.

I need to heal so I can kill them, so I let them drag me away even though I hate it.

I'm brought into one of the medical rooms, but instead of a bed, there is a chair one would see in a dentist's office. I'm tossed into it, and my arms and legs are quickly strapped down. Struggling against my need to fight, I relax into the leather and blink.

"What, no breakfast?" I taunt.

The guards ignore me, stepping back against the wall, and look at the opposite wall as if to avoid even looking at me. I'm forced to wait, and I grow bored. I test the restraints. I could snap them if need be, but for now, I leave them on, and sometime later, the door opens, admitting my father.

"Novaleen," he snaps in annoyance, the door shutting behind him. His tone is angry, and he looks tired, probably from the fire last night. His suit is slightly wrinkled, which tells me all I need to know. He's stressed and hasn't slept.

"Looking bad, Pops," I taunt. "Now, what's on today's agenda? Teeth pulling?"

"There was an explosion last night."

"I did hear something." I shrug as much as the bindings will allow. "What's your point?"

"We know it was you." My father sniffs, looking irritated.

"Are you sure?" I smirk. "I was in my room, you know, being a prisoner and all."

"Are you trying to make me believe that one of the most intellectual minds of our time couldn't have timed that?" he snaps.

"I think you have a problem in your house, Father, and it isn't me. After all, I'm injured and a prisoner. Maybe you should look at your staff." I see him falter just for a moment, but it's enough to let me know he's worried about that, worried about being betrayed from the inside.

It's another crack in the armour, which is something else I can use.

"Punish her!" he snaps as he turns and storms out.

The guards step forward almost as one, and I let out a low breath and force a smile. This is going to be bad, but I can survive it. "So, what do you guys think about—" My breath whooshes out of my lungs as one man slams his fist into my stomach. I feel my stitches rip, but not enough to cover the tearing of the wound from yesterday. It hurts like a motherfucker though. That's when I realise that if I can make him do it again, I can cover my ripped stitches.

"Pussy," I rasp, and just like I expected, he winds his fist up and slams it into my stomach, rupturing the wound. Blood pours from my flesh, and agony courses through me, but I smile as I wheeze. He played right into it, giving me exactly what I wanted.

"I'm going to enjoy this," another says as he steps up, and my heart stills as he grins. Winding a cloth between his hands, he kicks his foot into the chair, and my head slams back. He places the cloth he was holding over my mouth, and then ice-cold water pours across it, spraying over my mouth and face. I can't see, and my ears buzz. I struggle to breathe, my lungs on fire as I writhe in the straps, feeling blood slide across my stomach and chest. Just when I'm about to pass out from choking on water, he stops, allowing me to suck in desperate, painful breaths, only to repeat the action again.

It continues until my throat feels like razors are cutting into it from the inside and my lungs are so desperate for air each breath hurts. My stomach competes for a close second. Drenched, shivering, and coughing, I force my eyes open, waiting to see what will happen next.

He called it a punishment, but this isn't punishment.

This is a lesson.

This is a warning.

Their warnings come back to me. I have no buffer anymore, and this shows me just that. A scream slips free as something red-hot presses into the bottom of my foot, making me contort in the bindings. My toes burn and throb like pins and needles but a hundred times worse. All I can do is just lie here as they beat the bottoms of my feet with something hot. I could break free and kill them, but it would be for nothing, and I would be punished more.

No, I need to bide my time.

Never before have I come so close to breaking as they tear my body apart one sensation at a time. After my feet, I'm woozy, but I refuse to pass out.

"They say she's strong, so let's see how strong." A guard laughs, but I can no longer tell them apart. I jerk when my shirt is ripped away, leaving me in a grey cotton sports bra, and when I lift my head, I watch as they tear the gauze from my injury and dig their fingers into the wound, tearing it back open.

The howl of agony that leaves my lips is animalistic, and despite my best intentions, blackness claims me.

I wake with a jerk as something sharp pierces my stomach. "Fucking animals. This was sewn perfectly, now look at the mess," someone mutters.

I blink, trying to bring the room into focus, but it takes too long and my brain is sluggish. Eventually, I realise I'm in the same room, still shivering both from shock and temperature. Rolling my head down, I see the guards are gone and there is a man in a lab coat bent over my stomach, stitching up the mess they made of my wound.

"Such a waste," he mutters as he starts to staple me.

"I know you." My voice is little more than a whisper, but he jerks and looks up, freezing. I cough, clearing my throat, and he watches me struggle. "I know you," I repeat stronger once I catch my breath.

"I would hope so." He looks back down at his work and carries on. It hurts, but it's clear he is here to help, not to cause pain. "You spared my life once."

Blinking, I stare at his face until it comes to me. He was the head of the lab, the one we let go free before the plane crash. "You bastard!" I surge towards him, but he pushes me down with a glare at me then the door.

"Shut up. If they hear you are awake, they will come back in and hurt you. I was only supposed to stitch you up so you didn't die," he hisses, and we both stare at the door before he sighs and hurries to seal my wound.

"You bastard. I let you live, and you came back to him," I snap.

"It's not what you think," he mutters, ducking his head. "We don't have time to discuss it." He quickly cleans my stomach and looks me over, shaking his head. I see something almost haunted and sad in his eyes before he shakes it off. "Believe me, if I had any other choice, I would take it."

"You do."

"No, I don't, Nova," he replies sadly. "None of us do, least of all you. You, more than anyone, understand obligation and chains that bind us." He stands quickly, shoving his stuff back into his bag before pulling out a needle. He sticks it into a bottle, drawing up a dose and testing it before turning to me.

"This is all I can do. I'm sorry." He injects me with something, and I gape as he hurries to the door and rushes out.

My blood heats, and the guards step back in. "Look who's awake." One grins. "Time to continue with our punishment, shall we?"

Lying back like I'm at a spa, I smile like I'm in charge. "Of course, where were we?"

They have to bring the doctor back in three times before he announces that if I lose any more blood or am hurt again, I will die. It's a lie, well, close to a lie. I do feel like I'm dying, but I wouldn't give them the satisfaction. I can't decide if he's trying to help me or if he just feels guilty since he won't meet my eyes as I'm carried back to my room and tossed onto my bed.

I lie here, unable to move or feel thanks to the meds the doc keeps pushing. I'm guessing it's morphine. It let me drift while they tortured me, but it pissed them off more since they didn't get the reaction they wanted, so they had to get more creative. The last time the doctor came in, they did too, and he couldn't give me anything, hence the agony now.

But anything is better than the pain in my soul and the fact that I almost slipped away.

My men never would have known. They are all I think about. I hate it. I hate that I can't see them. I hate it and miss them, hoping wherever they are, it's better than this. It's all that keeps me going. I close my eyes now and imagine them here, needing their warmth and comfort.

It dashes away when the door opens. I groan and try to sit up, expecting more guards to haul me away, or even my father or a doctor. What I don't expect is him.

It's one single guard, and with one look into his cruel, mocking eyes, and I know his intentions. I leap to my feet, stumbling as I try to head to the bathroom to put a door between us, but I'm slow, the drugs and pain slowing me down.

He grips my hair and yanks me back until I'm pinned beneath him again.

"You know what your daddy said?" he says into my hair, pulling me back tighter to let me feel his hard cock against my ass. "That you are free game now. He doesn't need your cunt for anything, and he wants us to feel motivated, so I figured why don't I sample it? It seems like such a waste, don't you agree? Be a good girl and take it, and I'll get you extra food and some pain meds."

"Fuck you!" I yell, slamming my elbow back. "I'll fight you every step of the fucking way, you disgusting pig."

His fist slams into my face, the force knocking my head into the floor, and for a moment, my ears ring and my vision blurs. He rips at my clothes and when his hands reach into my underwear, I come back online. I turn over and slam my foot into his face. He falls back with a roar, so I do it again, blood pouring from his nose as we stare at each other, breathing heavily until his radio crackles.

"Omar, we need you in Lockdown One. Omar, repeat, where are you? He's mad you aren't at your post."

"Better get going, Omar," I choke out.

With one last look at me, he climbs to his feet, wiping his nose on his sleeve, and answers the radio. "I'm on my way." He grins at me. "This isn't over. There's no one to protect you, little girl."

"I don't need them to, but the next time you touch me, I'm going to cut your hands off and shove them down your throat," I promise.

He leaves me, slamming my door shut, and I curl into a ball, unable to move as the reality of what almost happened hits home.

Screaming, I slam my feet into the floor, roaring out my agony as tears begin to fall.

Sobbing on the floor, I wrap my arms protectively around me until anger starts to take over. I crawl to the bathroom, drag myself up by the sink, and stare at my reflection. I have one black eye, a split lip, bruised cheeks, a gaunt face, and . . . my hair.

I once loved my hair. It almost falls to my ass, wavy and black, but now all I can think about is how he used it against me. It could have been the difference between me getting away or being trapped.

Smashing my fist into the mirror, I watch cracks form, splintering like my soul, so I do it again until it shatters. Picking up a shard, I start to hack at my hair. Clumps of the black mass fall into the sink with the shards until I drop my shaky hand. My head hangs forward as tears slide down my cheeks.

I lift my head and meet my eyes once more.

My hair now falls to my shoulders in black waves, and I smile through the curtain. It's a bloodied, wavering smile, but it's there.

They will not break me.

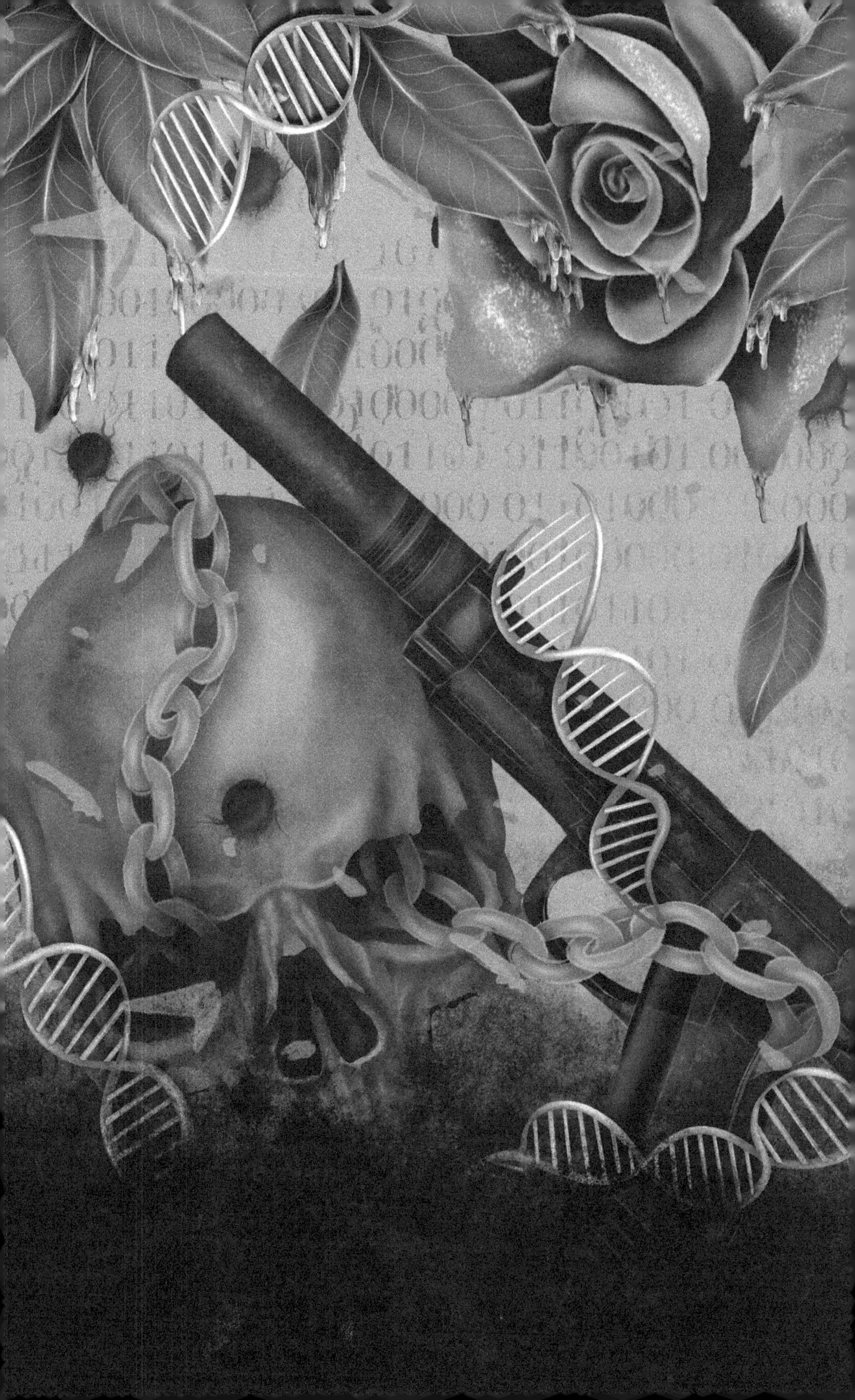

"How are you doing?" I ask into the comms in Nico's ear. We are all perched in different areas around the base, but he has to enter for his new job an old acquaintance we bribed got him at the lab. He shaved his head and with that, the guard's uniform, and the fake scars we added, he shouldn't be too noticeable unless they look closely. Dimitri even created a very convincing background as a marine and paid mercenary. He just went inside the compound, and I hate not having eyes on him.

I remind myself it isn't for long, since he's going to plant the external remote so Dimitri can hack into their systems. From there, we can come up with a better plan, but none of us are willing to leave Nova alone another day, so we need someone on the inside.

His grunt echoes through my mic, and I smirk as I peer down the scope, watching the guards' movements up top.

"This way. What did they say your name was, grunt?" another voice says through the mic.

"Jones," Nico mumbles, lowering his voice even more to make it less familiar.

"Right," someone retorts with a sarcastic tone and lowers his voice, but

I can hear it through the mic. "All fucking muscle, brawn, and no brain. Like we don't have enough of them already."

I wait, counting the seconds of the guards' rotations as they patrol from one side of the fence to the other. When I do, I scan the jungle, but I can't spot any of the others at all, even though I know they are there.

"Right, this way, Jones. I'll take you to security, who will check you all over and give you your job rotation. Bunks are up top if you are stationed here. You'll get a number, you'll either be nights or days, and we all eat in the cafeteria."

"What about days off?" Nico asks haughtily.

The man snorts. "Not for a while, dumbass. They are on the verge of something big here, and it's all hands. And don't go asking questions. It's a sure-fire way to get us all in trouble. Do your job, keep your head down, and get the massive paycheque you've been offered. After all, that's why we are all here. Got it?"

"Got it," Nico responds, seemingly put out, but it appears to assuage the man.

"Okay, here is the upper security office. There is another one deep within the compound in the underground structure. You will receive a tour if you are assigned there. I know they wanted more guards after a . . . security breach."

"What kind?" Nico asks.

"The bad kind," is all the man replies. "Yo, T, I've got a newbie for you." I hear the sound of retreating footsteps.

"Name," a bored sounding woman with a thick accent says.

"Rob Jones, Robert for full," Nico replies, and then there's typing and no more conversation until Nico breaks it. "Been here long, T?"

"Long enough," she mutters. "Okay, lucky you, you have been assigned to the underground, or as we call it, hell. Here is your key card. Show it to the security officers down there and they will get you settled. Usually, you would bunk up here, but some officers get to bunk underground if they don't mind it—most do."

"I don't," he says quickly, too quickly.

"Play it cool," I snap down the mic.

"Fucking military weirdos, always so eager," T mutters. "Fine, I'll assign you one underground. You'll get a tour and all the other information down there. We don't have many rules here, but stay silent. You see and hear nothing of what happens there except for security. Also, the only way out is in a body bag, got it, Robert?"

"Got it."

"Here. Take the elevator all the way down. Oh, and Robert? Welcome to hell."

NICO

The elevator is a service one, big enough to fit equipment, beds, or even a small army. The buttons tell me I'm at level one, and they only go down, so I hit the very bottom one labelled B10 and scan the key card. I checked the cameras as soon as I got in here, so I make sure I look bored, and I don't speak into the earpiece, although I can hear the others wondering what it's like. The small screen shows me the numbers as we drop, and I make sure to stand at attention, my hands clasped behind my back and legs spread. My duffle bag is tossed over my shoulder, and I'm wearing a black button-up to hide my distinctive tattoos as well as boots that are slightly plat-formed to change my height ever so slightly. I want to itch my head and the lack of hair there, but I ignore that too.

I wonder what Nova will think. She loved my hair, but it will grow back. I would do much worse things to be near her again.

The door dings as it slides open, and I don't know what I expected, but it isn't a plain white corridor leading farther into the underground labora-tory. A guard turns the corner at the end and hurries my way.

"New guy?" he asks as if anyone else would have gotten down here. Plus, I know they checked me via camera before they even let the lift descend.

I incline my head, and he jerks his. "Follow me. They didn't want you getting lost."

Or wandering around, more likely, and seeing things I shouldn't.

I follow him down the hall, my eyes bouncing around in fake interest, but really, I'm clocking all possible areas for attack and exits, needing to memorise it for the others.

"Nico, you good?" Jonas asks.

I can't respond with the man walking at my side, peering down at an iPad, so instead I clear my throat. "This is far underground. What kind of research is conducted here? I wasn't told."

"For a reason." The guard snorts and doesn't even look up. "It's our job to keep it that way, so no one outside of these walls knows anything, understood?" He looks up at me. "Don't go getting a conscience, merc. There is a reason we hire certain kinds here. We don't need your morals or brain, just your brawn, got it?"

"Got it," I respond slowly as if having to think about it. "Do you get reception down here? I want to watch the games." I shrug.

He chuckles. "Oh yeah, we do. We have the best connections in the world here, all thanks to the trusty scientists. You take care of them, they take care of you, if you know what I mean." I nod like I do.

We turn a corner, and I peek into open doorways, but they all seem to be empty labs.

"This level is mostly just for the entrance. All the fun happens below, and those levels are only accessible by stairs. This is level one. Level two has living quarters as well as some medical rooms, and level three is the security base, as well as more labs and medical rooms. Level four is recreation and offices."

"Is there a level five?" I ask.

He peers at me and clears his throat. "No questions," he reminds me, and I bite my tongue. He leads me to some stairs at the end and down we go. The concrete walls are only interrupted by cameras, lights, and black stencilled level numbers beside sealed doors we have to scan to get into. At level three, we exit into a corridor. Most of the doors are shut, and I only see some guards milling around in a small kitchen, living room area, but to the right is a security office, which I'm led into.

"New guy. Jones. He's yours." The guard I'm with slaps my back. "See you around, man." I just nod and quickly scan the room as the bored guard turns to the computer and starts typing, ignoring me too. The whole wall is filled with screens of all the floors and labs. This is where I will need to plant the bug, so I step forward, knocking into the chair he's sitting on as my hand slips into my pocket. When he turns to yell, I practically stumble back into the desk, placing it underneath and holding up my hands. "Sorry."

"Clumsy bastard," he snaps, turning back to the computer.

I click my fingers twice to let Dimitri know and then refocus on my surroundings. This might be the only chance I have to look around in here, so I need to make the most of it.

I'm scanning the cameras for any signs or traces of her when a conversation from guards outside has me stiffening.

"Did you see the beating she took? No wonder the doc is so interested."

"I saw her fight that military guy. She kicked his ass."

"She's hot as hell too. I might try and sneak into her room."

"Don't be stupid. The doc is her father." He lowers his voice then, and I can't hear more, but it's enough.

She's here.

Nova is here.

I hear the others cheering down the mic, and I smile but quickly school my features as the guard turns back to me with the rotations schedule. My heart hurts at the beatings they mentioned, but my girl can take it. She can survive anything, and she isn't alone anymore.

I'm here.

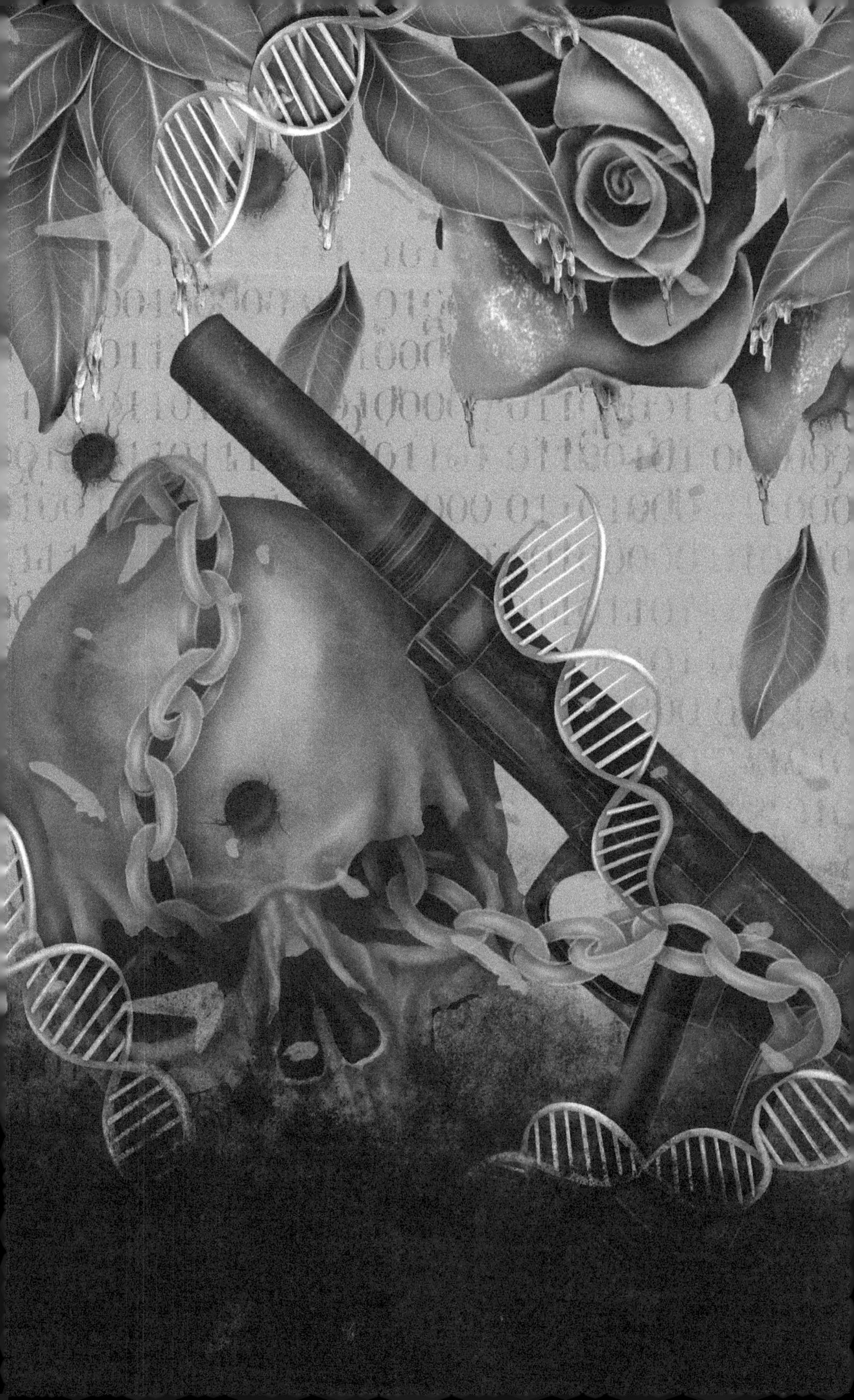

TWENTY-SIX

"Now, Novaleen," my father begins as he sits down opposite me. This could almost be called a meeting if you overlooked the fact that my hands are strapped to the electric chair. "Shall we begin?"

"It's Nova," I reply conversationally.

He frowns, his eyes roving over my hair like they did when I was first dragged in here. "I was told you broke the mirror in your room and cut your hair. May I ask why, Novaleen?"

"I felt like a change. You know how it is, got to spice up your life a little. The round-the-clock torture can get a little tiresome." I'm hurting all over, mind, body, heart, and soul, and yes, I'm taking it out on him. I don't know what he wants from me this time, and I don't fucking care.

He won't get it.

"I thought your punishment might make you more amenable, Novaleen. I simply wish to talk today."

"Of course," I mock. "Hence the electric chair."

"I have learned that sometimes you need to be persuaded. Do not make me the bad guy." He leans back, his arms crossed. "I'd like to talk to you about what you did while we were apart."

"When I ran away from home so I wasn't your prisoner, or when I thought you were dead, or both?" He goes to answer, but I cut him off. "Oh, I'm sorry, time's up, and I simply do not give a fuck."

The buzz zaps me, short and quick, and I narrow my eyes.

"I had one hell of a party when I thought you were dead, with Jell-O shots and a bullseye with your face on the board—" My words cut off with a snap of my teeth as the electricity pulses through me again, harder this time. When it cuts off, I sag a little.

"Now, how about we start elsewhere since you seem averse to talking about anything with your past, your . . . friends, or your sister."

"Do not speak her name," I warn, nostrils flaring as my nails dig into the chair, wishing they could carve into his face instead.

"You are still upset about her death. While I do hate the force I had to use, and she was very bright, it was necessary, Nova, you must see that. I had to free you from that bond. She was holding you back. You could never reach your full potential while you were worried about her or her reaction," he explains as if it's a logical decision.

I simply look over his shoulder to the glass screen where some other scientists are monitoring us. "Novaleen," he snaps, hating when I don't give him the attention he thinks he deserves.

"Did you spend years building this little hideout of yours?"

"Yes," he responds carefully.

"And white paint was the best you could go for?" I taunt.

The chair buzzes again, and when it cuts off, I laugh.

"Fine, let us talk about those men you are with. Failed experiments. I looked into their files. Most of them offered a lot of potential, but in the end, they failed, unlike you. Why do you think you felt so connected to them? Was it simply circumstance or because you felt like you could be somewhat free with them when it came to your past and abilities? Do you think that affects the way you saw them? Did it create an artificial bond?"

"It was not artificial," I snap. "They are my family."

"I am your family," he murmurs. "We do not have a bond."

"You are a sadistic fuck who dresses like a person in a toothpaste commercial," I spit. "They knew that. We had been through the same things."

"Ah, trauma bonded." He makes a quick note, which I hate.

"No, it is more than that," I hiss angrily at him before blowing out a breath and calming myself, knowing he wants a reaction. "I do not need to defend my relationships to you or explain them. It was fate that brought them to me, and what we have cannot be replicated or explained with science."

"Ah, that is where you are wrong. After all, I brought them to you, and I plan to repeat it. If we are to create solid, cohesive units of soldiers, then they will need a similar bond of trust. Maybe I should have taken them after all." He sighs. "A pity we can't find them."

I jerk at the slip of information, hanging onto his every word. I want to know more. Why can't he find them? Are they lying low? Hiding? Or worse, hunting?

"I would be interested to see what curated a bond faster—fear or loyalty," he murmurs to himself then blinks at me. "Never mind. Tell me how you have been since leaving me. Stronger? Faster? What other changes have you noticed?"

"Well, there was that time I felt a burning sensation when I peed, but that turned out to be an STD—"

Zap, and so it goes.

He asks question after question, which I answer with angrier and sassier answers, infuriating him. I just suffered a particularly bad shock when my head lolls back and my eyes go to the glass, and I swear I see a flash of a familiar, haunted gaze, but it is just wishful thinking, so I close my eyes, not wanting to hurt my heart more than it already does.

After the shock therapy, as Father called it, there is a cruel twist to his lips. He is angry that I refused to play his game. I know whatever comes next will be a punishment that I have no choice but to take. I'm escorted to a lab and tied down on the examination table. My eyes close for a moment as I try to rein back my panic, remembering the last time I was like this and I burnt out my insides. Still, I'm sore and healing, so surely they wouldn't—

A scream escapes my throat.

Their warnings were correct. They don't need me alive anymore, and the proof is in his eyes. His gloved hand slices open my healing stomach, cutting right through the stitches and tearing me open once more. There is a dangerous glint in his eyes. This is more than a punishment. This is a warning to give him what he needs or I will beg for death just like those other kids did.

When his gloved hand starts to force the wound open, I can't control my reactions anymore.

Gritting my teeth, I swallow the taste of my own blood, my nails breaking as I claw at the arms of the bed. My legs and arms thrash against the restraints, and I throw my head back in agony as pain blisters through me like a flame.

The blade slides deeper into my stomach, and I lift to watch the blood welling from my abdomen before I glare at the scientists and Father above me.

He doesn't spare me a look.

"You're dead," I warn, my voice choked.

He ignores me as he plunges his hand into my stomach, making me fall back, and the trapped howl of agony finally rips through the lab before I pass out.

When I wake up, I feel him there, watching and judging.

He pulled me apart like a cat playing with a spider, ripping off its legs to see if they still kick. Forcing my swollen, grimy eyes open, I find my stomach stapled, but I'm still tied down and coated in sweat and blood.

My father stands there with a pen poised above a notebook. "How do you feel, Novaleen?"

"Fuck you," I croak, my throat raw from screaming.

His eyes narrow before he repeats the question harder.

"How do I feel?" I repeat, my tongue thick. "Like when I get free, I'm going to rip you apart to see how you like it."

Dropping the pen, he leans in with a cruel twist of his lips, his familiar eyes meeting mine. "Oh, but you won't be getting free, will you? Not again."

And then he leaves.
I scream and fight, trapped once more.
I have been reduced to an experiment—again.

523

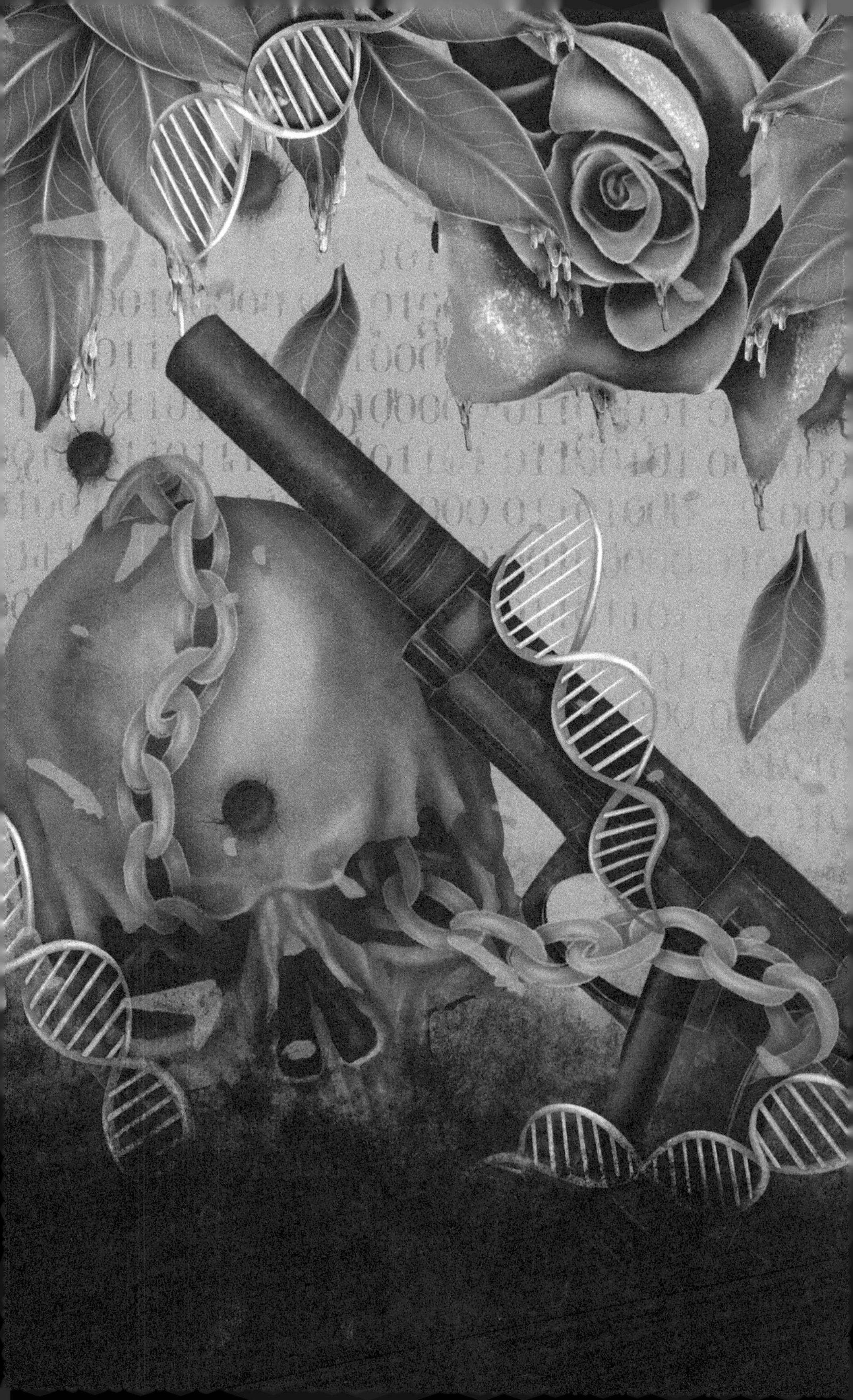

TWENTY-SEVEN

I'm stitched back up and pumped full of a drug cocktail that instantly makes me feel better. I overheard the scientist say that what they did was to test my healing, but that's bullshit. It was a warning through and through, and it has only made me angrier, but I have to play this smart. Even though I want to tear through them, I have to stick to the plan, which seems stupider the longer I'm down here.

I should just make my move, but I worry I will fail.

I hear Louis's voice in my head, telling me to be smart and plan.

Jonas tells me to gather weapons.

Dimitri advises me to gain access to their systems and tear them apart from the inside.

Isaac's voice says to allow myself to heal.

Nico tells me to use their weaknesses against them.

The only problem is, I don't know their weaknesses.

I'm escorted back to my room where I lie on the cot, debating my thoughts. They have to have a weakness, and I have to find it, which means action, because today taught me that they won't be happy until I'm ripped apart. I need to end this and soon.

Tilting my head, I see the door lock is off-kilter, so I get to my feet thanks to the drugs and I hurry over, sliding my nails between it until it catches. The dumbasses didn't even lock it properly. I could have gone through the tunnel, but it will hurt more, and honestly, they don't even seem to care. Surely, they have to know it's me fucking with them by now.

What else could they possibly do to me?

I need to find a weakness, which means going deeper into the facility than I ever have. I can't use the elevator because it requires a key card I don't have—I heard them mention it once. They force the guards to use the stairs, and I know they are for emergencies and will no doubt register if I open them.

I hesitate before rounding my shoulders and stepping out. When no guards come running or alarms go off, I walk down the corridor. Maybe they don't see me, or maybe they are just curious about where I will go. Either way, I have time.

I don't bother going down to the security room or the labs, since they hold nothing I want. Instead, I move to the elevator and press the button. It opens. Once inside, I look at the cameras and grin. It wouldn't surprise me if Father was watching as another test.

Determined to find something before he cuts me off, I jump and catch the ceiling tile. Pressing my feet to the wall, I push up and slide it to the side, and then I swing up into the elevator shaft, hoping there are no cameras. There's no way out that I can see. The cables for the elevator go all the way up, but there is only darkness. However, there are metal beams to the left and they go down, so I leap onto one. Ignoring the pulling in my stomach, I begin to climb down. I really hope the elevator doesn't move and crush me while I'm doing this. I have to walk across to the end of one beam. There's a gap where the elevator goes and then the door. Judging the distance, I step back and leap, catching the lip and forcing the door open. The weight makes me sweat, but I manage to get it open far enough for me to roll through and out onto another floor.

This one seems empty, and even the lights are off until I step farther in and they flicker on. The first two doors are locked, but I peer through their windows to see sheet-covered objects inside, clearly not in use.

Worried I won't find anything, I hurry down the corridor. I need to find a weakness to make this worthwhile. The farther I go in the corridor, the weirder this floor gets. There are no labs, bedrooms, or experimentation rooms that I can see, but at the end of the corridor, there is a huge glass window, and a terrible feeling starts deep inside of me.

Flashbacks of a similar window, of a dead kid in the middle of a blood-soaked experimentation room fill my vision. The guys were with me then, so I had their support. I was on the right side, and I had the power to stop it. Still, I am fearful of what I will find, but fear won't stop it from happening or make it better. Burying my head and pretending I don't see anything won't stop the truth. It just makes me weak, and I refuse to be weak.

On slow, unsure feet, I step closer to the glass, alarm bells screaming in my head, but I ignore them. I ignore it all. I am so focused on the glass that I don't even notice anyone else is here until a hand catches my arm.

I react on instinct, turning and smashing that person into the wall, snarling into the face of the man in the guard's uniform. He has a hat pulled low over his face, but when I get a good look at him, I freeze. "Nico?" I whisper, unsure if I'm seeing things or if I'm high or finally dead.

"Hey, baby," he murmurs, but he doesn't touch me.

"Are you real?" I whisper, my arm still pressed to his throat, pinning him to the wall.

"I'm real, baby. I want to fucking touch you so badly to prove it, but if they see on the cameras, I'll be useless and they'll know who I am. I have a role to play, so make it real, baby, and knock me out or some shit."

"No." I start to back away, and he snarls.

"I'm not leaving you alone here, baby. We have a lot to talk about. The others are close, but right now you need to make this look real. Smash me in the balls and then I'll escort you back." His eyes are telling me to play along, while my heart is leaping in joy. I want to collapse into his arms, sob, and let him make this all better, but he's right.

He winces. "Sorry. The guys are blowing up my ear trying to talk to you. She cannot fucking hear you, idiots," he hisses.

I grin, ducking my head to hide it. Tears form in my eyes, but the longer I stand here, the weirder it looks. "Sorry, babe," I whisper as I drive my knee up into his balls.

I step back, smirking like I'm happy as he crumples to the ground, cupping his cock and groaning. I want to help him, but I quickly step to the window like I'm worried about him stopping me. It's all about appearances now. We were caught before, but we won't be ever again.

Despite how angry and worried I am for what their presence means for my plan, I'm also relieved and happy that they came for me.

But that all fades when I get a look into that room.

Hundreds of bunk beds fill the room, with perfectly fitted white sheets and one single pillow. A lot of them are empty, while some have kids sitting atop them—kids of all ages, sizes, and races. Drawings are scattered on the walls, and some are even sketching now. One is reading in the corner, and one is asleep. Two are playing chess. I count fifteen altogether.

Fifteen innocent children are locked up in a gilded cage.

Is he experimenting on them?

Oh, God.

I cover my mouth as I look, my hand going to the window. They wear the same jumpsuits I do, but smaller. They seem clean and healthy, but that doesn't mean anything. I know how looks can be deceiving.

A hand grips my arm.

Nico.

I feel him freezing next to me as he gets his first look in the room. "Fuck, we have a problem," he mutters to the others.

"Nico!" I gasp in horror.

He shudders next to me, his grip tightening. "I know, baby, I see, but we have to get back. We'll help them, I promise, but we can't if we are caught."

He's right, I know he's right, but I'm also a zombie as he leads me back to the elevator, knowing my father wanted me to see this. I feel overwhelmed, and sickness claws at my throat. The pain starts to seep back in a little, the bone-deep, soul-wrenching pain. I was so dumb to think he would stop now that he had me.

I was going to blow this place up, and they would have been killed. I'm so thankful something stopped me. Maybe deep down, I knew, but this changes everything.

"Nico," I whisper in the elevator, and he tightens his hand, lowering his head so the camera can't catch his lips.

"Not yet," he snaps.

Knowing I'm pale and probably in shock, I let him drag me from the elevator.

A guard approaches. "Boss wants her back in her room." He looks at me and smirks. "Saw what you wanted, did you?"

I was right. He let me find that.

It was all another game.

I simply stare through him, my brain overloaded.

He will do what he did to us to those kids.

I have to swallow back my vomit, but then I think fuck it and heave forward, spilling it on the other guard's shoes. He yells and stumbles back.

"That's my girl," Nico mutters before tightening his grip. "I'll take her back and remind her to behave."

"You do that before I do," the guard snarls. "Fucking animal. Make it hurt, but not where they can see, if you know what I mean." He picks up his radio. "Turn off the cameras in her room. It's time for payback."

Payback, right. At least this works in our favour, but holy shit.

Nico smirks. "Thanks, man. Don't want to get fired too quickly, you know?"

Without waiting, he drags me back down the corridor to my room. Once there, we both glance at the cameras before he looks at me. "Fuck it, let them catch me." I'm in his arms in a minute. He turns me and presses me to the wall, his lips descending on mine. One hand comes up and rips out his earpiece, and he tosses it away—even I can hear shouting coming from it. Groaning, I grip his hat and rip it off, only to freeze at his shaved head. Pulling back, I gawk and he winces. I can see the worry there, so I rub my hand across it and grin.

"I like it. You look meaner," I murmur.

"I've missed you so much, baby," he says, dragging his lips across mine again as if he can't decide if he's going to kiss me or talk, so he does both. "So fucking much. I'm so angry at you for leaving, and when we blow this joint, I'm going to spend the rest of our lives proving it. But fuck, I'm so fucking happy to see you."

"I missed you too," I reply, but it cuts off as he kisses me again. I whimper when he pushes me back and my stomach protests. He pulls away immediately, dropping me.

"Nova," he says, his voice shaking.

"It's fine. I'm okay," I promise, but I wince as the pain slowly trickles back in. Before I can grab my shirt, he pulls it up and hisses. He goes to rush out of the door, but I stop him.

"Breathe, big guy, and think smart. I promise I'm okay."

"You have a massive fucking wound on your stomach, and you are covered in bruises. How is this okay?" he snarls. "I was so happy to see you, I didn't even notice your hair or how skinny you look. Nova, I'm going to fucking kill them. Tell me who did this, or is it all of them? Either way, they are dead." He rushes to the bed, picks up his earpiece, and puts it in. "Yeah, I'm here. Get in here, we are killing all of them."

Laughing, I take the earpiece. Luckily, he lets me, clearly worried about fighting me. "Hi, guys," I say nervously. It's silent for a second, and then there's a rush of voices all at once. Tears form in my eyes as I smile. "Okay, one at a time."

Louis's voice comes first. "What does he mean you're hurt?"

"I'm okay, just a procedure. I'll tell you later." I worry then, eyeing Nico. They came after me, but what if they are too angry at me?

Even just looking at Nico reminds me of that night, the one that stained my soul.

Ana.

"Fuck, I missed you so much," Jonas says.

"Talk more, I need to hear your voice," Dimitri murmurs.

"Are you okay?" Isaac asks.

"Tell us everything," Louis says before his voice softens. "We've missed you so much. We haven't stopped looking, not even for a second, and after this, we will be sitting down to discuss you sacrificing yourself for us and the appropriate punishment." I shiver from his tone and the promise in the words, and a spark of desire forms in me despite everything.

Sitting heavily on the bed, I sigh when Nico wraps himself around me, his big arms feeling like home. We don't have long, we need to use the time wisely, but I ache to hear their voices too. Seeing him and hearing them made it all real, and I just want them here with me, but that's foolish.

"Before I forget, there's a hole in the cupboard on this level. It leads to the ducts beyond to get in and out. I blew it a few days ago. I turned the cameras to avoid it and I will make sure to note some access points."

"Clever fucking girl," Dimitri purrs.

"I dropped a bug so Dimitri could access their systems and give us control," Nico explains, making me nod. Of course they did. Of course they planned.

"Louis, there are kids here. Whatever you have planned, it has to change, okay? They come first. We need to save them."

"Nova—"

"No, they come first, promise me. I can live with pain or staying longer or being punished by them, but I can't live with knowing kids are being hurt or worse. Promise me."

"I promise," he responds reluctantly, and I slump in relief.

"We don't have long." I grip Nico tighter, not wanting to let go. "It's not usual for them to punish me like this, and if Father finds out, he won't be happy, even if he will let it happen. There's a soldier here who survived the experiments. Avoid him at all costs. He's good, very good, and completely on Father's side." I have so much to tell them, but some of it won't even come out. I choke on my words. Right now, those kids have to be our first priority. "Whatever you have planned, I want in. I have access to the ducts through this bathroom, and I'm pretty sure they are watching me. Whatever timeline you have thought out needs to be moved up. He's losing his patience with me, and I don't know how much longer he will keep me alive when he can't get what he wants."

"What do you mean?" Isaac asks. "Are you okay?"

I hesitate, and Nico glances at the wound, a worried look in his eyes. "Baby, tell me they didn't . . ."

"They wanted my kids," I whisper before hardening my voice. "I stopped them from ever getting that from me."

There's silence then, and I wait with bated breath. Nico lifts his eyes, and I see so much pain there it staggers me. "I'm so sorry, Nova." He grips me tighter, kissing my stomach. "I'm so sorry you had to do that. You're so strong, baby. We'll make them pay."

"Nova," Isaac whispers.

"Don't, okay? Please." I can't afford to break down now. "I'm okay. I made a decision, one I can live with. I couldn't live with knowing that they would use my body and my children for his gains. I would never let another go through what I did. I'll probably break down after." If I survive, not that I planned to, but I have a feeling they don't want to hear that so I leave it out. "But for now, I need to be strong, okay? It's the only way I'm getting through this."

Luckily, Louis chimes in, giving me the escape I need. "Okay. Dimitri is accessing their system now. Nico, go back to guard duty and give us the information we need. We are coming, baby, just hold on, okay? Just a little bit longer. Then we will stop this bastard once and for all, and then I'm taking you home and never letting you out of my sight again."

I swallow. "Louis, I need you to promise me." My eyes are for Nico though. I know they will all fight me, but I need them to hear this. "If it's between saving me and saving the kids, save the kids."

Voices explode in my ear again, and Nico snarls, ready to fight me. "No. I mean it. We all make sacrifices. I will never forgive you if you choose me and they die. Promise me that they'll come first and you will save them. I can't—" I look away. "I cannot lose anyone else, so I need you to promise me this."

There's a moment of hesitation where I don't think they will. "I promise, Nova." He seems determined. "Nova, I'm sorry about An—"

"Don't say her name," I snap before I close my eyes. "Please, I can't . . . I can't, okay?"

"Of course, Nova," Isaac says, his voice reassuring. "We are right here, okay? You're not alone now."

"We're coming, baby, just hang on, and I will kill every last motherfucker in there for you," Jonas adds. I can't help but smile.

"I didn't want you to come after me, you know?" I hear them responding angrily, so I quickly hurry on. "I didn't want you to get caught or be in danger. I just wanted you to be happy, to find a life."

"You are our life, and we can't be happy without you," Nico snaps. "Do not ever think otherwise. There is no us without you. Baby, where you go, we go. There is no happiness, no life, and no future without you. I would suffer a hundred years of torture and die a thousand times simply to be at your side. Live or die, we do it together."

"He's right. Before you, we were a team, then after you, we became a family, and you are the heart of our family, Nova. We cannot function without you. You beat for us, so don't you even dare," Louis warns. "Now give Nico the mic, baby, kiss him, promise him you're okay so he doesn't go off the rails and kill everyone for the marks on your body, and remind him we will do that together."

"Yes, sir," I tease, handing the mic back over. My spirits are lifted, and love for them runs through me, along with worry. Nico puts the earpiece back in and grunts at whatever they are saying.

"I've got to go, baby."

Leaning forward, I cup his cheeks and kiss him soundly. "We will end this together. Louis is right. No killing anyone yet."

"No promises," he mutters, but I can tell he won't risk me or the kids. Standing, he gives me one last lingering look before turning away, but panic winds through me.

Catching his hand, I tug him back. "Don't you dare get caught or no one here is safe, do you understand me? I'll kill them if they so much as think about hurting you."

"Back at you, baby," he murmurs, kissing me hard before hurrying out the door like he doesn't trust himself to stay.

I'm alone once more, knowing they are out there. They are close, and that gives me hope.

It gives me renewed determination.

This isn't just about me or ending this or even the kids. It's about keeping my lovers safe.

I will not lose anyone else.

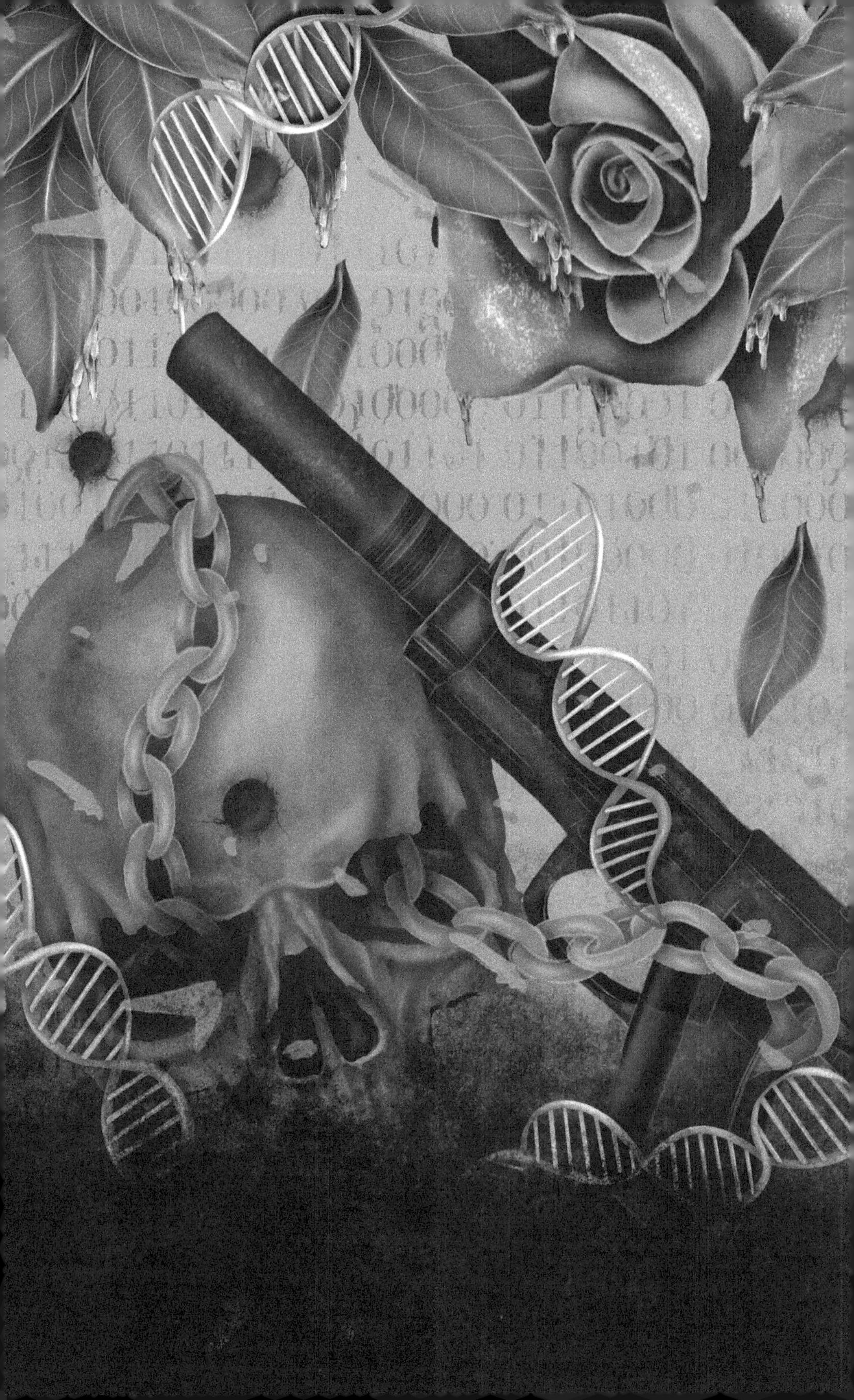

TWENTY-EIGHT

Ripping out the earpiece, I give in to a moment of weakness, my head pressed to the sniper rifle. I know my position, and I know what I should do, but it wars with my need to see my girl and protect her. She's hurting beyond the wounds she has suffered since we have been apart. I heard it in her voice. The others might not have, too focused on their own joy, but I did. I heard the truth in her words.

She's struggling, and part of her wants to die there, but I will not ever let that happen.

If she dies, then I die. It's that simple.

I quickly come up with a different plan, putting the earpiece in once more.

"Fuck this, I'm going in," I snap, not as collected as I wish, but it's too late to take it back.

"What?" Dimitri demands. "What about the plan?"

"No, he's right." I bet Isaac knew it the moment he spoke to her. "She needs him. She needs someone with her right now even if she won't admit it. I think she had a plan that we interrupted, one we wouldn't have liked very much, and I think, given the chance, she will still follow through."

"What do you mean?" Jonas snarls.

"No," Dimitri mutters, "she wouldn't. She knows how much that would . . . after Bas."

"She felt like she had no choice. She's grieving and not thinking properly. Coupled with whatever they are doing to her, she was doing what she thought was best with no way out. I will not allow that to happen, but someone needs to be there to remind her. Nico can't be compromised; we need him. Dimitri needs to stay here to get us in. Jonas wouldn't control himself, and Isaac would be taken away for his brain. It has to be me. It makes sense."

"He's right. So what's the plan?" Jonas sounds calm, which worries me, but I have no choice but to roll with it. I can only worry about so much.

"I'll get myself captured and make it look like I'm poking around for her. They might keep us together if they want information and for us to behave. I won't give them a choice. This will also mean that there are two working from the inside. Nico, I want you to check out that opening she mentioned. Jonas, when he relays where, I want you inside the perimeter and making us an exit. Dimitri, I want in that system now and I want complete control. Isaac, research every fucking option for our girl and what she mentioned about her choice. Do you understand?"

"Yes," they reply instantly.

"And I want safe spaces for the kids when they are out. You know your jobs, so do them." I rip out my earpiece, stowing it with my gun and other weapons, knowing they won't be allowed inside. I do keep a few knives and a small gun, just to make it look real.

I'm coming, my love, I tell her, even though she can't hear me.

I will not lose her, not like I lost Bas, Ana, and Sam. Fuck the mission. She comes first.

It doesn't take me long to get into position. I don't dare do it too close to their base in case they start to look around for the others. I can't draw attention to the guys. Instead, I head into the nearest town and begin to ask questions like I'm a forward scout, knowing it will get back to them. Nico already mentioned some guards live and work from here, so it's only a matter of time.

Four hours later, they take the bait. "I know the place you're looking for," a stern-faced man in jeans and a big coat says. "Follow me."

Dumb move, but it's exactly what I want, so I finish my drink at the bar and hurry outside after him. "Where is it?" I demand, trying to play the part, scanning the area. I can't go too easily or they will know it's a trap.

"This way. We can't be too careful. You never know who's listening," he mutters with a smirk. It's blatant, but I let it slide as he leads me around the back of the tiny pub. There's a black Escalade idling there, and five men jump out, their guns aimed at me.

Snarling, I quickly pull mine and grab the man leading me, pulling his back to my front as I press my gun to his head. After all, I have to give them a good show. "Where is she?" I demand.

"Come with us and you'll see," one says, his gun still aimed at me. "You're an idiot for coming alone."

Good, they fell for it.

"Don't move," I snap as they inch forward, "or he's dead." I start to back away. I hear the crunch of the gravel behind me as another approaches, but I pretend not to notice. Fuck, I'm a good actor. "You'll bring her to me."

"Now, let's talk about this," the leader says, holding his gun out in surrender, glancing behind me just for a second. The barrel of a gun presses to the back of my head. I could duck and shoot, I could win this easily, but I freeze instead. "You want to see her, correct?"

I simply grind my teeth as if debating my options, my instincts screaming at me to kill them, but I ignore it.

"I thought so. We can take you to her. Just stay nice and calm, drop the gun, and you'll be with her soon."

I hesitate, looking them over as if debating taking them on, and then the gun prods harder into my head. "Now!" the voice behind me snaps.

Releasing the man in my hold, I drop the gun, and they quickly bind my wrists and shove a black bag over my head before tossing me into the SUV, and then we are on our way. Even disoriented with the bag, I keep track of the turns we make to ensure they are, in fact, taking me to the base and not somewhere else. I'd have to kill them and try this again, which would waste precious time.

The general is getting itchy for updates, and Nova needs to be out of there. So much is riding on this plan. I have to trust the guys to do their part as well. It's up to Jonas, Dimitri, and Isaac now to find us a way in and out and to bring their systems down. Keeping Nova alive and okay is my job. Nico has infiltrated the inside.

Hopefully, this will work because one way or another, this ends now.

After thirty minutes, we turn up at the base. This time, I'm inside the SUV and driven straight to the front door. I overhear them talk about how glad the boss will be. Idiots. After a few stops and starts to check security, we come to a complete stop. Doors slam, and then I'm yanked from the vehicle. I stumble before righting myself. My eyes strain, so I shut them and focus on my other senses. I feel a burning sensation on my neck that lets me know my men are still out there watching.

Good.

My boots hit hard concrete which suddenly changes as we pass into a warmer area inside. There's some muttering as I'm groped, and then a few minutes later, we are moving again. When a woosh sounds and we start to descend, I realise I'm in an elevator.

The same one Nico went in?

I guess only time will tell. Hopefully, it means they are bringing me where I want to be. These idiots are so excited to bring me to the boss, thinking it's all their idea, that they haven't got a clue they are playing right into my hands. The elevator jerks to a stop, and they yank my arm. The air is cooler here, and it has a clinical scent, one I'm familiar with from my childhood. It's almost stuffy under the hood, and the bindings dig into my wrists, but I don't speak as their boots echo with mine down what I assume is a corridor. Another door opens, and I'm led inside what seems to be a room. It feels closed in, the air almost stale, as if it's not used much. I'm pushed into a chair, and my hands are rebound behind me, then the boot steps fade away as I'm left here.

Time passes oddly under the hood, and instead of trying to figure it out, I run through my list and plan. Convincing them to pair me with Nova should be hard but doable. Then, I'll ensure she is okay and check in with Nico—again, hard but doable. After that, we just need to find the research, destroy it, kill her father, and get out of here.

Easy, right?

I run through the pros and cons of my options since I have nothing else to do, and that's when I hear the door click, followed by soft footsteps. Not boots, more like soft-soled shoes. A scientist? A worker? A chair screeches in front of me, but I don't move, focusing on the sound to pinpoint the person. The breathing is soft, slow, and calm, and the scent is familiar.

Like pine needles and bleach.

"Hello, Dr. Davis," I murmur.

He chuckles, and the hood is pulled away. He's sitting before me, wearing a lab coat and looking exactly the same as he did when we saw him in the house, except now he has no blood on him. "Louis, I would say it's nice to see you, but . . ." He shrugs.

I roll my shoulders as I watch him, glancing around the room, noting the camera, the one exit and entrance, and the two guards behind me with guns and batons before I focus back on him. "The feeling is mutual."

"I'm sure. But then again, you were looking for me, not the other way around." His eyes narrow slightly as he works through my motivations. He could never believe it's just because I love his daughter since love eludes him. It makes him blind to how far people are willing to go.

It's something I can use against them.

"I wasn't looking for you, but for Nova."

He snorts, clearly not believing me. "Leave us. Keep the door open but stand outside." He waits for the guards to do just that, and he doesn't even spare them a look because he believes they are so beneath him. It gives me some hope that Nico will slip through without detection if he plays it smart.

"Why are you here?" Dr. Davis asks me, eyeing me warily.

"I was looking for Nova when your goons found me," I snap, repeating myself as I tug on the bindings. "Where is she? Is she okay? Is she alive?" I demand, pretending to panic when I know full well she is. Still, there's a moment of hesitation inside of me. What if he hurt her between the time I took the earpiece out and now?

"She's alive. I need her, after all, but I never needed you." He opens a folder. "You did show great promise though, and she clearly cares for you and you for her, so maybe we can still use you and get her to do what we need by hurting you. She's been somewhat . . . uncooperative."

That's my girl.

"But then again, you were always problematic. You had issues following orders." He shuts the folder with a dramatic sigh once more as if I've displeased him. "Sad really, you showed great promise. I was almost reluctant to end your experiment and label you a failure, but . . ."

"You did." I shrug. "What a shame. I want to see Nova."

"Yes, well, I need to decide if I'm going to kill you or use you. It has to be a thought-out decision, you see."

Shit, we have no time to waste. I lean back, projecting calm and mirroring him—a tried and true psychological movement.

"I did, but I never had anything on the line. We both know I am clearly willing to risk everything for her. She would do the same for me. You want us both to cooperate? Put us together." I shrug like it's easy.

"And why would I give you what you want? Neither of you have any options."

"You think we have no options truly? I thought you were smarter than that, Dr. Davis," I mock. "You created us, after all. What was it you used to say? To expand the human potential? You think the reason that you explored and widened to new possibilities truly could not outthink you? Either you are dumber than I imagined or simply not very imaginative. I could kill you right now and be gone before your guards even get here." Leaning forward, I watch him lean back. Fear flashes in his eyes for the first time as he understands the truth of his creation. "You created it, so don't doubt us. Put us together if you wish for us to cooperate. Otherwise, life will get very, very hard for you."

He doesn't like to be outplayed. He will find a way to take it out on us, but for now, he has no choice. He can't be sure I don't have something up my sleeve, and he's already admitted that he needs my help with Nova.

Standing, he glares down at me. "You're a means to an end. I'll make her aware of that. Soon, I won't need either of you. Remember that, Louis."

Stiffening at his clear threat, I incline my head as he storms out the door. If he doesn't need us anymore, then that means he got what he wants, or he's close to replicating the process without years of mental and physical torture and stimulation.

Not good, not good at all.

"Take him to her cell. Make them both aware of the consequences if they are to misbehave."

"But, sir," one of the guards begins, "I think—"

"I don't employ you to think! Do as you are ordered or you will be gone in a blink."

I watch the guards enter, ready to unbind my hands. I simply stand, yanking my hands apart and snapping the bindings. I take great joy in watching them pale in fear and reach for their guns. "Shall we?" I mock.

They share a look, and one pulls out his baton and presses it to my chest. "Try something, I dare you," he mutters. "I'd love to beat the shit out of you like we did that girl of yours."

I stiffen, my eyes narrowing. "You touched her?" I ask.

"Touched her? Oh, I would do so much more—"

Before he can speak his next words, I take the baton and slam it against his windpipe. He crumples to the ground, choking as he dies. Dropping the baton, I look at the guard pulling his gun. He glances from me to the guard and sighs, putting it away. "I haven't touched her. I don't get paid enough for this. Come on." He jerks his head.

He's smart. He can live for now.

Needing to check on her myself, I follow him. No one even mentioned the dying guard, so I guess they don't really care. It makes me wonder how much I can push it but first, I need to see her.

I'm led through a maze, but I memorise it, and then we stop before a closed door. After leaning in to open it, the guard lowers his voice, his mouth turned away from the camera. "If you love this woman, find a way to get her out. He's not going to stop until she's dead. It's been bad." With that, he opens the door, stopping any questions I might have, but I'll remember his face. He can live.

Stepping in, I almost drop to my knees right then and there at the sight before me.

"Nova."

TWENTY-NINE

I watch Louis be led inside with a soft sigh. He's crazy, but I understand why. It doesn't stop me from wishing I were him, though, so I could be at her side, but I know my place. I'm the best bet for getting into their systems, and that's how I help them. It's what I intend to do even as I listen carefully to Nico's conversations with the guards as they take a break. He's prying for information without being obvious. He's good; I'll give him that.

Glancing back down at the laptop on the grass, I refocus on getting into their systems. I have the cameras and alarms so far, but there are firewalls around folders and files that I want to break. I want full access, and anything less than that is not acceptable. There is no room for error when it comes to my family.

We all have our roles. Louis's phone rings then, and I purse my lips. I must groan out loud because the earpiece crackles with their voices.

"What is it?" Jonas mutters as I swear. "Are they okay? Is Nova?"

"Yeah, sorry, it's the general again," I mutter.

"Again?"

Nodding even though he can't see, I work through the responses to him. "Yeah, Louis had me feeding him false leads so he didn't get suspicious and try to stop us from going after Nova. He also didn't want them following us and giving away our positions. This isn't sanctioned."

"But why?" Isaac asks, sounding confused. "He trusts them, doesn't he?"

"As much as you can trust the government." I cough, relaxing back into my computer once it's done. They will eventually come looking, maybe even at the manor, but for now, we are safe. "How's it going, Isaac?"

He's taken the spare laptop to follow Louis's orders while we wait for me to get into the systems and for Nico to report back on the opening for Jonas. We need to wait for the night to sneak in anyway, so we have time—time Isaac is utilising for Nova's benefit. After all, he's the doctor, so he knows best.

The long silence tells me all I need to know. It's not good. "Without seeing the damage, I'm not sure, but . . . It is probably permanent."

"Fuck," I mutter.

I never asked her if she wanted kids. I never thought about it. I was always too focused on the mission, on the next invention, the next moment, but I won't ever admit to her that the idea of a little Nova running around doesn't appeal to me. What would our child be like after all we have gone through? Maybe it is for the best, but if it hurts her, I will find a way.

Come hell or high water, money would be no option. I will give her what she wants.

No matter how impossible it seems.

"And for the kids when we get them out?" I know he's looking into that too. He's locating the best safe places for them. It's important to us and to her that they are safe and happy and that they never have to suffer again. Who knows what they are doing to them in there. I mean, look what they did to us. The cycle stops with us.

"I have some options. I don't know if they are orphans, but I am assuming they are since either no one is looking for them or he paid to adopt them. Either way, I'm assuming they have no family, which makes it easier. Psychologically, he uses patterns to repeat his experiments. There are homes we can get them into, although it might be hard without revealing why they have no details or documents, but I'm still looking."

"Okay," I murmur. "I can always erase their pasts, but they might talk about it."

"True, kids are kids. You remember what we were like?" He chuckles before going quiet. "Do you think they are okay?"

"Of course," Jonas responds. "Dimitri can see them. He would tell us—"

"I mean mentally. Who knows what she has been through again, and coupled with the loss of her sister, I'm worried," Isaac admits.

"We will get her out, and then we'll have the rest of our lives to heal her hurt and help her," I offer. "We will not lose her like Bas."

"Want me to just storm in there and kill them?" Jonas mutters. I can hear him moving, no doubt changing to a better position to be near the base.

"Later maybe." I grin as I scan the cameras. I can see Nico in the break room, and then I flip through and find Nova. The door opens, admitting Louis. The pure shock and happiness on her face lets me know she's going to be okay. I want to stare, to memorise her face and reaction, but I turn that camera off for a moment to give them their privacy, not letting anyone else see. They won't know, but I do.

I refocus on the alarms and reprogramming them to do what I want. They don't even know I'm in their systems, destroying it all from the inside out while also trying to crack into their mainframe files. I'll get there eventually. It will just take some time.

"I'm hitting the head," Nico calls to his friends and moves away. Instead of the toilet, however, he moves down the corridor. "Okay, heading to the hole," he mutters to me. "Is she okay? Is Louis safe?"

"They are both good, brother. Keep going forward, and I'll call out any issues." I track his movements on the camera and tilt the one away from the janitor's door so they can't see him coming and going. It's not enough to draw attention, but enough to satisfy us.

"Yup, that level." I watch him ride the elevator. "Okay, forward. If Nova was correct, two lefts, one right."

Tracking him, I spot some guards ahead. "Slip into the next room." Silently, he moves into the room and we wait. "Okay, go." He's back out. "Hurry. Rotation changes soon," I say, and he speeds up without running.

Finally, he reaches the door and steps inside. I scan the cameras for any issues while he works. "It's a mess in here. Whatever she used, she did a good job. They tried to board it up. If I can get the boards off, I think I can get an opening, but I will need a noise to cover it."

"Got you." I trigger a fire alarm, covering the noise. I hear him grunting, snapping, and yanking as he removes the boards. I watch the guards run. "Almost disabling," I tell him when I see the guards in the control room, trying to switch it off.

"One more," he says, and just as the alarm cuts out, he speaks again. "Got it. Shit."

"What?" I demand.

"Erm, nothing, nothing. I've got this."

"Nico?" I ask, confused by the sudden tightness of his voice.

"Just keep checking on everyone else. Buy me time. I'll be there soon."

"Got you, man," I say even as I frown, wondering what is wrong.

THIRTY

"Nova," he murmurs as he stares at me. I'm sitting on the edge of the bed, hardly able to believe it's him.

How?

Why?

"Louis?" I murmur, rubbing at my eyes as if to wipe away the vision of him. The door shuts behind him, the noise snapping us into motion. He rushes to me as I rush to him. We meet midway, our lips coming together in a sloppy kiss as he lifts me into the air.

"I've got you, baby. I've got you," he promises as he kisses me and holds me tight.

"What are you doing here?" I murmur as I rain kisses across his face, unable to stop touching him.

"You needed us, you needed someone here, so I got captured. Don't worry, we have a plan." His grin is wide as he holds me tight, as if he will never let me go again.

I hope he doesn't.

Pulling back, I eye him in shock. "You got kidnapped because I needed you?"

"Of course, baby, I'd do anything for you." He groans, gripping me tighter and kissing me.

"I love you. I love you so much," I mumble against his lips. "I've missed you so much."

I'm slammed to the bed, my legs thrown over his arms. "I know you're hurt, my love, so stop me if I make it worse, but I need to be inside of you. I need to feel that you're alive. I've been going out of my mind."

Gripping his face, I tug him close as he rips at my pants, his eyes desperate. "I'm yours," I tell him, and I am. Fuck the pain. I want him to remind me of who I am and that I'm more than this living, breathing wound. I'm Nova. I'm okay. Just for a moment, I want to lose myself in his body.

Groaning, he yanks off the cheap underwear. His eyes flick back to my face and with a dirty grin, he spits on his fingers. He thrusts them into me, making me cry out as he works them inside of me, stretching me while his lips meet mine and swallow my moan. His thumb rubs my clit as desire slams through me, making my back arch off the bed. Grunting, he pulls his fingers from my wet pussy then shoves his pants down, and with one hard kiss, he thrusts into me. His cock stretches me as he sinks deeply inside me. The slight pain makes me groan as my body adjusts, and he moans as his head falls to mine.

"God, baby, I missed you so much. I was so fucking worried. Don't you ever do that again," he snarls as he pulls out and slams back in. "Say it, say you won't leave us again."

"Louis," I beg, biting his lip.

Snarling, he lifts and drops me on his dick as he reaches between us, rubbing my clit harshly. The sudden desire and pleasure makes my eyes close as I jerk.

"Say it," he orders, and just when I'm about to come, he stops. His cock is still inside me. Rocking, I try to get off, but he stills me and I slump. "Say it, Nova."

"I won't leave you again," I snap. "Please."

"Good girl," he purrs, kissing me as he rubs my clit while rocking into me, making sure to slide over those nerves that have me clawing at his shoulders and gasping into his mouth. It's too much. All the pain I've had fades into pleasure that explodes through me like fireworks. I scream into his lips, my body jack-knifing, and pain hits me from the movement in my stomach, but I don't let him stop.

I lock my legs behind him to keep him inside of me as he kisses me through my release. "Such a good girl, Nova," he murmurs as I shudder. He slowly pulls out of my pussy and shoves back in, hard and fast.

His other hand comes up and rips my shirt off to bare me to his gaze. I freeze then, and his eyes widen when he sees my new scars. I wait for his anger or disgust, but he slows, making sure I meet his eyes before he leans down and trails his lips over every single one until my throat is tight with tears.

"You are so perfect, my girl," he promises, "then and now. No matter what, I will spend our lives kissing these better and loving the story they tell of my girl surviving to get back to us."

Closing my eyes, I let him heal the wounds with his words and touch as his lips move up and down my chest. He licks my nipples before sucking them into his mouth. The zap of pleasure makes me fall back, and I grip the edge of the bed as he continues his assault.

His thrusts speed up. One hand holds me, while the other slides softly across my dripping clit. His mouth switches between my breasts as he murmurs, "Come for me, Nova. I need to feel it again. I need my girl's cum on my cock, and I need to fill you with mine so deeply, we can never be separated again."

"Louis!" I scream, uncaring who hears. Gripping his hair, I pull his mouth to mine as I fall off that cliff. He follows me this time, bellowing into my mouth as his hips flex, filling me to the point of pain as I feel him jerk and come inside me.

Shuddering, I suck in desperate breaths, my body alight with pleasure as he kisses my lips. "I love you. I love you so much, Nova," he murmurs. "I told you that I would always come for you, and I will. There isn't anywhere in this world where you could hide from me. It's you and me, Nova, forever. No matter what."

Whimpering, I fall into the kiss.

"I've got you, my love," he promises, our bodies still joined as pleasure continues to course through me. "I've always got you."

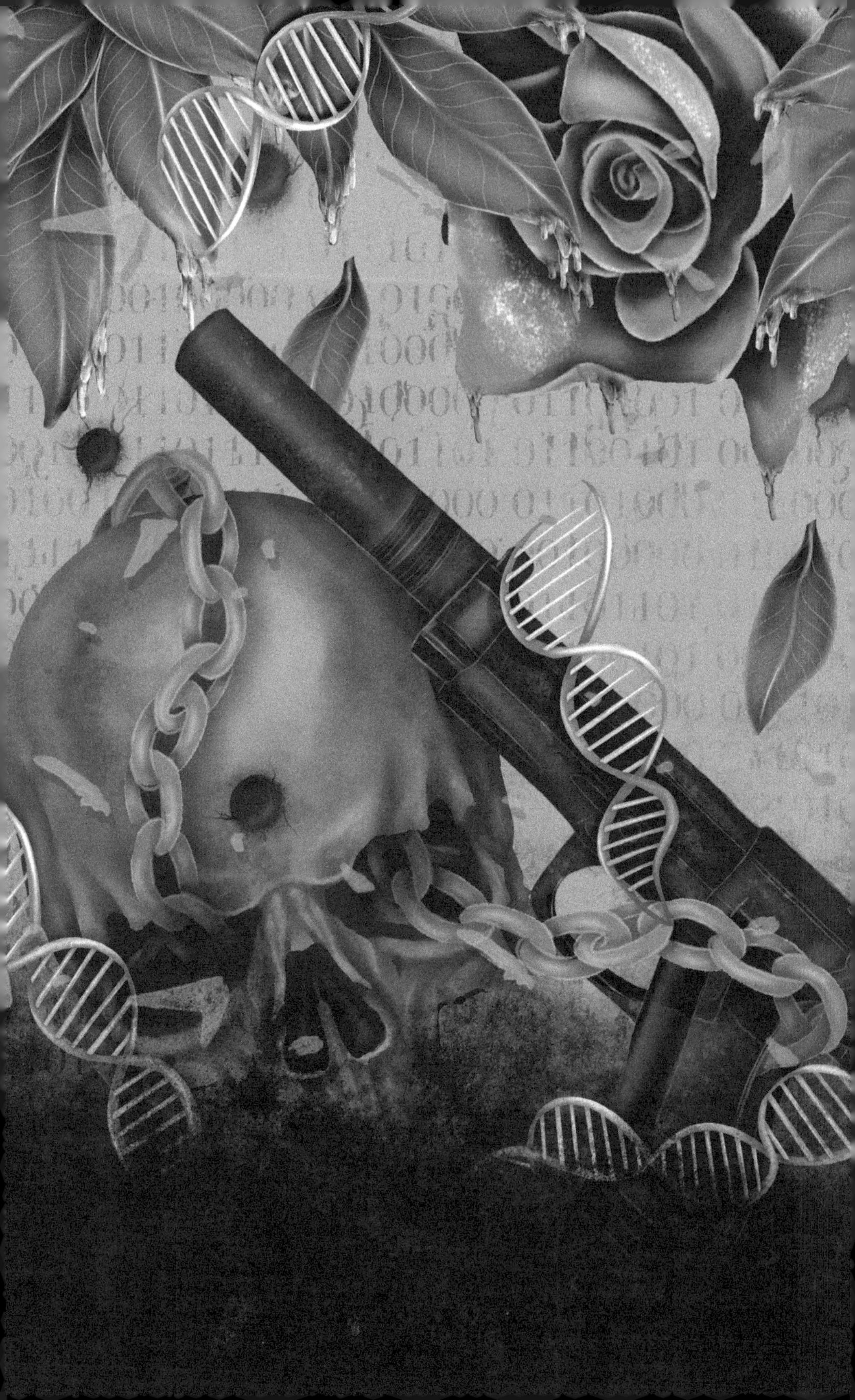

THIRTY-ONE

I tug out the earpiece for a moment, laying my hands on the cool, jagged metal of the hole our girl blew. I need to breathe through the panic because I don't want them to hear and make it a problem. There is no one else who can do this, only me, so I need to fucking get over it. I peer back into the black hole. It is a small, tight space.

It's the very fucking thing I fear more than anything.

It's another fucking scar, thanks to her dad, only this one is internal. If the others knew, they would try to figure another way out, but there is no other way. I need to do this for her and my family. Without giving myself time to overthink it, I cram myself into the hole, grunting and groaning as I contort my body into a weird angle until I finally fit. Closing my eyes for a moment, I slow my breathing like Isaac taught me. He has been working with me on triggers and how to control them, and although it hasn't worked, I wish I had tried harder now. I know I need to get moving, but I'm stuck, hesitating in the darkness. My body locks up with fear.

It's a stupid, irrational fear, but it doesn't stop me from sweating or my breaths from picking up even as I try to control it. Squeezing my eyes shut, I manage to lift a shaky hand and put the earpiece back in. "I need her."

I can't do this without her. I know she's with Louis, and I know she can't get here, but it doesn't matter.

"What?" Jonas asks, but Isaac is faster.

"Nico, why do you need Nova?"

"Tunnel is small," is all I can grit out. "I need her voice."

"Okay, that we can do," Dimitri responds, not questioning if I can do this. They simply hear my need and respond. My family, my brothers, always try to give me what I need. "So, it's a recording, but it's the best I have. Ignore the shit she's saying, since it is from when we were in the lab, but it's her, big guy. It's your Nova."

Her voice mercifully fills my ear then, the familiar cadence making my locked-up muscles relax as my shaking slows to a stop and I can finally suck in a lungful of clean, unpanicked air.

"How boring, yet another day—" She's talking. I don't even know about what, but it doesn't matter. She's here with me, and she needs me.

It gets me moving.

My panic over saving her takes precedence over my own fear.

"You want me to solve the problem? Fine." Even her sass translates, urging me on. Her anger becomes my own, and it's another reminder that I cannot leave her down here, not even for another day. I move faster, sliding my hands up the metal tubing, my back to the other side as I climb. I don't give myself time to think about where I am.

Instead, I focus on the motions of my body and her voice in my ear. It's an arduous process, and I don't know how much time passes until I reach a dead end. I turn to face what I presume is the outside world and blow out a breath.

"There, I'm done. Are you happy?" she snaps.

"I'll be happy when you're home, baby," I respond without meaning to and have to clear my throat. "Jonas, I'm here."

"Okay, the GPS signal in the earpiece should let us find you now that you are above ground. Here, Jonas, I have sent it to your phone. Go. Nico, you are going to have to wait there while he locates it, is that okay?"

Nodding, I close my eyes, realising he can't see me. "Yeah, just keep her voice in my ear."

"Got it, brother, hold on. You are doing amazing."

Her voice starts in a different clip this time. She's laughing, and then I hear Ana. "Annie, no, you'll get us in trouble."

"You are always in trouble anyway." Annie laughs, and then there's a bang.

"What is the meaning of this?" It's her father. "Well, who did this? Ana, was this you?"

"No, it was me." I can almost see my girl's defensive stance in front of her sister as she takes the blame. It switches again, this time to random clips of my girl's life from the labs and house footage. It's always her voice, and she's always calm or angry, never sad or screaming, thank God.

"One day, I'm going to get my revenge on you. You know that, right?"

I smile at that. That's my girl.

"There will come a day when there is nothing else you can do to me. You will look into my eyes as I make sure you can never hurt me again. One day, Father, you will regret your choices, and that's a promise."

That's my girl, and I intend to keep that promise with her. Before this week is through, this place will be dust, we will be home, and she will be in my arms where she belongs.

"Okay, drawing closer. Sorry, brother, I keep having to stop to avoid guards," Jonas mutters, no doubt moving through the base in the dark. I'm guessing D cut the alarms and turned the cameras away from him, or maybe Jonas just took it as a game and broke in—it wouldn't be the first time. "Question, if I blow you up by mistake, will you be mad?"

"Yes," I grumble.

He hesitates. "Okay."

"Jonas, you measured the explosives, right?" I demand.

"Sure, sure, totally measured them. This is the correct amount. I'm positive. Hundred percent. Okay, maybe like sixty percent, but it should be okay."

"Fucking hell." My eyes close once more. "If you kill me, Nova will kick your ass."

"Then she will kiss it better. I'm like forty percent sure this is the right amount. Maybe you should leave once I place it if you don't want to die because you're boring."

"I'm boring because I don't want to die in a fiery explosion?" I retort.

"Yep, exactly, think how exciting it would be—"

"I don't know if you're being serious or trying to distract me," I grumble.

"Maybe a bit of both. Me, personally, I'd like to die in a shark attack. I very much like being eaten, and those grey bastards are cute, so when I'm old and grey, feed me to the sharks."

Isaac sighs. "We are not feeding you to the sharks."

"I will," D adds.

"It's my dying wish!" Jonas snaps.

"You aren't dying!" I practically yell.

"Not yet, but one day, and when I die, I want to be surrounded by sharks. I want to die how I lived—with madness."

"You're mad, that's for sure," I mutter as something hits the side of the vent.

"See? All set. Oh, I forgot the timer. I better run, you too, Nico!"

Fuck!

I hear him sprinting away, so I release my hands from the side and let myself plummet, knowing it's the fastest way. At the bottom, I grab the side with a grunt and slide out of the hole, catching my shoulder and almost ripping the uniform. I've barely made it out of the hole when the base shakes.

It goes quiet for a moment. "Nico, tell me you're alive," Isaac demands.

"I'm good. Did it work?"

Coughing, Jonas replies, "Oh, it worked. There's a hole big enough even for your fat ass. Okay, let me cover it quickly before the guards get here. You better get back to work, soldier boy."

"Fucking idiot," I snap, even as I cover the hole but leave it loose enough for them to break through and slip out of the cupboard. The alarms up top are screaming, and I blend into the soldiers passing by.

"What was that?" I ask.

"Who knows? Someone said it was an attack, but it is probably just those idiot scientists experimenting again."

"Nothing to worry about then?" I question.

"Probably not. Better get back to your station. They will send up an alert if anything is wrong."

Nodding, I slip away. I don't want to just lie low in case they find the hole and realise we are close, but I have to trust that my brothers know what they are doing. "That's a good idea. Jonas, set another explosion in a bin and make it look like one of the scientists threw out chemicals."

I hear him moving to do just that, and after patrolling the corridor like I'm supposed to be doing, I see the guards heading back down and relax. It looks like they bought our ruse, and we are one step closer to getting our girl out of here.

"I'm fully in the system. I probably need twelve hours to plan, and then we'll make our move."

"Got it," I mutter.

Twelve hours until my girl is mine again.

Twelve hours until all this is over.

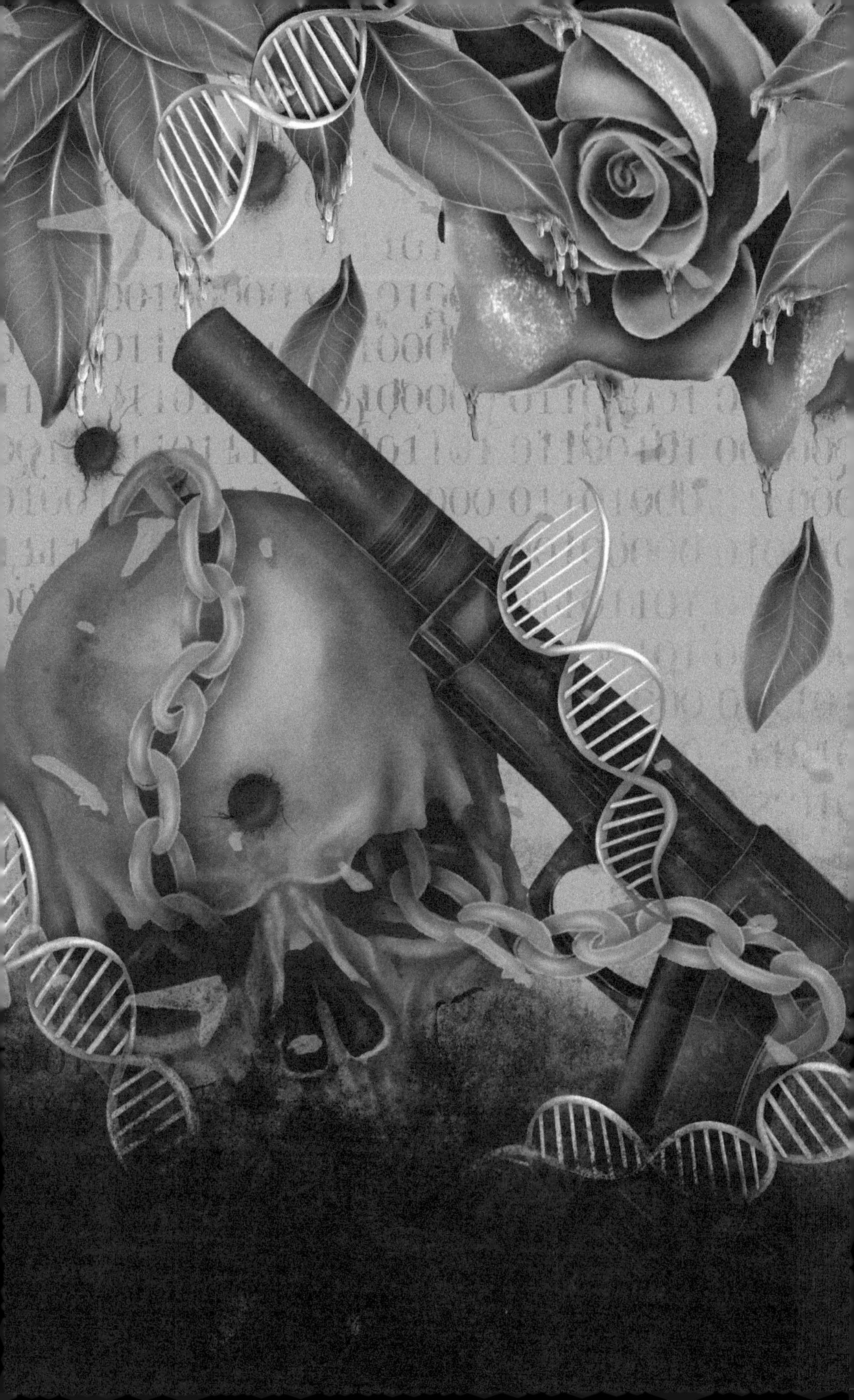

THIRTY-TWO

I'm wrapped in Louis's arms, soaking in his warmth and strength. His hand is tangled possessively in my hair, and his leg is tossed over mine. The cot is small, not made for two people, but neither of us care. We are as close as we can get.

"Tell me everything I've missed," I murmur against his bare chest, rubbing my face there. I feel him hesitate and sigh. "Everything, Louis."

"There she is." He chuckles. "Okay, well, we tried to track you—" I listen as he tells me about their efforts, my heart squeezing as I realise they didn't give up once. They didn't even think about it. All the while I was here, numb, and hurting, hoping they had forgotten me as I planned how to bring this place down and, in the process, kill myself.

I'm a selfish bastard.

I don't want that now. Seeing them again has brought back my desire to keep going, but it hurts that I even thought about leaving them. It's clear my leaving really hurt them, and that's something I have to live with. I wouldn't change my decision, and I can't. The past can only hurt us if we allow it. Instead, I need to learn from it and learn to trust them, to love them, and know they will always come for me.

"I wasn't sure," I whisper when he's done. "Part of me hoped you would forget me and move on, be happy . . . It would have been easier."

"How could you even think that?" he demands, jerking my chin up until I peer into his eyes.

"Because I can't lose any more people I love," I admit.

"You won't, I won't let you, but don't you ever dare think for a minute that we will give up on you. We could never walk away from you. Never mind the mission, baby, you're our whole life. This might have started as five fucked-up kids seeking revenge, but it is so much more now, and you know that. We are a family. You are our fucking heart, and without you, we cannot exist. We need you, and you need us. I love you, Nova. I've never loved anyone the way I love you, and I will not lose you ever again. A month was long enough. It was fucking agony each day, even more than your father ever managed to cause us. I will not spend another second away from you, do you hear me? It's us, Nova. It's always been us. Tell me you understand. Tell me you won't ever think that again, that you will never leave us again."

"I can't," I reply, and he narrows his eyes so I rush on. "Not if it means saving you because I love you too. I love you so much I'm willing to die to protect you. I won't lie to you, Louis, and I know you would do the same, so it has to be enough. It has to be enough that we are here and that we are together again and that I love you."

"You are infuriating," he snaps but softens, pressing his head to mine. "I have our whole lives to convince you we are better together."

"I know we are." My breath brushes his lips. "Sometimes it just hurts so much because I know . . ." I swallow as my darkest fears come out. "I know if I lost you like I lost Ana, I wouldn't go on, I couldn't, and that makes me so fucking weak."

"You could never be weak, Nova, and despite what your father said, love isn't a weakness. It is our strength, and without it, what is the point? Without it, we would just be like him. Love makes us stronger than we ever could be. It makes us believe in a future, in a better world. Love is the reason we fight and never give up, even when it looks bleak. Love gives us a reason to be a better person."

"When did you get so smart?" I mutter. "But what if I love you all too much? I mean, look what my father is capable of. If he knows of my love for you, he will use it against me . . . against you."

"Let him try. It's us against the world, baby, and I'm not going anywhere ever again, believe that. Your father, the experiments, the military, and even the fucking end of the world itself couldn't tear me from you."

"You are so hot when you get all riled up." I smirk, making him chuckle.

"Good, remember that for when we get out of here and I tan your ass red for daring to leave us."

"Promises, promises," I murmur, dragging my lips along his. "But I'll hold you to that."

Things are just about to get interesting when the door opens. We both freeze and lift up, seeing the guards. "Time to go, love birds." One smirks. "The doc wants you."

"Of course he does." Slowly, I slide from the bed. Louis helps me, keeping a hold of my hand as the guard comes towards us.

"It stinks of sex in here." Another laughs. "Is she good?"

Before I can react, Louis knocks out the guard and is back at my side. The remaining two guards look from their friend to us, and each grab an arm and drag us from the room. "You'll pay for that," one mutters, and once we are out of sight of the cameras around the corner, he slams his baton into Louis's stomach, causing him to bend over, gasping.

Snarling, I elbow the man holding me but then freeze when Louis holds up his hand. "Don't. Let them, baby."

"Yeah, baby," the one in my ear croons, and Louis's eyes turn molten as he glares at the man.

"If you so much as look at my girlfriend wrong one more time, I'll rip you apart limb from limb, and we both know I can. I'm being nice so far, and you don't want to see me when I'm not."

The man listens, thank fuck, and instead, they drag us silently down the corridor and thrust us into a room with a few tables and chairs and then stand at the door at attention.

"You okay?" I ask, shooting the guard who hurt him a glare that promises retribution.

"I'm fine, baby," Louis mutters, but I still glare at the man.

"You're dead for touching what's mine," I warn him. He laughs it off with his friend but I'm serious. Nobody hurts my men and gets away with it.

Not even me.

My father makes us wait, and when he enters, he places his tablet on the table and sits, watching us for a while. "I have a different kind of experiment today. We are getting close to locating a better way to open the mind without—"

"Torture?" I supply.

"Experimentation. We are synthesising a serum, but we'll need to test it. However, I still want to know the exact parameters of what I am creating. You understand, yes?"

I want to ask if the serum is being used on the children, how he is creating and testing it, but I can't without looking interested, and that would give him exactly what he wants.

"Oh, of course," I mutter. "Quit the crazy mumbo jumbo. What the fuck do you want?"

"I would remain polite, Nova. After all, I let your friend survive when I could have killed him. Remember that."

Grinding my teeth, I don't respond, and he smirks.

"Good girl."

Pulling something from his pocket, he places a gun on the table between us, not even sparing Louis a look.

I glance from the gun to him, but his face doesn't even move. He knows I could kill him with it.

"Kill one of the guards," my father orders, "or I'll kill him."

I don't even hesitate. After all, he deserves it. I pick up the gun and for a moment, I aim it at my father. He doesn't even flinch, and I know then he has a fail-safe plan in place, so instead, I turn it to the guard and fire. I shoot the one who hurt Louis. I know he's doing it to use Louis against me, to see how far he can push me and get me to follow orders, but I got what I wanted, so I don't fucking care.

"You did not shoot me," he muses as I place the gun back on the table.

"It wouldn't do me any good yet. When I kill you, Father, it will not be at the expense of one of your games. It will hurt, and I will be there to watch the life drain from your eyes."

Taking the gun, he doesn't even spare the dead guard a look. "So you say, yet you need a weapon in your hand to even feel that level of commitment."

"I do not need a weapon to kill, Father," I tell him honestly. "I never did. I never needed anything to be strong, but you've given me more than enough reason to be now." I leave it at that, not giving away our plan.

"Come, I have some things I wish to show you, though I assume you already know." Louis and I share a look but stand, moving to the door where the other guard is pale-faced and glancing between his buddy and me.

"Let that be a warning to you all," I say with a smirk as I pass, and he actually flinches.

Pussy.

"So fucking sexy," Louis murmurs to me as he takes my hand, and we follow my father. We could overpower him right now, but it would be a mistake. I can almost hear Louis telling me, *We stick to the plan*, and a moment later, more guards round the corner, waiting for us.

It's a trap. He was seeing if we would take our shot.

Once again, he's testing us. Good, let him think we are subdued. Instead, we follow blindly until we end up before the room where I found the children. The beds are filled with sleeping bodies now, and my heart stutters as I see them.

"These are my next line in experiments, naturally. Although the soldier aspect offered a good basis, since they were already trained, they were too . . . limited. Too many died from the experiments, but I think I finally have it right. For that, I had to go back to the beginning. To kids. To the malleable mind. They will be the next best thing in this world—highly intelligent and trained to respond. I will sell them to the highest bidder to fund my next line of experiments."

"Bullshit, you just want the money," I snap. "All this talk about science and expanding the human mind and saving mankind is bullshit. You just want money, you greedy bastard. I will never let you hurt those children the way you hurt us."

"You cannot stop me." He smirks. "Once I have what I need from you, you'll be useless. I just wanted to show you what you will be saving by following orders and giving me what I need. If I get what I need from you to make the serum successful, then I do not have to hurt them, do I? But let me show you how serious I am." He mutters something into a mic, and I watch, horrified, as a guard moves to the closest bed and covers the child's face with a pillow.

"Stop it!" I demand. He does, lifting the pillow only to repeat the action. He's not killing him, but he's making the poor, screaming, half-asleep child wish for death.

Something snaps deep inside me.

Before I've made the conscious decision, I've grabbed the pen from his pad and pressed it to his neck. "Tell him to stop now or I'll gouge out your jugular," I threaten. The place is silent bar the child's screams, the others huddling together and crying as they watch.

"You kill me and you are as good as dead," my father reasons, but his eyes are a touch too wide—fear.

"True, but I'll take you with me. Your choice, Father. Look at you. You're afraid. Do you like it? I'll admit that I like seeing the terror in your eyes, now see the truth in mine. I'm willing to die here, are you?"

Gritting his teeth, he nods, and I watch the man walk away. I should drop the pen, but I'm so fucking angry. Instead, I swipe it across his cheek, slicing it open as he shouts and falls back, covering it with his hand. I drop the pen as the guards surge towards me, and I grin at him.

"Now you'll always wear a reminder. Now you are as ugly on the outside as you are on the inside."

"Take her away now!" he howls, covering his cheek as I spit at his feet. Louis tries to grab me, but the guards drag me away as I see my father stumble down the corridor, no doubt looking for help. I laugh as we are thrown back into our cell.

Still laughing, I kick the door and then turn to the camera. "How do you like that, asshole? How do you like being on the other end? I will gut you!" I howl.

"Shh, I've got you." Louis wraps his arms around me and leads me to the bed. "Try to calm down, Nova. We have to be smart."

"Fuck smart. I want him to suffer now."

"Soon," he promises.

"No, now!" I yell, and before I know it, I'm flipped and pinned. His snarling face looms above me, and the strength in his grip makes my pussy clench, even in my anger.

"If you won't listen, then you clearly need an outlet. I will oblige, so be a good girl and come for me."

Keeping me pinned with one hand, he rips down the joggers, yanks my legs open, and slams his fingers into me. The bite of pain makes my back bow, even as I fight to get free.

He smacks my clit, making me cry out. The sharp pain brings my focus back to his snarling face. "That's it, love, focus on me. Take it all out on me."

His fingers twist inside me, curling around that spot that feels so good it hurts, all while his thumb rubs my clit. Against my own wants, I come with a cry, clenching around him with the force. Louis grins, not slowing as he continues to attack my body, forcing me to focus on him.

Use it, he said.

Use him.

Gripping his hands, I flip us and shove his joggers down as his head hits the bed, his eyes narrowed in desire. His blond hair is spread across my pillow, and his muscles clench. "That's it, Nova, use me. Come on, baby, I can take it."

I slide my hand across his abs and grip his cock. Tightening my hand, I stroke his hard length, feeling him jerk. His head drops back as he arches his hips up to thrust into my fist. "Nova," he groans needily. "Baby."

Feeling mean, I lean down and lick the tip of his cock, channelling all my anger and frustration into the desire between us.

His mouth parts on a moan, and he closes his eyes in bliss.

Seeing this huge, strong man weak below me is a heady feeling.

I lap at the tip of his cock, tasting his salty precum, and surrender. I suck the tip of him deep as he writhes with a bellow, and then I release him with a pop.

"Nova," he snarls, opening his glittering eyes. "Get your perky ass on my cock right this second."

"Or what?" I purr, leaning down and sweeping my tongue along his cock, keeping my mouth open so he can watch as I slide him to the back of my throat and rub him and his precum all over my mouth.

"I mean it, Nova. Don't be a brat or you'll be face down and my cock will be in that pretty ass instead of your pussy until you're screaming to come, and I won't let you."

"I'd like to see you try," I retort as I slide my tongue inside the tip of his cock with a hum.

"Last chance, brat," he warns, his jaw flexing.

Moving up his body, I press my lips to his. "Taste how much you want me, Louis."

"I always fucking want you," he says as he grips the back of my head, drags me down, and tangles his tongue with mine, tasting his own need. His other hand slides down my back and grips my ass, dragging my pussy along his cock, trying to get me to ride it.

Pulling away, I wag my finger at him. "Bad Louis."

Moving out of his grip, I slide up his body and seat myself on his face. "I'm sick of hearing you talk," I purr. "Use your mouth for better things and make me come on that silver tongue."

He grips my hips. "Gladly, love." He yanks me down, sitting me heavily on his face with a groan. His tongue instantly darts out and laps at my pussy.

I almost fall back from the bliss, one hand hitting the wall next to the tiny bed as it creaks with my rocking. I ride his face, grinding into his mouth as his tongue thrusts inside me, and his nose presses to my throbbing clit.

I circle my hips, finding the pressure I need, while I sit harder on his face as his nails dig into my ass cheeks, spreading it as he laps at my hole and thrusts inside it.

Moaning, I slap my hand into the wall, grinding down. I'm so close again, I'm already shaking. When he begins to hum, I'm lost. I cry out my release and fall forward to curl around him as I shudder, winding my hips through my release until I fall back.

Lifting my head, I meet his dark, hungry eyes. His face is coated in my glistening cream, and he laps greedily at his lips while reaching for me.

"Fuck, baby, bring that pretty pussy back here. Let me fucking suffocate between those thighs, drinking nothing but your cream for the rest of my life. They could come in right now and they would have to fight to get me off you."

Crawling up his body, I grab his hands and press them to my breasts as I rock into his cock. Lifting up, I grip his length and meet his eyes once more. "How about I fuck you instead? I want to see you come. I want to feel it," I tell him as I press the bulbous head of his cock to my entrance.

"Then ride me, baby, and make me come," he growls. "Ride my big fat cock. It's hard for you, always for you, waiting to be used, to be fucked."

"That's because you're mine," I say as I slam myself down, taking his full length. His hands grip my breasts, squeezing as I start to move, chasing another release. I use him like he demanded, taking it all out on his body. My head drops back as I ride him, making sure to swivel and hit my throbbing clit.

Each thrust pushes me higher as he sits up, shoving my shirt up and sucking my nipple into his mouth. He pushes me higher and higher until I spiral and explode.

Snarling, he rolls us until we fall from the bed and my back hits the floor. He grips my hair and hammers into my body, taking what he wants. He takes the control away, leaving me breathless as I cry out.

He pulls out of my body, making me whimper, then he flips me over and yanks my hips up. Slamming back inside of me, he slaps against my ass with each brutal thrust. My head is pulled back by his hand in my hair, and the slight pain makes me moan loudly.

"You're mine, Nova, never forget that," he snaps, smacking my ass with an open hand. The sting makes me jerk before it fades into a fire that burns through me, scorching away my anger. "All of you. I'm never letting you go. I will always be here, protecting you. We will get our revenge, love, together. Until then, take your man. Take every hard inch of me and know it's all for you."

His voice is feral as he smacks my ass once more, pummelling into me.

His hips stutter and I know he's close. I want to drain him dry. "Come, love, now."

"I can't," I admit, my body on the threshold.

"You can and you will," he growls.

Pushing me down, he grinds my pussy into the cold, rough floor, and I shatter once more as he moans, bowing over me as he fills me to the brim with his cum.

I'm boneless, my eyes closing as he turns us and wraps his arms around me. "Good girl, Nova. That's it, relax. We'll get him and our revenge together. Just hold on a little longer, my love."

Panting, I relax into his arms, knowing he did the right thing, but it doesn't stop me from feeling anger or guilt. What if he takes it out on the kids?

We need to move.

THIRTY-THREE

That night when the door opens, I expect the worst, but when a figure slips in and Nico grins, I relax.

"Sorry, I had to wait. Your father was on a warpath."

"How's the bastard doing?" I mutter as Louis glances over at Nico.

"His face is cut up pretty good and he's angry about it. I heard it was your work." Nico smirks, running his tongue across his lips as I nod in response. "That's my girl."

"I thought I was your favourite girl. You lied!" I hear Jonas cry out, making me laugh as I fall back.

Pushing away from the door, he heads over. Louis moves away, sitting up on the edge of the bed so Nico can cup my face. He kisses me softly and when my eyes flutter open, I see his are closed and his head is pressed to mine.

"I just need a minute, baby, to soak you up so I can go back out there. I just need a reminder of why the fuck I haven't killed them yet and taken you away."

"A reminder?" Smirking, I cup his face, sliding my hands up into his hair before yanking his head back as he groans, his eyes fluttering open. "I'll remind you, my love."

I turn my energy, my anger, into this . . . into something good.

I know Louis is watching, but neither Nico nor I care. It isn't the first, nor will it be the last time, and he gives us a moment of privacy together even though he's close enough to touch.

"Shit, wait, I want the cameras on, Dimitri."

Nico yanks the earpiece out and puts it in my ear.

"Scream for them, baby, so while they are out there working, they will get a reminder, too, and they will remember what they are fighting for."

"Fuck, D, show me the cameras," Jonas whines in my ear.

"I'm busy." Dimitri huffs. "But do as Nico says, Nova. Give me a reason to work harder."

"I agree. It would be good for morale," Isaac says, and I can almost see his smile.

"You heard him," Louis murmurs, leaning back and getting comfy to watch.

They want a show? They'll get one.

Using his short hair, I yank Nico down to me. "Suck," I demand, and Nico gladly wraps his lips around my nipple through my shirt, sucking hard. I groan, my eyes sliding to Louis for a moment to see him smirking. When Nico turns his head to suck my other nipple, there's a wet patch over my breast.

Wanting skin on skin, I push him back and stand. "Get undressed. I want you naked. I want all that skin on me," I tell him, and meeting his dark eyes, I slip from my clothes and sit on the edge of the bed.

Snarling, he rips off his belt and drops his weapons. His trousers are next, getting caught in his boots. He toes them off and reaches behind him, tugging his shirt up and off as I watch the flex of muscles with a moan. Desire courses through me at the sight of all those muscles, hard lines, golden skin, and thick scars.

When he moves closer, I press my bare foot into his chest. His dark eyebrow arches and he steps closer, bending my leg at the knee until he's nearly touching me.

Bending down, he drags his lips across my foot before sliding back down with his teeth. "Show me that pretty pussy, baby. I've been dreaming about it since I last had you, and it doesn't fucking compare."

Smirking, I kick him back, and he allows me to. My foot hits the floor once more, and I spread my thighs nice and wide, letting him see my wet pussy. I slide my hand down to tug at my nipples, then over my abs to cup my pussy, where I grind into my own touch. "Is this what you want?" I purr.

His eyes are locked on my touch as he nods jerkily.

"Then get down on your knees. Show me how badly you want it. Crawl to me. Crawl to my pussy."

Without pausing, he drops to his knees, keeping those dark, wicked eyes locked on me. Nico is huge, and when he starts to crawl, I watch the pull and play of all that muscle. His arms and back flex and bulge. He doesn't stop until he can run his tongue up my thigh to my pussy, sliding it across my hand and down my other leg.

"Show me, Nova, show me why I fight. Show me why I can't sleep or look at myself. Show me what's ours," he begs, his voice needy. His huge, hard cock bobs for attention, and he wraps his thick, tattooed hand around it, stroking himself as he waits.

I peel my hand from my pussy and he groans, falling forward at the sight. His tongue swipes between my folds as I fall back with a moan. My hands slide up my body to play with my breasts, but then his big ones are there, smacking my own away as he tweaks my nipples.

"Shit." I hear someone moan down the mic. "Louder, baby. Make him suck that needy clit until you scream."

Panting, I close my eyes. I can feel Louis's eyes on me and Nico's touch. The others' voices express their own need to hear my pleasure and know I'm alive. I feel it as well. I need Nico to remind me.

I need him to touch every inch of me, to kiss me and make it better.

To remake me as theirs as if no time has passed.

To love me as they once did.

His tongue curls around my clit, lashing it as I groan, allowing every little sound to slip out. Two big fingers slide into my pussy, stretching me as he fucks me with them. He sets a fast, hard pace as he greedily eats me, licking every drop of cream as if he can't get enough. I cry out and grind into his face for more, pushed higher and higher until I tumble and fall with a scream, shattering for him.

With a beautiful moan, he pulls his fingers free and licks them clean before shoving them back into me and licking them once more.

"Nico," I whine. He tweaks my overly sore nipples, and electricity goes right to my clit.

Chuckling, he wets his fingers once more, but instead of licking them clean like I expected, he slides them down and circles my asshole before slowly thrusting them inside me there.

"I'm going to make you come on my cock, princess. I'm going to fuck you hard and fast, and then Louis is going to claim this pretty little ass, isn't he?"

"Fuck, please," I whine as he slowly fucks my ass with his fingers, only to pull away once more, leaving me needy.

Slapping my pussy with his other hand, he hoists me farther up the bed. "Hold on, baby," he warns as his cock drags along my wet centre, and when his lips meet mine, he impales me.

My eyes almost cross.

Nico is so big, it borders on painful but in the best kind of way. With that one thrust, I forget everything. I focus only on him, biting at his lips as he pulls out and hammers back in, fucking me hard and fast just like he promised.

The bed squeaks with the force as he hammers me across the bedding. Snarling, he slides down and bites my sore nipples until I whine.

"Nico," I beg, lifting my hips to meet his thrusts.

His hand slides up to grip my neck in a collar, a reminder, a promise that I am still his and he is still mine.

Nothing has changed, even though everything has.

The world could fall apart right now, and I would gladly stand in the decimation, begging him not to stop . . .

And I do loudly, for the others to hear.

Their pants and grunts of pleasure reach my ears as they no doubt touch themselves while Nico fucks me.

"That's it, baby. Fuck, you're so goddamn beautiful. Look at you, taking me so good. That's it, tighten on me, come for your man," he demands, nipping my nipple as he twists his hips to drag his length along those nerves that have me seeing stars. I am so close it hurts, but with one more brutal nip of his teeth on my nipple, I tumble over the edge, gripping his cock like a vice as I do, screaming into the mic.

I hear someone moan their own pleasure, but I'm lost, barely able to move or make a noise as Nico pulls from my clinging body and guides me to my knees on the hard floor. Placing a pillow under my head, he guides me onto Louis's waiting cock. I slide down his hard length and turn to see him as Nico slides his wet cock across my ass, taunting me as Louis stills.

When I push back, Nico slides his cock in an inch, letting me clench on his tip until I slam myself back, impaling my ass on his cock as he roars.

Gripping my hips roughly, he yanks me back, fucking me hard and fast. One hand slides up my body, collaring my neck once more, while Louis's lips find mine.

They work me between them, fucking me in tandem. Hands caress every inch of me, reclaiming my body for themselves and me.

I'm pushed and pulled between them, and another release builds inside of me. Louis rubs my clit and with a shout, I come hard, clenching around them and dragging them with me. Louis moans in my ear as he pumps his cum deep inside my pussy.

Nico roars, thrusting into my ass until I feel his hot release splatter inside me. We all pant, locked together.

"I love you," I whisper to them both.

Lips caress my back. "We love you too, and we always will, baby."

We lie like that for a while, them just holding me until they eventually pull out of my body and help me clean up and dress before holding me on the bed.

"So beautiful," Dimitri murmurs down the mic, reminding me they are there.

"I love you all too. I can't wait until I get to touch you again," I admit.

"Us also," Isaac offers softly, his voice tense.

"Are you okay?" I ask Isaac, needing to check on him.

He sucks in a breath and releases it slowly. "I will be, sweetheart, when you're back in my arms."

"How's Bert?" I ask, afraid of the answer.

"He's going to be just fine. I promise."

"Thank you," I murmur, "for saving him."

"I . . . God, Nova, I'm so sorry I couldn't save them," Isaac whispers, and my eyes close. "I'm so fucking sorry for everything he did to us. I couldn't save them, and I'm just so fucking sorry."

"I know, but it's not your fault, so don't feel guilty. My father did this, not you." Handing the earpiece back over, I curl into the bed. I'm suddenly exhausted and hurting at the reminder of my sister and Sam. Nico watches me carefully as he plugs it back in then crouches, taking my hand as he looks between Louis and me.

"So, here is the plan." Keeping our hands clasped together, Nico explains in detail every step of it. Louis asks questions, and they change little details until he's finished, and then they both look at me.

"Is that okay with you, Nova?"

I nod. "As long as I get to kill my father and we free the kids, I don't care about anything else."

They share a look before Nico leans in and kisses me. "It's almost over, okay?"

I nod again, unsure what to say. I feel like this has been a dream. Like I've been here underground for so long, yet I achieved nothing, then suddenly it's all going to be over. It has to be. My father won't forgive me for today, and if I survive the night, I will be dead tomorrow, my brain and body used for this final experiment.

Tomorrow, we'll end this lifelong mission.

But what will be left after?

"You just have to hold on a little longer, baby, okay?"

"Okay." I press my face to his side, just soaking in his warmth. "I can do that."

"I know you can."

THIRTY-FOUR

I have no way of knowing if the guys are in position.

Today is the day.

Dimitri will bring down the alarms, Jonas will enter through the hole they made, and Isaac will come in after him. Isaac's job is to get to the kids, while Jonas's is to clear us a path. Nico will take down the guards and free us, and then we will finish my father. I know how wrong plans can go, though, and as soon as I wake up, I know this one will go wrong.

It's in the air.

All the guards come in pairs to drop off food, their eyes hard and wary as if they know something. Do they? Or am I simply overthinking all of this? Possibly, but after I shower and dress, doing some quick warm-ups with Louis to prepare for the day, I know I'm not wrong when the door opens and five guards storm in, their weapons pointed at us as if they are expecting trouble.

I share a silent look with Louis, in which we quickly adapt and allow them to take us. Nico will have to find us, but we can easily take these five out. We are led down the corridor once more, this time to the gym. Once inside, the guards spread out before the door, and then I realise they are in full protective gear.

Do they know something is wrong?

My question is answered when the door opens and Joel steps out. Unlike the guards, he's in simple jeans and a shirt, and he smirks as he comes to a stop a few feet away from us. "Your father asked me to question you while he's occupied."

"Occupied with what?" Louis asks.

No doubt he's worried that one of ours has been caught. I am too, but I have to trust them to look after themselves the way they are trusting me to be ready.

He ignores Louis completely and focuses on me. "Do you know anything about the loss of control over the alarms and cameras?" I just stare at him, waiting. "Nova, your father wants answers, and I have been given free rein to do anything to get those answers. Do you understand me? We both know you cannot survive another beating and round of torture."

Tilting my chin back, I smile tauntingly. "You want answers? Come and get them."

Joel smirks. "I was kind of hoping you would say that."

Louis steps closer, and Joel's gaze moves to him. "Don't worry, I'll let you watch. The guard can hold you. If you feel like giving answers at any point, just let me know."

He's trying to use us against each other. Clearly, they have noticed something is wrong, but they aren't sure if we are behind it or if it's something else. Father is taking precautions, but he should have taken more. This won't save him, and instead, he's given me the perfect opportunity to kill the one man I want to eradicate alongside my father.

Once we are given the signal, all bets are off.

Gone is the compliant prisoner, and in her place will be the super soldier he created.

Me.

I want revenge. I want to bathe in their blood. I want to drown in their bodies and screams, and I will have it. For a moment, my sister flickers in my mind, and I embrace it, letting her screams fill my head. It sends energy vibrating through me, and my fingers twitch at my sides, preparing to fight.

We need time, though, because if I fight now, I won't stop and the plan will fail. No, I need to be smart one last time, so when he advances on me, I don't move. I let him smash his fist into my stomach, curling around it for a moment and breathing through the pain before straightening. He meets my eyes, his own narrowing before he slaps me. My head jerks to the side from the force, and I spit out blood as I meet Louis's enraged gaze.

I silently tell him this one is mine and that I have to wait. I shake my head slightly. He wants to kill the man, but I can take this, and it will buy us the time we need. If they are focused on us, then they aren't focused on what else is happening, so for now, I accept the pain without fighting back.

Turning to Joel, I straighten and meet his angry gaze. "Fight back," he hisses in my face.

I simply stare coldly at him, waiting.

Shaking his head, he slaps his hands over my ears. The clap is loud, and my ears ring as I stumble. When his voice comes back, it's enraged, and he points at Louis. "What? So scared you won't even defend her? I thought you loved her. Isn't that why you came here? To protect her? Look at you just standing there. So weak. You won't even stop me if I do this." He slams his fist into my wound once more, and I grit my teeth to stop a cry from escaping my lips, narrowing my gaze on Louis who twitches. He's as still as a statue, but there is death in his eyes, and when he glances at me, his expression warns that he won't hold back much longer.

Despite the plan, despite the fact that Louis plans every move to the last second, he won't this time. He would ruin the plan simply to protect me.

If that isn't love, I don't know what is.

Fuck, I hope the guys hurry up or Louis is going to kill everyone before they get near us. When Louis doesn't answer, giving him what he wants, Joel turns back to me.

"Are you doing this?" he demands once more. Again, I say nothing, and his thumb digs into my wound. I bend inwards slightly, my eyes narrowing as agony spreads through me. He watches me from inches away, noting every expression. "Answer me and I'll stop. Make this easy on yourself. He doesn't want you dead just yet. If you answer, I'll make it quick when it's time, not like the brutal agony he will make you feel."

I say nothing, breathing through the pain, and he steps back with a snarl. I straighten despite the pain, and he attacks quickly, slamming his foot into the wound. I stumble back but right myself, knowing if I fall to the ground, it will be much worse. I refuse to fall ever.

"Fight back!" he roars as he grips my hair and throws me onto the mat. I'm just climbing to my feet when our signal comes.

An explosion rocks us, causing us to sprawl on the floor. I quickly leap up and know this is go time, so using their disorientation and confusion to my advantage, I point at the guards, telling Louis to take them.

Joel is mine.

"You want me to fight back?" I grin down at him. "You got it." I rush him with a silent roar.

He actually falls back as I advance, and I don't blame him. I let it all loose. All my anger, hurt, and grief. I embrace every dark part of myself. Power courses through my body, and my mind opens completely, making me work faster than ever before. I'm on him before he can even raise his hands.

I slam my fist into his face. "Fight back," I yell at him, mocking him as I slam my hands onto either side of his head, disorienting him before I bitch-slap him. He flies through the air, and I spare Louis a glance to see him ripping through the guards. He tears out someone's throat with his teeth before whirling to the next man, and desire and love pulse through me before I turn back to see Joel getting to his feet.

Wiping blood from his lips, he grins. "Finally, a fight."

I duck his punch and slam my fist up, breaking his ribs. He grunts but grips me and tosses me aside. I whirl, landing on my feet, and lunge at him. I wrap my legs around his neck as I spin upside down and then slam downward, rolling him to the ground. I hammer my fist into his face as he struggles and yells. Releasing him when his hand reaches for my wound once more, I roll back with a grin.

"Come on, is that all you've got?" I challenge.

"You're dead. Fuck what your father said. He doesn't need you. I'm the better one here," he spits.

"I'm the better one," I mock. "Yet you can't even beat a wounded female."

His nostrils flare, and he relies on emotion rather than logic as he rushes me. I know he's going for the face, so I duck, and then his knee comes up, but I was expecting it. I drive my own into his cock and when he stumbles, I leap up and ride him to the floor, hammering into his face. He brings his arms up to try and stop me, but he's slowing while I am only speeding up.

With a roar, I beat his face in, feeling bones break. Blood coats my split knuckles, but I still don't stop, not even as he twitches and then stops moving. Heaving, I sit back and take him in. His face is a bloody pulp.

"I think he's dead, love." Louis grins, and I look over to see him covered in blood, surrounded by dead guards. He tosses me a baton and a gun from a holster. I catch them and stand, and then I fire at Joel's face and chest at least five times.

"Now he is." Gripping the gun and the baton, I walk over to him, scanning for injuries. He does the same to me.

"I say we get out there. Fuck the plan, let's just hunt these bastards down. The more sides we attack from, the better. Fucking corral them like sheep." I expect him to turn me down but he nods.

"I say let's do it. We will meet with the others. Come on. Let's show them what they created."

JONAS

I hurry down the shoot that leads from the outside. I kick the boards Nico placed at the bottom, and then I wait in the cupboard with my eyes on my watch, and just as it hits zero, I whisper, "Boom."

The explosions I placed up top go off right on time. The gate goes down, and all the cars, entrances, and buildings explode. I spent all night crawling around the base, setting the charges with Isaac while Dimitri watched us and got into the last of the files. Thirty minutes before, he brought down all the cameras and alarms. Soldiers poured outside, looking for the source, but I was already inside.

"Damn, you should see the flames." Dimitri chuckles. "Okay, all systems are locked out permanently. Isaac and I are coming through the back gate while they flood the front. I'll be down in the elevator, but don't wait for us. Nico says Louis and Nova were taken somewhere and he can't find them. He's searching levels one and two, so you need to search the others. We will join you."

"Got it, and kill any I find on the way," I murmur, already pulling my gun before putting it back and palming two blades instead.

"Open season," he murmurs down the mic.

Grinning widely, I flip the knives happily and open the door. It's about time. I step out into the corridor and crack my neck. I plan to find my girl and kiss the everloving shit out of her, but first, it's time for a little payback.

They touched her.

They took her away from me.

I'll rip them to pieces until their screams echo through these corridors as a warning to whoever might try that again. Moving silently, I open each door to make sure my girl isn't in there, frowning in displeasure when I don't see anyone to kill. I want to give her a pile of hearts. In fact, I grab a bag and sling it over my shoulder just for that purpose, and then I step back into the hallway.

"Yoo-hoo, anyone home? Invader at the door!" When that doesn't work, I cock my head. "Oh look, I'm about to touch the experiments. Better come stop me!"

Still nothing.

What does a guy have to do to be attacked around here?

I mean, really.

Rolling my eyes, I pull my gun and fire at the wall, busting a pipe.

Whoops.

It does the trick, though, and I holster the gun just as two guards come skidding around the corner. "Only two, really?" I frown and point the knife at one. "Could you call the others on the radio? I'm starting to feel a little insulted. I need to show off for my girl."

Dimitri sighs. "Jonas."

"Can you record this for her?" I ask him as one calls into the mic. "Thank you, that was very kind. For that, you can die quickly."

He blanches and looks at his friend next to him, clearly scared. "Don't worry, we can wait for your backup. I want this to be fair," I tell them as I start to pick my nails with my knife, whistling as I wait.

"Erm, if you come with us, we won't hurt you?" the other offers.

I raise a brow at him, and he swallows.

"I'm sorry, that was stupid."

"It was, but it's okay. I bet it's your first time, right? Everyone is bad their first time. I mean, I wasn't, but I'm amazing." I shrug.

"I . . ." They share a look. "Maybe we can figure something out."

"Sorry, no can do. It's work, you understand." I wince as I hear boots before more guards emerge behind them and behind me, surrounding me. Grinning, I roll my neck. "This is more my speed. Don't shoot and cheat now, boys. Don't want to ruin the merchandise for my girl. Actually, she might give me head for a few bullet wounds. Feel free, but just avoid the face. She likes to sit on that."

"Doc says we can kill him," one calls, smacking his baton against his other hand as he grins at me. "Let's make it hurt. I've always wanted to kill one of these freaks."

"Oh, tough guy." I fake shiver. "I'm so scared. Please don't hurt me." Cackling, I crook my finger. "Bring it."

They surge towards me. Laughing, I dodge their weak attempts and slash. I twirl and slice through skin as I do. I hear screams as throats, arms, and legs are cut. I don't even see it anymore. I just keep moving as I dice them to pieces. Batons hit me, but I barely even feel them as I cut them down for my girl.

I do jerk as a bullet slams into my leg, but when I glance down, I see it's through and through and it hasn't hit anything important. It does, however, lodge in the femoral of a guard who goes down with a scream.

"Dummies," I chastise them. Spinning, I slam my knife into his neck and pull it out. Blood spurts across my face as I laugh crazily. Some are starting to retreat, and I follow them with my bloody knife held out.

"Here, here, scaredy cat," I call as they back away. "Do you want to know why the doc says you can kill me?"

When no one answers, I cock my head. "They called me damaged. Insane. I guess he wasn't wrong." Leaping onto the wall, I kick off it and come down on them. I slam my knife into one, turning my head and ripping my teeth into another. I use everything I have. When I turn back, there are only three left. One's hand is shaking as he aims a gun at me.

The other two are standing amongst the carnage in shock. Picking the one with the gun as my next target, I get to my feet. He shoots, and I duck under it. His hands are shaking so badly, he keeps missing as I walk calmly towards him, and once I reach him, I pull the pouch from my side, take the gun, and replace it with that.

"Can you hold this?" I ask him. He grabs the bag, his eyes wide as I race down the corridor and dive around the corner as it explodes. Laughing, I roll to my feet to meet the incoming guards.

The more the merrier.

There are ten of them in a pretty little row, all waiting to be killed.

"Duck, duck, goose," I call, pointing at one. "You're first."

I race towards them. They fire, but I manage to avoid being hit too badly, and I slide my knife in a figure eight fashion in the first man. He falls, and I turn to the next, slamming my knife into his thigh as I swivel on my knees and flip up and over him, ripping out the neck of another.

Ducking a punch, I turn and snap the neck of the next one.

I pull his baton and slam it across another's head, beating him until he falls, then I pluck the knife from the still screaming guard's thigh and make quick work of the others until they are all either dead or dying.

Crouching, I rip the shirt off the first male and stab him in the chest with my knife. He jerks, and his eyes widen. Oops, still alive. Oh well. Carving into his skin, I break his ribs, carefully extract his heart, and add it to the bag before moving to the next. I work my way through the ten soldiers. The last one is pressed against the wall, covering a bleeding wound on his thigh with his hand. With a grin, I uncover the wound and watch the blood squirt as he dies. Once he is gone, I do the same to him, carving out his heart.

I don't know which ones hurt my girl, but they are all complicit, so they died and will now be given to her as a sacrifice for their treachery.

Getting to my feet, I frown down at my bleeding leg. It's bothersome more than anything, so I use some of the ripped shirts to bind the wound. It will heal quickly enough and doesn't stop me from walking back to the other bodies and taking their hearts. I leave all their chests ripped open, the precious white walls sprayed with blood.

An idea comes to mind, so I move over to one wall and, after dipping my fingers into the closest soldier's neck wound, I begin to carefully write out words, stepping back once I'm done to check it out.

Perfect.

I LOVE YOU, NOVA.

There's a gagging noise, and I turn to see a soldier. They rip off their helmet and throw up. It's a female, her long, sweaty hair stuck to her face. She glances at me and then at the bodies. Her face is pale but determined as she straightens, pulling her weapon.

The woman stops before me, gripping her baton. "Look, I'm not sexist, okay? So I'm going to kill you the exact same way," I warn her. "I'll leave your heart though. I don't want my girl getting worried about me cutting through your shirt."

Before she can even speak, I slice her throat and watch her fall. I hesitate because I want more hearts for my collection, but I don't want Nova to be jealous, so I step over her and head off in search of more.

And my girl.

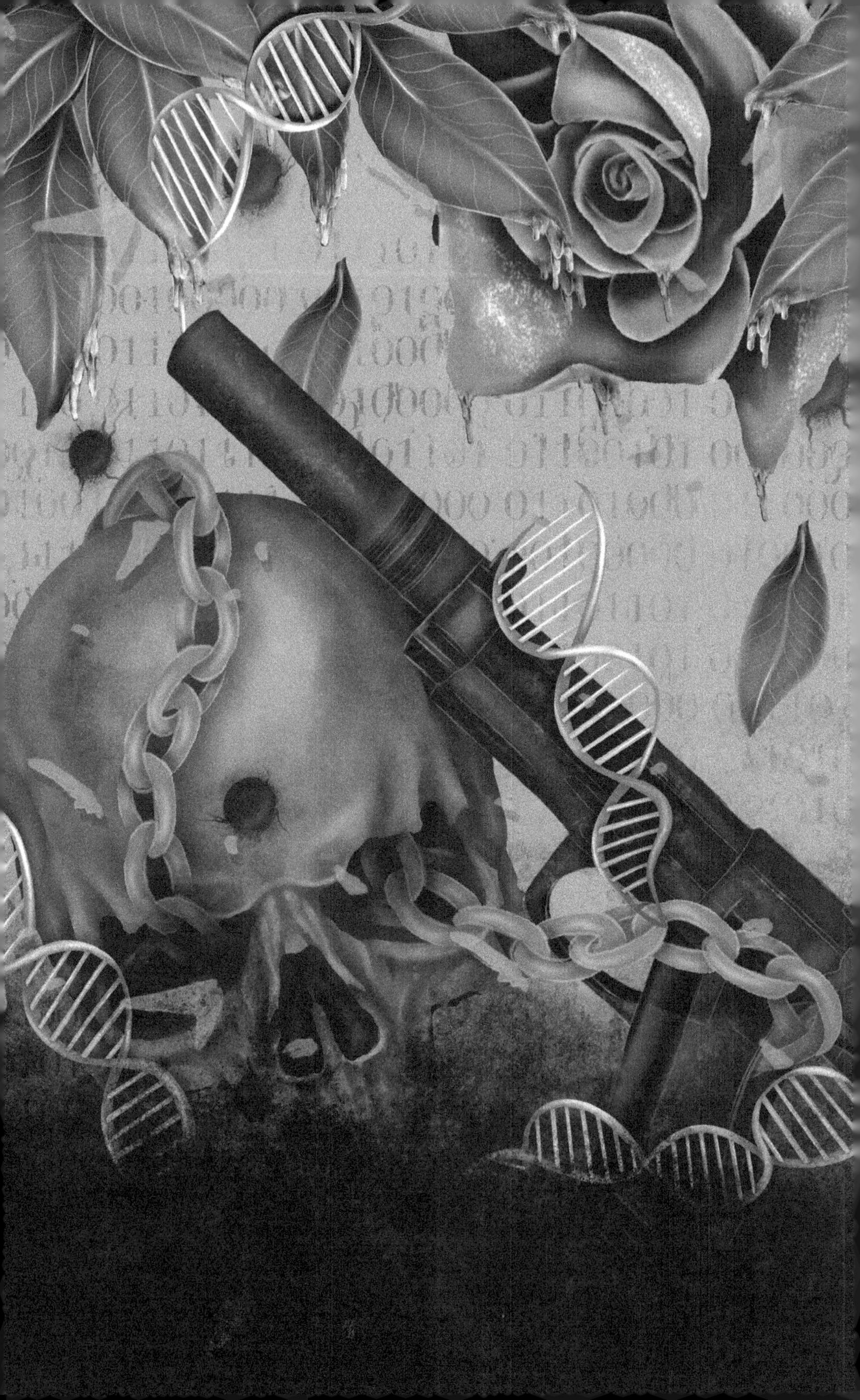

THIRTY-FIVE

The plan went wrong. I don't know how, but I blame Jonas. I was heading to Nova's cell when the alarms blared and the explosion rocked the structure . . . two whole hours early. Fuck. It doesn't help that the guards were all on high alert, but I didn't know why. I just knew I had to get to her. I bided my time, dressing in the gear provided and then slipping away when they started to move to their posts.

Pressing my hand to the wall to steady myself, I wait for the explosions to stop before ripping open Nova's cell door—only to find it empty.

Fuck!

Where is she? She has to be okay, I know that, but where did they take her?

Spinning, I search the corridor. "Any location on Nova and Louis?" I demand.

"They were being taken to the gym," Dimitri tells me. "Jonas is, erm, busy, but we are coming in. Meet you there."

"Got it. I'm free to take action?" I ask carefully. I've wanted to start taking them out since the moment I was brought down here. The things I have seen and the things they have done to my Nova have been burning in my gut since that moment, but I held it back and stuck to the plan.

"Free to act," Isaac tells me.

Smirking, I yank off the hat and toss it aside, rolling my shoulders. I might have been one of the guards, but I'm now their worst nightmare.

As I make my way to the gym to find my girl and make sure she is okay, I run into a mass of guards. "We are to report back to the doctor for protection. We've been breached," one tells me, clapping me on the shoulder.

Gripping the hand that touches me, I meet his eyes. "Yes, yes you have," I inform him, watching his eyes blow wide just before I snap his wrist. He screams, and I quickly break his neck. The guards scatter, trying to pull guns but unsure whom to shoot as I duck into their writhing masses and decimate them from the inside out.

I don't bother wasting my time because dead is dead. The longer I take here, the longer I am away from Nova—something I never want to be again. Pulling my gun, I fire again and again until it clicks empty. Bodies lie all around me, so I pick up a dead man's gun and continue until there is no one left standing but me.

Selecting another gun, I scavenge more clips and add them to my pockets, adding blades and everything else I might need, even a radio. The doc will want reports regarding his guards' whereabouts, and I'll be ready to answer when the time is right.

He's weak and scared right now, knowing we are coming for him.

Let him. He's our last point of call.

He's the end of all of this.

Stepping over the bodies, I carefully move through the maze of tunnels and head to the gym. Once I'm there, I find nothing but more bodies. "The gym is empty. No sign of her?"

"One sec," Dimitri mutters. "Let me check the portable camera."

I eye the corridors, debating which one I would take if I were Nova. She will want to protect the kids and get to her father—left to the kids, right to his main lab.

Blowing out a breath, I choose life or death . . .

Would her need for revenge outweigh her need to save innocents?

No, I don't think it would. I turn to the left and move to the elevator just as it opens for Dimitri and Isaac.

"She's in the labs," Dimitri tells me. "Isaac is heading down to the kids.

I'll go with him while you find her and her father. Oh, and if you see Jonas, stop him."

"What's he doing?" I ask, eyeing our surroundings.

"Erm . . . you know what? It's better not to ask," Dimitri says with a smile in his voice. "Get our girl. Let's end this."

Nodding, I step back and turn away as the elevator shuts once more. I have to trust them to protect the kids. They are the best at it. I would probably just scare them, and no doubt Jonas would terrify them. Isaac is soft spoken, and both he and Dimitri look kind and can talk with them. Moving through the halls, I stop when I find a mass of bodies littering the ground. There's something weird about them, and when I look closer, I realise it's because their chests are pried open and their hearts are gone.

Oh, God.

Running around the corner, I see the words written in blood and my head falls back with a groan. Jonas!

A noise has me lifting my head, and I see two guards come around the corridor, sweeping the area with their guns. Sighing, I fire and hit both between the eyes, stepping over them to continue.

"Trust me, it's better me than him," I inform them. There are more bodies with their hearts missing, and I follow the trail, needing to find him before I find Nova. She would never forgive me if I didn't.

The body trail lightens, with only one or two dotted around as if they were caught at the wrong time. They were probably sweeping or securing labs when he found them. I find one strapped down, his face completely carved away with a scalpel, and another is pinned to the wall like a bug, both hearts taken once more. How many has he taken, and what is he going to do with them?

I dread to think about it, but when I round the next corner, I have my answer. Jonas is whistling away, coated head to toe in blood, as he carves out the heart of a man who lies on the ground.

"Jonas!" I snap, seeing the open backpack next to him filled with the organs. His head whips up, his snarl turning into a welcoming smile.

"Hey, bro. Come help me. This one is tricky."

"Not a chance. Come on, Nova and Louis are in the labs," I order.

"But the heart . . ." Jonas pouts. "It's for Nova."

"Uh-uh, I think you have enough, come on." I clap his shoulder carefully.

He climbs to his feet, kicking the body before closing his bag and hefting it up. "Okay, let's go. You okay?" he asks me, smiling widely.

"Sure, are you?" I query warily. It is hard to tell under all the blood.

"Peachy. Isn't this great? It's been so long since I got to use so many skills." He sighs wistfully. "The only thing that would make it better would be if Nova was at my side. Do you think she will be impressed? I tried to get as many as I could."

"I think . . . I think she will be very shocked."

I grab his arm when he starts to wander away and pull him down the corridor to the labs where I hear smashing, and then I see her.

My raging fury.

My goddess.

My girl.

Her face is contorted in anger as she stands on a counter, smashing the shit out of computers with a metal pipe in her hand. Louis is gathering something into a bag, leaving her to it.

"Isn't she beautiful?" Jonas sighs before he rushes over.

Shaking my head, I decide to join them. After all, if you can't beat them, join them.

ISAAC

Riding in the elevator with Dimitri, I bounce nervously on my toes, worried about how everyone is. Nova in particular. I will need to talk to everyone individually, assess them, and make sure they are all okay. This is a tough situation, and it's clearly taken its toll on Jonas, whose sanity is questionable at the best of times, but right now, I need to focus on the kids. It's what she wants, and if it helps her, then I'll do anything, not to mention my need to save the innocent kids.

"Anything?" I ask Dimitri. He's trying to locate her father and check on the kids.

"Nothing. The cameras have either been destroyed or covered. They probably know we have access. Looks like we are doing this the old-fashioned way." He drops the portal computer and pulls out his gun.

I grip my own tighter, adrenaline pumping through me. This is what we are used to—working missions together—but this one has a high price tag and is more important than any other.

We can't afford to make mistakes. We must adapt to the situation and overcome it.

The ride seems to take forever, but it must only be a minute or so, and when the doors open, bullets fly. We flatten ourselves against the sides, and the doors shut as Dimitri hits the emergency button, keeping us stationary.

"What the fuck?" I demand. "How many are out there?"

"I don't know." He tosses me a mask from his hip. "Put this on. The gas will clear the immediate vicinity so we can get out and regroup." Tugging his own mask down, he pulls a gas grenade from his bag and when I nod, he turns off the alarm and allows the doors to open.

Tossing the grenade out, he jerks back as bullets whiz by us.

Our only protection is the shuddering metal of the elevator, which is being embedded with more and more bullets as the gas pumps into the corridor, fogging my mask.

We wait, our breathing loud as the hiss of the gas reaches us. Gradually, the bullets start to slow. The sounds of coughing reach us, and then we hear thumps. I nod at Dimitri and we roll out together. Luckily, no one is shooting. Most are passing out, and although it won't keep them down long, it still gives us enough time to clear it. They made a barricade, and there are at least ten guards here, their guns tossed to the floor when the gas hit.

As a doctor, I vowed to do no harm. I wanted to save lives, but they don't deserve saving. Not after what they have done.

No, my oath went out the window the moment they turned their devilish eyes to my girl.

Gritting my teeth as my instincts batter me, I raise my gun and fire with Dimitri, killing them as they choke and wheeze.

"Clear," I tell him. The gas starts to dissipate, but I keep my mask on for now as we peer over the barricade. It's made of everything and anything they could find, and I don't spot anyone over it. Dimitri told me the doors are at the end of this level, so we climb over and keep moving, but the next corridor is no better. Doors are ripped off, ready to be used as barricades, and guards quickly turn towards us.

Bullets fly and I roll, ripping off my mask and seeing Dimitri doing the same a few feet back.

"We have Nova and Louis. Everything okay?" Nico asks, his voice barking in my ear.

"We have run into a little trouble," I admit, taking shelter behind an overturned door as more bullets fly.

I wait for them to reload and pop my gun over, firing into their masses without looking. I hear someone scream, and I know I hit my mark. Climbing to my knees, I peer over only to duck. I glance back at Dimitri, who's reloading, then hold up my hand and close it.

Ten.

He nods and gets to his knees, counting down on his fingers, and at zero, we both stand and fire as we move, working as a unit. He takes left, and I take right. We watch the bodies fall. A bullet grazes my cheek and my ear, but I still don't stop. My heartbeat slows as time seems to still as we fire, until my gun clicks empty, and then I duck behind the next door with Dimitri next to me.

"Only three left," I tell him calmly as I reload, then I speak into the earpiece where I hear them talking. "Guards before the kids. We are taking care of them. Any luck on the doc?"

"Not yet." Louis grunts. "Keep us updated."

"Got it."

I love how he doesn't ask if we are okay. He knows better. If we needed help, we would call for it. His trust is what has me sitting taller.

Dimitri and I wait. We can hear their feet crunching over broken glass as they head our way. I reload as we bide our time. When they draw closer, we pop up and fire. Three fall just as quickly as they came, and we keep moving. There are no barricades down the next corridor, and it's unusually quiet, which isn't a good sign.

"D," I murmur.

"I know," he mutters as we open empty rooms, needing to check every single one on our way. All it would take is one guard to sneak up on us and we would be fucked. We can't have that. I need to live for my girl. It's time-consuming though, and when we reach the next corner, the hair on the back of my neck rises. I hold out my arm to stop D and cock my head.

He narrows his gaze, and I shake my head, unsure.

There's only one way to find out. Playing it smart, I crouch and peer around the corner, my eyes widening at what I find.

A fucking army.

Shit.

Sliding down the wall, I sigh as I talk quietly into the earpiece. "Guys, we've found the doc."

"Where?" they all ask, making me wince at the mix of voices.

"Here, behind a wall of guards. He's hiding with the kids. It's a last fucking stand. Get your asses down here." I rip out my earpiece and check my mag. I don't have enough.

We're fucked.

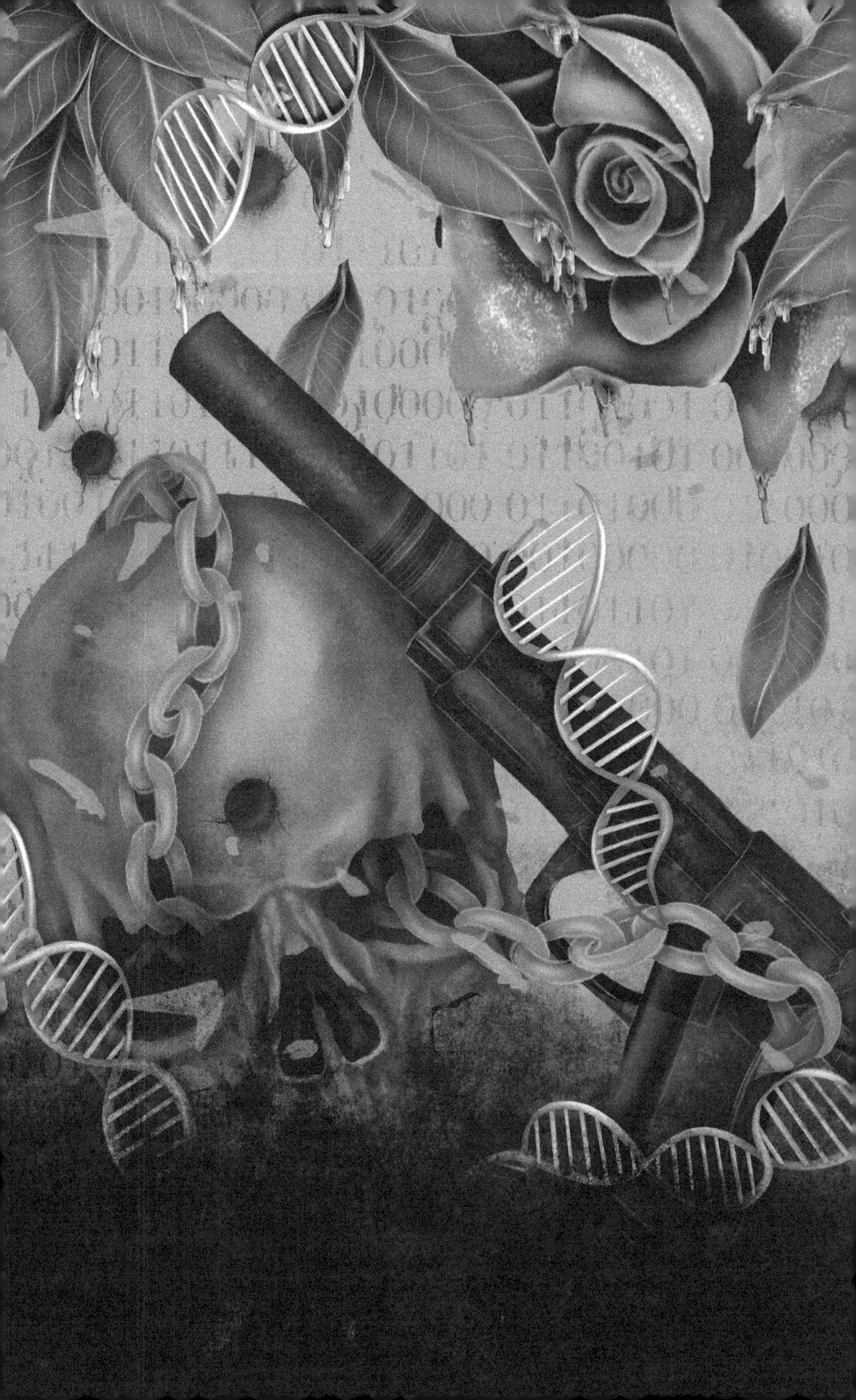

THIRTY-SIX

I let her smash anything she wants. It seems to be keeping her occupied. She wanted to find her father, but I wanted to secure the research first, knowing they could hide it or get rid of it at any time. It's just as important as he is. We cannot let this fall into the wrong hands. She understands that, even though she's frustrated, hence the smashing.

Whirling, I bring up my gun when I hear a noise, only to relax at the sight of Jonas and Nico standing in the doorway of the lab. "Dimitri and Isaac?" I ask.

"Heading down to the kids." Nico tosses me an earpiece. "Baby, are you okay?"

Panting, she presses the pipe she was using behind her shoulders, covered in blood. Her gaze goes to Jonas, and then her eyes widen. I follow her gaze, noting the blood. "Jonas, what happened?"

"Oh, it's not mine." He grins. "Hey, beautiful. I've missed you so fucking much."

"Me too." She leaps down, destruction forgotten, and Jonas catches her. He lays her back onto the desk and kisses her hard and fast, while Nico moves over to me.

"Here, help me. We are locking up the research just in case."

Nodding in understanding, he helps me gather the paperwork and copy the drives, piling everything in the lockbox I found.

Finally, Jonas and Nova come up for air, and I see him swing a bag around. Frowning, I watch in confusion as he hands it to Nova.

He sighs in bliss. "For you, beautiful."

She opens the bag and then just stares.

"What's in it?" I ask Nico. Knowing Jonas, it could be anything. Guns, bombs . . . whatever he feels like.

"You don't want to know," Nico mutters.

I move closer and peer inside, and my mouth drops open. "Are those . . ."

"Hearts." Jonas grins at her. "Of every single guard I killed. I made them pay for everything they did to you."

"Jonas," I sputter.

"Told you," Nico says, laughing behind me.

"Jonas," Nova whispers, and I wince. "That's so romantic. Thank you, baby. I love you!" She throws her arms around him and yanks him down, peppering his bloody face with kisses as he grins at us.

"Fucking hell, maybe we are the crazy ones and he has it all figured out," Nico mutters.

Shaking my head, I move back over to help him, wondering how the hell I can beat a bag full of hearts to impress my girl, and it's clear Nico is thinking the same thing.

Moaning, Jonas climbs up on top of the desk and pins her down, grinding into her as he swallows her moans.

"Should we do something?" Nico asks, jerking his head at the pair.

"No, it's stopping them from doing something bad." I grin, adding more to the box and then locking it up before moving to the next.

I check in with Isaac as they kiss, and when he tells me he's okay, I keep sorting the research with Nico. When we are done, we both just stare at Jonas and Nova who are practically fucking.

Nico looks at me. "Break it up."

"No, you." I snort and share a grin with him just as my earpiece crackles.

"Guys, we've found the doc."

"Where?" we all ask, and it even breaks Jonas and Nova apart.

"Here, behind a wall of guards. He's hiding with the kids. It's a last fucking stand. Get your asses down here." Then there's silence, but I heard the panic in his voice.

They are in the line of fire.

"Time to go, kids," I order, reloading and grabbing my weapons before heading towards the door, trusting my family to follow.

It is time to end this.

DIMITRI

"They are on their way," I whisper to Isaac. "We should wait. We are good, but not good enough to take down all of them, especially without hurting the kids or ourselves."

Isaac nods just as a shot rings out. "We know you're there. Step out or we'll start shooting the kids one by one. Do you really want their blood on your hands?"

I share a look with Isaac and stand. Swearing, he stands too. With another shared look, we step out, unwilling to risk the kids. All weapons are trained on us, but they don't instantly shoot, which is their first mistake.

"Drop the weapons!" one yells.

I'm not sure why they haven't killed us on sight. Maybe he wants us alive or plans on using us to flush the others out, but it's working in our favour. They have a gun pressed against the head of a small girl in a blue outfit in the back. She's crying but she's brave, standing tall.

"Okay, stay calm. It's going to be okay." I soften my voice for her. She nods but winces when the gun digs in deeper.

"Now!" one roars as I scan them, counting and looking at entrances and exits, noting everything.

I share a look with Isaac.

"Stop looking at him and drop them now."

With my eyes on the girl once more, I release my gun from my hand.

I hear running footsteps and know the others are coming. They are close. Time slows as I grin at the guards, who are relaxing, thinking they have us. Diving, I catch the falling gun, and before I even hit the floor, I come up shooting, hitting the two holding the kid, who runs, and then hitting three more before grabbing Isaac and diving back around the corner.

"Shit, that was epic." Isaac grins just as Nico, Louis, Jonas, and Nova skid to a stop before us, all panting.

Standing, I grab Nova and kiss her hard.

"Later," she murmurs, and I nod.

"Later," I promise as I look at Louis.

"Report," he demands. I move over so Isaac can have a moment with Nova.

"At least forty soldiers, now thirty-five. They are holding the kids hostage and know we are here. Two barriers to the left and the right. They have tactical rifles, helmets, and vests. I can't see her father, but for them all to have been called back here, I'm betting he's hiding with the kids, looking for a way out. He's not expecting us to risk the kids' safety."

"He's right though. We can't," Nova says, holding Isaac's hand. Jonas is in the corner with Nico just in case they move around or attack us while we talk.

Louis lowers his voice so they can't hear him. "I have a plan. It's crazy, but it just might work."

"Everything we do is crazy." I grin.

"True." He smirks. "So let's show them that."

THIRTY-SEVEN

Dimitri nods at me, and I step closer, kissing him soundly. "Be ready."

"Always. I've got you," he tells me.

"I'm coming out!" I call. "It's Nova, Dr. Davis's daughter. Don't shoot."

I wait and hear murmuring. "Step out unarmed or we will."

"Coming!" I look back and grin, blowing them a kiss.

Trusting my guys, I step out with my hands up, no weapons on display. I stop halfway down the corridor, far enough away not to die but also close enough to do what I need to.

"See? Not armed. Where is my father?" I demand.

"We will search you," someone else yells. "The others with you will reveal themselves, also unarmed, or we will shoot you."

"That's rude." I frown, stepping closer. "Where is my father?"

"Step out!" he orders, ignoring me.

"Is he with the kids? Are they okay?"

"For now." He smirks. "If your friends want you and the kids alive, do as I order."

"Here's the thing." I grin. "They really don't like following orders unless they are mine and in the bedroom." Winking, I close my fist and drop.

Bullets whiz over me as the lights cut out, thanks to Dimitri. There's a crash and I peer up through the door, seeing Louis and Jonas drop from the vents in the ceiling and onto the waiting mass. It turns the guards' focus inwards. I leap to my feet as Nico and Dimitri race past me, and then we leap into the fray.

Grabbing the gun taped to my back, I spray bullets at those closest to me before putting the gun away and using the knife I stole from Jonas. Screams ring out as the guns go off. I duck under a punch and keep moving until there is no one else but the darkness I'm fighting against.

Twenty men against five. They didn't even stand a chance. We are super soldiers for a reason, and the crazy plan worked. After all, they couldn't even imagine we would use one of our own as a distraction.

Morons.

The lights come back on. We are all panting as we stand in the mess of dead soldiers and guards. Smirking, I step over them and bang a bloodied hand on the window that looks into the glass of the children's room.

"Come out, Father. Your guards are dead. There is no one else to hide behind."

"That's where you're wrong." He steps out, holding a knife to a little boy's throat.

Snarling, I hit the button to open the door and descend the stairs, stopping before him, my men spreading out.

"Ah, that's close enough, Novaleen," he snaps, tightening his hold on the child.

Grinding my teeth, I scan the room, seeing the others hiding.

"Isaac." I nod and without a word, he and Dimitri head off to protect the kids. Jonas moves left, and Nico goes right, trying to circle my father, while Louis stands with me, side by side. My father cannot take us all, and his eyes flicker around as he realises that.

He wanted a super soldier unit, and he got one.

Shame it will be his death.

"Impressive unit," he remarks. "I guess I was wrong about them being failures. Maybe I was too harsh. We can sit down and talk about this—"

"Let the kid go." I ignore his silver tongue. His words mean nothing.

"No. You want me dead, Novaleen? Fine, but this kid will die with me, and you will have to live with more innocent blood on your hands. Just like Ana's."

"Do not!" I snarl. "You killed her! You are the one with blood on your hands," I yell. Anger flares inside me, along with guilt.

"No, Novaleen. I might have pulled the trigger, but you put her in the crosshairs. She was there for you. She trusted you to protect her. How foolish was that? You couldn't save her. All that training, all that money and time, and you couldn't even save the one person you wanted to. Maybe you were never what I needed. Never mind, I can start again."

"Shut up," I hiss.

"Don't listen to him, Nova," Louis mutters. "He's trying to make you react irrationally so he can get free."

I know he is, but it's working. Any mention of Ana and I become an unthinking, open, raw wound, and he knows it. He knows she is my weakness, alongside the kids.

"Let me go. Let me walk out of here, and I'll release the child," he offers, invading my conflicting mind. "Your choice, Nova. You can kill me now, but you'll be killing this innocent child, or you can let me go and save him."

"Nova," Louis snaps as I met the child's eyes.

All this time, blood, and pain got me here, but can I live with the stain on my soul if I do this?

It's a choice between life and death.

Between right and wrong.

Revenge and letting go.

I know what Ana would want me to do, and in the end, that's what I go with. I can live with him going free. I found him once, so I can do it again despite how angry I'll be. I cannot live with this child's innocent blood on my hands. I just can't.

I turn away from revenge and choose life instead.

I drop my gun to the floor, and he grins triumphantly. "Good, now I'm going to walk past you. Once up top, I will release the child and leave. Do not follow me."

He moves closer, and I turn with him as he starts to walk to the door, but when he's almost level with me, the kid drops to the floor and manages to slip his grip.

His only leverage is gone.

He quickly realises that and looks at me as I reach for another weapon to end this. Something settles in his eyes, and he rushes towards me.

Maybe he realises he's never getting out of this, or maybe he genuinely thinks killing me will distract them long enough for him to escape, but I see the knife rise, and then he drives it into my stomach, ramming it home. I let him, but I grab his hand as he tries to run, holding him to me as I snarl in his face. Using his hand, I yank the knife out, gritting my teeth at the agony.

His eyes flare as I pull the blade free and turn it. His hand resists and he struggles, but he's no match for me. I slowly drive it towards his own stomach, aiming for the kill shot.

He struggles in my grip. He's so weak.

"Nova, wait, Nova," he says, but I ignore his pleading as, inch by inch, I drive the knife closer until it starts to pierce his skin. His voice turns into a wail, and I slam it all the way home and let go. He stumbles back, covering the wound with his hands.

Even if at one time, he seemed like a god to me, now he is nothing but a weak, bleeding mess at my feet.

Isaac rushes over, putting pressure on my wound as I stare at my father. He peers down at the blade and then back to me in shock before falling to his knees. Despite knowing better, he pulls it free and drops it with clumsy, shaking hands before he falls back. Ignoring Isaac, I move to my father's side and kneel. My own blood mixes with his in a puddle beneath him.

Matching wounds.

Killing blows.

The only thing that saves me is my own healing ability and adrenaline as Isaac starts to inject me with something as I watch my father. His eyes blink rapidly, and his mouth opens and shuts as he covers the wound.

His hand lifts, reaching out, and I grip it. He thought he was unstoppable, but he was wrong.

"You thought you were unstoppable, but look at you now. You are weak and mortal. You are dying."

"Novaleen, please," he begs, coughing.

"You are just a weak old man surrounded by enemies. I'll leave your body here in the rubble to be burned and forgotten. No one will ever know what you did. I will make sure of it. All your research will be destroyed, and everything you did, everything you sacrificed, will be for nothing. Your life will be for nothing."

"Not nothing," he says. "You are alive."

"And I will never be anything but a normal person after this. Your research will die with us."

"No." He shakes his head.

Whatever Isaac injected me with is working. I feel nothing, and he's packing the wound and bandaging it as I squeeze my dad's hand to the point of pain to keep his eyes on me as he dies. I need to see it.

Leaning in, I press a kiss to his forehead.

"This is for Ana, Sam, Bas, and for every single person you have hurt and killed. They will be avenged here, and you? You will be nothing but a liar for all your bold claims and half-truths. Was it worth it? Was all the death and pain worth it, old man?"

He squeaks, losing too much blood.

"Was it?" I scream.

"Yes," he says. "You're alive and so is my research. It was worth it. I would do it all again."

Dropping his hand in anger, I sit back and watch as he dies scared, alone, and in agony. It isn't quick, and when his lungs rattle, I smile. When he takes his last breath, I almost laugh.

It's over.

It's done.

I check his pulse to be sure. "There's no coming back for you this time, Dr. Davis. It is over. It is done." Standing carefully, I lean into Isaac as weakness spreads through me. They are all watching me worriedly, the kids sheltered behind them.

"Let's go home," I demand. "Take me home, let me die, and then place me at her side."

I fall, my own wound getting the better of me.
It's too deep, and I lost too much blood.
The sacrifice was worth it, though, I think as my eyes close.
I am ready to be reunited with my sister.

THIRTY-EIGHT

The base has everything we need, so we move fast.

We will not lose her.

Not again.

Isaac barks out orders as Nico lifts her and rushes up the stairs to the lab. Isaac runs with him, holding pressure on the wound. "Stay with the kids."

"But—" Dimitri steps forward, looking heartbroken.

"Do it!" I order him and Jonas. I run after Nico, sliding into the elevator at the last moment. I don't have time to think about anything else. We reach the lab in under a minute and lay her down.

"Tell us what you need," I beg Isaac, swallowing my panic, knowing they are looking at me right now. I cannot afford to fall apart.

"Scrub up. I'm going to need to go in and cauterise what was hit, then we'll need blood. Luckily, she's the same type as Nico. Next, we'll seal and dress the wound." He starts putting an IV up and sliding it in as we quickly scrub up and gown, then he does the same. I take her hand as Isaac unpacks the wound.

"Nico, take your own blood. Louis, I'll need your help."

Nodding, I drop her hand and focus on the wicked wound he's unveiling. It is about five inches long, but it must be deep. He swiftly spreads it with a tool, and blood pours out.

"Wipe it," he demands. "I need to see."

I mop it up with the gauze on the table before he dives back in with some other tools, his eyes hard and determined.

"Don't you dare fucking die on me, my love," he grits out. "Don't you fucking dare. I'll bring you back."

"Isaac—"

"Don't, I can save her. I can save her."

"Tell us what you need," Dimitri demands, and I glare at him, looking over to see him in the doorway.

"The kids—"

"Are safe for now. What do you need, Isaac?"

"Help Nico," Isaac says, focused on his work.

Jonas hesitates in the doorway, tears dripping down his face.

"Is she going to die?" It's a heartbroken plea from the child inside him.

"Not today." I practically spit the words, speaking them into existence. "Talk to her, hold her."

Nodding, he hurries over and crouches at her head. He pushes her hair back, his voice low and soothing as he talks to her.

"Isaac?" I question. His eyes are narrowed on the wound I'm mopping up, his teeth gritted. His full concentration is on her, but I need to know.

"He nicked an artery somewhere. I need to find it," he mutters.

I quiet down then, looking at Nova whose face is pale, her lips growing blue.

She's dying. I know it.

"Isaac," I demand in panic.

"One fucking second," he barks. "Come on, baby. Where are you? Just show me." He digs into the wound and Nova screams, the sound echoing around us. Her eyes snap open for a second. I hold her down with Jonas as she struggles, her gaze completely unseeing until her eyes slide shut and she collapses.

Isaac doesn't even hesitate. He dives in harder, searching for the artery. "Isaac, we are losing her," I snap, needing something to do. "What do we do?"

"Give me a fucking second!" he roars before shouting, "I got it." He quickly clamps the artery before fixing it as I mop around the wound. He carefully pulls the tools out and drops the blood-covered metal onto the table. When he glances at Nova, his face pales at how still and weak she is.

She is close to death.

"Louis, attach the monitoring machines please. I need her blood pressure and heart rate, now. Nico, give me the line." He hurries around, quickly adding a line into her arm and directly pushing Nico's blood to her since she has lost so much. It drips down from her stomach and onto the floor as I attach the machines, the telltale beeping filling the air.

"Her heart is giving up," he whispers as he rushes to the wound, grabbing a staple gun. Pinching her skin, he starts to put her back together. "I'll need to recheck this, but for now, we need to close her and pump her with drugs and blood to keep her alive."

Every eye is on her, on her pale, sweaty face, until the machine suddenly begins to blare. Isaac's head jerks up, and he eyes her erratic heartbeat that suddenly stops.

Snarling, he rushes to her side and starts to perform CPR as I watch, feeling useless, my hand gripping hers.

"Don't you fucking dare," Isaac snaps as he gets in her face, even though her eyes are closed. "Don't you dare fucking leave me, do you hear me, Nova?" His voice is cruel, hard, and loud, unlike our soft-spoken Isaac, but I can't even protest around the lump in my throat. For all my plans and my strength, I cannot save her this time. "If you try to leave me, I'll bring you back from the fucking dead myself, so you hold the fuck on and help me save you, understood?" He rams his hands into her chest, his eyes going from her to the monitor.

"Come on, baby," I mutter. "You can do it."

"Don't you fucking dare," he says as he pushes on her chest. "Not today, not ever. You do not get to die."

Tears spill from my eyes as the machine continues to flat line. "Isaac—"

"No! She can't do this!" he roars, his eyes wild as he looks at me. "Mouth to mouth, now!"

I rush to do as he says, working in sync with him. He never stops working on her chest, and finally, a beep fills the air. We all turn, scared it isn't real, until it comes again.

Her heart is beating.

I must say it out loud because the room fills with joyous, relieved sighs.

"Nico will need orange juice," Isaac mutters as he double-checks the monitor and her pulse before cleaning the wound on her stomach. He applies something to it and then bandages it before covering her up. He's coated in blood as he rips the gloves off, tossing them into the bin. "I need a minute. Get me if anything changes," he mutters, and then he's gone, but I saw the look in his eyes.

I can't leave my girl though.

Not yet. My eyes go to Dimitri, who is hesitating near Nico, and he nods before going after Isaac as we work as a team to stay strong for her. Taking her hand once more, I lean down and brush a kiss over her forehead. "It's going to be okay, baby. We've got you. Just stay with us, okay? Please . . . Please don't give up on us. I promise we will never give up on you. We need you, Nova. Stay. Please, just fight one last time. That's it, Nova, one last fight. I promise."

DIMITRI

Rushing after Isaac, I find him around the corner, sinking to his knees, his blood-soaked face in his hands as he sobs. Turning away for a moment, I move to the closest room, grab what looks to be a bedpan and some cloths, and fill it with warm water before I return to find him in the same position. Dropping to my knees before him, I wet the cloths, and when he lifts his head, I smile sadly at him.

My heart aches. I want to be with Nova, to watch every single breath she takes, but my family needs me. She needs them. I need them.

When one of us falters, we have to be there for them. It's how we survive.

"Are you okay?" I ask. It's something I've heard her ask him a million times. Usually, he smiles that soft smile just for her, but this time, his eyes close for a millisecond and when they open, they blaze with agony. His lips tremble as tears carve a path through the blood on his face.

"No, no, I'm not." His voice is barely above a whisper.

"Me either," I admit as I start to wipe his face clean. "I've got you, brother. Let me take care of you for once."

"She . . ." His eyes close again as I meticulously wash his face. "She could die."

"She won't," I lie. I don't know if she will or not. I'm just praying with blind hope to a god I don't believe in.

He catches my hand, his eyes hardening. "She could, Dimitri. The wound . . . If she doesn't want to come back—"

"Shh." Twisting my wrist, I release it from his grip and continue to clean his face. When it's done, I sit back, dropping the cloth on the floor and taking his hand. "We have to be strong right now, okay? We are not losing anyone else." My voice hardens. "We can't. So, no matter how much it hurts right now, no matter how angry, sad, and worried we are, we keep it together for her. We give her a reason to fight. We keep our girl alive. We give everything for her like she did for us, okay? This isn't how our story ends. It can't be."

"What if it is?" he whispers dejectedly. I've never seen him like this before. Usually, he's the one who's comforting others and full of hope.

"Then we end it together just like it should be. No matter what, Isaac, we do everything we can. She deserves nothing less." Standing, I take his hand. "Come on, let's check on her."

I escort him back, and we all carefully watch as he checks her over. He hangs up the bags of Nico's blood. Isaac checks on Nico and covers him with a blanket as he grumbles before Louis orders Isaac to go shower. We can all see the toll this is having on Isaac, and I truly think this might scar him for life.

Nico and Jonas stay with her as I check on the kids and grab some food. They are all either asleep or in bed in the spare rooms we found. Despite what they saw, they don't seem overly upset. They are scared, that's for sure, but they are alive, and that's enough for now. We can deal with everyone else once we know Nova is stable.

I leave the food for Isaac and Louis, and then I head back to check on Nova.

I hesitate at the doorway. Nico is asleep next to her, or at least his eyes are closed, and Isaac is showering and eating under Louis's watchful gaze. Jonas is holding Nova's hand and talking quietly. I should give them privacy, but I find myself leaning closer to hear.

"I know you're hurting, baby, not just your body, but your heart. I know you miss your sister, but please don't do this to us, okay? I can't live without you. I can't. If you die, I die. It's that simple. There is no place in this world for Jonas without Nova, so even though it hurts, even though it would be easier to give in, come back to us because without you, there is no us. Not anymore. Please, baby, don't break our hearts. They've been yours since the moment we met you. Where you go, we go, so if this is the end, if you go, so do we. You hear me?"

"J—" Moving closer, I lay a hand on his shoulder as he wipes at his face, dashing away the tears. "She'll be okay. I know it. She's strong."

I don't. It's a fucking lie. I'm terrified down to my very soul that she won't make it through . . . that she doesn't want to, just like Bas. I can't lose someone else I love. Like Jonas, I would simply lock us all down here and end us all so we could be with her again.

He's right—where she goes, we go.

Nova's heart skips a beat like she hears us and agrees, or at least I like to think so.

Sinking to the ground next to her, we sit and wait, watching our love and hoping we can save her this time.

This time, we won't lose the only person we love.

THIRTY-NINE

It's been twenty-four hours since Nova last opened her eyes. I panic continually, thinking that I did something wrong, that I didn't do enough, that I missed something else. Louis informs me she probably just needs rest and time to heal. He's probably right, but it doesn't stop me from checking on her every thirty minutes. Nico is resting once more after giving more blood so we could do another transfusion since she lost so much. Louis and Jonas gently washed and dressed her while I put up more IVs. We've done everything we can, and it's up to her now. I know that, but it doesn't stop me from worrying.

Louis is staying busy, and between him and Dimitri, they have gotten all of the kids' information, as well as feeding them and checking them over, since I refused to leave Nova. Dimitri has started to look into their pasts. They probably won't have family, just like us, but I think it gives him something to do. They seem happy enough to be left to play in their new rooms, and as soon as we can move Nova, we can figure something out for them.

For now, we are here, watching our girl in the place where she nearly died.

Her father's body rots a few floors down. He doesn't get to be buried, after all. When we leave together, which we will, we plan on blowing this place sky-high, incinerating his body and every horrible thing he did here. Fuck, I'll even toast marshmallows in the fire with my girl.

Sighing, I tighten my hold on her hand, stopping myself from checking her vitals once more or uncovering the wound. She needs time, but it doesn't stop my constant need to assure myself that she is okay. Never before have I been more thankful to be a doctor, but I also know everything that could go wrong.

It so very nearly did. I almost lost her during surgery.

I will never forget that.

Not ever.

I must fall asleep because something makes my head snap up—a noise. I blink into the shadowed room, noticing a lamp is on in the corner that someone must have switched on. Nico is still snoring away, his blanket kicked off. Sighing, I close my eyes once more when the hand I'm holding twitches.

My gaze goes to Nova to see her blinking her eyes open and turning her head. Leaping to my feet, I grab a glass of water with a straw. "Shh, drink this," I whisper, holding both to her mouth. She sips it before turning away, and I put it back before checking her eyes and pulse.

"Is—" She winces in pain.

"It's okay, baby, just hold on," I murmur, my heart racing so fast it's hard to hear. "Vitals are good, no concussion or reaction in the eyes. I think you're going to be okay."

I almost slump at that. She's going to be okay.

"Am I dead?" she whispers.

"No, you are very much alive, sweetheart," I murmur, kissing the back of her hand and almost collapsing with relief. "You'll need to rest and take time to heal, but I think you'll be okay."

My eyes lock on hers once more, greedy for every word, touch, and look, which is why I don't wake Nico or shout for the others. I don't want to end this moment since I came so close to losing her.

"Are you okay, Isaac?" she croaks. Her eyes search mine worriedly, even though she is in a hospital bed in a bunker where she was tortured and kept alive to be experimented on.

This girl.

"Am I okay? Am I okay? You almost died on my fucking table, Nova, so no, I'm not okay. I almost lost the woman I love more than anything else in this fucking world. I almost . . . I almost couldn't save you and that killed me!" I laugh bitterly as Nico jerks awake.

"What, what?" He falls to the floor in confusion, searching for a threat before his eyes land on Nova. "Baby!" He rushes over and kisses her. She kisses him back, smiling as he hurries to the door to tell the others, but he turns back to focus on me.

"I'm sorry," she whispers, tightening her grip on my hand.

"Don't." I shake my head, trying to suck back all my emotions. I need to be okay, for her and for them.

"I'm so sorry you had to deal with that, Isaac," she whispers as I hear pounding feet. "I love you so much."

"I love you too," I promise. "Don't ever do that to me again," I order as I lean in to kiss her softly.

"Never," she vows just as the others slide into the room and surround her. There are so many voices, touches, and kisses that I end up pushing them back.

"Give her space. She needs to rest and relax, not be moved or jostled," I snap.

"Yes, doctor," Jonas teases, even as he grins brightly at her. "You missed so much." He hurries to tell her everything, and she smiles, but it turns into a wince, and he slows to a stop. "Are you okay?"

"Just tired and hurting," she admits. For Nova to admit that she's in pain, it must be bad.

"Let me give you something." I hurry to inject her, and she relaxes, smiling at us.

"I still can't believe you came for me."

"Of course we did," Louis murmurs. "We love you. There is nothing we wouldn't do for you, Nova."

"Now rest," Dimitri orders.

"It's over, baby. He's dead, and you're alive. Just rest. There's nothing else to do," Nico says, and under our watchful gazes, her eyes start to slide shut.

"Are you all just going to watch me sleep?" she mutters, making surprised laughter tumble from us.

"Yes," Jonas answers without a care.

"I was debating it," I mutter.

Huffing, she narrows her eyes once more. "Louis, get them to rest. They look exhausted, and that includes you. Oh, and fucking eat and shower, you stink." With that, she shuts her eyes once more, leaving me grinning like a madman.

Our girl is going to be just fine.

It looks like we finally get the ending we deserve.

FORTY

I sleep for a while. I know because when I wake up, the big lights are on and the guys are milling around. Luckily, they look better. They've clearly showered and slept a little, even if Isaac is checking my wound when I wake.

"How's it look, doc?" I croak, my throat sore from sleeping and screaming.

He smiles softly as he covers it and moves to my side. "Good," he murmurs. "It's healing fast, though that shouldn't surprise me. I'd still like you to rest for a few days. I don't want to irritate the healing process or the staples, and your body has been through a lot of trauma, but you'll be okay."

I can see the question in his eyes. My body will heal, but will my soul and heart mend? I don't have the answer, so I look away, meeting Louis's eyes as he leans against the doorway, wearing a soft smile directed at me.

"Can I sit up?" I ask.

Isaac frowns but moves my pillows and helps me sit. It tugs on the wound, and I bite back a moan of pain. I'm used to it by now, after all, and I don't want them to worry. The quicker we can get the hell away from here, the better. Leaning back into the pillows, I eye them warily.

"The kids?" I ask. The last thing I remember is seeing them before my father attacked. "The one my father held?"

"All okay. They are a little shaken up, confused, and scared, but they will be fine. I don't know what was done to them yet, but I will find out. I promise," Louis murmurs. "Everyone else is fine, just focus on you."

"Where are they—"

"Nova," Louis and Isaac admonish.

Rolling my eyes, I relax as much as I can, but every look around at the white, sterile room makes me antsy. "Are we sure they are all dead, including my father?" I question, needing to know, needing to be sure.

"I checked and double-checked them all myself." Louis pushes from the door and takes my hand. "He's dead, Nova, for good this time. You're free; we all are. It's done. Our mission is over. We stopped him."

"It doesn't feel real," I admit.

"It will take some time. A lot has happened over the last few days," he says, kissing the back of my hand. "Just take a little bit of time to relax and let your mind and body heal, okay?" I groan, and he chuckles. "I know it's hard, but it's for the best."

"I hate bed rest unless it's for fun stuff," I mutter as Isaac grins at me, checking my vitals once more. I need to have a talk with him about those shadows in his eyes, but not with anyone else here. "The others?"

"Dimitri is wiping everything and copying all the files, Jonas is on patrol up top, and Nico is with the kids." My eyebrows rise at that, making Louis smirk. "Surprisingly, they seem to like him. He hates it, or so he says."

"Sure he does." I smile, closing my eyes. I am exhausted, but I know I can never fully relax while we are here. It doesn't feel like it's over while this place still stands. It's a reminder of what my father was capable of and can still do while his research exists. He might be dead, but his findings are not, which is something we need to discuss, but from the glint in Louis's eyes, I can tell he won't let me—not now when they are determined for me to relax and rest.

Isaac leans down and kisses me softly. "The more you rest, the quicker we can get out of here."

Grumbling to myself, I close my eyes once more, even though I hate leaving them to deal with everything. I expect to struggle to sleep, but before I know it, blackness claims me.

I jerk awake with a scream, the nightmare trapped on a loop in my brain until I fight against the hands on me, only to realise it's the bedding. Lights blare on, blinding me for a moment before I blink it away and realise I'm in bed, hooked to machines after killing my father.

I am not trapped by them as they cut me open.

My guys rush into the room, their weapons held up, and they only relax when I wave them away. Ignoring their protests, I sit up and suck in some air as hands rub my back.

"Are you okay?" Nico asks.

"Just a bad dream," I tell him, feeling embarrassed. "Sorry."

"Don't ever be sorry for that," he reassures me softly, wrapping me in his arms.

I fight it at first, not wanting to give in to the comfort and warmth, knowing I will break, but he's so hard to resist, and I slump into his hold. Tears form in my eyes. It feels like I've cried enough for a lifetime, but I can't stop them from coming.

"Annie and you guys were there, and I couldn't save you," I admit in a whisper, more tears flowing down. "She's dead."

"I know," he murmurs, kissing my head. "I know, baby. Let it all out."

"She's dead, and I'm alive. She's fucking dead." I smack my fists into his chest and he lets me. "She's dead. I lost her. I couldn't stop them. I couldn't do anything." I don't even know what I'm saying other than it all pours out. My nightmare brought on everything that has happened, and it spills from me like a tidal wave of pain. He holds me the entire time, stroking my hair. Their warmth, their comfort surrounds me, protecting me as I break, wishing they could take it away.

"I'm so sorry, babe," Nico whispers, his voice thick with pain. "We should have known. We should have protected you and Ana better. We are so very fucking sorry."

"It isn't your fault. It's his, and he's gone. We can't change it, but it hurts," I admit. "It hurts so fucking much that I feel like I'm dying sometimes." I lift my head to see his eyes filled with tears. "Will it ever stop? Will I ever stop feeling like my chest is in a vice and I can't get a breath without choking? Will it ever feel like I can live again?"

"No, but it gets easier."

I turn my head to meet Dimitri's sad eyes.

"Each day, it grows a little easier to breathe. There will still be moments where you remember them and it breaks you apart . . . Something little can catch you off-guard. But each day, it gets easier to get up, easier to move and carry on. You never truly forget them, not really. It's always there, waiting for you to remember, and sometimes you just . . . lose track of that for a time. It could be days, weeks, or even months, but then it's there again. The pain never goes away with time; it just gets easier to manage. Eventually, you'll forget all the bad stuff, and even though it hurts, you'll remember the good. You'll remember the happy times and smile and tell us about them to keep her alive within us. It doesn't mean you stop loving her by going on, Nova. It simply means you love her enough to keep moving despite losing her. That's how you keep her alive with us, and that's how you survive this. One foot in front of the other, one breath, one second at a time. Eventually, those seconds add up to minutes, hours, days, weeks, months, and finally years, until you've lived longer without them than you did with them. It still fucking hurts, but you're not alone. I wish I could change the past and save her, but I can't. I'm here though. *We* are here. You won't go through this alone. Even in the darkness, we will hold your hands, and I know Ana would want you to be happy. She loved you so much, Nova. You are her big sister, you will always be her big sister, and when the time comes, you will see each other again. Until that day, it's okay to struggle and forget what she smelled like. It's okay to let go, Nova. We will be right here to catch you."

Tears stream down my face as I take his hand, his own pain matching mine. It's the pain that only someone who has lost somebody they love so deeply can understand.

"You loved her, and she loved you, Nova, and that's all that matters," he whispers as he squeezes my hand. "I promise that we will love you until the very end. We will help you heal in every way we can, and one day, you'll tell me everything about her and I'll tell you all about Bas. Deal?"

"Deal," I croak as they shuffle closer, offering me their comfort as I cry for the sister I lost and the future she could have had and the torture I have experienced since childhood. I finally get it all out, enveloped by my men, my family.

My lovers hold me together as I break apart, giving me their strength when I am weak.

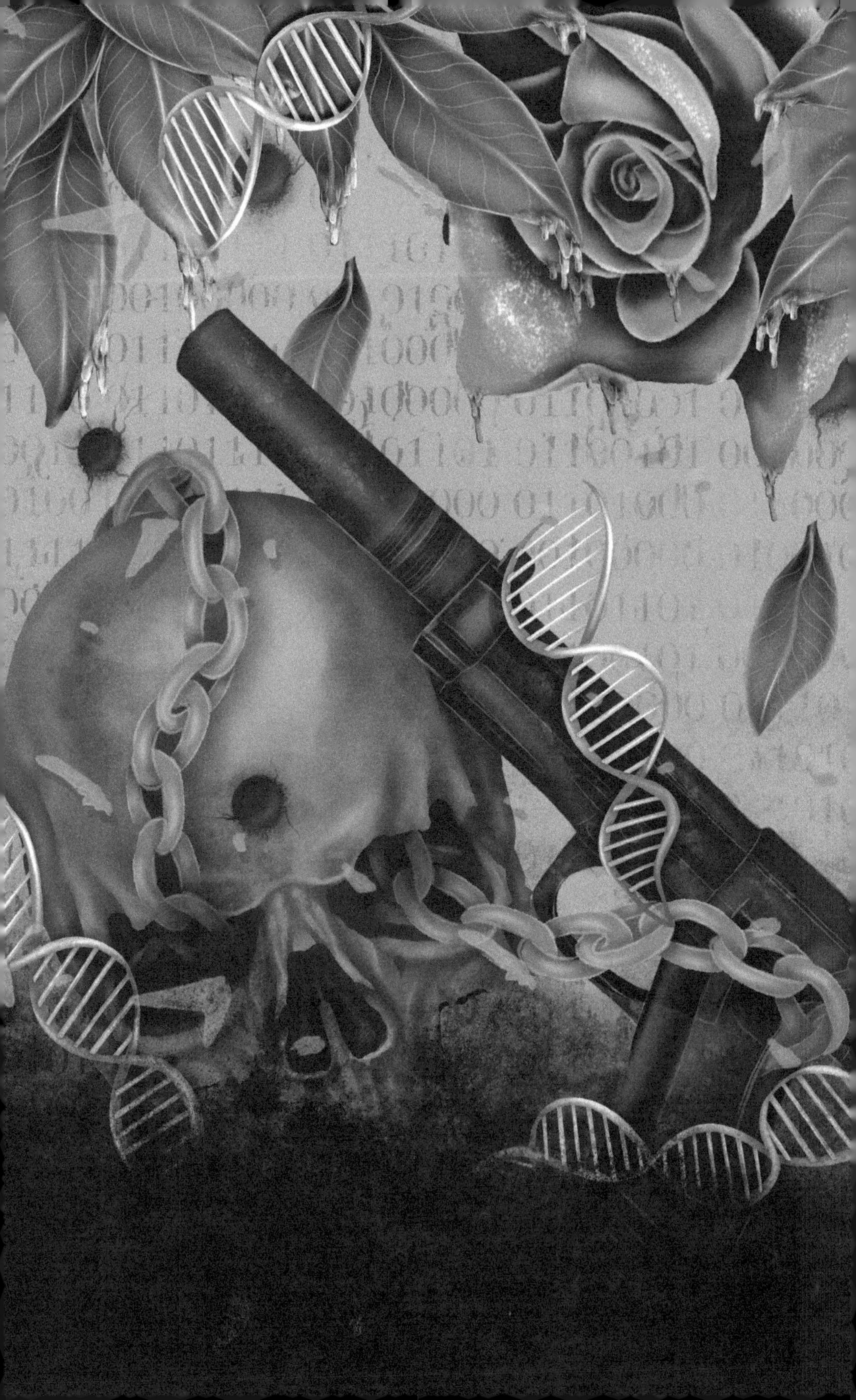

FORTY-ONE

I let them look after me. I could say it's just to ease their nerves and stop them from worrying, but honestly, it's kind of nice. I've been through so much recently, so not having to worry about taking care of myself is . . . enjoyable. I love them for it even more. I still cannot believe they came for me. They could have left me and said fuck the mission. They could have even still carried on the mission, since I was never the priority, but they made me their priority because they love me. I see it in every touch, every look, and every action. I never thought about our future past this place and what it would mean.

I love them, I know that, but love hurts.

Love has the ability to destroy you. Look at Ana. But every time I think about pulling away to stop myself from being hurt in the future, they pull me back in. They won't allow us to end our relationship. They call us family. Didn't I call us that once as well? Can I have that again? I hope so. I hope I'm not too fucked up in the head to ruin this because this thing we have is good.

It's great.

It's not perfect, but it's a reason to live.

I loved them enough to sacrifice myself, but can I love them enough to keep living?

I guess only time will tell. There are some moments when I'm fine, driving towards the future and smiling with them as they flutter around me like nurses. Other times, the pain of everything I've lost and endured becomes too much and I drown in it, blinded to those helping hands reaching out to hold me.

They tell me time will help.

One breath, one second turns into minutes. Dimitri's words come back to me, and I force air into my lungs. I repeat it until I can see once more and I understand what he meant. Seconds can turn into minutes if you simply remember to breathe and let the pain wash through you rather than drown you under its waves. A mere second can change everything if we let it.

The darkness that plagues me won't be easily defeated. It will come back, and it will linger and wait for when I'm weak, but with them at my side, I hope it's enough that I will be strong enough to fight it.

I'm strong enough not to give in to its comforting lull, to not be selfish enough to take that leap that would destroy them the way my sister's death did me.

Death is easy, but living is fucking hard.

I have regrets, but when I look into their eyes, I wouldn't change anything I did because it brought me to them—these five, wonderful men who are so willing to travel across the world to find me and kill anyone who gets in their way.

I always thought being strong meant standing alone, just like my father thought, but I was wrong. Being strong means allowing others in, knowing they might hurt you. It's trusting them to stand at your back and catch you when you fall. We are stronger together than we ever could be alone.

We are just six fucked-up experiments with endless possibilities for a future.

It's kind of terrifying not knowing what we will be doing tomorrow.

For so long, surviving has been my mission, followed by stopping my father, but now the world is waiting for us.

"Hey, love," Louis murmurs, leaning against the door of the room they put me in. "You okay? Are you in any pain? I can get Isaac."

"Stop, I'm fine." I smile to soften my words. I know he's worried. His pinched features show his concern, as does the fact he checks on me every five minutes. If it wasn't so sweet, it would be annoying. "How's everyone?"

"We're fine, just worried about you," he admits, pushing away from the door and heading my way, cupping my cheeks with a sigh. Leaning into his warmth, I shut my eyes as I soak in his comforting, grounding touch. "The kids are leaving soon."

"What? Where to?" My eyes open as I struggle to my feet. With an annoyed frown, he stops me, preventing me from tearing open my wound.

"Somewhere safe for now until Dimitri can determine their backgrounds and what we should do to prevent this from ever happening again."

"We cannot leave them alone, Louis. They've been through enough," I argue.

For the first time since I woke up, his eyes flash like they used to. "We don't plan on it if you'd listen for one minute, brat." He huffs, a smirk playing on his lips. Desire flares through me, but I push it back because now is definitely not the time.

My eyes narrow on him, his narrow on me, and we just stare each other down until he grins.

"God, I missed that fucking look. I never thought I would see it again." His grin grows as I roll my eyes. "Dimitri hired a private plane with security. Bert is on the plane, and he will be escorting them to a safe house, ensuring they settle in. We have some of the best doctors available on staff to monitor them, and Dimitri has the place wired so we can watch them at all times."

"Oh." I relax at that. Of course they thought of everything.

"You really thought I would send them somewhere alone and scared?" he asks. It's a joke, but I see the pain in his eyes over the fact that I wouldn't trust him to sort this out.

Sighing to myself, I lean my head against his chest, listening to his steady, strong heartbeat and letting it ground me. "I didn't. You know that. I guess I'm just used to dealing with everything myself."

"One day you won't be. I cannot wait for that," he whispers, stroking the back of my head. "I promise they will be safe, Nova. I would die before I let anyone hurt them again."

"I know." I got so used to depending on myself down here, but Louis has proven himself over and over again. He's a capable leader, an excellent soldier, and a brilliant man. If he promises something, he will keep it. He's trying to help. It's just an old habit that I need to break so I can trust them to handle things without worrying about it. Fucking independence and stubbornness. "I'm sorry."

"You don't have to be, my love. I cannot begin to imagine what has happened to you since the last time I saw you." I start to stiffen, but he doesn't let me go. "We are here if and when you are ever ready to talk about it. If you never are, that's okay too. But know this, Nova." He tilts my head up to meet his gaze. "We are never going anywhere again. It's us and you, so get used to it, my love." He kisses me softly, making my eyes shut once more before he pulls away. "I'm going to check on them."

"May I come?" I murmur hopefully.

He frowns, and I know he's about to protest.

"You could carry me." It's a low move because I know he would give me anything I want, and honestly, Louis loves protecting me, so he scoops me into his arms, holding me tight.

"Brat," he mutters, but it is spoken in a loving way.

"You know it." I snuggle into his shoulder, wrapping my arms around him. How many nights did I wish I could have this again? I refuse to let my issues ruin this.

He walks confidently through the corridors, and I close my eyes. The pain is distant, thanks to the pain meds Isaac keeps pumping me with even though I say no, so I'm relaxed, and when we stop before the elevator, I see all the kids there, dressed in warm clothing, ready to go. They turn to us as we approach, and Nico steps from their masses. My mouth drops open with a laugh at the first sight of him.

He's covered in glitter and drawings, but it's the sheet tied to his waist like a tutu that causes me to laugh. The kids around him giggle, especially one little girl who hides behind him.

Not the least bit bothered to be caught like this, he winks at me. "I'll keep it on for later, baby."

Laughing harder, I slide down Louis's body and stay propped against his side. "You better." I grin as I look the kids over. They are all so young. I know they must have seen, heard, and experienced some horrible stuff, but looking into their hopeful, happy eyes, I'm reminded of why we did this. "I'm Nova," I introduce myself with a little wave.

"We know." The little girl peeks from behind Nico. "Nicky was telling us about you. He said he's going to marry you." She giggles harder.

"Is that right?" My eyes go to him, and Nico simply grins at me. "Do you think I should?"

"He's funny, plus he gave us piggyback rides and has juice boxes. I think you should," she replies.

"And what about me? Can she marry me?" Louis asks.

"I don't know," the girl hedges. "Do you have juice?"

"I have something better. I have chocolate," he whispers like it's a secret.

She nods. "Then you can marry him too."

"Why, thank you for your permission." I'm unable to stop smiling, and my heart is light as I look around. "You'll all be okay. We promise. We'll take care of you now."

"We know," a little boy says, holding the hand of a girl at his side. "Thank you for saving us." He's clearly the oldest here, and although he's no older than ten, the way he looks at me as he speaks shows knowledge way beyond his age—one that is only put there by pain and horror.

"Okay, kids, the plane is here," Nico calls, clapping. "Remember what we talked about. Hold onto your friend until you're on board, and once there, what do we do?"

"Listen to Bert," they repeat in innocent voices with big, fluttering eyes. Something in my heart cracks, and I swallow my pain as I look at them, knowing this is as close to having kids as I will ever get, and although I'm happy, it hurts.

"Good, let's go!" The elevator opens, and they all file inside. Nico hangs back before darting over to me and kissing me soundly.

"I'll make sure they get on board safely. Bert is dying to see you, but he knows this is important to you. Go rest, baby." He steps into the elevator with the kids, bringing them up top and to safety.

"He's right. You need to rest," Louis murmurs, shouldering my weight.

"Not yet. Can we just walk around for a bit? I don't want to be trapped in that bed again. It reminds me too much of the beds my father tied me to." It's a low blow but true, and he jerks next to me.

"We will move you. What would be easier?"

"Louis, Louis, stop." He's about to go into leader mode. "It is fine. I know I need to rest, so it doesn't bother me too much, but I just want to be out of bed for a little while, okay?"

"Are you sure?" He frowns down at me as he lifts me into his arms once more. I could walk, but I don't protest, and he doesn't offer to let me.

"Yes." I press my lips to his neck, feeling him shiver. "Then I'll rest, and we can get the fuck out of here. The sooner I never have to see this place again, the better."

Louis falters but then turns. "I know a place." I let him take me without question, my eyes sliding shut as I soak in his love and warmth. I only open them again when he sets me down on a sofa in what looks to be a canteen. Jonas is stuffing food in his mouth, but he waves and grins at me before offering his plate to me. Grinning, I shake my head just as Dimitri comes in, holding a tablet in one hand.

"They are off. Nico is coming back down, then he and Jonas will wire the—" He jerks to a stop when he sees me. "You're out of bed. Are you—"

"She's gone! Where is she?" Isaac yells, frantically running into the room, his eyes wild until he sees me. "Oh, you're okay? You're okay," he says.

"I'm fine, I just wanted to see the kids off. I didn't walk, doc, so don't worry." I wink at him as he collapses next to me.

"Thank fuck," he mutters as I lean into his side, and he relaxes. Not too long after, Nico joins us as Dimitri looks between me and the tablet.

"You can carry on. I should know the plan," I grumble when they just keep staring.

"Sorry, babe." Dimitri winces. "Jonas and Nico are going to wire the whole facility. I checked everywhere and gathered all the data I could. The backups will be deleted and incinerated. No trace will be left behind."

"And we're sure there's no one else down here or up top?" I ask.

"We dealt with everyone up top after. They were preparing an assault team, which delayed them. Some had come down when ordered, so only a few remained," Louis explains. "We have searched every room down here for any others who might have hidden and found nothing."

"There was a doctor, the one we spared last time. He was here. He helped me," I tell them. "Is he okay?"

They share a look, and Louis sighs. "We found him. His neck was broken. It appeared to have happened hours before we even attacked. From what we saw, it looked like he was trying to gather his things to escape."

"Oh." I don't really know what else to say. He helped me, but that didn't make him a good guy, even if I know why he was doing it. There has been so much death here, it's hard to work through it all. He made his choice, though, and so did we. "When do we leave?"

"When Isaac says you're okay to travel." Louis narrows his eyes on me. "And I agree, no rushing this. We aren't letting you hurt yourself. A few more days won't change anything."

"It will for me. I want out of here," I mutter, but I know they won't budge, so I relax. "What can I do to help?"

"You've done everything, babe, just rest," Jonas says. "Or I can keep you occupied—"

"No sex," Isaac and Louis say at the same time.

"Spoilsports. I was going to suggest cuddling, or maybe I could carry her around while I wire up the place and she can watch my back." He becomes serious. "I know how badly I would hate doing nothing while being stuck in a place where I was held captive."

"Well shit." Nico chuckles. "Jonas is being all emotionally intelligent."

"Leave him alone." I point at Nico. "Or I'll kick your ass when I'm better."

"I can't wait," he purrs with a wink.

"Thank you, Jonas." I hold out my hand, and forgetting his food, even though I know it's a trigger for him, he hurries over. He sits at my feet, and I pull him closer to me. "You're right. It is hard to be here, but I've lasted this long, so I can last a few more days." Leaning down, I lay a gentle kiss on my lover's head. "Thank you for trying to protect me."

"Always, baby," he says, turning to kiss my hand and holding it to him, his eyes solemn for once until he suddenly perks up. "When we get home,

I'll make you the biggest stack of pancakes with Bert. That always cheers me up."

God, I love this man.

"Alright, alright, she needs to rest," Isaac declares, his voice stern, leaving no room for argument.

"Can I rest here with you guys?" I plead with him. "I hate lying there." I hate the panic in my tone, but now that I'm fully awake, being trapped in that room feels too much like being trapped on those tables and cut apart.

"Of course," he tells me, "but you'll need to lie down."

"Sure thing, doc."

He stands, and they help me lie down, covering me up and giving me a pillow as Nico and Jonas kiss me goodbye and go to wire up the place. Isaac sits with me, checking my vitals and playing with my fingers as if he's loath to be parted from me. Dimitri watches the tablet carefully, but he brings me some food and water with a soft smile.

Louis is about to leave when his phone rings. He frowns down at it but answers, then he puts it on the table, pressing speaker as he leans back. "General."

"We have been trying to get ahold of you for days," the general snaps, making me roll my eyes. This might have started with them putting us on this mission, but it turned into much more.

"I have been busy," Louis drawls. "Would you like a report?"

There is a long pause. "You have one minute."

"We have located Dr. Davis and dealt with the threat. His experiments have ceased, and the research has been gathered for safekeeping." He leaves out anything else that's personal, and I send him a silent *thank you* for that. I don't want this dick knowing my business.

"Dr. Davis is dead?" His voice is carefully cold.

Louis frowns. "Yes."

"But you have the research with you?" he continues.

"We do . . ." Louis frowns over at me. "To keep it safe, although we will probably destroy it."

"No, don't destroy it. Bring it here with you," he says quickly.

Too quickly.

"For what?" Louis demands as I stiffen.

"Don't question things above your paygrade. Dr. Davis might have been a madman, but some of his research was cutting edge."

"It was insane and inhumane," Louis snaps. "Why do you want the research?"

"That is none of your business. I expect your team and the research at the bunker by next week. Understood?"

Louis's eyes harden, and he stares at the phone for a moment. "Understood," he replies then hangs up, meeting my eyes. "I don't like that."

"Me either." I look around. "You don't think he would try to use the research, do you? My father mentioned super soldiers. Hell, he even had soldiers. I never thought to question how he got them, but the general was against my father . . . wasn't he?"

"He said so from the get-go," Louis mutters. "That's why we trusted him. We even did our own background checks. He was clean, but I don't particularly want him or the government to get their hands on this research."

"Neither do I," I agree as Dimitri and Isaac nod. "So what do we do?"

Louis looks at the phone again before sitting taller. "We follow our plan for now. Rest, and then we'll go home when you're ready. Let me deal with this for now. I need to think some things over." Grabbing his phone, Louis strides from the room, and I share a look with Dimitri who quickly goes after him.

"Isaac, if he tries to use my father's research—"

"We won't let that happen. You know that, Nova," he promises, kissing my hand. "Rest, everything will be okay."

My mind whirls a mile a minute. I thought this was over. I thought this ended with my father. He never once mentioned any connection to the military, but how did he get soldiers? It could be a coincidence, and Dimitri said he's clean—they wouldn't have trusted him otherwise. The general said he thought my father was a monster, a traitor, but then why would he want his research?

To protect it or use it?

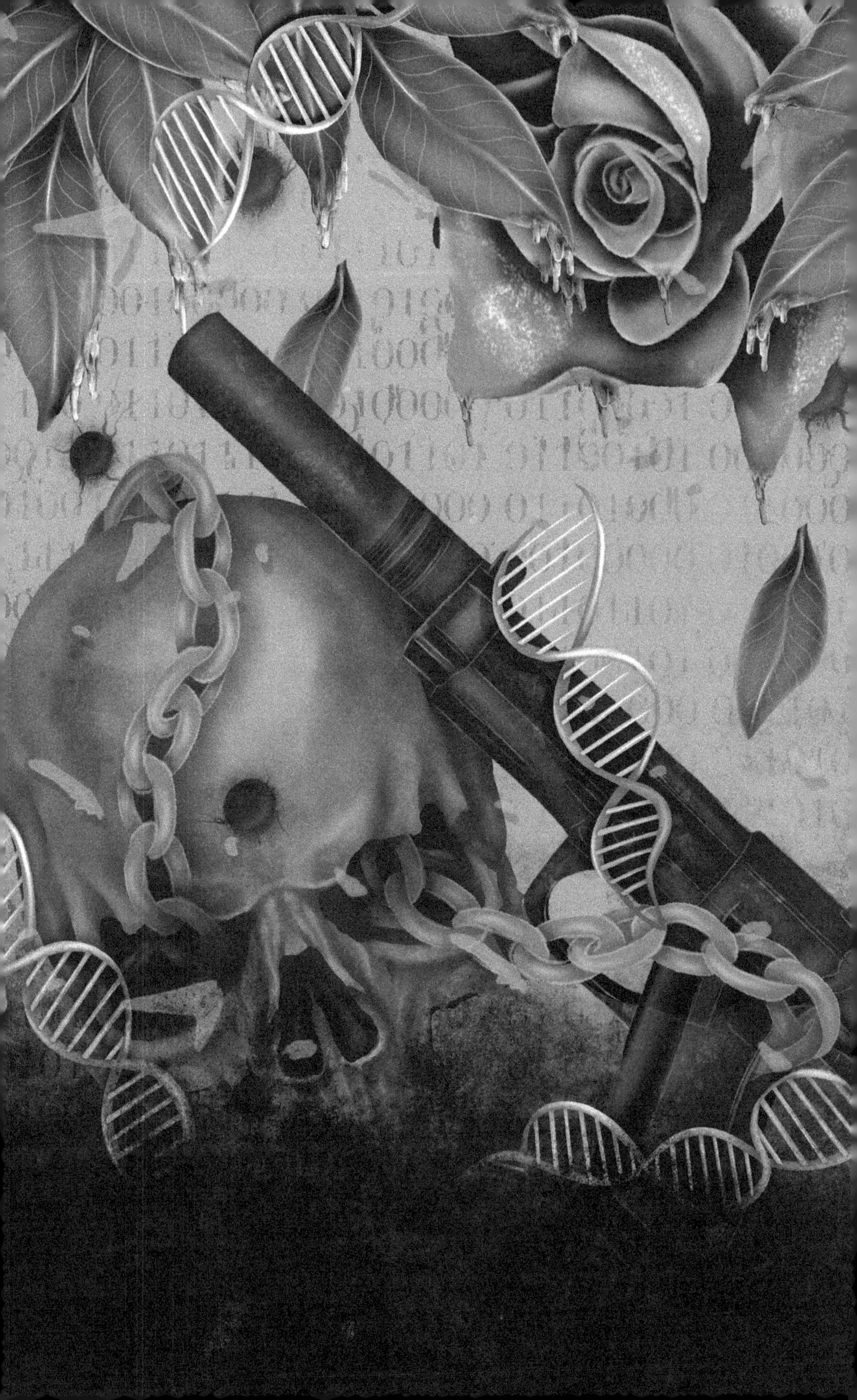

FORTY-TWO

I'm over this shit.

I know they want to take care of me because they love me, but I'm over it. I want out. I want fresh air. I want away from this bunker and the stench of dead bodies that has lingered over the last two days. They've been so busy, I barely see them. Instead, I take the time to stretch out my body, careful of my wound since I don't want to stay here longer than I need to. I do some basic exercises. I walk and jog, I do some push-ups, and I eat and shower and repeat. By the second day, I'm going insane. At least I had a purpose before, and I had things to keep me busy. Granted, that was usually round-the-clock torture, but hey, beggars can't be choosers.

I'm fed up, to say the least, and when I stride into the kitchen we've claimed as our command post and find Louis, I decide it's time to tell him that.

He spins his chair around, and I watch his grin turn into a groan. "Baby," he starts.

"No, I'm fine. We are leaving. Today. Now. I want out!" I snap. "I will be fine on the plane. I will rest and relax and do everything you fuckers want, but if I spend one more goddamn hour down here, I'm going to go crazy—okay, crazier—and take it out on you bitches. So either be a good boy and give the order or I'm breaking out of here and you can follow. Either way, we are leaving, understood?"

"Nova, we are trying to take care of you," he says calmly, sounding completely rational.

"Aww, that's cute. I don't give a fuck. We are leaving," I retort unreasonably, but it doesn't stop him from chuckling or pulling me closer and kissing me, even as I keep my arms crossed, not willing to back down.

"If you are sure, I can tell the others," he begins.

"I am. I'm sure. I couldn't be surer. I need to get out of here, Louis." I let him see the truth. I'm afraid I'll go crazy if I stay down here another minute. There are too many ghosts, too much pain, and too many nightmares that plague me here. "Please." I'll beg if I need to.

"Okay," he says, standing and kissing my head. "I'll tell the others. Go get dressed and we can leave."

"Really?" I would leap up and down if it wouldn't tear my wound.

"Really." He grins. "We only stayed to help you. I would never ignore your desire to leave, my love. Let's go home."

"Let's." Leaning up, I kiss him harder. "Thank you."

"Always, Nova."

Now that we're standing down the road, the base looks small. How could one place house such horrors? Yet it did, and as I watch Jonas flip open the switch, nothing but relief fills me.

"Boom." He grins and two seconds later, the explosives they wired into the building blow it sky-high, incinerating everything.

The guards' bodies, my father's body, the labs, the results, and the rooms and all the pain they held.

The whole base goes up in flames, climbing into the sky. Nothing will be left but the scars on my body and soul from what happened here. It almost pisses me off. They should have suffered more, but I can't change that now. Turning away, I get into the Jeep we stole and watch the flames as we drive to the nearby airfield where Dimitri's plane is.

Nobody is waiting for me at home this time. There will be no little sister ready to welcome me back and share all my secrets with. It seems to hit me then, and tears fall from my eyes. I hide my face as we speed to the airplane.

Breaking down now will solve nothing.

Instead, I close my eyes and let the smell of smoke and the bump of the car lull me into a place between sleep and wakefulness where it doesn't hurt so badly.

I slept the entire plane ride home. I can see the worry on my men's faces, but I cannot bring myself to comfort them and let them know I'm okay. I'm not okay, and it couldn't be more evident than when we pull up at the manor and Bert opens the door.

I'm out of the car before they even stop, rushing into his open arms. "Nova!" he cries when he sees me, catching me as I fling myself at him. We sink to the ground as I bury my head in his chest, my tears falling once more.

"Miss Nova, I'm so sorry," he whispers, rubbing my back, his own tears wetting my hair as we hold each other. "I'm so very sorry."

"Me too," I murmur. "Is she . . ."

"We buried her." He pulls back, brushing my tears away. "I insisted on it. Your men dug the holes, and they made sure she was with Sam under the shelter of the tree so she wouldn't be alone. I made sure it was finished."

What does it matter? She's dead, but I simply nod, turning my head to see the two graves hidden under the canopy of the old tree. Pain splinters me apart, and I don't even notice him helping me to my feet and heading inside, not until I'm looking around the foyer, as if waiting for her to jump out.

She doesn't, of course.

This place is as empty as when I first arrived and filled with two more ghosts.

"I can make some food. I bet you must be hungry," Bert offers at my side but doesn't let go. "Or I can—"

"She's really gone." I don't know why I'm saying it. I knew she was.

I saw her die. I felt it. I held her.

Why did a small part of me expect to see her smiling face inside this house? Looking up at Bert, I see the same pain reflected in his eyes. Bert was never our father, but he sure as fuck loved us like one.

Loved Ana like one.

He lost two daughters that day, and now one is back. We share a grieving look for the good that was stolen from the world because she was the best. She was kind, sweet, strong, and sure. Ana was so intelligent, it was scary, and she was determined to make the world a better place. It should be her who's here, not me. She was going places, she had things to do, and she would have changed everything.

Me? I'm just a scarred, fucked-up individual who can take a lot of pain. Despite my father's beliefs, I'm nothing special. Not really. I'm just what he created. Ana? She was so much more.

But life is a bitch like that. I lived, she died, and it hurts.

They say that everyone was born with a purpose or they find their destiny, something they were created for, but if I believed that, then I would have to believe that my sister's reason for being born was to die. I refuse to consider that. It's a load of shit. We are born, we suffer through life, and if we are lucky enough, we find someone to suffer through it with us. I don't believe we are all born with a great destiny, I believe we make one.

Hers? Hers is in the legacy she leaves me with.

"I know," he whispers. "It's almost too hard to be here. I see a memory of her everywhere I look. It hurts, Miss Nova, but she wouldn't want us to stop. She wouldn't want us to be unhappy. She loved you so much, Nova. She loved you, and you did everything you could. If you couldn't save her, then nobody could, and she knew that. Your mission is over. You did it. Now it's time to live. We have to."

"I don't know if I can," I admit out loud for the first time.

"You can do anything you put your mind to. You always could," he responds with a squeeze.

"I spent my whole life protecting her and carrying on for her. Now what? What do I do, Bert?" I look up at him. "What do I do without her?"

"We remember her and honour her in the way we live."

Bert is right, and when he takes my hand, I let him lead me outside to the tree. There, chiselled in stone, is her name, right next to Sam's. The tears continue to fall as I struggle to breathe, holding Bert's hand tightly in mine.

"It's over, Annie. It's over. He's gone. He can't hurt anyone else anymore. I thought you should know." My voice is choked, and I swallow around my agony that is still as fresh as the moment her eyes closed. "I love you, Annie, and I'm so sorry."

I turn away because I can't take it anymore, then I leave Bert there and head back inside where my men are waiting for me, but if they hold me, I will break down further. I'm tired of crying. I'm tired of being weak.

"We should hide the research for now and check in on the children."

"Of course." Louis nods. "Are you okay?"

"I'm fine. I'll be fine," I reply. "I just need to stay busy, okay? Just let me do that."

"Okay, well, you can help Dimitri and Nico hide the research. Isaac and I will check on the kids." Nodding, I follow Nico to the car. He does let me help, but he carries the boxes in while I carry the hard drives with Dimitri.

"Any ideas?" D asks, looking around.

"One," I reply. It's a place I forgot about until now.

Grabbing a bag, I head upstairs, past my and Annie's rooms, to the formal sitting room on this level we never used. A panelled wall runs all the way around it. Moving to the bookcase on the right, I see the gap is still there. I used to fit behind it, but now I have to nudge it out of the way with Nico's help. Hidden behind it is a trapdoor Bert cut for us when we told him what we wanted, and it leads into the space that used to be a cupboard before it was sealed, so this is the only way in and out.

Crouching, I open the door and peek inside, seeing the torch waiting there. Books lie discarded in the blankets, and there are glow-in-the-dark stickers on the cupboard ceiling and drawings on the wall. It was a place for us to hide when we needed to. It was our place.

It seems only right that I hide this here, leaving her to protect it.

Crawling inside, since the others will be too big, I crouch and look around, a sad smile curling my lips. "Only Annie and I knew about this place. It was our hiding spot." Lifting my hand, I trace a drawing she made of us and Bert. Turning away, I drag my bag in and hold my hands out for the rest. "It will be safe here for now."

They don't question me, and I pile it all in here and cover it in a blanket just in case before sliding out. Nico helps me up, and Dimitri double-checks, adding something before straightening and moving the bookcase back. If you weren't looking, you wouldn't have a clue it was there.

"I set a camera and a motion sensor inside as well. It's not on the house plans, so that's good." He nods. "Okay, how about we get some food, take showers, and then crash? It's late."

"Sure." I look back at the spot as he takes my hand, and I allow him to lead me away. It's yet another reminder of what I have lost, but I know she's there, guarding the research for me.

I'm picking at my food. The table is quiet, and no one seems to want to disturb it, not even Bert. My eyes keep going to the two empty chairs opposite me. Is this what my life will be like? Sad, quiet meals with empty chairs?

I give them all a tight smile as I stand. "I'm going to bed. I'm tired."

"Are you okay?" Isaac asks worriedly.

"I'm fine, just tired," I lie and then move from the table. "Goodnight." I don't give them time to question me, nor do I ask them to join me, and they don't offer.

Are we broken beyond repair, or am I simply too broken to love anymore?

I don't know, but when I collapse, it's in her bed, not mine. I suck in her scent as I cry, wrapping her cold sheets around me and wishing she were here.

I wish they had taken me, not her.

Sam would have loved her through her pain. They would have stopped

Father, grown old, and had kids. They would have made this place a home. She would have been happy. She would have been better than me.

But everyone is right. I need to live for her now.

I cannot change the past nor can I take the pain away.

I just need to learn to live with it if I can and hope they love me enough to stay by my side as I try to heal my broken heart and lonely soul.

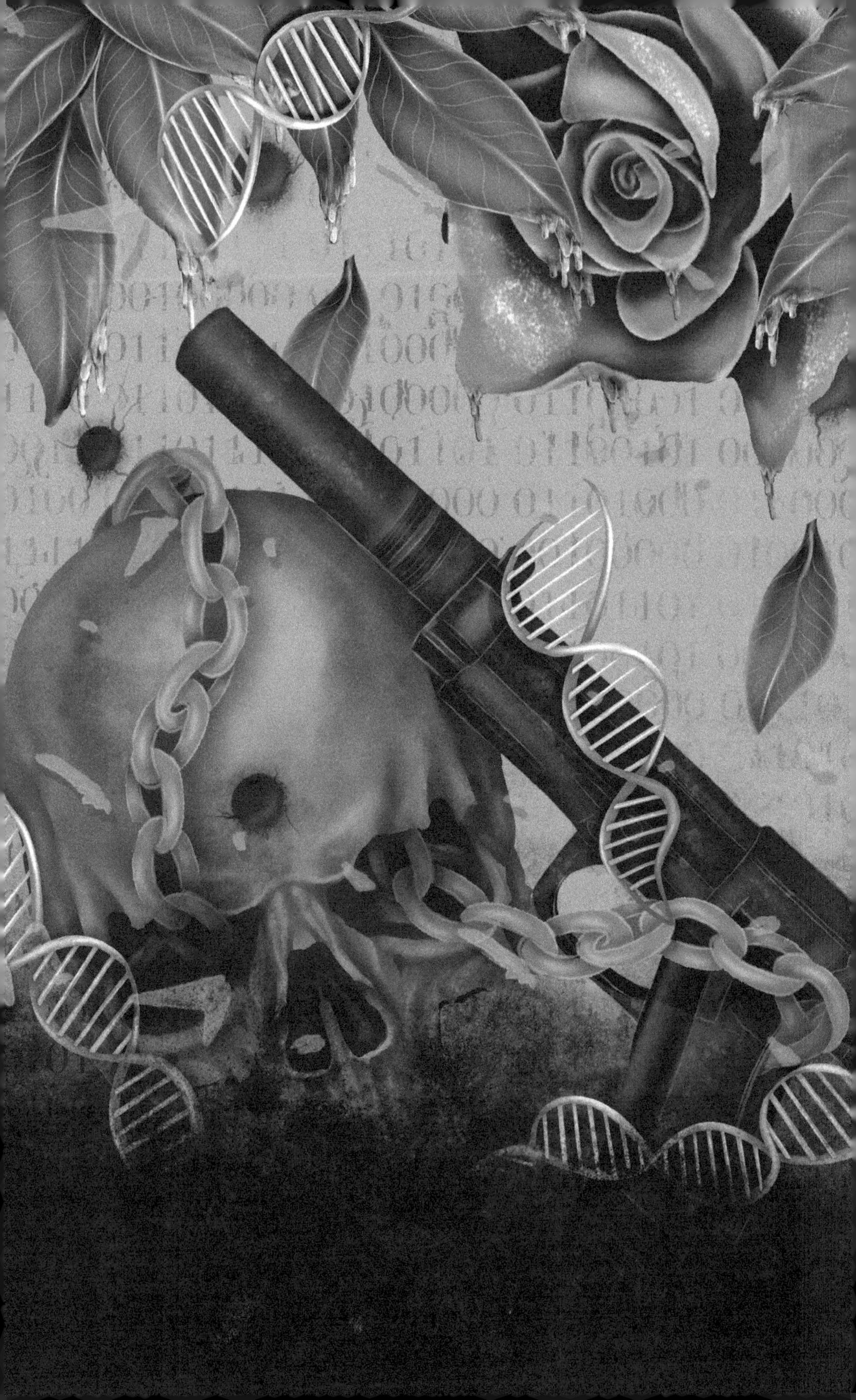

FORTY-THREE

The crack of lightning wakes me up, and I jerk upright in Ana's darkened room. There's a quilt over me, some water next to the bed, and clothes laid out. My guys were here, but they left me alone like I wanted, and I feel bad for a moment before my gaze moves to the window to see the rain coming down hard, the night sky lighting up with sparks of lightning as rumbles of thunder rock the house.

A storm.

Annie.

I jump up and walk out of the bedroom door, intent on getting to her.

I slip on some shoes at the front door and head outside without hesitating. Stilling as the rain lashes me, I feel it chill me to the bone as it causes the oversized shirt and shorts to stick to my body. Ignoring it, I hurry to the graves below the tree.

The cold makes me shiver, but I don't stop until I drop to my knees before her grave. The wet mud gives slightly, chilling me through.

Ana.

"Hey, Annie," I call softly, wiping the rain from my face as lightning arcs through the sky, lighting up the darkness like she always did for me. "I know you hate storms, so I'll sit with you, okay?" I whisper, the wind catching my words and taking them to her.

Pain bubbles in my throat until I choke on it and a sob breaks free. "I woke up and you weren't there. For a moment, I forgot you were dead," I admit, my voice cracking. Pain builds inside of me, and I have to let it out. "It's not fair." I slam my hand into the mud. "It's not fucking fair."

Tipping my head back, I release my pain in a scream.

The storm catches it, wrapping my pain and fury up in its depths and using it.

"I miss you so much," I whisper, crawling closer, shivering from the cold rain.

Sliding under the tree and the protection it offers, I lean against the trunk, watching the night sky for a while as pain swallows me. "I always loved storms. They reminded me of you and the times you would sneak into my bed and let me hold you through them, no matter how old you got. Whenever I see lightning, I smile," I admit, even as tears drip down my face, a smile curling my lips. "It reminds me that no matter what happens, love doesn't stop. It just changes. The lightning is my reminder you existed, Ana, and that you loved me and I loved you. Isn't that the most beautiful thing you have ever heard?" Looking down at her grave, I let my tears fall steadily, blending with the rain.

"Storms are my favourite thing now because of you. Every time it storms, I will be right here with you until the end, Annie, until the day they have to wheel me out here. Then, I'll be in the ground right next to you."

My head falls back to the wood, and I watch the sky light up with it, knowing she's right here with me. My hand curls around air where hers would be, my shoulder almost heavy from her head. I can feel her with me, and for the first time since I lost her, I breathe without pain.

I know it's going to be okay.

The storm tells me that.

She might be gone, but there will always be the memories and love I have of her. I close my eyes, letting the tears fall even as a smile curls my lips. She's right here with me as I say goodbye.

As I let her go and hold her heart with my own.

When my eyes open, I freeze.

My men stand before me, half asleep but concerned.

"She hated to be alone during storms," I tell them, shivering in the cold. "I couldn't let her be alone."

I worry what they will do, but I shouldn't have.

They don't complain or speak. They wrap me in a coat and blanket before sitting next to me under the canopy, keeping me warm with their bodies, and that's when I know they aren't going anywhere.

No matter what happens, we are family.

Forever.

They take my hand and settle at my sides, until we sit shoulder to shoulder under the canopy, protecting my sister through the storm. I break apart with the lightning and put myself back together again with their help.

Hours pass this way until my shaking gets to be too much, and then I stand, looking at them. "She will be okay now. The worst of the storm has passed, I think." I hold out my hand. "Take me inside."

Louis is the first to stand, covered head to toe in rainwater, but he never once complained. His hand is muddy like my own as he takes it. "Are you sure?"

Looking back at her grave, I nod with a smile. "I'm sure. She is going to be okay. It's going to be okay. I'm going to be okay," I reply, looking at him with a sad smile. "Take me to bed."

As he searches my gaze, I see lightning flash across his eyes, but I shudder again and he quickly herds me inside, the others following closely. The door shuts with a bang the thunder covers swiftly. Shivering, I kick off the wet shoes and drop the blanket and coat to the floor, watching them plop them into a puddle.

I run to the stairs and hurry up to my room, knowing they are following. Once inside, I turn to face them as they cross the threshold and shut the door behind them.

Sliding my wet clothes away, I drop them to the floor, shivering as they stare at me. "Nova," Isaac starts, but I shake my head and step back.

"Warm me up," I order.

"Let us get towels, and we can go back to sleep," Louis offers.

"No, I've slept enough. I need you to remind me I'm alive," I say. "I need to be held and touched. I need to be loved. I need you to remind me that you aren't going anywhere. I need you all so much. Please."

Nico is the first to move, following me to bed.

I lie back, shivering. "Warm me up," I call, and Nico crawls up the mattress, covering me with his body as his lips find mine in the dark. His kiss is soft, gentle, and loving. His hands slide across my naked body, infusing me with his heat and strong touch, offering me his comfort and love.

Other hands join his, gliding over my body, and I realise they have towels. They are drying and warming every inch of me until Nico pulls away and gets to his knees. "Up, baby," he orders. I kneel, and Louis slides behind me, drying my neck and face with soft, sure strokes before drying my hair as best as he can. All the while, Nico's eyes hold me prisoner, and when Louis reaches down with the towel and cups my breasts, I groan. Louis tweaks my nipples as pleasure sweeps through me.

Crawling to me, Nico runs his tongue along my thigh and up, chasing some water before stroking across my pussy. "Lie back, baby." Swallowing, I do as he says, lying back on Louis. He's naked and hard behind me, his hands still playing with my breasts, tweaking my nipples until they are hard and pointed, waiting for their touches and mouths.

There's a noise beside me, and I look over to see Jonas crawling up the bed on my right, his eyes on me as he lies by my side, wrapping his lips around my nipple. I gasp as he sucks. Another head joins his and I jerk, turning left to see Isaac doing the same on my other side as Nico traces my pussy with teasing licks, chasing water.

Dimitri is watching and waiting patiently for his turn, so I keep my eyes on him as they tease me and bring me back to life. "I need you all," I admit.

"You've got us, so just relax, baby, and let us look after you," Nico murmurs.

My eyes slide closed in bliss as they weave a spell around me. Pleasure mounts when Nico's tongue slides over my clit, and I almost come off the bed. He holds me down, and Dimitri slides in alongside him. My mouth parts on a moan as Nico moves farther down, leaving room for Dimitri as his tongue joins in, curling around my clit as Nico's thrusts into me.

I cry out, trying to pull away, but they don't let me. They up their assault until I moan beneath them, grinding back into Louis's hard cock.

"Please," I whimper.

With each of their touches, I come back to life, and when Jonas and Isaac bite my nipples, Nico thrusts into me with his tongue, and Dimitri bites my clit, I fly over the edge, screaming into the night.

"That's it, Nova. Give us everything. Let that big brain rest. I just want you to feel. Feel our love for you. Let us guide you. Let us love you," Louis murmurs in my ear. "Look at them, look at how much they love you and how much they want you."

My eyes open as I pant, seeing them spread around me.

"We are all yours, the best killers in the world, and you brought us to our knees. You made us obsessed with you. You made us wild with it and so crazed, we would kill anyone who took you from us. Let us love you as much as we can, let the storm feel it."

Oh fuck.

I can't even put into words how much I love them. I was dead before them. They aren't just bringing me back to life tonight, but every day since I met them.

I hear them murmuring, but I remain reclined, trusting them like they asked. When I'm turned, I open my eyes and peer down at Dimitri, who's below me as he smirks. Hands grip my hips and lift me, then they slide me down his cock, making us both groan. I fall forward, kissing him as she slowly fills me. Hands slide over my ass and lift me, then another cock is at my entrance, and my eyes widen as it pushes in, stretching me. They rock into me as I catch my breath and push back, and they work in tandem, thrusting into me. When I glance over my shoulder, I find Isaac there with love blazing in his eyes. Panting, I rock into their touches as a finger presses against my chin and turns my head. I roll my eyes up to Jonas, who smiles softly and kisses me before kneeling once more, holding his cock in his hand. I open my mouth, wanting to taste, and he obliges.

He slowly slides his length into my mouth. I suck, sliding up and down as they fuck me. Hands slide over my body, Louis and Nico no doubt, and I cry out around Jonas's cock. Dimitri groans, running his lips along my chest and neck. Others kiss my back and sides as we make slow, unhurried love.

Dimitri is the first to fall, groaning into my chest as I feel him come, taking me with him. Isaac groans as he and Dimitri pull out of me, then I'm turned. Isaac kneels before me, cock in hand, and when he slides back into me as I'm wrapped in Dimitri's arms, I cry out.

Jonas grips my mouth once more and fills it, my head turned.

"That's it. Good girl, Nova. Just feel," Louis whispers in my ear. "Just feel their love, feel the pleasure winding through you. Let it carry you away and trust us to be here to catch you."

Whimpering, I do just that, lifting my hips to take Isaac as he makes love to me, all while sucking Jonas's big cock as he speeds up, unable to resist. He takes my mouth hard and fast until he jerks, thrusting deeply as he explodes down my throat, and I have no choice but to swallow.

Panting, I become dizzy when I'm turned once more. Isaac is still in my pussy as Nico slides beneath me and working with Isaac, he slides across my pussy. When Isaac pulls out, Nico thrusts in, and then they are both fucking me.

"Louis," I beg.

"I'm here, my love. I'm right here. We all are, look."

Lightning arcs beyond the window, illuminating the room. The sight makes me cry out. My head falls forward, but I lift it when I sense Louis. He waits, but I'm ready for him, and he comes gladly. His leaking length slides across my lips, staining them and my soul with his need and love.

"Beautiful," he murmurs as thunder rocks the house. "Wild and unpredictable, but a goddamn beauty of nature, just like this storm."

I suck him into my mouth, needing to show him how I feel because no words will do it justice. I slide him across my tongue, hollowing my cheeks as he fills my mouth, working with Nico and Isaac to keep me filled while building pleasure once more.

There is nothing but love and need inside me.

I feel so alive, it almost hurts, as if electricity from the storm flows through me, guided by their touch and bringing me back to life.

Jonas and Dimitri wrap their lips around my nipples and suck as every single one of them touches me, loving me.

I can't do anything but fall once more.

I cry out my release, and just like always, they follow me.

Isaac and Nico groan, and Isaac splashes his cum inside me as Nico pulls out and sprays it across my legs and pussy. Louis grips my chin and takes my mouth hard and fast as I shake, trapped by the force, and with an audible bellow that matches the thunder, he fills my mouth.

Tears slide down my cheeks. I'm happy.

I collapse in their midst, my strings cut, but for the first time in a long time, I know tomorrow will bring nothing but joy.

How could it not with them surrounding me? They heal my soul with each touch.

Lightning fills the sky as I close my eyes once more, surrounded by my loves, my heart beginning to heal along with my body.

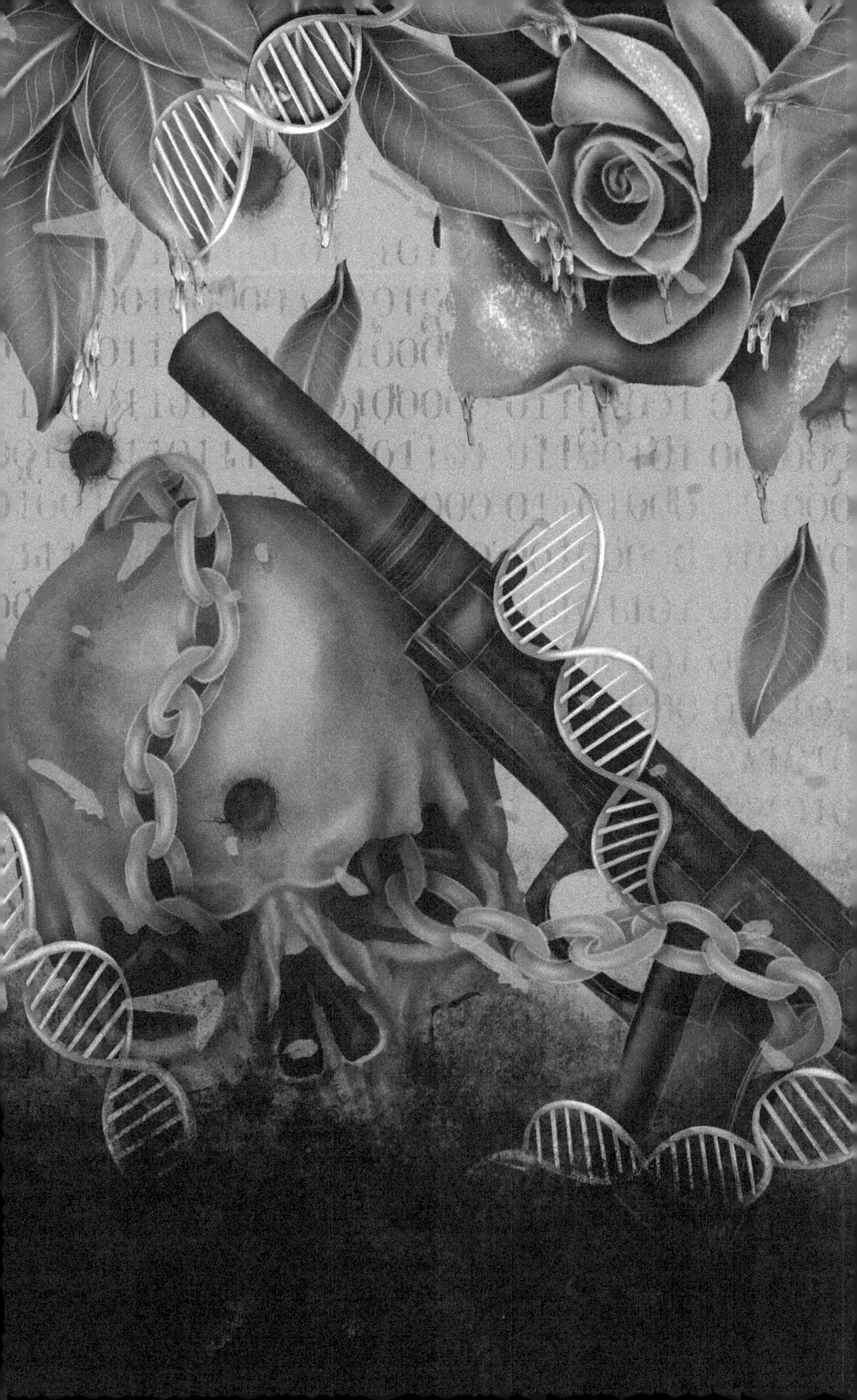

FORTY-FOUR

NOVA

I wake to an empty bed, warm and satisfied. I can hear them downstairs, though, so I don't worry. I roll over and just relax, soaking in their scents, thinking about everything we need to do.

We need to deal with the kids and find them someplace happy and safe to live. We also need to deal with the military.

They expect us to hand over the research next week, but I've already decided we won't. I need to broach it with Louis and the others, but I'm hesitant to break the peace we have found, so for a few more days, I will pretend and enjoy what we have.

Getting up, I head to the bathroom and crank on the shower. They warmed me up last night, but I still feel disgusting after sitting in the mud. Careful of my wounds, I wash my hair twice and scrub my body before sliding into one of their shirts and some leggings, adding fluffy socks. I leave my hair down to dry and head downstairs to find them.

I still at the kitchen door, a smile curling my lips. Bert and Jonas are cooking side by side. It's clear Bert is teaching Jonas how to make pancakes. Jonas's face is locked in concentration, his tongue caught between his teeth. "That's it, Master Jonas, just like that!" Bert praises as Jonas manages to flip it. "You'll be a chef in no time!"

My heart clenches with pure joy as Jonas grins at Bert, so carefree and happy.

"They better be for me," I call as I move to the dining table where Isaac is sipping tea.

He smiles at me. "Are you okay?" we say at the same time and giggle.

I sit in his lap, and he sighs as I snuggle closer, watching Jonas and Bert plate the food.

"I'm okay," he says. "How are you feeling? We didn't push you too much last night, did we?" His voice is quiet so we aren't overheard.

"I'm fine," I murmur, kissing his cheek.

"We haven't eaten yet. We waited for you," Bert tells me as he lays the food out with Jonas. "Master Louis is with Dimitri and Nico. I will call for them."

"Thank you, Bert." I catch his hand and kiss it. My gratitude is meant for so much more than the food he just gave me. He makes Jonas smile, and he is always here for us.

"Of course, Miss Nova." He smiles softly. "Quite the storm last night."

"It was." I look at the window where the sun is shining. "They say storms wash everything clean. I don't know about you, but I'm hoping that's true. I think it's going to be a beautiful day."

"I believe so," he whispers. "I truly do. I saw a rainbow this morning. That means good luck, but I hope it means a good future."

Meeting his eyes, I smile sadly. "I hope so too." Releasing his hand, I let him find the others as Jonas serves me a pancake and nervously hands me a fork.

"Well?" he asks hopefully. "Is it good?"

I hurriedly take a bite, and I don't even fake a moan. "So good." I lower my voice. "Don't tell Bert, but they might even be better than his, babe."

"I heard that!" Bert calls, making me laugh as Jonas grins, puffing up with pride.

Louis kisses me as he sits, sorting himself a plate before adding more to mine. Nico is sweaty when he drops into a seat, and Dimitri smiles at me as he sits and Jonas gives them pancakes. Bert sits with us, and we eat in comfortable silence. When I'm done, I lean back.

"So, what were you guys doing?"

"Updating security," Nico replies. "It means climbing all over the house."

"Ignore him, he drew the short straw." Louis laughs. "These pancakes are amazing. Congratulations, Jonas."

Jonas grins under the praise, sitting up taller as I blow him a kiss.

"How are the kids?" I ask.

"They are okay. They are settling into the apartment building well, so it should work until we find a permanent solution. Did you sleep well?" Dimitri asks.

"I did." I wink. "So, what's the plan for today?" I'm hesitant to bring up my suspicion about the military or what we will do, and it seems they are as well, so I let it slide for another day. It's not urgent, and I want to enjoy our time together since I spent so much time apart from them.

"We are going to finish updating the security on the house. It might take us a while, but you can help Dimitri organise it if you want. Isaac wanted to check you and Bert over once more, and then he's going to double-check all the research since he has the most knowledge. Jonas is working on a project for me," Louis explains.

I smile. "Sounds like a plan."

"Okay, so the new cameras will be here, here, here, and here," Dimitri tells me. "We are also adding motion sensors throughout the grounds. All the windows will eventually be replaced by the bulletproof kind the military uses, and we are also going to update the fence, gate, and alarms."

"Wow, sounds like a lot." It's clear they are doing this because of what happened last time.

"Nothing's too much when it comes to protecting my family." He grins at me. "Is there anything else you can think of?"

"Yeah, there is actually." I grab his face and yank him down to me, kissing him hard.

"What are you doing, Nova?" he murmurs as he tries to pull back.

Sliding from my chair, I plop onto his lap, grinding against his hard cock. They brought me back to life last night, and it seems my desire came with it.

"I thought it was obvious. Maybe you need a demonstration," I tease as I reach down and unzip his jeans. He struggles between us, trying to move me gently, but I grip his hard cock and he stills.

I stroke his huge length while grinding into his jean-clad thigh. "Still confused?" Standing, I kick off my leggings, leaving the shirt since it's cold, and then I straddle him once more. Lifting the shirt, I meet his eyes as I slide my hand up my thigh to my pussy, circling my hole. "Your cock goes here—"

His hand darts out and grips my neck, making me groan. "Louis is right. You are such a brat."

"Very true," I retort, desire making my heart race and my thighs slick. "Why don't you fuck it out of me?"

He smacks my hand away as he yanks me back to his mouth. Kissing me hard and fast, he sweeps his tongue against mine as he dominates me. The chair creaks as we grind together, so he sits me on the edge of the desk, kicking my thighs open.

"D, I need your cock." I groan as he leans down and swipes his tongue across my clit.

"You get what I give you. Now, Nova, be a good brat and scream for me. I heard that through the mic while I was working and it drove me crazy. Do it again with my tongue buried in this pretty pussy and you can have my cock. You can ride it until you are filled with my cum and they realise what we are doing in here."

His radio crackles. "Dimitri, can you check the positions of the cameras?"

He completely ignores it as I tangle my hand in his hair, tugging his head closer as my torso falls back. My nipples brush against the fabric of the top, making me moan. His talented tongue curls around my clit, and he finds a quick rhythm that has my hips jerking up as I grind into his face, but just as I'm about to come, he moves down and thrusts his tongue into me.

"Dimitri," I whine, sounding just like the brat he accused me of being.

He groans, and the sound vibrates through me, making me jerk below him. When he pulls his tongue out, I meet his eyes. "I forgot that you taste like fucking heaven. I've changed my mind. Cover my face in your cum. I don't care if you scream or don't. I just want to taste you with every breath I take. I want to drown in it."

"D." I hold his hair tighter, watching his pupils blow in pleasure and pain. "You better make me then."

With a wicked grin, he grabs my thighs and throws them over his shoulders, eating me like a madman.

His tongue dips inside me, fucking me before rubbing my clit. The fast pace drives me crazy as I roll my hips, wanting more. He gives me what I want, thrusting two fingers inside me and stretching them as I cry out.

My release takes me by surprise. His fingers pull free then his mouth seals on my pussy, swallowing every drop of my cum before his fingers are back inside me, rubbing my G-spot. My legs jerk as one orgasm rolls into the next while he abuses my poor pussy, draining every drop of my release from me. When he sits back sometime later, his face drips with my cream, and he grins so broadly, it must hurt.

Legs shaking, I try to relearn how to breathe.

"Dimitri?" Louis snaps.

Reaching out, Dimitri grabs the mic. "Looking good, keep going," he says without taking his eyes off me as he stands. He pushes his jeans down and with a wicked grin, he wipes his hand across his face, gathering my cream and stroking his cock with it before stepping between my shaking thighs.

"Scream for me," he orders as he pulls me down and impales me on his length.

I do, my head falling back with a scream as he pounds into me. The desk creaks from the force of his thrusts as he grips my hip to work me onto his hard length. My legs are floppy, but I manage to wrap them around his waist and lift my hips for his punishing thrusts.

I want more.

He moans, gripping my hips as he drives into me harder, and the radio crackles again. "Dimitri? How about now?"

"So fucking good," he tells them.

"What?" Louis asks in confusion, and then he presses the radio against me and twists his hips, smacking my clit at the same time, and I cry out.

"Oh, never mind." Louis chuckles.

Dropping it, he smirks at me. "They all know you are in here getting fucked like the good girl you are, coming for your man. Fuck, baby, I can feel you gripping me. You're so ready to come again, aren't you?"

"Fuck, fuck, please, D." I can't help but beg as the pleasure inside of me grows.

"Good girl, just like that. You're taking me so well," he praises, spiralling me higher as he groans and hammers into me. "I'm close. That's it, baby. Now come for me. Milk my cock."

His words send me over the edge, and I cry out my release as he follows me, bellowing his pleasure as he thrusts into me, filling me with his cum just like he promised.

When he collapses over me, I wrap my arms around him, breathing heavily and grinning. He kisses my chest over my racing heart. "Isaac is going to kill me."

FORTY-FIVE

"I'm here for my checkup, doc!" Nova sings as she saunters into the lab. Unlike the first time we were here, she doesn't even glance around. Her eyes don't darken, nor is she held back by any ghosts, but her mental health is precarious at the moment with her sister's death and what she went through in the bunker. It's my job to ensure she is okay. She's all that matters.

Bert is healing well, and I'm happy with his progress, so now my sole focus is my love.

I pat the medical bed I moved in here, and she hops up, wearing a cheeky grin on her face. "Oh, kinky," she purrs. "How do you want me, doc? Want me to bend over and cough?"

Grinning, I strap on the BP machine and wait. It's great for someone who endured such a bad stab wound. I want to take some blood too, but she seems to be healing well. "Shirt up," I order.

"Sure thing." She simply rips it off, leaving her breasts free, and my mouth goes dry and I forget how to move or speak. "Doc?" she purrs.

I duck my head and lift the gauze to check her wound, trying to ignore the way her silken skin feels against my knuckles as I touch her. She's my patient here, after all.

I clean and redress it. "You can put your shirt on now, babe," I say, even as my eyes catch on her breasts, my cock hardening as it always does around my girl. "Now, let's talk about you. How are you feeling?"

"Needy. Want to play doctor?" she whispers. "Because I do."

"This is a perfectly normal response to trauma. You are finding ways to make yourself happy. I love you, Nova, but I don't want you to ignore what happened to you."

"Hmm, sure, you're a great doctor. So smart," she teases, rubbing her bare chest against me. "What else?" She reaches down and grips my cock, making me groan and jerk.

"You—" My head falls back as she starts to massage my hard length. "You need to be able to talk about what happened so you can deal with it and we can be aware of any triggers—fuck it."

She giggles. "Thank God. I thought you would talk all day."

"Nova." I really try to remember why this can't happen, but I've never just been her doctor. I'm her lover as well, and I'm helpless when it comes to her.

Sliding from the bed, she stops before me. "Isaac, I know you worry, but I'm fine. We both know we need this. We need some fun and a whole lot of pleasure, so lay your sexy ass down on the table and let me play nurse." The wicked grin she gives me melts all my defences, and when she slides her leggings down, I'm lost in the beauty that is Nova.

Grabbing her hair when she leans in, I tug on the shorter strands. She stiffens for a moment before relaxing. "I love your shorter hair," I tell her, seeing the edge of panic in her eyes. She probably needs this control, so I kiss her softly before shucking off my joggers and shirt as she watches. I throw myself onto the table and lean back, placing an arm under my head. "Go ahead, Nurse Nova."

Her eyes trace my body, making my cock jerk and stand at attention. I stretch to showcase my muscles, loving the way she moans. I've never been more thankful for the drills Louis puts us through than when I see my girl's appreciation for my body. Sliding on top of me, she straddles my thighs as her eyes sweep over me once more like she doesn't know where to start.

"I'm so goddamn lucky," she murmurs.

"No, that's me, sweetheart," I say without even a moment's hesitation.

Sitting on top of me is a goddamn angel, or maybe a devil—all wicked grins, dark hair, tanned muscles, and tattoos. She looks fucking incredible, and as she slides her body across me, I lift so I can kiss around her new scar. The flash of love in her eyes makes me smile as I lie back.

"I'm yours, Nova, have your wicked way with me."

"Oh, I plan to," she promises, pressing her pussy against my bare thigh and grinding into me, letting me feel her wetness. My hands curl into fists so I don't reach for her and drag that pretty pussy up here so she can sit on my face instead. This is her show at her pace. If she wants to be in control, then she's got it.

She could spend hours here, teasing me and working me up, and then leave and I would let her, as long as she keeps looking at me like I'm her goddamn saviour. So despite my need to bend her over and fuck her raw until she screams my name, I wait patiently.

I'm rewarded because my girl isn't cruel. Her lips slide down my throat, and she nips my skin here and there, the sharp pain making me jerk up. Soothing it better, she kisses down and across my chest.

"Nova."

"Shh, you said I could play," she murmurs, rolling her eyes up to mine as her taunting lips slide across my length. I want to throw my arm across my face because it's too much, but I can't look away as she licks up and down my length like it's a fucking ice cream cone. Pleasure spirals through me, and she hasn't even touched me yet.

Giggling, she grips my length and slides her lips down my cock, sucking me all the way to the back of her throat. I see fucking stars. I can't help thrusting into her mouth, trying to take control. She smacks me away, pinning me down as she taunts me, licking and sucking my length until I'm a panting, sweaty mess below her, trying to resist blowing my load before I even get into her glistening pussy.

"Sweetness, swing around. The doctor wants to play too." Her eyes heat and she turns, placing that beautiful ass on my face, and I finally get what I want.

Grabbing her perfect hips, I drag her back, sealing my lips around her engorged clit. Her moans echo around the room as she sucks my cock harder. I'm helpless to do anything but thrust into her hot, wet mouth, fucking it like I will her pussy. All the while, she grinds against my waiting tongue, her taste exploding across it.

Perfection.

I let her rock onto me, her moans and gasps getting louder, and I know she's close. I want her nice and wet before I get inside her because I know I won't last. I never do, not with her. She makes it impossible.

"Baby, if you don't stop, I'm going to come," I warn her.

"Good," she purrs, sucking my cock like a fucking Hoover.

Fuck.

Fighting back the tightening of my balls, I nip her clit before sucking hard. She falls forward with a cry as she comes, smothering me with her pussy and cum just like I wanted.

When she slumps, I lap at her pussy, tasting as much of her as I can before she turns. "I wanted to play."

"Play now." Circling my length, I hold it for her. "Ride me and see how goddamn crazy you make me, sweetheart. I'm on the verge of spilling as it is, but I want inside you before that, so sit that pretty cunt on my cock and ride."

Pouting, she lifts her pussy over me, dragging it across my cock until I growl. She slides down, sitting on my length before working her hips to take me all the way. My head falls back with a thump, a guttural groan escaping my lips as I fight my release. It's fucking hard, worse than any torture and better than any pleasure. Her tight, wet heat grips me so good, it's painful not to move.

"Eyes on me, Isaac," she commands, not moving, so when I force them open and meet hers, she rewards me by lifting up on her knees and dropping back down, swallowing my cock as she bounces.

"Fuck!" I yell, lifting my hips off the bed to bury myself deeper in her. My chest heaves and sweat pours down my body as I fight to last as long as I can.

My back almost bows from the need to empty my balls inside her. "That's it. Watch me, doctor," she flirts, sliding her hands up her body to grip her swaying tits. My eyes lock on her as she tweaks and twists her nipples, her cunt tightening around me as she chases her own pleasure.

"Feed them to me," I demand breathlessly. "Let me taste them."

"Say please," she purrs, riding me harder.

"Please, sweetheart," I beg.

She leans forward, and my cock slides deeper into her as she feeds me her pretty rosy nipples. I suck and attack them like a madman, unable to stop. She rocks harder on my length before sitting up. I reach for her but she slaps me away, sliding her hand down and rubbing her clit as she lifts and drops.

"I'm so close," she says. "Isaac, I want you to come with me. I want to feel it."

"Baby, I've been there since the moment you walked in here. Make yourself come, use me, I'm yours."

"I know." Her cunt pulses around me, and I know she's close. "God, I love you. I love you so much."

"I love you, sweetheart, now come for me. I want to feel you milk my release. Let go." Whimpering, she closes her eyes and her body jerks. Not a moment later, her pussy clamps down around me and her scream bursts free as she milks my cock, shaking and twisting as she comes.

Snarling, I reach down and grab her thighs, hauling her back and forth on my cock until I follow her into oblivion. My release splashes inside of her as she whines. I keep her there, impaled on my cock, as I fill her, and then she collapses forward onto my chest. Wrapping my arms around her, I try to get my racing heart to slow, even as our bodies are still locked together in bliss.

I kiss her sweaty head and hold her tighter. "We've got the rest of our lives to play, Nova."

Grinning, she places a kiss over my heart. "I can't wait, doctor."

Me fucking too.

FORTY-SIX

"So, Jonas has been working on this for me, but I thought you should all know that I don't plan to give the military what they want."

Nova's head jerks up, but the others don't look surprised as Louis leans back on the sofa.

"I don't like what they plan to use the research for, nor do I like being used for other motives. They won't accept this, so we are planning for the worst-case scenario. They expect us next week, but we are going early—the element of surprise. I'm thinking one last mission, but only if we all agree."

Nico nods. "Fuck yeah."

"I agree." Isaac worries on his lips, glancing at Nova. "I was worried about what it would mean for all of us if they had the research. His notes are substantial, so they could continue where he stopped."

"You know I'm in." Dimitri shrugs.

"Nova?" I ask worriedly. I won't do anything she doesn't want.

"I've been worried but unsure how to bring it up. I think they wanted to take the research from us all along. So, what's the plan?"

Grinning, I lean closer. "We break in, baby. We sneak into the super-secret bunker we helped booby-trap and give them our polite answer of fuck off."

She smiles. "And if he says no to our polite answer?"

"Then we say it not so politely." Louis grins. "We are sneaking in to show them they are weak against us. They have forgotten why they hired us, so it's time to show them. One last mission to protect the research and our family."

"Fuck yeah." Nova nods.

"I get to do the killing!" I call, my hand shooting up.

"No killing," Louis snaps. "We don't need the military on our asses for the rest of our lives."

"Why? I've heard there are some nice no extradition countries," I mutter but deflate. "Fine, no killing unless they try to kill me or you, then all bets are off."

"Thank you." Louis sighs, knowing that's as good as he will get.

"Want to see the project?" I wiggle my eyebrows at Nova, and she grins.

"You know I do."

Rushing around the table, I throw her over my shoulder as the others simply watch us and then continue planning.

Planning is boring anyway. I much prefer this.

I drop her to her feet in the room I claimed. It's a bit of a mess, with weapons and clothes everywhere, but she doesn't care as I wrap my arms around her and show her the device I built to Dimitri's specifications.

"What is it?" she asks, reaching out to touch it.

"An EMP, just in case." I chuckle, running my nose up her neck. "But I really just wanted to have you all to myself."

"Is that right?" She grins up at me. "And what could you want to do all alone up here with me?"

Backing her into the nearest wall, I press my hand above her, grinning down at my girl. I love seeing her so happy. "I can think of some things, but they all lead to the same thing."

"And what's that?" she murmurs as I reach down and hoist her up, wrapping those perfect legs around me as I grind her against my hardness.

I run my nose along her neck once more, inhaling the scent that is all my girl, and when I reach her ear, I bite down on the lobe as she moans. "You screaming for me," I whisper as she shudders.

"Then make me," she demands.

"Oh, I plan to." I grin, rocking into her cunt and letting her feel my desire for her. "I want you on your knees, and I want that pretty ass. I know they have all been in this greedy cunt this week."

"Jonas," she whimpers, rocking into me.

"That's it, get nice and wet for me because you'll be taking my big, fat cock in that pretty little ass until you can't walk. We are taking back every single inch of you, baby, so hold on."

Her eyes flare. She knows what I mean and she wants it. She doesn't want there to be any part of her we have not touched. Turning, I toss her on the bed, watching her bounce, and before she can roll away, I pounce. I roll her onto her stomach, yank her pants down, and slide my fingers through her wet folds.

"So fucking wet," I growl. "Is this all for me, baby? Have you been waiting for me to pin you down and fuck you like you want?"

"Yes." She pushes back into my hand, but I don't let her move as I pinch her clit, her ragged scream filling the air as I abuse it. I keep her there until she's on the verge of coming, and then I pull back, leaving her snarling.

Chuckling, I slide my trousers down, kicking them off the bed before I drag my cock along her pussy. "Don't you dare come yet," I warn her. "I'm going to get my cock nice and wet. If you come, I'll get myself off and leave you here without getting my cock."

"Fucking hell," she grumbles, burying her face in the pillow even as she pushes her ass out.

Sliding my cock along her folds, I get my length nice and wet, purposely bumping her clit until she's whining and fighting not to come. Grinning at how fucking cute she is, I slip my cock inside her, working it into her pussy with slow, soft thrusts that have her rocking back, and when she's about to come again, I slide out.

"Jonas," she screams, pounding her fist into the bed. "If you don't make me come, I'm going to kill you."

"I'd love it, and you know that," I purr as I lift her hips, pressing her ass back and pushing her thighs farther open. "But okay, baby."

Pressing against her ass, I force my cock inside her, watching her stretch around it. She pushes back to take more, and feeling mean, I slam all the way into her. She screams as she tries to jerk away, but I don't let her. I make her feel every hard inch of my cock in her little ass. When I start to move, she whines and fights to get off my cock, but I don't let her, instead sliding my hand down and pinching her clit again.

"Come," I snarl.

She detonates at my command, almost squirting as she cries out. Groaning at the sight, I rub her clit mercilessly as I hammer into her ass, mixing pain and pleasure.

I pummel into her little ass, watching her cheeks jiggle from the force. Her dripping pussy clenches, wanting to be filled too, so I slide my fingers down and work them into her, stretching her with my hand and cock. She cries out and pushes back to take more, fighting me as she claws at the bed.

She's a perfect fucking sight.

I'd win a thousand missions or wars to come back to her.

"Fuck, baby," I growl, hammering into her as I fuck her with my fingers. "I fucking love this so much. I love the way you take me. I love how nothing is ever too much. I'm going to fill you with so much cum, it's going to overflow, and then later, I'm going to take that pretty mouth too. I will fill every single one of your holes with it. Fuck, I even saw a video where they fucked someone's urethra. I might even try that. I don't want any part of you to go untouched by me. I want to own every inch like you own every inch of me."

"Jonas!" she screams as I work another finger inside her.

My words turn to a growl as she clenches around me. I know she's close, but I want this to last forever. I want to be locked inside of her until the day I die, my name on her lips and her taste on my tongue.

"Don't you fucking dare." I smack her ass hard, making her cry out. "Not yet. Don't you dare. I want you like this."

"Please." Her nails rip at the bedding. "Fuck, J, I can't." Her words slur as she pushes back, impaling herself on my hand and cock. I feel her clenching tighter, needing to come.

"Fuck." I fight my own, feeling it building at the base of my spine. I fight as hard as I can, but I should have known that I always lose when it comes to us. She will always win, and I love it that way.

Roaring, I press into her ass, my release exploding out of me. It sends her off the edge like she was waiting for it, her ass tightening around me and dragging more from me as I spurt and rock into her tight little hole.

Groaning, I pull out and slam back in, fucking my release into her as she whines, her cunt fluttering around my fingers as I pull them out. Her breathing is ragged as she slumps beneath me. I slowly pull my cock out, watching my release spill from her ass, and I almost come again at the sight.

Sliding my fingers through my mess, I watch our combined cum glisten, and I know nothing will ever be more beautiful.

I thrust my fingers into her pussy, coated in her cream, and stroke her as she comes for me again. Groaning, she lies beneath me, shaking with aftershocks, her eyes closed in bliss.

I lie down next to her and let her spoon me, both of us covered in cum and sweat. "That's what I wanted to show you."

"I'm so glad you did." She giggles, burying her head against my neck.

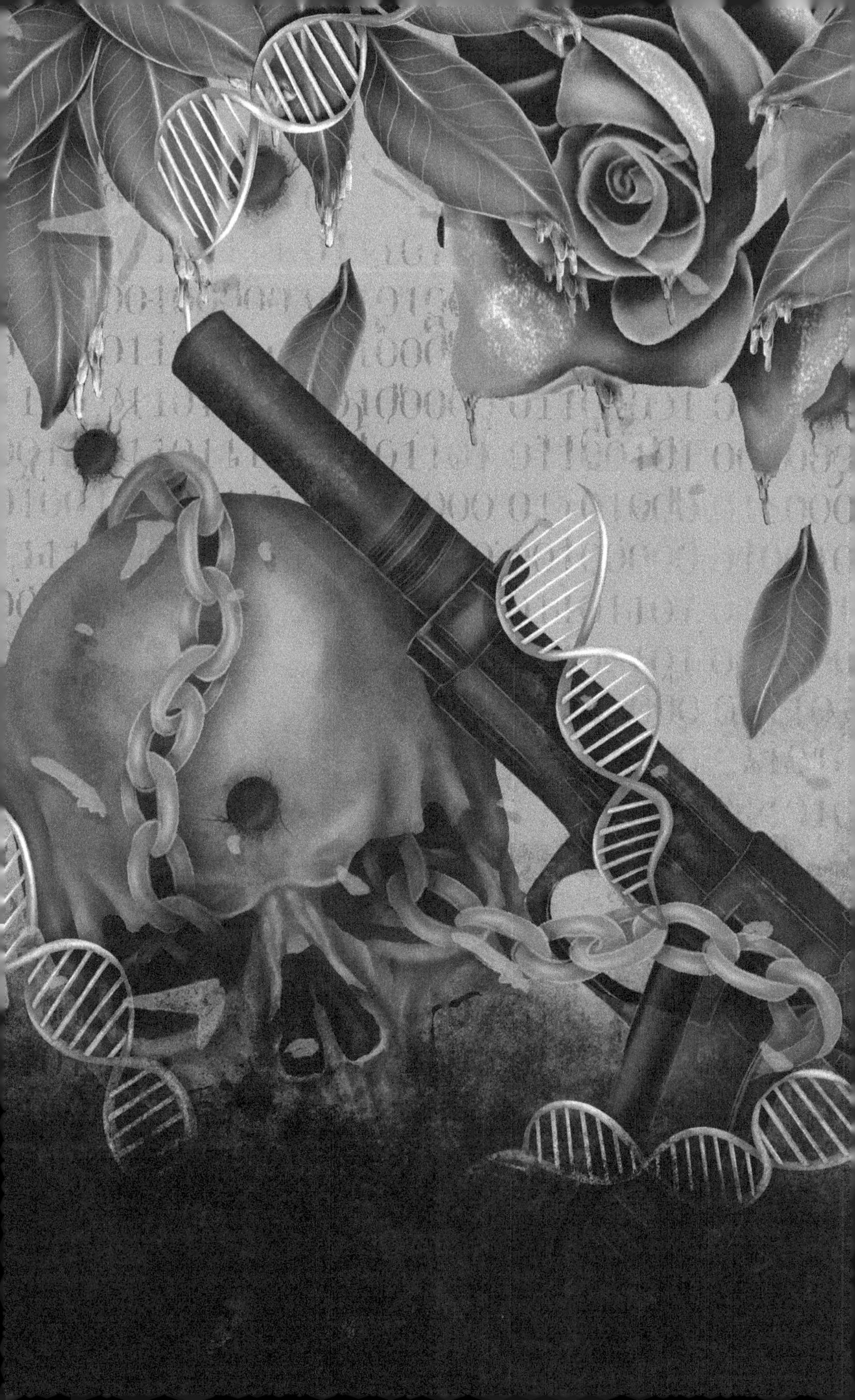

FORTY-SEVEN

It's been a while since I saw the base, months in fact, but so much has changed since then that it feels like a lifetime ago. When I first came here, I was an angry, lost little girl, and now I'm a scarred, hard woman protecting the men she loves. I'm part of a family, a unit, and I'm fighting for something much bigger than petty revenge.

I am fighting for love.

They don't know that we are here this time. Dimitri knows the layout, as well as every trap and alarm in the bunker. Although there is only one way in, we have ways of getting around without being seen. Last time, Jonas happily showed me traps and tricks, but now we are sneaking in.

One last mission together.

One against our very own military.

This won't be like breaking into my father's place. They had soldiers there, sure, but this place is meant to be a fortress, and the soldiers here are active duty and waiting for a fight.

We park as far away as we can so the cameras don't see us beforehand. When we are close enough, Dimitri loops the footage so the alarms don't sound, causing them to go into lockdown. In the darkness, wearing matching black outfits, we share a grin. Adrenaline pumps through me, along with excitement.

I was made for this, and as much as I hate it, it couldn't be more obvious as we effortlessly weave through the many booby traps. We avoid the barn, knowing it's the most heavily guarded area. The scrapyard looks even more abandoned and maze-like in the dark. Jonas points out any areas that are rigged with bombs and sensors and we avoid them, luckily knowing the path through without even making a noise. We simply hop over the landmines and hope they haven't set anymore. Jonas assures me they wouldn't have because before they came along, apparently their security was shit. The guys helped them upgrade it, which works in our favour now.

Once we're through the hill, we head up the sharp incline, which is open ground, to the bunker. We don't spot any guards here, but to be sure, we stay low to the ground. No words are exchanged, since all of us know our roles and how important this is. At the top, I crouch and wait, knowing Dimitri is going to manually open the bunker so we don't alert anyone. I scan our surroundings, watching our backs.

Once we reach the elevator that takes us down, Dimitri pops open a panel as we crouch and protect his back, the night giving us good coverage. We work silently and in a moment, the doors open and we drop to the platform. Unlike last time, there's no escort waiting, and we rush off. We need to find the general before they find us. We want answers, and we want him to understand.

Guns up, we sweep the corridors. Dimitri turned the cameras off, and Jonas plants the EMP while we protect him. We see some soldiers ahead, so we duck into the side rooms and wait for them to pass. My breathing is calm and even as Nico presses against my back. I feel his hardness, even through his suit, and try to focus as desire builds within me.

"Behave," I mutter with a grin.

"Clear," Dimitri murmurs, and I open the door, moving left as Nico moves right, walking backwards to watch our backs. The general should be sleeping at this time, but when we reach the stairs to his room, Dimitri halts us.

"He's in his office. Looks like he fell asleep there. Change of plan."

His office is through the base's hub, but we have no choice. We head that way instead and find a few bored, tired soldiers monitoring the screens, even as they loop.

In the glass office up top, the general reclines back in his chair, his mouth open on a snore. "Target acquired," I murmur. "Five bogies, backs to the door. Unprepared," I report as I move backwards and press my back to the wall.

"Ideas?" Louis asks.

"Three of us sneak in and knock them out." I shrug. "Easy and silent."

Louis frowns, clearly not liking it, but he nods. "Nova, Nico, you're with me. D, you're on cameras. Jonas, watch our backs. Isaac, make sure he doesn't kill anyone."

"Ah, man," Jonas mutters, but we are already moving.

Louis counts down, and when his fist clenches, Nico rips the door open and we move in quickly and silently, sliding behind some desks as one guy turns to look. The door is shut once more and he frowns, searching the room before looking back at the cameras. I point to the two huddled together on the left, playing cards. Nico nods to the middle one, and Louis gestures to the two on the right. I move into position as they do the same.

Once we are all in place, I count down, and on one, I surge into action, stepping behind my two targets and trusting them to do the same. I slam two injections into their necks as they start to turn. "What?" one mumbles before the drug takes hold, and then they slump.

I glance over to see the others were quickly taken care of as well and grin. It's good having a doctor who has access to sedatives on staff. These soldiers should be out cold for a while. The doors open, and the others join us. Isaac and Jonas instantly bar it as we head to the general's office.

We file in and take up our positions. I sit in the opposite chair, lifting my feet and kicking the general's off the desk. They fall with a thump and he windmills his arms to keep his balance as he wakes. His eyes widen when he sees me, and I wave.

"What the fuck is the meaning of this?" he snarls, and when he sees all of us, he looks for his men, all of whom are sleeping. "Why didn't you tell us that you were here?"

"We wanted to have this conversation privately." Louis shrugs, sitting on the edge of the desk. "Ah, don't press that button, sir. I would hate to have to break your hand."

"He will," I say helpfully. "Or I will."

The general moves his hand from the emergency button, crossing his arms as he glares at us. "Where's the research?" he demands, still thinking he's in charge.

The fool.

"Not with us," Louis answers. "We want to know why you want it. Before you snap or answer in anger, know that your life depends on how you answer, general, and we will know if you are lying. After all, we were created to be the best."

"It is none of your business. It's a matter of national security." He huffs. "Now hand over the research. It belongs to the government."

"Do you plan to use it?" I demand, leaning forward. "Think carefully."

"All research will be contained and tested to ensure its safety." He narrows his eyes. "It's better that we use it than some other country. Think of the lives we could save in battle. Dr. Davis went about it wrong, but we can do better—"

"Who else is helping you with it?"

"No one so far. I will present it to the ruling body for testing. You must understand. After all, look at you—"

I lift my gun and blow out his brains before looking at Louis. "No one will ever use that research. This ends with him." Standing, I put my gun away as the alarms blare.

"Fuck, I thought you said no killing. Why did she get to?" Jonas whines just as soldiers burst through the door, and I grin as Louis shakes his head but holds up his hands.

"Do as I say and we'll make it out of this alive," he says.

I grin at him. "Where's the fun in that?" I hold my hands up anyway as soldiers surge into the office. We are ordered to kneel and then handcuffed and led into the room below. A half-dressed man storms into the room. I remember him from our first time here. He's second-in-command, I believe, but I leave the talking to Louis since I tend to shoot first.

"Who the fuck killed the general, and how the fuck did they get in here?" He turns his glare on us. "Answers!" he barks.

Yup, military all the way through.

"We have intelligence that the general was working with Dr. Davis on the banned experimental program to expand the human brain. We were simply doing as we were ordered and executing the mission." Louis is a good liar.

"Do you have proof? You just cannot go around assassinating generals!" he roars.

"We had proof, yes, and we did our mission. Are you going back on your terms now? We did as ordered."

"Dr. Davis?" he asks, his arms crossed. It's clear his general hasn't kept him in the loop.

"Dead."

"The research?"

We all try not to stiffen at that, but it's just genuine curiosity on his part.

"Dead and burned with his body," Louis replies. "It's all gone. The mission is done."

"Fucking hell. This is a clusterfuck. I want these idiots fired" —he points at the drugged men— "and anyone on the perimeter brought up on charges. You six, get the fuck out of my sight. The general might have wanted to work with you, but I sure as shit did not, and when they come around asking questions, I will not protect you. Get out of here now."

"We are free to go?" Louis queries, making damn sure.

"Yes, go before I change my mind. If the general was involved, then you did as ordered. It doesn't mean I fucking like it, but we keep our deals. You're hired mercs, though, and nothing else. Go." Our hands are unlocked, and we are shoved to our feet.

Before we can get into any more trouble, Nico grabs me, and Louis grabs Jonas, and they drag us out. Soldiers escort us up top, where I breathe in the fresh air of the night as sunlight streaks through the sky.

"I guess we didn't need the EMP," I remark.

"Nah, I'll set it off just for fun." Jonas giggles.

Dimitri groans. "Oh, God, get us out of here before we are arrested and thrown into a dark cell somewhere."

The soldiers escort us down the hill just as we see a troop doing early-morning drills and exercises. I guess they didn't hear the alarms, or they have been given the all-clear.

When we get closer, it's clear they are on weapons training, with open crates holding grenades and rocket launchers.

We stop to watch them, but when I glance over, Jonas has a rocket launcher on his shoulder and is pointing it at the drilling soldiers.

"Jonas!" I snap.

He glances between me and the men behind me and pouts. "But they said I could play with it."

I groan. "They didn't mean to shoot them."

"Well, then they should have said that." Pulling the launcher down off his shoulder, he drops it back into the box, still pouting, and stomps away. "I never get to kill anyone anymore."

Wincing at the soldiers who are unsure whether to shoot or laugh, I follow Jonas, and we reach the car in ten minutes. Once there, our escort disappears back up the hill.

We just got away with espionage and murder, but the research is safe and so are we.

When we reach the car, I look over at Louis. "Now what?" I ask.

Before I can react, he grabs the back of my head, yanks me over, and slams his lips to mine. Groaning into the kiss, I return it as the others whistle and cheer, and when he pulls away, he says, "Now, baby? We plan the rest of our lives."

FORTY-EIGHT

As I sit at the table, my eyes once more go to the empty chair left for Ana. I love this house and the memories I have here, but in the few days since we have been back, I haven't been able to relax. I wake up with my heart hurting, and I look in every room for her. It almost feels like I'm trapped in the past once more.

Maybe I am.

Maybe I have always been trapped here in one way or another.

As a child, it was my father who kept me here, but as an adult, it was my duty and love for my sister.

Now that both are gone, I'm left in the empty shell and surrounded by ghosts, but the living must live. I don't think I can do that here. I left once, but I was running, knowing the rubber band between me and this place would snap me back one day. This time, I know it won't be a forever goodbye, but it will be an ending. I'll finally be putting my past to rest, which will allow me to move on.

At the moment, we linger in purgatory, but it's time to rejoin the world.

Louis is talking with the guys as they debate house options for the children. Dimitri has found that they are all orphans, either stolen from bad situations, the street, or from a broken system. Nobody misses them, and nobody is looking for them. They have nothing to go back to. We are determined to leave them better off than we found them. Since my father's death, I've become extremely wealthy, not that I give a shit, but now that Ana is . . . Yeah, I'm the sole benefactor of the Davis estate and everything that entails.

Well, fuck him and fuck his money.

An idea comes to me, one that instantly makes me grin and lifts my heart. "I can't stay here." Every eye turns to me, but my focus is on the chair where my sister should sit. "I can't. I can't be trapped here anymore. I have been tied to this house in one way or another since birth. It's time to let go of the ghosts and truly live like you keep telling me." I meet their gazes, seeing their confusion. "I can't stay, but I refuse to leave Annie here alone. If she wasn't here, I'd let this place rot for everything he did, but it's just a house, a house my sister loved and grew up in. A house we became a family in."

I reach over and take Bert's hand. "A house where I learned what love really is. I can't stay, and she can't leave." I look at the maps of choices. "But they can. Let's give him one last fuck you and make this their house. There are enough rooms, and we can get staff for them and fund it with his blood money. He owes them that. Give them a better chance at life and give Annie some company. Let it be filled with laughter and love once more."

"Miss Nova, are you sure?" Bert whispers.

"I want nothing from him. Not this house, not a pound of his money. I've always made my own way, and I always will, but it should be used for good and to make up for what he's done. He'd turn in his grave if he knew, so yeah, I'm sure. Let's bring this old, haunted house back to life. Let's give it a purpose." I smile sadly at Bert. "I know you love this place despite everything. You are always welcome to stay and work—"

"My home is where you are," he says. "I only ever stayed for you and Miss Ana. It was never the job or the house; it was you. If you will have me, I will go with you." He looks at my men. "I like to take care of you. You are my family now as much as Miss Nova, as long as it's okay with you."

"You are always welcome wherever we go," I tell him as the others nod.

"You always have a place with us." Louis smiles. "Wherever that is. Nova?"

"I don't know. I just know that there has to be something for us out there. A place where we can learn to live again and heal from the horrors in our pasts. Where we can just . . . thrive." Smiling at them, I reach out and lay my hand on the table. "When I was down in the bunker, it's all I thought about—a place of our own, a place for a family."

"Then we will find it," Louis murmurs.

"We can still . . . work on the side, right?" Jonas asks worriedly.

Laughing, I wink at him. "I think we will need to in order to stop us all from going completely insane. We can't change who we are, but I think we can afford a little slice of peace, don't you? Besides, it's now our mission to protect that research."

"I'm in." Dimitri shrugs. "Where you go, I go."

"I agree. I think I'd like somewhere warm for a change." Isaac grins.

"Fuck it, I'm in. I'd just stalk you anyways." Jonas chuckles.

I look at Nico, who rolls his eyes like he can't believe I have to ask. "We're a family."

"Louis?" I query.

"I agree. Where you go, we go. I think you're right though. We deserve a slice of peace. We have spent so much time tracking your father and getting our revenge, we never truly got to live, not even as kids. We deserve it, and you deserve it as well, Nova. Let's go find our home together."

Their hands cover mine until we are one.

One family.

My eyes go back to the chair, and I know she would like this decision. I know she would be happy with me finally letting go and moving on. It doesn't mean I'll forget her. It just means I'll carry her with me on my adventures, wherever they may take us.

It didn't take us long to pack up our stuff. We are so used to being on the go, everything is already packed and we travel light. Bert, on the other hand, took longer, and we had to help him pack everything, but after Jonas threw his clothes in a bag, he kicked him out, refolding everything and tightly packing it in little cubes that blew my mind. We've set plans into motion for the house. Bert was the one to interview his replacement, and he was happy with the lady he chose. She will help maintain the house and care for the children and report back to us. There will also be other staff on hand, such as teachers and everything they could ever need. They will all turn up tomorrow, and we want to be gone before then.

I leave the guys to pack the car under Bert's watchful gaze and head to the tree, my hands twisting before me. "I can't leave without saying good-bye, though it's not goodbye forever. I'll come back and visit and check on the house . . . and you, but I can't stay here forever, not even for you. I know you'd be happy that I'm putting myself first for once and giving life a go, as you used to say. And of course, they are by my side. I love them, Annie. I really do. I'm glad you got to know that before . . ." Swallowing hard, I close my eyes for a moment and feel the sun on my face. "I'm going to miss you so much. I don't think it will ever stop hurting, but I'm taking you with me. Wherever we wander, wherever we go, you'll be there. I'll live enough for both of us, and when the time comes, I'll meet you beyond." Leaning down, I brush away some dirt from the headstone and smile sadly, tears once more filling my eyes, but I don't let them fall.

"I love you, Annie. I always have. Thank you for being my little sister. Thank you for teaching me that it's okay to love again." Standing, I wipe off my hands and glance over to see them all waiting. Nico is perched at the open door with his shades on. "I promise to show you one hell of a life, and maybe a few more missions." I chuckle. "Watch over them for me, Annie." I glance back down at her. "Take care of Sam. Bye."

I force my feet to the car, each step lighter than the last, and when a light breeze brushes over me, pushing me towards it, I smile, knowing she's there. Nico slides inside, and before I follow, I glance back at the house. I'll come back to check on the kids, but I'll never live here again.

This manor holds so much pain and so many ghosts for me—both good and bad. It's where I lived. It's where I hurt, grieved, and loved. It's where

I learned I was unbreakable and where I learned I could be unstoppable. It will always be where I grew up, but now it's time to find a home, not just a house.

It's time to find my forever with them.

With my family.

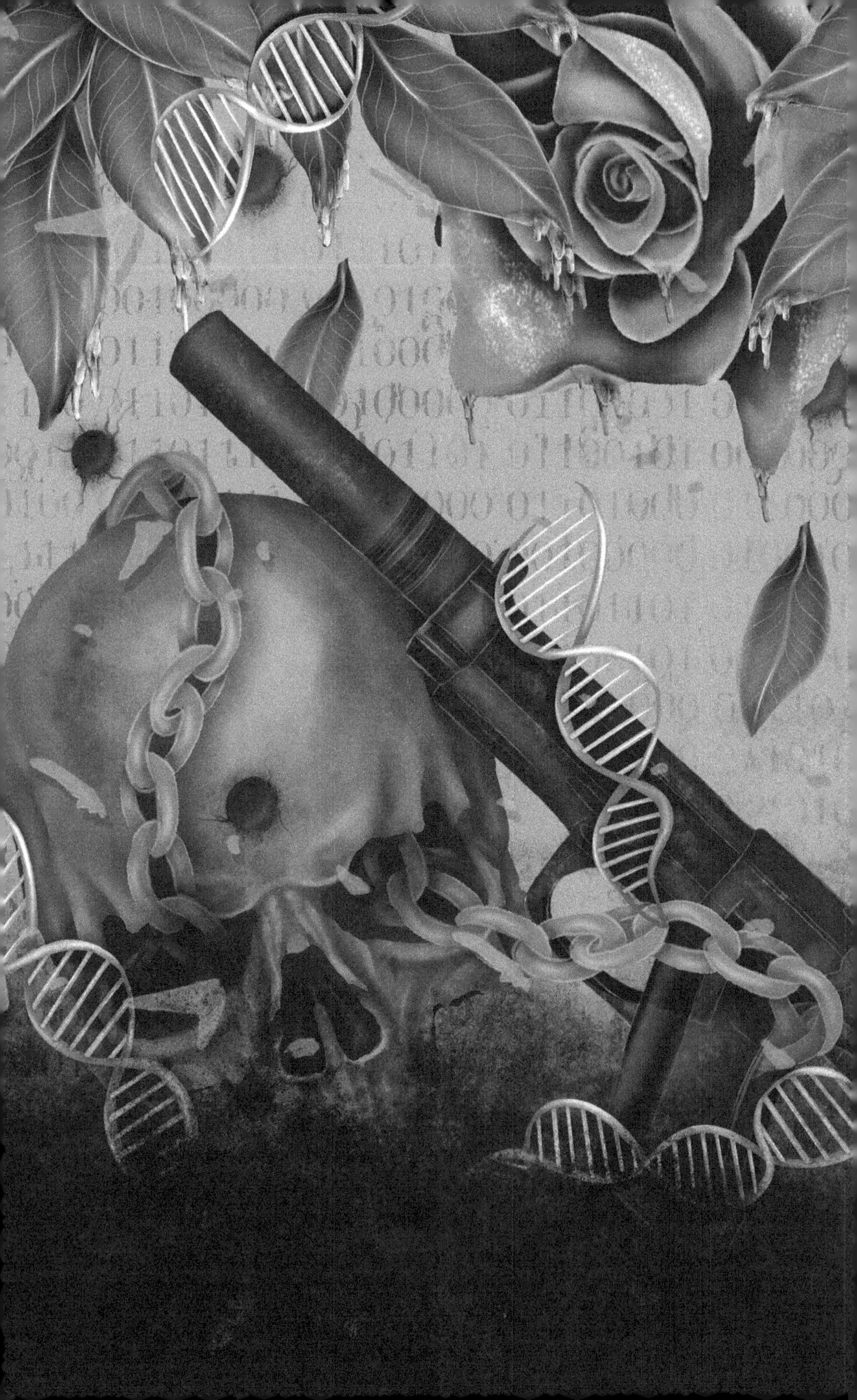

FORTY-NINE

"**A**re you sure you want to go this way?" I ask for the tenth time, glancing back at Nova who's staring out of the window. She has a look in her eye that I can't describe, like she knows something we don't. When she turns to me with a soft smile, I know she does.

"I can almost feel it. Keep going," she demands.

Over the last month, we have travelled around Paris so Isaac could see his old home like he never did before, but she didn't want to live anywhere in France. We then explored Spain, Germany, Norway, Poland, and hell, even Iceland. When you have a private plane, you can go wherever you want, and it seems like Nova wants something very specific. She's smiling more, and she's starting to heal. I love seeing my girl so happy, but she hasn't found somewhere to settle down like she wants.

Not until the plane landed in Italy.

The last places were chosen at random, just by placing a finger on the map, but as soon as she stepped out here, something changed in her. It's like she looked out at the view and said this is it. For the last few days, we have been driving around Italy, exploring the scenery, experiencing the culture, and evaluating all it has to offer. Every time, she gets this look in her eye and tells us to keep going.

I don't care where we stay, just as long as it's with her, so I turn down the dirt road she randomly told me to stop at. There's a little village sign posted not far from here. We passed some old chateaus and wineries, and the rolling hills are beyond beautiful. There's something so pure and real about where we are, but this dirt road looks like it leads to nowhere.

Dimitri has a physical map open. She wouldn't even let him use his satellites or computers, which is making him cranky, but we are all determined to find the place where she wants to spend the rest of our lives, to make our family, our future. Fuck, I'll travel the world twice over to find it if that's what it takes.

I just want her to be happy and for us to be together.

Keeping my hands on the wheel as the SUV bumps over the dirt road, I glance to either side of us. I only see rolling fields until we crest a hill, and on the other side is a house. It appears to be an older chateau with a few outbuildings surrounding it. It almost looks like a farm, and up front is a for sale sign.

Nova leans forward, smiling at it. "This is it. I can feel it. Can you?"

I nod as I look at her smiling face. "I can, baby."

"Then let's go!"

I rev the engine and we drive the rest of the way. When we pull up outside of the house, I cringe. It needs a lot of work, but as I get out and survey the land, I realise it clearly has potential.

"It needs work," Louis comments.

"Eh, so do we." Nova shrugs. "Perfect would be boring." She smiles at the house just as the two front doors open and an older lady in a summer dress peers out.

"Are you here for the viewing?" she asks, glancing over at us.

"We are," Nova replies and heads her way. "I hope that's okay. I couldn't just drive past." She peers around. "This place is beautiful."

"It was my grandmother's and hers before it." She smiles at Nova. "It was here before most of the rest of the world was. Come on in."

We troop in after the older lady, and my jaw drops at the inside of the house. It's beautiful. Huge windows framed by old-style curtains with gauze allow the sunlight to hit the brick walls, and the floors are a mix of old styles that somehow seem warm and homey. The lady guides us around, showing us a grand dining room big enough for us. There are old carved fireplaces and even a library with a sitting room, all done in robin's-egg blue and white, with comfy-looking sofas and gorgeous paintings and rugs. I tune out her voice as I walk around, imagining us here. There is room for us outside to spar and train, and there are enough bedrooms for all of us, but the master is my favourite.

Double doors lead out onto a veranda, and the bed itself is huge and up on a small platform. White sofas face a roaring fire with a painting above it. The en suite has a gigantic tub with a window before it, looking out over the hills. Every room is clearly well-loved and has been designed for the people living here. It feels like a fairy tale. Bert gets excited about the kitchen, oohing and aahing over the appliances and talking with the lady about recipes as we wander around and explore.

It's a strange mix of old Italian and updated tastes, and honestly, Nova is right. It's incredible. The outside needs work, but all the best things do. I could imagine us here, curled up together before the fire, laughing and joking at the dining table, and exploring the land.

I could see us here.

I could see Nova here, and when I turn to her, it's clear she can too. She's smiling in a way I've never seen before, appearing almost hopeful.

There's a pool out back, overlooking the valley, surrounded by perfectly manicured bushes and roses, and when we join them again, Bert smiles at us widely. He's clearly already in love with the place, and the older lady showing us looks hopeful.

"This place is incredible," Nova gushes.

"It is. It needs some work, since I've not been able to keep up with it since my husband died, but I just want the next owners to enjoy their lives here like my children and I have. I want it to be filled with laughter again."

"That's exactly what we are looking for," Nova tells her. "A home, a place where we can just live and enjoy life."

"I've raised all my children here, and I can tell you that no matter where you go in the world, there is no place like home, and when you feel it, you know it," she says wisely.

"I couldn't agree more. My name is Nova, by the way. It's nice to meet you." Nova reaches out to shake her hand.

"Hi, Nova, I'm Anabel."

We all freeze, and Nova's eyes widen as she shakes the older lady's hand. "Anabel?" she repeats.

"Yes, Anabel." She seems confused.

"A beautiful name," Nova says and glances back at us with a knowing smile. "Almost like it led us home."

"I'm sorry?" Anabel asks.

"I said we'll take it," Nova replies. "This is where we are meant to be. This is home."

LOUIS

Dimitri is more than happy to buy the house with the money he says is ours. Nova is hesitant, but he insists. Anabel suggested a price that I was pretty sure was nowhere near what we should be paying, but when we asked, she simply said that some things were meant to be, and seeing her family house loved and restored once more would be enough.

We get the keys the very next day.

It only took us a few hours after we moved in to find a place to hide the research. There's a wine cellar under the house, which can only be accessed through a trapdoor in the kitchen. Dimitri starts to heighten security, but we lock the research down there and leave it to be forgotten.

All we ever wanted was to stop this from happening to anyone else. We succeeded, and now we get to live. It won't be easy to settle into civilian life, but we deserve it. That doesn't mean I won't keep my eyes peeled for anything we can help with—after all, old habits die hard—but for now, it's time for us to enjoy our lives.

Here, we are not super soldiers or experiments. Here, we just get to be, and as I sip my coffee, watching the beautiful sunrise, my family's laughter reaching me, I can't help but let the tension roll from my shoulders for the first time ever.

No enemies or missions.

No responsibilities.

My only purpose is to be happy.

Arms slide around me from behind, making me grin as I close my eyes. "Morning, beautiful."

"Morning." She sighs. "I woke up and you were gone."

"I couldn't miss this." Putting down my coffee, I turn and wrap my arms around her, turning us once more to face the sunrise as she picks up my coffee and starts to drink it. We always seem to share, so I've started taking it how she likes it, even if it's too sweet for me. I kiss the top of her head as I hold the love of my life in my arms in our new forever home.

"It's beautiful, isn't it?" she whispers.

"It is, but it will never be as beautiful as you."

She giggles, elbowing me. "Corny bastard."

"You love it." I grin, kissing her head once more. "We get forever, Nova, but I promise it won't be long enough with you." She turns to peer up at me, and I smile softly down at her, my heart leaping with joy. "Promise me this is it—us, this house, our family . . . If you try to leave us again, I'll chain you to us forever."

"It's us, baby. I promise." She leans up, coffee forgotten, and interlaces her hands behind my neck. The feel of her warm body against mine makes my dick harden but I ignore it, soaking in her comfort as I press my head to hers.

"What shall we do with all the time we have?" I grin.

"Oh, I don't know. I can think of a few things," she teases just as the sounds of Jonas's maniacal laughter and Nico's swearing reach us.

I groan as she laughs. "It's a good thing I'm stuck with them," I mutter as she kisses me and grabs the coffee, sliding past me.

"Well, when they get to be too much, you could always just hide away with me," she purrs as she slides backwards into the house. "Like right now, I plan on taking a very long, very hot bath."

Before she can run, I have her draped over my shoulder as I stride through the house. "Bert, the kids are yours for an hour."

"Yay!" Jonas yells as Nico groans loudly.

She laughs as I spank her and bring her back to our bedroom to spend the next fifty years ravishing the love of my life.

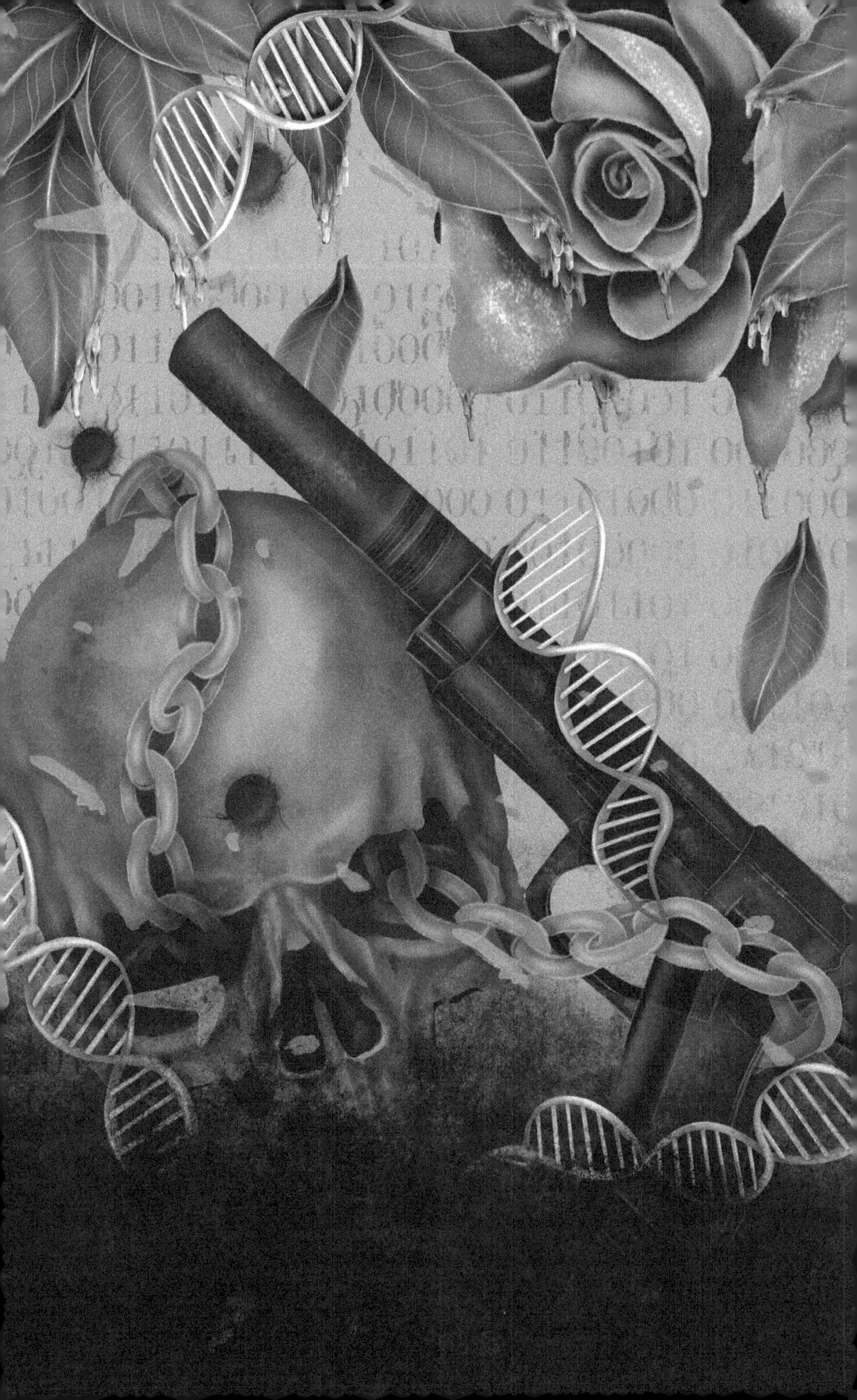

FIFTY

"Isaac!"

I jerk awake, and I'm out of the empty bed where my love should be quicker than I can blink. Thundering down the stairs in search of her panicked scream, I pick up a weapon on the way. Jonas has hidden them around the entire house—old habits. We might be settling into civilian life, but we cannot change who we are.

We are still soldiers.

It's been a week since we've moved in and we've settled into bliss, apart from now, when my heart races in worry. I don't hear the guys, only Nova's scream echoing in my head. What if she's hurt? What if someone came after us?

I smash through the front door, frantically searching for her. "Nova!" I scream.

"Isaac!"

I follow the sound around the house and slide to a stop when I find Nova. She's almost crying, staring down at a donkey lying before her with its leg in her lap.

"Isaac. Help him. He broke his leg." She pouts as I continue to stare, my adrenaline pumping through me.

"You screamed because you found a donkey that has a broken leg?" I scrub the back of my head in confusion, sliding my knife into my pants. "Babe, I'm a doctor, not a vet."

"You're a hero." She widens her eyes. "Please, Isaac? We can't leave him in pain."

I blink before dropping to my knees before her. "Okay, go get my bag."

She nods. "It's going to be okay," she tells the donkey, who whines and gently places his foot down as she rushes inside.

Scratching my head, I stare at the donkey. "It can't be too different from a human, right?" I tell him. "I guess we'll find out."

Taking hold of its legs, I wince when it cries. "Shh, it's going to be okay," I say. "I just have to check this fracture." I talk to it like it's one of my patients, and when Nova comes back, I prop up the leg as best as I can and give him some pain meds before leaning back.

"We can move him into the old barn. There's still hay there, and we can give him food until he gets—" My voice cuts off as she knocks me to the floor, kissing my face.

"My hero!" She grins down at me.

"Always," I reply, smiling up at her.

DIMITRI

"Why the fuck is there a donkey in the barn?" I hear Nico yell, and I shake my head with a laugh.

I focus on the screens before me. I've checked on the kids every day. They seem to be settling in well, and I'm glad for that. I also check on my investments. We have enough money for this lifetime and ten over, so our girl will never want for anything since she refuses to touch any of her father's money.

A message comes through just then, an old contact of mine offering us a job. Smiling, I hit accept before turning the computers off and getting to my feet. My eyes linger on the photo of Bas and me. We were so young.

Pressing my fingers to my lips, I kiss the tips and then press them to the photo. "Love you," I tell him.

"D, come see this!" Nova laughs.

Grinning, I turn to the stairs. "Coming, my love." Glancing back at Bas, I smile. "I'll take care of her for us." I go to join my family, leaving the screens I once claimed as home behind and joining the real world instead.

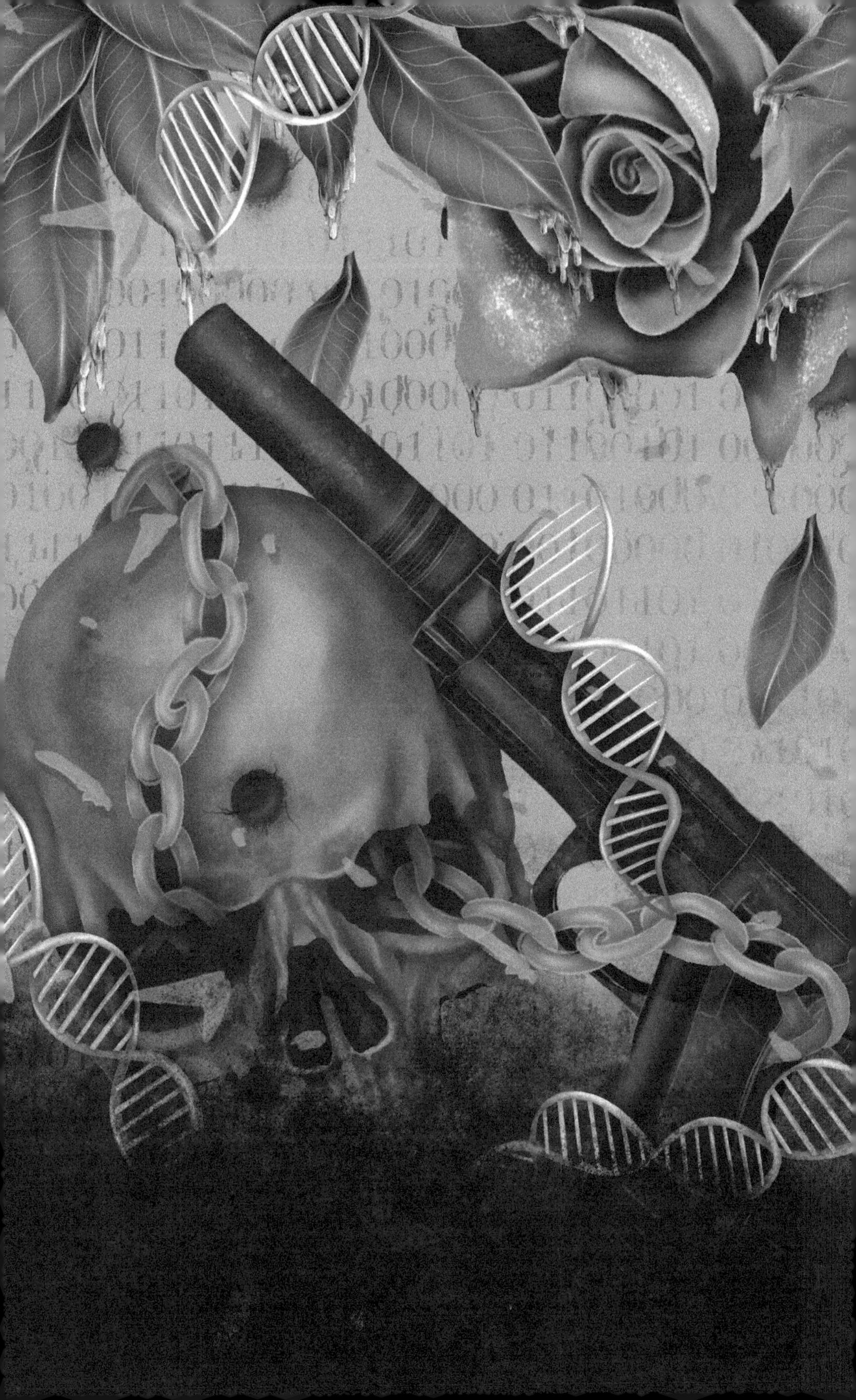

FIFTY-ONE

Two months later . . .

"I got him." I grin, my eye on the scope. "Let me know when you're clear, baby."

"Got it," she says just before the door bursts open and my girl emerges, a backpack slung over her shoulder with the stolen gear. Nico isn't far behind, and Louis is on their tail, slamming and blocking the door.

Dimitri sighs at my side. "Incoming," he says, and I don't glance away from the scope as I hit the detonator and the building explodes, throwing them to the floor before they roll to their feet and run.

"You were only supposed to distract them, not blow up the building," Isaac deadpans from my left, his first-aid kit ready.

"Oops." I grin just as they burst from the door, and we start picking them off as my girl and brothers race to our vehicle. Once they are clear, we pack up. Slinging the bag over my shoulder, I clap Dimitri on the back and head to meet them.

We don't take missions often anymore, only enough to keep us from growing bored, but this was a fun one for sure. We stole some important documents for the US government, and although no country admits to using us, that's fine. It works well for us.

At the car, Nova grins up at me. "Big fire, babe."

"You know it." I kiss her, moaning as her taste spreads through me. I never thought I could love someone as much as I do her, and my obsession only gets worse the longer we are together.

Sliding her down my body, I let her feet hit the floor as the others climb in and the car roars to life.

"Let's go home." She grins at me. "I've got some new toys to show you." She wiggles her brows, making me groan.

Smacking her ass, I haul her into the car and hit the hood through the window. "Fast as you can, we've got things to do."

"Hopefully not rescuing more animals," Nico grumbles, even though the big bastard is up every morning, feeding every single animal Nova has rescued. She turned our home into a rescue centre. She said they are like us, and we couldn't argue with that, especially when she named the pig Davis.

Otherwise, life is fucking good.

I'm not broken.

I'm not psychotic . . . Okay, I am a little, but only for her.

My girl.

My love.

My family.

Forever.

NOVA

"Don't," I warn, pointing my finger at a grinning Dimitri. I turn to keep Jonas in my sights as he tracks me. Shit. I turn to see Nico at the door, his muscles flexing. Louis is sipping his coffee as he watches with glowing eyes, and Isaac winks at me as he climbs to his feet. "I mean it," I warn. "I just showered."

"I'll clean you . . . with my tongue," Jonas says. "You just look so pretty today."

"It is your own fault, coming down like that and expecting us to behave," Dimitri remarks.

Bert just sings along to his music, carrying on cooking breakfast.

"Bert, I claim sanctuary!" I call.

"Nope, sorry, Miss Nova." He waves a spatula at me. "I will put the food in the oven to stay warm though."

"Fuck!" I snap, turning to the open windows and dashing to them.

I hear them give chase, their laughter urging me on. Gritting my teeth, I run as fast as I can. I slide across dirt as I wind around the house, searching for an advantage. My brain processes like a computer, discarding route options and highlighting better ones, but theirs are doing the same.

I skid to a stop when I see a grinning Nico standing near the pool, waiting for me. Turning, I find Jonas skipping after me, and when there's a thud, I whirl to find Louis landing below the balcony he jumped from. Groaning, I scan for Dimitri and Isaac, and when I don't see them, I start to back away slowly.

"You think I'll make it that easy?" I chuckle. I feint left and then turn and race right, ducking under Louis's reaching hands. They don't want to catch me yet, though. That much is obvious. When I skirt the windows, I see Dimitri and Isaac chatting, holding coffee cups in their hands as they stroll from the kitchen. They blow me kisses as I race by.

Bastards.

Annoyance flares in me. I want to win, even though I know they are five of the best soldiers in the entire world and it's me against them.

I have an advantage though. I know how they think. Louis will hang back, letting them track me while trying to create a net around me to corner me in, and then he will take the kill shot. If I can cause enough chaos and confusion, I might just manage to evade them.

If I want to.

I slow slightly when arms suddenly wrap around me, lifting me into the air. A warm breath wafts over my ear as I shudder with desire, and some-one's hard cock grinds into my ass tauntingly.

"Got you."

Jonas.

"Do you?" I purr, leaning back as I relax, and when he lowers me slightly, I slide from his grip, turn, and knee him in the cock. With a howl, he drops to his knees.

"Sorry, babe." I giggle as I back away.

"That was so fucking hot. Shit, baby, my balls," he groans as he stumbles to his feet. "Better run," he growls as he hounds my steps. "She's over by the barn!" he calls to the others.

"Traitor," I hiss.

"For your pussy, baby? Absolutely."

Done with talking, I duck through the barn and burst out of the other end, racing towards the fields. Maybe I can lose them in the overgrown grass. Diving into the long foliage, I hold my arm out to block it as I race forward. I hear some shouts behind me and put on a burst of speed to outrun them, but the grass suddenly parts before me, revealing a grinning Dimitri. "Hey, beautiful."

"Fuck." I start to back away when hands grab me from behind once more.

"Got you," Nico says.

"You put up a good fight, but we both know you wanted to be caught, love," Louis murmurs as he wanders forward and stops before me, jerking his head at Nico. "Take her back."

"Bastards," I hiss as I flail and kick, but I moan when Nico grips my pussy.

"Behave, brat," he warns before tossing me over his shoulder and racing for the house. Part of me wants to give in—after all, it's exactly what I want—but then again, I never did know how to concede.

Once we are out in the open, heading towards Isaac and Jonas, I make my move. I unbalance Nico, which allows me to fall from his shoulder, but before I take two steps, I'm hauled back up.

A hand comes down on my ass in a hard slap. "If you carry on, I'll let Jonas play."

"You are threatening me with a good time," I remind him, wiggling on his shoulder to get him to spank me again, and he does. The sting fades into a burn, making me moan.

I lift my head as we move into the house. Bert waves at me as he sits and reads his paper.

"I claim sanctuary."

"Nope, have fun," he replies without even lifting his head, and when we hit the stairs, I see him putting on some headphones.

We reach our room within seconds, and Nico tosses me on the bed. I bounce and dart to the door, but the others file in, blocking my way. Backing away, I make my way towards the balcony without looking, but Isaac moves behind me, stopping that route too.

"Fine, you caught me." I huff. "Now what do you plan to do?"

The smile Louis aims at me is cruel and possessive. "Clothes," he orders, and I tilt my head in confusion, but my clothes are ripped off from behind. I spin to find Isaac backing away with a grin.

I narrow my gaze on him when my bra and knickers are cut away. Growling, I kick them off, and they hit Jonas's chest where he plucks them up with the knife he used to remove them and stuffs my underwear into his mouth.

The shudder that passes through me isn't healthy, nor the clenching of my thighs as desire hammers through me.

"Bed," Louis commands.

Shit. Before I can dart away, Nico strides over and hauls me to the bed, lying down with me pinned on top of him. His ankles catch my kicking legs and press them down to the bed. One hand grips my throat; the other grabs my hands.

I twist and buck, but he's too fucking strong, and all it does is rub his hard cock against me, leaving me wet and panting. When I still, chest heaving, Louis looks at Dimitri. "You caught her. You get her first."

Chuckling, D grins as he unzips his jeans and palms his hard cock. "The question is, is she wet enough to take us all?"

"Why don't you find out?" I snarl.

His grin widens at my words as he strokes himself. The adrenaline from the chase changes to raw, primal need as I watch him touch himself, and when I can't take it anymore, I widen my thighs to try and entice him. I see the victory in his eyes at my submission before he presses a knee to the bed and crawls between my pinned legs. His eyes are only for me as his hands slide up my thighs and grip them, yanking them farther open.

He lies down between my legs, nudging his wide shoulders there, and drags his tongue across my pussy. I jerk and cry out, twisting in Nico's hold, who tightens his grip on my throat.

"Oh, she's wet, but let me make sure," he coos, and his dark eyes close as he attacks me. His tongue laps at my clit before thrusting inside me, fucking me like we both know he will soon. Groaning, I try to lift my hips and grind into him, but I'm caught between them with no other choice but to take it.

My breath catches as he wraps his lips around my clit and sucks. My back tries to bow, and my eyes close as I cry out. I feel all of their eyes on me, intent on my pleasure and making me theirs.

I fucking want it.

I want it all, dirty, hard, and raw.

Dimitri's fingers slide into me, curling and stroking as he sucks and bites until it's too much. With a scream, I explode, gushing over his fingers and tongue. When the pleasure ebbs, I slump and feel him pull away. I don't even manage to open my eyes before he's driving into me.

Nico's hand keeps me anchored as my eyes snap open, clashing with Dimitri's as he moves above me, and with a growl, he pulls out and slams back in, taking me hard and fast. My name is a hissed word on his lips as his body presses against mine, all hard edges and perfection.

His gaze holds mine, forcing me to see every inch of his love, devotion, and obsession as he fucks me. "Look at you," he growls as I lift my hips to meet his thrusts, wordlessly begging for more.

I only feel alive when I am with them.

"Look at how perfect you are. We caught you, Nova, and we are never letting you go, not ever. You are ours for eternity."

Whimpering his name, I turn my hands and slash my nails into Nico, hearing him grunt, but he still doesn't release me, and I realise that was their plan all along—no escape, not even an inch of space.

"I love you, Nova, so much it hurts, and when I thought I lost you, I didn't see the point of going on. I live only for you. Do you understand? Without you, I am just another computer," he growls, his thrusts speeding up.

It's bordering on painful but so fucking delicious I cry out, clenching around him. It's too much. It's not enough.

I'm lost to it, to him, to them.

"Nova," he whispers as he drives into me. His long, hard thrusts hit that spot inside me, making me see stars.

My heart skips, and fire races through my veins until I can't take any more.

"Come for me again," he demands. "Come with me, together."

As always, they ensure my pleasure first, and his words send me over the edge once more. Crying out my release, I clamp on his cock as he hammers into me twice more before stilling, his forehead hitting mine as he pants and jerks. His cum drips from me as we both breathe raggedly.

"I love you," I tell him.

Grinning, he kisses me softly. "I love you too." He pulls from my body, and with one last, lingering kiss, he moves away.

Isaac crawls up my body, trailing kisses along my skin as he goes. His soft smile is firmly in place when he reaches my lips.

"Hi." He grins.

"Hi." I giggle.

"Are you okay?" he asks with a naughty grin.

"No, but you can make it better by fucking me," I taunt, rubbing against him.

"Gladly," he purrs, sliding down my body. He stops to lick and suck my nipples until I moan loudly. His cock slides across my pussy and the mess there, and then his mouth meets mine once more and he swallows my gasp as he pushes into me.

He kisses me leisurely, softly, and builds the heat inside me with love.

His hips pull back and roll forward.

Unlike Dimitri, Isaac is soft and loving. He rains kisses across every inch of me he can reach. Pleasure arcs through me, leaving me gasping and writhing. His slow thrusts never change, and then I shatter, pulling him with me, his groan echoed in my chest as he fills me with his release.

When I open my eyes, he places a soft kiss over my heart before pulling from my body and sliding away. Their cum drips from me, my legs shake with aftershocks, and I'm covered in sweat, yet they look at me like I'm the most beautiful woman in the world.

Louis is next, which surprises me.

His dark eyes lock me in place like always. Louis has this strange power over me that constantly makes me either want to fight him or give into him. "Be a good girl and ride my cock, love," he purrs, sliding farther up until he consumes my vision. His hands jerk my hips up so I'm rubbing my pussy along his length, and with each rub, his mushroom head smacks my clit, making me groan. I roll my hips, chasing my release, and just when I'm about to come, he pulls away.

"Asshole." I pout.

"Brat," he counters, but it's said lovingly. He frees one leg from Nico, holding it hostage as he tosses it over his shoulder, bending me as his cock presses to my entrance. "Scream for me," he orders.

"How about you make—" My retort ends in a high-pitched howl as he drives into me. The force shifts me back on Nico. Chuckling, Louis tightens his grip on my leg, turning his head to bite my thigh as he pulls out and hammers in.

"What was that?" he taunts, his voice silky against my skin. "Want me to do it again, love?"

"You couldn't even if you tried—" He smacks my clit so hard, I see stars, a scream slipping free once more.

"That's what I thought, brat. Now be a good girl and don't come until I say so." Before I can respond, he's fucking me in earnest. The bed shakes from the force as he rubs my clit, driving me towards my release despite his words.

I hold it back, gritting my teeth as I fight the pleasure spiralling through me as he fucks me.

He grinds me back into Nico, who grunts in pain, his hard cock notched against my ass, and with each thrust, I slide across it.

"I can't," I whine. "Louis, please, I need to—" I can barely speak over the roaring blood in my veins, and with one last twist of his hips, Louis smacks my clit.

"Now," he orders.

Like a perfect soldier, I howl as my release flows through me. My legs kick and shake as he fucks me through it, growling. With a groan, he stills, and his cum splashes inside me.

When he pulls back, he falls to the side. "Go easy on her. No fucked-up shit this time," he warns Jonas, his voice rough, and pleasure fills me at how I affected him, but I don't have long to think about it because Jonas consumes my vision.

He pouts. "He said we have to behave, Nova."

"When do you ever?" I reply.

"True." He tugs me down, freeing my legs until Nico is just holding my hands. He presses my legs to his chest, lifting me into the air, and with a wicked grin, his cock slides across my pussy. I tense, preparing myself for his invasion, but when he's covered in cum, he slides lower.

My eyes close as he presses to my ass. "If I cannot have your madness, I want your screams," he snarls, and with a brutal twist of his hips, he buries himself in my ass. He works himself as deep as he can, our mixed cum helping him slide inside before he pulls out and thrusts back in, forcing me up and onto his cock.

I cry out from the sharp pain, but then his fingers thrust into my pussy, curling to rub that spot that has my cries turning into screams as he begins to claim my ass. Pain and pleasure mixes like it always does with him.

I close my eyes, unable to handle it, my body his to master, and when I scream my release, he roars his, pumping it into my ass before pulling out and spraying the rest across my chest and pussy.

"Fucking perfect," he praises.

"Isn't she just?" Isaac says.

Their attacks disarm me. They love on every inch of me until all I can do is take their praise and love as it rebuilds every inch of me that has been torn down before them.

Arms drag me back up.

Nico.

Spent, I slump into Nico. "Shh, I've got you, baby," he promises, lifting me slightly, and all I can manage is a whine as he slides me down onto his waiting cock. Arms wrap around me from behind as he fucks me from below.

My breasts bounce with the force, and my eyes close in bliss as I let him carry me away.

"Mine, my Nova."

"Yours," I agree, arching back and rolling into his touch.

His hand slides down my body and across my clit. "I'm close already. Watching you get fucked and feeling it on top of me almost had me spilling, baby," he admits. "So come for me, let me feel it before I can't hold back anymore."

He pinches my clit, making me scream in pain and pleasure as a surprise orgasm slams through me. When I come back to, he's groaning so sexily in my ear and filling me with his release.

I can barely breathe, and I definitely can't move. Long after the sweat starts to cool on my body, Nico pulls free, leaving me sticky and satisfied.

"We've got you," Louis murmurs, climbing onto the bed. Someone wipes my pussy and thighs, but I don't look, just lax with pleasure and so happy I could cry.

Arms wrap around me once more, different ones sliding across my body until they are all touching me.

I want every day to be like this.

I cuddle closer to my men, a satisfied smile on my lips as I close my eyes. My body is sweaty, my pussy is sore in the best way, and my heart is full and overflowing. "I love you all," I murmur.

Louis sighs happily. "I love you too."

"I love you too. Now sleep, you've worn me out," Jonas mumbles, making me giggle as I bury my head deeper into Nico's chest. Isaac pulls me closer as Dimitri presses a kiss to my leg.

I fade into a dreamless sleep, just as I always do when they are here.

The crack of lightning wakes me just before thunder rattles the shutters of our house. My men wake instantly. I smile at them as I slip from the bed. Unlike before, I wait for them. Nico wraps a robe around me, and I put my slippers on as we head downstairs. Opening the veranda doors we installed, we gather on the sofas there. Dimitri wraps blankets around us as Bert makes trays of herbal tea and sets them out, joining us as we watch the storm.

A tradition to honour the woman who gave her life for us.

Somewhere, Ana is watching this storm with us, her grave decorated with flowers and drawings from the kids we saved. We also started a soldiers' rehab program in her and Sam's names, and I know every person there tonight will be looking at the sky, thinking of the woman they owe that to.

Hands hold me close, and although it hurts, a smile tilts my lips as I watch the rain hit the windows of my new home. Storms will always make me think of my sister, of the woman I loved so deeply, I gave up everything for her, but life has a funny way of ripping you apart and putting you back together.

It certainly did that to me. I often wondered when I would break and give into the darkness, and more than once, I debated doing just that. It would have been easier, but I never liked the easy option. It doesn't mean I don't carry my scars with me because I do. I still struggle sometimes, but on nights like this, I remember why I fight to get up every day.

For her.

For every child my father hurt.

For every child they killed.

For the soldiers who were just doing their duty.

I live for them, my family, and for myself.

"Do you remember the night before we met you?" Dimitri murmurs.

It brings me out of my thoughts, and he smiles brightly. "It was a stormy night just like this. I checked. I guess storms have always been our thing as well as hers."

"I guess so," I whisper. "Maybe that's why I always loved them so much."

I take his hand and turn back to the windows, a brighter smile on my face. Somewhere out there, destiny is laughing at me. Only a few years ago, on a night like this, I was trapped in a cheap hotel room, completely alone, guided by anger and revenge, and now here I am, in love and happier than I've ever been.

I have a new life and a new future I plan to fully embrace.

I guess I was just a pretty liar when I said revenge was all there was to live for.

The world still has its dark days, and there are still those who would come for the research, but that is our mission now. We will protect it and those children. My father's experiments end with us. We will never let another suffer under the same experiments, and one day, it will be forgotten just like him. We will be forgotten as well, but that's okay with me. We know what we did, we know what we are capable of, and we will stand here as a reminder and a promise until the very end because we are unbreakable.

We are unstoppable.

EPILOGUE

Two years later . . .

Like I do every morning, I sip my coffee as I watch the sunrise. The house and our land are quiet. Not even the animals are awake yet. The dogs are snoring on top of Nico and waiting for him to feed them. Dimitri's computers are turned off and have been for days, since he prefers to spend his time with us now. Jonas continues to build weapons, only now he sells them to the good guys. Louis, as it turns out, is very good at restoration, and we updated our house and started on the property together. Maybe in time, we'll make that a business, but for now, we are just enjoying life. Isaac fully embraced his role as vet and qualified in it. His days of being a doctor are behind him—unless Jonas and I get too rough during sex—and he now spends his days helping animals rather than patching bullet wounds.

And me?

My smile grows as I watch the colours spread across the sky. I got everything I wanted. I'm never alone anymore. I have a family who loves me more than anything else in this world. I have men willing to kill for me. I still train, but not religiously. I'm more than my body and what it's capable of, after all. I still haven't figured out what I'll do with the rest of my life, but I have plenty of time.

"Baby?" comes a sleepy voice behind me.

I open my eyes as I glance down at my ring, the ring they all had made for me, before I turn to see Louis. "Hey," I whisper. "Go back to sleep. I'll be there in a second."

"You better or we'll find you," he warns.

I nod, knowing they will.

They prove how much they love me every day, and I finally started to believe it and let go of my pain and my past. My heart still aches when I think of everything we lost, including my sister, but I'm more determined than ever to enjoy the life we have because nothing is guaranteed.

So, I stop and watch the sunrise, feel the breeze, and dance in storms and remember . . .

Life is so much more than what others want for us. There is a big, wide world out there just waiting for us to find our happiness in whatever shape or form that comes in.

My happiness just so happens to be in an old Italian villa with six incredible men, a father I never lost, five dogs, three cats, a donkey, two horses, a pig, and a llama.

I head inside our home and back to my men where my heart pulls me, the floor under me protecting the very thing that created us.

Our secret we will always protect.

Together.

ACKNOWLEDGMENTS

This book was so hard to write in some places, it took me to a very dark place and as darkness plagued me and my loved ones, I turned the pain into ink. Luckily, for every stormy, shadowed night, there is a bright sunshine morning.

I cannot begin to thank everyone who makes my work possible but for especially trusting me through the process of this one. From my incredible betas who's hearts I break daily to my phenomenal editor and proofreader who make my madness legible. To my PAs who understand the craziness and help me get it out into the world . . . and then finally to you.

My readers.

I would not be here today without you all. I never forget that and I'm truly so thankful every time you take a chance on a book I have written. I hope you love Nova's story as much as I did and remember, Pretty Liars, you are never alone.

ABOUT K.A. KNIGHT

K.A Knight is an USA Today bestselling indie author trying to get all of the stories and characters out of her head, writing the monsters that you love to hate. She loves reading and devours every book she can get her hands on, and she also has a worrying caffeine addiction.

She leads her double life in a sleepy English town, where she spends her days writing like a crazy person.

Read more at K.A Knight's website or join her Facebook Reader Group.
Sign up for exclusive content and my newsletter here
http://eepurl.com/drLLoj

ALSO BY K.A. KNIGHT

THEIR CHAMPION SERIES *Dystopian RH*

The Wasteland

The Summit

The Cities

The Nations

Their Champion Coloring Book

Their Champion - the omnibus

The Forgotten

The Lost

The Damned

Their Champion Companion - the omnibus

DAWNBREAKER SERIES *SCI FI RH*

Voyage to Ayama

Dreaming of Ayama

THE LOST COVEN SERIES *PNR RH*

Aurora's Coven

Aurora's Betrayal

HER MONSTERS SERIES *PNR RH*

Rage

Hate

Book 3 coming soon..

THE FALLEN GODS SERIES *PNR*

Pretty Painful

Pretty Bloody

Pretty Stormy

Pretty Wild

Pretty Hot

Pretty Faces

Pretty Spelled

Fallen Gods - the omnibus 1

Fallen Gods - the omnibus 2

COURTS AND KINGS *PNR RH*

Court of Nightmares

Court of Death

FORBIDDEN READS (STANDALONES)

CONTEMPORARY

Daddy's Angel

CONTEMPORARY RH

Stepbrothers' Darling

LEGENDS AND LOVE *CONTEMPORARY*

Revolt

PRETTY LIARS *CONTEMPORARY RH*

Unstoppable

Unbreakable

FORGOTTEN CITY *PNR*

Monstrous Lies

Monstrous Truths

Monstrous Ends

STANDALONES

IN DEN OF VIPERS' UNIVERSE - CONTEMPORARY

Scarlett Limerence

Nadia's Salvation

Alena's Revenge

Den of Vipers *CONTEMPORARY RH*

Gangsters and Guns (Co-Write with Loxley Savage)

CONTEMPORARY

The Standby

Diver's Heart *CONTEMPORARY RH*

SCI FI RH

Crown of Stars

AUDIOBOOKS

The Wasteland

The Summit

Rage

Hate

Den of Vipers *(From Podium Audio)*

Gangsters and Guns *(From Podium Audio)*

Daddy's Angel *(From Podium Audio)*

Stepbrothers' Darling *(From Podium Audio)*

Blade of Iris *(From Podium Audio)*

Deadly Affair *(From Podium Audio)*

Deadly Match *(From Podium Audio)*

Deadly Encounter *(From Podium Audio)*

Stolen Trophy *(From Podium Audio)*

Crown of Stars *(From Podium Audio)*

Monstrous Lies *(From Podium Audio)*

Monstrous Truth *(From Podium Audio)*

Monstrous Ends *(From Podium Audio)*

Court of Nightmares *(From Podium Audio)*

Unstoppable *(From Podium Audio)*

Unbreakable *(From Podium Audio)*

Fractured Shadows *(From Podium Audio)*

SHARED WORLD PROJECTS

Blade of Iris - Mafia Wars *CONTEMPORARY*

CO-AUTHOR PROJECTS - *Erin O'Kane*

HER FREAKS SERIES *PNR Dystopian RH*

Circus Save Me

Taming The Ringmaster

Walking the Tightrope

Her Freaks Series - the omnibus

STANDALONES

PNR RH

The Hero Complex

Collection of Short Stories

Dark Temptations (contains One Night Only and Circus Saves Christmas)

THE WILD BOYS SERIES *CONTEMPORARY RH*

The Wild Interview

The Wild Tour

The Wild Finale

The Wild Boys - the omnibus

CO-AUTHOR PROJECTS - *Ivy Fox*

Deadly Love Series *CONTEMPORARY*

Deadly Affair

Deadly Match

Deadly Encounter

CO-AUTHOR PROJECTS - *Kendra Moreno*

STANDALONES

CONTEMPORARY RH

Stolen Trophy

PNR RH

Fractured Shadows

PNR

Burn Me

CO-AUTHOR PROJECTS - *Loxley Savage*

THE FORSAKEN SERIES *SCI FI RH*

Capturing Carmen

Stealing Shiloh

Harboring Harlow

STANDALONES

CONTEMPORARY

Gangsters and Guns - IN DEN OF VIPERS' UNIVERSE

OTHER CO-WRITES

Shipwreck Souls *(with Kendra Moreno & Poppy Woods)*

The Horror Emporium *(with Kendra Moreno & Poppy Woods)*

FIND AN ERROR?

Please email the author name, title of the book and a screenshot of the error to thenuttyformatter1@gmail.com